THE MAHABHARATA

PRAISE FOR THE SERIES

'The modernization of language is visible, it's easier on the mind, through expressions that are somewhat familiar. The detailing of the story is intact, the varying tempo maintained, with no deviations from the original. The short introduction reflects a brilliant mind. For those who passionately love the Mahabharata and want to explore it to its depths, Debroy's translation offers great promise . . .'

—*Hindustan Times*

'[Debroy] has really carved out a niche for himself in crafting and presenting a translation of the Mahabharata . . . The book takes us on a great journey with admirable ease.'

—*Indian Express*

'The first thing that appeals to one is the simplicity with which Debroy has been able to express himself and infuse the right kind of meanings . . . Considering that Sanskrit is not the simplest of languages to translate a text from, Debroy exhibits his deep understanding and appreciation of the medium.'

—*The Hindu*

'Overwhelmingly impressive . . . Bibek is a truly eclectic scholar.'

—*Business Line*

'Debroy's lucid and nuanced retelling of the original makes the masterpiece even more enjoyably accessible.'

—*Open*

'The quality of translation is excellent. The lucid language makes it a pleasure to read the various stories, digressions and parables.'

—*Tribune*

'Extremely well-organized, and has a substantial and helpful Introduction, plot summaries and notes . . . beautiful example of a well thought-out layout which makes for much easier reading.'

—*Book Review*

'The dispassionate vision [Debroy] brings to this endeavour will surely earn him merit in the three worlds.'

—*Mail Today*

'Thoroughly enjoyable and impressively scholarly . . .'

—*DNA*

'Debroy's is not the only English translation available in the market, but where he scores and others fail is that his is the closest rendering of the original text in modern English without unduly complicating the readers' understanding of the epic.'

—*Business Standard*

'The brilliance of Ved Vysya comes through.'

—*Hindustan Times*

THE MAHABHARATA

Volume 9

(Sections 86 to 87)

Translated by

BIBEK DEBROY

PENGUIN BOOKS

An imprint of Penguin Random House

PENGUIN BOOKS

USA | Canada | UK | Ireland | Australia
New Zealand | India | South Africa | China

Penguin Books is part of the Penguin Random House group of companies whose addresses can be found at global.penguinrandomhouse.com

Published by Penguin Random House India Pvt. Ltd
7th Floor, Infinity Tower C, DLF Cyber City,
Gurgaon 122 002, Haryana, India

First published by Penguin Books India 2014
This edition published 2015

10 9 8 7 6 5 4 3 2

ISBN 9780143425229

Typeset in Sabon by Eleven Arts, New Delhi
Printed at Repro India Limited

www.penguin.co.in

For my wife, Suparna Banerjee (Debroy),
who has walked this path of dharma with me

Ardha bhāryā manuṣyasya bhāryā śreṣṭhatamaḥ sakhā
Bhāryā mulam trivargasya bhāryā mitram mariṣyataḥ
Mahabharata (1/68/40)

Nāsti bhāryāsamo bandhurnāsti bhāryasamā gatiḥ
Nāsti bhāryasamo loke sahāyo dharmasādhanaḥ
Mahabharata (12/142/10)

Contents

FAMILY TREE

Bharata/Puru Lineage

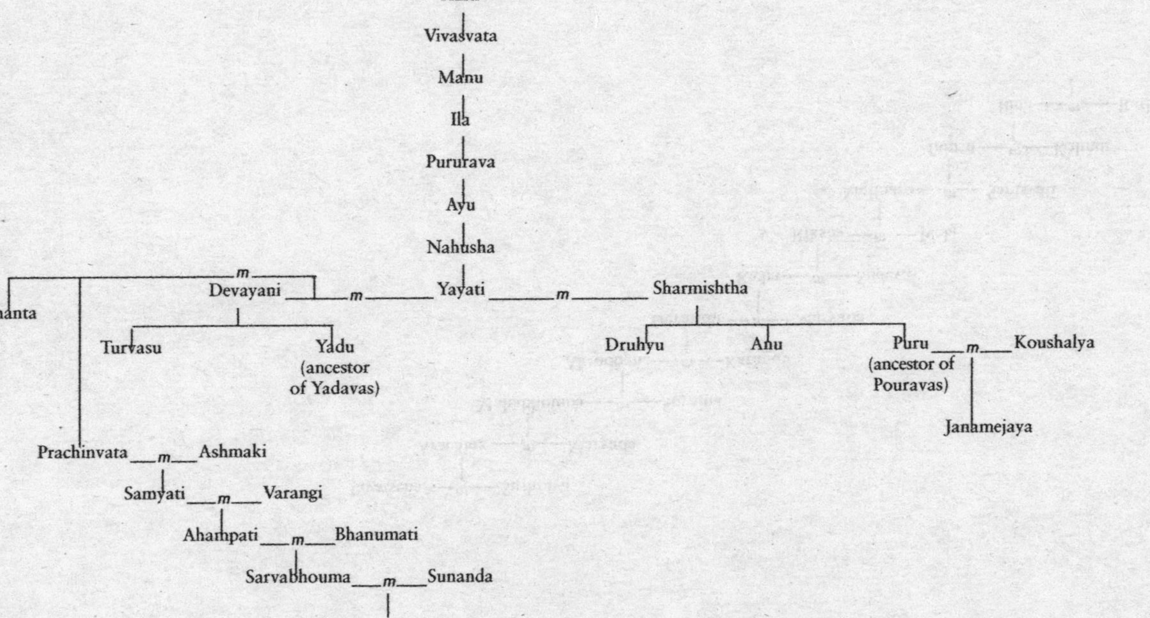

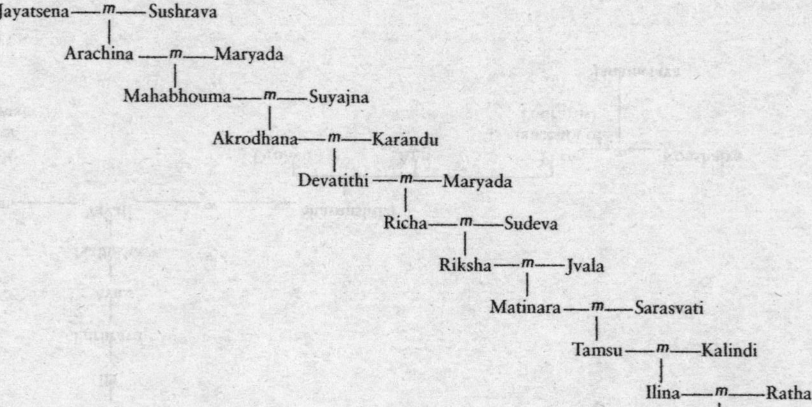
Jayatsena —m— Sushrava
Arachina —m— Maryada
Mahabhouma —m— Suyajna
Akrodhana —m— Karandu
Devatithi —m— Maryada
Richa —m— Sudeva
Riksha —m— Jvala
Matinara —m— Sarasvati
Tamsu —m— Kalindi
Ilina —m— Rathantari

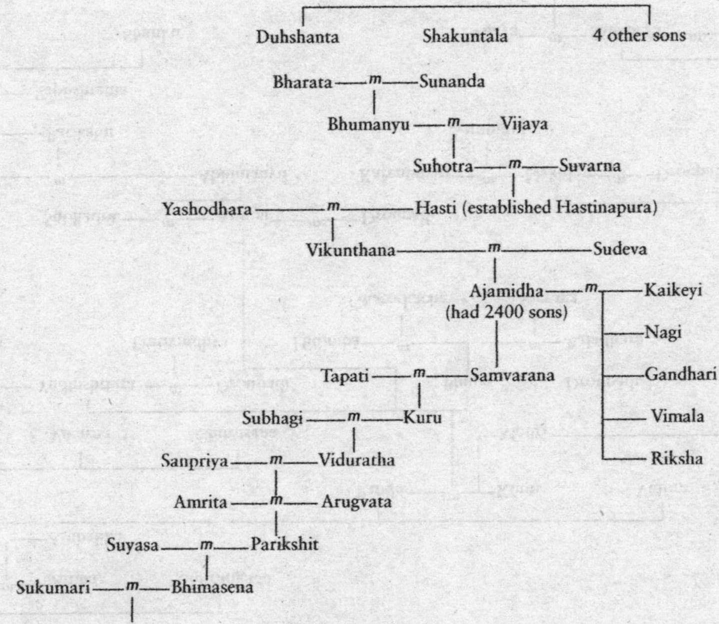

Duhshanta
Shakuntala
4 other sons
Bharata
m
Sunanda
Bhumanyu
Vijaya
Suhotra
Suvarna
Yashodhara
Hasti (established Hastinapura)
Vikunthana
Sudeva
Ajamidha
(had 2400 sons)
Kaikeyi
Nagi
Gandhari
Vimala
Riksha
Tapati
Samvarana
Subhagi
Kuru
Sanpriya
Viduratha
Amrita
Arugvata
Suyasa
Parikshit
Sukumari
Bhimasena

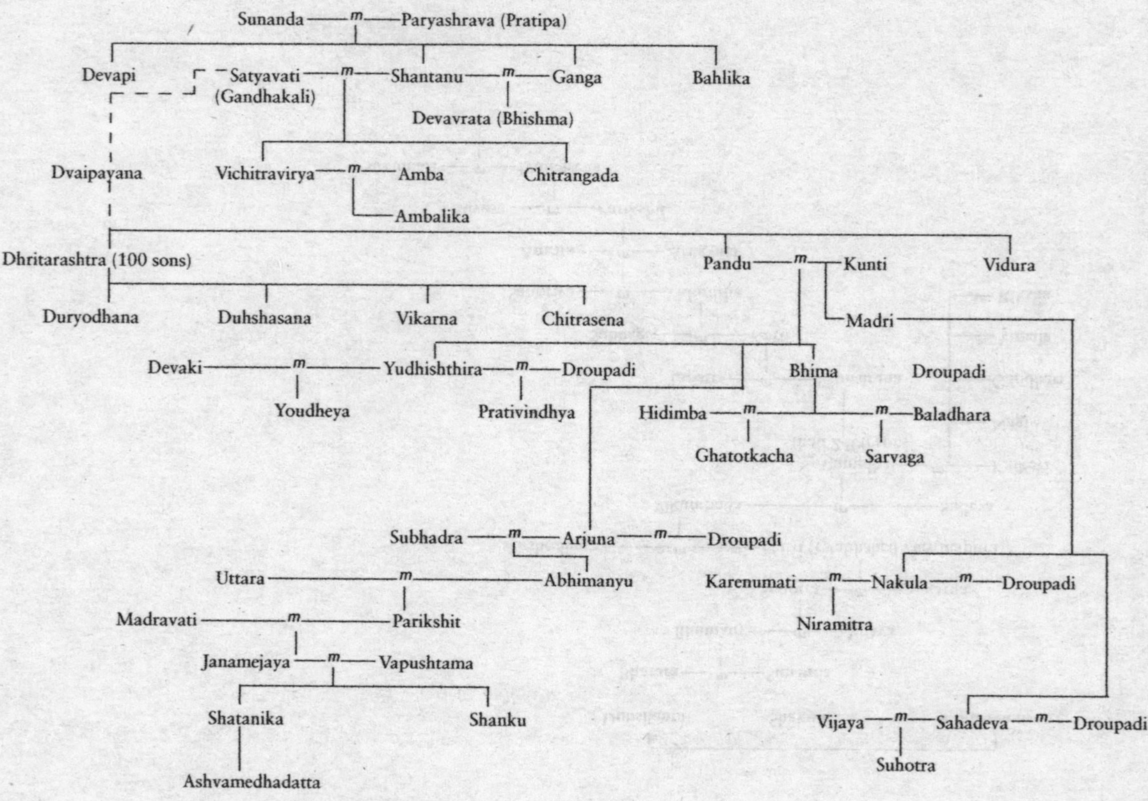

Sunanda — m — Paryashrava (Pratipa)
Devapi
Satyavati (Gandhakali) — m — Shantanu — m — Ganga
Bahlika
Devavrata (Bhishma)
Dvaipayana
Vichitravirya — m — Amba
Chitrangada
Ambalika
Dhritarashtra (100 sons)
Pandu — m — Kunti
Vidura
Madri
Duryodhana
Duhshasana
Vikarna
Chitrasena
Devaki — m — Yudhishthira — m — Droupadi
Bhima
Droupadi
Youdheya
Prativindhya
Hidimba — m — Baladhara
Ghatotkacha
Sarvaga
Subhadra — m — Arjuna — m — Droupadi
Uttara — m — Abhimanyu
Karenumati — m — Nakula — m — Droupadi
Madravati — m — Parikshit
Niramitra
Janamejaya — m — Vapushtama
Shatanika
Shanku
Vijaya — m — Sahadeva — m — Droupadi
Ashvamedhadatta
Suhotra

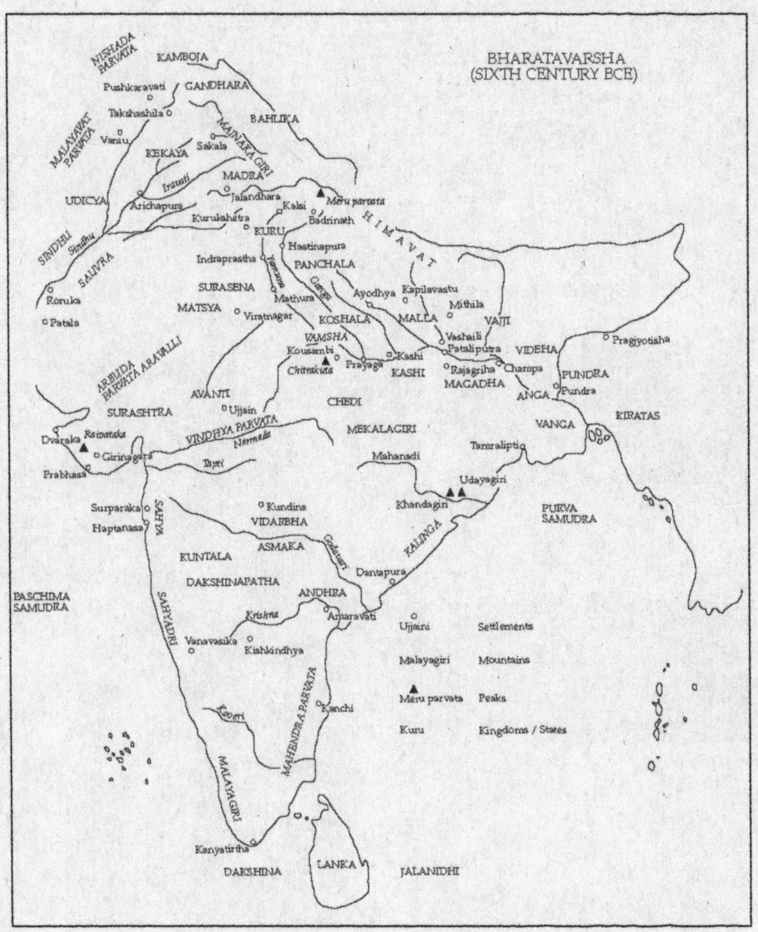

BHARATAVARSHA
(SIXTH CENTURY BCE)
NISHADA PARVATA
KAMBOJA
Pushkaravati
GANDHARA
Takshashila
BAHLIKA
MALAYAVAT PARVATA
Vaniu
MAINAKA GIRI
Sakala
KEKAYA
MADRA
Iravati
UDICYA
Arichapura
Jalandhara
Meru parvata
Kalsi
Kurukshetra
Badrinath
HIMAVAT
KURU
SINDHU
Sindhu
SALIVRA
Hastinapura
Indraprastha
PANCHALA
Yamuna
Ganga
SURASENA
Mathura
Ayodhya
Kapilavastu
Roruka
MATSYA
Viratnagar
Mithila
Patala
KOSHALA
MALLA
VAJJI
VAMSHA
Vashaili
Pataliputra
VIDEHA
Pragjyotisha
Kousambi
Kashi
Chitrakuta
Prayaga
KASHI
Rajagriha
Champa
ARBUDA PARVATA ARAVALLI
PUNDRA
Pundra
AVANTI
MAGADHA
ANGA
CHEDI
Ujjain
SURASHTRA
KIRATAS
VINDHYA PARVATA
MEKALAGIRI
VANGA
Narmada
Dvaraka
Raivataka
Tamralipti
Girinagara
Mahanadi
Tapti
Prabhasa
Udayagiri
Khandagiri
Surparaka
SAHYA
Kundina
PURVA SAMUDRA
Haptanasa
VIDARBHA
KALINGA
ASMAKA
Godavari
KUNTALA
Dantapura
DAKSHINAPATHA
PASCHIMA SAMUDRA
ANDHRA
SAHYADRI
Krishna
Amaravati
Ujjaini
Settlements
Vanavasika
Kishkindhya
Malayagiri
Mountains
MAHENDRA PARVATA
Meru parvata
Peaks
Kanchi
Kaveri
Kuru
Kingdoms / States
MALAYAGIRI
Kanyatirtha
LANKA
DAKSHINA
JALANIDHI

Acknowledgements

Carving time out from one's regular schedule and work engagements to embark on such a mammoth work of translation has been difficult. It has been a journey of six years, ten volumes and something like 2.25 million words. Sometimes, I wish I had been born in nineteenth-century Bengal, with a benefactor funding me for doing nothing but this. But alas, the days of gentlemen of leisure are long over. The time could not be carved out from professional engagements, barring of course assorted television channels, who must have wondered why I have been so reluctant to head for their studios in the evenings. It was ascribed to health, interpreted as adverse health. It was certainly health, but not in an adverse sense. Reading the Mahabharata is good for one's mental health and is an activity to be recommended, without any statutory warnings. When I embarked on the hazardous journey, a friend, an author interested in Sanskrit and the Mahabharata, sent me an email. She asked me to be careful, since the track record of those who embarked on unabridged translations of the Mahabharata hasn't always been desirable. Thankfully, I survived, to finish telling the tale.

The time was stolen in the evenings and over weekends. The cost was therefore borne by one's immediate family, and to a lesser extent by friends. Socializing was reduced, since every dinner meant one less chapter done. The family has first claim on the debt, though I am sure it also has claim on whatever merits are due. At least my wife, Suparna Banerjee (Debroy) does, and these volumes are therefore dedicated to her. For six long years, she has walked this path of dharma along with me, providing the conducive home cum family environment that made undistracted work possible. I suspect Sirius has no claim on the merits, though he has been remarkably patient at the times when he has been curled up near my feet and I have been translating away. There is some allegory there about a dog keeping company when the Mahabharata is being read and translated.

Most people have thought I was mad, even if they never quite said that. Among those who believed and thought it was worthwhile, beyond immediate family, are M. Veerappa Moily, Pratap Bhanu Mehta and Laveesh Bhandari. And my sons, Nihshanka and Vidroha. The various reviewers of different volumes have also been extremely kind and many readers have communicated kind words through email and Twitter, enquiring about progress.

Penguin also believed. My initial hesitation about being able to deliver was brushed aside by R. Sivapriya, who pushed me after the series had been commissioned by V. Karthika. And then Sumitra Srinivasan became the editor, followed by Paloma Dutta. The enthusiasm of these ladies was so infectious that everything just snowballed and Paloma ensured that the final product of the volumes was much more readable than what I had initially produced.

When I first embarked on what was also a personal voyage of sorts, the end was never in sight and seemed to stretch to infinity. There were moments of self-doubt and frustration. Now that it is all done, it leaves a vacuum, a hole. That's not simply because you haven't figured out what the new project is. It is also because characters who have been part of your life for several years are dead and gone. I don't mean the ones who died in the course of the actual war, but the others. Most of them faced rather tragic and unenviable ends. Along that personal voyage, the Mahabharata changes you, or so my wife tells me. I am no longer the person I was when I started it, as an individual. That sounds cryptic, deliberately so. Anyone who reads the Mahabharata carefully is bound to change, discount the temporary and place a premium on the permanent.

To all those who have been part of that journey, including the readers, thank you.

The original ten volumes were published sequentially, as they were completed, between 2010 and 2014.

Introduction

The Hindu tradition has an amazingly large corpus of religious texts, spanning Vedas, Vedanta (*brahmanas*,[1] *aranyakas*,[2] Upanishads,), Vedangas,[3] *smritis*, Puranas, dharmashastras and *itihasa*. For most of these texts, especially if one excludes classical Sanskrit literature, we don't quite know when they were composed and by whom, not that one is looking for single authors. Some of the minor Puranas (Upa Purana) are of later vintage. For instance, the Bhavishya Purana (which is often listed as a major Purana or Maha Purana) mentions Queen Victoria.

In the listing of the corpus above figures itihasa, translated into English as history. History doesn't entirely capture the nuance of itihasa, which is better translated as 'this is indeed what happened'. Itihasa isn't myth or fiction. It is a chronicle of what happened; it is fact. Or so runs the belief. And itihasa consists of India's two major epics, the Ramayana and the Mahabharata. The former is believed to have been composed as poetry and the latter as prose. This isn't quite correct. The Ramayana has segments in prose and the Mahabharata has segments in poetry. Itihasa doesn't quite belong to the category of religious texts in a way that the Vedas and Vedanta are religious. However, the dividing line between what is religious and what is not is fuzzy. After all, itihasa is also about attaining the objectives of *dharma*,[4]

[1] Brahmana is a text and also the word used for the highest caste.

[2] A class of religious and philosophical texts that are composed in the forest, or are meant to be studied when one retires to the forest.

[3] The six Vedangas are *shiksha* (articulation and pronunciation), *chhanda* (prosody), *vyakarana* (grammar), *nirukta* (etymology), *jyotisha* (astronomy) and *kalpa* (rituals).

[4] Religion, duty.

artha,[5] *kama*[6] and *moksha*[7] and the Mahabharata includes Hinduism's most important spiritual text—the Bhagavad Gita.

The epics are not part of the *shruti* tradition. That tradition is like revelation, without any composer. The epics are part of the *smriti* tradition. At the time they were composed, there was no question of texts being written down. They were recited, heard, memorized and passed down through the generations. But the smriti tradition had composers. The Ramayana was composed by Valmiki, regarded as the first poet or *kavi*. The word kavi has a secondary meaning as poet or rhymer. The primary meaning of kavi is someone who is wise.

And in that sense, the composer of the Mahabharata was no less wise. This was Vedavyasa or Vyasadeva. He was so named because he classified (*vyasa*) the Vedas. Vedavyasa or Vyasadeva isn't a proper name. It is a title. Once in a while, in accordance with the needs of the era, the Vedas need to be classified. Each such person obtains the title and there have been twenty-eight Vyasadevas so far.

At one level, the question about who composed the Mahabharata is pointless. According to popular belief and according to what the Mahabharata itself states, it was composed by Krishna Dvaipayana Vedavyasa (Vyasadeva). But the text was not composed and cast in stone at a single point in time. Multiple authors kept adding layers and embellishing it. Sections just kept getting added and it is no one's suggestion that Krishna Dvaipayana Vedavyasa composed the text of the Mahabharata as it stands today.

Consequently, the Mahabharata is far more unstructured than the Ramayana. The major sections of the Ramayana are known as *kanda*s and one meaning of the word kanda is the stem or trunk of a tree, suggesting solidity. The major sections of the Mahabharata are known as *parva*s and while one meaning of the word parva is limb or member or joint, in its nuance there is greater fluidity in the word parva than in kanda.

The Vyasadeva we are concerned with had a proper name of Krishna

[5] Wealth. But in general, any object of the senses.
[6] Desire.
[7] Release from the cycle of rebirth.

Dvaipayana. He was born on an island (*dvipa*). That explains the Dvaipayana part of the name. He was dark. That explains the Krishna part of the name. (It wasn't only the incarnation of Vishnu who had the name of Krishna.) Krishna Dvaipayana Vedavyasa was also related to the protagonists of the Mahabharata story. To go back to the origins, the Ramayana is about the solar dynasty, while the Mahabharata is about the lunar dynasty. As is to be expected, the lunar dynasty begins with Soma (the moon) and goes down through Pururava (who married the famous apsara Urvashi), Nahusha and Yayati. Yayati became old, but wasn't ready to give up the pleasures of life. He asked his sons to temporarily loan him their youth. All but one refused. The ones who refused were cursed that they would never be kings, and this includes the Yadavas (descended from Yadu). The one who agreed was Puru and the lunar dynasty continued through him. Puru's son Duhshanta was made famous by Kalidasa in the Duhshanta–Shakuntala story and their son was Bharata, contributing to the name of Bharatavarsha. Bharata's grandson was Kuru. We often tend to think of the Kouravas as the evil protagonists in the Mahabharata story and the Pandavas as the good protagonists. Since Kuru was a common ancestor, the appellation Kourava applies equally to Yudhishthira and his brothers and Duryodhana and his brothers. Kuru's grandson was Shantanu. Through Satyavati, Shantanu fathered Chitrangada and Vichitravirya. However, the sage Parashara had already fathered Krishna Dvaipayana through Satyavati. And Shantanu had already fathered Bhishma through Ganga. Dhritarasthra and Pandu were fathered on Vichitravirya's wives by Krishna Dvaipayana.

The story of the epic is also about these antecedents and consequents. The core Mahabharata story is known to every Indian and is normally understood as a dispute between the Kouravas (descended from Dhritarashtra) and the Pandavas (descended from Pandu). However, this is a distilled version, which really begins with Shantanu. The non-distilled version takes us to the roots of the genealogical tree and at several points along this tree we confront a problem with impotence/sterility/death, resulting in offspring through a surrogate father. Such sons were accepted in that day and age. Nor was this a lunar dynasty problem alone. In the Ramayana, Dasharatha of the solar dynasty also had an infertility problem, corrected through a sacrifice. To return to the genealogical tree, the Pandavas won the Kurukshetra war. However, their five sons through Droupadi were killed. So was Bhima's son Ghatotkacha, fathered on Hidimba. As was Arjuna's son Abhimanyu, fathered on Subhadra. Abhimanyu's son Parikshit inherited the throne in Hastinapura, but was killed by a serpent. Parikshit's son was Janamejaya.

Krishna Dvaipayana Vedavyasa's powers of composition were remarkable. Having classified the Vedas, he composed the Mahabharata in 100,000 shlokas or couplets. Today's Mahabharata text doesn't have that many shlokas, even if the Hari Vamsha (regarded as the epilogue to the Mahabharata) is included. One reaches around 90,000 shlokas. That too, is a gigantic number. (The Mahabharata is almost four times the size of the Ramayana and is longer than any other epic anywhere in the world.) For a count of 90,000 Sanskrit shlokas, we are talking about something in the neighbourhood of two million words. The text of the Mahabharata tells us that Krishna Dvaipayana finished this composition in three years. This doesn't necessarily mean that he composed 90,000 shlokas. The text also tells us that there are three versions to the Mahabharata. The original version was called Jaya and had 8,800 shlokas. This was expanded to 24,000 shlokas and called Bharata. Finally, it was expanded to 90,000 (or 100,000) shlokas and called Mahabharata.

Krishna Dvaipayana didn't rest even after that. He composed the eighteen Maha Puranas, adding another 400,000 shlokas. Having composed the Mahabharata, he taught it to his disciple Vaishampayana. When Parikshit was killed by a serpent, Janamejaya organized a snake-sacrifice to destroy the serpents. With all the sages assembled there, Vaishampayana turned up and the assembled sages wanted to know the story of the Mahabharata, as composed by Krishna Dvaipayana. Janamejaya also wanted to know why Parikshit had been killed by the serpent. That's the background against which the epic is recited. However, there is another round of recounting too. Much later, the sages assembled for a sacrifice in Naimisharanya and asked Lomaharshana (alternatively, Romaharshana) to recite what he had heard at Janamejaya's snake-sacrifice. Lomaharshana was a *suta*, the sutas being charioteers and bards or raconteurs. As the son of a suta, Lomaharshana is also referred to as Souti. But Souti or Lomaharshana aren't quite his proper names. His proper name is Ugrashrava. Souti refers to his birth. He owes the name Lomaharshana to the fact that the body-hair (*loma* or *roma*) stood up (*harshana*) on hearing his tales. Within the text therefore, two people are telling the tale. Sometimes it is Vaishampayana and sometimes it is Lomaharshana. Incidentally, the stories of the Puranas are recounted by Lomaharshana, without Vaishampayana intruding. Having composed the Puranas, Krishna Dvaipayana taught them to his disciple Lomaharshana. For what it is worth, there are scholars who have used statistical tests to try and identify the multiple authors of the Mahabharata.

As we are certain there were multiple authors rather than a single one, the question of when the Mahabharata was composed is somewhat pointless. It wasn't composed on a single date. It was composed over a span of more than 1000 years, perhaps between 800 BCE and 400 ACE. It is impossible to be more accurate than that. There is a difference between dating the composition and dating the incidents, such as the date of the Kurukshetra war. Dating the incidents is both subjective and controversial and irrelevant for the purposes of this translation. A timeline of 1000 years isn't short. But even then, the size of the corpus is nothing short of amazing.

* * *

Familiarity with Sanskrit is dying out. The first decades of the twenty-first century are quite unlike the first decades of the twentieth. Lamentation over what is inevitable serves no purpose. English is increasingly becoming the global language, courtesy colonies (North America, South Asia, East Asia, Australia, New Zealand, Africa) rather than the former colonizer. If familiarity with the corpus is not to die out, it needs to be accessible in English.

There are many different versions or recensions of the Mahabharata. However, between 1919 and 1966, the Bhandarkar Oriental Research Institute (BORI) in Pune produced what has come to be known as the critical edition. This is an authenticated text produced by a board of scholars and seeks to eliminate later interpolations, unifying the text across the various regional versions. This is the text followed in this translation. One should also mention that the critical edition's text is not invariably smooth. Sometimes, the transition from one shloka to another is abrupt, because the intervening shloka has been weeded out. With the intervening shloka included, a non-critical version of the text sometimes makes better sense. On a few occasions, I have had the temerity to point this out in the notes which I have included in my translation. On a slightly different note, the quality of the text in something like Dana Dharma Parva is clearly inferior. It couldn't have been 'composed' by the same person.

It took a long time for this critical edition to be put together. The exercise began in 1919. Without the Hari Vamsha, the complete critical edition became available in 1966. And with the Hari Vamsha, the complete critical edition became available in 1970. Before this, there were regional variations in the text and the main versions were available from Bengal, Bombay and the south. However, now, one should stick to the critical edition, though there are occasional instances where there are reasons for dissatisfaction with what the scholars of the Bhandarkar Oriental Research Institute have accomplished. But in all fairness, there are two published versions of the critical edition. The first one has the bare bones of the critical edition's text. The second has all the regional versions collated, with copious notes. The former is for the ordinary reader, assuming he/she knows Sanskrit. And the latter is for the scholar. Consequently, some popular beliefs no longer find a place in the critical edition's text. For example, it is believed that Vedavyasa dictated the text to Ganesha, who wrote it down. But Ganesha had a condition before accepting. Vedavyasa would have to dictate continuously, without stopping. Vedavyasa threw in a counter-condition. Ganesha would have to understand each couplet before he wrote it down. To flummox Ganesha and give himself time to think, Vedavyasa threw in some cryptic verses. This attractive anecdote has been excised from the critical edition's text. Barring material that is completely religious (specific hymns or the Bhagavad Gita), the Sanskrit text is reasonably easy to understand. Oddly, I have had the most difficulty with things that Vidura has sometimes said, other than parts of Anushasana Parva. Arya has today come to connote ethnicity. Originally, it meant language. That is, those who spoke Sanskrit were Aryas. Those who did not speak Sanskrit were mlecchas. Vidura is supposed to have been skilled in the mlechha language. Is that the reason why some of Vidura's statements seem obscure? In similar vein, in popular renderings, when Droupadi is being disrobed, she prays to Krishna. Krishna provides the never-ending stream of garments that stump Duhshasana. The critical edition has excised the prayer to Krishna. The never-ending stream of garments is given as an extraordinary event. However, there is no intervention from Krishna.

How is the Mahabharata classified? The core component is the couplet or shloka. Several such shlokas form a chapter or *adhyaya*. Several adhyayas form a parva. Most people probably think that the Mahabharata has eighteen parvas. This is true, but there is another 100-parva classification that is indicated in the text itself. That is, the adhyayas can be classified either according to eighteen parvas or according to 100 parvas. The table (given on pp. xxiii–xxvi), based on the critical edition, should make this clear. As the table shows, the present critical edition only has ninety-eight parvas of the 100-parva classification, though the 100 parvas are named in the text.

Eighteen-parva classification	*100-parva classification*	*Number of adhyayas*	*Number of shlokas*
(1) Adi	1) Anukramanika[8]	1	210
	2) Parvasamgraha	1	243
	3) Poushya	1	195
	4) Pouloma	9	153
	5) Astika	41	1025
	6) Adi-vamshavatarana	5	257
	7) Sambhava	65	2394
	8) Jatugriha-daha	15	373
	9) Hidimba-vadha	6	169
	10) Baka-vadha	8	206
	11) Chaitraratha	21	557
	12) Droupadi-svayamvara	12	263
	13) Vaivahika	6	155

[8] Anukramanika is sometimes called anukramani.

Eighteen-parva classification	*100-parva classification*	*Number of adhyayas*	*Number of shlokas*
	14) Viduragamana	7	174
	15) Rajya-labha	1	50
	16) Arjuna-vanavasa	11	298
	17) Subhadra-harana	2	57
	18) Harana harika	1	82
	19) Khandava-daha	12	344
		Total = 225	Total = 7205
(2) Sabha	20) Sabha	11	429
	21) Mantra	6	222
	22) Jarasandha-vadha	5	195
	23) Digvijaya	7	191
	24) Rajasuya	3	97
	25) Arghabhiharana	4	99
	26) Shishupala-vadha	6	191
	27) Dyuta	23	734
	28) Anudyuta	7	232
		Total = 72	Total = 2387
(3) Aranyaka	29) Aranyaka	11	327
	30) Kirmira-vadha	1	75
	31) Kairata	30	1158
	32) Indralokabhigamana	37	1175
	33) Tirtha-yatra	74	2293
	34) Jatasura-vadha	1	61
	35) Yaksha-yuddha	18	727
	36) Ajagara	6	201
	37) Markandeya-samasya	43	1694
	38) Droupadi-Satyabhama-sambada	3	88
	39) Ghosha-yatra	19	519
	40) Mriga-svapna-bhaya	1	16
	41) Vrihi-drounika	3	117
	42) Droupadi-harana	36	1247
	43) Kundala-harana	11	294
	44) Araneya	5	191
		Total = 299	Total = 10239
(4) Virata	45) Vairata	12	282
	46) Kichaka-vadha	11	353
	47) Go-grahana	39	1009
	48) Vaivahika	5	179
		Total = 67	Total = 1736

Eighteen-parva classification	*100-parva classification*	*Number of adhyayas*	*Number of shlokas*
(5) Udyoga	49) Udyoga	21	575
	50) Sanjaya-yana	11	311
	51) Prajagara	9	541
	52) Sanatsujata	4	121
	53) Yana-sandhi	24	726
	54) Bhagavat-yana	65	2055
	55) Karna-upanivada	14	351
	56) Abhiniryana	4	169
	57) Bhishma-abhishechana	4	122
	58) Uluka-yana	4	101
	59) Ratha-atiratha-samkhya	9	231
	60) Amba-upakhyana	28	755
		Total = 197	Total = 6001
(6) Bhishma	61) Jambukhanda-vinirmana	11	378
	62) Bhumi	2	87
	63) Bhagavad Gita	27	994
	64) Bhishma vadha	77	3947
		Total = 117	Total = 5381
(7) Drona	65) Dronabhisheka	15	634
	66) Samshaptaka-vadha	16	717
	67) Abhimanyu-vadha	20	643
	68) Pratijna	9	365
	69) Jayadratha-vadha	61	2914
	70) Ghatotkacha-vadha	33	1642
	71) Drona-vadha	11	692
	72) Narayanastra-moksha	8	538
		Total = 173	Total = 8069
(8) Karna	73) Karna-vadha	69	3870
(9) Shalya	74) Shalya-vadha	16	844
	75) Hrada pravesha	12	664
	76) Tirtha yatra	25	1261
	77) Gada yuddha	11	546
		Total = 64	Total = 3315
(10) Souptika	78) Souptika	9	515
	79) Aishika	9	257
		Total = 18	Total = 771

Eighteen-parva classification	*100-parva classification*	*Number of adhyayas*	*Number of shlokas*
(11) Stri	80) Vishoka	8	194
	81) Stri	17	468
	82) Shraddha	1	44
	83) Jala-pradanika	1	24
		Total = 27	Total = 713
(12) Shanti	84) Raja-dharma	128	4509
	85) Apad-dharma	39	1560
	86) Moksha Dharma	186	6935
		Total = 353	Total = 13006
(13) Anushasana	87) Dana Dharma	152	6450
	88) Bhishma-svargarohana	2	84
		Total = 154	T otal = 6493
(14) Ashva-medhika	89) Ashvamedhika	96	2743
(15) Ashra-mavasika	90) Ashrama-vasa	35	737
	91) Putra Darshana	9	234
	92) Naradagamana	3	91
		Total = 47	Total = 1061
(16) Mousala	93) Mousala	9	273
(17) Mahapra-sthanika	94) Maha-Prasthanika	3	106
(18) Svargarohana	95) Svargarohana	5	194
Hari Vamsha	96) Hari-vamsha	45	2442
	97) Vishnu	68	3426
	98) Bhavishya	5	205
		Total = 118	Total = 6073
Grand total = 19	Grand total = 98 (95 + 3)	Grand total = 2113 (1995 + 118)	Grand total = 79,860 (73787 + 6073)

Thus, interpreted in terms of BORI's critical edition, the Mahabharata no longer possesses the 100,000 shlokas it is supposed to have. The figure is a little short of 75,000 (73,787 to be precise). Should the Hari Vamsha be included in a translation of the Mahabharata? It doesn't quite belong. Yet, it is described as a *khila* or supplement to the Mahabharata and BORI includes it as part of the critical edition, though in a separate volume. In this case also, the translation of the Hari Vamsha will be published in a separate and independent volume. With the Hari Vamsha, the number of shlokas increases to a shade less than 80,000 (79,860 to be precise). However, in some of the regional versions the text of the Mahabharata proper is closer to 85,000 shlokas and with the Hari Vamsha included, one approaches 95,000, though one doesn't quite touch 100,000.

Why should there be another translation of the Mahabharata? Surely, it must have been translated innumerable times. Contrary to popular impression, unabridged translations of the Mahabharata in English are extremely rare. One should not confuse abridged translations with unabridged versions. There are only five unabridged translations—by Kisori Mohan Ganguly (1883–96), by Manmatha Nath Dutt (1895–1905), by the University of Chicago and J.A.B. van Buitenen (1973 onwards), by P. Lal and Writers Workshop (2005 onwards) and the Clay Sanskrit Library edition (2005 onwards). Of these, P. Lal is more a poetic trans-creation than a translation. The Clay Sanskrit Library edition is not based on the critical edition, deliberately so. In the days of Ganguly and Dutt, the critical edition didn't exist. The language in these two versions is now archaic and there are some shlokas that these two translators decided not to include, believing them to be untranslatable in that day and age. Almost three decades later, the Chicago version is still not complete, and the Clay edition, not being translated in sequence, is still in progress. However, the primary reason for venturing into yet another translation is not just the vacuum that exists, but also reason for dissatisfaction with other attempts. Stated more explicitly, this translation, I believe, is better and more authentic—but I leave it to the reader to be the final judge. (While translating 80,000 shlokas is a hazardous venture, since Ganguly and Dutt were Bengalis, and P. Lal was one for many purposes, though not by birth, surely a fourth Bengali must also be pre-eminently qualified to embark on this venture!)

A few comments on the translation are now in order. First, there is the vexed question of diacritical marks—should they be used or not? Diacritical marks make the translation and pronunciation more accurate, but often put readers off. Sacrificing academic purity, there is thus a conscious decision to avoid diacritical marks. Second, since diacritical marks are not being used, Sanskrit words and proper names are written in what seems to be phonetically natural and the closest—such as, Droupadi rather than Draupadi. There are rare instances where avoidance of diacritical marks can cause minor confusion, for example, between Krishna (Krishnaa) as in Droupadi[8] and Krishna as in Vaasudeva. However, such instances are extremely rare and the context should make these differences, which are mostly of the gender kind, clear. Third, there are some words that simply cannot be translated. One such word is dharma. More accurately, such words are translated the first time they occur. But on subsequent occasions, they are romanized in the text. Fourth, the translation sticks to the Sanskrit text as closely as possible. If the text uses the word Kounteya, this translation will leave it as Kounteya or Kunti's son and not attempt to replace it with Arjuna. Instead, there will be a note explaining that in that specific context Kounteya refers to Arjuna or, somewhat more rarely, Yudhishthira or Bhima. This is also the case in the structure of the English sentences. To cite an instance, if a metaphor occurs towards the beginning of the Sanskrit shloka, the English sentence attempts to retain it at the beginning too. Had this not been done, the English might have read smoother. But to the extent there is a trade-off, one has stuck to what is most accurate, rather than attempting to make the English smooth and less stilted.

As the table shows, the parvas (in the eighteen-parva classification) vary widely in length. The gigantic Aranyaka or Shanti Parva can be contrasted with the slim Mousala Parva. Breaking up the translation into separate volumes based on this eighteen-parva classification therefore doesn't work. The volumes will not be remotely similar in size. Most translators seem to keep a target of ten to twelve volumes when translating all the parvas. Assuming ten volumes, 10 per cent means roughly 200 chapters and 7000 shlokas. This works rather well for Adi Parva, but collapses thereafter. Most translators therefore have Adi Parva as the first volume and then handle the heterogeneity

[9] Krishna or Krishnaa is another name for Droupadi.

across the eighteen parvas in subsequent volumes. This translation approaches the break-up of volumes somewhat differently, in the sense that roughly 10 per cent of the text is covered in each volume. The complete text, as explained earlier, is roughly 200 chapters and 7,000 shlokas per volume. For example, then, this first volume has been cut off at 199 chapters and a little less than 6,500 shlokas. It includes 90 per cent of Adi Parva, but not all of it and covers the first fifteen parvas of the 100- (or 98-) parva classification.

* * *

The Mahabharata is one of the greatest stories ever told. It has plots and subplots and meanderings and digressions. It is much more than the core story of a war between the Kouravas and the Pandavas, which everyone is familiar with, the culmination of which was the battle in Kurukshetra. In the Adi Parva, there is a lot more which happens before the Kouravas and the Pandavas actually arrive on the scene. In the 100-parva classification, the Kouravas and the Pandavas don't arrive on the scene until Section 6.

From the Vedas and Vedanta literature, we know that Janamejaya and Parikshit were historical persons. From Patanjali's grammar and other contemporary texts, we know that the Mahabharata text existed by around 400 BCE. This need not of course be the final text of Mahabharata, but could have been the original text of Jaya. The Hindu eras or *yuga*s are four in number—Satya (or Krita) Yuga, Treta Yuga, Dvapara Yuga and Kali Yuga. This cycle then repeats itself, with another Satya Yuga following Kali Yuga. The events of the Ramayana occurred in Treta Yuga. The events of the Mahabharata occurred in Dvapara Yuga. This is in line with Rama being Vishnu's seventh incarnation and Krishna being the eighth. (The ninth is Buddha and the tenth is Kalki.) We are now in Kali Yuga. Kali Yuga didn't begin with the Kurukshetra war. It began with Krishna's death, an event that occurred thirty-six years after the Kurukshetra war. Astronomical data do exist in the epic. These can be used to date the Kurukshetra war, or the advent of Kali Yuga. However, if the text was composed at different points in time, with additions and interpolations, internal consistency in astronomical data is unlikely. In popular belief, following two alternative astronomers, the Kurukshetra war has been dated to 3102 BCE (following Aryabhatta) and 2449 BCE (following Varahamihira). This doesn't mesh with the timelines of Indian history. Mahapadma Nanda ascended the throne in 382 BCE, a historical fact on which there is no dispute. The Puranas have genealogical lists. Some of these state that 1050 years elapsed between Parikshit's birth and Mahapadma Nanda's ascension. Others state that 1015 years elapsed. (When numerals are written in words, it is easy to confuse 15 with 50.) This takes Parikshit's birth and the Kurukshetra war to around 1400 BCE. This is probably the best we can do, since we also know that the Kuru kingdom flourished between 1200 BCE and 800 BCE. To keep the record straight, archaeological material has been used to bring forward the date of the Kurukshetra war to around 900 BCE, the period of the Iron Age.

As was mentioned, in popular belief, the incidents of the Ramayana took place before the incidents of the Mahabharata. The Ramayana story also figures in the Mahabharata. However, there is no reference to any significant Mahabharata detail in the Ramayana. Nevertheless, from reading the text, one gets the sense that the Mahabharata represents a more primitive society than the Ramayana. The fighting in the Ramayana is more genteel and civilized. You don't have people hurling rocks and stones at each other, or fighting with trees and bare arms. Nor do people rip apart the enemy's chest and drink blood. The geographical knowledge in the Mahabharata is also more limited than in the Ramayana, both towards the east and towards the south. In popular belief, the Kurukshetra war occurred as a result of a dispute over land and the kingdom. That is true, in so far as the present text is concerned. However, another fight over cattle took place in the Virata Parva and the Pandavas were victorious in that too. This is not the place to expand on the argument. But it is possible to construct a plausible hypothesis that this was the core dispute. Everything else was added as later embellishments. The property dispute was over cattle and not land. In human evolution, cattle represents a more primitive form of property than land. In that stage, humankind is still partly nomadic and not completely settled. If this hypothesis is true, the Mahabharata again represents an earlier period compared to the Ramayana. This leads to the following kind of proposition. In its final form, the Mahabharata was indeed composed after the Ramayana. But the earliest version of the Mahabharata was composed before the earliest version of the Ramayana. And the events of the Mahabharata occurred before the events of the Ramayana, despite popular belief. The proposition about the feud ending with Virata Parva illustrates the endless speculation that is possible with the Mahabharata material. Did Arjuna, Nakula and Sahadeva ever exist? Nakula and Sahadeva have limited roles to play in the story. Arjuna's induction could have been an attempt to assert Indra's supremacy. Arjuna represents such an integral strand in the story (and of the Bhagavad Gita), that such a suggestion is likely to be dismissed out of hand. But consider the following. Droupadi loved Arjuna a little bit more than the others. That's the reason she was denied admission to heaven. Throughout the text, there are innumerable instances where Droupadi faces difficulties. Does she ever summon Arjuna for help on such occasions? No, she does not. She summons Bhima. Therefore, did Arjuna exist at all? Or were there simply two original Pandava brothers—one powerful and strong, and the other weak and useless in physical terms. Incidentally, the eighteen-parva classification is clearly something that was done much later. The 100-parva classification seems to be older.

The Mahabharata is much more real than the Ramayana. And, therefore, much more fascinating. Every conceivable human emotion figures in it, which is the reason why it is possible to identify with it even today. The text itself states that what is not found in the Mahabharata, will not be found anywhere else. Unlike the Ramayana, India is littered with real places that have identifications with the Mahabharata. (Ayodhya or Lanka or Chitrakuta are identifications that are less certain.) Kurukshetra, Hastinapura, Indraprastha, Karnal, Mathura, Dvaraka, Gurgaon, Girivraja are real places: the list is endless. In all kinds of unlikely places, one comes across temples erected by the Pandavas when they were exiled to the forest. In some of these places, archaeological excavations have substantiated the stories. The war for regional supremacy in the Ganga–Yamuna belt is also a plausible one. The Vrishnis and the

Shurasenas (the Yadavas) are isolated, they have no clear alliance (before the Pandavas) with the powerful Kurus. There is the powerful Magadha kingdom under Jarasandha and Jarasandha had made life difficult for the Yadavas. He chased them away from Mathura to Dvaraka. Shishupala of the Chedi kingdom doesn't like Krishna and the Yadavas either. Through Kunti, Krishna has a matrimonial alliance with the Pandavas. Through Subhadra, the Yadavas have another matrimonial alliance with the Pandavas. Through another matrimonial alliance, the Pandavas obtain Drupada of Panchala as an ally. In the course of the royal sacrifice, Shishupala and Jarasandha are eliminated. Finally, there is yet another matrimonial alliance with Virata of the Matsya kingdom, through Abhimanyu. When the two sides face each other on the field of battle, they are more than evenly matched. Other than the Yadavas, the Pandavas have Panchala, Kashi, Magadha, Matsya and Chedi on their side. The Kouravas have Pragjyotisha, Anga, Kekaya, Sindhu, Avanti, Gandhara, Shalva, Bahlika and Kamboja as allies. At the end of the war, all these kings are slain and the entire geographical expanse comes under the control of the Pandavas and the Yadavas. Only Kripacharya, Ashvatthama and Kritavarma survive on the Kourava side.

Reading the Mahabharata, one forms the impression that it is based on some real incidents. That does not mean that a war on the scale that is described took place. Or that miraculous weapons and chariots were the norm. But there is such a lot of trivia, unconnected with the main story, that their inclusion seems to serve no purpose unless they were true depictions. For instance, what does the physical description of Kripa's sister and Drona's wife, Kripi, have to do with the main story? It is also more real than the Ramayana because nothing, especially the treatment of human emotions and behaviour, exists in black and white. Everything is in shades of grey. The Uttara Kanda of the Ramayana is believed to have been a later interpolation. If one excludes the Uttara Kanda, we generally know what is good. We know who is good. We know what is bad. We know who is bad. This is never the case with the Mahabharata. However, a qualification is necessary. Most of us are aware of the Mahabharata story because we have read some version or the other, typically an abridged one. Every abridged version simplifies and condenses, distills out the core story. And in doing that, it tends to paint things in black and white, fitting everything into the mould of good and bad. The Kouravas are bad. The Pandavas are good. And good eventually triumphs. The unabridged Mahabharata is anything but that. It is much more nuanced. Duryodhana isn't invariably bad. He is referred to as Suyodhana as well, and not just by his father. History is always written from the point of view of the victors. While the Mahabharata is generally laudatory towards the Pandavas, there are several places where the text has a pro-Kourava stance. There are several places where the text has an anti-Krishna stance. That's yet another reason why one should read an unabridged version, so as not to miss out on these nuances. Take the simple point about inheritance of the kingdom. Dhritarashtra was blind. Consequently, the king was Pandu. On Pandu's death, who should inherit the kingdom? Yudhishthira was the eldest among the brothers. (Actually, Karna was, though it didn't become known until later.) We thus tend to assume that the kingdom was Yudhishthira's by right, because he was the eldest. (The division of the kingdom into two, Hastinapura and Indraprastha, is a separate matter.) But such primogeniture was not universally clear. A case can also be established for Duryodhana, because he was Dhritarashtra's son. If primogeniture was the rule, the eldest son of the Pandavas was Ghatotkacha, not Abhimanyu. Before both were killed, Ghatotkacha should have had a claim to the throne. However, there is no such suggestion anywhere. The argument that Ghatotkacha was the son of a rakshasa or demon will not wash. He never exhibited any demonic qualities and was a dutiful and loving son. Karna saved up a weapon for Arjuna and this was eventually used to kill Ghatotkacha. At that time, we have the unseemly sight of Krishna dancing around in glee at Ghatotkacha being killed.

In the Mahabharata, because it is nuanced, we never quite know what is good and what is bad, who is good and who is bad. Yes, there are degrees along a continuum. But there are no watertight and neat compartments. The four objectives of human existence are dharma, artha, kama and moksha. Etymologically, dharma is that which upholds. If one goes by the Bhagavad Gita, pursuit of these four are also transient diversions. Because the fundamental objective is to transcend these four, even moksha. Within these four, the Mahabharata is about a conflict of dharma. Dharma has been reduced to *varnashrama* dharma, according to the four classes (*varna*s) and four stages of life (*ashrama*s). However, these are collective interpretations of dharma, in the sense that a Kshatriya in the *garhasthya* (householder) stage has certain duties. Dharma in the Mahabharata is individual too. Given an identical situation, a Kshatriya in the garhasthya stage might adopt a course of action that is different from that adopted by another Kshatriya in the garhasthya stage, and who is to judge what is wrong and what is right? Bhishma adopted a life of celibacy. So did Arjuna, for a limited period. In that stage of celibacy, both were approached by women who had fallen in love with them. And if those desires were not satisfied, the respective women would face difficulties, even death. Bhishma spurned the advance, but Arjuna accepted it. The conflict over dharma is not only the law versus morality conflict made famous by Krishna and Arjuna in the Bhagavad Gita. It pervades the Mahabharata, in terms of a conflict over two different notions of dharma. Having collectively married Droupadi, the Pandavas have agreed that when one of them is closeted with Droupadi, the other four will not intrude. And if there is such an instance of intrusion, they will go into self-exile. Along comes a Brahmana whose cattle have been stolen by thieves. Arjuna's weapons are in the room where Droupadi and Yudhishthira are. Which is the higher dharma? Providing succour to the Brahmana or adhering to the oath? Throughout the Mahabharata, we have such conflicts, with no clear normative indications of what is wrong and what is right, because there are indeed no absolute answers. Depending on one's decisions, one faces the consequences and this brings in the unsolvable riddle of the tension between free will and determinism, the so-called karma concept. The boundaries of philosophy and religion blur.

These conflicts over dharma are easy to identify with. It is easy to empathize with the protagonists, because we face such conflicts every day. That is precisely the reason why the Mahabharata is read even today. And the reason one says every conceivable human emotion figures in the story. Everyone familiar with the Mahabharata has thought about the decisions taken and about the characters. Why was life so unfair to Karna? Why was Krishna partial to the Pandavas? Why didn't he prevent the war? Why was Abhimanyu killed so unfairly? Why did the spirited and dark Droupadi, so unlike the Sita of the Ramayana, have to be humiliated publicly?

* * *

It is impossible to pinpoint when and how my interest in the Mahabharata started. As a mere toddler, my maternal grandmother used to tell me stories from *Chandi*, part of the Markandeya Purana. I still vividly recollect pictures from her copy of *Chandi*: Kali licking the demon Raktavija's blood. Much later, in my early teens, at school in Ramakrishna Mission, Narendrapur, I first read the Bhagavad Gita, without understanding much of what I read. The alliteration and poetry in the first chapter was attractive enough for me to learn it by heart. Perhaps the seeds were sown there. In my late teens, I stumbled upon Bankimchandra Chattopadhyay's *Krishna Charitra*, written in 1886. Bankimchandra was not only a famous novelist, he was a brilliant essayist. For a long time, *Krishna Charitra* was not available other than in Bengali. It has now been translated into English, but deserves better dissemination. A little later, when in college, I encountered Buddhadeb Bose's *Mahabharater Katha*. That was another brilliant collection of essays, first serialized in a magazine and then published as a book in 1974. This too was originally in Bengali, but is now available in English. Unlike my sons, my first exposure to the Mahabharata story came not through television serials but comic books. Upendrakishore Raychowdhury's Mahabharata (and Ramayana) for children was staple diet, later supplanted by Rajshekhar Basu's abridged versions of both epics, written for adults. Both were in Bengali. In English, there was Chakravarti Rajagopalachari's abridged translation, still a perennial favourite. Later, Chakravarthi Narasimhan's selective unabridged translation gave a flavour of what the Mahabharata actually contained. In Bengal, the Kashiram Das version of the Mahabharata, written in the seventeenth century, was quite popular. I never found this appealing. But in the late 1970s, I stumbled upon a treasure. Kolkata's famous College Street was a storehouse of old and second-hand books in those days. You never knew what you would discover when browsing. In the nineteenth century, an unabridged translation of the Mahabharata had been done in Bengali under the editorship of Kaliprasanna Singha (1840–70). I picked this up for the princely sum of Rs 5. The year may have been 1979, but Rs 5 was still amazing. This was my first complete reading of the unabridged version of the Mahabharata. This particular copy probably had antiquarian value. The pages would crumble in my hands and I soon replaced my treasured possession with a republished reprint. Not longer after, I acquired the Aryashastra version of the Mahabharata, with both the Sanskrit and the Bengali together. In the early 1980s, I was also exposed to three Marathi writers writing on the Mahabharata. There was Iravati Karve's *Yuganta*. This was available in both English and in Marathi. I read the English one first, followed by the Marathi. The English version isn't an exact translation of the Marathi and the Marathi version is far superior. Then there was Durga Bhagwat's *Vyas Parva*. This was in Marathi and I am not aware of an English translation. Finally, there was Shivaji Sawant's *Mritunjaya*, a kind of autobiography for Karna. This was available both in English and in Marathi. Incidentally, one should mention John Smith's excellent abridged translation, based on the Critical Edition, and published while this unabridged translation was going on.

In the early 1980s, quite by chance, I encountered two shlokas, one from Valmiki's Ramayana, the other from Kalidasa's *Meghadutam*. These were two poets separated by anything between 500 to 1,000 years, the exact period being an uncertain one. The shloka in *Meghadutam* is right towards the beginning, the second shloka to be precise. It is the first day in the month of Ashada. The yaksha has been cursed and has been separated from his beloved. The mountains are covered with clouds. These clouds are like elephants, bent down as if in play. The shloka in the Valmiki Ramayana occurs in Sundara Kanda. Rama now knows that Sita is in Lanka. But the monsoon stands in the way of the invasion. The clouds are streaked with flags of lightning and garlanded with geese. They are like mountain peaks and are thundering, like elephants fighting. At that time, I did not know that elephants were a standard metaphor for clouds in Sanskrit literature. I found it amazing that two different poets separated by time had thought of elephants. And because the yaksha was pining for his beloved, the elephants were playing. But because Rama was impatient to fight, the elephants were fighting. I resolved that I must read all this in the original. It was a resolution I have never regretted. I think that anyone who has not read *Meghadutam* in Sanskrit has missed out on a thing of beauty that will continue to be a joy for generations to come.

In the early 1980s, Professor Ashok Rudra was a professor of economics in Visva-Bharati, Santiniketan. I used to teach in Presidency College, Kolkata, and we sometimes met. Professor Rudra was a left-wing economist and didn't think much of my economics. I dare say the feeling was reciprocated. By tacit agreement, we never discussed economics. Instead, we discussed Indological subjects. At that point, Professor Rudra used to write essays on such subjects in Bengali. I casually remarked, 'I want to do a statistical test on the frequency with which the five Pandavas used various weapons in the Kurukshetra war.' Most sensible men would have dismissed the thought as crazy. But Professor Rudra wasn't sensible by usual norms of behaviour and he was also a trained statistician. He encouraged me to do the paper, written and published in Bengali, using the Aryashastra edition. Several similar papers followed, written in Bengali. In 1983, I moved to Pune, to the Gokhale Institute of Politics and Economics, a stone's throw away from BORI. *Annals of the Bhandarkar Oriental Research Institute (ABORI)* is one of the most respected journals in Indology. Professor G.B. Palsule was then the editor of ABORI and later went on to become Director of BORI. I translated one of the Bengali essays into English and went and met Professor Palsule, hoping to get it published in ABORI. To Professor Palsule's eternal credit, he didn't throw the dilettante out. Instead, he said he would get the paper refereed. The referee's substantive criticism was that the paper should have been based on the critical edition, which is how I came to know about it. Eventually, this paper (and a few more) were published in ABORI. In 1989, these became a book titled *Essays on the Ramayana and the Mahabharata*, published when the Mahabharata frenzy had reached a peak on television. The book got excellent reviews, but hardly sold. It is now out of print. As an aside, the book was jointly dedicated to Professor Rudra and Professor Palsule, a famous economist and a famous Indologist respectively. Both were flattered. However, when I gave him a copy, Professor Rudra said, 'Thank you very much. But who is Professor Palsule?' And Professor Palsule remarked, 'Thank you very much. But who is Professor Rudra?'

While the research interest in the Mahabharata remained, I got sidetracked into translating. Through the 1990s, there were abridged translations of the Maha Puranas, the Vedas and the eleven major Upanishads. I found that I enjoyed translating from the Sanskrit to English and since these volumes were well received, perhaps I did do a good job. With Penguin as publisher, I did a translation of the Bhagavad Gita, something I had always wanted to do. *Sarama and Her Children*, a book on attitudes towards dogs in India, also with Penguin, followed. I kept thinking about doing an unabridged translation of the Mahabharata and waited to muster up the courage. That courage now exists, though the task is daunting. With something like two million words and ten volumes expected, the exercise seems open-ended. But why translate the Mahabharata? In 1924, George Mallory, with his fellow climber Andrew Irvine, may or may not have climbed Mount Everest. They were last seen a few hundred metres from the summit, before they died. Mallory was once asked why he wanted to climb Everest and he answered, 'Because it's there.' Taken out of context, there is no better reason for wanting to translate the Mahabharata. There is a steep mountain to climb. And I would not have dared had I not been able to stand on the shoulders of the three intellectual giants who have preceded me—Kisori Mohan Ganguli, Manmatha Nath Dutt and J.A.B. van Buitenen.

Bibek Debroy

Shanti Parva

Shanti Parva is a parva that is about peace, *shanti* meaning peace. In the 18-parva classification, Shanti Parva is the twelfth and is the longest parva of the Mahabharata. In the 100-parva classification, Shanti Parva constitutes sections 84 to 86. Shanti Parva has 353 chapters. In the numbering of the chapters in Shanti Parva, the first number is a consecutive one, starting with the beginning of the Mahabharata. And the second number, within brackets, is the numbering of the chapter within Shanti Parva.

SECTION EIGHTY-SIX

Moksha Dharma Parva

This parva has 6,935 shlokas and 186 chapters.

Chapter 1496(168): 53 shlokas
Chapter 1497(169): 37 shlokas
Chapter 1498(170): 23 shlokas
Chapter 1499(171): 61 shlokas
Chapter 1500(172): 37 shlokas
Chapter 1501(173): 52 shlokas
Chapter 1502(174): 20 shlokas
Chapter 1503(175): 37 shlokas
Chapter 1504(176): 17 shlokas
Chapter 1505(177): 39 shlokas
Chapter 1506(178): 17 shlokas
Chapter 1507(179): 15 shlokas
Chapter 1508(180): 30 shlokas
Chapter 1509(181): 20 shlokas
Chapter 1510(182): 17 shlokas
Chapter 1511(183): 16 shlokas
Chapter 1512(184): 18 shlokas
Chapter 1513(185): 27 shlokas
Chapter 1514(186): 32 shlokas
Chapter 1515(187): 60 shlokas
Chapter 1516(188): 22 shlokas
Chapter 1517(189): 21 shlokas
Chapter 1518(190): 13 shlokas
Chapter 1519(191): 11 shlokas
Chapter 1520(192): 127 shlokas
Chapter 1521(193): 32 shlokas
Chapter 1522(194): 24 shlokas
Chapter 1523(195): 23 shlokas
Chapter 1524(196): 23 shlokas
Chapter 1525(197): 20 shlokas
Chapter 1526(198): 18 shlokas
Chapter 1527(199): 32 shlokas
Chapter 1528(200): 46 shlokas
Chapter 1529(201): 35 shlokas
Chapter 1530(202): 33 shlokas
Chapter 1531(203): 43 shlokas
Chapter 1532(204): 16 shlokas
Chapter 1533(205): 33 shlokas
Chapter 1534(206): 21 shlokas
Chapter 1535(207): 29 shlokas
Chapter 1536(208): 26 shlokas
Chapter 1537(209): 20 shlokas

Chapter 1538(210): 36 shlokas
Chapter 1539(211): 48 shlokas
Chapter 1540(212): 52 shlokas
Chapter 1541(213): 18 shlokas
Chapter 1542(214): 16 shlokas
Chapter 1543(215): 37 shlokas
Chapter 1544(216): 28 shlokas
Chapter 1545(217): 59 shlokas
Chapter 1546(218): 38 shlokas
Chapter 1547(219): 23 shlokas
Chapter 1548(220): 118 shlokas
Chapter 1549(221): 94 shlokas
Chapter 1550(222): 24 shlokas
Chapter 1551(223): 23 shlokas
Chapter 1552(224): 75 shlokas
Chapter 1553(225): 16 shlokas
Chapter 1554(226): 38 shlokas
Chapter 1555(227): 31 shlokas
Chapter 1556(228): 38 shlokas
Chapter 1557(229): 25 shlokas
Chapter 1558(230): 21 shlokas
Chapter 1559(231): 34 shlokas
Chapter 1560(232): 34 shlokas
Chapter 1561(233): 20 shlokas
Chapter 1562(234): 29 shlokas
Chapter 1563(235): 27 shlokas
Chapter 1564(236): 30 shlokas
Chapter 1565(237): 36 shlokas
Chapter 1566(238): 20 shlokas
Chapter 1567(239): 25 shlokas
Chapter 1568(240): 22 shlokas
Chapter 1569(241): 14 shlokas
Chapter 1570(242): 25 shlokas
Chapter 1571(243): 23 shlokas
Chapter 1572(244): 12 shlokas
Chapter 1573(245): 14 shlokas
Chapter 1574(246): 15 shlokas
Chapter 1575(247): 13 shlokas
Chapter 1576(248): 21 shlokas
Chapter 1577(249): 22 shlokas
Chapter 1578(250): 41 shlokas
Chapter 1579(251): 26 shlokas
Chapter 1580(252): 20 shlokas
Chapter 1581(253): 51 shlokas
Chapter 1582(254): 52 shlokas
Chapter 1583(255): 41 shlokas
Chapter 1584(256): 22 shlokas
Chapter 1585(257): 13 shlokas
Chapter 1586(258): 75 shlokas
Chapter 1587(259): 35 shlokas
Chapter 1588(260): 39 shlokas
Chapter 1589(261): 61 shlokas
Chapter 1590(262): 45 shlokas
Chapter 1591(263): 55 shlokas
Chapter 1592(264): 19 shlokas
Chapter 1593(265): 23 shlokas
Chapter 1594(266): 19 shlokas
Chapter 1595(267): 38 shlokas
Chapter 1596(268): 14 shlokas
Chapter 1597(269): 20 shlokas
Chapter 1598(270): 34 shlokas
Chapter 1599(271): 69 shlokas
Chapter 1600(272): 44 shlokas
Chapter 1601(273): 63 shlokas
Chapter 1602(274): 60 shlokas
Chapter 1603(275): 21 shlokas
Chapter 1604(276): 58 shlokas
Chapter 1605(277): 47 shlokas
Chapter 1606(278): 38 shlokas
Chapter 1607(279): 25 shlokas

Chapter 1608(280): 23 shlokas
Chapter 1609(281): 23 shlokas
Chapter 1610(282): 21 shlokas
Chapter 1611(283): 30 shlokas
Chapter 1612(284): 39 shlokas
Chapter 1613(285): 39 shlokas
Chapter 1614(286): 41 shlokas
Chapter 1615(287): 45 shlokas
Chapter 1616(288): 45 shlokas
Chapter 1617(289): 62 shlokas
Chapter 1618(290): 110 shlokas
Chapter 1619(291): 48 shlokas
Chapter 1620(292): 48 shlokas
Chapter 1621(293): 50 shlokas
Chapter 1622(294): 49 shlokas
Chapter 1623(295): 46 shlokas
Chapter 1624(296): 50 shlokas
Chapter 1625(297): 25 shlokas
Chapter 1626(298): 26 shlokas
Chapter 1627(299): 18 shlokas
Chapter 1628(300): 17 shlokas
Chapter 1629(301): 27 shlokas
Chapter 1630(302): 18 shlokas
Chapter 1631(303): 21 shlokas
Chapter 1632(304): 27 shlokas
Chapter 1633(305): 21 shlokas
Chapter 1634(306): 108 shlokas
Chapter 1635(307): 14 shlokas
Chapter 1636(308): 191 shlokas
Chapter 1637(309): 52 shlokas
Chapter 1638(310): 29 shlokas
Chapter 1639(311): 27 shlokas
Chapter 1640(312): 46 shlokas
Chapter 1641(313): 51 shlokas
Chapter 1642(314): 49 shlokas
Chapter 1643(315): 57 shlokas
Chapter 1644(316): 59 shlokas
Chapter 1645(317): 30 shlokas
Chapter 1646(318): 63 shlokas
Chapter 1647(319): 29 shlokas
Chapter 1648(320): 41 shlokas
Chapter 1649(321): 43 shlokas
Chapter 1650(322): 52 shlokas
Chapter 1651(323): 57 shlokas
Chapter 1652(324): 39 shlokas
Chapter 1653(325): 4 shlokas
Chapter 1654(326): 124 shlokas
Chapter 1655(327): 107 shlokas
Chapter 1656(328): 53 shlokas
Chapter 1657(329): 50 shlokas
Chapter 1658(330):71 shlokas
Chapter 1659(331): 52 shlokas
Chapter 1660(332): 26 shlokas
Chapter 1661(333): 25 shlokas
Chapter 1662(334): 17 shlokas
Chapter 1663(335): 89 shlokas
Chapter 1664(336): 82 shlokas
Chapter 1665(337): 69 shlokas
Chapter 1666(338): 25 shlokas
Chapter 1667(339): 21 shlokas
Chapter 1668(340): 11 shlokas
Chapter 1669(341): 9 shlokas
Chapter 1670(342): 16 shlokas
Chapter 1671(343): 11 shlokas
Chapter 1672(344): 10 shlokas
Chapter 1673(345): 13 shlokas
Chapter 1674(346): 13 shlokas
Chapter 1675(347): 16 shlokas
Chapter 1676(348): 20 shlokas
Chapter 1677(349): 16 shlokas

Moksha means liberation, as opposed to the pursuit of dharma, artha and kama.

Chapter 1528(200)

'Yudhishthira said, "O grandfather! O immensely wise one! O best among the Bharata lineage! I wish to hear the truth about Pundarikaksha, Achyuta, the creator who himself has not been created, Vishnu, from whom all beings originate and into whom they all return, Narayana, Hrishikesha, the unvanquished Govinda, Keshava."

'Bhishma replied, "I have heard the truth about this from Jamadagni's son, Rama,[1] when he spoke about it, from *devarshi* Narada and from Krishna Dvaipayana.[2] O son! Asita-Devala,[3] the immensely ascetic Valmiki and Markandeya have spoken about the extraordinarily great Govinda. O foremost among the Bharata lineage! Keshava is the illustrious almighty lord. He is Purusha and pervades everything. The lord is heard of in many ways. O mighty-armed one! O Yudhishthira! He is the wielder of the *sharnga* bow.[4] Learned brahmanas in the world have spoken about his greatness. Listen to this. O Indra among men! People who know about the ancient accounts speak about this. Govinda's qualities are infinite and I will recount them to you. He is the great being. He is in all beings. Purushottama is great in his soul. He created wind, energy, water, space and the earth. The lord, the god of all beings, looked at the earth. The great-souled Purushottama proceeded to lie down on

[1]Parashurama.

[2]Vedavyasa.

[3]Famous sages, Asita and Devala, but often referred to together as Asita-Devala.

the water. The first among all the beings was full of energy and lay down on that supreme bed and created attraction.[5] We have heard that the soul of all beings created this refuge of all beings through his mental powers and this sustains both the past and the future. O mighty-armed one! After that had been created, a celestial lotus sprouted from the great-souled one's navel and it had the radiance of the sun. O son! The illustrious god Brahma, the grandfather of all beings, was created from that lotus and the directions shone with his radiance. O mighty-armed one! When that great-souled one manifested himself, there was a great asura named Madhu, who had earlier been born from darkness. He was fierce. He was fierce in his deeds and his resolution was fierce.[6] To ensure Brahma's welfare, Purushottama slew him. O son! Because of this act of slaying, all the gods, *danava*s and humans came to call that bull among all the Satvatas by the name of Madhusudana.[7]

'"Through his mental powers, Brahma created seven sons, Daksha and the others—Marichi, Atri, Angiras, Pulastya, Pulaha and Kratu.[8] O son! Through his mental powers, Marichi created his first son, Kashyapa. He was like Brahma in his energy. O foremost among the Bharata lineage! Even before Marichi had been created, from his toe, Brahma created the Prajapati named Daksha.[9] O descendant of the Bharata lineage! Thirteen daughters were first born to him. The eldest of Prajapati's daughters was Diti. O son! Marichi's son, Kashyapa, knew about all forms of dharma, was immensely illustrious and auspicious in his deeds. He became a husband to all of them. Daksha Prajapati, the immensely fortunate one, who knew about dharma, then had ten other daughters and gave them to Dharma. O descendant of the Bharata lineage! Dharma's sons

[4]Bow made of horn. Vishnu and Krishna's bow.

[5]The text uses the word *samkarshana*. This is also interpreted as consciousness.

[6]Madhu wished to kill Brahma.

[7]Madhusudana means the slayer of Madhu. The Satvatas are Yadavas and Krishna is the bull among the Satvatas. Krishna is being equated with Vishnu.

[8]Accounts of creation and names differ and are not always consistent.

[9]Prajapati literally means the lord of beings. The term is applied to those of Brahma's sons who had offspring and became lords of their creations.

were the Vasus, the infinitely energetic Rudras, the Vishvadevas, the Sadhyas and the Maruts. He[10] then had twenty-seven younger daughters. The immensely fortunate Soma[11] became a husband to all of them. The others[12] gave birth to *gandharvas*,[13] horses, birds, cattle, *kimpurushas*,[14] fish, plants and trees. Aditi gave birth to the Adityas, the immensely strong ones who were foremost among the gods. The lord Vishnu, also known as Govinda, was born among them as a dwarf.[15] Through his valour, the prosperity of the gods increased and the danavas were vanquished. Diti's offspring were the *asuras*.[16] Danu gave birth to danavas and Viprachitti was foremost among them. Diti gave birth to all the great-spirited asuras.

'"Madhusudana also created day and night, the proper reckoning of time, forenoon and afternoon. Using his intelligence, he created clouds from the water and mobile and immobile objects. The immensely energetic one created the earth and its directions. O Yudhishthira! O bull among the Bharata lineage! The mighty-armed lord Krishna, Keshava, then again created one hundred brahmanas from his mouth, one hundred kshatriyas from his arms, one hundred vaishyas from his thighs and one hundred shudras from his feet. The immensely illustrious one thus created the four varnas. The lord made Dhata the supervisor of all beings.[17] In those days, men could

[10]Daksha.

[11]The moon.

[12]Kashyapa's other wives.

[13]Gandharvas are celestial musicians and are semi-divine.

[14]*Kinnaras* or kimpurushas are mythical beings who were followers of Kubera and could sing well. They were also physically deformed, sometimes described as possessing human heads and bodies of horses.

[15]Vishnu's *vamana* (dwarf) incarnation. In this incarnation, Vishnu tricked the demon king, Bali, and took his kingdom away.

[16]There are three terms for demons, often used synonomously. Asura is actually the antithesis of *sura*, god. Danavas are the offspring of Danu, while *daityas* are the offspring of Diti.

[17]Meaning Brahma. The words Dhata and Vidhata are used synonymously, but have slightly different nuances. Vidhata is more like creator, while Dhata is more like presever.

live for as long as they wished to and there was no fear on account of Yama. O bull among the Bharata lineage! At that time, offspring were generated from resolution alone and there was no need to resort to the dharma of sexual intercourse. O lord of men! During the period of *treta yuga* too, offspring resulted from resolution and there was no need for the dharma of sexual intercourse.[18] O king! During dvapara, offspring were generated through the dharma of sexual intercourse. O king! In kali yuga, people began to live in pairs. O son! I have told you about the lord of all beings, the one who rules himself. O Kounteya! I will now tell you about the ones who cannot be controlled—all those who are born in the southern regions, the Talavaras, the Andhrakas, the Utsas, the Pulindas, the Shabaras, the Chuchupas and the Mandapas. I will also recount to you those born in the northern regions, the Younas, the Kambojas, the Gandharas, the Kiratas and the Barbaras. O son! These are the performers of wicked deeds and roam around on earth. O lord of men! They follow the dharma of dogs, crows, ravens and vultures. O son! They did not roam around on earth during krita yuga. O bull among the Bharata lineage! Such people originated during treta yuga. When that extremely terrible intervening period that comes at the end of a yuga arrived,[19] the kings approached each other and began

[18]Yuga is an era or epoch. Each of Brahma's days consists of four yugas—*satya*, treta, *dvapara* and *kali*. But before that, time is not the same for the gods and humans. Six human months correspond to a divine day and six human months correspond to a divine night. Therefore, 360 human years are equivalent to one divine year. Measured in divine years, satya yuga is 4,000 years, treta yuga is 3,000 years, dvapara yuga is 2,000 years and kali yuga is 1,000 years, giving a total of 10,000 years. But there are also some years as transition periods from one yuga to another, so a four-yuga cycle actually consists of 12,000 divine years. A four-yuga cycle, known as *mahayuga*, is therefore 4,320,000 human years, satya yuga contributing 1,728,000, treta yuga 1,296,000, dvapara yuga 864,000 and kali yuga 432,000 years. one thousand mahayugas are Brahma's day and another 1,000 mahayugas are Brahma's night. Each of Brahma's days is called a *kalpa*. The beginning of a kalpa is when creation occurs and at the end of the kalpa, there is destruction.

[19]Probably the intervening period between treta yuga and dvapara yuga.

to fight. O best of the Kuru lineage! In this way, the great-souled one created everything. Devarshi Narada has spoken about the god as the creator of all the worlds. O lord of men! O mighty-armed one! O bull among the Bharata lineage! Narada thinks that Krishna is supreme and eternal. This is the nature of Keshava, for whom, truth is his valour. Pundarikaksha is not only a man. He is inconceivable."'

Chapter 1529(201)

'Yudhishthira asked, "O bull among the Bharata lineage! Who were the first Prajapatis? Who are the immensely fortunate rishis and what directions do they preside over?"

'Bhishma replied, "O best among the Bharata lineage! I will tell you about what you have asked. Listen to the Prajapatis and the directions that each of them was said to preside over. There was the single, illustrious, original and eternal Svayambhu Brahma. The great-souled Svayambhu Brahma had seven sons—Marichi, Atri, Angiras, Pulastya, Pulaha, Kratu and the immensely illustrious Vasishtha, who was like Svayambhu himself. The Puranas refer to them as the seven brahmanas. These were the first. I will now tell you about all the other Prajapatis. In Atri's lineage was born the illustrious, eternal and ancient Barhi, descended from Brahma himself. The ten Prachetas were descended from him and those ten only had a single son—the Prajapati named Daksha. In this world, Daksha is known by both the names. Marichi's son, Kashyapa, is also known by two names. Some learned ones know him as Arishtanemi.[20] The handsome and valiant Bhouma was born to Angiras. He performed worship for one thousand divine yugas. O lord! The illustrious Aryama and others were his sons. They are famous as ones who laid down ordinances and created beings. O one without decay! Shashabindu[21] had ten

[20]The other name being Kashyapa.

[21]Clearly, another of Bhouma's sons.

thousand wives. Through each of them, he had one thousand sons. In this way, the great-souled one had one million sons. These sons did not allow anyone else to be a Prajapati. The ancient brahmanas addressed Shashabindu's offspring by this name and from that great lineage of Prajapatis originated the Vrishni lineage. I have told you about the illustrious Prajapatis.

'"I will now tell you about the gods who are the rulers of the three worlds—Bhaga, Amsha, Aryama, Mitra, Varuna, Savita, Dhata, the immensely strong Vivasvat, Pusha, Tvashta, Indra and Vishnu is said to be the twelfth. These twelve Adityas were descended from Kashyapa. Nasatya and Dasra are known as the two Ashvins. They were the sons of Martanda, the eighth of the Prajapatis.[22] Tvashta had handsome and immensely illustrious sons—Vishvarupa, Aja-Ekapada, Ahi, Budha, Virupaksha, Raivata, Hara, Bahurupa, Tryambaka as the lord of the gods, Savitra, Jayanta and the unvanquished Pinaki.The immensely illustrious eight Vasus have already been mentioned earlier. At the time of Prajapati Manu, these were the different kinds of gods. At first, they were known as both gods and ancestors. Among the Siddhas and the Sadhyas, depending on conduct and beauty, there were different types. The Ribhus and Maruts are categories of gods. In this way, the Vishvadevas and the Ashvins are revered. The Adityas are kshatriyas and the Maruts are vaishyas. The Ashvins are held to be shudras and performed fierce austerities. The gods descended from Angiras have certainly been determined to be brahmanas. I have thus recounted the four varnas among all the gods. If a person gets up in the morning and recites the names of the gods, he is freed from all sins, regardless of whether they have been committed by him or by others.[23] Yavakriti, Raibhya, Arvavasu, Paravasu, Oushija, Kakshivat and Bala were the sons of Angiras. O son! These, Kanva, the son of rishi Medhatithi,

[22]Meaning, the eighth in the list of Adityas. The eighth is Vivasvat or Martanda, the sun god, and the Ashvins were descended from him.

[23]A person can also be tainted by the sins of others.

[24]The seven great sages.

Barhishada and the *saptarshis*[24] who created the three worlds are in the east. Unmucha, Vimucha, the valiant Svastyatreya, Pramucha, Idhmavaha, the illustrious Dridavrata and Agastya, the son of Mitra-Varuna—these brahmana rishis always resort to the southern direction. Rushadgu, Kavasha, Dhoumya, the valiant Parivyadha, the *maharshis* known as Ekata, Dvita and Trita and Atri's son, the illustrious lord Sarasvata—these nine great-souled ones resort to the western direction. Atreya, Vasishtha, the great rishi Kashyapa, Goutama, Bharadvaja, Koushika Vishvamitra and Jamadagni, the great-souled and illustrious son of Richika—these seven resort to the northern direction. I have recounted to you the fiercely engertic ones in all the directions. These great-souled ones are the creators of beings and are witnesses. In this way, these great-souled ones are established in each of the directions. If one recites their names, one is freed from all sins. If a person seeks refuge in a direction that they preside over, he is freed from all sins and safely returns home."'

Chapter 1530(202)

'Yudhishthira said, "O grandfather! O immensely wise one! O one who has the valour of truth in battle! I wish to hear everything about lord Krishna, who is without decay. He has performed extremely great and energetic deeds in ancient times. O bull among the Bharata lineage! Accurately tell me everything about them. Why did Hari assume the form of an inferior species? What tasks did he accomplish? O grandfather! Tell me this."

'Bhishma replied, "Earlier, I went out on a hunt and went to Markandeya's hermitage. There I saw many hermits seated, in their thousands. They honoured me by offering me *madhuparka*.[25] Accepting that, I worshipped and honoured the rishis back in return.

[25]A respectful offering made to guests or bridegrooms, consisting of honey and curd.

What I will recount was stated by maharshi Kashyapa there. It is divine and delights the mind. Listen attentively. In ancient times, the foremost danavas were full of anger and avarice. There were also hundreds of giant asuras, intoxicated by their strength, Naraka and the others. There were many other danavas too, invincible in battle. They could not tolerate the supreme prosperity of the gods. The gods and devarshis were oppressed by the danavas. O king! They could not find any peace and fled in different directions. The residents of heaven saw that the earth was in a miserable state. It was full of danavas who were terrible in form and were extremely strong. Afflicted by the load of that burden, it was miserable and submerged.[26] The Adityas were terrified. They went to Brahma and said, 'O Brahma! How will we continue to bear the depredations of the danavas?' Svayambhu replied, 'I have already ordained what needs to be done. They are powerful and intoxicated because of boons. Those stupid ones do not know that Vishnu, whose form cannot be seen, has assumed the form of a boar.[27] That god cannot be assailed, even by all the immortals together. He will swiftly go to the spot where those worst among danavas are. Thousands of those terrible ones reside inside the bowels of the earth. He will pacify them all.' Hearing this, the supreme ones among the gods were delighted. The immensely energetic Vishnu assumed the form of a boar. He penetrated the nether regions and advanced against Diti's offspring. On seeing that superhuman being, all the daityas united. Goaded by destiny, all of them advanced violently and encircled him. From every direction, they rushed against the boar and seized it. From every direction, they angrily tugged at the boar. The Indras among the danavas were gigantic in form. They were immensely valorous and full of strength. O lord! But they were not able to do anything at all. Those Indras among the danavas were then terrified and overcome by fear. Though there were thousands of them, they were full of doubt in their minds. The god of the gods is the soul of yoga and the charioteer of yoga. O supreme among the Bharata lineage! The illustrious one resorted to yoga. He emitted a mighty roar

[26]Dragged down into the nether regions.

[27]Vishnu in his boar (*varaha*) incarnation.

and agitated those daityas and danavas. The worlds and all the ten directions seemed to resound with these roars. At the sounds of those roars, all the worlds were agitated. The directions, and all the gods, with Shakra[28] at the forefront, were frightened. The entire universe was severely afflicted and became immobile. Mobile and immobile objects were confused by that roar. All the danavas were terrified by that noise. They lost their lives and fell down, confused by Vishnu's energy. Those who hated the thirty gods sought refuge in *rasatala*.[29] But the boar tore into them with his hooves and mangled their flesh, fat and bones. Because of that great roar, he came to be known as Sanatana.[30] He is Padmanabha,[31] the great yogi, the preceptor of all beings and the king of all beings. All the large number of gods went to the grandfather and asked, 'O lord! O god! Who is roaring like this? We cannot understand this. Who is this? Whom does this roar belong to? It has paralysed the universe.' At that time, Vishnu was in his form of a boar and the maharshis praised the great god. The grandfather replied, 'He has slain the lords among the danavas. He is great in his form and great in his strength. This god is the great yogi. He is the soul of all beings and the creator of all beings. He is the yogi who is the lord of all beings. He is the womb. He is the atman. Be steady. He is Krishna, the destroyer of all sins. He is the immensely radiant one and has accomplished a task that others would have found impossible to undertake. He has now returned to his own atman. He is immensely fortunate and immensely radiant. He is Padmanabha, the great yogi. He is the soul of all beings and the creator of all beings. O supreme among the gods! You should not be tormented. Nor should you be frightened, or grieve. He is the one who ordains. He is the creator. He is time, the destroyer of everything. He is the one who holds up the worlds. He is the great-souled one who emitted the roar. He is

[28]Indra.

[29]Nether region. There are seven nether regions—*atala, vitala, sutala*, rasatala, *talatala, mahatala* and *patala*.

[30]This is contrived. *Sanaṭana* means eternal. *Nadana* means sound and *Sanadana* would mean someone with a sound.

[31]With a lotus in the navel.

the immensely fortunate one, revered by the worlds. He is Achyuta Pundarikaksha,[32] the origin of all beings.'"'

Chapter 1531(203)

'Yudhishthira said, "O father![33] O descendant of the Bharata lineage! Tell me about the supreme yoga of moksha. O supreme among eloquent ones! I wish to know the truth about this."

'Bhishma replied, "In this connection, an ancient history is recounted about a conversation on moksha between a preceptor and a disciple. There was a supreme brahmana rishi who was a preceptor. His disciple was extremely intelligent and desirous of welfare. While the preceptor was seated, the disciple controlled himself and touched his feet. With hands joined in salutation, he said, 'O illustrious one! I have a great doubt in my mind. If you are satisfied with my worship, you should explain this. Where have I come from? Where have you come from? What happens thereafter? Tell me accurately. O supreme among brahmanas! If all beings are the same and if their driving force is the same, why are their origin and destruction so different from each other? There are also detailed words in the Vedas about different kinds of people.[34] You know the truth about this and you should explain all this to me.'

'"The preceptor said, 'O disciple! O immensely wise one! Listen to the supreme mystery about the brahman, described in the sacred texts. This is *adhyatma* and represents wealth for all beings. Vasudeva is everything in the universe. He is the mouth of the brahman. He is truthfulness, generosity, sacrifices, renunciation, self-control and

[32]Respectively, the one without decay and the lotus-eyed one.

[33]The word used is *tata*. This means father, but is affectionately used towards anyone who is older or senior.

[34]If people are the same, why are there different ordinances for different people?

uprightness. He is the eternal Purusha. Those who know the Vedas know him as Vishnu. He is the cause of creation and destruction. He is the eternal brahman, who is not manifest. That brahman was born in the Vrishni lineage. Listen to the history. Brahmanas should hear this from brahmanas and kings from kshatriyas. This is about the greatness of the god of the gods, the infinitely energetic Vishnu. You should hear about the supreme Varshneya, since that will ensure your welfare. He is the wheel of time. He is without beginning and without end. His signs are both existence and non-existence. He is the one who makes all beings in the three worlds revolve on the wheel. He is Akshara.[35] He is Avyakta.[36] He is Amrita.[37] He is the eternal brahman. Keshava is spoken of as a tiger among men and a bull among men. The supreme and undecaying one created the ancestors, the gods, the rishis, the *yakshas*,[38] the danavas, the serpents, the asuras and human beings. In that way, the lord created the sacred texts of the Vedas and the eternal dharma of the worlds. Having destroyed everything, at the beginning of a new yuga, he creates nature.[39] As seasons with their many different signs and forms progressively come into being, these are also seen at the end of Brahma's night. Through the progress of time, different yugas come into being. For the advance of the worlds, different kinds of knowledge are also decreed. At the end of a yuga, the Vedas and the histories also disappear. However, having obtained Svayambhu's prior permission, the maharshis get them back through their austerities. The illustrious Brihaspati knew about the Vedas and the Vedangas.[40]

[35]Literally, the syllable or the word. *Akshara* also means the brahman and is one of Vishnu's names. The word also means immutable.

[36]Not manifest.

[37]Immortal.

[38]Yakshas are semi-divine species and companions of Kubera, the god of treasure.

[39]The text uses the word *prakriti*, which also has nuances other than nature.

[40]The six Vedangas are *shiksha* (articulation and pronunciation), *chhanda* (prosody), *vyakarana* (grammar), *nirukta* (etymology), *jyotisha* (astronomy) and *kalpa* (rituals).

For the sake of the universe and for the welfare of the universe, Bhargava obtained the sacred texts about good policy.[41] Narada accepted the knowledge about gandharva[42]and Bharadvaja about bows.[43] Gargya learnt about the conduct of the devarshis and Krishnatreya about medicine. There were many others who were learned and spoke about *nyaya*,[44] *tantra*, reasoning and the sacred texts. Let him[45] be worshipped through good conduct.'

'"Neither the gods nor the rishis were capacble of comprehending the supreme brahman. The illustrious lord, Dhata Narayana, was the only one who comprehended him. From Narayana, the large numbers of rishis, the foremost among the gods and the asuras and the ancient *rajarshi*s got to know about the supreme one, who is the medication for all misery. With the appropriate cause, prakriti always brings forth, urged by the sentiments of *purusha*, and the entire universe begins to whirl around.[46] This is like thousands of lamps being lit from another lamp. In that way, prakriti creates many other things, but is not exhausted. Though it is not manifest, it creates intelligence and ego, which lead to acts. Space results from ego and wind results from space. Energy results from wind. Water results from energy and the earth is created from water. These are the eight foundations of prakriti and the universe is established on these.[47] The five senses of knowledge, the five organs of action, the five objects of the senses and the mind, as the sixteenth, result from transformations of these. The ears, the skin, the eyes, the tongue

[41]Bhargava means Shukra or Shukracharya. We have translated *niti* as good policy. Shukracharya was descended from Bhrigu.

[42]Singing, dancing and music.

[43]Archery and the science of fighting.

[44]Logical principles, or the school of philosophy known as Nyaya.

[45]Brahma.

[46]In *sankhya* philosophy, prakriti is the original source of the material world and is active. Purusha is inert or inactive.

[47]Intelligence, ego, space, wind, energy, water and earth add up to seven. Prakriti must be added to get eight. More plausibly, mind has been missed out in the listing.

and the nose are the five senses. The feet, the anus, the genitals, the mouth and the hands are the five organs of action. Sound, touch, form, taste and smell are what are to be known and pervade the consciousness, the mind going everywhere. It[48] knows taste through the tongue and is said to become words. United with the senses, the mind is engaged in everything. In their various forms, these sixteen should be known as divinities. They bring about knowledge within the body and are worshipped by those who know about worshipping. The tongue represents the qualities of water, smell the qualities of the earth, hearing the qualities of sound[49] and touch the qualities of the wind. This is always known to be the case with all beings. It is said that the mind is the quality of existence. Existence arises from that which is not manifest. Those who are intelligent know that it[50] is there in all beings, as the soul of beings. Its attributes are borne by the entire universe, by mobile and immobile objects. The blazing radiance of that god is said to be the supreme objective. This sacred city with nine gates[51] possesses all these characteristics. The great atman pervades and lies down inside and is known as purusha. It is without decay. It is immortal. It knows about what is manifest and also about what is not manifest. It is pervasive, with qualities, and subtle. It is the refuge of all beings and their qualities. A lamp shows whether a person is small or large. In that way, in all creatures, one can know the purusha through the knowledge of the atman. It is the one who knows what is to be known. It is the one who hears and sees. It is the reason behind this body. It is the doer of all the deeds. There is fire in wood, but it cannot be seen if the wood is cut. In that way, the atman is inside the body, but it can only be seen through yoga.

[48]The mind.

[49]The Critical edition uses the word *shabda* (sound). Non-critical versions have *nabha* (space), which fits better.

[50]The brahman.

[51]The body. The nine gates of the body are two eyes, two ears, two nostrils, the mouth, the anus and the genital organ.

The river has water and there are rays attached to the sun. In that way, it[52] goes where the body goes. Where there is the body, the soul is there. When a person dreams, the atman and the five senses leave the body. Like that, when the body is cast aside,[53] the atman departs and obtains another. It is bound down by its earlier acts and obtains the consequences of those acts. The powerful force of its own deeds conveys it elsewhere. Having left one body, it obtains another body and another one after that. I will now tell you about how beings naturally follow their own acts."'

Chapter 1532(204)

'"The preceptor said, 'All mobile and immobile beings belong to four categories. They are not manifest, alive, manifest and dead. Know that the mind exists in the atman, which is not manifest. It[54] is not manifest and it is destroyed. A giant tree may be hidden inside the small blossom of an *ashvattha* flower. It is seen only when it has emerged. Like that, the manifest is created from what is not manifest. A piece of iron has no consciousness, but advances towards a lodestone. Some reasons and attributes are natural. But others are not like that.[55] Having become manifest, those attributes provide reasons and objectives to the doer. However, there are also unconscious attributes that provide reasons for the consciousness to be collected.[56] The earth, the sky, heaven, beings, the rishis, the gods, the asuras and nothing else existed, with the exception of

[52]The atman.

[53]Because of death.

[54]The mind.

[55]This is difficult to understand, since it is left dangling. The sense probably is that one can transcend the natural propensities.

[56]This shloka is also difficult to understand. The plain meaning seems to be that there are inferior propensities and superior propensities.

the soul. It conveys everything. It goes everywhere. It is the cause behind the mind, which then possesses attributes. It has been said that reasons and characteristics are based on ignorant deeds. Because of being united with those reasons, it is made to engage in deeds again and the great wheel continues to revolve, without beginning and without end. That which is not manifest is the nave, while the manifest transformations represent the circumference. As the smooth axles revolve, the *kshetrajna* is certainly established in that wheel.[57] Those who extract oil crush sesamum seed in presses. Like that, because of the sentiments of desire and ignorance, the entire universe is crushed in that wheel. Having been seized by ego, the being performs acts. In the combination of acts and reasons, further reasons are generated.[58] There are no reasons behind acts. Nor are acts associated with reasons. In what is thought to be deeds and effects, it is time which is actually the doer. But prakriti is united with the reasons and the transformations work against each other. They transgress each other. However, the purusha is always established over them. Like dust following the wind, dust, darkness, impure sentiments and powerful reasons follow the kshetrajna. But they do not touch or effect the great-souled one. It is like the wind, which bears dust, but is itself without dust. Just as the two[59] are different, a learned person knows the difference between kshetra and kshetrajna. If one practises, one does not have to go to prakriti again.'[60]

'"The illustrious rishi thus severed the doubt that had arisen. Having considered this view, which has all the signs of accomplishment, the seeds[61] must be burnt, so that they do not sprout again. If they are burnt through knowledge, the atman is not tied down to hardships again."'

[57]The *kshetra* is the body. The kshetrajna is someone who knows the body, that is, the soul.

[58]Because of ignorance, further reasons for acts.

[59]Wind and dust.

[60]The text does not state this. But Bhishma clearly takes over again.

[61]Of ignorance and desire.

Chapter 1533(205)

'"The preceptor said, 'Those who exhibit signs of being engaged in action think that they are obtaining dharma through this. But others who are devoted to knowledge find no delight in them. Those who know about the Vedas and base themselves on what the Vedas have said are extremely rare. In this case, those who are learned, desire to follow the superior path.[62] Those who are of virtuous conduct practise this praiseworthy behaviour. These intelligent ones advance towards the supreme objective. Having obtained a body, everyone is seized by delusion. Such a person is overcome by desire and anger and *rajas* and *tamas*.[63] Therefore, one should not perform impure acts and should desire disassociation from the body. Having driven deeds into a hole, one obtains the auspicious worlds. When gold is mixed with iron, it becomes impure and does not shine. In that way, if mixed with the impure and the astringent,[64] knowledge no longer shines. Because of confusion, desire and avarice, if one follows *adharma*, one transgresses the path of dharma and is continuously destroyed. Therefore, one must not have attachment towards sound and the others[65] and material objects. Anger, delight and misery feed on each other. The five elements are in the body and so are *sattva*,[66] rajas and tamas. Who will one censure? Who will one praise? What will one say? Foolish people follow attachment towards things like touch, form and the others. Because of their ignorance, they do not realize that the bodies only represent earthy qualities. A house made of earth is plastered with earth. Like that, this body is made out of earth and is attached to earth.[67] Honey, oil, milk, butter, meat, salt,

[62]The Vedas talk about both action and abstention from action. But absention from action is superior, because it leads to emancipation.

[63]Rajas and tamas are the qualities of passion and darkness respectively.

[64]These are material objects and possessions.

[65]That is, the senses.

[66]The quality of purity.

[67]This earth means food, which is a manifestation of earth.

molasses, grain, fruits and roots are modifications of earth, mixed with water. There are those who resort to the wilderness. They are not interested in roaming around with other men. They obtain food with difficulty and taste it only for remaining alive. That is the way one should dwell in this world, which is also a wilderness. One must make efforts and take food only for the journey, like medicine by a patient.[68] Using truth, purity, uprightness, renunciation, fame, valour, forgiveness, fortitude, intelligence, the mind and austerities, one must search out the proper nature of everything, in due order. One must desire tranquility and not be distressed in the soul. One must restrain the senses. In their ignorance, beings are confused by sattva, rajas and tamas and are severely whirled around on the wheel. Therefore, one must properly examine all the sins that arise from ignorance. One must always cast aside the power of ignorance and ego. The great elements, the senses, the qualities of sattva, rajas and tamas and the three worlds and their lord are all established in the ego.[69] Time always shows afflicted people its qualities. In that way, know that, in all beings, it is the ego that makes beings embark on action. Know that tamas is responsible for confusion. It represents darkness and results from ignorance. All joys and sorrows are attached to the three qualities of sattva, rajas and tamas. Listen to them. Lack of confusion, delight, affection, lack of doubt, fortitude and memory—know that these are the virtuous qualities associated with sattva. Desire, anger, distraction, avarice, confusion, fear, exhaustion, despondency, sorrow, excessive pride, insolence, lack of nobility—without any distress, the severity or lack of severity of these faults must be examined. Each of these must always be tested, to the extent that they exist in the atman.'

'"The disciple asked, 'To loosen the bonds,[70] which sins do intelligent people banish from their minds? Like the fruits of confusion, which are the ones that keep on recurring? Using reasoning and intellect, which are the strong and weak faults an intelligent

[68]The journey is the progress of life.

[69]The ego has a base in ignorance.

[70]Of this world and life.

person should think about? O lord! Tell me about all this and instruct knowledge to me.'

'"The preceptor replied, 'A person who is pure in his soul severs the sins from their roots and is freed. An axe made of steel can destroy an object made of steel. That is the way a person who has cleansed his soul easily destroys the sins associated with rajas. In all bodies with the atman, rajas, tamas and those which give rise to pure deeds[71] are like seeds. Therefore, the atman in the body must discard rajas and tamas. Having been freed from rajas and tamas, the sattva will make it clean. There are those who say that sacrifices and rites, when performed with mantras, are instruments in following pure dharma. However, if one performs acts of dharma driven by rajas, or if one performs them with a desire for artha, all these amount to a serving of kama. When tamas is united with avarice, one serves anger and one becomes full of violence, addicted to pleasure, lassitude and sleep. However, one who is based in sattva is virtuous. He sees, and resorts to, only what is virtuous. Such a being is sparkling, handsome, pure and full of learning.'"'

Chapter 1534(206)

'"The preceptor said, 'O bull among men! Delusion is brought about by rajas. Anger, avarice, fear and insolence—these are brought about by tamas. Purity[72] leads to the supreme *paramatman*, the god who is without decay and without change. This is Vishnu, who is not manifest, but pervades everything. He is the supreme god. It is because of his skilful maya that the bodies of men are dislodged from knowledge and the beneficial. With their knowledge confounded, they are led towards desire. Desire leads to

[71]Sattva.

[72]Sattva.

anger, avarice and delusion in men and they perform deeds full of pride, insolence, ego and selfishness. From deeds, bonds of attachment arise and that attachment then leads to sorrow. Because these are undertaken, there is happiness and unhappiness and one is liable to birth and death. Since one is born from the mixture of semen and blood, one resides in the womb and that abode is full of excrement, urine, moisture and blood. Overcome by thirst, the being is flooded by these. One must know that women are the strands through which this cycle[73] is borne along. They are naturally the kshetra and men possess the qualities of kshetrajna. Therefore, learned men in particular must not follow young women. They are sorceresses,[74] terrible in form, and confuse those who are not learned. They are immersed in rajas and are the eternal embodiment of the senses. It is because of attraction for them that semen is created and beings are born. There are worms that get attached to one's body. One knows that these are not really part of one's body and flings them away. In that way, one should know that the offspring are also not really part of one's body and should cast them aside, like worms. Beings are born from semen, juices and affection, determined naturally by the acts that they have performed earlier. An intelligent person ignores them. Rajas is established in tamas and sattva also bases itself on tamas.[75] Know that knowledge is based on ignorance and that there are signs of ego. There is a seed in beings and that seed is known as the *jiva* of consciousness.[76] Because of deeds performed and because of time, it is whirled around in this cycle. It takes pleasure in this body, like the mind does in a dream. Because there are qualities of a womb in those deeds, the living being obtains a womb. The seeds of deeds performed goad the senses in beings.[77] Ego, attachment and

[73]We have translated *samsara*, the cycle of worldly existence, as cycle.

[74]*Kritya*, evil female spirits.

[75]Tamas clouds both sattva and rajas.

[76]Jiva has multiple meanings. Here, it means the principle of life in beings and intelligence and consciousness. For present purposes, jiva can be equated with the atman.

[77]There is the implied suggestion that the atman remembers these past deeds in the womb.

consciousness are generated. The attachment to sound leads to the atman obtaining ears. Because of the attachment to form, the eyes result and desire for scent leads to the nose. There is touch and the five kinds of wind, *prana*, *apana*, *vyana*, *udana* and *samana*, which lead to the sustaining of the body. The limbs are created because of attachment and the brahman[78] is engaged in action. In the body and in the mind, in the beginning, the middle and the end, there is sorrow and nothing but grief. Know that misery is inherent in birth and ego enhances it. It can be restrained through renunciation and a person who knows about renunciation is freed. Both the creation and the destruction of the senses result from rajas. Using the sight obtained from the sacred texts, a learned person must act so as to test them. Even if one accomplishes the objective of satisfying the senses, a person who knows can use the senses of knowledge to determine the reasons. Such a being does not have to accept a body again.'"'

Chapter 1535(207)

'"The preceptor said, 'I will now tell you about the means one can use, if one uses the sight obtained from the sacred texts. Using that knowledge, a wise person can attain the supreme objective. Among all beings, humans are said to be the best, brahmanas among humans and brahmanas who know the mantras among brahmanas. Brahmanas who know the truth about the Vedas can determine the purpose and progress of everything. They know everything and can see everything. They are special among all beings. A blind man who is travelling alone experiences hardships. It is like that for people devoid of knowledge. Therefore, those with knowledge are known to be superior. Thus, those who

[78]Being used here for the atman.

[79]The text uses the word *lingam*. While this has diverse meanings, given the context, the male genital organ is the obvious one.

are blind about dharma, but yet desire to follow dharma, go by the sacred texts. But they only accomplish limited objectives and I will soon describe those qualities. Purity in words, body and mind, forgiveness, truthfulness, fortitude, learning—among all kinds of dharma, these are described as the qualities of those who know about dharma. The form of the brahman is said to be there in *brahmacharya*. This is the supreme way for all beings and takes one towards the supreme objective. This means the avoidance of any association with the genital organ.[79] It also means the avoidance of touch by the body, hearing by the ears, sight by the eyes and taste by the tongue. All these are to be cast aside. Using the intelligence, one follows the unblemished conduct of brahmacharya. A person who follows this conduct in its entirety obtains Brahma's world. A person who follows it in an average way obtains the world of the gods. A person who resorts to such conduct in an inferior kind of way is born learned, as a foremost one among the brahmanas. It is extremely difficult to follow the methods of brahmacharya. Listen to this. A brahmana who engages in this must control his mind. He must not speak to women, nor hear them. He must not look at them when they are naked. Sometimes, when one looks at them, passion arises in those who are weak. If there is attraction, one must follow a vow of hardship,[80] enter the water and spend three days there. If this happens when one is asleep, one must mentally recite *aghamarshana* thrice.[81] One must burn down the sins of passion that are inside. Using knowledge, the discriminating person controls his mind. Excrement and filth exist in ducts that are inside the body. Like that, know that the atman is also bound down inside the body. There are arteries inside the human body, with bile, phlegm, blood, skin, flesh, bones, marrow and nets of veins. These bear juices. Know that there are ten arteries that convey the qualities of

[80]Such as fasting.

[81]This is a reference to the Aghamarshana *suktam* (after the sage Aghamarshana) from the Rig Veda. This is used for consecration ceremonies, ablutions and at times of bathing.

the five senses.[82] From those arteries, thousands of others emanate out and those are subtler in form. The veins are like rivers that convey juices to the ocean of the body. In the midst, attached to the heart, there is a vein known as *manovaha.* When men think of it, it collects semen from all parts of the body and releases it. There are veins that follow it and extend to every part of the body. They also convey the quality of energy and terminate at the eyes. There is butter hidden inside milk and that is churned up through churning rods. Like that, when there is resolution, churning rods churn out semen from the body. Even when one is asleep, passion can lead to resolution in the mind. The semen is touched by manovaha and is released from the body. The illustrious maharshi Atri knows about the generation of semen. There are three seeds, Indra is the associated divinity and this is spoken of as indriya.[83] Know that the progress of the semen is the reason behind an admixture of species. Detachment can burn these sins and such men do not have to take up a body again. When it is the time to die and give up the functions of the body, if a person pacifies the qualities[84] and uses his mind to draw them into manovaha, he is freed.[85] The mind then obtains knowledge and everything proceeds from the mind. Such great-souled persons become successful and divine and blaze like stellar bodies. Therefore, one must undertake unblemished deeds. One must sever rajas and tamas and ascend upwards. The knowledge one has obtained when one is young becomes weak with old age. However, when one's intelligence matures with age, one can regain it through one's mental strength. But this is an extremely difficult

[82]The text uses the word *dhamani*, which is really an artery. *Shira* is technically a vein. The number of arteries is actually described as twenty-four, but ten of those (two each) are associated with sound, sight, smell, taste and speech.

[83]The three seeds, as in reasons, behind semen have to be deduced. They probably are food, desire and manovaha. Semen is *shukra* and there may be a pun with Indra's name of Shakra. *Indriya* means senses and there may thus be another pun with Indra.

[84]Sattva, rajas and tamas.

[85]Manovaha is also known as *sushumna.*

path to follow and involves transcending the bonds of qualities. However, if one sees the sins, one can transcend them and obtain immortality.'"'

Chapter 1536(208)

'"The preceptor said, 'Beings come to a bad end because they are lazy and addicted to the objects of the senses. However, not being attached to these, great-souled ones attain the supreme objective. Birth, death, old age, misery, disease and mental anguish—seeing that the world is always overwhelmed by these, an intelligent person seeks to bring about his emancipation. He must be pure and without ego in his words, mind and body. He must be tranquil, learned and a mendicant who is indifferent. He will then roam around happily. However, if there is attachment in his mind because of compassion towards beings, he must ignore this, knowing that everything in this universe is because of the fruits of earlier deeds. Whether good or bad deeds have been committed earlier, those results must be borne. In words, intelligence and action—one must peform auspicious deeds. Non-violence, truthfulness in speech, uprightness towards all beings, forgiveness and lack of distraction—a person who follows this is happy. This is supreme dharma and brings joy to all beings. Know that this eliminates all misery. A person who knows the truth about this is happy. One must use one's intelligence to control one's mind and sustain all beings. One must not desire to injure them and one must not allow one's thoughts to bind one down. One should direct one's words and mind towards such action. He should always speak virtuous words, looking towards the subtleties of dharma, and speak words that do not censure, but are truthful and do not cause injury. Evil results from harsh and violent words which are cruel and condemning, as it does from excessive speech. One's consciousness is then distracted. Words lead to attachment. If one is detached, that should be reflected in words too. One should avoid tamas in intelligence, mind and deeds. If a person resorts to action because of rajas, he will reap the consequences. He will obtain misery in this world and hell thereafter. Therefore, one must exhibit patience in one's mind, words and body and act accordingly. Bandits who are carrying loads of sheep always opt for directions that are adverse.[86] Know that ignorant people in the world are like that. If the bandits wish to follow desirable directions, they have to fling aside their burdens. Like that, to obtain happiness, one has to cast aside acts based on rajas and tamas. Such a person is not suspicious. He doesn't desire anything. He has freed himself from possessions. He lives alone. He has attained all his desires. He is an ascetic. He is in control of his senses. He has burnt his hardships through knowledge. He has controlled his atman. Having withdrawn his mind, he obtains the supreme. There is no doubt that a patient man who has cleansed his soul must control his intelligence. The mind must be controlled with intelligence and desire for objects controlled with the mind. When the senses have been restrained and the mind is under subjugation, the god manifests himself and one cheerfully advances towards that lord. When the mind has been controlled, Brahma manifests himself. One must not engage in yoga and tantra, in any form at all. Instead, one must act so that one's conduct is permeated by the warp of that tantra.[87] One should seek to sustain oneself on broken bits of grain, seeds from which oil has been extracted, inferior kinds of grain,[88] vegetables, barley, coarsely ground meal, roots and fruit that have been obtained through begging. Depending on the time and the place, a virtuous person will be restrained in his diet. Having examined it, he will follow the appropriate conduct. This is like gradually kindling a fire. One must

[86]These are stolen sheep and the king's soldiers will catch them along the way.

[87]This presumably means that yoga and tantra must not be practised so as to obtain any special powers. They are not an end. They are the means to the end of good conduct.

[88]*Kulmasha*. Alternatively, a kind of bean.

gently use the kindling of knowledge and the sun of knowledge will manifest itself. Ignorance is actually based on knowledge and the three worlds are based on that.[89] *Jnana* follows *vijnana*[90] and destroys the ignorance. One does not know the eternal because they seem to be separate.[91] A person who knows about renunciation is devoid of attachment and is freed. Having overcome age, old age and death, he wins the eternal brahman. He obtains immortality, the Akshara who is without change.'"'

Chapter 1537(209)

'"The preceptor said, 'One must always desire to follow unblemished brahmacharya. Considering the sins that arise from dreaming, one must wholeheartedly try to give up sleep.[92] In sleep, the embodied being is overcome by rajas and tamas. Having lost its memory, it wanders around outside the body. Practising knowledge and thereafter enquiring about objectives, one must remain awake. Concentrating on vijnana, one must always remain awake at night. On this, there are feelings whereby one thinks about material objects during dreams. While the senses are suspended, the being behaves as if it still possesses a body. It has been said that Hari, the lord of yoga, knows how this occurs. The maharshis have said that what he has described is the truth. The learned say that when the senses are exhausted, everyone sees dreams. The mind has not been exhausted and it is said that is the reason. The mind is addicted to action and resolution is awake. That is the reason mental desire for prosperity surfaces in the mind during dreams. In

[89]There is ignorance because the knowledge is clouded.

[90]External and internal knowledge, respectively. The former is learnt from teachers, the latter from one's own self.

[91]Presumably the atman and the brahman.

[92]*Svapnadosha*, in general, refers to sins that arise from dreaming. But more specifically, it means seminal discharge in sleep.

this cycle, there are innumerable desires a being faces.[93] They may seem to have disappeared from the mind, but the supreme being inside knows them all. The qualities of those deeds become known and present themselves.[94] They affect the minds of beings and influence them. Those qualities of rajas, sattva and tamas present themselves. This is even if one has engaged in virtuous deeds that yield infinite fruits. The ignorant see images that excite wind, bile and phlegm. It has been said that sentiments of rajas and tamas are difficult to cast aside. Even when one's senses are tranquil, there are resolutions in the mind. In the course of dreams, the mind perceives these through its sight. The mind is pervasive and unrestrained in all beings. The mind is based in the body. The door that is the mind does disappear.[95] Everything that exists and does not exist becomes manifest in that state of sleep. But the learned person becomes acquainted with the quality of adhyatma,[96] which is inside all beings. At that time, the mind only has the resolution to be attached to the qualities of the supreme god and objective. Through the powers of his own atman, he knows everything and knows himself to be divinity. He is engaged in austerities. He is as radiant as the sun and is beyond darkness. Because of the austerities, the being becomes like Maheshvara and like the prakriti of the three worlds. These are the kinds of austerities the gods engaged in. The asuras represented tamas and destroyed those austerities. This is what was respectively protected by the gods and the asuras. This is said to be the signs of ignorance.[97] Know that the qualities of sattva, rajas and tamas also characterize the gods and the asuras. Know that sattva is the quality of the gods and that the other two[98] represent the qualities of the asuras. Know that Brahma

[93]The cycle of life. This is thus not just about desires in this life, but about desires in earlier lives too.

[94]The qualities of sattva, rajas and tamas and earlier deeds.

[95]It disappears in some cases. This is known as *sushupti*, as opposed to ordinary sleep. Sushupti is deep slumber. The body sleeps. But though the mind is awake, there are no dreams.

[96]The spiritual, concerning the supreme spirit.

[97]The conduct of the asuras.

[98]Rajas and tamas.

is beyond all this. He is immortal, radiant and Akshara. Those who are learned and have cleansed their souls go to that supreme objective. With the sight of knowledge, one is capable of recounting reasons about this. It is only through withdrawal that one is capable of knowing the brahman, which is not manifest.'"'

Chapter 1538(210)

'"The preceptor said, 'A person who does not know about those four things does not know supreme dharma.[99] The supreme rishi obtained the manifest, and that which is not manifest, as *tattvam*.[100] That which is manifest is in the jaws of death. Know that which is not manifest is the immortal objective. The rishi Narayana has spoken about the signs of inclination.[101] Everything in the three worlds, the mobile and the immobile, is established on this. The traits of the dharma of renunciation[102] are that this leads to the eternal brahman, who is not manifest. Prajapati has spoken about the characteristics of the dharma of pravritti. From pravritti, one has to return again.[103]Nivritti leads to the supreme objective. A supreme sage who is engaged in nivritti attains that supreme end. He is devoted to knowledge and always discriminates between what is auspicious and what is inauspicious. For that, one must know both the unmanifest and purusha. One must also know the one who is greater than the unmanifest and the purusha. One who is accomplished must specially look towards the differences between

[99]The number four is left dangling and it's not immediately obvious which four are meant. In all probability, this means the brahman with qualities, the brahman without qualities, that which is manifest and that which is not manifest.

[100]As will soon be evident, this supreme rishi is the sage Narayana. Tattvam means the truth, the real state, the essence.

[101]Inclination towards, and attachment for, action and its fruits, *pravritti*.

[102]Detachment from fruits and renunciation of action, *nivritti*.

[103]Rebirth.

them. The signs of both of them[104] are that they are without beginning and without end. They are both always subtler than the subtlest and greater than the greatest. They are similar in this way. But there are also differences between them. Prakriti's dharma is creation and it has three kinds of traits.[105] Know that the traits of the kshetrajna are the converse.[106] Because of the qualities, prakriti is seen to have transformations. But purusha and the more powerful one[107] are incapable of being comprehended. Creation results from the union[108] and the attributes of action enable one to understand. A doer is characterized by action and withdrawal from action. Though words like 'who', 'I' and 'this' are used, they are meaningless. It is like a person who wears a headdress made out of three pieces of cloth. The embodied being is enveloped in sattva, rajas and tamas. Therefore, one must understand four subjects and aspects.[109] Someone who knows this will not be confused, even when his time draws to an end. If one desires the celestial prosperity of the brahman, one must be pure in words and mind. For the body, one must observe fierce rituals and be engaged in unblemished austerities. The three worlds are illuminated and pervaded by austerities performed by the inner being. The radiance of the sun and the moon in the sky is because of austerities. The power of austerities is in knowledge. Austerities are praised in the world. Because of its attributes, austerities free a person from acts committed because of rajas and tamas. Brahmacharya and non-violence are said to be the austerities of the body. Control over words and the mind and tranquility are said to be austerities of the mind. In particular, following the ordinances, one must receive food from brahmanas. If one is restrained in food, the sins that result from rajas are destroyed. In one's mind, one must withdraw from

[104]Purusha and prakriti.

[105]Sattva, rajas and tamas.

[106]In the sense that the kshetrajna or purusha is inactive and is beyond the three qualities.

[107]The brahman.

[108]Between purusha and prakriti.

[109]Similarities between purusha and prakriti, differences between them, similarities between purusha and the brahman and differences between them.

material objects and action. Thus, one must only accept that much of food as is necessary.

'""When one is afflicted by old age and one's end has arrived, one must act without any distress. One must confront it by fixing one's mind on knowledge. Divested from rajas and the body, the embodied being silently moves around. When one is freed from action and one's intelligence turns to lack of attachment, one is based in prakriti.[110] When one is freed from the distraction of the body, one can also be freed from what comes after the end of the body.[111] The creation and destruction of beings always has a reason. However, if one has belief in the supreme reason behind creation, one is freed from the compulsion to return.[112] But there are those who are ignorant about the forces behind the end of the world and creation and destruction. They use their patience to hold up their bodies and use their intelligence to withdraw their minds. They withdraw from places and objects that are destructible and worship what is subtle. They know everything that should be known from the sacred texts. After death, some of them, with cleansed souls, attain the ultimate resort. Some virtuous ones worship the object of meditation.[113] The supreme god cannot be destroyed and has been described as a flash of lightning. When the end comes, some have burnt their sins through austerities. All these great-souled ones go towards the supreme objective. The attributes[114] are subtle and one must look at them with sight gained from the sacred texts. Freed from all possessions, one knows that supreme body. One has fixed one's mind on dharana and has penetrated into what is inside. With the mind united with knowledge, one is then freed from the

[110]Freed from the senses. But this does not mean that one has attained moksha.

[111]There are subtleties left implicit in the text. These concern transitions, after death, from the gross body to the subtle body and so on. When one is truly emancipated, one is freed from these subtler forms of the body too.

[112]Rebirth.

[113]The text uses the word *dharana*, which is concentrated meditation. Dharana is one of the steps in the eight components of yoga.

[114]Of the brahman.

mortal world. Pure and having obtained the brahman, one attains the supreme objective. One obtains the knowledge that is free from folly and cannot be dislodged. This is the divine and illustrious one, without origin. This is Vishnu, who has the attributes of not being manifest. Those whose sentiments are pure have no desires and become content with that knowledge. With that knowledge, they base themselves in Hari. They suffer no decay and do not return. They obtain the supreme resort and take delight in the one who is without decay and without destruction. This is said to be knowledge and there is nothing else. The entire universe is bound down by thirst and is whirled around on a wheel. The strands of a lotus plant penetrate everywhere within the lotus. In that way, for those who are thirsty,[115] it always penetrates everything in the body, from the beginning to the end. This is like a weaver using his needle and thread to move around everywhere in a garment. Like that, the threads of this cycle are bound down by the needle of desire. Prakriti is subject to transformation. Purusha is eternal. A person who knows this is freed from desire. The illustrious rishi Narayana, the refuge of the universe, revealed all this, driven by compassion for beings and for the welfare of the universe. This is immortality.'"'

Chapter 1539(211)

'Yudhishthira asked, "O one who knows about conduct! O one who knows about dharma! After discarding human objects of pleasure, what conduct did Janaka, the lord of Mithila,[116] follow, so as to advance towards emancipation?"

'Bhishma replied, "In this connection, an ancient history is recounted. By following this conduct, the one who knew about conduct, advanced towards great happiness. In Mithila, there was a

[115]With desire.

[116]This Janaka is not to be confused with Sita's father. This Janaka was descended from that Janaka's lineage and is also referred to as Janaka.

lord of men named Janadeva and he was descended from Janaka. He thought about the dharma that would uplift him beyond the body. One hundred preceptors always dwelt in his residence. They showed him different kinds of dharma and some of them were heretical. But basing himself on the sacred texts, he was not satisfied with what they repeatedly told him about their determinations about death, birth after death and the nature of the atman. There was a great sage named Panchashikha, the son of Kapila. Having travelled the entire earth, he came to Mithila. He had ascertained the true knowledge about all kinds of dharma connected with renunciation. He had settled all the meanings, was free from opposite sentiments,[117] and all his doubts had been dispelled. He was said to be the only rishi who was beyond the desire that characterizes humans. He desired the ultimate and eternal happiness that was so difficult to obtain. People were astounded at his form and thought that he was the supreme rishi, Prajapati Kapila, who expounded samkhya,[118] himself. He was the first disciple of Asuri and was said to be immortal. For one thousand years, he[119] had performed the sacrifice known as *panchasrota*.[120] There was a circle of the followers of Kapila and they were seated. They wished to hear from him about the supreme being, who was not manifest. Because of his own sacrifices and austerities, the sage had become successful. He had obtained divine sight and had understood the difference between kshetra and kshetrajna. The single Akshara of the brahman is seen in many different forms. In that circle, Asuri spoke about the one who is not manifest. There was a brahmana lady by the name of Kapila[121] and she was Asuri's wife. Panchashikha became his[122] disciple and suckled milk at her breast. Because he suckled milk from the breasts of Kapila's wife, he came to be known as his son and obtained supreme intelligence. The illustrious one told

[117]Like pleasure and pain, happiness and unhappiness.

[118]One of the six schools of philosophy.

[119]As will be evident, this is a reference to Asuri and not to Panchashikha. Kapila was also known as Asuri.

[120]Literally, the one with five flows, a description of the mind.

[121]That is, Kapilaa.

[122]Asuri's.

me about how he became Kapila's son.[123] He also told me about how Kapila's son obtained every kind of supreme prosperity.

'"Kapila's son knew about supreme forms of dharma and also knew that those one hundred ordinary preceptors were confused about the reasons. Kapila[124] therefore presented himself there and Janaka became devoted to him. He abandoned those one hundred preceptors and started to follow him. For the sake of supreme welfare, following dharma, he bowed down before him. He taught him about supreme emancipation, described as samkhya. He spoke to him about being free from birth and about being free from action. Having spoken to him about being free from action, he spoke to him about being free from everything. He spoke about being attached to action, and about the fruits those acts lead to. 'These cannot be trusted, since they are certain to be temporary and subject to destruction.[125] There are some who argue that people can directly witness the destruction. They therefore say that the supreme words of the sacred texts have evidently been defeated.[126] They say that there is no atman and one's self is subject to death, hardship, death,[127] old age and decay. A person who holds the view that the atman is different is completely confused. If something that does not exist is thought of as without decay and without death, then the king should also be thought of in that way.[128] Whether something exists or does not exist should be determined by the signs of its existence. How can the progress of people be determined to be based on such an object? The foundations of a conclusion must be based on what can be directly seen. Even if the sacred texts hold a different view, without direct evidence, one cannot arrive at such a conclusion. One's sentiments cannot be influenced by guesses. Thus, the view that there is another being in

[123]It is not clear who told Bhishma the story. It is presumed to have been Markandeya or Sanatkumara.

[124]Panchashikha.

[125]The text does not indicate this clearly. But this seems to be the place where Panchashikha's quote begins.

[126]Since the body is destroyed, nothing beyond the body can exist.

[127]The word death is used twice, one for the body, the second for the atman.

[128]If a non-existent entity is thought of in that way, an existent entity must also be thought of in a similar way.

the body should actually be held to be the view of non-believers.[129] A banyan tree results from a single seed. Clarified butter results from the process of cooking. These are said to be properties of different species. Lodestone and the sun-crystal[130] drink up water.[131] When one is dead, why should there be a being that approaches the gods? There is certain proof that once one is dead, there is a cessation of action. However, these are not valid arguments for something that does not have a form. The immortal cannot be realized by ordinary mortals. There are some who say that rebirth is because of ignorance and because of the attempt to undertake action. The reasons are avarice and confusion and inclination towards sin. Ignorance is said to be the field, and deeds performed earlier are like the seed. Thirst generates affection and that leads to rebirth. It lies hidden in the consciousness. When the mortal body is burnt, it is born again in a different body, preserving the spirit.[132] This has been heard from some as the truth. However, since the body that one is born in may be a completely different one, how can there be an association between the two? In this case, what desire can there be for donations, learning and the strength of austerities, since the results of all such deeds are held to be obtained by someone else?[133] There are others who are miserable because of the deeds that they have performed earlier. One must arrive at a determination after looking towards this misery and joy. When the body is crushed by a club and is born again, it is sometimes held that the consciousness that results is a different one. This is held to be like seasons, years, lunar days, cold, heat, the pleasant and the unpleasant. Like these, one passes on,[134] but the spirit is preserved. However, this[135] will be overcome by old age and be destroyed by

[129]Instead of the other way round. The word used is *nastika*. The various arguments advanced here are those of non-believers, specifically, some aspects of Buddhism.

[130]*Ayaskanta* and *suryakanta* respectively.

[131]These instances illustrate that though there are tranformations, there is some direct evidence.

[132]As distinct from the atman.

[133]The next body.

[134]From one body to another.

[135]The spirit, distinct from the atman.

death. Like a house that is progressively weakened, it will eventually be destroyed. The senses, the mind, the wind, the blood, the flesh and the bones are all progressively destroyed and enter the elements that created them. There are many reasons that arise in the mind about the paths followed by people, the obtaining of the fruits from the dharma of donations, the meaning of the words in the Vedas and the conduct of people. But none of these would be valid.[136] Reflecting on such things, different people head in different directions. Some submerge in them and obtain intelligence. Others age like trees. Every being is made miserable because of good and bad deeds. The sacred texts bring them back, like elephants by those who control elephants. Thus, there are many who desire happiness, but are unwilling to pay the price. They are overcome by greater misery and like people who have been separated from their meat,[137] come under the subjugation of death. Everyone is certain to be destroyed. What is the point of relatives, friends and possessions? If one abandons these in an instant and then departs, one does not return. Earth, space, water, fire and the wind always nourish the body. If one thinks of this, how can one be freed of desire? However, these are also destroyed and there is no happiness in these.' These words were supreme and were without deception. With the atman only as a witness, they were beyond disease. Hearing them, the king was astounded. He glanced towards him[138] and got ready to ask him once again."'

Chapter 1540(212)

'Bhishma said, "Janadeva, Janaka's descendant, was thus instructed by the supreme rishi. He again asked him about existence and non-existence after death. 'O illustrious one![139]

[136]If one believed the non-believers.

[137]There is an implicit image of carnivores craving for meat.

[138]Panchashikha.

[139]The text does not clearly indicate the beginning of a quote. But it is obvious.

If there is indeed a consciousness after death, then what is ignorance and what is knowledge? What does one do? O supreme among brahmanas! If it is seen that all good deeds are destroyed, then what is the difference between being distracted and not being distracted? Whether there is attachment, or whether there is lack of attachment, a being is destroyed. Why should one undertake acts? What should one determine and resolve? What is the truth about this?' He was thus confused, foolish and enveloped in darkness.[140]

'"The wise Panchashika pacified him by speaking these words to him. 'There is no destruction in that excellence.[141] Nor is there any existence in that excellence. This is an accumulation of the body, the senses and consciousness. They circle independently, but also influence each other and lead to action. The five branches are the elements of space, wind, fire, water and earth. They follow their own natures and are naturally distinct. Space, wind, heat, liquids and earth—these five come together in the body and become one. Knowledge, heat and wind—these are the three that give rise to action. The senses, the objects of the senses, natural consciousness, the mind, prana, apana and transformations flow from the elements. Hearing, touch, taste, sight and scent are the five senses and their qualities result from consciousness. When this is united with knowledge, three kinds of pain are said to be certain—happiness, unhappiness and the absence of both unhappiness and happiness. Sound, touch, form, taste and smell—these five exist in the body until the time of death. With the sixth quality of knowledge, they bring about everything. All acts, renunciation and all determinations about the truth depend on these. Intelligence is said to be the supreme, great and imperishable seed.[142] If a person sees the atman in this accumulation of qualities, then his sight is faulty and his infinite misery will not be destroyed. If a person looks on these as not being the atman, then he has no sense of ownership.

[140]The darkness of ignorance.

[141]A reference to the state of emancipation.

[142]Because it leads to emancipation.

In such a case, sorrow lacks a foundation to which it can attach itself. That is the reason there is the supreme sacred text known as *samyangamana.*[143] I will expound this to you. For the sake of your moksha, listen attentively. Renunciation is recommended for all those who wish to be free of their deeds. However, those who have always been versed in false views have to undergo hardship and sorrow. Deeds are for renouncing objects. Vows are for renouncing objects of pleasure. The yoga of austerities involves the renunciation of happiness and terminates in the renunciation of everything. I will tell you about what the learned have described as the path for renouncing everything. That leads to the alleviation of misery. Anything else leads to hardship. The five senses of knowledge, and the mind as the sixth, are based in consciousness. I have spoken of the mind as the sixth and there are the five organs of action. Know that the two hands are the organs of action and the two feet are the organs of movement. The penis is the organ for procreation and pleasure and the anus is the organ for release. The mouth is specially for uttering words. Know the movements of these five. With intelligence, there are eleven[144] and these must be cast away from the mind. The ears, sound and consciousness—these three are required for hearing. It is the same for touch, form, taste and smell. These fifteen[145] are required for the reception of the qualities. Three kinds of sentiments also present themselves. These three are sattva, rajas and tamas. In all kinds of attempts, they lead to three kinds of pain. Jubiliation, delight, happiness, joy, tranquility in consciousness, irrespective of whether a reason is present or absent for this state of consciousness—these are the qualities of sattva. Dissatisfaction, repentance, sorrow, avarice, lack of forgiveness, irrespective of whether a reason is present or absent—these are the signs of rajas. Lack of judgement, confusion,

[143]Literallly, the right state of mind.

[144]Five organs of sense, five organs of action, and intelligence.

[145]Each of the five senses being associated with three attributes. Consciousness is a constant. In addition, there is an organ and something that triggers the organ.

distraction, dreaming and excessive sleep, irrespective of how these have been caused—these are the many qualities of tamas. If there are any signs of delight in the body or the mind, these should truly be known as the attributes of sattva. If there is any association of repentance or sorrow in a person, without any reflection, this can be identified to have been caused by rajas. Thus, if there is any confusion in the body or in the mind, even if it is incomprehensible or indiscernible, that has been caused by tamas. Hearing originates with sound and the ears base themselves on it. In the science of hearing, one cannot discern any difference between the two.[146] The skin, the eyes, the tongue and the nose, as the fifth, are also like that. Touch, form, taste, smell and consciousness are based on the mind. The ten[147] undertake their own tasks, separately and collectively. Know that consciousness is the eleventh and intelligence is the twelfth. As long as these work together, tamas cannot be destroyed.Their simultaneous operation is commonly known as conduct. The learning of the sacred texts has earlier determined the working of the senses and the three kinds of qualities have been thought of. Confused by them, consciousness swiftly roams around amidst what is impermanent. Even at the best of times, this is said to be tamas happiness. If one does not serve what has been described in all the sacred texts, then one is enveloped in darkness and serves what is false and manifest. These are the thoughts on how dependence on the qualities leads to individual action. Some follow them completely and some not at all. There are those who have thought about adhyatma. They speak of this accumulation as kshetra and what exists in the mind as kshetrajna. This being the case, what is destroyed? What is eternal? All beings are driven by these reasons and their natures. Once a river has entered an ocean, it gives up its name. The spirit is destroyed in that way and no longer has an individuality. This being the case, after death, how can consciousness again be born? The *jivatma* merges and nothing in

[146]Hearing and sound.

[147]Five organs of sense and five organs of action.

the middle can be grasped.[148] If a person possesses intelligence and knowledge about moksha, without any distraction, he then desires his own atman and does not get tainted by the fruits of any evil acts. He is like the leaf of a lotus, sprinkled with water. He is freed from the many firm bonds, whether these arise from offspring or from the gods.[149] He abandons both happiness and unhappiness. He is freed and goes to the foremost one, who is without any signs. This is the auspicious one. Accepting the proofs of the sacred texts, he then lies down, beyond old age, death and fear. His good deeds are destroyed. He is beyond the sins too. Therefore, the fruits of these are also destroyed. The great one is pure, free and without signs. He sees and gets attached to that greatness. When the strands are severed, a spider that has been stationed there, falls down. Like that, he is freed from his miseries, which are crushed like rocks on a mountain. A *ruru* deer casts aside its old horns and a snake its old skin. Like that, he goes beyond what can be seen and casting aside his miseries, is free. When a tree is about to fall down on water, a bird abandons it. In that way, he casts aside his happiness and unhappiness. He is free and goes to the supreme one, who is without any signs. A song is sung about the king of Mithila.[150] When he saw that his city was being burnt by a fire, he said, "Not even a chaff of mine is being burnt here."[151] The lord of the earth had himself said this.' Having heard these words about the immortal objective, spoken by Panchashikha himself, the king of Videha looked at everything. He ascertained the truth about everything and roamed around in great happiness, bereft of sorrow. He who reads this, determined to pursue moksha, always considers this and never decays. He does not suffer miseries because of any calamities. He is freed, like the lord of Mithila after meeting Kapila."'

[148]Most of this is directed at Buddhist philosophy. The middle is a reference to consciousness, as distinct from the atman.

[149]Sacrifices performed for the gods.

[150]This king was Janaka, Janadeva's ancestor.

[151]Janaka had renounced everything.

Chapter 1541(213)

'Yudhishthira asked, "What action enables one to obtain happiness? What action leads one to obtain unhappiness? What action frees one from fear in this world? O descendant of the Bharata lineage! What conduct ensures success?"

'Bhishma replied, "The intelligence of the ancient ones was based on the sacred texts and they praised self-control for all the varnas, but especially for brahmanas. A person who is not self-controlled does not obtain success in his rites. Rites, austerities and the Vedas are all based on self-control. Self-control increases energy and that is the reason self-control is said to be sacred. A person who is self-controlled is free from fear, is cleansed of sins and attains greatness. A self-controlled person sleeps in happiness and awakes in happiness. He roams around happily in the world and is cheerful in his mind. Self-control leads to restraint and one is not overcome by fierceness of energy. Such a person always sees his many enemies[152] as distinct from the atman. Those without self-control are like predatory beasts and always cause fear among beings. It was to control them that Svayambhu created kings. Among all the ashramas, self-control is special. The fruits of self-control are said to be greater than the dharma obtained through these. I will now tell you about the signs of those among whom self-control has arisen—lack of miserliness, lack of excitement, satisfaction, faithfulness, forgiveness, lack of anger, constant uprightness, lack of excessive speech, lack of pride, worship of seniors, lack of envy, compassion towards all beings, absence of slander, refraining from speaking too much in public, lack of false speech and abstention from praise and censure. Among men, such a person is convinced about being virtuous and does not wish to pursue desire. He is not driven by enmity and possesses no deceit. He regards praise and censure equally. He immerses himself in good conduct. He is cheerful in his atman and is learned. He obtains reverence in this world. After death, he goes to heaven. He is

[152]These enemies are vices.

engaged in the welfare of all beings and does not hate people. He is like a giant and calm lake. He is cheerful and content in his wisdom. He has no fear of any being and they are also not frightened of him. He bows down before all beings. Such a self-controlled person is learned. He is not delighted if he obtains great prosperity. He does not sorrow during a hardship. If a brahmana is thus accomplished in his wisdom, he is said to be self-controlled. His deeds are informed by the sacred texts. He follows the auspicious conduct of virtuous people. He is always full of self-restraint and enjoys great fruits. He has lack of jealousy, forgiveness, tranquility, satisfaction, pleasantness in speech, truthfulness, generosity and ease. That path is not for an evil-souled person. A brahmachari conquers his senses, having subjugated his desire and anger. Rigid in his vows, such a brahmana performs valiant and terrible austerities. He roams around in this world, waiting for his time.[153] He possesses no evil and is full of his atman."'

Chapter 1542(214)

'Yudhishthira asked, "Brahmanas who observe vows sometimes eat the food that is offered as an oblation. O grandfather! What happens if a brahmana possesses this desire?"

'Bhishma replied, "O Yudhishthira! If one eats after following the Vedas, it is different. But if one commits the act of eating in violation of the three Vedas, then one's vows are destroyed."

'Yudhishthira asked, "Ordinary people say that fasting is like austerities. O great king! Is this really austerity? What are austerities?"

'Bhishma replied, "People think that fasting for months or fortnights are austerities. But the virtuous do not regard them as austerities. Instead, they are an impediment in getting to

[153]Awaiting death.

know about the atman. Renunciation and becoming the disciple of a virtuous person is the supreme austerity. Such a person is always fasting and such a person is always a brahmachari. Such a brahmana will always become a sage and will always worship the gods. O descendant of the Bharata lineage! Even if he lives in a family,[154] he will always desire and dream of dharma. He will never eat flesh and will always meditate on the auspicious. He will always desire amrita and will never cause violence for food. He will always be devoted to guests and will always be like one who survives on leftovers."

'Yudhishthira asked, "How can one fast and be a brahmachari all the time? How can one always be devoted to guests and survive on leftovers?"

'Bhishma replied, "If a person eats in the morning and eats again in the evening, without eating anything in between, he will be regarded as fasting all the time. If a brahmana goes to his wife only at the time of her season, he is a brahmachari, as long as that man always speaks the truth and is always devoted to wisdom. A person who does not pointlessly eat meat is said to be a vegetarian.[155] He will always be generous and pure by not dreaming or sleeping during the day. O Yudhishthira! Know that if a person only eats what has been left after the servants and guests have eaten is like a person who subsists on amrita. If a brahmana never eats until they[156] have eaten, through that act of not eating, he conquers heaven. If one survives on the leftovers after gods, ancestors, servants and guests have eaten, that is said to be like surviving on what is left at a sacrifice. They always obtain infinite worlds. With Brahma, the apsaras and the residents of heaven present themselves in their homes. They share their food with the gods and the ancestors. They find delight with their sons and grandsons and obtain the supreme objective."'

[154]That is, even if he is a householder.

[155]The interpretation is that the eating of the flesh of animals killed at sacrifices is acceptable.

[156]Gods, ancestors, guests and servants.

Chapter 1543(215)

'Yudhishthira asked, "O descendant of the Bharata lineage! In this world, men are united with their good and bad deeds, for the sake of reaping the fruits. But is a man actually the doer or not? I have a doubt about this. O grandfather! I wish to hear the complete truth about this. I wish to hear the truth."

'Bhishma replied, "O Yudhishthira! In this connection, the ancient history of a conversation between Prahlada and Indra is recounted. Though he[157] was born in an evil lineage, he was extremely learned and was unattached. His sins had been cleansed and he was bereft of confusion and insolence. He was virtuous and engaged in the observance of vows. Praise and censure were the same to him and he was self-controlled. It was as if he dwelt in an empty house. He knew about the creation and destruction of all beings, mobile and immobile. He was not enraged at objects that caused displeasure. Nor did he find delight in objects that caused pleasure. He looked upon gold and a lump of earth in the same way. He was patient and had resolved to fix his determination on the supreme knowledge about the atman. He knew everything, superior and inferior, about beings and looked upon them equally. He was in control of his senses.

'"Once, when Prahlada was seated alone, Shakra approached him, wishing to dislodge him from his wisdom, and spoke these words. 'In this world, there are qualities that are revered among men. All of those qualities are seen to be present in you. Your intelligence is seen to be like that of a child. You know about the atman. What do you think is the supreme? You are now tied down in bonds. You have been dislodged from your place and have come under the subjugation of your enemies. O Prahlada! You are devoid of prosperity. Though you should grieve, you are not sorrowing. O son of Diti![158] Is this because of the wisdom that you have obtained or is it because of your fortitude? O Prahlada! You seem to be well. But behold the state of

[157]Prahlada. Prahlada, or Prahrada, was devoted to Vishnu and there are no stories about his being deprived of his prosperity.

[158]The daityas were the sons of Diti, who was married to the sage Kashyapa.

your hardship.' The patient one, who knew about what had to be determined, was thus urged. He used gentle words to describe his own state of wisdom. 'He who does not understand the origin and destruction of all beings is confused because of that foolishness. But someone who sees this is not confused. Origin and destruction happen because of nature. In either existence or non-existence, no enterprise can be seen. There is no enterprise in non-existence and there is nothing that is the doer. Though the person never actually does anything in this world, there is a sense of vanity. If a person thinks himself to be the doer of good or bad deeds, he does not know his own self and his wisdom is tainted. That is my view. O Shakra! If a person is himself the doer, then it is certain that all the deeds he begins for the sake of his benefit will be successful. There will never be any defeat. It is seen that despite the best of efforts, there is no cessation of the unpleasant and no existence of the pleasant. Where is the scope for enterprise? It is seen that though some do not make any efforts, there is nothing unpleasant and they are covered by the pleasant. This must be because of nature. It is seen that some extremely intelligent people confront adversity and have to seek riches from those who are malformed and limited in intelligence. Indeed, all the qualities, good and bad, penetrate a person because of nature. Therefore, where is the scope for pride? Everything is because of nature. That is my determined view. Thus, my wisdom is based on the atman and there is nothing else. In this world, I think that the fruits of all good and bad deeds become attached. I will now tell you everything about action. Listen. When a crow eats, the presence of the food is known because of its cawing. In that way, all deeds are the manifestations of nature. A person who knows about the appearances of nature, but does not know about supreme nature, is confused because of his foolishness. He looks at everything through this foolishness. Everything flows from nature. A person who has comprehended all these manifestations has understood. What will he do with pride and insolence? I know everything about the rites of dharma and that all beings are not permanent. O Shakra! Therefore, I do not sorrow. I know that everything has an end. I have no sense of ownership. I am without insolence. I do not belong to this world. I am free of all bonds. I see that all beings have a beginning and an end and I am well. O Shakra! For a person who is accomplished in his wisdom, self-controlled, without thirst, without hope and without effort, everything in this world is looked at with the light of that knowledge. These are manifestations of nature and I do not love them or hate them. I do not see anyone who hates me. Nor do I see anyone who is my own. O Shakra! I do not desire anything above or below, or in the transverse directions.[159] There is no delight to be obtained[160] from knowledge, lack of knowledge, or the object of knowledge.' Shakra asked, 'O Prahlada! I am asking you. Tell me the means whereby one can obtain this kind of wisdom and this kind of tranquility.' Prahlada said, 'O Shakra! A man attains greatness through uprightness, lack of distraction, calmness, being immersed in the atman and serving the elders. One then obtains wisdom from nature and tranquility from nature. Everything that you see is obtained from nature.' Thus addressed by the lord of the daityas, Shakra was astounded. O king! Delighted, he then honoured these words. The lord of the three worlds[161] worshipped the Indra among the daityas. Having taken the permission of the Indra among the asuras, he returned to his own abode."'

Chapter 1544(216)

'Yudhishthira asked, "O grandfather! There may be a lord of the earth who has been dislodged from his prosperity and is roaming around the earth. He may have been crushed by the rod of destiny. What intelligence should he resort to? Tell me."

'Bhishma replied, "In this connection, the ancient history of a conversation between Vasava[162] and Bali, Virochana's son,

[159]Above probably means heaven, while below means the nether regions. In that case, transverse may be used in the sense of the earth.

[160]By the soul.

[161]Indra.

[162]Indra.

is recounted. Having defeated all the asuras, Vasava went to the grandfather,[163] joined his hands in salutation and bowing down before him, asked him about Bali. 'O Brahma! I do not see Bali, whose wealth did not dimish, despite his giving it away liberally.[164] Tell me where Bali is. He was the one who set and arose, lighting up the directions. He was the one who attentively showered down at the right time. I do not see Bali. O Brahma! Tell me where Bali is. He was Vayu, Varuna, Ravi,[165] Chandrama[166] and Agni, who heated beings and the earth. I do not see Bali. O Brahma! Tell me where Bali is.'

'"Brahma replied, 'O Maghavan![167] It is not proper that you should ask about him now.[168] However, if one is asked, one should not utter a falsehood. I will tell you about Bali. O Shachi's lord![169] He may be[170] among camels, cows, asses or horses. He may be the best among those animals[171] and may be alone in his apartment.'

'"Shakra asked, 'O Brahma! If I meet Bali, alone in his apartment, should I kill him, or should I not kill him? O Brahma! Instruct me about that.'

'"Brahma replied, 'O Shakra! You should not cause injury to Bali. Bali does not deserve to be killed. O Shakra! You should ask him about good policy. O Vasava! But you should do as you wish.'"

'Bhishma replied, "Having been addressed by the illustrious one, the great Indra went to the earth. He was surrounded by great

[163]Brahma.

[164]Bali was extremely generous. He was Virochana's son and Prahlada's grandson. He conquered the three worlds and dislodged Indra from heaven. In his dwarf (vamana) incarnation, Vishnu took advantage of Bali's generosity and robbed him of the three worlds. According to some stories, Bali was thereafter tied down by Varuna's nooses.

[165]The sun.

[166]The moon.

[167]Indra.

[168]Since Indra had defeated Bali.

[169]Shachi is Indra's wife.

[170]Having been reborn.

[171]This probably means that Bali may have been reborn as a man.

prosperity and was ascended on Airavata's[172] shoulder. He saw Bali, in the form of an ass. As the illustrious one had said, he was alone in that abode.

'"Shakra said, 'O danava! You have now obtained the form of an ass and are subsisting on chaff. You have been born as an inferior species. Are you grieving or are you not grieving? I see what I have not seen earlier. You have been brought under the subjugation of your enemies. You are devoid of your prosperity and friends. You have been dislodged from your energy and valour. Earlier, when you advanced, you used to be surrounded by thousands of your relatives. You scorched all the worlds and did not think that we were worth considering. The daityas looked towards you and subjected themselves to your rule. It is because of your prosperity that the earth yielded crops, even when it had not been tilled. You have now been reduced to this hardship. Are you grieving or are you not grieving? In earlier times, you were full of pride and stationed yourself on the eastern shores of the ocean, dividing your riches amongst your relatives. What was the state of your mind then? You were honoured by thousands of celestial women, who danced before you. For thousands of years, you sported in blazing prosperity. All of them[173] were adorned in garlands made out of lotuses and all of them were golden in complexion. O lord of the danavas! What was the state of your mind then and what is it now? You used to possess a great and golden umbrella and it was adorned with gems. In seven different ways, sixty thousand gandharvas danced before you. In your sacrifices, there used to be a gigantic altar that was completely made out of gold. There, you gave away thousands and millions of cattle. You roamed around the entire earth, hurling the *shamya* according to the prescribed rites and performing sacrifices.[174] What was the state of your mind then? I do not see the vessel now, nor the umbrella or the whisks. O lord of the asuras! Nor do I see the garland that was given to you by Brahma.'

[172]The name of Indra's elephant.

[173]The celestial damsels.

[174]A shamya is a wooden rod. It is hurled from the hand and a sacrifice is performed wherever it happens to land. In this way, the entire earth is covered.

'"Bali replied, 'You do not see the vessel, the umbrella or the whisks. O Vasava! Nor do you see the garland that was given by Brahma. You have asked me about my gems. They have now been hidden inside a cave. When my time arrives, you will see them again. However, this conduct of yours is not appropriate for your fame or your lineage. When you see me amidst this adversity, why are you boasting about your prosperity? Learned ones who are accomplished in wisdom, virtuous, content in their wisdom and tranquil, do not grieve in misery and find delight in happiness. O Purandara! You are boasting because of your common knowledge. When your sentiments become like mine, you will not speak in this way.'"'

Chapter 1545(217)

'Bhishma said, "O descendant of the Bharata lineage. He[175] was sighing like a serpent. Shakra laughed at him and again spoke words that were more piercing than those uttered earlier. 'When you advanced earlier, you were surrounded by one thousand vehicles and relatives. You scorched all the worlds and disregarded all of us. O Bali! Behold your extremely miserable state now. Your relatives have abandoned you. Are you grieving or are you not grieving? You obtained unsurpassed delight earlier. You were stationed, with all the worlds under your subjugation. You have been brought down now. Are you grieving or are you not grieving?'

'"Bali replied, 'I see that all of this is transient and is because of what the progress of time has wrought on me. O Shakra! Since I know the truth about all of this, I do not sorrow. O lord of the immortals! These bodies of beings have an end. O Shakra! That is the reason I do not grieve. This is not because of any crime that I have committed. This life force and the physical body are born together and last till death. They grow up together and they are

[175]Bali.

destroyed together. Having obtained this existence,[176] I am powerless only temporarily. Since I know this, because of that knowledge, I suffer no pain. Just as all flows head towards the ocean, all beings end in death. O wielder of the *vajra*! Men who know this are never confused. Those who do not know this are overcome by rajas and confusion. They sink down when they face hardships and their intelligence is destroyed. A man who gains intelligence destroys all his sins. Bereft of sins, one obtains virtue. Such a person is hale and delighted. Those who retreat from it[177] are born again and again. They are tormented by misery and are goaded by that which does not lead to welfare. Whether there is success in obtaining prosperity, whether there is adversity, whether one is alive or dead and whether there are fruits of joy or misery, I do not hate them. Nor do I crave them. There is a slayer and there is someone who is slain. But if a man thinks that he is the slayer, he is himself slain. Whether it is the slain or whether it is the slayer, neither of them truly knows. O Maghavan! A person who kills and is victorious and then boasts about his manliness, is not actually the doer. The actor who has done this is elsewhere. Who is the one who has brought about the creation and the destruction of the worlds? It may be thought that this task has been accomplished by a doer. But the actual doer is someone else. All beings are generated from earth, wind, space, water and light, as the fifth. Therefore, where is the scope for sorrow? Realize this great knowledge—a weak person, a strong one, a malformed person, a handsome one, an unfortunate person and a fortunate one, are all afflicted by time, deep in its own energy. Since I know that I have come under the subjugation of time, why should I be pained? What is being burnt is something that has already been burnt.[178] What is being slain is something that has already been slain. What is being destroyed is something that has been destroyed earlier. A man gets what has already been obtained for him. There is no island.[179] Where

[176]Of an ass.

[177]From virtue.

[178]Because of destiny.

[179]Destiny is being compared to an ocean.

is the further shore? No boundary can be seen. This destiny is divine. Though I think about it, I do not see an end to it. O lord of Shachi! Had I not seen that time is behind the destruction of beings, then I might have felt delight, insolence and anger. I subsist on chaff. I have been abandoned by the people of the household and am in the form of a donkey. Knowing this, you are condemning me. If I so desire, even now, I can assume many kinds of forms that are so terrible that, looking at them, you will run away from me. But it is time that gives everything and it is time that takes everything away. Time pervades everything. O Shakra! Do not boast about your manliness. O Purandara! Earlier, everyone was distressed because of my rage. O Shakra! I know about the eternal dharma of the worlds. Like me, know about this and do not be overcome with amazement. Power and influence are never due to one's own self. Your consciousness is like that of a child. It is just as it was in ancient times.[180] O Maghavan! Glance towards everything with your intelligence and obtain what is best for you. The gods, men, the ancestors, the gandharvas, the serpents and the *rakshasas*—all of them used to be under my subjugation earlier. O Vasava! You know this. "We bow down before the directions where Bali, Virochana's son, is stationed." Their intelligence confused because of envy, this is what they used to say to me. O lord of Shachi! I do not sorrow because of that reverence that was shown to me. My intelligence is firm and I will remain under the subjugation of the one who ordains. One may see a person who has been born in a noble lineage. He is handsome and influential. But with his advisers, he lives in misery. This can be nothing other than destiny. O Shakra! On the other hand, one may see a person who has been born in an inferior lineage and is stupid. Despite his inferior birth, with his advisers, he may live in happiness. This can be nothing other than destiny. O Shakra! An auspicious and beautiful woman will be seen to suffer from misfortune. O Shakra! An inauspicious and ugly woman will be seen to be fortunate. O Shakra! My state is not

[180]It has not progressed.

because of anything I have done. O Shakra! My state is not because of anything you have done. O wielder of the vajra! Your state is not because of you and our state is not because of us. O Shatakratu! This is not because of anything you have done, not to speak of something I have done. Progressively, prosperity and adversity do not come about because of deeds. I see you in your resplendence, stationed as the king of the gods. You are handsome and radiant and are roaring at me. This would not have happened had time not attacked me and remained stationed here. Had that not been the case, despite your holding the vajra, I would have used my bare fists to bring you down now. But this is not the time for exhibiting valour. The time for exhibiting forgiveness has arrived. Everything is established in time and time cooks everything. There was a time when I was the lord of the danavas and was worshipped. I roared and tormented and there was no one who could advance against me. O king of the gods! I single-handedly robbed the twelve great-souled Adityas of their energy, with you included in that group. O Vasava! I was the one who soaked up the water and released it again.[181] I was the one who offered heat and light to the three worlds. I was the one who protected and I was the one who destroyed. I was the one who gave and I was the one who took away. I was the one who restrained and I was the one who released. I was the lord and master of the worlds. O lord of the immortals! That lordship has now been taken away. I have been assailed by the soldiers of time and none of that can be seen in me. O lord of Shachi! I am not the doer. You are not the doer. No one else is the doer. O Shakra! It is time that progressively destroys the worlds, as it desires. People who are learned about the Vedas say that the year is his mouth.[182] The months and the fortnights are his body and days and nights are his attire. The seasons are the gates.[183] There are also people who, because of their learning, say that

[181]Bali had become Indra then.

[182]Time is being equated with Brahma.

[183]Interpreted as the senses.

everything should be thought of as him. The five sheaths one thinks of are nothing but his five aspects.[184] Brahma is deep and fathomless, like a gigantic ocean. He is without beginning and without destruction. He is said to be supreme and without decay. Though he himself possesses no attributes, he assumes attributes in beings. Men who have comprehended the truth certainly think of him in this way. They think that he brings about the progression and regression of beings. But there is no progression for that which is inside.[185] It is above nature. He is the resort of all beings. Where can one go, other than to that resort? One cannot avoid this by running, or by remaining stationary. All the five senses are incapable of seeing him. Some speak of him as Agni and some speak of him as Prajapati. Others say he is the seasons, the fortnights, the months, the days and the moments. There are others who say he is the forenoon, the afternoon, or midday, or an instant. Virtuous ones speak of him as one and many. Know him as time, the one who has everything under his subjugation. O Vasava! There have been many thousands of Indras. O lord of Shachi! Their strength and valour were just like your own. O Shakra! You are extremely strong. You are the king of the gods and are proud of your strength. However, when it is time, immensely valorous time will pacify you. It takes away everything. O Shakra! Therefore, be steady. Neither I, nor you, nor those who have come before us, are capable of transgressing it. You have obtained this supreme royal prosperity now. Know that it was earlier vested in me. It is not real and does not remain with one person alone. It was established in one thousand Indras before this and all of them were superior to you. O lord of the gods! It is unstable. It abandoned me and has approached you now. O Shakra! You should not boast again. You should be tranquil. If you have such sentiments, it will abandon you and swiftly go to someone else.'"'

[184]These five sheaths cover the atman and are *annamaya* (related to food), *pranamaya* (related to energy), *manomaya* (related to the mind), *vijnanamaya* (related to knowledge) and *anandamaya* (related to bliss).

[185]The atman.

Chapter 1546(218)

'Bhishma said, "Shatakratu then saw the blazing Shri,[186] in her own form, emerge from the body of the great-souled Bali. The illustrious chastiser of Paka[187] saw her resplendent power. Vasava's eyes dilated with wonder and he asked Bali. 'Who is this one who is emerging, blazing in her own energy? Her bracelets and diadem are beautiful.'

'"Bali replied, 'I do not know whether she is an asura maiden, a goddess or a human. O Vasava! Do as you wish and ask her yourself.'

'"Shakra asked, 'O one with the beautiful smiles! O one with the diadem! O radiant one who is emerging from Bali! Who are you? I do not know you. Tell me your name. You are stationed here like Maya,[188] resplendent in your own energy. Who are you? O one with the beautiful eyebrows! You have abandoned the lord of the daityas. Tell me your true nature.'

'"Shri replied, 'Virochana did not know me. Virochana's son, Bali, does not know me. I am known as Duhsaha and the learned know me as Vidhitsa.[189] O Vasava! I am also known by the names Bhuti, Lakshmi and Shri.[190] O Shakra! You do not know me. All the gods don't know me.'

'"Shakra asked, 'O Duhsaha! You have dwelt with Bali for a long time. Why are you abandoning him now? Is it because of his acts or because of mine?'

'"Shri replied, 'Dhata and Vidhata[191] cannot control me. O Shakra! Time determines my progressive movement. O Shakra! Do not show disrespect.'[192]

[186]The embodied form of prosperity, in particular, royal prosperity.

[187]Indra killed a demon named Paka.

[188]Maya was the architect of the demons.

[189]Respectively, someone who is difficult to withstand and the desire for action.

[190]All three names mean plenty and prosperity.

[191]Respectively, the creator and the ordainer.

[192]Towards Bali.

'"Shakra asked, 'O one with the diadem! Why have you abandoned Bali? Why are you approaching me? O one with the sweet smiles! Tell me this.'

'"Shri replied, 'I am established in truth, donations, vows, austerities, valour and dharma. Bali has deviated from these. He was devoted to brahmanas. He was truthful and in control of his senses. But he began to hate brahmanas and touched clarified butter with soiled hands.[193] Earlier, he was devoted to the performance of sacrifices. However, he was afflicted by destiny and became foolish. He began to boast to people that he was capable of performing sacrifices to me.[194] O Shakra! O Vasava! I will therefore abandon him and dwell with you. Bear me up without distraction and through austerities and valour.'

'"Shakra said, 'O one whose abode is a lotus! There is no single man amongst gods, humans or amongst all beings, who is capable of bearing you for ever.'

'"Shri replied, 'O Purandara! Indeed, there is no single one amongst gods, gandharvas, asuras or rakshasas who is capable of bearing me for ever.'

'"Shakra said, 'O auspicious one! Tell me the means whereby you will always remain with me. You should tell me truthfully and I will act in accordance with those words.'

'"Shri replied, 'O Indra of the gods! I will tell you the means whereby I am always established with you. Listen. Following the ordinances of the Vedas, divide me into four parts.'

'"Shakra said, 'According to their capacity and their strength, I will determine abodes for you. O Lakshmi! When you are with me, I will never transgress you. O creator of all beings! Among men, let the earth bear you. It is my view that she is capable of bearing one quarter of you.'

[193]The text uses the word *ucchishta*. This means, he touched clarified butter while eating. Or, having eaten, he touched clarified butter without having washed his hands first.

[194]Probably implying that Bali did not need priests any longer.

'"Shri replied, 'This is one quarter of me. Let it be established on earth. O Shakra! Now make arrangements for the second of my four quarters.'

'"Shakra said, 'Among men, the water tends to them in liquid form. Let the clear waters bear a quarter. They have the capacity to bear.'

'"Shri replied, 'This is one quarter of me. Let it be established in the waters. O Shakra! Now make arrangements for the third of my four quarters.'

'"Shakra said, 'The gods, the sacrifices and the Vedas are established in the fire. Let it bear the third quarter, since it is capable of bearing well.'

'"Shri replied, 'This is one quarter of me. Let it be established in the fire. O Shakra! Now make arrangements for the fourth of my four quarters.'

'"Shakra said, 'There are virtuous men who are truthful in speech and are devoted to brahmanas. Those unblemished and virtuous ones have the capacity to bear. Let them bear a quarter.'

'"Shri replied, 'This is one quarter of me. Let it be established in the virtuous. O Shakra! With I having been distributed among beings, protect me.'

'"Shakra said, 'I have thus caused a distribution among beings. Listen to my words. I will kill those who injure you.'"

'Bhishma said, "Having been thus abandoned by Shri, Bali, the king of the daityas, spoke these words. 'The sun heats in front[195] and in the southern direction, in the west, as well as in the east. However, when the midday sun shines and does not set, there will again be a battle between the gods and the asuras and I will defeat you.[196] Amidst all the worlds, the sun will then heat only one spot.

[195]The north.

[196]This is given the following interpretation. Mount Meru is in the centre of the earth. The sun travels around Meru and shines everywhere. But this is during the present *manvantara* of Vaivasvata. When this is followed by Savarni manvantara, the sun will only shine on Mount Meru and there will be darkness everywhere else.

O Shatakratu! There will then be a battle between the gods and the asuras and I will vanquish you.'

"'Shakra replied, 'Brahma instructed me that you should not be killed by me. O Bali! That is the reason I am not releasing the vajra at your head. O Indra among the daityas! O great asura! Go wherever you wish and may you be at peace. There will be no occasion when the sun will only be stationed at the midpoint and heat there. Svayambhu[197] has earlier laid down the course of time it must follow. It follows that truth and heats subjects incessantly. It follows six months of a northward and southward course each. That is the way the sun creates cold and heat for all the worlds.'"

'Bhishma replied, "O descendant of the Bharata lineage! Thus addressed by Indra, Bali, the Indra among the daityas, left for the southern direction. Purandara went towards the north. Bali sang this song, which was without any trace of pride. Having heard his words, the one with the thousand eyes rose up into the sky."'

Chapter 1547(219)

'Bhishma said, "O Yudhishthira! In this connection, the ancient history of a conversation between Shatakratu and Namuchi is recounted. He[198] was seated, bereft of prosperity, like an ocean that wasn't agitated, knowledgable about the creation and destruction of all beings. Purandara spoke to him. 'O Namuchi! You have been tied down in bonds. You have been dislodged from your place. You are under the subjugation of your enemies. You are devoid of prosperity. Are you grieving, or are you not grieving?'

"'Namuchi replied, 'Nothing changes because of sorrow. The body alone is afflicted and enemies are delighted. No help is brought by grieving. O Shakra! I know that everything has an end. Therefore,

[197]Brahma.

[198]Namuchi.

I am not sorrowing. O lord of the gods! Grief destroys beauty and dharma. One must indeed subdue the sorrow that arises in one's mind. Knowing what is beneficial, one must meditate on that in one's mind and in one's heart. There is no doubt that this is capable of ensuring success in everything. There is one ordainer. There is no second ordainer. The ordainer ordains the man, as he lies down in the womb. I am instructed by him, like water flowing downwards. I flow as I am appointed. I know about existence and non-existence and about that which is superior.[199] However, despite knowing what is best, I do not act in that way. Submerged in hopes, dharma and well-wishers, I do good deeds and their reverse. I flow as I am appointed. Whatever can be obtained is what will be obtained. Whatever is meant to happen is what will happen. As has been decided by the creator, one will repeatedly dwell in different wombs. One doesn't go there because of one's own wishes. The existence that I have obtained is because of my destiny. A person whose sentiments are like this will never be confused. Respect and the lack of a name occur progressively. Only a person who thinks his own self to be the actor sees unhappiness in this.[200] In this world, who is not afflicted by catastrophes—the sages, the gods, the great asuras, the aged ones who know the three Vedas and hermits in the forest? Those who know the supreme are not frightened by this. No anger is generated in a learned person. He does not suffer. Nor is he delighted. He does not sorrow if there is a hardship on account of lack of riches, or some other kind of difficulty. He is established, as naturally immobile as the Himalayas. If riches and success do not delight him and a time of hardship does not confuse him, such a person is superior. A man who can bear the burden when faced with happiness or unhappiness is medium. A man must always be cheerful and must not torment himself, even when he confronts a downfall. He must control the torment that grows in his mind, because that harms the body. If there is an assembly with virtuous people gathered there and if, on entering it, a person

[199]Moksha or emancipation.

[200]A wise person doesn't regard himself as an actor and thinks of this as destiny. But a foolish person is miserable because he ascribes it to his own action.

is not freed from fear, then that is not a virtuous assembly.[201] If an intelligent man immerses himself in dharma and then decides, he is capable of bearing a burden. The deeds of a wise man are difficult to fathom. Even when it is a time for confusion, a wise person is not confused. Even when he is dislodged from his position and faces a hardship and a disaster because of this, like Goutama in his old age, he is not confused.[202] In the world of the mortal, one cannot obtain what is not meant to be obtained through mantras, strength, valour, wisdom and manliness. Why should one sorrow on account of that? In ancient times, the creator ordained this, before I was born. What was ordained has happened. What can death do to me? One obtains what was meant to be obtained. One goes where one is meant to go. One gets what is meant to be got, unhappiness or happiness. A man who knows all of this is not confused. He is skilled in the midst of joy and misery and is the lord of all riches.'"'

Chapter 1548(220)

'Yudhishthira asked, "What is best for a man when he is immersed in hardships and difficulties? O lord of the earth! What about when his relatives are destroyed and his kingdom is destroyed? O bull among the Bharata lineage! In this world, you are the supreme speaker for us. I am asking you about this. You should tell me about it."

'Bhishma replied, "O king! If a person has been separated from his sons, wives, happiness and riches and is immersed in hardships and difficulties, fortitude is the best for him. For a person who has

[201]This sentence hangs loose and there is no obvious connection with what comes before or after.

[202]The sage Goutama's wife, Ahalya, was seduced by Indra, who adopted Goutama's form. Goutama cursed Ahalya that she would turn to stone. However, in the process, Goutama also suffered.

patience, the body does not suffer. Because the body is healthy, he again obtains prosperity. If a king or a man resorts to righteous conduct, his patience and steadfastness will manifest themselves in all the tasks he is engaged in. O Yudhishthira! In this connection, an ancient history is recounted, about the conversation that again took place between Bali and Vasava. There was a battle between the gods and the asuras and this lead to a destruction of daityas and danavas. Vishnu obtained the worlds and the kingship of the gods for Shatakratu.[203] Sacrifices were performed to the gods and the four varnas were established. The three worlds were prosperous and Svayambhu was filled with delight. Shakra was ascended on Airavata, which had four excellent tusks and was an Indra among elephants. Surrounded by prosperity, the lord travelled through the three worlds. He was surrounded by the Rudras, the Vasus, the Adityas, the Ashvins, the rishis, the gandharvas, the Indras among the serpents, the Siddhas and others. On one such occasion, on the frontiers of the ocean and in a cavern inside a mountain, the wielder of the vajra saw Bali, Virochana's son, and approached him. Despite seeing Indra, the lord of the gods, seated on Airavata's shoulder, surrounded by large numbers of gods, the Indra among the daityas was not distressed and did not sorrow. Shatakratu was seated on that best of elephants and saw that Bali was stationed there, without any fear and without any agitation. He asked, 'O daitya! You are not distressed. Is this because of your valour or is this because you have served your seniors? Is it because you have been cleaned through austerities? In every respect, this is a very difficult state to attain. You have been brought down from a supreme position and are now under the subjugation of your enemies. O Virochana's son! What is the support that enables you not to grieve, though you should sorrow? With your relatives, you attained the best state possible and enjoyed supreme objects of pleasure. You have now been deprived of your army and your kingdom. Tell me. Why aren't you mourning? Earlier, you were a god, occupying the seat of your father and

[203]In his vamana incarnation, Vishnu obtained the worlds from Bali and gave them to Indra.

grandfather. You have now seen that robbed by your rivals. Why aren't you mourning? You have been tied down in Varuna's nooses and have been struck by the vajra. You have been robbed of your wives. You have been robbed of your wealth. Tell me. Why aren't you mourning? You have been dislodged from your prosperity. You have been dislodged from your riches. Yet, you are not sorrowing, and this is an extremely difficult thing to do. If the kingdom of the three worlds has been destroyed, who else would be interested in remaining alive?' He spoke these and other harsh words, intending to subdue him.

'"However, Virochana's son, Bali, heard these words cheerfully. Without being frightened, he replied, 'O Shakra! When I have been severely afflicted, why are you boasting? O Purandara! I see you standing here now, with the vajra upraised. Earlier, you were incapable of doing this. How have you acquired the capacity now? Indeed, who other than you could have spoken such extremely cruel words? The learned say that if someone has brought a brave enemy under his subjugation and control, but has the capacity to show mercy, that person is indeed a man. When two people quarrel and fight, the outcome is uncertain. One of them obtains victory and the other one obtains defeat. O bull among the gods! You should not exhibit such a temperament towards me. Do not think that you have become the lord by defeating all the beings with your valour and strength. O Shakra! This state is not because of anything we have done. O Shakra! Nor is it because of what you have done. O wielder of the vajra! This state is not because of you or because of us. You will become what I am now. You will become like us. Do not think that my state is because of my wicked deeds or because of what you have done. Progressively, a man encounters happiness and unhappiness. O Shakra! You have obtained the state of Shakra because of progression, not because of your deeds. As time elapsed, time conveyed me. It is time again that conveys you. Happiness does not come to a man because of serving the mother and the father, worshipping the gods, or because of following other good qualities. When a man is afflicted by time, learning, austerities, donations, friends and relatives are not capable of saving him. Even if one counters in one hundred different ways, calamities strike back. Men are incapable of fighting them back through intelligence and strength. One is afflicted through this progression and there is no one who is a saviour. O Shakra! This is a reason for sorrow only if you think of yourself as the doer. If the doer is actually the doer, then no one else would have made the doer do anything. However, because someone else makes the doer do things, that other entity is a lord over the apparent doer. I defeated you through the aid of time. It is through the aid of time that you have vanquished me. Time is the force behind all movement. Time drives all beings. O Indra! Your intelligence is ordinary and you do not comprehend the destruction. Some show you a great deal of reverence because of the superiority you have obtained through your own deeds. But there are those like us, who know the progress of the worlds. When we are afflicted by time, why should we grieve? Why should we be confused and frightened? Even when I am constantly afflicted by time and suffer a calamity, shall my intelligence, or that of someone like me, be destroyed, like a shattered boat? O Shakra! I, you, and all the future lords of the gods, will have to traverse the path followed by hundreds of Indras earlier. You are now extremely unassailable and are blazing in supreme prosperity. But when your time comes, time will destroy you, just as it has destroyed me. From one yuga to another yuga, there have been many thousands of Indras and daityas. They have been carried away by time. Time is extremely difficult to cross. Having obtained this state, you have an extremely high opinion of yourself, as if you are the eternal god Brahma, the creator of all beings. But this state is not immobile. Nor is this state eternal. However, because of your foolish intelligence, you think it to be thus. You trust something that should not be trusted. You think that something temporary is permanent. Because of your delusion, you think that the royal prosperity that you desire is yours. Know this to be a fact that this is not yours, nor ours, nor that of others. There are many others who have obtained this state. But they have all passed on. O Vasava! This fickle position will stay with you for some time. Like a cow abandoning one drinking spot for another, it will then go to someone else. There are so many kings who have passed through this world earlier, that I am not even interested in enumerating them. O Purandara! There will be many others after you too. This earth possesses trees, herbs, jewels, rivers and mountains. I no longer see those who have enjoyed it in earlier times. Prithu, Aila, Maya, Bhima, Naraka, Shambara, Asvagriva, Puloma, Svarbhanu, with an infinitely long standard, Prahlada, Namuchi, Daksha, Viprachitti, Virochana, Hrinishedha, Suhotra, Bhuriha, Pushpavan, Vrisha, Satyeshu, Rishabha, Rahu, Kapilashva, Virupaksha, Bana, Kartasvara, Vahni, Vishvadamshtra, Nairrita, Rittha, Ahuttha, Viratamra, Varahashva, Ruchi, Prabhu, Vishvajit, Agratishouri, Vrishanda, Vishkara, Madhu, Hiranyakashipu, the danava Kaitabha, the daitya Kalakhanja, with all the Nairritas—there were these Indras among daityas and Indras among danavas. These came earlier and even before that. We have heard their names and those of others. There were many Indras among daityas earlier. They have abandoned the earth and have gone. They have all been afflicted by time. Time is the strongest. O Shatakratu! All of them performed hundreds of sacrifices and rites. You are not the only one. All of them were devoted to dharma. All of them always performed sacrifices. All of them could roam around in the sky. All of them never showed their backs in the field of battle. All of them were capable of tolerating. All of them possessed arms like clubs. All of them could show one hundred different kinds of maya. All of them could go wherever they desired. We have not heard of any of them being defeated, once they embarked on a battle. All of them were devoted to the vow of truth. All of them could sport as they willed. All of them were devoted to the vows of the Vedas. All of them were extremely learned. All of them could withstand. All of them obtained riches and lordship. However, none of those great-souled ones who came earlier was proud because of his wealth. All of them were truly generous. All of them were devoid of malice. Each of them behaved towards all beings exactly as they should have. All of them were the sons of Dakshayani and Prajapati.[204] All of them were extremely strong. They blazed and

[204]Prajapati means the sage Kashyapa, who was married to several of Daksha's daughters.

scorched. But time carried them away. Once you have enjoyed the earth, you will again have to give it up. O Shakra! You will be incapable of restraining your grief then. Free yourself from this desire for objects of pleasure. Free yourself from this pride that comes from prosperity. If you do that, when your own kingdom is destroyed, you will be able to bear the sorrow. You should not sorrow when it is a time for grief. You should not be delighted when it is a time for joy. Forget the past and the future and act in accordance with what has presented itself. Time never sleeps and it presented itself before me. O Indra! Pardon me. But it will also present itself before you. O Indra of the gods! You have spoken such words to me with the object of piercing and frightening me. Seeing that I am controlled, there is no doubt that you think extremely highly of me. Time struck me first and will follow you later. O Indra of the gods! Who are you roaring at? I have already been struck by time. When I used to rage in battle, who in this world was capable of standing before me? O Vasava! You are stationed here because time has proved to be more powerful. Those one thousand years meant for you will be completed.[205] You will then be dislodged from your state and be robbed of your energy, just as all my limbs are now. I am an Indra who has been dislodged from his status and you have naturally become an Indra in heaven. Because of the progress of time, you are now worshipped in this extremely wonderful world of the living. O Indra! But what is it exactly that you have done? And what have we done to be dislodged? Time is the doer and the undoer. There is nothing else that is the cause. Decay, destruction, riches, happiness, unhappiness, existence and non-existence—when a learned person confronts any of these, he is neither delighted, nor distressed. O Indra! You know us. O Vasava! We know you too. I have been disarmed and bound by time. Why are you then boasting before me? You know the manliness that I exhibited earlier. The valour that I exhibited in battle is sufficient proof. O lord of Shachi! The Adityas, the Rudras, the Sadhyas, together with the Vasus, and all the Maruts were vanquished by me. O Shakra! You also know what happened

[205]Indra was destined to rule for one thousand divine years.

in the encounter between the gods and the asuras. All the assembled gods were swiftly shattered by me in the battle. In that terrible battle, I angrily struck you on the head with mountains, with their forests and those who lived in those forests. I struck with you with summits and peaks. What could I not have done then? But time is impossible to cross. That is the reason I am not interested in killing you, holding that vajra, with my fists. This is not the time for exhibiting valour. The time for showing forgiveness has arrived. O Shakra! That is the reason I am being tolerant, though I am less tolerant than you are. My time has matured and I have been cooked by the flames of time. O Shakra! I have been restrained and bound by the nooses of time and you are boasting before me. This is the dark being whom the worlds find impossible to cross.[206] This terrible one has bound me, like an animal with ropes, and is standing here. Gain, loss, happiness, unhappiness, desire, anger, existence, non-existence, slaughter, bondage, freedom—all of these are obtained because of time. I am not the doer. You are not the doer. The doer is always the one who is the lord. Time has cooked me, like a fruit that has appeared on a tree. Despite being yoked to time, there are things a man can do to obtain happiness. Despite being yoked to time, there are again things that can be done to obtain misery. When a person who knows about time has been touched by time, that person should not grieve. O Shakra! That is the reason I am not grieving. That is of no help at a time of sorrow. If one grieves at a time of sorrow, the hardship is not ameliorated. There is no capability in that grief. That is the reason I am not sorrowing now.' He spoke in this way to the thousand-eyed and illustrious chastiser of Paka.

'"Having been thus addressed, Shatakratu controlled his anger and spoke these words. 'You have seen my upraised arm with the vajra and Varuna's nooses. Who with intelligence will not be distressed at this, including Death, the destroyer of everything? However, you are not distressed at this. Your intelligence is not fickle and you have seen the truth. O one with truth as his valour! You have spoken words to the effect that you are not distressed. On

[206]The personification of time.

seeing that everything in this universe is transient, which embodied being in this world will be interested or capable of reposing his faith in anything that pertains to the body? I also know that everything in this world is temporary. Although it cannot be seen, everything is constantly being borne by time's eternal and terrible fire. When one has been touched by time, there is no salvation. The subtlest and the greatest of beings are cooked. Without any master and without any distraction, it constantly cooks beings. The decay due to time cannot be withdrawn. Once one has attained it, there is no freedom. One may not realize this. But ever attentive, time is awake in beings. No one has earlier been seen to have made efforts and escaped it. It is the ancient and eternal dharma. It looks on all living beings in the same way. Time cannot be avoided and there is no exception to what it does. Like a moneylender computing interest, time calculates days, nights, months, *kshana*s, *kashtha*s, *kala*s and *lava*s for us. There are those who say, "I will do this today. I will do that tomorrow." Time approaches and bears them away, like a raft on the current of a river. "I saw him just now. How can he be dead?" While men are heard to lament in this way, time robs them. Riches, objects of pleasure, status and prosperity are all temporary and uncertain. It is extremely difficult to conduct oneself. Everything is brought down and so are existence and non-existence. But you are not distressed by this. Your intelligence is not fickle and you have seen the truth. Even in your mind, you are not bothered about what you have been before. Time afflicts this world and being stronger, cooks it. It sweeps away, regardless of whether a person is young or old. Addicted to jealousy, pride, greed, desire, anger, fright, wishes, confusion and pride, people are deluded. But you know the truth about existence. You are learned in wisdom and austerities. You look at time extremely well, as if it was a myrobalan fruit in your hand. You know the truth about the character of time. You are accomplished in all the sacred texts. O son of Virochana! You have cleansed your soul. You are desired by those who know. I think that with your intelligence, you have comprehended all the worlds. You roam around, free in every way. You have not been tainted by anything. You have conquered your senses and the qualities of rajas and tamas do not touch you.

You are without affection. You have destroyed all sorrow. You worship your atman alone. You are a well-wisher to all beings. You are without enmity. You are tranquil in your mind. On seeing you in this state, my mind turns to compassion. Because of the progress of time, you are bound in Varuna's noose and you will be freed from them, because of the evil conduct of subjects. O great asura! May you be safe. When daughters-in-law will engage aged mothers-in-law in work, when deluded sons will send their fathers to work, when *vrishala*s will make brahmanas wash their feet, when shudras will fearlessly serve brahmana wives, when men will release their seeds into vaginas that should be avoided, when sacrifices will be carried in brass vessels, those made out of mixed metal and other inferior vessels, when the four varnas will transgress all restraints, then, one by one, you will progressively be freed from these bonds. There will be no fear from me. Adhere to this agreement. Be safe and without any restraint. Be hale and healthy.' Having spoken these words, the illustrious Shatakratu departed, with that king among elephants as his mount. The lord of the gods had vanquished all the asuras. He was delighted and happy and was the single king. The maharshis chanted words of praise in the name of Vrishakapi, the lord of all mobile and immobile objects. The fire god bore all the oblations and the amrita that was offered to the lord. The supreme among brahmanas performed sacrifices in every way. The lord[207] lost all his rage and his mind was tranquil. Vasava blazed in his energy and cheerfully returned to his own abode in heaven and found pleasure there."'

Chapter 1549(221)

'Yudhishthira said, "O king! O grandfather! Tell me about a man's earlier form and his subsequent downfall."

'Bhishma replied, "O fortunate one! The mind indicates a man's

[207]Indra.

earlier form and what will happen and not happen to him in the future. On this, an ancient history is recounted about a conversation between Shri and Shakra. O Yudhishthira! Listen to this. As he wished, Narada roamed around in the three worlds. He was great in his austerities and could see this world and the supreme one. Though he was an ordinary rishi, he was the equal of those who resided in Brahma's world. He was a great ascetic and was tranquil in his soul. His infinitely blazing energy was like that of Brahma himself. On one occasion, he arose in the morning and wished to purify himself with water. He went to where the Ganga emerges through the gate known as Dhruva.[208] The one with the thousand eyes, the wielder of the vajra and the slayer of Shambara and Paka, also happened to come to the spot where the devarshi was. Both of them were in control of their souls. Having performed their ablutions and meditations, they sat down together. They were seated on the banks of the river, with sand as fine as gold. The devarshi recounted stories of auspicious deeds, tales about good conduct. They were attentive and spoke to each other about these ancient accounts. The sun arose and its net of rays was spread before them. On seeing that full solar disc, they arose. They worshipped the supreme sun, whose task it was to dispel the darkness. At that time, on the further side of the sky, they saw a body of light arise and it blazed like the sun. O descendant of the Bharata lineage! They saw that it was approaching them. There was this unmatched radiance that illuminated the three worlds and it was astride Vishnu's vehicle, with both Suparna[209] and the sun situated there. There was a divine form, attended by apsaras. She was like a gigantic sun or fire herself, with large rays radiating out. Her ornaments were like nakshatras and her garlands dazzled with stars. They saw the goddess Padma Shri herself, stationed on a lotus. The supreme lady descended from her celestial vehicle and approached Shakra, the lord of the three worlds, and rishi Narada. Followed by Narada, Maghavan approached. He joined his hands in salutation and offered himself to the goddess. The one who knew

[208]In heaven, the Ganga flows in Brahma's world and Dhruva is the pole star.
[209]Garuda, Vishnu's mount.

about everything[210] also worshipped the supreme one. O king! The lord of the gods spoke these words to Shri. 'O one with the beautiful smile! Who are you? For what purpose have you come here? O one with the excellent brows! O fortunate one! From where have you come and where are you going?'

'"Shri said, 'In the three worlds, all the mobile and immobile objects, those with supreme souls desire to be united with me and make efforts. I have been born from a lotus and awake at the rays of the sun. I bring prosperity to all beings. I am Padma Shri and I wear a garland of lotuses. O slayer of Bala! I am Lakshmi. I am Bhuti.[211] I am Shri. I am Shraddha and Medha.[212] I am Sannati, Vijiti and Sthiti.[213] I am Dhriti.[214] I am Siddhi.[215] I am Tvidbhuti.[216] I am Svaha and Svadha. I am Samstuti, Niyati and Kriti.[217] I station myself on the standards and at the forefront of the soldiers of victorious kings. I dwell in the abodes, material objects and cities of those who are devoted to dharma. O slayer of Bala! I always dwell with Indras among men, those brave ones who desire victory and do not retreat from the field of battle. There are those who are always devoted to dharma, extremely intelligent ones who are devoted to brahmanas and speak the truth. I always dwell with those who are modest and generous in their conduct. I earlier used to dwell with the asuras, when they were bound down by the dharma of truth. However, since their intelligence has turned perverse, it no longer pleases me to live with them.'

'"Shakra asked, 'O one with the beautiful face! What was the conduct of the daityas when you dwelt with them? What did you see that you abandoned the daityas and the danavas?'

'"Shri replied, 'There are those who based themselves on their

[210]Narada.

[211]*Bhuti* means wealth and prosperity.

[212]*Shraddha* means faith, *medha* means wisdom.

[213]Respectively, humility, victory and permanence.

[214]Resolution.

[215]Success.

[216]Blazing prosperity.

[217]Respectively, praise, fortune and deeds.

own dharma. They are not dislodged from patience. They take delight in the paths that lead to heaven. I am always attached to those spirited ones. There are those who are engaged in donations, studying, sacrifices and the serving of seniors, gods, brahmanas and guests. I always dwell with them. They[218] kept their houses clean. Their women were under control and they offered oblations to the fire. They were self-controlled and served their superiors and brahmanas. They were truthful in speech. They were faithful and conquered their anger. They were generous and did not suffer from jealousy. They never wished to be intolerant towards each other. They were patient and were not tormented at the prosperity of others. They donated and accumulated. They were noble and compassionate. They were extremely content and upright. They were firm in their devotion and had conquered their senses. Their servants and advisers were satisfied. They were grateful and pleasant in speech. They did what should be done and did not cause any injury. They were modest and sought to ensure their vows. On auspicious occasions, they always bathed well, smeared themselves well and ornamented themselves. They were devoted to fasting and austerities. They were cheerful and knowledgable about the brahman. They awoke before the sun arose. They did not sleep before it was night. In the night, they always avoided curds and pounded ground meal.[219] They were brahmacharis. At the right time, they looked at clarified butter and other auspicious objects. They worshipped the brahmanas. They always observed dharma and donated, and always received back in turn. They slept when it was midnight and never slept during the day. They always found delight in giving a share of their possessions to the distressed, those who were without protectors, the aged, the weak, the diseased and women. They always comforted those who were miserable, frightened, anxious, terrified, afflicted by disease, those who had been robbed and those who suffered from calamities. They followed what was dharma and did not injure each other. They undertook favourable tasks and served preceptors and the aged. As is

[218]This is a reference to the danavas earlier, before they deviated.

[219]*Saktu*, colloquially known as *sattu*.

appropriate, they worshipped the ancestors, the gods and guests. They ate leftovers and were always devoted to truth and austerities. No one ate alone. No one went to another person's wife. They exhibited compassion towards every being, as if towards one's own self. They never found delight in releasing semen into space, animals, forbidden vaginas, or on sacred days. They were always accomplished in donating and were always upright. They were enthusiastic, without arrogance, extremely affectionate and forgiving. O lord! Truthfulness, generosity, austerities, purity, compassion, gentle speech and lack of injury towards friends—they possessed all these. They were not penetrated by excessive sleep, procrastination, lack of affection, jealousy, rashness, discontent, sorrow and desire. In earlier times, the danavas possessed these qualtiies and I dwelt with them, since the time beings were created. But once the era changed, time turned adverse and they lost those qualities. I saw that they had lost dharma and that their selves had been taken over by desire and anger. There were aged advisers who spoke about what was right and the truth. But they repeatedly laughed at these aged ones, who were superior in all the qualities. When they were seated and the aged ones arrived, they did not stand up and greet and worship them, as they used to earlier. Sons displayed their own power in the presence of the fathers. Enemies became servants and shamelessly proclaimed this fact. They desired to obtain great riches through the performance of reprehensible deeds that were not in accordance with dharma. They spoke loudly in the night. The fire began to blaze downwards.[220] Sons prevailed over their fathers and wives over their husbands. Mothers, fathers, the aged, preceptors, guests and seniors were no longer respected because of their seniority. Children were no longer protected. Without giving away as alms and sacrifices and without apportioning shares for ancestors, gods, guests and seniors, people started to eat. The cooks no longer faithfully observed requirements of purity in minds, words or deeds. They ate what was not covered. Grain was scattered around and became food for crows and rats. Milk was left uncovered. They arose with unwashed hands and

[220]An auspicious sacrificial fire has a flame that blazes upwards.

touched clarified butter.[221] Spades, plants, garments and brass vessels were scattered around and so were all the other objects and implements, with the housewives taking no notice of these. Walls and storehouses were destroyed and no care was taken to repair these. The tethered animals were not given grass and water. While the children and all the servants looked on, the danavas ate, and it was food that should not be eaten. They cooked *payasa*,[222] *krisara*,[223] meat and *shashkuli*[224] for themselves.[225] They cooked what should not be cooked and ate pointless flesh. All of them slept after the sun arose and before it was night. There were quarrels in every house, day and night. Though noble ones were seated there, the ignoble ones were worshipped. They deviated from the tasks of the ashramas and hated each other. There was a mixture[226] and no sorrow on account of this. No difference could be seen between brahmanas who knew about the Vedas and those who were unclear about the chants, those who deserved a great deal of respect and those who deserved no respect. No difference could be seen in behaviour, ornaments, attire, movement or status. There was enjoyment without service and the rites and conduct of bad people were followed. Women wore the attire of men. Men wore the attire of women. They obtained supreme delight in sporting, pleasure and roaming around. Earlier, the prosperous ones had only given to heirs who were deserving. But that was no longer the case. Those who were non-believers became powerful. In a time of difficulty, a friend sought the support of a friend. However, even if there was the slightest bit of selfish gain a friend could obtain, he acted against his friend. People were interested in obtaining the riches of others. Even the noble varnas were seen to take up the livelihood of traders. Shudras became rich in austerities. There were others who followed futile

[221]The text uses the word ucchishta. This means, having eaten, one touches clarified butter without having washed the hands first.

[222]Rice cooked in sweetened milk.

[223]Dish of milk, sesamum and rice, kind of dessert.

[224]Cakes made out of rice or barley.

[225]Not as sacrificial offerings.

[226]Of the varnas.

rules of studying, without observing any vows. Students no longer served their preceptors. Some preceptors became friends to their students. Fathers and mothers became exhausted from trying to earn a livelihood. The aged no longer had protectors and had to beg food from their sons. There were wise ones there, knowledgable about the Vedas and as deep as the ocean. However, they resorted to agriculture and similar pursuits and ignorant ones started to eat at funeral ceremonies.[227] Every morning, students no longer went to preceptors and asked them excellent questions about the tasks that should be performed. Instead, the roles were reversed. In the presence of the father-in-law and the mother-in-law, daughters-in-law summoned, chastised and instructed their husbands, or having summoned them, conversed with them. Fathers had to take great care to ensure that their sons were kindly disposed. Having divided up the property, they dwelt there in great misery. On seeing that the riches of others were burnt by the fire, stolen by thieves and seized by kings, they laughed from a sense of enmity, even if those others happened to be well-wishers. All of them were ungrateful, non-believers, wicked and intolerant and had intercourse with the wives of their preceptors. They ate what should not be eaten. They were without restraints and violated pledges. They became distressed because of their conduct and walked the path of catastrophe. O Indra of the gods! It is my view that I will not dwell with the danavas. O lord of Shachi! I have myself come before you. Welcome me. O lord of the gods! If you worship me from the forefront, so will the other gods. Seven other goddesses exist wherever I am. They are devoted to me. They follow my instructions and have given themselves to me. There is an eighth, and these eight desire to dwell with me here—Asha, Shraddha, Dhriti, Kanti, Vijiti, Sannati and Kshama.[228] O chastiser of Paka! The eighth, Vritti,[229] is at

[227]Instead of learned brahmanas.

[228]Respectively, hope, faith, resolution, radiance, victory, humility and forgiveness.

[229]Conduct.

their forefront. They and I have abandoned the asuras and come to your dominion. We will reside with the thirty gods, who possess steadfast dharma in their souls.'"

'Bhishma said, "Having been addressed by the goddess in these words, Narada, the rishi of the three worlds, and Vasava, the slayer of Vritra, delighted her by welcoming her. The wind, the friend of the fire, began to blow in the abodes of the gods. It bore auspicious fragrances and was pleasant to the touch, bringing happiness to all the senses. The thirty gods stationed themselves in that auspicious spot, desiring to worship her. They wished to see Maghavan seated with Lakshmi. The one with the thousand eyes obtained divinity. He was with Shri and with his well-wisher, the celestial rishi.[230] The bull among the gods arrived there, on a chariot that was yoked to tawny horses and was immediately honoured by all the gods. The powerful Narada noticed the sign that the wielder of the vajra made, one that was mentally approved of by the goddess Shri. The immensely wise one praised the arrival of Shri there as an auspicious event. The firmament was radiant and showered down amrita on the abode of Svayambhu, the grandfather. Drums sounded, though they had not been struck. All the directions were pleasant. As was appropriate, Vasava showered down rain on the crops. No one deviated from the path of dharma. The earth was ornamented with many stores of jewels. Victorious sounds, voiced and unvoiced, resounded on earth and in heaven. Illustrious men found delight in the rites, performed auspicious deeds and remained established in the path of virtue. Illustrious men, immortals, kinnaras, yakshas and rakshasas were happy and prosperous. Even if there was a wind, flowers, not to speak of fruits, did not drop down from trees before it was the right time. Cows yielded tasty milk whenever it was desired. There was no one who ever spoke fierce words. Such were all the objects of desire that were brought to the gods, with Shakra at the forefront, by Shri. If a person reads this account at an assembly of brahmanas and worships it, desiring prosperity, he

[230]Narada.

will obtain prosperity. O supreme among the Kurus! I was urged by you. These are the supreme indications of prosperity and adversity. I have recounted all of this to you. You should examine the truth about this and follow it."'

Chapter 1550(222)

'Yudhishthira asked, "Through what behaviour, what conduct, what learning and what devotion can one obtain Brahma's abode, which is certainly beyond nature?"[231]

'Bhishma replied, "If one is engaged in the dharma of moksha, is controlled and limited in diet and controls his senses, then he obtains Brahma's abode, which is certainly beyond nature. O descendant of the Bharata lineage! In this connection, an ancient history is recounted, about the conversation between Jaigishavya and Asita. Jaigishavya was immensely wise and knew about the path of dharma. Asita-Devala spoke to the great rishi, who was never enraged. 'You are not delighted when you are praised. You are not angered when you are criticized. What is this wisdom and whence has it come? How have you found refuge in it?' Having been thus addressed, the great ascetic replied. Those great and auspicious words left no doubt and were full of deep import. 'O brahmana! You have asked me about the supreme objective, devotion, tranquility and the performance of auspicious deeds. I will tell you. O Devala! There are those who regard censure and praise equally. They hide their vows and good deeds. They do not hurt through words. Nor are they engaged in speaking anything injurious. They do not wish to strike back those who strike them. Such people are learned. They do not grieve over what is yet to come. They act in

[231]We have translated prakriti as nature. Brahma is not affected by the transformations of prakriti.

accordance with what has presented itself. They do not sorrow over what is past and do not even remember it. O Devala! For both kama and artha, they honour what has presented itself. They accomplish their vows and forcefully act in accordance with what has presented itself. Their learning is mature and they are immensely wise. They have conquered anger and have vanquished their senses. They never commit any crimes, in mind, deeds and words. They never desire harm or injury to anyone else. Those patient ones are not tormented at someone else being prosperous. They do not speak words of praise or censure about others. Nor do they ever react to words of praise or censure about their own selves. They are tranquil in every way and are engaged in the welfare of all beings. They are not angered or delighted. They do not cause injury to others. They have released themselves from all the bonds that bind the heart down and are happy. They have no friends. Nor are they friends to others. They have no enemies. Nor are they enemies to others. Mortal ones who act in this way always live happily. O supreme among brahmanas! They know about dharma and observe dharma. They are happy, but that is not true of those who have deviated from the path. I have resorted to that path. What else is there to say? Whether I am criticized or praised, that is no cause for any joy. Depending on what they desire, men advance along different paths. However, censure and praise cannot affect my growth or decay. A person who knows about the truth is content with this, as if it is amrita. An accomplished person will always regard the two[232] equally and treat them like poison. He will then be freed from all sins. If a person ignores this, he will be destroyed. There are some learned ones who desire the supreme objective. Those people, who seek refuge in this vow, obtain happiness. A person who has conquered his senses is regarded as having performed all the sacrifices. He obtains Brahma's abode, which is certainly beyond nature. Gods, gandharvas, pishachas and rakshasas are incapable of climbing up to that objective and obtaining that supreme end.'"'

[232]Censure and praise.

Chapter 1551(223)

'Yudhisthira asked, "On this earth, who is the man who is loved by all the worlds, is unblemished and possesses all the spirits and also has every kind of quality?"

'Bhishma replied, "O bull among the Bharata lineage! You have asked me a question. In this connection, there was a conversation between Ugrasena and Keshava about Narada.[233]

'"Ugrasena said, 'Behold. All the worlds have resolved to praise Narada. I think that he possesses all the qualities. I am asking you. Tell me.'

'"Vasudeva replied, 'O lord of the Kukkuras! Listen to me and I will tell you what you have asked me. O lord of men! I will briefly tell you about Narada's virtuous qualities. His character and conduct are such that he does not suffer from arrogance, destructive of the body. There is no gap in his learning and his character. That is the reason he is worshipped everywhere. The ascetic Narada is restrained in his speech and there is no exception to this. There is no desire and avarice in him. That is the reason he is worshipped everywhere. He knows the truth about adhyatma. He is tranquil, capable and in control of his senses. He is upright and truthful. That is the reason he is worshipped everywhere. He is energetic and illustrious. He possesses intelligence, policy and humility. Because of his birth, austerities and age, he is worshipped everywhere. He is cheerful in his conduct. He is excellent in his pleasures and food. He is considerate and pure. He speaks excellent words, devoid of malice. That is the reason he is worshipped everywhere. He firmly acts so as to ensure welfare. There is no sin in him. He is not pleased at the hardships of others. That is the reason he is worshipped everywhere. He desires to hear the objectives of the Vedas, the sacred texts and the accounts, and tolerates those who

[233]Ugrasena was the king of Mathura and belonged to the Kukkura clan. He was deprived of the kingdom by his son, Kamsa, and imprisoned. After Kamsa was killed by Krishna, Ugrasena became the king again. Krishna's father was married to Kamsa's sister, Devaki.

are ignorant. That is the reason he is worshipped everywhere. He behaves equally. There is no one he loves and no one he hates. He speaks what is pleasant to the mind. That is the reason he is worshipped everywhere. He is extremely learned and is colourful in his tales. He possesses knowledge. He is without laziness and without deceit. He is not distressed. He is without anger and without greed. That is the reason he is worshipped everywhere. He has never engaged in any quarrels for the sake of artha, dharma or kama. He has severed all taints. That is the reason he is worshipped everywhere. He is firm in his devotion. His soul has no blemish. He is learned and is devoid of cruelty. He is free from all sins of delusion. That is the reason he is worshipped everywhere. Though he is seen to be attached, he is actually detached from all the things that cause attachment. His doubts do not last for a long time. He is eloquent. That is the reason he is worshipped everywhere. For the sake of accomplishing any object or obtaining respect, he never praises himself. He is not envious and is mild in his speech. That is the reason he is worshipped everywhere. There are many kinds of ordinary conduct in this world. He is accomplished and knows about these. He associates with these people, but does not censure them. That is the reason he is worshipped everywhere. He does not hate any kind of knowledge and subsists on austerities. He does not allow himself to spend time fruitlessly. That is the reason he is worshipped everywhere. He has conquered exhaustion. He is accomplished in his wisdom. He is not content with meditation. He resorts to the rituals, without any distraction. That is the reason he is worshipped everywhere. Because his policies are good, he is never shamed. He is engaged in the supreme objective. He does not reveal the secrets of others. That is the reason he is worshipped everywhere. He is not delighted at obtaining wealth. Nor is he distressed when nothing is obtained. He is firm in his intelligence and his soul is not attached. That is the reason he is worshipped everywhere. He is vested with all the qualities. He is skilful and ceaseless in the pursuit of the auspicious. He knows about time. He knows about policy. He knows about the people to whom good things should not be done.'"'

Chapter 1552(224)

'Yudhishthira said, "O Kourava! I wish to hear about the origin and end of all beings. From one yuga to another yuga, what is the nature of meditation, deeds and time? What is the truth about all the worlds and beings, their coming and going? How do creation and destruction come about? O supreme among virtuous ones! I am asking you. If your intelligence is so disposed as to favour me, you should tell me. Earlier, I heard you recount the supreme words that Bhrigu spoke to the brahmana rishi Bharadvaja, supreme in his intelligence. Therefore, I have become supremely devoted to dharma and wish to find refuge in that celestial spot. Therefore, I am asking you again and you should tell me."

'Bhishma replied, "In this connection, an ancient history is recounted, about the illustrious Vyasa being asked by his son. Vyasa's son, Shuka, studied all the Vedas, Vedangas and Upanishads and having become accomplished about the knowledge of dharma, wished to find out about virtuous deeds. Vyasa's son thus asked Krishna Dvaipayana, so that his doubt and uncertainty about the purport of dharma might be dispelled. 'Who is the creator of all the categories of beings? How is the classification of time determined? What are the tasks that brahmanas should perform? You should tell me.' Having been thus asked by the son, the father told him about everything. He knew about everything and about all forms of dharma. He knew about the past and the future.

""'Brahma is without a beginning and without an end.[234] He is without origin and divine. He is without decay. He is permanent and without transformation. He cannot be thought of. He cannot be known. Before everything else, Brahma was there. Fifteen *nimeshas*[235] make a kashtha. Thirty kashthas are reckoned as a kala. Thirty kalas and an additional one tenth of a kala make a *muhurta*. Thirty muhurtas make up one day and one night. This is

[234]This is Vyasa speaking.

[235]The twinkling of the eye.

the enumeration given by the sages. Thirty days and nights are said to be one month. Twelve months are said to constitute one year. Those who know about numbers say that there are two *ayana*s in a year, *uttara* and *dakshina*.[236] In the world of men, the sun separates day from night. Beings make efforts to undertake tasks during the day and sleep during the night. One such month[237] is again one day and one night for the ancestors. *Krishnapaksha* is their day and they undertake action then, while *shuklapaksha* is their night and they sleep then.[238] One year[239] is again one day and one night for the gods. *Uttarayana* is their day and *dakshinayana* is their night. I have already recounted day and night in the world of the gods. I will now tell you about the number of years for Brahma. In due order, I will tell you about the number of years in krita, treta, dvapara and kali yuga. Four thousand years[240] is said to be the duration of krita yuga. There are another four hundred years as morning and four hundred as evening.[241] For the other three, the main is reduced by one fourth, or thousand, and the *sandhya* by hundred.[242] These measurements continuously hold up the eternal worlds. O son![243] Those who know about Brahma also know the eternal brahman. In krita yuga, all the four parts of dharma and truth exist. This is supreme and nothing is followed that is against dharma. In each of the others, dharma is seen to progressively reduce by one-fourth. Theft, falsehood, deceit

[236]Respectively, the sun's movement north of the equator and south of the equator.

[237]For men.

[238]Non-critical versions often reverse the order, with ancestors sleeping during krishnapaksha.

[239]For humans.

[240]Of the gods.

[241]Sandhya, the intervening period between two yugas. Krita yuga thus consists of four thousand and eight hundred divine years.

[242]Treta yuga has 3,000 main years and 300 years in each sandhya, with a total of 3,600 years. Dvapara yuga has 2,000 main years and 200 years in each sandhya, with a total of 2,400 years. Kali yuga has 1,000 main years and 100 hundred years in each sandhya, with a total of 1,200 years.

[243]The word used is tata.

and adharma flourish. In krita, there is no disease. There is success in all pursuits and the life span is four hundred years. In treta, the life span is reduced by a quarter. We have heard that the following of the Vedas, life spans, benedictions and the fruits of the Vedas also progressively decrease. There are different kinds of dharma for krita yuga, treta and dvapara. Dharma is also different for kali yuga, when one acts according to one's capacity. Austerities are supreme in krita yuga and knowledge is supreme in treta. Sacrifices are spoken of in dvapara and donations in kali yuga. Wise and learned ones say that twelve thousand years constitute a yuga.[244] A thousand of these[245] is said to be one of Brahma's days. Brahma's night is also like that. When it is day for the lord, the universe is created. When it is destroyed, he immerses himself in adhyatma.[246] At the end of the sleep, he awakes. People who know about night and day say that Brahma's day is for one thousand yugas and his night is also for one thousand yugas.

"''When the night is over, the unmanifest Brahma awakes. Though he is not manifest, he creates the great being that is his manifest mind. Brahma is the energetic seed and everything in the universe springs from that. From that single being, both mobile and immobile objects are created. When it is dawn, he awakes and creates the universe with his knowledge. At first, there is Mahabhuta.[247] This quickly becomes Mana,[248] the manifest form of the soul. Those overwhelming rays create those seven through mental powers.[249] Mana is far-reaching and flows in many different ways. There are determination and resolution to create and is done by transforming itself. Akasha[250] is

[244]Twelve thousand divine years represent one cycle of krita, treta, dvapara and kali and one such cycle is a mahayuga.

[245]Mahayugas.

[246]The universe is destroyed when it is Brahma's night. During the night, Brahma meditates.

[247]The great being, also known as Mahat. This is nothing but intelligence.

[248]Mind.

[249]Mahat, Mana and the five elements.

[250]Space.

generated and sound is held to be its quality. From Akasha is created the pure and powerful Vayu,[251] the bearer of all scents. Touch is held to be its quality. From Vayu is generated Jyoti,[252] the dispeller of darkness. Those rays are created and their qualities are held to be form. From Jyoti is created Apa,[253] with taste as its attribute. From Apa results Bhumi,[254] with scent as its quality. This is said to be the original creation. One after another, they receive the qualities of the preceding one. They are said to not only possess their own quality, but also of the one from which they were created.[255] If one discerns scent in water and takes that to be its quality, the person is ignorant. Scent is known to belong to earth, though it may also find a refuge in water or wind. These seven different entities have different forms of energy and exist separately, so that beings may be destroyed. But for the sake of creation, they come together. Those great-souled ones assemble and unite with each other. When they resort to a body, it is then said to be Purusha. When they resort to the body, there are sixteen forms.[256] With all the deeds,[257] Mahat enters the body. For the sake of austerities, it resorts to all beings. This is Mahabhuta, the original creator, and is known as Prajapati. He creates beings and is the supreme Purusha. Brahma is without orgin and generates gods, rishis, ancestors, humans, worlds, rivers, oceans, directions, mountains, trees, men,[258] kinnaras, rakshasas, birds, animals, wild animals,[259] serpents, unmanifest and manifest objects, both mobile and immobile. Each of those created obtains the legacy of its earlier

[251]Wind.

[252]Light.

[253]Water.

[254]Earth.

[255]Space only possesses the quality of sound, wind has the qualities of both sound and touch, light has the qualities of sound, touch and form, water has the qualities of sound, touch, form and taste and earth has the qualities of sound, touch, form, taste and scent.

[256]The five elements, the five senses, the five organs of action and the mind.

[257]Earlier deeds.

[258]Humans are mentioned twice.

[259]A difference is being drawn between domestic animals and wild animals.

deeds. Having obtained these, each is created again and again. Violence, non-violence, mildness, cruelty, dharma, adharma, truth, falsehood—the creator thinks of the qualities that had pleased the being earlier. Mahabhuta affixes the different senses to the bodies of beings and determines the constituent parts. Some learned ones speak of enterprise, others of earlier deeds. Some brahmanas think of destiny, others think of the natural traits of beings. Enterprise, deeds and destiny lead to fruits and this is helped by nature. Some say that thinking of these three as separate is not correct. Some say this is true. Others say that is true. Others speak of the uneven consequences of deeds. However, there are insightful ones who know about the being who created the universe and regard all these equally. Austerities bring the greatest benefit to beings and its foundations are self-control and tranquility. Through these, one obtains everything, all that one desires and wishes for. Through austerities, one obtains the being who created the universe. He is in all beings and is the lord who created beings. It is because of austerities that the rishis can study the Vedas, day and night. Svayambhu created those eternal words, which are without origin and are passed down. Though they go by the names of the rishis, he created the Vedas.[260] When it was the end of the night, he gave it to them. Nama, Bheda, Tapas, Karma, Yajna, Akhya, Loka-siddhi, Atma-siddhi and the ten kinds of techniques have been spoken of in the Vedas.[261] He[262] is mysterious and has been spoken about in the words of the Vedas. Those who have insight into

[260]The Vedas were only revealed to the rishis, not composed by them.

[261]This shloka is an extremely difficult one to translate and there are complicated issues of interpretation. For example, Nama is understood as referring to the Rig Veda and means the study of all the Vedas. Bheda is division and is here interpreted as half, that is, the wife, dharma being performed with the wife. Tapas is austerities. Karma stands for rituals and Yajna is sacrifices. Akhya means fame and is the undertaking of public works that bring one fame. Loka-siddhi is success in this world, while Atma-siddhi is success in the next world. This leaves the ten techniques. One possible interpretation is patience, forgiveness, self-control, honesty, purity, control of the senses, intelligence, learning, truthfulness and lack of anger—required for studying the Vedas.

[262]Brahma.

the Vedas know this. He has also been spoken about at the end[263] and can be realized by practising the rites. A person who is devoid of yoga has a sense of separateness and duality and is born because of his deeds. However, a person who knows about Atma-siddhi can generally drive that sense forcefully away. There are two Brahmas who should be known, Shabda-Brahma and Para-Brahma.[264] Having understood Shabda-Brahma, one can go to Para-Brahma.

'"'Slaughter represents sacrifice for kshatriyas. Offerings[265] represent sacrifice for vaishyas. Servitude represents sacrifice for shudras. Austerities represent sacrifice for brahmanas. There was no need for sacrifices in krita yuga, but they were recommended in treta yuga. There was an uprooting of sacrifices in dvapara yuga and this is also true of kali yuga. Mortals have come to regard Rig, Sama and Yajur as standing for different kinds of dharma. They desire their own prosperity and look upon austerities and the object of austerities as distinct. In treta, they were regarded as the same and there were extremely powerful ones, who controlled all mobile and immobile objects. In treta, sacrifices and the varnas co-existed together. However, because lifespans were reduced, these went into a decline in dvapara yuga. Even if one looks, in kali yuga, all the Vedas cannot be seen. With sacrifices, which are the bridges of dharma, they have been destroyed. The dharma of krita yuga can only be seen to be vested in some brahmanas who have cleansed their souls and are learned and are also devoted to austerities. Depending on the dharma of one yuga and another yuga, people are associated with rites of adharma. Though they know what the Vedas have described as being appropriate for a certain yuga, they sell their own dharma. When it rains repeatedly during the monsoon, a large number of beings and immobile objects are generated. From one yuga to another, dharma[266] is created in that fashion. As the seasons progress, many different

[263]End of the Vedas, Vedanta.

[264]Shabda means sound and Shabda-Brahma stands for the Vedas. Para-Brahma is beyond the Vedas and is supreme.

[265]Interpreted as agriculture.

[266]Understood as rituals.

kinds of forms are seen. In that fashion, different signs can be seen in Brahma, Hara and the third.[267] This has been ordained by time and it has neither a beginning, nor an end. It has been spoken about earlier and it creates and devours subjects. It is the controller who uses its powers to establish and restrain them. Because of their nature, they are repeatedly seen to be addicted to opposite sentiments. O son! I have told you everything that you have asked about—creation, time, rituals, the Vedas, doers, tasks, action and fruits. I will now tell you about how he[268] withdraws himself, when it is night and day is over. The subtle lord of the universe then immerses himself in adhyatma. In the firmament, the sun burns everything, with its seven crests of flames. Everything is pervaded by those rays and the entire universe starts to blaze.'"'

Chapter 1553(225)

'"Vyasa said, 'All beings on earth, mobile and immobile, are first destroyed and then merge into the earth. Everything, mobile and immobile, thus disappears. The ground is then seen to be without wood and without grass, like the back of a tortoise. Water then accepts the quality of the earth, that is, scent. Having been bereft of scent, the earth can then be thought of as having been destroyed. Water is then established, in the form of mighty waves that make giant roars. It pervades everything, staying still and moving around. O son! Light then accepts the quality of water. Having lost its own quality, water seeks refuge in light. The sun is stationed in the middle of the firmament. But crests of flames hide it. Everything is covered by those rays and the entire sky seems to be blazing. However, the wind then accepts the quality of light. Though light is pacified, a gigantic wind is whirled around. The

[267]Brahma, Shiva and Vishnu (the third) have different manifestations.
[268]Brahma.

wind creates itself, using its own foundation.[269] It moves upwards, downwards and diagonally, agitating the ten directions. Space then devours the wind's quality of touch. The wind is pacified. But basing itself in the sky, it continues to roar. The quality of space, sound, is then accepted by Mana, the soul of everything that is manifest. Whatever is made manifest by Mana, is withdrawn by the unmanifest Brahma. With its qualities, Mana is then submerged into Chandrama.[270] Mana is immersed in adhyatma and bases itself in Chandrama. After a long period of time, Sankalpa[271] is brought under subjugation. Chitta[272] devours Sankalpa and this is the supreme knowledge. Time devours knowledge and the sacred texts say that time is devoured by Bala.[273] But Bala is devoured by Time and is in turn brought under subjugation by Vidya.[274] The unmanifest and supreme Brahma then roars in the sky and brings Vidya into his soul. He is eternal and the greatest. In this fashion, all the beings are drawn into Brahma. This has certainly been spoken about properly. This is what should be known. This is knowledge. This has been seen by yogis who are supreme in their souls. Thus, the unmanifest Brahma repeatedly extends and withdraws. Thus do Brahma's night and day last for 1,000 yugas.'"'

Chapter 1554(226)

'"Vyasa said, 'I have recounted everything that you asked about, about how different categories of beings are appointed. I will now tell you about the tasks to be undertaken

[269]Sound.

[270]In a straightforward translation, Chandrama is the moon. However, the word has special meanings in yoga.

[271]Resolution, but being used as a synonym for Chandrama.

[272]Consciousness.

[273]Strength.

[274]Knowledge.

by brahmanas. There are *jatakarma* and other rituals, ending with *samavartana*.[275] These involve the payment of dakshina and require a preceptor who is knowledgable about the Vedas. One must be engaged in serving the preceptor and study all the Vedas. Having repaid the preceptor's debt,[276] one obtains knowledge about all the sacrifices, and graduates. Having taken the preceptor's permission, one must then adopt one of the four ashramas and follow its prescribed ordinances, until one is freed from one's body. One can accept a wife for generating offspring. Or one can adhere to brahmacharya. Or, with the preceptor, one can dwell in the forest. Or one can follow the dharma of a mendicant. The state of the householder is said to be the foundation for all four. Such a person, who is self-controlled and matures while he scrapes away,[277] is successful everywhere. Through offspring, studying and performing sacrifices, he is freed from the three divine debts.[278] Having purified himself through these deeds, he can then proceed to the other ashramas.[279] He must dwell in a place of learning that is the most sacred spot on earth. That will be the yardstick for his obtaining supreme fame. The fame of brahmanas increases through extremely great austerities, accomplishment in learning, performing sacrifices and donating. As long as his deeds and fame remain in this world, a man obtains eternal and sacred worlds in the hereafter. He must study and teach. He must officiate at a sacrifice and perform his own sacrifices. He must not receive or

[275]These are *samskara*s or sacraments and there are thirteen of these. The list varies a bit. But one list is *vivaha* (marriage), *garbhalambhana* (conception), *pumshavana* (engendering a male child), *simantonnayana* (parting the hair, performed in the fourth month of pregnancy), *jatakarma* (birth rites), *namakarana* (naming), *chudakarma* (tonsure), *annaprashana* (first solid food), *keshanta* (first shaving of the head), *upanayana* (sacred thread), *vidyarambha* (commencement of studies), *samavartana* (graduation) and *antyeshti* (funeral rites).

[276]By paying the fee due to the preceptor.

[277]Scrapes away all the attachments.

[278]Offspring repays the debt to ancestors, studying repays the debt to the sages and sacrifices repay the debt to gods.

[279]*Vanaprastha* and *sannyasa*.

give without reason. Great riches can be obtained by officiating at sacrifices, through pupils and through maidens.[280] Whatever has been obtained must not be enjoyed alone. For a person who is in the state of a householder, there is no option but to receive for the sake of gods, rishis, ancestors, preceptors, the aged, the diseased and the hungry.[281] For those who are afflicted and in disguise, one must give, including cooked food, to the best of one's capacity. One must indeed give in excess of one's capacity. To those who deserve to be given, there is nothing that cannot be given.

'"'The virtuous and learned must even be given Uchchaishrava.[282] Entreated by Kavya,[283] Satyasandha, great in his vows, gave up his own life for the sake of protecting a brahmana and went to heaven.[284] Samkriti's son, Rantideva, offered only lukewarm water to the great-souled Vasishtha and obtained greatness in the vault of heaven. Atri's son, Indradamana, was an intelligent lord of the earth. He gave many kinds of riches to deserving people and obtained worlds in the hereafter. Ushinara's son, Shibi, gave up his limbs and his beloved son for the sake of benefiting a brahmana and went to heaven.[285] Pratardana was the lord of Kashi and gave up his own eyes for the sake of a brahmana, obtaining umatched fame here and in the hereafter. The extremely intelligent Devavridha gave away a celestial umbrella, with eight golden ribs, and went to heaven with his entire kingdom. The immensely energetic Samkriti, from Atri's lineage, instructed his pupils about Brahma, who is without

[280]Maidens clearly refers to marriage. Anything beyond that is a matter of deduction, since the text doesn't elaborate. However, both dowry and brideprice were not approved of.

[281]The brahmana must receive for the sake of subsistence and for performing pious acts towards these.

[282]The name of Indra's horse. That is, everything can be given to them.

[283]Presumably Shukracharya.

[284]Nothing more is known about this incident. King Satyasandha occurs in the Skanda Purana, but that story is different.

[285]Shibi was a generous king. A hawk pursued a pigeon and Shibi gave up his own flesh to protect the pigeon from the hawk. But that story has nothing about a brahmana, or about Shibi's son.

qualities, and went to the supreme worlds. The powerful Ambarisha gave brahmanas eleven billion cows and went to heaven, with his entire kingdom. For the sake of brahmanas, Savitri gave away her earrings and Janamejaya gave away his body. Both of them went to the supreme worlds. Yuvanashva, the son of Vrishadarbha, gave away all his jewels, his beloved women and a beautiful residence, and obtained the supreme worlds. Nimi, the king of Videha, gave away his kingdom. Jamadagni's son[286] gave away the earth. Gaya gave away the earth, with its cities, to brahmanas. There was a time when it did not rain and Vasishtha sustained and kept all the beings alive, like Prajapati among the subjects. Karandhama's son was King Marutta. He gave away his daughter to Angiras and swiftly proceeded to heaven. King Brahmadatta of Panchala was supreme among intelligent ones. He gave away his treasure and a conch shell to the foremost among brahmanas and obtained the worlds.[287] King Mitrasaha gave away his beloved wife, Madayanti, to the great-souled Vasishtha and went to heaven with her. The immensely illustrious royal rishi, Sahasrajit, gave away his beloved life for the sake of a brahmana and went to the supreme worlds. The great king, Shatadyumna, gave Mudgala a golden residence that was full of all the objects of pleasure and went to heaven. The powerful king of Shalva was known by the name of Dyutiman. He gave his kingdom to Richika and went to the supreme worlds. The royal rishi, Madirashva, gave away his slender-waisted daughter to Hiranyahasta and went to worlds that the gods are content with. The lord and royal rishi, Lomapada, gave away his daughter Shanta to Rishyashringa and obtained all the great objects of desire. The immensely energetic King Prasenjit gave away one hundred thousand cows, with their calves, and went to the supreme worlds. There are many other such great-souled ones. They were virtuous in their souls

[286]Parashurama.

[287]This may be an inaccurate translation. The text uses the word *shankha*. A natural translation for this is conch shell. However, giving away a conch shell does not fit the context. Shankha also means a large number. So he may have given away a large amount of treasure.

and conquered their senses. Through their donations and austerities, they went to heaven. As long as the earth exists, their fame will remain established. They obtained heaven through donations, sacrifices and the generation of offspring.'"'

Chapter 1555(227)

'"Vyasa said, 'The knowledge known as *trayi*, mentioned in the Vedas and the Vedangas, must be experienced.[288] There are varnas and aksharas in the Rig and in the Sama, and in the Yajur and in the Atharva.[289] There are spirited and immensely fortunate ones who are accomplished in what is recounted in the Vedas and skilled about adhyatma. They can see the beginning and the end. A person who acts in a virtuous way must observe the rites laid down by dharma. A brahmana must desire to conduct himself so that he does not suppress any other being. He must obtain knowledge from virtuous and good people who are skilled in the sacred texts. He must be devoted to the truth and undertake all the acts in the world that are in accordance with his own dharma. Dwelling as a householder, a brahmana must perform the six tasks.[290] He must always faithfully perform the five sacrifices.[291] He must be patient and should not be distracted. He must be self-controlled, in control over his soul and knowledgable about dharma. A brahmana must be beyond joy, fear and anger and must not suffer from lassitude. Donations, studying, sacrifices, austerities, modesty,

[288]Trayi means three. Though the Atharva Veda is also mentioned here, trayi means the Rig Veda, the Sama Veda and the Yajur Veda.

[289]Varna is letter, while akshara is syllable.

[290]Studying, teaching, performing sacrifices, officiating at the sacrifices of others, giving and receiving.

[291]Studying, worshipping the gods, offering oblations to the ancestors, feeding other people and feeding other living beings.

uprightness and self-control increase energy and drive away sin. An intelligent person must cleanse his sins and be restrained in his diet. He must conquer his senses. Having subjugated desire and anger, he should seek to attain the brahman. He must worship the fire and brahmanas. He must bow down before the gods. He must discard hateful words and all violence that is not in accordance with dharma. This is the kind of conduct that has first been laid down for brahmanas. Later, when knowledge arrives, he must engage in tasks. It is tasks that bring success. An intelligent person will be able to cross the terrible river that is extremely difficult to traverse and is difficult to withstand. The five senses constitute the water. The banks are made out of greed. Intolerance constitutes the mud. It originates from desire and anger and always causes great delusion. The entire universe is always struck by that great force, ordained by destiny, and confused and whirled around by the flow of nature. Time is the single great river and the years are the eddy. The months are waves and the seasons are the current. The fortnights are moss and grass. The twinkling of the eyelids represents the foam. Day and night are the force. The terrible crocodiles are represented by desire. The Vedas and sacrifices are the rafts. For beings, dharma is like islands. Artha and kama are the springs. Truth represents the stairs along the banks. Non-violence represents the trees that flow along. The yugas are the pools in the middle of the course. This is as difficult to comprehend as the brahman. The creator creates beings and drags them along, towards Yama's abode. Those who are learned can cross it, using their wisdom and patience as rafts. But what can those of limited intelligence, those who possess no rafts, do? A wise person can cross it, but not an ordinary person. From a distance, the wise person sees everything, good and bad traits. However, a person with limited intelligence has doubt in his soul and desire in his soul. His senses are fickle. A person who is not wise cannot cross and cannot go to the further shore. He suffers from the great taint of not possessing a raft and advances towards delusion. There are also those who have knowledge, but are grasped by the crocodile of desire. They don't possess a raft either.

Therefore, an accomplished person must make efforts so that he does not submerge. A person who is not submerged in this way is a brahmana. A person who speaks about the three,[292] is born in a noble lineage and is without doubt and performs the three acts[293] is thus not submerged and crosses with the help of wisdom. A person who has refined himself, is self-restrained and controlled and has cleansed his soul is wise and subsequently obtains success in this world and in the next. Following the conduct of a householder, he must be without anger and without envy. He must perform the five sacrifices and always eat the leftovers from sacrifices. He must observe virtuous conduct and act in accordance with righteous rites. He must follow a conduct that does not obstruct dharma. Greed is censured for him. He must know the truth about learning and knowledge. He must be accomplished in virtuous conduct. He must observe the tasks of his own dharma and not mix up tasks.[294] He must faithfully perform the rites. He must be generous, wise and devoid of jealousy. If he knows the difference between dharma and adharma, he will be able to cross everything, even if it is difficult to traverse. He must possess fortitude and not be distracted. He must be restrained, knowledgable about dharma and immersed in his soul. He must be without delight, fear and anger. Such a brahmana does not suffer. This was the conduct that was laid down for brahmanas earlier. If he performs acts that bring him the wealth of knowledge, he is successful everywhere. Even if they desire dharma, those who are not accomplished observe adharma. Dharma becomes like adharma for him and he is made to grieve. Deciding to do dharma, he achieves adharma. Wishing to do adharma, he achieves dharma. Such a person is foolish and does not know these two kinds of acts. He adopts bodies and is born and dies.'"'[295]

[292]The three Vedas.

[293]The rituals connected with the three Vedas. Alternatively, teaching, officiating at sacrifices and accepting gifts.

[294]Mix up the tasks of different varnas.

[295]He goes through the cycle of birth and death.

Chapter 1556(228)

'"Vyasa said, 'Therefore, if one does not wish to be confused in one's mind, when one is immersed and submerged, one must resort to the raft of knowledge. Learned and patient ones use this raft, which is constructed out of wisdom, to cross over. Those who are not learned cannot save themselves, or others. Sages who are united with yoga sever themselves from the taints. They yoke themselves to the ten tasks that bring bliss and also to *anupaya* and *upaya*.[296] Those who are wise use their mental sight to control their eyes[297] and conduct. Those who desire supreme knowledge use their intelligence to control their speech and thoughts. Those who desire tranquility in the soul use their knowledge to control their souls. A man who follows this may be extremely terrible, knowledgable about the Vedas or ignorant about hymns and meditation, an observer of dharma and performer of sacrifices or one who commits wicked deeds, a tiger among men or a follower of the practices of eunuchs. But as long as he follows this, he will be able to cross the ocean of old age and death, which is so difficult to traverse. That is the reason one must single-mindedly devote oneself to yoga. One who enquires in this way obtains Shabda-Brahma. Dharma is the *upastha*.[298] Upaya is the *varutha* and apaya is the *kubara*.[299] Apana is the *aksha*, prana is

[296]There are thus twelve requirements and there is interpretation involved. These twelve are: (1) a clean place where yoga must be performed; (2) pure acts; (3) attachment towards others who are devoted to yoga; (4) sacred objects; (5) the methods used; (6) destruction of desire and attachment; (7) certainty of belief about yoga; (8) restraint of the senses; (9) purity in food; (10) suppression of attachment towards material objects; (11) regulation of the mind, or not resorting to bad practices (anupaya); and (12) contemplation, or strategy (upaya).

[297]As a surrogate for the senses.

[298]There is the imagery of a chariot and upastha is the seat on which the charioteer sits.

[299]Upaya means good practices, the opposite of anupaya. *Varutha* is the wooden bumper around a chariot. *Kubara* is the pole for attaching the yoke.

the yuga.[300] Wisdom represents the harnesses that are attached to the yoke. Consciousness is the *bandhura*.[301] Good conduct and the avoidance of bad conduct are the *nemi*.[302] Sight, touch, scent and hearing are the four mounts that bear it along. Wisdom is the *nabhi*.[303] All the sacred texts are the *pratoda*.[304] Knowledge is the charioteer. The patient kshetrajna is seated there and faith and self-control are at the front.[305] Renunciation follows at the rear, with tranquility. The path is of purification, and meditation is the objective. With the soul, the chariot then obtains radiance in the divine world of Brahma. There are means of yoking this chariot so that one speedily reaches Akshara[306] by observing mental ordinances. The chariot then travels fast. I will tell you about this. Altogether, there are seven kinds of dharana that a learned person practises.[307] There are dharanas to the rear, to the side and everywhere. Gradually, through these, he controls the earth, the wind, space, water, fire, ego and intelligence and obtains special powers.[308] He then gradually obtains power over the one who is not manifest. Those who are united with yoga obtain the power of conception. Those who are united with yoga obtain success and behold their own atmans. Instructed properly, he sees the subtlety of the atman. The firmament seems to be covered in a subtle substance, as if smoke has been mixed with dew. Initially, the soul seems to be freed from the body. When the smoke has disappeared, a second form can be seen. In the sky, he

[300]In *pranayama*, the breath of life is prana and this has five actions—prana (exhalation), apana (downward inhalation), vyana (diffusion through the body), udana (upward inhalation) and samana (digestive breath). Aksha is the wheel and yuga is the yoke.

[301]The part of the yoke attached to the pole.

[302]The circumference of the wheel.

[303]Central part of the chariot, where the warrior, as opposed to the charioteer, is seated.

[304]The goad.

[305]The two horses at the front.

[306]The one without decay, the brahman.

[307]Concerning the five elements, intelligence and consciousness.

[308]These shlokas are difficult to understand and some liberty has been taken.

then sees his atman in the form of water. When the water has passed, the form of fire manifests itself. When that has disappeared, there is the manifestation of a form that has the complexion of gossamer and is dressed in yellow garments. The yellow then becomes white and there is a form that is as subtle as the wind. The consciousness becomes white and subtle and this is nothing but the unmanifest brahman. There are diverse kinds of fruits that result from all these. Listen. If he is able to conquer the earth, he becomes like Prajapati, undisturbed, and with powers over creation and destruction. He can create beings from his own body. If he is able to control the quality of the wind, it is said that he can make the earth tremble with only his toe or finger, or with his hands and feet. If he immerses himself in the quality of space, he assumes the quality of space and differences between him and space vanish and he can make himself vanish. If he obtains the quality of water, as he wills, he can drink up all waterbodies. When his form is like that of the fire, he is seen to have a form that cannot be pacified. When the sense of ego has been conquered, these five[309] come under subjugation. When these and the sixth aspect of the atman, intelligence, have been conquered, he obtains all the powers and has a form that is not blemished. The manifest merges with the unmanifest and the unmanifest can be grasped. Everything in the world emerges from that[310] and obtains the trait of manifestation. I will explain to you in detail about how things become manifest. Listen. What is manifest has been spoken about in sankhya.[311] Listen. In both yoga[312]and sankhya, twenty-five kinds of truth have been spoken about and treated equally.[313] There is no difference between them. Listen. It has been said that anything that is manifest has birth, growth, decay and death. These are its four attributes. That which is the reverse of this is said to be the unmanifest. It is the determination of the Vedas that there are two kinds of atman. One has those four

[309]The five elements.

[310]The unmanifest.

[311]The sankhya school of philosophy.

[312]As a school of philosophy.

[313]The number twenty-five cannot quite be pinned down.

traits[314] and the four objectives[315] are prescribed for the other. The manifest comes out of the unmanifest and may have intelligence or may not have intelligence. I have told you about sattva and kshetrajna, which we have been instructed about.[316] The Vedas have said that both these atmans get attached to material objects. Sankhya says that withdrawal from material objects is the characteristic of success. One must be free from a sense of ownership and free from ego. One must be free from opposite sentiments and dispel all doubt. One must never be angered, nor hate. One must never utter a falsehood. Even if one is censured or struck, one must be friendly and not act in an adverse way. One must restrain all three kinds of chastisement in the form of speech, deeds and thoughts. One must look upon all beings in the same way. Such a person obtains the brahman. A person should not have desire, or lack of desire. He must only establish himself in the journey. He must not be greedy. He must not be distressed. He must be controlled. He must perform tasks and be indifferent to appearance. His senses must be brought together in his mind. He must not deviate from his wishes. He must show lack of injury towards all beings. According to sankhya, this is the kind of person who is emancipated. This is also the path of emancipation through yoga. Listen to the reasons for this. If one can progress beyond the powers obtained through yoga, one is freed. There is no doubt that I have spoken to you about different kinds of attributes of intelligence. If a person is free from opposite sentiments in this way, he attains the brahman.'""

Chapter 1557(229)

'"Vyasa said, 'In this way, a patient person accepts the raft of knowledge and accepts and bases himself on peace. He is immersed and submerged, but seeks refuge in knowledge.'

[314]Birth, growth, decay and death.

[315]Dharma, artha, kama and moksha.

[316]Sattva is the physical body (kshetra) and kshetrajna is the soul or jivatman.

'"Shuka asked, 'What is that knowledge? What is the learing that restrains opposite sentiments? According to dharma, what are the characteristics of attachment and detachment?'

'"Vyasa replied, 'A person who thinks that everything is because of nature, without being established in any other foundation,[317] does not obtain the means of emanicipation, because of his lack of wisdom. Those who hold the view that nature is the sole reason for existence are like sacred grass that has not been sprinkled. They obtain nothing. Foolish people who resort to either of these views[318] and regard nature as the cause do not get what is best for them. This belief in nature is an act that results from confusion in the mind and brings destruction. There are those who hold that things exist because of nature and others who hold that they flow from other entities.[319] Those who are full of learning engage in tasks like agriculture, accumulation of crops, generation of offspring, collection of means of transport, objects of pleasure, houses, seats and medicines. Those who speak about these are full of wisdom. Wisdom engages one in attaining objectives. Wisdom conveys one to what is most beneficial. Though kings are the equals of others in attributes, it is through wisdom that they enjoy kingdoms. It is because of learning that one can differentiate between superior and inferior beings. O son! Creation results from learning. Learning is the supreme objective. Four kinds of birth have been laid down for all beings—from wombs, from eggs, from sweat and plants. This can be discerned. Mobile entities are seen to be superior to the immobile. It is evident that enterprise is superior to material objects. It is said that there are two kinds of mobile entities, those with many legs and those with two legs, those with two legs being superior. Those with two legs are said to be of two kinds, those that live on land and those

[317]Implying a denial of the existence of the brahman.

[318]This is difficult to understand and needs explanation. In both views, nature is assumed to be everything and the cause. But in one case, nature is itself held to be an illusion. In the other case, nature is real and is not an illusion, but is regarded as the cause.

[319]But those other and preceding entities also originate with nature. Both doctrines thus ascribe nature alone to be the primordial cause.

that do not.[320] Those that live on land are superior and enjoy many kinds of food. Bipeds who live on land are of two kinds, medium and superior. Those who are medium follow the dharma of *jati*s and are better.[321] Among those who are medium, there are said to be two kinds—those who know about dharma and those who do not. Those who know about dharma are superior because they undertake what should be done and do not undertake what should not be done. Those who know about dharma are said to be of two kinds, those who are learned about the Vedas and those who are not. Those who are learned about the Vedas are superior because the Vedas are vested in them.[322] Those who are learned about the Vedas are said to be of two kinds—those who expound on them and those who do not. Those who expound on them are superior, because they uphold all kinds of dharma. They know about the Vedas and all the rites that lead to the fruits of dharma. The sacrifices and all the Vedas flow from those who expound about them. Those who expound about the Vedas are said to be of two types—those who know about the atman and those who do not. Those who know about the atman are superior, because they have comprehension about birth and lack of birth.[323] He who knows about both kinds of dharma[324] knows everything about all kinds of dharma. He is detached and firm in his resolution to the truth. He is pure. He is the lord.[325] The gods know such a brahmana as someone who is established in knowledge about

[320]By bipeds that do not live on land, one means birds.

[321]While jati is not varna, in this context, the dharma of jatis can be understood to be *varnashrama* dharma. Medium men follow this. Superior men have transcended the dictates of varnashrama dharma. Why should medium men be better? This seems contradictory. The resolution of this is a matter of interpretation. Medium men being better is a popular belief, but is not the truth. That is one possible line of reasoning.

[322]Speculatively, the Vedas were not in writing and were passed down through oral transmission. The Vedas were vested in them in the sense that they had learnt the Vedas by heart.

[323]They are freed from the cycle of birth and death.

[324]Attachment to tasks and detachment from tasks.

[325]In the sense of possessing powers.

dharma. He is firm in his determination about Shabda-Brahma and the one who is superior to that.[326] Such people know the soul both inside and outside.[327] O son![328] Such people are brahmanas. Such people are gods. The entire universe of beings and everything that is beneficial in the universe is based on them. There is nothing that is equal to their sentiments of greatness. They are beyond all deeds and beyond origin and destruction. They are like Svayambhu and the lords of the four kinds of beings.'"'

Chapter 1558(230)

'"Vyasa said, 'This is the conduct for brahmanas, as laid down earlier. If a learned person performs these tasks, he is successful in everything. He has no doubt in determining what acts should be undertaken. What are tasks that are mandatory and what are tasks that lead to knowledge?[329] For tasks that lead to knowledge in men, this is what I have deduced and experienced. I will describe this. Listen. Some say that tasks are undertaken by men because of enterprise. There are other people who praise natural destiny. There are also some who draw a distinction between the three—human enterprise, destiny and the natural fruits of conduct. Some pick on a single reason, others on their combination. In this way, people established in acts say that there is existence, or that there is non-existence, or that existence cannot be established, or that non-existence cannot be established, thus treating them differently. But there are those who know the truth and regard all these as equal.[330] Treta, dvapara and kali yugas are full of doubts. The ascetics of krita

[326]Para-Brahma.

[327]Inside their own selves and outside.

[328]The word used is tata.

[329]These are the kinds of questions that lead to doubts. Knowledge can be obtained other than through acts. Therefore, are acts mandatory?

[330]They know that everything results from the brahman.

yuga were tranquil and knew the truth. They did not look upon all the Rig, Sama and Yajur hymns differently.[331] They examined desire and hatred and only worshipped austerities. They were engaged in the dharma of austerities. They were firm in their observance and always devoted to austerities. They obtained everything, all that they desired and wished for in their minds. Through austerities, one becomes like the one who created the universe. One becomes like the lord who is the creator of all beings. He[332] has been spoken about in the words of the Vedas. He is difficult to fathom, even by those who have the sight of the Vedas. He has again been spoken about in Vedanta. He can be discerned through the yoga of tasks. It has been said that slaughter represents sacrifice for kshatriyas and oblations for vaishyas.[333] Servitude represents sacrifice for shudras and meditation represents sacrifice for brahmanas. One becomes a brahmana by diligently performing the tasks and studying. However, whether one performs the tasks or does not perform the tasks, by exhibiting friendliness,[334] one is said to be a brahmana. At the beginning of treta, all the Vedas, sacrifices and varnashrama existed. But as lifespans decreased, they went into a decline in dvapara yuga. The Vedas suffered during dvapara. It was like that in kali yuga too. At the end of kali, though they could be seen, yet they could not be seen.[335] One's own dharma went into a decline and dharma suffered. The juices disappeared from cows, the earth, water and herbs. Because of adharma, the Vedas vanished, and so did the dharma of the Vedas and the ashramas. All mobile and immobile objects deviated from their own dharma. Just as all the beings are sustained by the rain showering down on the ground, from one yuga to another, the Vedas and their *angas*[336] are created afresh. Time does this and it

[331]In treta, dvapara and kali yugas, people regarded one or the other of the Vedas as superior. But no such artificial differences were drawn during krita yuga.

[332]The brahman.

[333]The interpretation is that kshatriyas slaughter animals at sacrifices and vaishyas grow crops that are offered as oblations.

[334]Towards all beings.

[335]A roundabout way of stating that they became invisible.

[336]The Vedangas.

has no beginning and no end. I have recounted this to you earlier, about creation and destruction. Dhata is the creator of all beings and Yama controls them. Nature drives them into many kinds of opposite sentiments. O son![337] Creation, time, the upholding of the Vedas, the doer, tasks, rites and fruits—I have told you about these. This is what you had asked me.'"'

Chapter 1559(231)

'Bhishma said, "Having been thus addressed, he[338] praised the supreme rishi and asked him about the pursuit of moksha dharma.

'"Shuka asked, 'There may be a learned brahmana who has had offspring. He has performed sacrifices and has become old. He is wise and devoid of jealousy. How can he obtain the brahman, which is so difficult for the mind to grasp? Is it through austerities, brahmacharya, renouncing everything, intelligence, sankhya or yoga? I am asking you this. Instruct me. How can a man bring about unwavering attention in the mind and in the senses? You should explain this to me.'

'"Vyasa replied, 'There is nothing other than learning and austerities. There is nothing other than the control of the senses. There is nothing other than renouncing everything. Success cannot be obtained through any other means. Svayambhu created all the great elements first. These were then placed in the bodies of the living beings. It is said that the bodies come from the earth, the essence from water and the eyes from light. Prana and apana have the wind as their refuge and the vacant spots in the bodies have space as their refuge. Vishnu is in their steps, Shakra is in their strength and Agni is in their bowels, desiring to eat. The directions

[337]The word used is tata.

[338]Shuka.

are in the ears, with hearing. Sarasvati is in the tongue, with speech. The ears, the skin, the eyes and the nose as the fifth, are said to be the senses of sight and it is through using these that knowledge becomes successful. Sound, touch, form, taste and scent as the fifth are separate from the senses. They should be thought of as objects of sight. Like horses are controlled, the senses must be yoked by the mind. The atman in the heart must control the mind. The mind is the lord of all the senses and their objects. The atman and the mind ensure their creation and destruction. The senses, the objects of the senses, nature, consciousness, mind, prana, apana and the soul always reside in the bodies of embodied beings. But attributes, sound[339] and consciousness are not the base for knowledge. Knowledge is generated through energy, never through the qualities. In this way, in the body, the seventeenth is surrounded by the sixteen qualities.[340] Using his mind, a learned brahmana sees the atman inside himself. It cannot be seen through the eye or comprehended through all the senses. The great atman manifests itself through the lamp of the mind. It is without sound, touch, form, taste and scent. It is without decay. It is in the body, but is without a body. It is beyond the senses, but can be seen. It is not manifest, but exists in the manifest body. It is immortal, but resorts to a mortal body. A person who beholds it obtains the brahman after death. A learned person looks upon a learned brahmana, a cow, an elephant, a dog and an outcaste[341] equally. The great atman pervades everything and dwells in all beings, mobile and immobile. The atman is in all beings and all beings are in the atman. A person who sees the atman in all beings obtains the brahman. The extent to which one knows the atman in one's own self is the extent to which one knows the atman in the paramatman.[342]

[339]That is, the senses.

[340]The sixteen are the five senses, the five organs of action, the five elements and consciousness. The atman is the seventeenth.

[341]*Svapaka.*

[342]This is a cryptic and difficult shloka and some liberties have been taken. The sense is that knowledge of the paramatman is determined by knowledge of one's own atman.

A person who always knows this, obtains immortality. He regards all beings as his own self and is engaged in the welfare of all beings. He leaves no trail, like a bird in the sky or an aquatic creature in the water, and the gods themselves are confused in trying to follow his tracks. A person whose tracks cannot be seen is indeed extremely great-souled. Time cooks all beings, inside its own self. But that which cooks time[343] can never be known. It does not exist above, or diagonally, below, to the side, or in the middle. It does not exist anywhere. Nor has it come from anywhere. Everything in this world is inside it. There is nothing that is outside it. Even if one shoots one thousand arrows one after another, each endued with the speed of thought, even then one will not be able to obtain the extremities of that which is the cause of everything. It is subtler than the most subtle. It is larger than the largest. Its hands and feet extend in every direction. The eyes, heads and faces are everywhere. The ears are everywhere in the world. It is established, pervading everything. It is smaller than the smallest. It is larger than the largest. It is certainly seen to be established inside all beings. The atman has two attributes, indestructible and destructible. The destructible form is in all the beings. The indestructible form is divine and immortal. Having gone to the city with the nine gates,[344] Hamsa[345] restrains and controls it. It is the lord of all beings, mobile and immobile. Those who are accomplished speak of the truth—it resorts to the nine, subject to destruction and decay. But Hamsa is said to be without decay. It is mysterious and is Akshara.[346] The learned obtain Akshara and give up life and birth.'"'[347]

[343]The brahman.

[344]The body has nine gates—two eyes, two ears, one mouth, two nostrils, one anus and the genitals.

[345]We have deliberately not translated this. While hamsa means swan, it is also used as an expression for the soul.

[346]This is interpreted as signifying unity between the jivatman and the paramatman.

[347]They go beyond the cycle of birth and death.

Chapter 1560(232)

'"Vyasa said, 'O virtuous son! I was asked by you and have recounted the exact truth. I have recounted to you the philosophy of sankhya. I will now tell you everything about the tasks of yoga. Listen. The intelligence, the mind and all the senses must be united. O son! If one meditates on the atman, one will obtain supreme knowledge. One will obtain this through tranquility. One must be self-controlled and devote oneself to adhyatma. One must turn one's intelligence to finding pleasure in the atman. One must be pure in one's deeds. One will then know what should be known. The learned and the wise say that five taints associated with yoga must be severed. These are desire, anger, avarice, fear and sleep as the fifth. Anger is conquered through tranquility, desire by giving up all resolution. A patient person resorts to the truth and should give up all sleep. Through fortitude, the penis and the stomach must be controlled. The hands and the feet must be protected through the eyes. The eyes and the ears must be controlled through the mind, the mind through words and deeds. Fear can be conquered through attentiveness and greed by serving the wise. In this way, one must attentively conquer the taints associated with yoga. One must honour the fire and brahmanas and bow down before the gods. One must abandon hateful words, those that are full of violence and not pleasant to the mind. The brahman is the energetic seed and is the essence of everything. It is the single one in both kinds of beings, mobile and immobile. Meditation, studying, donations, truth, modesty, uprightness, forgiveness, purity in food, cleanliness and control of the senses—energy can be increased through these and sins cleansed. One is then successful in all one's pursuits, and knowledge arrives. One must behave equally towards all beings and towards what has been obtained and what has not been obtained. One will be cleansed of all sins, energetic, restrained in diet and in control over the senses. Having subjugated desire and anger, one must desire to attain the objective of the brahman. One must be single-minded and controlled in restraining the mind and the senses. Just before night, or just after night, one must fix one's mind on the atman.[348] If a person cannot control a single one of the five senses, that is a weakness in the senses, and wisdom drains out, as if through a hole at the bottom. The mind must first be subdued, like a fisherman drawing in the fish. A person engaged in yoga must then control the ears, the eyes, the tongue and the nose. Having restrained them, they must be fixed in the mind. With all resolution having ebbed away from the mind, it must then be fixed on the atman. The five[349] must be controlled and placed in the mind. After this, the mind, as the sixth, must be placed in the atman. When this has been done, the brahman is pleased and manifests itself. It blazes, like flames without smoke, or like the resplendent sun. Like fire in lightning in the sky, one then beholds the atman inside one's own self. Everything is then seen in it and it is seen in everything. Learned brahmanas see the great atman. They are immensely wise and persevering and are engaged in the welfare of all beings. If a person is rigid in his vows and observes them for a limited period of time,[350] seated alone, he obtains identity with Akshara. Infatuation, hallucination, the whirling around of scent, hearing and sight, wonders of taste and touch, pleasant, cool and warm breezes, powers and other phenomena—all these are obtained through yoga.[351] Knowing the truth about these, he must ignore them and return them to his atman. A restrained sage must ignore them. At three times,[352] he must engage himself in yoga—on the summit of a mountain, at a place of worship, or at the foot of a tree. He must control all his senses, like cattle in a cow pen in a village. He must always be single-minded in his thoughts and turn his mind to nothing other than yoga. In every way possible, one must restrain the fickle mind. He must be engaged in this and must never deviate.

[348]Meditation should be in the evening, or at dawn.

[349]The five senses.

[350]This is interpreted as a period of six months.

[351]Through yoga, several such powers are obtained. But these are distractions and must be ignored.

[352]Dawn, noon and evening.

Single-minded in attaining the objective, he must reside in deserted mountain caverns, temples to the gods or deserted houses. He should have no association with others, in words, deeds and thoughts. He must ignore everything and be restrained in his diet. He should look at what has been obtained and what has not been obtained as equal. He should not be delighted. Nor should he be distressed. Whether he is praised or whether he is reprimanded, he must look on both equally, and not desire good things for the former and bad things for the latter. He should not be delighted at obtaining something. He should not think about something that has not been obtained. He must behave equally towards all beings and must follow the dharma of the wind.[353] Such a virtuous person seeks everything in the atman and looks upon everything equally. If he is engaged in this way for six months, he obtains the Shabda-Brahma.[354] On seeing that subjects are afflicted by grief,[355] he must look upon a lump of earth and gold in the same way. He must withdraw from this path.[356] He must desist from it and be free of confusion. Even if one belongs to one of the inferior varnas and even if one happens to be a woman, as long as one desires dharma, one can resort to this path and obtain the supreme objective.[357] A man who controls his senses and is not fickle obtains the ancient and eternal one who is without birth and without decay. It is subtler than the most subtle. It is greater than the greatest. United with his own atman, he sees it inside himself. These are the words of the great-souled maharshis. They spoke about this and beheld it with their minds. In one's mind, one should follow the words that have been spoken and instructed. A learned person will then see the great being inside his own self, until the time comes for a living being to be destroyed.'"'

[353]The wind does not get attached to anything.

[354]This is interpreted as meaning that he no longer has to undertake any rites, but passes beyond them.

[355]Because of their attachments.

[356]Of acquisition.

[357]By implication, the Vedas and sankhya are prohibited to inferior varnas and women. But the path of yoga is available to everyone.

Chapter 1561(233)

'"Shuka asked, 'The words of the Vedas talk about undertaking tasks and also about renouncing them. Where do those who pursue knowledge go?[358] Where do those who act go? I wish to hear about this. Please tell me about this. These two kinds of instructions seem to be similar and also contradictory.'"

'Bhishma said, "Thus addressed, Parashara's son spoke these words to his son.[359] 'I will tell you about the paths of tasks and knowledge and also about the destructible and the indestructible, about where those who pursue knowledge go, and about the destination of those who undertake rites. O son! Listen single-mindedly to the mysteries of one and the other. Listen to dharma, as stated by the believers, and also to what the non-believers say.[360] Both sides may seem to be similar, but there are differences between them. There are two paths on which the Vedas are established. There is dharma with characteristics of pravritti, and nivritti is also well spoken of.[361] A being is bound down through deeds and is freed through knowledge. Therefore, those who are far-sighted do not undertake any tasks. After death, one is born again through deeds and adopts a form with the sixteen attributes. Through knowledge, one becomes part of the eternal and umanifest one, the one without decay and transformation. Therefore, men who are limited in intelligence praise deeds alone. They find pleasure and worship this net of bodily entities. However, there are also those who are supreme in intelligence, accomplished in the sight of dharma. They do not praise deeds, just as a person who drinks water does not praise wells and rivers. Deeds lead to fruits, happiness and unhappiness, existence and non-existence. However, a person who obtains knowledge reaches the spot where there is no reason to grieve. Once one goes

[358]That is, those who do not undertake the rites.

[359]Vedavyasa was the son of the sage Parashara.

[360]Believers in the rites and those who do not believe in the rites.

[361]In this context, pravritti is attachment to action and nivritti is detachment.

there, one does not die. Once one goes there, one is not born. Once once goes there, one does not decay. Once one goes there, one does not increase. That is the supreme brahman, eternal, unmanifest and without decay. It is without any obstructions. It is without any exertion. It is immortal. It is without destruction. Opposite sentiments do not bind down a person there, in thoughts or in deeds. He is equal and friendly towards everyone, engaged in the welfare of all beings. O son! There is a difference between a man who is full of knowledge and one who is full of deeds. Know that he[362] can be seen to be as subtle as the moon established in its *kala*.[363] The rishi[364] has spoken in detail about what has been inferred. A newborn moon can be seen in the firmament, like a bent sliver. O son! Know that a person is embodied with the qualities of his deeds and, with those eleven transformations in him, is endowed with the increase in kalas.[365] The kshetrajna is the divinity who finds refuge in the bodily form, like a drop of water on the petal of a lotus. A person who conquers his atman through renunciation always knows this. Know that all beings are united with the qualities of sattva, rajas and tamas. The jivatman has these qualities. But know the jivatman to be the paramatman. Consciousness is said to be the quality of living beings. It makes them endeavour in everything. Those who know speak about the supreme beyond the body. The seven worlds flow from that.'"'[366]

[362]A man who has obtained knowledge.

[363]The moon is made out of sixteen kalas. These wax and wane, during shuklapaksha and krishnapaksha. On the night of the new moon, the moon cannot be seen, but its kala still exists. A wise person is being compared to this.

[364]This is taken to be the sage Yajnavalka.

[365]A person engaged in tasks is being compared to the moon, with the fruits of those tasks contributing to growth and decay, like the kalas of the moon. A person who has knowledge is freed from the kalas and the growth and decay. The eleven transformations result from the five organs of sense, five organs of action and intelligence.

[366]There are actually fourteen worlds (*loka*s), seven above and seven below. This is a reference to the seven above—*bhurloka, kharloka, svarloka, maharloka, janarloka, taparloka* and *satyaloka (brahmaloka)*.

Chapter 1562(234)

'"Shuka said, 'I have understood that there is a creation that is destructible, one united with qualities and the senses. But there is another kind of auspicious and eternal creation that can be comprehended by meditating on the atman. However, I again wish to hear about the reasons for virtuous conduct in this world. That is what righteous ones have ordained. I desire to hear those described. The words of the Vedas say that tasks should be undertaken and also that they should be renounced. How will I know which is better? You should explain this to me. Once I have been purified through instructions from my preceptor, I will know the truth about conduct in the world. Using the intelligence to separate and delink my atman from my body, I will then obtain that which is without decay.'

'"Vyasa replied, 'In ancient times, Brahma himself laid down rules for conduct. The supreme and virtuous rishis followed this earlier. The supreme rishis conquered the worlds through brahmacharya. In their hearts, they placed their atmans in what was most beneficial. They placed their minds in their atmans. They dwelt in the forest and survived on roots and fruits. They tormented themselves through extremely great austerities. They dwelt in auspicious spots. They showed no injury towards living beings. At the right time, they went to seek alms from the abodes of those who were in the vanaprastha stage, when there was no smoke and when the pestles were silent.[367] They obtained the brahman. They did not praise. They did not bow down. They gave up both the good and the bad. They roamed around alone in the forest, surviving on whatever little was available.'

'"Shuka said, 'In the words of ordinary people, the words of the Vedas are contradictory. In matters of proof, when there is such a conflict, which is then the sacred text? I wish to hear about this. O illustrious one! Tell me about it. How should one act, so as not to violate any rites that have been laid down?'"

[367]That is, when the time for cooking was over.

'Bhishma said, "Having been thus addressed, Gandhavati's son[368] spoke to his son. The rishi honoured the words that his infinitely energetic son had spoken. 'Whether a person is a householder, a brahmachari, in the vanaprashta stage or a mendicant, if he undertakes all the prescribed tasks, he attains the supreme objective. Even if a person follows any one of these ashramas in the appropriate way and is free from desire and hatred, he will obtain greatness after death. These are four steps in a ladder that vests with the brahman. By resorting to this ladder, a person obtains greatness in Brahma's world. For one quarter of the life, a person should follow brahmacharya, without any malice. Learned about dharma and artha, he should dwell with his preceptor or with his preceptor's son. He must be compliant and must not censure anybody. Having performed all his tasks, he must study with his preceptor, but only when his preceptor has summoned him for a lesson. In his preceptor's house, he must eat and sleep after his preceptor, and awake before his preceptor does. A disciple must perform all the tasks that a servant would have. Having done all this, he must stand at the side. He must be like a servant who performs all tasks and is accomplished in all the duties. He must be pure and skilled. He must possess all the qualities. He must be limited and pleasant in speech. He must conquer his senses and must not look at his preceptor with fierce eyes. He must not eat before he has eaten. He must not drink before he has drunk. He must not be seated before he has sat down. He must not sleep before he has slept. He must gently touch his preceptor's feet with upturned palms and knead them, the right with the right and the left with the left. He must respectfully greet his preceptor and say, "O illustrious one! Instruct me. I have done this. O illustrious one! I will do whatever else you ask me to." Having told him all this, he must offer all his riches to the preceptor. He must again tell his preceptor about all the tasks that he has undertaken and ask about what needs to be done. There are some scents and tastes a brahmachari must refrain from. However, it is the determination of dharma that once he has graduated, he can use these again. These

[368]Vedavyasa was the son of Satyavati and she was also known as Gandhavati.

are the detailed rules that have been laid down for a brahmachari. Practising all these, he must remain near his preceptor. To the best of his strength, he must try to please his preceptor. Having done this, the disciple can move on from this ashrama to another ashrama and observe the duties of that. One quarter of his life will thus be spent on the vows of the Vedas and fasting. Having given the dakshina to the preceptor, following the prescribed ordinances, he will graduate. Desiring to accomplish dharma, he will follow dharma and ignite a fire,[369] accepting a wife. This is the state of a householder, in which, he spends the second quarter of his life.'"'

Chapter 1563(235)

'"Vyasa said, 'For the second quarter of his life, he will dwell in a house, in the state of a householder. Desiring to pursue dharma, he will follow good vows, ignite a fire and accept a wife. Wise and learned ones have laid down four kinds of conduct for a householder. The first of these is to maintain a store of grain, the second to maintain a pot of grain, the third is not to provide for tomorrow, while the last is to follow the conduct of pigeons.[370] If one desires to follow dharma and conquer the worlds, in progressive order, the succeeding one is superior to the preceding one.[371] A person who follows the first must undertake six tasks.[372] A person who follows the second must undertake three.[373] A person who

[369]The household fire.

[370]Feeding on whatever is available on the ground.

[371]That is, not saving grain is superior to saving grain.

[372]A person who maintains a store of grain must perform the six tasks of performing sacrifices for himself, officiating at sacrifices of others, teaching, studying, making gifts and receiving gifts.

[373]A person who maintains a pot of grain must perform the three tasks of studying, making gifts and receiving gifts.

follows the third must undertake two.[374] The fourth will only base himself on sacrifices to Brahma.[375] The dharma of a householder is said to be great. However, one must not cook only for one's own self. Nor should animals pointlessly be slaughtered.[376] If an animal or an inanimate being[377] is to be brought down, the ordinances of a sacrifice must be observed. He must not sleep during the day, or during the first part of the night and the last part. He must not eat in between.[378] When it is not her season, he must not summon his wife. In his house, there must never be a brahmana who is not fed or not worshipped. Guests who convey oblations at sacrifices, those who are learned in the Vedas and have bathed themselves in the vows, those who are accomplished and learned in the Vedas, those who are generous and live according to their own dharma, those who observe the rites and those who are ascetics must always be honoured. It is recommended that offerings meant for the gods and the ancestors are for people like these. It is instructed that a share should be given to all beings, even if they sport long nails and hair, even if they have been dislodged from dharma despite knowing it, even if they have deviated from *agnihotra* sacrifices and even if they have injured the old and the young. A person who is a householder must give food to all of them. The eating of leftovers is always like eating amrita. It is like eating the oblations that are left at the end of a sacrifice, like amrita. A person who eats after the servants have eaten is said to subsist on leftovers. He must be content with his own wife. He must be self-controlled. He must conquer his senses and be devoid of malice. He must not get into debates with officiating priests, priests, preceptors, maternal uncles, guests, dependants, the aged, the young, the distressed, physicians, kin, matrimonial allies, relatives, mothers, fathers, daughters-in-law, brothers, sons, wives,

[374]A person who does not provide for tomorrow must perform the two tasks of studying and making gifts.

[375]Interpreted as studying.

[376]Other than at sacrifices.

[377]Like a tree.

[378]The recommended meals are in the morning and in the evening.

daughters and the category of servants. Having been freed from such conversations, he is freed from all sins. If he can conquer this, there is no doubt that he wins all the worlds. The preceptor is the lord of Brahma's world, the father is the lord of Prajapati's world.[379] Guests are the lords of Indra's world, the officiating priest of the world of the gods. Daughters-in-law hold sway over the world of apsaras, kin over that of the Vishvadevas. Matrimonial allies and relatives control the directions and mothers and maternal uncles control the earth. The old, the young, the distressed and the weak hold sway over the sky and have a power like Vishnu. The elder brother is like a father. The wife and the son are like one's own body. The class of servants represents one's own shadow. The daughter is most loved. Therefore, one must always tolerate them, without any anxiety, and must never reprimand these. A person devoted to the dharma of a householder must be learned. He must always be devoted to dharma and must be free of exhaustion. He must perform any task because of considerations of artha. He must act in conformity with dharma. There are three kinds of conduct for a householder and in progressive order, each subsequent one is superior to the preceding one.[380] This is also said to be true of the four ashramas.[381] These are said to be the rules that ensure prosperity in all tasks. A kingdom prospers when those who dwell in it follow the conduct of those who store grain in pots, or glean them like pigeons from the ground.[382] If a person cheerfully follows the vows of a householder, ten generations of his ancestors and ten generations of his descendants attain the supreme objective. Acting in this way, he obtains worlds obtained by universal emperors. This is also the objective ordained for those who control their senses. The world of heaven is ordained for householders who are generous in their minds and engaged in welfare. That heaven is full of excellent blossoming flowers and has celestial vehicles. It has

[379]If these are pleased, those respective worlds can be won.

[380]This probably means kama, artha and dharma, in that order.

[381]Sannyasa is superior to vanaprastha, vanaprastha is superior to garhasthya and garhasthya is superior to brahmacharya.

[382]It is not obvious why these two modes have been singled out.

been spoken about in the Vedas. Householders who control their souls find a place in the world of heaven. The brahman is the ladder that frees them. By following this second mode,[383] one obtains greatness in the world of heaven. After this, there is the supremely great ashrama that is the third, spoken about for those who are ready to cast aside their bodies. Residing in the forest is superior to being a householder. They waste away their bodies there. Listen to this.'"'

Chapter 1564(236)

'Bhishma said, "You have been told what learned ones have ordained about the conduct of householders. O Yudhishthira! Listen to what has been spoken about next. In due order, a person must proceed to the third stage, one that is characterized by supreme conduct. This is the ashrama of vanaprastha, followed by those who are not distressed from observing vows. O Partha! Listen to the conduct of those fortunate ones, who follow this everywhere in the world. They reside in auspicious regions and follow this conduct after having examined it first.

'"Vyasa said, 'When a householder sees wrinkles on his body and white hair, and when he sees the children of his children, he should then resort to the forest. The third quarter of the life should be spent dwelling in vanaprastha. He must tend to the fires he used to tend to.[384] He must worship the residents of heaven. He must be controlled and restrained in his diet. Without any distraction, he must only eat at the sixth time indicated for taking meals.[385] He must maintain cows and other things required for agnihotra sacrifices. He must survive on rice or barley that grows wild and has not been tilled. He must offer oblations at the five kinds

[383]The householder stage is the second ashrama.

[384]As a householder.

[385]This means the evening.

of sacrifices.[386] Four kinds of conduct are recommended for those who are in the vanaprastha ashrama. Some only wash[387] what is needed immediately. Others store enough for a month. Some others store for a year and some others store for twelve years. To accomplish their objectives, they must perform the sacrifice of honouring guests. When it rains, they must only have the sky for a shelter. When it is autumn, they must find refuge in the water. When it is summer, they must torment themselves through the five austerities.[388] They must always be restrained in diet. Some roam around the earth. Others are seated or lie down on the bare ground. In the forest, some sprinkle their beds and seats with water. Some use their teeth as mortars for grinding grain. Others use stones for crushing grain. Some only drink a little bit of grain mixed with water during shuklapaksha. Some only drink[389] during krishnapaksha. Others eat what becomes available in the normal course of things. Some are rigid in their vows and subsist on roots, fruits and flowers. As is appropriate, they follow the mode revered by the Vaikhanasas.[390] That apart, there are many other learned ones who have been consecrated. The fourth stage[391] is generally referred to as the dharma of the Upanishads. This follows after garhasthya and vanaprastha. O son! Even in this yuga, brahmanas who know the truth about everything have followed this—Agastya, the saptarshis,[392] Madhucchanda, Aghamarshana, Samkriti, Sudiva, Tandi, who lived on barley and conquered his exhaustion, Ahovirya, Kavya, Tandya, the wise Medhatithi, Shala, Vaka, Nirvaka and Shunyapala, who conquered his exhaustion. They were learned in this kind of dharma and went to heaven. O

[386]Offerings at ritual sacrifices, offerings to gods, offerings to ancestors, offerings to guests and offerings to other animals.

[387]A reference to washing food.

[388]Four fires are lit in the north, the south, the east and the west, with the practitioner seated in the middle. The sun above the head is the fifth fire.

[389]That grain mixed with water.

[390]Class of hermit.

[391]Of sannyasa.

[392]The seven great rishis. While this list varies marginally, the standard one is Marichi, Atri, Angira, Pulastya, Pulaha, Kratu and Vasishtha.

son! There were large numbers of Yayavara[393] rishis, fierce in their austerities and accomplished and far-sighted about dharma. They immediately obtained the fruits of this dharma. There were so many brahmanas who resorted to the forest that it is impossible to speak about them. There were the Vaikhanasas, the Valakhilyas and Sikatas. They performed difficult deeds. They were always devoted to dharma. They conquered their senses. All of them went to the forest and immediately obtained the fruits of their dharma. Those fearless ones may not have become *nakshatras*,[394] but can be seen in the large number of stellar bodies. When one is overcome by old age and afflicted by disease, in the fourth quarter of one's life, one should abandon the vanaprastha stage. One should perform the sacrifice that can be performed in a single day and offer up everything as dakshina. One must perform one's own funeral rites.[395] One must take pleasure in one's own self and must not depend on anyone else. One must regard one's own self as the sacrificial fire and give up all possessions. One must perform the sacrifice that can be performed in a single day, which is the sacrifice of all sacrificies. When one sacrifices one's own self, all other sacrifices and rites can cease. This sacrifice for the sake of emancipation is like making sacrifices to the three fires.[396] One should not find fault with the food and only eat five or six mouthfuls for the sake of the five breaths of life.[397] At the end of vanaprastha, a sage will cut his hair, beard and nails. Having cleansed himself, he will then proceed from this ashrama to the next sacred ashrama. Such a brahmana departs, offering freedom from fear to all beings. After death, he obtains the eternal and energetic worlds. He is excellent in conduct and all his sins have been cleansed. He doesn't act so as to desire anything in this

[393]If this is not interpreted as a proper name, it means those who are mendicants, with no fixed abode.

[394]There are twenty-seven nakshatras, which are stars/constellations.

[395]Symbolically.

[396]The three sacred fires at any sacrifice—*ahavaniya* (to the east), *dakshinagni* (to the south) and *garhapatya* (the fire for the householder).

[397]Prana, apana, samana, udana and vyana.

world or in the next. He is without anger and without confusion. He is beyond friendship and enmity. Such a man is indifferent towards anything other than his own atman. He observes *yama* and that which follows.[398] He is not distressed at having to give up the principles, oblations and mantras of the sacred texts.[399] He is pursuing the objective of performing a sacrifice with his atman. He has conquered his senses and has no doubt about this supreme dharma. After the other three, this fourth ashrama is said to be supreme. It is the best and has all the good qualities. I will recount that supreme state to you. Listen.'"'

Chapter 1565(237)

'"Shuka said, 'You have spoken to me about what should be done in vanaprastha. When one is engaged in this,[400] to the best of one's ability, how should one engage the atman, so that one attains the supreme objective?'

'"Vyasa replied, 'A person must cleanse himself in the two ashramas.[401] Having done this, he must then engage in tasks for the supreme objective. Listen attentively to this. Having eliminated all taints in the first three stages, he must then resort to the supreme state of renunciation. Renunciation is the best stage. Listen to the conduct that must be followed in that state. One should always roam around alone and seek to accomplish the objective without any help. A person who roams around alone sees that there is nothing to be shunned and there is nothing that decays.

[398]That which follows yama is *niyama*. Though there are several principles, yama is good conduct vis-à-vis the external world and niyama is more like internal good conduct.

[399]He has passed beyond these.

[400]Sannyasa.

[401]A reference to *garhasthya* and vanaprastha. However, we have taken a call here. It could equally well be the brahmacharya and garhasthya stages.

He is without a fire. He is without an abode. At best, he enters a village for the sake of food. It is recommended that he should save nothing for the next day. His sentiments must be like that of a sage. He must eat little, be restrained in his diet and eat only once a day. The signs of a mendicant are a skull,[402] shelter under trees, old garments as attire, lack of companions and indifference towards all beings. Words penetrate him like stones hurled into a well[403] and do not return to the original speaker. Such a person is fit to dwell in the ashrama of isolation. He does not see others. He does not hear others. He never speaks injurious words, especially about brahmanas. He always speaks words that are pleasant to brahmanas. He is silent when he is censured and finds treatment for this within his own self. Though he is always alone, he fills the entire sky.[404] To him, a deserted spot seems to be full of people. The gods know such a person to be a brahmana. He covers himself with anything. He eats anything. He sleeps anywhere. The gods know such a person to be a brahmana. He is afraid of company, as if they are serpents. He regards anything that satiates as hell.[405] He regards women as corpses.[406] The gods know such a person to be a brahmana. He is not angered or delighted, regardless of whether he is honoured or insulted. He does not cause any being to be frightened. The gods know such a person to be a brahmana. He is not delighted at the prospect of death. Nor is he delighted at the prospect of remaining alive. He only waits for the time,[407] like a servant awaiting instructions. His consciousness has been cleansed. His food and words are clean. He is free from all sins. Since he is without enemies, what fear can he have? He has been

[402]For drinking.

[403]That is, they have no effect.

[404]The interpretation is that he sees himself in everything and everything in himself.

[405]This is interpreted as especially applying to food. One should eat only enough to survive and not seek to satiate oneself.

[406]*Kunapa*, alternatively, the name of a specific hell.

[407]Of death.

freed and has no cause for fear from anything that possesses a body. The footsteps of any animal that follows get lost in the footsteps of an elephant. Everything is absorbed in the footprints of an elephant.[408] In that fashion, all dharma and artha are absorbed in lack of injury towards all beings. A person who practises non-violence always resides in what is immortal. He is non-violent and looks on everything equally. He is truthful. He has fortitude and controls his senses. He is the refuge of all beings. He attains the supreme objective. In this way, learned ones are content in their wisdom and are not frightened. He has gone beyond death and the attributes of death do not affect him. Such a sage is free from all attachments and seems to be established in the sky. He wanders alone and tranquil. The gods know such a person to be a brahmana. His life is for the sake of dharma and his dharma is for the sake of others. His days and nights are for the sake of the auspicious. The gods know such a person to be a brahmana. He is without desire. He is without exertion. He does not bow down his head. He is without praise.[409] He does not engage in any inferior deeds. The gods know such a person to be a brahmana. He takes delight in the happiness of all beings. He is extremely distressed at the misery of everyone. If they are frightened, he sorrows. He faithfully undertakes his own tasks. Granting beings freedom from fear is superior to all donations and dakshina. A person who first gives up all injury to the bodies of beings grants these subjects eternal freedom from fear. From the navel of the world, the face is raised upwards and oblations are offered into it.[410] The head and the upper limbs of the fire receive everything, the good and the bad. In the confines of his heart, he offers his own life up as a libation. All the worlds and the gods are satisfied with his

[408]The fruits of yoga are like the footprints of an elephant and everything gets absorbed in them.

[409]He does not praise others, nor does he react to praise from others.

[410]There is the metaphor of a sacrificial altar and fire, being compared to the individual offering himself up as an oblation.

offering up his atman as oblation in that agnihotra. It is divine and golden. It has three shells and three parts.[411] It is the supreme objective and is foremost among things to be known. It is greatest in all the worlds. The gods and accomplished people with good deeds walk along that path. It has been spoken of as the greatest objective, the essence of what is to be known in the Vedas and all the rites. He who knows it as the atman in his own body is always loved by the gods. It is not attached to the earth and is divine. It cannot be measured. It is golden. It was born from an egg and resides in the egg.[412] It is like a winged bird in the firmament. Blazing in its rays, it can be known inside the atman. It whirls around and has no decay. It rotates on six naves, with twelve spokes and excellent joints.[413] The wheel of time is deep and mysterious and everything in the universe heads towards its gaping mouth. It pervades the body of everything in the universe and all the worlds progress towards it. That is spoken of as something that satisfies the gods. When they are satisfied, they gratify that open mouth. The body is ancient and eternal and is full of energy. It is the end of all the worlds and offers freedom from fear. Beings are never frightened of him and he never causes fright to beings.[414] He is not censured. Nor does he censure anyone. A brahmana who sees the paramatman in his own atman is like that. He is humble and without confusion. He is beyond all sins. He desires nothing in this world, nor in the other world. He is without anger and without confusion. He regards a lump of clay and gold in the same way. He is devoid of sorrow and is beyond friendship and enmity. He is beyond censure and praise and beyond liking and disliking. He wanders around indifferent, as a mendicant.'"'

[411]These are difficult shlokas to translate. Quite clearly, the brahman is being described. One of the three is presumably sattva, rajas and tamas. But the second three is not obvious, though it could mean the three worlds.

[412]The egg of creation.

[413]A reference to time, with six seasons and twelve months. The joints are the days.

[414]This is now about the person who knows the brahman.

Chapter 1566(238)

"'Vyasa said, 'The kshetrajna has to experience the transformations of nature. These don't know it,[415] but it knows them. It is made to undertake tasks because of the senses, with the mind as a sixth. Well-trained and excellent horses are firmly controlled.[416] The objects of the senses are superior to the senses and the mind is superior to these objects. Intelligence is superior to the mind and the mahat atman is superior to the mind. The unmanifest is superior to the mahat and the inmortal[417] is superior to the unmanifest. There is nothing that is superior to the immortal. It is the highest limit and the supreme objective. The atman is hidden inside all beings and cannot be seen. Only those who are sharp in their intelligence and can see the subtleties of the truth can fathom it. The intelligence must be used to collect all the senses, the many objects of the senses and the mind, as the sixth, into the atman. One must think about what should be thought about. Having used intelligence to goad the mind, one must meditate on the supreme. Realizing that he has no power, the person must seek to obtain the immortal objective through tranquility in his soul. But a person whose memory is fickle and whose self is under the subjugation of all the senses and who gives his atman up to them, is like a person who is dead and obtains nothing but death. Abandoning all resolution, the consciousness must be merged in the truth. When consciousness is vested in the truth, a person becomes like Kalanjara.[418] With the consciousness gratified, the sage goes beyond the good and the

[415]The atman.

[416]The atman should control the mind and the senses in that way.

[417]The brahman.

[418]Kalanjara is the name of a famous mountain. The obvious meaning is that one becomes as immobile as that mountain. But *kalanjara* is also a meeting point for mendicants. With a pun on the word kala (time), there may also be a sense of conquering time.

bad. He bases himself on the gratification of his atman and enjoys infinite happiness. A sign of that satisfaction is that he sleeps in contentment. He is like the flame of a lamp that is not stirred by the wind. In this way, at the beginning of the night and the end of the night,[419] he unites the atman with the atman.[420] He is virtuous in his diet and pure in his soul and beholds the atman in the atman.[421] This is the essence of all the Vedas and the sacred texts. O son! For realizing the atman, these are the instructions of the sacred texts. This is the essence of all dharma and all accounts about the truth. This amrita has been obtained by churning the ten thousand chants from the Rig Veda.[422] It is like wood and fire being used to churn butter from curds. O son! In that way, for you, I have given you the wisdom of the learned ones. O son! These are the words of the sacred texts, given as instructions to snatakas. These should not be given to people who are not tranquil, those who are not self-controlled and ascetics. Nor should they be given to those who are unacquainted with the words of the Vedas, or do not follow them. They should not be given to those who are malicious, not upright, those who are directionless in their tasks, those who slander and those who burn everything down in the science of argumentation. But they should be given to calm ascetics who are praised, or should be praised, and beloved sons and devoted disciples. The secrets of this dharma should be revealed to such people and not to anyone else. I think that even if a man is given the entire earth with all its treasures, this truth is superior to that gift. There is a greater and superhuman mystery about adhyatma. This was seen by the maharshis and sung about in Vedanta. You have asked me about it and I will tell you the truth about it.'"'

[419]Evening and dawn.

[420]The first atman is the jivatman and the second atman is the paramatman.

[421]Now the second atman is the jivatman and the first atman is the paramatman.

[422]There are different texts of the Rig Veda, with roughly 1,000 hymns and 10,000 chants (*richs*).

Chapter 1567(239)

'"Shuka asked, 'In detail, tell me about adhyatma again. O illustrious one! O supreme among the rishis! What is this adhyatma?'

'"Vyasa replied, 'O son! For men, there is something known as adhyatma. I will recount this to you. Listen to the explanation. Earth, water, fire, wind and space are the great elements in beings and are like the waves of the ocean.[423] A tortoise stretches out its limbs and draws them back again. Like that, the great elements extend and withdraw in beings. They pervade all the mobile and immobile objects. Creation and destruction are determined on the basis of these. The five great elements exist in all the beings that have been created. O son! But it is also seen that these exist unevenly in different beings.'

'"Shuka asked, 'How can one discern this in the bodies? What are senses? What are qualities? How can they be felt?'

'"Vyasa replied, 'I will accurately describe what has been comprehended about this. Listen attentively to the truth about how it occurs. Sound, hearing and space inside beings—these three originate in space. The breath of life, exertion and touch—these three are the qualities of the wind. Form, sight and digestion—these three are said to result from fire. Taste, tongue and juices—these three are the qualities of water. Scent, nose and the body—these three are the qualities of the earth. The five elements that I have described to you mix with the senses and undergo transformations. Touch is said to be associated with the wind, taste with water and form with fire. Sound is said to be created by space and smell is the attribute of the earth. The mind, intelligence and sentiments—these three are created by their own selves.[424] Though these are beyond the qualities, it is the view that they are not superior to the qualities. There are five senses in men and the mind is said to be the sixth. Intelligence is said

[423]They are like the waves of the ocean because while all the water in the ocean is one, the waves are regarded as separate and distinct.

[424]Because of the deeds undertaken in earlier lives.

to be the seventh and the kshetrajna is the eighth. Rajas, sattva and tamas—these three are created by their own selves. Those qualities are seen to exist equally in all beings. A tortoise extends its limbs and draws them back again. In that way, intelligence extends the qualities and draws them back. A person who is supreme in intelligence acts so as to look for it[425] above the feet, the hands, the face and the head. Intelligence is controlled by the qualities, and the senses are controlled by intelligence. Among all of these, the mind is the sixth. If there is no intelligence, how can there be qualities? When a person is full of cheerfulness and is seen to be tranquil in his soul and pure, that is held up by sattva. When a person is full of torment in deeds and thoughts, rajas is always the originator and this confuses beings. When a person is confused about the unmanifest and finds this imcomprehensible and impossible to know, this is driven by tamas. Delight, joy, bliss, peace and satisfaction in the consciousness, regardless of whether something unexpected occurs or does not occur—these are the qualities of sattva. Insolence, falsehood in words, greed, confusion, lack of forgiveness, whether there is a reason for this or whether there is no reason for this—are the signs of rajas. Delusion, distraction, lassitude, sleep and lack of exertion—whenever these are indulged in, that is known to be the quality of tamas.'"'

Chapter 1568(240)

'"Vyasa said, 'The mind creates sentiments, and intelligence chooses between them. The heart differentiates between the pleasant and the unpleasant. Know that there are three kinds of urges behind action. The objects of the senses are superior to the senses and the mind is superior to the objects of the senses. Intelligence is superior to the mind and it is held that the atman

[425]The atman.

is superior to intelligence. Intelligence is in the atman of men. Intelligence is in the atman that is inside. When it creates sentiments, it becomes the mind. Since the senses are different, the intelligence discriminates between them. When it hears, it becomes hearing. When it touches, it becomes touch. When it sees, it become sight. When it tastes, it becomes the tongue. When it smells, it becomes the nose. It is intelligence that creates a difference between these. What are called the senses in men are seen to be the three kinds of sentiments of the intelligence.[426] One is sometimes delighted. At other times, one grieves. There are times when a person is united with neither happiness, nor unhappiness. The ocean is the lord of the rivers and the giant shoreline withstands the waves. Like that, though driven by the three sentiments, it can transcend them.[427] Though thought of as existing separately, when it desires anything, intelligence is known as the mind. All the strong senses must be conquered. In due course, when each of these[428] overwhelms the intelligence, it exists in the mind. Rajas is excited and follows sattva. Just as the spokes are attached to the wheel of a chariot, those qualities are attached to those three.[429] A man must use his supreme intelligence like a lamp to control the senses and use yoga to be indifferent and immobilize desire. While qualities are natural, a learned person is not confused. He is always without sorrow and without delight and beyond jealousy. The senses pursue objects of desire and are incapable of seeing the atman. It is difficult for people with cleansed souls to see it in this way, not to speak of others. However, the mind can be used to control them,[430] as if through reins. The atman then manifests itself in all beings, like a lamp inside a pot, when the darkness has been overcome. An aquatic bird doesn't become wet, even when it roams around in

[426]Sattva, rajas and tamas.

[427]Through yoga, intelligence can transcend the qualities.

[428]The senses.

[429]Sattva, rajas and tamas attach themselves to the mind, intelligence and consciousness.

[430]The senses.

water. In that fashion, a person whose wisdom is accomplished is not tainted by material objects. Though he enjoys them, he is never attached to them. He has performed deeds earlier,[431] but only loves the atman now, which is inside all living beings. He has given up the path characterized by the qualities. For him, there are no qualities, other than those engendered by the sattva in his atman. The qualities are incapable of comprehending the atman, though it always knows them. It sees the qualities and is also their creator. Know that this is the subtle difference between understanding and the kshetrajna. One of them creates the qualities. But the qualities do not create that single one. They[432] are naturally different, but are always united. The fish that lives in water is different from the environment in which it lives. A gnat may be attached to a fig tree, but they are actually different. A blade of grass is also different from the clump of *munja* grass it is in. Like that, though they are united, they are actually established separately.'"'

Chapter 1569(241)

'"Vyasa said, 'Understanding creates the qualities and the kshetrajna is also established there. However, the lord[433] is indifferent towards all the qualities that have been created. All the qualities that have been created follow their own nature. This is like a spider creating strands that are the qualities. Despite pravritti, some are not felt, because they decay and are withdrawn. Others are destroyed because of nivritti.[434] One must think about both these

[431]Before opting for sannyasa.

[432]Understanding and the soul.

[433]The atman.

[434]Both of these result from the practice of yoga. In the case of pravritti, the qualities are not really destroyed. But their presence is no longer felt. In the case of nivritti, they are destroyed.

possibilities and try to do what is best. Following either principle, one can obtain the womb of greatness. A man must always act so as to obtain the one without beginning and without end.[435] He must not be angry. Nor should he be delighted. He must always be devoid of jealousy. He must firmly sever the strands in his heart that are due to intelligence and thoughts. Having overcome them, he will be free from doubt. He will be devoid of sorrow and obtain happiness. A man who is dislodged from the ground and falls down and is submerged in a full river is tormented. Know this world to be also like that. However, a learned man who knows the truth acts accordingly and it is as if he is on land. A person who knows the atman realizes that the atman is only knowledge. Such a person understands the origin and destruction of all beings. He looks on both[436] equally and soon obtains excellent and supreme tranquility. In particular, because of birth, this comes naturally to brahmanas. Knowledge of the atman and tranquility are sufficient to lead to emancipation. Having known this, one becomes enlightened.[437] What other qualities can there be of learning? Having known this, learned people accomplish their objectives and are emancipated. Those without learning suffer from great fear. But those with learning have no such great fear. There is no objective that is superior to this, the eternal end obtained by learned people. There are people who are afflicted with jealousy because of material objects.[438] There are others who glance at these and sorrow. However, an accomplished person looks at these and does not grieve at what has been obtained and what has not been obtained. Anything done without attachment destroys earlier deeds.[439] In this world, one must act so as to renounce[440] both the pleasant and the unpleasant.'"'

[435]The soul.

[436]Origin and destruction.

[437]The text uses the word Buddha, enlightened.

[438]At what others possess.

[439]Deeds, say, of past lives.

[440]Renounce attachment.

Chapter 1570(242)

'"Shuka asked, 'O illustrious one! Tell me about supreme dharma, to which nothing is superior. What is that special dharma?'

'"Vyasa replied, 'I will tell you about the dharma that was praised by the ancient rishis. This is special among all kinds of dharma. Listen single-mindedly to this. The senses cause agitation. One must carefully use one's intelligence to restrain them. This is like a father controlling his foolish and wayward sons. The concentration of the mind and the senses is the greatest austerity. Since all dharmas flow from this, this is regarded as supreme dharma. The intelligence must be used to restrain all of them, with the mind as the sixth. Thinking a lot about what it is difficult to think about, one must be satisfied in the atman. Just as cows return from pasture and return to their houses, when one is immersed in the atman, one can see the supreme and the eternal. Like a flame that is without smoke, great-souled and learned brahmanas can see the great atman[441]in all atmans. A giant tree with many branches and full of flowers and fruit does not itself know which are its flowers and which are its fruit. In that way, the atman does not know where it has come from and where it is going.[442] However, there is an inner atman that sees everything.[443] With the blazing lamp of knowledge, see the atman inside your own self. Having seen the atman inside your own self, know everything and know that you are not the body. Be cleansed from all sin, like a snake that has cast off its skin. With that supreme intelligence, be free of sin and free from anxiety. This terrible river[444] has currents that flow in every direction in this world. The five senses are crocodiles and the mind and resolution are embankments. It is

[441]The paramatman.

[442]Referrring to birth and death.

[443]The inner atman is obviously the jivatman, whereas the earlier reference to the atman is of the atman confounded by the ignorance of the mind, intelligence, consciousness and the senses.

[444]The river of life.

strewn with the grass of greed and confusion. Desire and anger are the reptiles. While truth constitutes the *tirtha*s, falsehood constitutes the waves. Wrath is the mud in that supreme river. It arises from the unmanifest and flows swiftly. A person who has not cleansed his soul is incapable of crossing it. It is full of desire in the form of crocodiles. Use your intelligence to cross it. It flows towards the ocean of life and its womb is in the nether regions. It is difficult to cross. O son! It flows from one's birth and in this world, its eddies are impossible to cross. Learned and persevering people, accomplished in wisdom, can cross it. Having crossed, you will be freed from everything. You will be pure and your soul will be cleansed. Having resorted to that superior intelligence, you will attain the brahman. After crossing, you will be free from all hardships. Your soul will be cheerful and devoid of sin. You will calmly look down on beings on this earth, as if from the top of a mountain. You will not be enraged. You will not be delighted. You will not possess any violent designs. You will behold the creation and destruction of all beings. The learned think that this is the best among all kinds of dharma. Sages who know about the truth and are the best among the upholders of dharma, say that this is dharma. This knowledge about the atman should be made known and instructed to one's son. It should be spoken about to someone who is self-controlled and devoted and has welfare in mind. This knowledge about the atman is a mystery. It is the greatest among all mysterious things. O son! The omnipresent atman is itself a witness to what I have spoken about. The brahman is not female, male or neuter. It doesn't experience misery and joy. It is the past, the present and the future. If one knows this, irrespective of whether one is male or female, one does not have to be born again. This has been ordained for obtaining freedom from birth. O son! Just as I have spoken about this to you, there are many other views and perceptions. But I have expounded what is proper. You are my son. You are a virtuous son, with qualities. Therefore, I have affectionately told you this excellent account. You asked me about it and for the sake of your welfare, I have lovingly told you. O son! I have told you what you asked me about.'"'

Chapter 1571(243)

'"Vyasa said, 'One should not be enamoured of fragrances, food and other objects that bring happiness. Nor should one accept ornaments. One should not desire for honour, deeds and fame. A brahmana is known from such conduct. There may be a person who has served,[445] observed brahmacharya and studied all the Vedas—the Rig, the Sama and the Yajur. But this does not make him a brahmana. There may be a person who looks upon all beings as kin, who knows everything and knows all the Vedas. But until lack of desire is generated in him, he does not become a brahmana, free from birth and death. There may be a person who has performed many kinds of sacrifices and rites, giving away a lot of dakshina. But until he is compassionate and without greed, he does not obtain the status of a brahmana. When a person does not frighten others and is himself not terrified by others, when he does not desire anything or hate anything, he attains the brahman. When he does not have wicked sentiments towards all beings, in deeds, thoughts and speech, he attains the brahman. Other than the single bondage of desire, there is no other bondage in this world. Someone who is free from the bondage of desire attains the brahman. Just as the moon is freed from misty clouds, he is freed from desire. Such a patient person is radiant and waits for his time[446] with fortitude. He is full, like waters flowing into the ocean. He is in a state that is not dislodged and is not overwhelmed by desire. He does not wish for any desires. In this body, he obtains the world of heaven. The Upanishads represent the truth of the Vedas. Self-control represents the truth of the Upanishads. Donations represent the self-control of the Upanishads. Austerities represent the donations of the Upanishads. Renunciation represents the austerities of the Upanishads. Happiness represents the renunciation of the Upanishads. Heaven represents the happiness of the Upanishads.

[445]The preceptor.

[446]Time of death.

Tranquility represents the heaven of the Upanishads. If you desire truth and contentment, their supreme signs are tranquility and the extinguishing of grief, sorrow in the mind, torment and thirst. Lack of sorrow, lack of ownership, tranquility, cheerfulness, immersion in the atman and lack of desire for riches—these again are said to be the six signs of completeness. The wise use these six qualities of sattva to become extremely learned. Those learned ones are established in the atman in this world and are also learned after death. It[447] has not been created, nor is it destroyed. It is natural and does not require cleansing. A wise person acts well, knows adhyatma and enjoys a happiness that is without decay. He restrains his mind from wandering around in every direction and fixes it.[448] Through this, he obtains a satisfaction that is incapable of being obtained through any other means. Through this, one is content without eating. Through this, one is content without riches. Through this, one is strong, despite lack of attachment. A person who knows this knows the Vedas. Such a person protects his atman and does not think about the various doors.[449] He is only devoted to the atman. Such a person is said to be a virtuous brahmana. Such a person is established, having extinguished his desire. He is controlled in the supreme truth. He is happy in every way, like the waxing moon. Because of his qualities, such a sage is honoured among beings as special. His happiness dispels sorrow, like the sun dispelling darkness. He transcends tamas. He transcends deeds. He transcends any decay in the qualities. He is not attached to material objects. He does not experience birth and death. He is free in every way and regards everything as equal. While still in his body, he transcends the senses and the objects of the senses. He obtains the supreme cause and transcends the reason for action.[450] Having obtained the greatest of the great, there is no return[451] for him.'"'

[447]The atman.

[448]On the atman.

[449]The gates of the body, a reference to the senses.

[450]The reason for action is interpreted as prakriti.

[451]Rebirth.

Chapter 1572(244)

'"Vyasa said, 'There may be a disciple with qualities, one who has been freed from opposite sentiments and having established himself in artha and dharma, is inquisitive. Such a person should be told, and made to hear, about this greatness. Space, wind, light, water and the earth as the fifth, existence, non-existence and time—these exist in all beings formed by the five elements. The gaps are space and the sense of hearing is formed by that. A person who knows about the ordinances of the sacred texts knows that sound is its quality. Movement and prana and apana are constituted by the wind. Know that the sense of touch and touch itself is its[452] essence. Heat and the light in the eyes are full of light. Know that its qualities are the warmth in the body. Liquid discharges, juices and fat are instructed as belonging to water. It is held that the sense of taste and the tongue represent qualities of water. Bones, teeth, nails, beard, body hair, hair, veins, arteries, skin and all solid objects are the essence of the earth. The nose is said to represent the sense of smell. The sense associated with scent is known to represent the essence of the earth. Each succeeding element possesses the qualities of the preceding one.[453] The sages know that everything flows from the aggregate of the five elements. The mind is the ninth and intelligence is said to be the tenth.[454] The eleventh is the atman inside and this is said to be superior to all the others. Intelligence tries to analyse the atman and the mind tries to explain the atman. Through deeds, it is possible to infer that the atman is inside the body.[455] All living beings are characterized by

[452]The wind's.

[453]This has been explained earlier.

[454]There is a gap which can only be plugged through interpretations. Other than the five elements, there are ignorance, desire and acts committed earlier. These account for eight.

[455]This is a very difficult shloka to translate and some liberties have been taken.

these[456] and time. But a wise person sees it[457] as untainted and does not suffer from confusion.'"'

Chapter 1573(245)

'"Vyasa said, 'It[458] is separate from the body and exists in a subtle form inside the body. Following the deeds mentioned in the sacred texts, those who are conscious of the secret texts, can see it. When the rays of the sun travel around, their coming and going cannot be seen. In that way, it is freed from the body and moves around, but it is beyond human powers to detect this.[459] However, the sun's radiance can be seen in an image in the water. In that fashion, the image of the soul can be seen in the gross body. In its subtle form, it is freed from the body. Those who have controlled their senses and know about the truth can perceive this. Whether asleep or awake, they always think about the atman. Primarily, they are free from opposites and abandon all tasks connected with rajas. Day is like night to them and night is like day. These yogis always practice yoga and have their atmans under control.[460] It is eternal. But because of qualities, it is not eternal in living beings. It is without birth and without decay and roams around in subtle form, with those seven.[461] If a man has not been able to conquer his mind and his intelligence even in his sleep, he distinguishes between his body and someone else's body and experiences happiness and unhappiness. That is the reason he obtains misery. That is also the

[456]Their earlier deeds.

[457]The atman, which is untouched by deeds and time.

[458]The atman.

[459]The atman assumes a subtle body and moves around, outside the gross body.

[460]Interpreting, they have control over the subtle bodies.

[461]The five elements, or senses, and mind and intelligence.

reason he obtains joy. He experiences anger and greed and acting in accordance with these, faces calamities. In his dreams, he obtains great riches and performs auspicious deeds. But when he awakes, these cannot be seen. The extremely energetic atman is located in the hearts of all beings. However, because of being enveloped with tamas and rajas, it cannot be seen in the bodies. But there are those who are devoted to the sacred texts and yoga, searching for their own atmans. They look for that other form, which is as firm as a vajra. Different beings have been created, with the four ashramas and their tasks. But of these, yoga is the foremost and it takes one to the supreme brahman. Meditating, immersed in yoga and tranquil, Shandilya spoke about the seven subtle ones and the six strands of Maheshvara.'"'[462]

Chapter 1574(246)

'"Vyasa said, 'There is a colourful tree of desire in the heart. It is generated from the store of confusion. Anger and insolence constitute its gigantic trunk. The desire for knowledge is the source of its liberation. Ignorance is its root and delusion sprinkles it with water. Jealousy makes up the leaves. Earlier acts provide the fertilizer. Lack of judgement and lack of thought are the branches. Sorrow makes up the terrible smaller branches. The thirst that seduces are the creepers that surround it from all sides. Those who are extremely greedy, desiring the fruit, worship that

[462]Shandilya was a famous sage. The seven subtle ones are interpreted as the senses, the objects of the senses, mind, intelligence, mahat, prakriti and purusha. Maheshvara simply means great lord or great power. In this context, it does not necessarily mean Shiva. The six strands are interpreted as omniscience, contentment, infinite intelligence, impartiality, constant vigil and omnipotence.

giant tree. They seek those fruits, tied up in bonds of effort. As long as one is tied down by those bonds, the tree attracts a person. But if a person endeavours, he can go beyond misery and transcend them both.[463] A person whose wisdom is accomplished and bursts forth burns down the tree, like the poison in a person afflicted with disease being destroyed. Aversion becomes his foundation and forcibly destroys its foundation.[464] Distraction is severed through renunciation and by resorting to supreme tranquility. A person who knows that desire only attracts, can use the knowledge of desire to kill it and go beyond misery. The body is described as a city and intelligence as its lord. For intelligence, which is based in the body, the entity known by the name of the mind is the one that thinks of the objectives. The senses are the subjects in the city and it is for them that tasks with objectives are performed. It is there that two terrible taints exist, known as tamas and rajas. With the lords of the city,[465] the citizens remain alive for this. Serving those two taints, the ones without the gates[466] also serve those objectives. It is difficult for intelligence to be conquered.[467] Nevertheless, its dharma is said to be the same as that of the mind. The citizens[468] are agitated by the mind and lose their stability. The intelligence strives for objectives that are damaged and are not successful. But despite not being accomplished, they are separately remembered and torment the mind. Though the mind alone is important, the intelligence is also separately afflicted. One is then enveloped by emptiness and covered by rajas. The mind meets this rajas and has a friendship with it. It gathers up the citizens of the city and hands them over to rajas.'"'

[463]Both misery and joy.

[464]Aversion to attachment is the foundation of yoga and destroys the tree's foundation.

[465]Mind, intelligence and consciousness.

[466]The body has gates. The ones without gates are mind, intelligence and consciousness.

[467]By rajas or tamas.

[468]The senses.

Chapter 1575(247)

'Bhishma said, "O son! Listen once again to an enumeration of the qualities in beings. O unblemished one! These are praiseworthy words, uttered from Dvaipayana's mouth. The words spoken by the illustrious one are like a blazing fire, with flames that have no smoke. O son! I am recounting these examples to you yet again. The earth has qualities of stability, gravity, hardness, productiveness, smell, heaviness, capacity, accumulation, establishment and fortitude. The water has qualities of being cool, juices, moisture, liquidity, softness, tranquility, taste, flowing and wetness in earthy objects. The qualities of fire are difficulty of resisting, energy, heat, capacity to cook, radiance, purification, affection, lightness, sharpness and the ability to rise upwards, as the tenth. The qualities of the wind are control, touch, the location of speech, independence, strength, speed, confusion, effort and the performance of tasks. The qualities of space are sound, expanse, ability to pervade, the lack of a foundation, the lack of a refuge, not being manifest, not being transformed, the ability of not being resisted and the ability to cause transformations in beings. Created by the five elements, it is said to possess fifty qualities.[469] Fickleness, argumentation, expression, detachment, imagination, forgiveness, propensity towards good, propensity towards evil and lack of readiness—these are the nine qualities of the mind. Thinking good and evil, enterprise, concentration, doubt and observation—these are the five qualities of intelligence.'"

'Yudhishthira asked, "How can intelligence have five qualities? How can the senses possess qualities? O grandfather! Tell me everything about this subtle knowledge."

'Bhishma replied, "There are said to be sixty qualities in beings.[470] Beings are always attached to those qualities. Beings, and what they

[469]Each of the five basic elements possesses ten qualities.

[470]The five elements have fifty qualities. Intelligence possesses five qualities. Evidently, five out of the mind's nine qualities are being singled out.

are attached to, have been created by Akshara. O son! That is what has always been spoken about in this world. O son! Everything present in this world is said to have been thought in his mind and created. That is the truth about the origin of all beings and about the origin and destruction of beings. Therefore, obtain tranquility in your intelligence."'

Chapter 1576(248)

'Yudhishthira said, "These lords of the earth are lying down on the surface of the ground. Those immensely strong ones have lost their lives in the midst of the armies. Each of them was terrible in strength, endowed with the might of ten thousand elephants. In the battle, they have been slain by men who were their equals in energy and strength. In earlier times, I have not seen any others who could have killed these people in battle. They were full of valour. They were full of energy and strength. O immensely wise one! Yet they are lying down here, bereft of their lives. When they have lost their lives, the word 'dead' is used about them. These dead kings were generally fierce in their valour. I have a doubt in this connection. Where do senses and death come from? Who dies?[471] Where does death come from? Why do subjects on earth confront death and are borne away by it? O one who is like the immortals! O grandfather! Tell me this."

'Bhishma replied, "O son! In ancient times, in krita yuga, there was a king named Avikampaka. With his mounts having been destroyed in a battle, he came under the subjugation of the enemy. His son was named Hari and he was Narayana's equal in strength. However, with his army and his followers, he was slain in the battle by the enemy. Having come under the subjugation of the enemy, the king was overcome by sorrow, because of his son.

[471]The body or the atman?

Desiring peace, he roamed around on earth[472] and saw Narada. The lord of men told him everything that had happened, about his being captured in the battle by the enemy and about his son's death. On hearing his words, Narada, the store of austerities, wished to dispel the sorrow on account of his son and told him an account. 'O king![473] Listen to this extremely detailed account. O lord of the earth! I heard this account earlier. Engaged in the creation of subjects, the immensely energetic grandfather[474] created a large number of subjects. They became extremely old, but did not die, and generated offspring. O unblemished one! There was not the slightest bit of space that was not covered with living beings. O king! The three worlds were covered with them and were unable to breathe. O lord of the earth! He[475] then began to think about how they might be destroyed. However, though he thought about it, he could not determine any reason for the destruction. O great king! From the fire of his rage, a fire arose out of his body. O king! The grandfather burnt down all the directions with this. O king! The fire that resulted from the illustrious one's anger burnt down heaven, earth, the firmament and the universe, with its mobile and immobile objects. When the great grandfather was enraged with the force of that great anger, living beings and immobile objects were certainly destroyed. Then the god Sthanu Shiva, the destroyer of enemy heroes and the lord of the Vedas, the one who has tawny and matted hair, wanted to ensure a refuge for the universe and went to Brahma. For the sake of the welfare of the subjects, Sthanu went to him. The blazing god, the granter of boons, spoke to Shiva. "It is my view that you should get a boon from me. What is your desire? I will accomplish it today. O Shambhu! I am the doer. I will ensure your pleasure and your growth."'"'

[472]He was defeated by the enemy, but was left free.

[473]Though the text does not explicitly state this, this is clearly a quote ascribed to Narada.

[474]Brahma.

[475]Brahma.

Chapter 1577(249)

'"'Sthanu said, "O lord! Everything that I have done is for the sake of the subjects who have been created. O grandfather! Know that you should not be angry with the ones you have created. O god! In every direction, the subjects are being burnt because of the fierceness of your fire. On seeing this, I feel compassion. O lord of the universe! Do not be enraged with them."

'"'Prajapati replied, "I am not enraged. Nor is it my desire that these subjects should cease to exist. I desire the destruction for the sake of making the burden of the earth lighter. The goddess[476] has been afflicted by the burden and has constantly urged me for the destruction. O Mahadeva! Because of the burden, she seems to be submerging in the water. Despite using my intelligence to reflect on this, I have not been able to understand what to do. Anger entered me because I wished to destroy this growth."

'"'Sthanu said, "O lord of the thirty gods! Be pacified about this destruction and do not be enraged. Do not destroy the subjects and the mobile and immobile objects. There are four kinds of categories of beings—all the waterbodies, all the grass and herbs, mobile objects and immobile objects. The entire universe is being robbed of these and all these created entities are being reduced to ashes. O illustrious one! Show your favours. O virtuous one! This is the boon that I seek from you. Once they are destroyed, these subjects will never return again. Therefore, let this infinite energy be countered with your own energy. With the welfare of the subjects in mind, think of some other means. O scorcher of enemies! Let all these living beings be able to return again. It is not desirable that all the created subjects should be destroyed, together with their offspring. O lord over lords of the worlds! I have been appointed by you as the one who presides over existence. O protector of the universe! All the mobile and immobile objects in the universe have sprung from you. O great god! With your favours, I desire that these subjects should return and find subsistence."'

[476]The earth.

'"Narada said, 'The god who was restrained in speech[477] heard Sthanu's words. He then restrained the energy that had originated from within himself. The illustrious one, worshipped by the worlds, restrained the fire. The lord began to think about creation and destruction. He restrained the fire that had resulted from his anger. At that time, from within the great-souled creator of the universe, a lady manifested herself. She was dark and dressed in red garments. Her eyes and palms were red. She was adorned with celestial earrings and wore divine ornaments. Having emerged from within him, she stood on his right. Those two lords of the universe[478] saw that celestial maiden. O lord of the earth![479] The original god of the worlds[480] addressed the goddess and said, "O Death! Slay the subjects. Using my intelligence and my rage, I have thought of you as the destroyer. Therefore, destroy all the subjects, whether they are dumb or learned. O beautiful one! Without any differentiation, destroy the subjects. You are thus appointed by me and you will obtain supreme prosperity." The goddess Death wore a garland of lotuses. Hearing this, the maiden was tormented by grief and began to shed tears. O lord of men! She joined her hands in salutation and wept. To ensure the welfare of men, she again entreated him.'"'

Chapter 1578(250)

'"Narada said, 'The large-eyed lady controlled her grief. She bent like a creeper, joined her hands in salutation and said, "O supreme among those who grant boons! I have been created by you. How can you engage a lady like me in such a terrible deed, one that is fearful to all living beings? I am terrified that I will act in

[477]Brahma.

[478]Brahma and Shiva.

[479]Meaning Avikampaka.

[480]Brahma.

accordance with adharma. Instruct me about a task of dharma. O lord of everything auspicious! You can see with your eyes that I am terrified. There are living beings who are children, young and aged, who have done me no injury. How will I take them away? O lord of living beings! I am bowing down before you. Show me your favours. There will be beloved sons, friends, brothers, mothers and fathers. O god! If I make them die, I am terrified that I will commit a crime. The tearful sorrow and compassion of the survivors will burn me for an eternal period. I am frightened of their power. That is the reason I seek refuge with you. O god! The performers of wicked deeds will go to Yama's abode. O granter of boons! O lord! Be pacified and show me your favours. O grandfather of the worlds! This is the desire that I wish you to satisfy. O lord of the gods! Through your favours, it is my wish that I should perform austerities."'

'"The grandfather replied, 'O Death! I have thought of you for the sake of destroying subjects. Do not think about this. Go and destroy all the subjects. This will certainly happen. It cannot be otherwise. O one with the unblemished limbs! O unblemished one! Act in accordance with my words.'

'"Narada said, 'O mighty-armed one! O vanquisher of enemy cities! Having been thus addressed, she did not reply. She stood there, raising her eyes up at the illustrious one. Though he repeatedly spoke to her, the beautiful one seemed to be bereft of her senses. The god of the gods, the lord of the lords,[481] was himself silent. Brahma then resorted within himself and became pacified. The lord of the worlds smiled and looked at all the worlds. The illustrious and unvanquished one controlled his rage. We have heard that the lady then departed. Having promised to destroy subjects, she withdrew. O Indra among kings! Mrityu[482] swiftly went to the spot known as Dhenuka. The goddess performed supreme austerities there, ones that are very difficult to accomplish. Standing on one foot, she performed austerities for fifteen billion years.[483] There, she performed austerities

[481]Brahma.

[482]Death.

[483]*Padma*. A padma is an unspecified large number, but is sometimes taken as equal to one billion.

that are extremely difficult to accomplish. After this, the immensely energetic Brahma again spoke these words to her. "O Death! Swiftly act in accordance with my instructions." But she ignored this. O son![484] O one who grants honours! She again performed austerities for eighteen billion years. O son! She roamed with the deer and again performed austerities for ten thousand billion years. O king! She went again and observed an extraordinary vow of silence. O king! During this, she immersed herself in water for eight thousand years. O bull among the Bharata lineage![485] The maiden then went to the river Koushiki. Subsisting on water and air, she practised the vows again. The immensely fortunate one then went to Ganga and Mount Meru. Desiring the welfare of living beings, she stood immobile there. She went to the summit of the Himalayas, where the gods had assembled. O Indra among kings! She stood on her toes for a billion years. She made careful efforts to pacify the grandfather. The creator of the worlds went and spoke to her there. "O daughter! Why are you acting in this way? Act in accordance with my words." Death then again spoke to the illustrious grandfather. "O god! I cannot take away the subjects. I am again seeking your favours." She was terrified because of the fear of adharma and again beseeched him. However, the god of the gods ignored her words and spoke to her. "O Death! There will be no adharma for you. O fortunate one! It is desirable that you should control the subjects. O fortunate one! The words that I have spoken can never be falsified. Eternal dharma will now penetrate you. I and all the gods will always be engaged in ensuring your welfare. I will also grant you the other wish you desire. Subjects will be afflicted by disease and no sin will accrue to you. You will be a man among men, a woman among women and the third sex among eunuchs." O great king! Having been thus addressed, she joined her hands in salutation and again spoke to the great-souled and undecaying one, to the effect that she could not do this. But the lord of the gods told the goddess, "O Death! Destroy men. O auspicious one! I am decreeing that no adharma will attach to you. In front of me, I can see that tears are dropping from your eyes and that you are holding

[484]The word used is tata.

[485]Since Narada is speaking to Avikampaka, this is a clear inconsistency.

them in your hands. These will become diseases among men, terrible in form. O Death! At the appropriate time, they will afflict them. When their end comes, all living beings will be united with desire and anger. Since you will not discriminate in your conduct, you will follow dharma and no adharma will be attached to you. Protect the dharma that I have spoken about. You will not immerse yourself in adharma. Therefore, you should find this desire agreeable. Engage yourself in destroying living beings." At this, Mrityu was frightened of his curse and agreed to follow the instructions. When the time of living beings was over, she started to dispatch desire and anger, so as to confound and destroy them. The tears that Mrityu had shed became diseases that afflicted the bodies of men. Therefore, one should not sorrow when the lives of living beings are extinguished. Instead, one should use one's intelligence to understand this. When their lives are over, all gods among beings depart and return again.[486] O lion among kings! In that way, when their lives are over, all men go away, like the gods. The wind is terrible and immensely energetic. It emits a mighty roar and is the breath of life in all living beings, following different courses in the bodies, until they are separated from their bodies. That is the reason the wind is special and is known as the god of the gods. All the gods are characterized by traits of mortality. There are traits of divinity in all mortals. O lion among kings! Therefore, do not sorrow over your son. Your son has obtained heaven and delight there. This is the way Mrityu was created by the god, so that she could appropriately destroy beings when the time arrives. The diseases are the tears that she shed. At the right time, they destroy living beings.'"'

Chapter 1579(251)

'Yudhishthira asked, "All these men have doubts about dharma. What is dharma? Where does dharma come from?

[486]Are born again.

O grandfather! Tell me this. Is dharma for objectives in this world, or is it for objectives in the world hereafter? Or is dharma for both objectives? O grandfather! Tell me this."

'Bhishma replied, "Good conduct, the sacred texts and the Vedas—these are the three signs of dharma. The wise say that the objective is a fourth indication of dharma. On this, superior and inferior deeds have been spoken about. The rules of dharma have been laid down for conduct in this world. They ensure happiness, both in this world and in the next. A wicked person who engages in evil is incapable of obtaining the subtle aspects of dharma. Some say that those who perform wicked deeds can never be freed from their sins. However, a person who speaks about sin may act like one who follows dharma.[487] Devotion to dharma is evident in the conduct of those who resort to it, not by speaking about it. A thief may steal riches and spend those on dharma. When there is no king, a thief may find delight in stealing the property of others. However, when others steal what he has stolen, he then wishes for a king. Even when his own property has been touched, he is not content with the riches that belong to him alone. Without any fear and without any uncertainty, he knocks at the king's doors, as if he is a pure person.[488] A person who is evil in conduct never thinks of himself in that way. Truthful words are virtuous and there is nothing that is superior to the truth. Truth holds everything up. Everything is established in truth. The perpetrators of wicked and terrible acts also separately have pledges of truth among themselves. They resort to the pledge of not acting violently towards each other. If they do not abide by these agreements, there is no doubt that they are destroyed. It is eternal dharma that the riches of others should not be stolen. Powerful ones think that this system has been instituted by the weak. However, when destiny makes them weak, they take

[487]Clearly, a distinction is being drawn between speaking of evil and acting wickedly.

[488]The reference is to a thief who goes and complains to the king about having become the victim of a theft himself.

pleasure in this system. Those who are extremely powerful are not necessarily happy. Therefore, never use your intelligence to embark on a task that is not upright. Then there is no reason for fear from wicked people, thieves, or kings. Since such a person has not done anything against anyone else, he is free from fear and dwells in purity. A thief is frightened of everything, like a deer that has come to a village. Having acted wickedly, he thinks that everyone's conduct is like that. A pure person is always delighted and is always fearless. Judging by his own self, he never sees any wicked conduct in others. Those who are engaged in the welfare of beings have said that donations represent dharma. Those who have riches think that this conduct has been laid down by those who are miserly. However, when destiny makes them poor, they find pleasure in this principle. However, those who are extremely rich aren't necessarily happy. A man should not act towards others in a way that he would not like to be acted against. Knowing what is not agreeable to himself, he should not act towards others in that way. If a person becomes the lover of someone else's wife, whom will he speak to? What does he deserve to say? Act towards others in ways that you are prepared to tolerate yourself. That is my view. If a person wishes to remain alive himself, how can he murder another? One should think about others on the basis of what one desires for one's own self. Extra objects of pleasure should be shared with others. That is the reason the Creator ordained the practice of moneylending. One must remain established in the pledges that have been made to the gods. When it is a time of gain, it is laudable to remain established in dharma. The learned have said that dharma is what is agreeable to everyone. O Yudhishthira! Behold. I have instructed you about the signs of dharma and adharma. This is what the Creator ordained in ancient times, for the sake of ensuring accumulation in the worlds. Virtuous people always pursue the subtle objectives of dharma and observe supreme conduct. O supreme among the Kuru lineage! I have recounted to you the signs of dharma. Therefore, never use your intelligence to embark on a task that is not upright."'

Chapter 1580(252)

'Yudhishthira said, "You have spoken about the subtle signs of dharma, which have been instructed by the virtuous. I have the power to differentiate between some of the things you have spoken about. There were several questions in my heart and you have answered them. O king! Without disputing what you have said, there is something else I want to say. But the beings that are created come and go. O descendant of the Bharata lineage! This is incapable of being understood by studying about dharma.[489] The dharma of those who flourish is of one kind. But it is different for those who face a hardship. In a time of adversity, how is a person capable of knowing through studies alone? It is the view that good conduct constitutes dharma. Conduct is the sign of the virtuous. But there is capability and there is incapability. How can good conduct then be taken to be a sign? It is seen that an ordinary person acts in accordance with adharma, though it is in the form of dharma. And an extraordinary person acts in accordance with dharma, though it is in the form of adharma. Those who are knowledgeable about the sacred texts have also laid down standards of proof. We have heard that the words of the Vedas decline from one yuga to another. There is one kind of dharma in krita yuga and another kind in treta and dvapara. There is another kind of dharma in kali yuga. So it seems to depend on capacity. The true words of the Vedas are for the sake of propagation of the worlds. The supreme words of the Vedas have extended in all the directions. They are said to constitute the proof, but the proof is not to be seen.[490] When one proof contradicts another proof, where does the sacred text come from? When dharma goes into a decline, evil-souled ones become powerful. Whatever they act against is destroyed and never obtains a foundation again. Whether we know it or not, whether we are capable of knowing it or not, this[491] is finer

[489]Dharma has been interpreted as good deeds and their fruits. But birth and death seem to have an element of nature, or destiny.

[490]The sense seems to be that the words of the Vedas are differentially applied across the yugas. So what is the truth?

than a razor's edge and larger than a mountain. At first, it seems to be as large as a city of the gandharvas. But then, when it is minutely scrutinized by the wise, it seems to become invisible. O descendant of the Bharata lineage! Cattle drink from small puddles in fields, which then dry up. Like that, when the eternal dharma of the sacred texts decays, it cannot be seen. There are some who follow desire. There are others who follow decay. There are others who follow other objectives. There are many others who are wicked and follow fruitless conduct. Even among virtuous people, dharma is seen to swiftly go into a decline. There are others who call it[492] madness and laugh at it. There are great ones who withdraw and follow the dharma of kings.[493] They are not seen to engage in conduct that ensures the welfare of everyone. Some become powerful through such conduct. Others are again seen to be constrained by it. There are others who do as they wish, but their status remains unchanged. Something increases the power of one person. But the same thing restrains another person. There are many kinds of conduct that are discerned among everyone, not always pursued single-mindedly. There are things that wise people have spoken about for a long time, as illustrative of eternal dharma. Their earlier conduct is the eternal foundation."'[494]

Chapter 1581(253)

'Bhishma said, "In this connection, an ancient history is recounted about words exchanged between Tuladhara and Jajali on dharma. There was a brahmana named Jajali. He lived in the forest, following the conduct of those who dwell in the forest. Once,

[491]The path of dharma.

[492]Dharma.

[493]Implying that brahmanas behave like kshatriyas.

[494]This is an argument in favour of absolute norms of dharma, as opposed to relative ones.

the immensely ascetic one went to the region near the ocean and tormented himself through austerities there. He controlled himself and was restrained in diet. He was dressed in tattered garments and skins and his hair was matted. He was covered in dirt and mud. The intelligent sage spent many years there. O lord of the earth! The immensely energetic one dwelt in the water. Wishing to see the worlds, he travelled around, with the speed of thought.[495] He saw the earth, right up to the frontiers of the ocean, with its forest and groves. Having done this, while he was inside the water, one day, the sage thought, 'In this world, with its mobile and immobile objects, there is no one like me. Who else can dwell in the water and roam around with me in this way?' While he said this in the water, the rakshasas noticed this. The pishachas said, 'You should not speak in this fashion. There is the immensely illustrious Tuladhara in Varanasi and he follows the dharma of a trader. O supreme among brahmanas! Even he should not speak the words that you have.' Having been thus addressed by the demons, Jajali, the great ascetic, replied, 'I will go and see the wise and illustrious Tuladhara.' When the rishi spoke in this way, the rakshasas arose from the ocean and said, 'O supreme among brahmanas! Go. Follow this road.' Thus addressed by the demons, Jajali departed, with distress in his mind. He went to Varanasi, met Tuladhara and spoke these words to him."

'Yudhishthira asked, "O father![496] What were the virtuous deeds that Jajali had performed earlier? How did he obtain supreme success? You should recount that to me."

'Bhishma replied, "He performed extreme and terrible austerities. The great ascetic was devoted to performing ablutions in the morning and in the evening. He tended to the fire properly. The brahmana was devoted to studying. Jajali knew about the ordinances of vanaprastha and blazed in his radiance. He was engaged in truth and austerities, but was still not able to comprehend dharma. When it rained, he slept under the open sky. During autumn, he immersed himself in water.

[495]Because of his powers, the gross body remained in the water, while the subtle body travelled around.

[496]The word used is tata.

During summer, he exposed himself to the heat and the wind. But he still did not obtain dharma. He lay down on many uncomfortable beds and on the ground and changed these around. When it rained, the sage would stand under the open sky. Rain showered down on his head from the sky and he repeatedly received this. The lord's hair became matted and filthy and the strands were tangled. He always went to the forest, covered in filth and dirt. Sometimes, the immensely ascetic one did not eat. Sometimes, he survived on air. Sometimes, he stood like a wooden pillar and did not move at all. O descendant of the Bharata lineage! O king! While he stood there, immobile like a pillar, two *kulinga* birds[497] built a nest on his head. However, the brahmana rishi was overcome with compassion for this couple. He allowed them to use grass to build a nest in his matted hair. The immensely ascetic one remained immobile, like a pillar. They[498] were reassured and lived there happily. The rains passed and autumn presented itself. Following Prajapati's rules, those carefree birds approached each other with desire. O king! Those birds laid eggs on his head. The energetic brahmana, rigid in his vows, realized this. However, despite knowing this, the immensely energetic Jajali did not move. His mind was always firm on upholding dharma, and adharma did not appeal to him. He was not going to harm anyone. O lord! They were thus assured and happily lived on his head. The eggs were nurtured and young birds developed inside them. They began to grow. But even then, Jajali did not move. Careful in his vows, he protected the eggs and the birds. Therefore, the one with dharma in his soul did not move and meditated. In the course of time, the birds emerged and the sage realized when the young birds developed wings. Thus, one day, the one who was rigid in his vows saw the birds. The supreme among intelligent ones was extremely delighted. He was happy to see them grow. The birds and their offspring were fearless there. Once the wings had developed, he saw that they would fly out and return again. The birds would go out in the morning and return in the evening. The

[497]A kulinga is a shrike or a sparrow. Subsequently, the word *chataka* is used, not to be confused with *chaataka*. A chataka is a sparrow, so sparrows are meant.

[498]The birds.

brahmana Jajali did not move. Sometimes, though the mother and the father were not present, they would return and then fly out again. Jajali did not move. O king! Then they began to go out and return again in the evening. The birds returned, to live there. After this, the birds went out for five days before they returned. Then it became six days. Jajali did not move. In the course of time, as they became strong, all the birds went out for many days at a time and did not return. Later, the birds did not return for a month. O king! Finally, when they did not return at all, Jajali left. Jajali was overcome with wonder at what had happened. He thought that he had obtained success, and pride penetrated him. The one who was careful in his vows saw that the birds, which had been born and reared on his head, finally left. He was full of delight. When the sun arose, the immensely ascetic one went to the river. He bathed there and offered oblations to the fire. Since those chataka birds had been born on his head, Jajali, supreme among ascetics, slapped his armpits and exclaimed, 'I have obtained dharma.' At this, Jajali heard an invisible voice speak in the sky. 'O Jajali! You are not Tuladhara's equal in dharma. The immensely wise Tuladhara lives in Varanasi. O brahmana! Though he deserves to, he does not speak the way you do.' On hearing these words, he became full of anger and wished to see Tuladhara. O king! The sage began to roam around the earth, without any fixed place of abode. After a long period of time, he reached the city of Varanasi and saw Tuladhara, selling his wares. On seeing the brahmana arrive, the one who earned a living from trading arose cheerfully and welcomed and honoured him. Tuladhara said, 'O brahmana! I knew for certain that you would come here. O supreme among brahmanas! Listen to the words that I tell you. You lived on the shores of the ocean and performed great austerities there. But earlier, you never had any sense of what was dharma. O brahmana! When you obtained success in your austerities, birds were soon born on your head and they were nurtured by you. When they developed wings, they flew around, here and there. O brahmana! Having given birth to those chatakas, you felt proud at having obtained dharma. O supreme among brahmanas! You then heard a voice in the sky and it spoke about me. At this, you felt anger and that is the reason you have come here. O supreme among brahmanas! What can I do to please you? Tell me.'"'

Chapter 1582(254)

'Bhishma said, "Having been thus addressed by the intelligent Tuladhara, the intelligent Jajali, supreme among ascetics, replied in these words. 'O trader! You sell all the juices and all the scents, trees and herbs and their roots and fruits. How has this steadiness in intelligence come to you? From where has this knowledge come? O immensely wise one! Tell me everything about this.' O king! Having been thus addressed by the illustrious brahmana, the vaishya Tuladhara, who knew about the true objectives of dharma and the subtleties of dharma, spoke to Jajali, who had performed difficult austerities, but was still not content with his knowledge. 'O Jajali! I know eternal and ancient dharma, with all its mysteries. People who know say that it is nothing but friendliness and being engaged in the welfare of all beings. There should be no violence towards living beings, or limited violence. O Jajali! Such conduct is said to follow supreme dharma and that is the way I live. My house is built with wood and grass that has been cut by other people. O brahmana rishi! Lac, lotus roots, lotus filaments, scents, the agents for cleaning, superior and inferior, and the juices and many other objects, with the exception of liquor, are bought by me from other people. I sell them again, without any deceit. O Jajali! If there is a person who regards everyone as a well-wisher and is engaged in everyone's welfare, in deeds, thoughts and words, he knows dharma. I do not praise or censure the deeds of others. O brahmana rishi! I look upon these colourful people, the way I look at the sky. I do not obstruct or oppose. I do not hate or desire. O Jajali! I look upon all beings as equal. That is my vow. I have been freed from good and bad. I have cast aside love and hatred. O Jajali! I hold up my pair of scales equally towards everyone. O Jajali! O best among intelligent ones! That is the way I look at you and at all the other people. A lump of earth, a piece of iron and gold are the same to me. The blind, the deaf and the mad, despite being adversely affected by destiny, are always full of joy. That is the way I look at everything. Those who are old, those who suffer from disease and those who are emaciated are indifferent towards objects of pleasure. In that way, I have lost all interest in objects of desire and pleasure. When a person is not frightened and no one is terrified of him, when he does not desire and does not hate, then he obtains success and becomes a brahmana. A person who does not harbour wicked sentiments towards all beings, in deeds, thoughts and words, attains the brahman. A person who grants fearlessness to all beings attains a state that is without fear. For him, there is no past and no future and no dharma. A person who agitates people through cruel words and harsh punishment, as if he is the face of death, suffers from great fear. Great-souled and aged ones observe the conduct of non-violence towards their sons and grandsons and I follow them. A person who knows, an ascetic or a powerful person can be deluded and from that confusion, eternal dharma and good conduct can be destroyed. However, if a wise person follows good conduct, he can swiftly obtain dharma. Such a virtuous person wanders around, self-controlled, without any violence in his consciousness. In a river, a piece of wood drifts along as it wishes and sometimes comes into contact with another piece of wood, which is also flowing along, as it wills. There are other pieces of wood that come together and then drift apart. Grass, wood and refuse are sometimes seen to come together. This is the nature of conduct, seen here and there. If there is a person who does not agitate any being and if he grants fearlessness to all beings, that person always attains the state of a sage. O learned one! There may also be a person who agitates all the people, like a wolf. Like an aquatic animal, he makes people shriek and climb onto the shore. A person who has aides is extremely fortunate and obtains riches, in this world and hereafter. That is what wise people have spoken about in the sacred texts. Some practise a little bit of what has been mentioned. Other accomplished ones follow it in entirety. All the fruits that are obtained through austerities, sacrifices, donations and wisdom can be obtained by ensuring fearlessness. In this world, a person who grants the dakshina of fearlessness to all beings accomplishes all the sacrifices and himself obtains the dakshina of fearlessness. There is no dharma that is the equal of non-violence towards beings. A person who never agitates beings and grants all beings fearlessness attains the state of a great sage. A person who agitates beings, like a snake that has arrived inside a house, does not obtain dharma, in this world or in the next. When a person looks on all beings as his own self and treats all beings equally, the gods themselves are confused when they try to follow his path and his footsteps. The donation of fearlessness to beings is the supreme among all donations. O Jajali! I am telling you the truth. Listen to it with devotion. A person who is fortunate is not born again. An unfortunate person is born again. Obsessed with their tasks, people are always seen to be asleep. There is nothing that is without a reason. O Jajali! Dharma is subtle. In the words of dharma, tasks have been ordained for the past and the future. There are subtleties and so many contradictions that one is incapable of knowing it. Some understand this internally. Others only comprehend conduct. There are those who kill bulls, making them bear heavy burdens, binding and restraining them, inserting rings in their noses. Why aren't these people killed? There are those who kill beings for eating them. Why are they not censured? Men make other men slaves and enjoy the results. They kill, bind and restrain them, making them work day and night. This is despite they themselves knowing the misery from killing and striking. The gods dwell in the five senses of all beings—Aditya, Chandrama, Vayu, Brahma, Prana, Kratu[499] and Yama. But there are those who kill and trade beings, without even thinking about it. O brahmana! I am not speaking about oil, clarified butter, honey, other objects and herbs.[500] There are many animals that are happily reared in regions where there are no gnats. Despite knowing that their mothers love them, many men oppress them. They take them to regions where there is a lot of mud, with many gnats. They make them mounts and beasts of burden. Others oppress them in other ways. I think that these deeds are no different from killing a foetus. Agriculture is regarded as a virtuous livelihood. But it is extremely terrible. Wooden implements with iron at the mouth injure the earth and kill beings that live in the ground. O Jajali! Look towards the bulls that have been yoked. Cows have been named as unslayable.

[499]Intelligence or a sacrificial rite, personified.

[500]Those are the objects Tuladhara trades in.

How can this person then kill them? The person who kills a cow for the sake of gain commits a great offence. Many rishis and ascetics spoke to Nahusha. "A cow is a mother. You have killed a bull, which is like Prajapati. O Nahusha! You have perpetrated a wicked deed and we are frightened on this account." They divided it[501] into a hundred and one parts and inflicted it as diseases on all living beings. O Jajali! The immensely fortunate rishis passed this on to the subjects and told Nahusha, who had committed a sin like that of killing a foetus, "We will not be able to offer oblations at your sacrifices." This is what those great-souled ones, who knew about the truth, said. However, the rishis and the ascetics got to know the truth and were quickly pacified.[502] O Jajali! These are the kinds of inauspicious and terrible conduct practised in this world. These are practised even by accomplished people who know, simply because these are norms of conduct. One should seek out the reasons behind dharma and not follow it because it is the conduct of the world. O Jajali! Listen to the conduct I follow towards those who hurt me or praise me. They are equal before me and I do not like or dislike either. This is the kind of dharma that is praised by the learned. This is full of reason and is practised by the ascetics. This is always seen among those who observe dharma in their conduct and are accomplished.'"'

Chapter 1583(255)

'"Jajali said, 'O Tuladhara! You have spoken about the dharma that has been laid down and about the supreme conduct that should be followed by beings to reach the gates of heaven. Crops results from agriculture and it is on the basis of those that you remain alive. O trader! It is with animals and herbs that mortal beings remain alive. Sacrifices flow from those. You speak like a

[501]The sin.

[502]They got to know that Nahusha had not killed the bull intentionally.

non-believer. This world will not be sustained and nothing will be left if these doctrines are followed.'

'"Tuladhara replied, 'O Jajali! O brahmana! I will speak about sustenance. I am not a non-believer. I am not criticizing sacrifices. But a person who knows about sacrifices is extremely rare. I bow down before the sacrifices of brahmanas and before people who know about sacrifices. Having abandoned their own sacrifices, brahmanas have resorted to the sacrifices meant for kshatriyas. O brahmana! Greedy for the riches of others, it is the non-believers who have led to such practices. Though they know about the words of the Vedas, they have disguised falsehood behind apparent truth. "This should be given. That should be given." There is no end to this kind of desire. O Jajali! Theft and undesirable acts result from this. An oblation obtained through good means is what satisfies the gods, such as bowing down, oblations, studying and herbs. The worship of gods should be in accordance with what is laid down in the sacred texts. Through their sacrifices, wicked people give rise to wicked offspring. The greedy give birth to the greedy. The contented give birth to the contented. The resultant offspring are just like the performer of the sacrifice and the officiating priest. Through sacrifices, offspring who are like the unblemished sky can result. O brahmana! Oblations offered into the fire rise up into the sun. Rain results from the sun. Crops result from rain and offspring come through these. Therefore, earlier, people performed their own sacrifices and obtained all the objects of desire. The earth yielded crops without tilling. Herbs resulted because of the benedictions. No sacrifices were seen to be undertaken with a view to obtaining selfish fruits. However, there were some who undertook sacrifices, despite having doubts about the fruits of sacrifices. Consequently, the wicked, the cunning, the greedy and those who felt a need for riches were born. Those who have performed wicked deeds go to the worlds earmarked for those with inauspicious deeds. Using arguments to counter arguments, a man performs inauspicious deeds. O supreme among brahmanas! Such people are always evil-souled and unaccomplished in wisdom. O brahmana! They take deeds to be misdeeds and the reverse. They do not also follow the deeds that Brahma laid down for the worlds. We have also heard that if deeds without qualities are performed, they lead to no fruits. If these are not countered, they injure all beings. Truth is sacrifice. Self-control is sacrifice. So are lack of jealousy towards everyone, contentment with one's own riches and lack of greed for riches. That is how a renouncer results. A person who knows the truth about kshetra and kshetrajna is engaged in his own sacrifice. He studies, wishing to know about the brahman, and is satisfied in his own self. All divinity is in the brahman. Everything finds a refuge in the brahman. O Jajali! When such a person is satisified, the gods are satisfied. When he is not satisfied, they are not satisfied. If a person is satisfied with all the juices, he finds no delight in anything in particular. In that way, a person who is satisified with wisdom is always satisfied and this gives rise to happiness. Dharma is comfort for him. Dharma is happiness and everything is established on that. Such a person knows the truth about existence and searches for wisdom. There are others who know about jnana and vijnana and can cross over to the further shore, which is always extremely auspicious and is full of sacred people. Having gone there, one does not grieve. Nor is there distress of any kind. That is the place of the brahman and virtuous people attain it. That is not for those who desire heaven, or for those who sacrifice for fame and riches. It is a path followed by the virtuous and their strength is non-violence. They know about trees, herbs, fruits and roots.[503] Those who sacrifice, and their officiating priests, are not greedy and do not desire riches. There are also brahmanas who have accomplished all their tasks. Nevertheless, driven by compassion for other subjects, they perform their own sacrifices. Subjects obtain heaven by pursuing their own dharma. O Jajali! Thus, because of my intelligence, my conduct towards everyone is identical. O bull among brahmanas! O great sage! The wise ones always engage themselves in these kinds of sacrifices and through these, go along the path trodden by the gods. Some have to return.[504] But there is

[503]That is, these are the only appropriate sacrificial offerings.

[504]Be reborn.

no return for the learned. O Jajali! However, both types go along the path trodden on by the gods. Using the resolution in their minds, they become successful, yoking their own selves and using their own selves as beasts of burden, and milking their own selves. They make their own selves the sacrificial altars and thus give away a lot of dakshina. A person who has cleansed himself in this fashion should not be greedy for cattle. O brahmana! He performs a sacrifice by bowing down, as if he was a herb. His intelligence places renunciation at the forefront. That is what I am describing to you. He is beyond desire and beyond starting anything. He is beyond honour and praise. His deeds have been extinguished, but he is without decay. The gods speak of such a person as a brahmana. A person who does not listen to the sacred texts, does not perform sacrifices and does not give to brahmanas is a person who follows common conduct. O Jajali! What end will he attain? By following this path, observed by the gods, it is as if he performs sacrifices.'

'"Jajali said, 'I have not heard this truth from the sages. O trader! I am therefore asking you about a difficulty. The rishis who came earlier did not consider this.[505] Nor did those who came later establish this. O trader! If animals are capable of obtaining happiness by serving the tirtha of the atman, then why do they obtain misery because of their deeds? O immensely wise one! Instruct me about this. I have great faith in you.'

'"Tuladhara replied, 'There are some sacrifices that do not actually become sacrifices.[506] They should not sacrifice. A cow can be used for all the oblations at a sacrifice, because of milk, curds, clarified butter, hair, horns, feet and everything that comes from the mouth.[507] It has been ordained that one should not embark on a sacrifice without a wife. The sacrificial cake has been spoken of as representing sacrifices

[505]Meaning yoga.

[506]Because they are not properly performed, and this refers to both internal and external sacrifices.

[507]For external sacrifices, the yield from a cow offers sufficient oblations. For those who are poor, the dust from the hooves and the water, in which the tail and the horns have been washed, will suffice.

of all animals. This is like all the rivers being akin to Sarasvati and all mountains being sacred. O Jajali! The atman is a tirtha and one does not have to become a guest at different places.[508] O Jajali! If one follows this kind of dharma, without searching for reasons behind dharma, one will obtain the auspicious worlds.'"

'Bhishma said, "This was the kind of dharma that was praised by Tuladhara. This is always full of reason and is followed by the virtuous."'

Chapter 1584(256)

'"Tuladhara said, 'Those who are virtuous live in this way. Those who are virtuous resort to this path. Look at the deeds performed by the virtuous and you will know the truth. There are many birds that roam around in every direction. There are some that were born on your head. There are also hawks and others of different species. O great brahmana! Here and there, they are seeking to enter.[509] Behold. They have contracted their wings, feet and bodies everywhere. Summon them. Though they have been born through their father, they have also been generated from you. There is no doubt that you are their father. O Jajali! Therefore, summon your sons.'"

'Bhishma said, "At this, Jajali summoned the birds. They replied in divine words, words that were full of dharma. 'For this world and for the next, one must perform acts of non-violence. O brahmana! Desire destroys and with that, men are also destroyed. When faith declines in words and thoughts, no sacrifices can lead to salvation. In this connection, Brahma recited a song and it is chanted by those who know about the sacred accounts. The gods regard the sacrificial deeds of those who have purity, but lack faith, and those who have

[508] In search of places of pilgrimage.

[509] The birds are seeking to enter their own nests.

faith, but lack purity, equally and ignore them both. The gods have also held that a miserly and learned brahmana and an eloquent and prosperous person are equal. However, Prajapati told them that they had erred in treating two unequal things equally. "Faith purifies a prosperous person. Lack of faith destroys him. Even if there is only one person in the world and he is without faith, the gods do not accept his oblations. Those learned about dharma also know that his food should not be eaten. Lack of faith is a supreme sin. Faith releases from all sin. A faithful person discards sin, like a snake casting off its skin."[510] Renunciation with faith is superior to all sacred deeds. If a person refrains from all evil conduct and is faithful, he is purified. What need does he have of austerities, deeds or conduct? There can be a man with faith and there can be a man without faith. This is what virtuous and knowledgable people who know about the purpose of dharma have said about dharma. We were curious and obtained this insight about dharma. O immensely wise one! If you conquer the urge to compete, you will obtain the supreme. The trader possesses faith and follows the dharma of faith. O Jajali! A person established in his own path is superior.'[511] In this way, Tuladhara told him about many things and he obtained a complete realization of what has been spoken of as eternal dharma. O Kounteya! Having heard those famous and valorous words spoken by Tuladhara, the brahmana obtained tranquility. In a short while, he and Tuladhara, those two immensely wise ones, went to heaven and found delight in the happiness there. Having earned the fruits of their own deeds, they went to their respective places. A person who looks at everything equally, is faithful and controlled and possesses an excellent intelligence, performs sacrifices in this way. Without sacrifices, a person is not taken there. O king! Faith is the virtuous goddess Savitri, the daughter of the sun. She is the one who gives birth to faith in the world of the living. I have instructed you appropriately. What more do you wish to hear?"'

[510]The text does not indicate which part is Brahma's song, so these quotation marks are somewhat arbitrary.

[511]There is abruptness in the text, with the words of the birds ending suddenly.

Chapter 1585(257)

'Bhishma said, "In this connection, an ancient history is recounted, about what King Vichakhanna sung, driven by compassion for subjects. He saw the mangled body of a bull and heard the extremely piteous cries of cattle. The king saw a sacrificial enclosure where cows were being slaughtered. He said, 'May there be safety to all the cattle in this world.' When the violence had started, these words of benediction were heard. 'Those who have deviated from the ordinances, those who are non-believers and confused, those who have doubts within themselves, are the men who applaud of violence. Manu, with dharma in his soul, said that there should be non-violence in all deeds. Driven by attachment to desire, men cause violence to animals outside the sacrificial enclosure.[512] Therefore, one should follow the instructions and know the subtle nature of dharma. It has been held that non-violence is superior to all kinds of dharma. They dwell near sacred places, but have abandoned the learning of the Vedas. These misers are driven by desire for the fruits and follow bad conduct, in the disguise of good conduct. Pointing to sacrifices, trees and sacrificial altars, men pointlessly eat flesh.[513] This kind of dharma is not praised. Flesh, *madhu, sura*, fish, *asava* and krisara have been thought of by cunning people.[514] They were not thought of in the Vedas. Desire, confusion and greed led to these temptations being introduced. The brahmanas note that Vishnu is present in all sacrifices. It has been said that, with an excellent mind, he should only be offered payasa.[515] In the Vedas, trees have been thought of as sacrificial offerings. These are the kinds of things that should properly be offered to the great god, with pure sentiments. All these deserve to be offered to that god.'"

[512]They are slaughtered outside the enclosure.

[513]Implying that the flesh of animals killed at sacrifices is also not recommended.

[514]While madhu does mean honey, given the context, madhu, sura and asava are kinds of liquor. Krisara is made out of wheat flour, rice and sesamum.

[515]Payasa is rice cooked in milk and sugar.

'Yudhishthira asked, "The body and various difficulties always quarrel and cause injury to each other. If one abstains from all work, how will it be possible to sustain the body?"

'Bhishma replied, "One must act so that the body does not suffer and so that one does not come under the subjugation of death. According to capacity, one's conduct should follow the norms of dharma."'

Chapter 1586(258)

'Yudhishthira asked, "O supreme teacher! In determining what task to pursue, should one decide quickly or take time over the decision? We are always confronted with extremely difficult tasks."

'Bhishma replied, "In this connection, an ancient history is recounted about what happened earlier, concerning the conduct of Chirakara, born in the lineage of Angiras.[516] A person who acts after a long time is fortunate. A fortunate person is one who acts after a long time. A person who acts after a long time is intelligent and does not commit a sin in his acts. Goutama's son acted after a long time and was immensely wise.[517] He took a long time to decide on all tasks. He thought about the objective for a long time. He remained awake for a long time. He slept for a long time. He completed tasks after a long time. Therefore, he was known as Chirakara. He was also spoken of as lazy and limited in intelligence. People said that he was foolish in intelligence and lacked far-sightedness. On one occasion, his father was angry at his mother's promiscuous behaviour.[518] Ignoring

[516]Chirakara means a person who acts after a long time, so there is a pun.

[517]Chirakara was the sage Goutama's son and Goutama was born in the Angiras lineage.

[518]Goutama's wife was Ahalya and she was seduced by Indra. Since Indra did this in Goutama's disguise, this wasn't quite Ahalya's fault. In the standard story, Ahalya was cursed by Goutama that she would turn to stone and be eventually liberated by Rama.

the other sons, he told him, 'Kill this mother of yours.' Though he agreed when he was asked, as was his nature, Chirakara thought about this for a long time.[519] He was cautious and always thought for a long time about what should be done. 'How will I follow the instructions of my father and yet not kill my mother? While apparently following dharma, how will I avoid being submerged, like a wicked person? Following the instructions of the father is supreme dharma. Yet, protecting my mother is my own dharma. Since a son is not independent, how can I avoid being afflicted? How can one be happy after killing a woman and a mother? How can one obtain status after ignoring a father's orders? I cannot ignore what my father has said. I must nurture and protect my mother. How will I resist suffering on either score? How will I not cross either? The father's own self enters the wife and is born, so that conduct, character, lineage and family can be sustained.[520] I am my father's own self. But I am also my mother's son. Since I know how I have been born, why should I not possess knowledge about this?[521] My father spoke words at the time of my jatakarma and other minor rites. Those are sufficient to firmly establish the reverence that is due to my father. Because the father nurtures and instructs, it is supreme dharma to regard him as the foremost among instructors. That is dharma, conclusively determined in the Vedas. The only source of delight to the father is the son. The father is everything for the son. The body and everything else have been given by the father alone. Therefore, one must act in accordance with one's father's words and not think about it at all. If one acts in accordance with one's father's words, all one's sins are cleansed. In sight of all the worlds, he provided fortune and objects of pleasure at the time of delivery. He was a party to the union and acknowledged this is the

[519]Here, the text uses the word Chirakarika. But Chirakarika and Chirakara mean the same thing.

[520]The son is believed to be part of the father's own self, born through the mother.

[521]That is, there is no doubt about the father or the mother.

simantonnayana ceremony.[522] The father is heaven. The father is dharma. The father is the supreme of austerities. When the father is pleased, all the gods are pleased. Any benedictions pronounced by a father serve a man. When the father praises, there is cleansing of all sins. The flower is severed from the stalk. The fruit is also severed from the stalk. But even if the son's affection decreases, the father's affection remains.' These were the son's thoughts about the reverence that was due to the father. 'The father does not occupy an inferior station. Let me now think about my mother. I have been born on earth as a compound of the five elements. But my mother was the origin, like the two pieces of wood used to create a fire. For the body of any man, the mother represents those sticks and saves him from all hardships. When she is there, there is no reason for sorrow. When she is not there, there is hardship. Even when a person is divested of riches, his mother is there in the house. Even if a person has many sons and grandsons, even if he is one hundred years old, when he approaches his mother, he behaves like a two-year-old. Whether a person is capable or incapable, whether a person is fat or thin, the mother protects the son. According to the ordinances, there is no one else who sustains in that way. When he is separated from his mother, he ages, he is distressed and the entire world seems to be empty. There is no shelter that is equal to a mother. There is no objective that is equal to a mother. There is no sanctuary equal to a mother. There is no protection equal to a mother. Because she bears him in her womb, she is known as Dhatri. Because she gives birth, she is known as Janani. Because she nurtures his limbs, she is known as Amba. Because she gives birth to a brave one, she is known as Virasu. Because she nurtures the child, she is known as Sushru. There is no difference between a mother and one's own body. Unless his head is empty and he is devoid of his senses, which man will kill such a person? When a couple unites to bear life, there is resolution

[522]These are references to the father accepting paternity before the son is born. Simantonnayana is parting of the hair and the husband applies colour (usualy vermilion) to the parting on his wife's hair. Before delivery, this is done in the fourth, sixth or eighth month.

in both the mother and the father, but success in accomplishing that objective depends on the mother. The mother knows the gotra and the mother knows whom he has been born from.[523] The mother's pleasure comes from nurturing alone. The father's affection is from a desire to have offspring. If a man himself accepts a woman's hand for the sake of following dharma together and then goes to another woman, he is not slain on those grounds. A husband is known as Bharta because he sustains his wife. He is known as Pati because he protects his wife. When these two traits disappear, a husband is neither a Bharta nor a Pati. A woman cannot commit a crime. It is the man who commits the crime. While adultery is a great crime, it is the man who has commited the crime.[524] For the wife, it has been said that the husband is the greatest protector and the supreme god. She gave herself up to someone who was in the form of that supreme person.[525] In all acts that involve crimes, women never commit the crimes. We have been given the injunction that women are never satisfied with intercourse.[526] There is no doubt about this evident nature of dharma and it should be remembered. She is a woman and a mother and occupies a position of greatest reverence. Even brutish animals know that such a person should not be killed. It is known that the father is alone a collection of all the gods. But because of her affection, the mother is a collection of all mortal beings and the gods.' In this way, because he took a long time to act, he reflected a lot.

'"After a long period of time had elapsed, Goutama returned. After having engaged in austerities, the immensely wise Medhatithi Goutama returned. He had also thought about it for a long time and had decided that what he had proposed for his wife was improper. He was tormented by great grief and tears flowed from his eyes. Because

[523]The implied suggestion is that Chirakara knows that Goutama is his father only because his mother has told him that.

[524]One can speculate about why this should be the case. In all probability, this is because of the patriarchal view that a man was committing a crime against another man's property. Hence, the woman was absolved of guilt.

[525]Indra in Goutama's disguise.

[526]Given this proclivity, they cannot be blamed.

of the effects of his learning, he was overcome with repentance. 'Purandara, the lord of the three worlds, came to my hermitage. He was in the form of a brahmana, following the vow of being a guest. At that time, I comforted him with words. I welcomed and honoured him. As is proper, I gave him the gift due to a guest and water for washing the feet.[527] As is proper, I bowed down before him and spoke to him obediently. A woman belongs to an incompetent species and cannot be held to have committed a transgression. Thus I, my wife, or the lord of the thirty gods, did not commit a crime.[528] It is dharma's fault that delusion led to the offence. Those who hold up their seeds have said that all hardships emanate from envy. It is because of jealousy[529] that I have been destroyed and flung into this ocean of great grief. I confront this hardship because I have had a virtuous and beloved woman killed. I should have protected my wife. Who will save me now? I acted hastily and commanded the intelligent Chirakara. But because he takes a long time to act, perhaps he can still save me from this sin. A person who takes a long time to act is fortunate. A fortunate person takes a long time to act. If you have taken a long time to act now, you will truly be Chirakara. Save me, your mother and all the austerities that I have accomplished. If you also save yourself from that sin, you will truly be Chirakarika. You naturally take a long time to act and this long time is indicative of your wisdom. Make the truth about your name successful today and be Chirakarika. Your mother expected you for a long time. She bore you in her womb for a long time. Make that long period of time you take also true today. Be Chirakarika. Is he taking a long time[530] because of repentance? Has he been delayed because he has slept for a long time? Perhaps Chirakarika is not showing himself because of the great torment it will cause to both

[527]*Arghya* and *padya* respectively.

[528]Why is Indra not being blamed? Probably because Goutama did not wish to blame anyone else, especially a guest. Alternatively, Indra had lost his senses and was therefore not in control over himself.

[529]Indra's jealousy.

[530]To come and greet Goutama on return.

of us.' O king! In this fashion, maharshi Goutama was miserable at the time. Then he saw his son, Chirakarika, standing close to him. On seeing his father, Chirakarika was extremely miserable. He threw the weapon away and bowed his head down, to seek favours. Goutama saw that his son was prostrate before him on the ground, with his head bowing down. He was extremely delighted to see that his wife was without harm. The great-souled one had gone away alone, separating himself from his wife and his intelligent son in that hermitage. The son stood there humbly, with the weapon in his hand, expecting to be reprimanded.[531] He asked if he should complete the task that had been assigned to him. The father saw that the intelligent son was still prostrate at his feet. He was terrified and was seeking his pardon for at all having picked up the weapon. The father praised him for a long time and inhaled the fragrance of his head for a long time. He embraced him for a long time and said, 'May you live for a long time.' Because of his son, Goutama was thus filled with joy and delight.

'"The immensely wise one praised him and spoke these words. 'O fortunate one! O Chirakarika! For a long time, may you take a long time to act. Because of the long time you took, I have been saved from great misery for a long period of time.' The learned one, supreme among sages, then sung this chant. 'Patient people, should take a long time to act, because that course is full of qualities. One should take a long time before severing a friendship. One should act so as to discard him, only after a long period of time. One should take a long time before making a friend. But having done this, one should sustain him for a long time. Whether it is in anger, insolence, pride, hatred, wicked deeds or unpleasant tasks, a person who takes a long time is praised. When an accusation against a relative, a well-wisher, a servant or a woman has not been proved, a person who takes a long time is praised.' O descendant of the Bharata lineage! Thus was Goutama pleased with his son. O Kouravya! Therefore, on any task, you should also take a long time. If a man thus thinks about every task for a long time and then

[531]However, we were earlier told that the son had flung the weapon away.

makes up his mind, he will not be tormented for a long time. If a man holds his anger for a long time and if he embarks on action after a long time, he does not suffer repentance because of his deeds. The aged must be worshipped for a long time. One must sit near them for a long time. One must serve dharma for a long time. One must spend a long time in enquiry. One must serve the learned for a long time. One must attend to the virtuous for a long time. One must restrain one's atman for a long time. Then, one will be respected for a long time. When one is asked by others, one must spend a long time in replying, in words that are full of dharma. One must think for a long time before answering. Then, one will not be subjugated for a long time. The extremely great ascetic[532] performed a lot of worship in his hermitage for many years. With his son, the brahmana then went to heaven."'

Chapter 1587(259)

'Yudhishthira asked, "Without oppressing even a little, how should a king protect? O best among virtuous ones! I am asking you. O grandfather! Tell me."

'Bhishma replied, "In this connection, an ancient history is recounted about a conversation between Dyumatsena and King Satyavat. We have heard that on the instructions of his father,[533] some men were to be executed and Satyavat spoke words, the likes of which, had never been spoken earlier. 'Dharma becomes adharma and adharma seems to be dharma. Execution has assumed the form of dharma. But it should not be that way.'[534]

'"Dyumatsena said, 'If one does not execute in accordance with dharma, how will one be able to differentiate dharma? O Satyavat! These are bandits who should be killed. Otherwise, there will be a

[532]Goutama.

[533]Dyumatsena was Satyavat's father.

[534]Bhishma is quoting Satyavat, who has argued against capital punishment.

mixing up.[535] If I do not act this way, I will bring about the advent of kali yuga. If you know how the world can progress without this, then tell me.'

'"Satyavat replied, 'It is the task of the brahmanas to keep the other three varnas under restraint. If they are bound in the noose of dharma, then there will be little deviation. The others look towards the conduct followed by brahmanas. When they do not listen, it is only then that the king should restrain them. He will differentiate according to the sacred texts, but there should not be any execution. In such action, one should follow the tasks appropriately laid down in the sacred texts of policy. By slaying a single bandit, the king kills those who are innocent. When that man is slain, his wife, mother, father and son are also killed. When a king has been injured, he must impose appropriate punishment. Sometimes, there may be a wicked person who imbibes good conduct from someone virtuous. From wicked subjects, virtuous offspring can be born. The roots should not be severed. That is not eternal dharma. They should be punished lightly and atonement is recommended. Such people can be imprisoned and disfigured. Their riches can be taken away. But the relatives should not be made to suffer through capital punishment. They may seek refuge with a priest and say, "O brahmana! I will not commit such a wicked act again." O king! The instructions are that in such cases, they should be released. If a brahmana wears deerskin, holds a staff and has shaved his head, he should nevertheless be punished, if he commits a crime. A great person's crime should be considered against his greatness. However, unlike the first offence, if a person commits a crime repeatedly, he does not deserve to be released.'

'"Dyumatsena said, 'As long as subjects remain within the agreements, that is said to be dharma, but not when those boundaries are transgressed. If they are not killed, everything will break down. In earlier times, light punishments were sufficient to ensure good rule.[536] They were mild and established in truth and their enmity

[535]Of dharma and adharma.

[536]Because people were naturally virtuous.

was also light. In earlier times, shaming was sufficient chastisement. Later, harsh words and censure became punishment. Still later, seizure of property became punishment. Finally, chastisement through execution became common. Despite the threat of execution, there are people who are incapable of being restrained. Bandits pay no attention to the sacred texts of men, gods, gandharvas and ancestors. Such a person does not belong to anyone. Nor does anyone belong to him. He does not hesitate to steal ornaments from cremation grounds frequented by demons.[537] A person who depends on an agreement with them is ignorant and is bereft of his senses.'

'"Satyavat replied, 'If there is no means of making them virtuous other than through violence, then act so that one can at least gain through a sacrifice.'[538]

'"Dyumatsena said, 'For the sake of the progress of the world, kings perform supreme austerities. When they[539] proliferate, everyone follows that kind of conduct. They must be terrified to ensure good conduct. Evildoers are not slain because of any other desire. Having ensured good deeds, a king can then rule his subjects. When he follows superior conduct, the better people also follow him. Men always follow the conduct of superior people. A person who controls himself is able to control others. However, if he is himself addicted to material objects and the senses, men laugh at him. If there is a person who acts against the king, driven by arrogance or delusion, he must be restrained through every possible means, so that he is checked from evil. He[540] must restrain himself, so that he can control evildoers. But he must also use the staff of severe punishment, even against those who are relatives and intimate. If a person who has committed a grave sin is not confronted with a great calamity, it is certain that wickedness will proliferate there and dharma go into a decline. A learned brahmana who possessed good conduct instructed

[537]He steals from dead bodies too.

[538]Instead of simply executing them, execute them through a sacrifice. They will then be cleansed of their sins and ascend to heaven.

[539]Bandits.

[540]The king.

me about this earlier. O son! I have also been instructed this by your grandfather. They were driven by great compassion and gave this assurance to virtuous people. In the first era of krita yuga, this is what was thought of for kings. During treta yuga, dharma diminished by one quarter. In the subsequent dvapara yuga, there was another decrease by one quarter and only two quarters were left. When kali yuga set in, kings became wicked in conduct. With the progress of time, only one-sixteenth of dharma's kalas remains.[541] O Satyavat! If one follows the norms of the first era, there will be confusion. It has been instructed that punishments should be in proportion to lifespans,[542] strength and era. Out of compassion for beings, Svayambhu Manu said that for the sake of emancipation, there are great fruits from following dharma.'"'

Chapter 1588(260)

'Yudhishthira said, "O grandfather! You have already told me about lack of injury and renunciation among beings, those that have the six characteristics.[543] Tell me about the two kinds of dharma now, the dharma of the householder and the dharma of a person who renounces. O grandfather! For those who wish to travel a long distance, which of these two is superior?"

'Bhishma replied, "Both kinds of dharma lead to great fortune and both are extremely difficult to follow. O son! Both lead to great fruits and both are followed by the virtuous. I will tell you about the proofs

[541]The whole is made out of sixteen kalas. One quarter means four kalas and kali yuga should have four kalas of dharma. But because of the wickedness of kings, a stronger assertion is being made that only one kala out of sixteen kalas is left in kali yuga.

[542]Down the eras, lifespans also decline.

[543]This is probably a reference to the six signs of completeness—lack of sorrow, lack of ownership, tranquility, cheerfulness, immersion in the atman and lack of desire for riches.

that have been cited for both. O Partha! Listen single-mindedly, so that your doubts about dharma can be severed. O Yudhishthira! In this connection, the ancient history of a conversation between Kapila and a cow is recounted. Listen to it. We have heard that when Tvashtri[544] came to visit Nahusha in earlier times, he saw that he[545] was following the certain and ancient practice of the sacred texts and was about to kill a cow. Kapila was cheerful in spirit and was engaged in the pledges of truth. He was learned and restrained in diet. He possessed the supreme intelligence of faith. When he saw this, he said, 'I remember the truth of the Vedas, which have become lax now.' At that time, a rishi and mendicant named Syumarashmi penetrated the cow's body and said, 'What is this? If it is the view that the Vedas constitute dharma, how can there be a different kind of view?[546] Patient ascetics use the knowledge of the sacred texts to obtain insight. All of them know about the atman and are regarded as rishis. They are devoid of thirst and without anxiety. They desire nothing. All of them have no resolutions. This is what the Vedas have proclaimed.'

'"Kapila replied, 'I am not censuring the Vedas, or saying anything against them. We have heard that for the same objective different kinds of duties have been laid down for different ashramas. The renouncer[547] goes there. The one who is in vanaprastha goes there. The ones who are in garhasthya or brahmacharya also go there. It has been the eternal view that all the four modes represent paths followed by the gods. Their superiority and inferiority, strength and weakness, have been spoken about in terms of the fruits obtained. Knowing this, the Vedas have advocated tasks to accomplish all the objectives. But elsewhere, we have faithfully heard the sacred texts to state that there need be no tasks at all. There seem to be taints with beginning tasks. But there also seem to

[544]Tvashtri has different meanings, such as the creator. Here, it is being used for Kapila.

[545]Nahusha.

[546]If the Vedas sanction animal slaughter, why should one hold a contrary view?

[547]The sannyasi.

be great taints with not beginning tasks. This being the state of the sacred texts, it is difficult to comprehend strengths and weaknesses. With the exception of these sacred texts, if you see any view that holds something to be superior to non-violence, tell me about it. What do you see?'

'"Syumarashmi said, 'We have always heard the sacred texts say that sacrifices must be performed for the sake of heaven. One first thinks of the fruits and then embarks on a sacrifice. The sacred texts have said that goats, horses, sheep, cows, different kinds of birds, wild and domesticated, and herbs are meant for sustaining life.[548] Every day, food must be eaten in the morning and in the evening. The sacred texts have said that animals and grain are the limbs of a sacrifice. Prajapati created them and sacrifices together. The lord Prajapati made the gods and others perform sacrifices with their help. All animals have been divided into seven categories each and a succeeding one is inferior to a preceding one.[549] The entire universe has been spoken of as a supreme sacrificial altar. From earlier times, this is what has progressively been followed. According to his strength, which learned man doesn't choose a living form for a sacrifice? Animals, humans, trees and herbs also desire to go to heaven and with the exception of sacrifices, there is no means of reaching heaven. Oblations like herbs, animals, trees, creepers, clarified butter, milk, curds, the earth,[550] the directions, faith and the time—these are the twelve components.[551] When the hymns of the Rig, Yajur and Sama Veda and the person performing the sacrifice are added, there is a total of sixteen. The fire that burns in the household is said to be the seventeenth. These are said to be the limbs of a sacrifice and the foundations of the sacrifice. Clarified butter, milk, curds mixed

[548]They are eaten by other living beings.

[549]This is very terse. Seven kinds of domestic animals and seven kinds of wild animals have been recommended as fit for sacrificing. The seven wild ones are lions, tigers, boars, buffaloes, elephants, bears and monkeys, lions being the best and monkeys being the worst. The seven domestic ones are cows, goats, men, horses, sheep, mules and donkeys.

[550]The sacrificial ground.

[551]Of a sacrifice.

with sugar, skin, hair,[552] horns and hooves—a cow can provide everything for a sacrifice. Each of these is a recommended object. With officiating priests and dakshina, they can sustain sacrifices. People collect all of these and perform sacrifices. It has been heard in the sacred texts that they[553] have been created for sacrifices. Since ancient times, this is how men have progressively conducted themselves. However, there are some who do not wish to cause any injury or lead to any violence. They perform sacrifices because of conviction and not because they desire the fruits of sacrifices. There is no doubt that what have been stated constitute the limbs of a sacrifice. Following the ordinances, they must be appropriately used and support each other. I see the sacred texts of the rishis and the Vedas are established in them. Those learned ones see the instructions that have been laid down by the Brahmanas.[554] Sacrifices have been created by the Brahmanas and they are based on the Brahmanas. The entire universe is based on sacrifices and sacrifices are based on the universe. The learned say that if a person has sacrificed to the best of his capacity and has uttered the words "Om", the womb of the brahman, "Namah", "Svaha", "Svadha" and "Vashat", he has nothing to fear in the three worlds and in the world hereafter. The Vedas, the Siddhas and the supreme rishis say this. A person in whom all the hymns of the Rig, the Yajur and the Sama are vested, invoked in the proper way, is truly a brahmana. O brahmana! You know the results of an agnihotra and *soma* sacrifice. O illustrious one! You also know the consequences of the other great sacrifices. O brahmana! Therefore, you should not think at all about sacrifices or about officiating at them. Sacrifices performed properly lead to heaven and after death, lead to great fruits in heaven. It is certain that those who do not perform sacrifices do not obtain any worlds here, or in the hereafter. Those who know about the words of the Vedas know that there are proofs about both.'"'[555]

[552]Hair in the tail.

[553]Cows.

[554]The Brahmana texts.

[555]Performing acts and abstaining from action.

Chapter 1589(261)

'"Kapila said, 'Ascetics see these are the outcomes and there is nothing in the three worlds that can obstruct them.[556] Those learned ones are without opposite sentiments. They do not bow down. They are not bound down by any hopes. They are free from all kinds of sins. They roam around, pure and unblemished. They are firm in their resolution that renunciation represents emancipation. They base themselves in the brahman. They are full of the brahman. They have made the brahman their abode. They are devoid of sorrow and have destroyed rajas. They obtain the eternal worlds. They obtain the supreme objective. Why do they need garhasthya?'[557]

'"Syumarashmi said, 'Even for those with supreme faith, even for those who seek the supreme objective, there is no option but to resort to garhasthya. All other ashramas depend on it. All living beings sustain themselves by depending on their mothers. In that way, all the other ashramas are possible because they are based on garhasthya. The householder performs sacrifices. The householder observes austerities. Any dharma that one wishes to pursue has garhasthya as its foundation. O sage! Everything that has life is engaged in procreation. It is not possible to generate offspring in any other mode. O brahmana! All grass and grain, in plains and mountains, depend on this mode. And life is sustained on those grass and grain. Therefore, how can any eloquent person say that there can be emancipation without the householder stage? Those who are without faith, those who are without wisdom, those who are devoid of subtle insight, those who are without hope, those who are lazy and exhausted and those who are tormented because of their own deeds—even though they may be regarded as learned—these are the only ones who regard renunciation as the supreme ashrama. The firm and eternal injunctions are for the sake of the three worlds. That is the reason an illustrious brahmana is

[556]The sense has to be deduced. Ascetics can see that the outcomes of all acts lead to temporary fruits that are not permanent.

[557]Since being a householder seems to be inferior to renunciation.

worshipped from the time of his birth.[558] Even before the ceremony of conception has been performed, mantras exist in brahmanas and enable them to perform, without any uncertainty, direct and indirect acts. In cremations, renewed attachment,[559] using vessels for food, donating cattle and other animals and immersing funeral cakes in water, these[560] become necessary. There are three kinds of ancestors—*archishmat*s, *barhishad*s and *kravyad*s.[561] After death, they grant permission for mantras to be chanted. Mantras are thus the reason.[562] When this has been pronounced in the Vedas, how can mortals obtain emancipation without repaying their debts to ancestors, gods and brahmanas? There are indeed the speculations of some learned people. But they are lazy and devoid of prosperity. They may say that they know about the words of the Vedas. But they speak lies in the guise of truth.[563] If a brahmana performs sacrifices in accordance with the sacred texts of the Vedas, he is never afflicted by sin. With his sacrifices, the animals that have been killed and his dharma, he ascends upwards. He satisfies his desires and satisfies them.[564] A man cannot obtain greatness by ignoring the Vedas, deceit or illusion. The brahman is obtained through the practices of brahmanas.'

'"Kapila said, 'There are *darsha, pournamasa,* agnihotra and *chaturmasya*.[565] These are eternal sacrifices for intelligent people. There are those who no longer have any resolutions and are extremely firm in their fortitude. They are pure and have sought refuge in the brahman. They desire immortality and through the brahman, can

[558]Presumably because brahmanas uphold those injunctions.

[559]Probably rebirth in a new body.

[560]The mantras.

[561]Respectively meaning bright, those who are seated on sacrificial grass and those who eat flesh.

[562]Reason for success in rites.

[563]Clearly those who denigrate garhasthya and uphold sannyasa.

[564]By deduction, the animals killed in the sacrifices.

[565]These are names of sacrifices. Darsha is the day of the new moon and the sacrifice performed on that day. Pournamasa is likewise the sacrifice on the day of the full moon. A chaturmasya sacrifice is performed once every four months.

satisfy the gods and the ancestors. They see their own selves in all beings and all beings in their own selves.[566] The gods are themselves confused when they try to follow in their footsteps. The being inside has four gates and four faces. Therefore, censure can also come from four directions. The gatekeeper has those four gates of the two arms, the organ of speech, the stomach and the genital organ.[567] One should not gamble with dice and take the riches that belong to others. One should not accept cooked food from those who have not been born in a womb.[568] An intelligent person will not come under the influence of anger and strike others with hands and feet, thus protecting these well. He will not loudly indulge in verbal abuse, nor will he indulge in slander and rumour. He will be devoted to the truth and restrained in speech. He will not be distracted. Thus, he will protect the gate that is the organ of speech extremely well. He will not refrain from food. But nor will he eat a lot. He will not be greedy and solicit the companionship of the virtuous. He will eat just enough to sustain the progress of life. Thus will he protect the gate that is the stomach. When there is a brave wife, he will not have intercourse with another woman. Nor will he summon a woman when it is not her season. He will devote himself to the vow of serving his wife. The gate of the genital organ will be protected in this way. The learned brahmanas protect all the gates of the genital organs, the stomach, the arms and the organ of speech, as the fourth, extremely well. If all these gates are not guarded, there will be failure. What will such a person obtain through austerities? What will be accomplished through sacrifices or his atman? If a person casts aside his upper garment, if he sleeps on the bare ground, using his arm as a pillow and if he is tranquil, the gods know such a person to be a brahmana. Such a sage finds pleasure alone and is comfortable with all the opposite sentiments. He does not think about others. The gods know such a

[566]Such people don't need to sacrifice animals.

[567]The being inside is the atman. If the four gates are not kept in check, there can be censure on account of all four. The four faces refer to the atman's properties of being all-embracing, extremely fine, omniscient and unblemished.

[568]This probably means those who have had inferior birth.

person to be a brahmana. He knows everything about nature and its transformations. He knows about the objectives of all beings. The gods know such a person to be a brahmana. He grants fearlessness to all beings and is engaged in being free of fear from everyone. He sees himself inside all beings. The gods know such a person to be a brahmana.[569] He is not concerned with the Vedas and the fruits of rites. However, following the sanctions of all these, he takes delight in the absence of fruits. But it is certain that his tasks bring the rewards of fruits. They are seen to be without qualities and are obtained alone and in private. Those qualities are extremely difficult to comprehend and extremely difficult to obtain. But the fruits of rites come to an end. That is what you should see.'

'"Syumarashmi said, 'The Vedas provide support for both renunciation and fruits.[570] Both those paths are evident. O illustrious one! Tell me about this.'

'"Kapila replied, 'You should see it as evident that you should resort to the path of the virtuous. What is evident about the one that you wish to follow?'[571]

'"Syumarashmi replied, 'I am Syumarashmi. I have come here to ask you about the brahman. I desire what is beneficial for me. That is the reason, in an upright way, I started this conversation. My intention wasn't a debate. O illustrious one! It is just that I have this terrible doubt. Explain it to me. You have said that, for those who resort to virtuous paths, the benefits can directly be seen. For the path that you follow, what can be directly seen? There are sacred texts about argumentation and there are the other sacred texts. Avoiding the sacred texts about argumentation, I have studied the other sacred texts, which bring success. Those sacred texts are the words of the Vedas. It can be seen that those sacred texts have determined that the signs of success are directly manifest. This is like a boat that has been tethered, so that it cannot be borne along by the tide. O brahmana! How can we be dragged away? If we possess wicked intelligence,

[569]That is, he is not interested in temporary fruits, but in emancipation.

[570]Fruits of action.

[571]The fruits of yoga are evident. But what is evident about the fruits of rites?

how can we cross it?[572] O illustrious one! Tell me about this. I have resorted to you. Instruct me. There is no one who has completely renounced, is completely content, is completely without sorrow and disease, and is completely free from desire, resolution and action. You indulge in joy and misery, just as we do. You are no different from all the other animals in serving the objects of the senses. Conduct has accordingly been laid down for the four varnas and ashramas and they follow this. How does one determine what brings happiness?'

'"Kapila replied, 'If one acts according to the sacred texts and follows all the injunctions and rites, there will always be happiness. For a person who pursues knowledge, knowledge saves from everything. Any conduct that deviates from knowledge destroys subjects. That is the reason learned people are always happy in every way. Sometimes, one obtains the sense of complete unity.[573] Without understanding the truth about the sacred texts, some weak people come under the subjugation of desire and anger and are overwhelmed by arrogance. They do not know the truth about the sacred texts. They are like bandits who rob the sacred texts. Their intelligence has not ripened and they are inauspicious. They do not seek to attain the brahman. They see the lack of qualities. Their bodies are based on the qualities of tamas and they are devoted to tamas. Any being follows the inherent traits of his natural characteristics. Because of the qualities that are always generated by their nature, they are overcome by hatred, desire, wrath, insolence, falsehood and arrogance. However, there are those who use their intelligence and abandon both the good and the bad. They desire the supreme objective and endeavour to remain engaged in self-restraint.'

'"Syumarashmi said, 'O brahmana! Everything that I have said has been recounted in the sacred texts. If one does not understand the true purport of the sacred texts, one engages in rites. It has been heard that learning is that which is in conformity with the sacred texts. It has also been determined that not following the rites is against the sacred texts. The words of the Vedas represent the

[572]The image of a river.

[573]Unity with the universe.

learning of the sacred texts. However, it is seen that many insolent people act against the sacred texts. For both this world and for the next, they see faults in the sacred texts. Ignorance destroys their wisdom and with wisdom in decay, they become enveloped in tamas. A person who resorts to this and roams around in every direction, basing himself on the words of the Vedas, is alone capable of being emancipated and being successful in every possible way. He is said to be liberated. This is an extremely difficult task for someone who lives in a household. Even if he indulges in donations, studying, sacrifices, generating offspring and uprightness, he is not capable of being freed. Shame on the doer and the tasks and on the futile exertions. However, if one turns one's back on the rites of the Vedas, one becomes a non-believer. O illustrious one! This is what I quickly wish to hear about. O brahmana! Tell me about this. I have sought refuge with you. Instruct me. I wish to learn everything that is known to you about emancipation.'"'

Chapter 1590(262)

'"Kapila said, 'People regard the Vedas as proof and one should not turn one's back on the rites in the Vedas. Know that there are two brahmans, Shabda-Brahma and Para-Brahma. Having attained Shabda-Brahma, one can then proceed towards Para-Brahma. Having created the body, he follows the Vedas and creates the body.[574] When the body has thus been purified, that vessel becomes a brahmana. After this, other tasks must be undertaken and I will tell you about them. Only the person can directly know whether there has been detachment in the mind. Other people cannot bear witness to this fact. Dharma is followed by those who sacrifice without any desires.

[574]This is cryptic and is a reference to the father. Having physically created the body, at the ceremony following conception, he chants mantras from the Vedas and endorses the creation of the body.

They are those who renounce and are not greedy. They are devoid of sentiments of compassion or envy. Even when they are engaged in the path of riches, they use it for visting places of pilgrimage. They never indulge in wicked deeds and resort to the rites prescribed by birth. They are firm in their minds and resolutions. They have decided to pursue pure wisdom. They are not enraged. They do not suffer from malice. They have no sense of ego and do not indulge in jealousy. They faithfully pursue unsullied knowledge. They are engaged in the welfare of all beings. There were many such householders, following their own tasks. There were kings and brahmanas who practised the indicated rites. For a long time, they followed uprightness. They were content, firm in their pursuit of knowledge. Those faithful and pure people clearly followed dharma, both Para and the other kind.[575] They first cleaned their souls and then acted in accordance with the vows. They acted according to that dharma, even when it was very difficult to follow and involved hardships. Earlier, they followed that dharma collectively and earned happiness. Since they had no doubts, they did not have to perform atonements. They truly depended on dharma. Their minds were such that they could not be dislodged. They did not transgress the norms and showed no deceit in the practice of dharma. Collectively, those initial ones followed such conduct and because of this, they had no need of atonements. The sacred texts say that atonements became necessary when the souls became weak. In earlier times, there were many brahmanas like this. They performed sacrifices. They possessed the wisdom of the three.[576] They were pure, good in conduct and illustrious. Those learned ones continuously performed sacrifices, but without being tied down by the bonds of desire. Their sacrifices and rites from the Vedas were in conformity with the sacred texts, appropriate for the time, appropriate for their resolutions and appropriate for their vows. They had overcome desire and anger and were naturally firm in their souls. They were upright and always tranquil. They were engaged in their own tasks. In every way, they followed what we have come to know as the eternal

[575]Para-Brahma and Shabda-Brahma.

[576]The three Vedas.

sacred texts. They were cheerful in their spirits. They performed tasks that were extremely difficult to accomplish. They were engaged in their own tasks and performed terrible austerities. That ancient and eternal conduct was certainly extraordinary. They acted without any uncertainty in their intelligence, clear about the signs of dharma. They were safe in the practice of dharma. They were not distracted and not vanquished. All the varnas were engaged in this way and there was no exception to this. Those bulls among men followed that single dharma which has four quarters. Having followed it in the proper way, those virtuous ones went to the supreme objective. They left their houses and resorted to the forest. There were others who remained in their houses and became brahmacharis. Learned brahmanas know that dharma consists of four ashramas. Those who attain the brahman's eternal abode are certainly brahmanas. There were thus many ancient brahmanas who followed dharma. Those brahmanas can be seen in the firmament, shining as stellar bodies. Some are nakshatras and many are large numbers of stars. Following the Vedas, they are content and have obtained the infinite. If they happen to be reborn in this cycle of life, since they are not tainted by wicked deeds, they rarely perform tasks that require births in wombs. Such people are brahmanas. How else can one be a brahmana? It is good and evil acts that enable the determination. We have learnt in the sacred texts that all of them obtain the infinite in this way and that their wisdom has been ripened. They have auspicious souls and only thirst for emancipation. The four kinds of dharma in the Upanishads is generally said to apply to everyone.[577] Those brahmanas who control their souls are Siddhas and are always successful. They are said to base themselves on knowledge, with contentment as the foundation. They possess renunciation in their souls. This eternal search for the brahman has always been the dharma of mendicants. Sometimes

[577]The four stages of life. However, an alternative interpretation of the number 'four' is possible, referring to the four stages of sleep—wakefulness, sleep with dreams, dreamless slumber and *turiya* or *samadhi*. The sense would then be that while everyone has to go through the four stages, yogis go straight into samadhi.

others also pursue this, but only according to capacity. Whether one reaches that objective, or whether one only moves towards it because one is weak, the brahman is the auspicious object of desire and frees a person from the cycle of life.'

'"Syumarashmi said, 'There are those who enjoy, donate, perform sacrifices, study and resort to a life of renunciation, after having pursued the dharma of serving the senses. Among these, when they die, who attains supreme heaven? O brahmana! I am asking you about this. Tell me the exact truth.'

'"Kapila replied, 'All those auspicious ones who enjoy have all the qualities.[578] However, they do not obtain the bliss that comes through renunciation. You can see this.'

'"Syumarashmi said, 'You based yourself on knowledge. Householders have determined to perform acts. However, it has been stated that the objective of all the ashramas is the same. No difference is seen between them, singly or collectively. Which is superior or inferior? O illustrious one! Tell me this.'

'"Kapila replied, 'Acts clean the body, but knowledge is the ultimate objective. When sins have been thrown out and one has tasted knowledge, non-violence, forgiveness, peace, lack of injury, truth, uprightness, lack of enmity, lack of pride, modesty, renunciation and tranquility result. Through this path, one obtains the supreme objective of the brahman. A learned person knows this in his mind and determines to act accordingly. There are brahmanas who are always tranquil, pure, firm in the pursuit of knowledge and content. They are said to progress towards the supreme objective. Those who know what it is to be known in the Vedas and also the contexts are said to know the Vedas. The others are like bellows.[579] Since everything is established in the Vedas, a person who knows the Vedas knows everything. All the faith is established in the Vedas and everything that exists and does not exist.[580] All the faith exists

[578]A reference to householders.

[579]Bellows that blow wind. That is, they are only full of wind.

[580]The present is interpreted as what exists and the past and the future as what do not exist.

in this and everything that exists and does not exist.[581] Those who realize know that it is the end and the middle and everything that is true and everything that is false.[582] When everything has been renounced, there is tranquility and peace. There is contentment, and auspicious emancipation is based on this. There is lack of falsehood in this. There is truth in this. This is everything that is to be known. This[583] is inside all mobile and immobile objects. The unmanifest brahman does not decay and is the source of creation. This gives all kinds of happiness and is the supreme objective. Energy, forgiveness and unadulterated and auspicious tranquility—these are certainly the eternal reasons for bliss. If the sight of knowledge is used, one reaches Shabda-Brahma. For the sake of the brahman, I bow down in obeisance before Brahma.'"'

Chapter 1591(263)

'Yudhishthira said, "O descendant of the Bharata lineage! The Vedas praise dharma, artha and kama. But which gain is special? O grandfather! Tell me this."

'Bhishma replied, "In this connection, an ancient history is recounted, about what Kundadhara had affectionately done for someone who had done him a good turn earlier. There was a brahmana who did not possess any riches. But he desired to pursue dharma and use the wealth for the purpose of conducting sacrifices. He tormented himself through fierce austerities. Having made up his mind, he worshipped the gods. But though he worshipped the gods with devotion, he failed to obtain riches. He then began to think, 'Which is the god who has not so far been worshipped by men, who can be speedily pleased?' He then saw a follower of the

[581]The sentence is repeated again, almost exactly.

[582]True and false in the sense of existence and non-existence.

[583]The brahman.

gods, Kundadhara, standing near him, with a tranquil form that was in the form of the cloud. On seeing that great-souled one, devotion was generated in him. 'This one, with a body like this, will bring prosperity for me. He lives near the gods and has not been worshipped by men earlier. He will quickly grant me a lot of riches.' The brahmana then used incense, fragrances, superior garlands and many kinds of offerings to worship him. The cloud was pleased within a short period of time. Wishing to benefit him, he spoke these words to the one who had controlled himself. 'The virtuous ones have decreed methods of salvation for those who kill brahmanas, those who are drunkards, those who are thieves and those who have broken their vows. But there is no salvation for those who are ungrateful. Desire has a son named adharma. Anger is said to be the son of jealousy. Greed is the son of deceit. But ungratefulness has no offspring.' The brahmana lay down on a bed of kusha grass. Kundadhara's energy penetrated him and he saw all the beings in a dream. He was tranquil and he had cleansed himself with austerities and devotion. The brahmana's atman was pure and in the night, he saw these signs. O Yudhishthira! He saw the immensely radiant and great-souled Manibhadra standing amongst the gods, issuing instructions. The gods were granting kingdoms and riches to those who performed good deeds and were taking them away in the case of bad deeds. O bull among the Bharata lineage! In the midst of the yakshas, he saw Kundadhara prostrate himself on the ground before the gods. Instructed by the words of the gods, the immensely illustrious Manibhadra asked, 'Why is Kundadhara prostrate on the ground? What does he want?'

'"Kundadhara said, 'That brahmana is devoted to me. If the gods are pleased with me, I desire that favours should be shown to him, so that he can obtain happiness.'"

'Bhishma said, "Instructed by the words of the gods, Manibhadra again spoke these words to the immensely radiant Kundadhara. 'O fortunate one! Arise. You have been successful. Be happy. Whatever riches are desired by this brahmana, your friend, on the instructions of the gods, I will give those riches to him, because of your friendship with him.' But Kundadhara thought that the sentiments of men were certainly fickle. Therefore, the illustrious one thought that he should turn the brahmana's mind towards austerities.

'"Kundadhara said, 'O granter of riches! I am not seeking riches for the brahmana. For this devotee, I desire that you should act so as to show him another favour. For this devotee, I do not desire the earth, full of riches, or a great store of wealth. Instead, let him follow dharma. Let him find delight in dharma. Let his intelligence be such that he earns a living through dharma. Let dharma be the most important thing for him. It is my view that this should be the favour shown.'

'"Manibhadra replied, 'The fruits of dharma are many kinds of kingdoms and happiness. Let him enjoy those fruits and let him be free of all physical hardships.'"

'Bhishma said, "However, the immensely illustrious Kundadhara repeatedly entreated that he should only be driven to practise dharma. At this, the gods were satisfied.

'"Manibhadra replied, 'The gods are pleased with you and with this brahmana. He will have dharma in his soul and his mind will turn towards dharma.'"

'Bhishma said, "O Yudhishthira! The cloud was delighted at having been successful. He had obtained the boon that he desired in his mind, one that was extremely difficult to get. The supreme among brahmanas saw that many fine pieces of cloth were scattered around near him. But he was indifferent towards them.

'"The brahmana said, 'Since he has not paid any attention to my good deeds, no one else will.[584] I will therefore go to the forest and live a life of supreme dharma.'"

'Bhishma said, "The supreme among brahmanas was indifferent and the gods had also shown him their favours. He entered the forest and started great austerities. The brahmana subsisted on whatever fruits and roots were left after serving the gods and the guests. O great king! There was great love in his mind for dharma.

[584]Kundadhara has not rewarded the brahmana's good deeds by asking for riches for him. However, the brahmana has also expressed indifference towards the fine garments.

The brahmana then discarded all roots and fruits and subsisted only on leaves. The supreme among brahmanas gave up leaves and subsisted on water. Thereafter, he subsisted for a large number of years on air alone. Despite this, it was extraordinary that the breath of his life did not fade. He was faithful towards dharma and performed fierce austerities. After a long period of time, he obtained divine sight. He thought, 'If I am pleased with someone and my mind turns towards giving him great riches, my words will never be false.'[585] Cheerfully, he continued with more austerities. Having been successful, he again thought about what would come next. 'If I am satisfied with someone and wish to grant him a kingdom, he will become a king and my words will not be false.' O descendant of the Bharata lineage! At this, Kundadhara showed himself before him, both because of his friendship and because the brahmana had been successful in his yoga of austerities. O king! The brahmana was surprised to see Kundadhara, but met him and honoured him according to the prescribed rites. Kundadhara said, 'O brahmana! Use your divine and supreme sight to see the ends that kings come to and also use your sight to look at the worlds.' With his divine sight, the brahmana could see a long distance away and saw that thousands of kings were submerged in hell.

'"Kundadhara said, 'If after worshipping me faithfully you had only obtained misery, what would I have given you and how would I have shown you favours?[586] Look and look again at what happens to the desire that men possess. In particular, the gate of heaven is barred to men.'"

'Bhishma said, "He saw[587] men stationed there, enveloped in desire, anger, greed, fear, intoxication, sleep, laziness and procrastination.

'"Kundadhara said, 'People are bound by these. Gods are frightened of men because they always act contrary to the words of the gods, in every way. Without the permission of the gods, no one

585Because of the powers he obtained through his austerities.

586Had Kundadhara only wanted riches for the brahmana.

587The brahmana saw.

can follow dharma. Through the strength of austerities, you can bestow kingdoms and riches.'"

'Bhishma said, "At this, the brahmana bowed his head down before that store of water. The great-souled one said, 'You have shown me a great favour. Earlier, I was bound down by desire and avarice and did not realize your affection for me. Therefore, you should pardon me.' Kundadhara told the bull among brahmanas, 'I have forgiven you.' He embraced him with his arms and disappeared from there. In ancient time, thus did the brahmana roam through all the worlds, having been united with austerities through Kundadhara's favours. Through the strength of dharma and yoga, one attains the supreme objective. One can roam around as one wishes and obtain success in all one's desires. A person who follows dharma is worshipped by gods, brahmanas, virtuous people, yakshas, men and *charanas* .[588] But this is not true of those who desire riches and other things. If a person's mind is such that loves dharma and practises it, the gods are extremely pleased with him. The happiness obtained through riches lasts for a short time. Dharma brings supreme happiness."'

Chapter 1592(264)

'Yudhishthira asked, "O grandfather! There are many sacrifices and austerities, all with a single objective. Which of these sacrifices is recommended for dharma and not for the sake of happiness alone?"

'Bhishma replied, "In this connection, Narada recounted the ancient account of a brahmana. For the sake of performing sacrifices, he resorted to *unchhavritti.*[589] The brahmana lived in Vidarbha, best among kingdoms in the practice of dharma. Surviving on unchhavritti, that rishi worshipped Vishnu. He ate *shyamaka*,

[588]Celestial singers.

[589]There are grains left after a crop has been harvested, or after grain has been milled. If one subsists on these leftovers, that is known as unchhavritti.

suryapatni and *suvarchala*.[590] But because of his austerities, those bitter and tasteless herbs also tasted succulent. Having gone to the forest, he refrained from injury towards all beings on earth. O scorcher of enemies! Desiring to go to heaven, he offered roots and fruits in those sacrifices. His wife's name was Pushkaracharini and she was pure and thin through the practising of vows. Satya[591] instructed her to join him in the sacrifice as a wife. Though she did not approve of this, she was terrified of his curse and her nature was also to follow.[592] Her garments consisted of feathers that peacocks had cast aside. Though she was unwilling, she was summoned to the sacrifice by the officiating priest.[593] In that forest, not very far away, dwelt a person who was descended from Shukra's lineage. He was in the form of a deer. He was also jealous and a follower of adharma.[594] He spoke these words to Satya. 'You are trying to perform an extremely difficult task. If a sacrifice is devoid of its mantras and other limbs, it will be performed improperly. Therefore, fling me there as an oblation and without any distractions, go to heaven.' At this, Savitri herself manifested at the sacrifice and counselled him to do this. But though invited, he replied, 'I will not slay my neighbour.' Having been restrained, she[595] entered the flames of the sacrifice. She did not wish to see a sacrifice that was improperly performed and wished to enter the nether worlds. However, the deer again joined its hands in salutation and entreated Satya. But Satya embraced it and asked it to go away. The deer departed. But having gone eight steps, it returned and said, 'O Satya! If you slay me, you will perform a good deed. Slay me and attain a virtuous end. I am granting you divine sight. Look at those apsaras. Look at those wonderful *vimana*s and

[590]Shyamaka is a kind of millet, suryapatni (also known as *mashaparni*) is a kind of herb used in traditional medicine and suvarchala is linseed.

[591]The brahmana's name.

[592]Though there has been nothing to indicate this so far, she disapproved of the idea of slaughtering animals for a sacrifice.

[593]Satya was the officiating priest.

[594]Since the deer is later described as a form of Dharma, there is no reason for it to be jealous or a follower of adharma. The inconsistency cannot be explained.

[595]Savitri.

the great-souled gandharvas.' With that sight, he glanced at those extremely beautiful worlds and he was touched by desire. He looked at the deer and thought that he was capable of dwelling in heaven through violence. It was Dharma himself who had spent many years in the forest in the form of a deer. Wishing to ensure his salvation, he said, 'In your mind, you should not think of a sacrifice that involves the killing of a deer. Your great austerities will thereby be destroyed. Sacrifices should not involve any violence.' The illustrious Dharma himself accepted an officiating role at that sacrifice. He obtained the state of meditation and supreme austerities that his wife had already obtained. All dharma involves non-violence. Violence does not bring success in a sacrifice. This is the truth that Dharma spoke to Satya and I have told you about it."'

Chapter 1593(265)

'Yudhishthira asked, "How does a man become wicked? How does he follow dharma? How does he obtain emancipation and where does he go?"

'Bhishma replied, "You know everything about dharma. You are only asking to confirm your belief. Hear about emancipation and renunciation and the foundations of wickedness and dharma. On knowing about the five,[596] wishes first run after them. O bull among the Bharata lineage! Having obtained these, desire and anger are generated. To accomplish these, he then takes delight in performing tasks. Form, taste and the others attract as desirable objectives. From this, attachment results and aversion follows after that. Greed follows and confusion comes after that. When one is overcome with greed, confusion, attachment and aversion, no dharma is generated. The intelligence turns to acts of adharma. One uses

[596]The five senses.

deceit to practise dharma. One finds delight in using deceit to pursue artha. O descendant of the Kuru lineage! Through deceit, one tries to be successful in obtaining riches. The intelligence turns to this and wickedness becomes attractive. O descendant of the Bharata lineage! This is despite well-wishers and learned people trying to restrain him. He replies to them in words that seem to be full of reason, supported by the ordinances. Because of attachment and confusion, three kinds of adharma increase. He thinks of sin, speaks of it and does it. When he thus engages in adharma, the virtuous perceive his taints. But those who have similar dispositions become his friends and serve the evildoer. He does not obtain happiness here, not to speak of the hereafter. This is how one has evil in his soul. Now hear about the person who has dharma in his soul. He is accomplished in dharma and obtains benefits. Because of his wisdom, he can see the sins in advance. He is skilled in ascertaining happiness and unhappiness and serves virtuous people. Because he consorts with those who are righteous, his proclivity towards such conduct also increases. He finds delight in wisdom and dharma. He sustains himself through dharma. Even if his mind turns towards obtaining riches, he does this only through dharma. He sprinkles his foundations only with those things where there are qualities. He has dharma in his soul and obtains friends who are good. Having obtained friends and riches, he finds delight in this world and in the next. O descendant of the Bharata lineage! The learned know that as the fruits of dharma, a living being obtains lordship over sound, touch, form, taste and scent.[597] O Yudhishthira! However, having obtained the fruits of dharma, he is not satisfied. Through the sight of learning, he is not content until he has renounced. Through the sight of wisdom, he sees sins in desire. He no longer finds delight in desire, and dharma liberates him. On seeing that everything in the world is destroyed, he strives to give up everything.[598] He uses every means possible for emancipation and avoids those that

[597]Through yoga, one obtains the objects of desire.

[598]All fruits are destroyed. Therefore, he is no longer interested in the fruits.

are against it. He quickly resorts to renunciation and abandons all wicked deeds. He has dharma in his soul and obtains supreme emancipation. O son! O descendant of the Bharata lineage! I have told you what you asked me about—sin, dharma, emancipation and renunciation. O Yudhishthira! Therefore, in every situation, you must practise dharma. O Kounteya! If you base yourself in dharma, you will obtain eternal success."'

Chapter 1594(266)

'Yudhishthira said, "O grandfather! You have said that emancipation can be obtained through some means and not by others. O descendant of the Bharata lineage! I wish to hear what those appropriate means are."

'Bhishma replied, "O immensely wise one! What you have asked requires accomplished sight. O unblemished one! You must always seek to hunt out the appropriate means in everything. O unblemished one! When one turns one's intelligence towards fashioning a pot, once the pot has been done, it vanishes.[599] In that way, the reasons for pursuing dharma are no longer there once one has obtained dharma.[600] The road that goes to the eastern ocean doesn't go to the western one. There is only one path for emancipation. Listen to that in detail. One should practise forgiveness, eliminate anger and abandon all desire and resolution. One must patiently follow sattva and conquer sleep. By being attentive, one must protect oneself against fear. The atman must be used to control the breath. Patience must be used to restrain wishes, hatred and desire. Practice must be used to control errors

599 The objective having been accomplished, there is no need for the resolution any more.

600 Dharma is pursued through acts, for the fruits, known as pravritti. However, once one pursues dharma in the sense of nivritti or renunciation, those reasons cease to exist.

and the whirl of confusion. Through practice of knowledge, one must ascertain the truth about important and unimportant things. Through restrained diet, one must ward off digestive disorders and disease. Contentment and knowledge of the truth must be used to control greed, confusion and hatred. Through the dharma of compassion, one should conquer the adharma of indifference. Through tranquility and abandoning of attachment, one must control the desire to obtain things. Through yoga, a learned person realizes that affection and hunger are temporary. Compassion and contentment are used to control pride and thirst. Enterprise is used to conquer lassitude. Certainty is used to conquer doubt. Loquaciousness is conquered through silence and fear through valour. Words and thoughts are controlled through intelligence and intelligence through the sight of knowledge. Knowledge about the great paramatman is used to control the jivatman.[601] Finally, that[602] can be known by those who are tranquil and pure in deeds. The wise know how to control the five taints associated with yoga. These are desire, anger, greed, fear and laziness as the fifth. These must be discarded and yoga must be practised. Meditation, studying, donations, truthfulness, modesty, uprightness, forgiveness, purity in intake of food and control over the senses—these are the means used to increase energy and dispel sins. Thus, resolution becomes successful and knowledge is obtained. Such a person is energetic and has cleansed his sins. He is restrained in diet and has conquered his senses. Having subjugated desire and anger, he attains the state of the brahman. He is without folly and without attachment. He has cast aside desire and anger. He bases himself on lack of distress, lack of insolence and lack of anxiety. He is cheerful, unblemished and pure. This is the path of emancipation. He controls his words and thoughts and all desire."'[603]

[601]The text uses the word atman for both. But we have translated it in this way to make comprehension easier.

[602]The paramatman.

[603]The desire for obtaining powers through yoga is controlled. Otherwise, one will deviate from the objective.

Chapter 1595(267)

'Bhishma said, "In this connection, an ancient history is recounted about a conversation between Narada and Asita-Devala. The aged Devala, supreme among intelligent ones, was seated. Narada asked him about the creation and destruction of beings. 'O brahmana! Where was this universe, with its mobile and immobile objects, created from? Where do they go at the time of destruction? Tell me about this.'

'"Asita replied, 'It is said that when the time comes, the creator of all beings thinks about existence and brings into being the five great elements. Time urges itself to create beings from these. There is no doubt that those who say that there is anything else[604] utter a falsehood. O Narada! Know that these five are eternal, indestructible and fixed. These naturally possess great energy and time is the sixth. Water, space, earth, wind and fire are the elements. Do not entertain the doubt that there is anything superior to these. There are no texts or arguments to substantiate that doubt. Know that the accumulation or withdrawal of these six leads to everything. These five, time, the eight strands are the only eternal reason behind the creation and destruction of all beings.[605] When beings are destroyed, it is into these that merger takes place. When beings are created, they emerge from these. When a creature is destroyed, it is divided into five parts, and is also created from these. The body comes from earth, hearing from space. The eyes come from fire, life from the wind and blood from water. The eyes, the nose, the ears, the skin and the tongue as the fifth are the senses of knowledge and the wise know that these are for attaining the objects of the senses. Sight, hearing, smell, touch and taste are known to be the qualities of the senses. There are five senses, five qualities and five connections. Form, scent, taste, touch and sound are the qualities that are obtained through the senses. There are five each of senses, qualities and connections. The senses don't actually comprehend the qualities of form, scent, taste, touch and sound. These are actually understood by

[604]Other than the five great elements, time and the creator of all beings.

[605]This needs explanation. The five elements and time add up to six. The other two, making up eight, are past deeds and the resolution to create.

the kshetrajna. Consciousness is superior to the accumulation of the senses. The mind is superior to consciousness. Intelligence is superior to the mind. The kshetrajna is superior to intelligence. Initially, creatures consider all material objects through separate senses. Subsequently, the mind reflects and resorts to intelligence. One then comprehends the truth about all the objects perceived by the senses. Consciousness and mind interact with the accumulation of the senses, and intelligence is the eighth. Those who have thought about adhyatma and have thought about it know these eight to be the organs of knowledge. Know that the hands, the feet, the anus, the penis and the mouth as the fifth are the organs of action. The mouth is said to be the organ that is used for speaking and eating. The feet are the organs for moving and the hand are the organs for doing something. The anus and the penis are similar in action and are both organs for discharge. One is for the discharge of excrement, while the other is for discharge at the time of sexual desire. However, it has rightly been said that there is a sixth organ of action and that is strength. I have spoken to you about all the senses of knowledge, organs of action and their attributes. When the organs are exhausted, they cannot perform their own tasks. Since the action of the organs is suspended, a man sleeps. However, though the senses are under suspension, if the mind is awake and concerns itself with material objects, this is known as a state of dreaming. There are three attributes of sattva, rajas and tamas. When engaged in action, the state of sattva is praised. Joy, success in tasks, power and the supreme objective are said to be the signs of those who have resorted to sattva. The sentiments that any creature properly resorts to and the sentiments that it aspires for, are always evident in its coming and going.[606] It is said that there are seventeen characteristics of the qualities and the senses.[607] The eighteenth one[608] that dwells in the

[606]In interpretations, this is explained in the following way. If one is emancipated, there is no difference in sentiments between states of being awake and dreaming. But in others, those sentiments differ.

[607]Five organs of knowledge, five organs of action, consciousness, mind, intelligence, strength and sattva, rajas and tamas.

[608]The atman.

body is eternal. All those qualities adhere to the one who assumes a body and dwells in the body. When he no longer dwells in the body, they are also disassociated from the body. The body is reduced to the five elements. There are eighteen qualities in the body.[609] Heat is the twentieth and all this comes about through an interaction between the five elements. Together with the breath of life, mahat sustains these in the body. That is the reason for creation and destruction of the body. When those good and bad deeds are exhausted, the body is reduced to the five elements. In due course of time, depending on the good and bad deeds that have been performed, another body is entered. Through a process of death and rebirth, he repeatedly gives up one body and resorts to another body. He is urged on by time, like a person abandoning a dilapidated house for a new house. Those who are wise and firm in their resolution are not tormented because of this. Foolish people, those who are proud of relationships, are the only ones who grieve on account of this. There is no one to whom he belongs. There is no one who belongs to him. He is always alone, enjoying joy and misery in the body. Some creatures are born again. There are others who are not reborn. Some are freed from their bodies and attain the supreme objective. Having abandoned the body, the store of good and bad deeds, when the body is destroyed, such people attain the brahman. Knowledge of sankhya is recommended for the destruction of good and bad deeds. Once those are destroyed, learned ones can see that the state of the brahman is the supreme objective."'

Chapter 1596(268)

'Yudhishthira said, "Brothers, fathers, sons, relatives and well-wishers have been slain for the sake of accomplishing objectives. We have been driven by wicked resolutions and

[609]Ignorance has been added to the earlier tally of seventeen. The atman is now being counted as the nineteenth.

have been cruel. O grandfather! How can this thirst for riches be removed? Following that thirst, we have perpetrated wicked deeds."

'Bhishma replied, "In this connection, an ancient history is recounted about a song sung by the king of Videha, when he was asked by Mandavya. 'I possess nothing, but I live my life in great happiness. Though Mithila[610] is blazing, nothing that belongs to me is burning. Riches indeed bring prosperity. But those who know, regard these as misery. Objects that bring little prosperity always confuse those who are not accomplished. Whatever happiness satisfaction brings in this world and whatever great happiness is obtained in heaven are not even one-sixteenth of the happiness that comes about from the extinguishment of thirst. With the progress of time, a cow grows and so does its horns. In that way, with more and more riches, the thirst also increases. If one has a sense of ownership in anything, then, when that object is destroyed, one suffers from torment. One should not be driven by desire. Attachment to desire brings misery. When desired riches have been obtained, they should be used for dharma. But even then, desire must be shunned. A learned person regards all beings as equal, as equal as a tiger and a lump of flesh.[611] Having been successful in purifying his soul, he renounces everything. He discards both truth and falsehood, sorrow and joy, the pleasant and the unpleasant, fear and freedom from fear. Having abandoned everything, he is tranquil and healthy. This[612] is difficult to be given up by those who are evil in their intelligence. Even when the body decays, it does not decrease. It is like a disease that destroys life. The casting aside of thirst brings happiness. A person who has dharma in his soul beholds his own atman, like the sparkling and unblemished moon. He obtains happiness in this world and fame in the hereafter.' On hearing the king's words, the brahmana was pleased. Mandavya, who had earlier been confused, honoured those words."'

[610]Mithila was the capital of Videha.

[611]There is no difference between a tiger and its food, the lump of flesh.

[612]The thirst.

Chapter 1597(269)

'Yudhishthira asked, "What kind of conduct, what kind of behaviour, what kind of knowledge and what kind of faith enable one to obtain the state of the brahman, which is permament and is beyond nature?"

'Bhishma replied, "A person who is devoted to the dharma of moksha must be restrained in diet and must conquer his senses. He will then obtain the supreme state, which is permanent and is beyond nature. The sage will depart from his home and regard gain and loss as equal. He will be indifferent to objects of desire, even when they present themselves. He will become a mendicant. He will not hurt anyone through sight, thoughts or words. He will not display any harsh conduct, whether the person is present or absent. He will not cause injury to any being. He will roam around like the sun.[613] He should lead a life so that he does not commit an act of injury. He must tolerate harsh words and never be arrogant. Even when he is enraged, he will speak pleasant words. When he is censured, he will reply agreeably. When he roams around in the midst of a village, he should not show either excessive friendship or enmity. When searching for alms, he should not go to a house that he has visited earlier. Even when he is reviled, he must protect himself well and not speak unpleasant words in reply. He must be mild and not injure someone who has injured him. He must control fear and rage. The sage should desire alms when the smoke has gone out, when the pestle has been laid down, when the fire has been extinguished, when food has been eaten and when the vessels are no longer laid out.[614] He should only accept what is required for subsistence and ignore anything in excess. He should not be distressed at not getting something. Nor should he be delighted at getting something. He should not desire what ordinary people want. He should not eat when he is respectfully invited.[615] In a similar way, he should refuse anything that is offered as a mark of

[613]Meaning that he will not reside in any fixed abode.

[614]When the house is through with the meals.

[615]If he is invited to eat in a house, he should refuse it.

honour. He must not find fault with the food that has been offered, nor should he praise its qualities. He must always refuse a bed or a seat offered as a mark of honour. He should reside in an empty house, at the foot of a tree, in a forest or in a cave. His conduct should not be known to others. If others come there, he should go somewhere else.[616] He should treat requests and obstructions equally. He will be certain and fixed. He will not be bound down by either good deeds or bad ones. He will control the force of words, his mind and the force of anger. He will control the urge to know and the force of the stomach and the penis. The ascetic will control these urges. No censure will be allowed to afflict his heart. He will be neutral, regarding praise and censure as equal. This is the supremely sacred ashrama of a mendicant. He is great in soul and excellent in his vows. He is controlled and is detached in every way. He doesn't go to earlier places.[617] He is tranquil. He is without an abode. He is controlled. He does not consort with those who are in vanaprastha or garhasthya stages. He should not unwittingly fall prey to desire. Nor should he succumb to delight. Know that this is the ashrama of moksha, known to those who are learned. Everything about moksha was spoken about by the learned Harita. If a person departs from his house and grants fearlessness to all beings, he obtains worlds that are full of energy."'

Chapter 1598(270)

'Yudhishthira said, "All the people speak of ourselves as being blessed. However, there is no man who is more miserable than we are. O supreme among the Kurus! O grandfather! We have been born as men, but have been born from the gods. The worlds honour us, but we have obtained misery. When will we resort to sannyasa and destroy this sorrow? O supreme among the Kuru lineage! Taking

[616]This is also interpreted as retreating inside his own self.
[617]Earlier places refer to his former life as a householder.

life in these bodies is a matter of sorrow. We will free ourselves of the seventeen attributes[618] and merge with the five elements. O great grandfather! We will also free ourselves from the eight objects of the senses and the qualities.[619] The sages, who are firm in their vows, are not born again. O scorcher of enemies! When will we be in a position to abandon the kingdom?"

'Bhishma replied, "O great king! Everything can be counted and everything has an end. The number of rebirths can also be counted.[620] Nothing in this world is fixed. O king! In connection with what we are talking about, no sin has been associated with you. O one who knows about dharma! Endeavour and in the course of time, you will follow that path. O king! In this body, the atman is the lord of good and bad deeds. But the rising darkness obstructs the vision. The wind has no dust or colour in it. But when it is tinged with a pigment, that colour penetrates it and this is also seen to colour the directions. In that way, because of the fruits of deeds, the atman is tinged and enveloped in darkness. It fades, adopts that colour and circles around amidst bodies. In any creature, knowledge destroys the ignorance that causes darkness. When that is dispelled, the eternal brahman manifests itself. The sages say that this cannot be accomplished through acts. Those who have been liberated should be worshipped, even by the worlds of the immortals. The large numbers of maharshis are also not content.[621] In this connection, there is an ancient song. O king! Listen to it attentively. The daitya Vritra was dislodged from his prosperity and sung this. O descendant of the Bharata lineage! He was vanquished and was without aides. His kingdom was lost. However, despite being in the midst of enemies, he resorted to his intelligence alone and did not grieve. In those ancient times, Vritra lost his riches and Ushanas[622] spoke to him. 'O danava! Now that you have been defeated, are you distressed?'

[618]The five senses, the five organs of action, the five kinds of breaths of life, mind and intelligence.

[619]The five objects of the senses and the qualities of sattva, rajas and tamas.

[620]There is an end to the cycle of rebirth.

[621]Without having attained the brahman.

[622]Shukracharya, the preceptor of the demons.

'"Vritra said, 'Because of truth and austerities, I know about destruction. I do not sorrow or rejoice at the creation and destruction of beings. Goaded by time, beings are subjugated and submerged in hell. Some say that all the learned ones go to heaven. Goaded by time, they spend the computed durations of time there. However, when that duration is over, they are born again and again. They are born as thousands of inferior species and go to hell. Bound by the nooses of time, beings are helpless and go there. I have seen that creatures circle around in this way. The sacred texts have said that gains are commensurate with deeds. Creatures are born as inferior species, men and gods and go to hell. After that unhappiness and happiness and misery and joy is over, they return to their earlier conduct.[623] All the worlds are bound down by the injunctions of Yama. All beings are travellers along a path that has been travelled before.'"

'Bhishma said, "He knew about time and its enumeration, about what cannot be enumerated and about creation and stability. When he spoke in this way, the illustrious Ushanas replied, 'O son![624] Why are you speaking these terrible, wicked and insane words?'

'"Vritra said, 'You and the other learned ones have directly seen the great austerities I tormented myself with in earlier times and the sacrifices that I performed out of greed. I brought fragrances, beings and diverse kinds of scents. I grew in my energy and transcended the three worlds. I roamed around with my companions, showering garlands of rays. I could not be defeated by any being and I was never frightened of anyone. However, the prosperity that I earned through my austerities was destroyed through my own deeds. O illustrious one! But resorting to my fortitude, I am not sorrowing over that. In earlier times, when I was fighting with the great-souled and great Indra, I saw the illustrious lord, Hari Narayana. He is Vaikuntha, Purusha, Vishnu, Shukla, Ananta, Sanatana, Munjakesha, Harishmashru and the grandfather of all

[623]The cycle of death and rebirth.

[624]The word used is tata.

beings.[625] There is no doubt that a little bit of those austerities are still left for me.[626] Therefore, I wish to ask you about the fruits of deeds. For which varna has Brahma decreed the greatest prosperity? Why is that supreme prosperity lost? How are beings created? How do they live? Who makes them act? What are the supreme fruits obtained by living for an eternal period? What can be achieved through deeds and what can be achieved through knowledge? What fruits are obtained? O brahmana rishi! You should explain this to me.'"

'Bhishma said, "O lion among kings! Having been thus addressed, the sage replied. O bull among men! Together with your brothers, listen attentively to what he said."'

Chapter 1599(271)

'"Ushanas said, 'I bow before the illustrious and powerful god Vishnu. O son! He holds up the surface of the earth and the sky in his hands. O supreme among danavas! His head is the eternal region. I will tell you about Vishnu's supreme greatness.'"

'Bhishma said, "While they were conversing in this way, the great sage Sanatkumara, with dharma in his soul, arrived there, to dispel their doubts. The Indra among the asuras and the sage Ushanas worshipped him. O king! The bull among sages then sat down on an expensive seat. When the immensely wise one was seated, Ushanas spoke these words to him. 'For the sake of the Indra among the danavas, tell him about Vishnu's supreme greatness.' On hearing

[625]All of these are Vishnu's names, Vaikuntha being his abode, as well as his name. Shukla means pure or white. Ananta means infinite, Sanatana means eternal. Munjakesha is one with yellow hair, while Harishmashru is one with a tawny beard.

[626]The original austerities, as well as the rewards from seeing Hari. Since some of those fruits are still left, Vritra is entitled to ask Shukracharya about auspicious things.

this, Sanatkumara spoke words that were full of grave import. He told the intelligent Indra among the danavas about Vishnu's greatness. 'O daitya! Listen to everything about Vishnu's supreme greatness. O scorcher of enemies! Know that everything in the universe is established in Vishnu. O mighty-armed one! He is the one who creates all beings, mobile and immobile. In the course of time, it is he who withdraws them back and creates them again when the time arises. At the time of destruction, everything enters him. Everything is created from him. Danavas are incapable of obtaining him through austerities or through sacrifices. One is capable of obtaining him by restraining the senses. Both internal and external acts must be based in the mind.[627] If they are purified through intelligence, one can obtain eternity. This is like a goldsmith purifying gold in the fire, using a great deal of different efforts. A being may purify himself through one hundred births. But through limited deeds and a great effort, another being may purify himself in a single birth. If the filth on the body is cleansed before it has become thick, it requires only a little effort. In that way, one must make a great deal of effort to remove the taints. If a few garlands are mixed with sesamum seeds, they do not shed their scent and become fragrant. This is the subtlety of knowledge. A large number of garlands must repeatedly be mixed. Then the scent[628] goes away and the fragrance of the garlands is established. Through hundreds of lives, one must seek for the qualities. One must use one's intelligence to restrain the taints and endeavour and practise. O danava! Listen to the reasons behind deeds, whereby creatures become addicted to, or detached from, the consequences of those deeds. O lord! Listen with single-minded attention. In due course, I will explain how creatures engage in action and refrain from it. The illustrious lord, Hari Narayana, is without a beginning and without an end. He creates all the beings, mobile and immobile. He is in all beings that are mutable and immutable. He uses his rays to drink up the universe through his

[627]External acts are sacrifices and rites. Internal acts are in the form of purification inside. Provided these are done well, they do help.

[628]Of the sesamum seeds.

eleven transformations.[629] Know that his feet are the earth and the firmament is his head. O daitya! His arms are the directions and his ears are the sky. His energy is the sun and his mind is established in the moon. His intelligence is always in knowledge and his juices are in the water. O supreme among the danavas! The planets are in the midst of his eyebrows. O danava! The nakshatras are his eyes and the earth constitutes his feet. Know that rajas, tamas and sattva are Narayana's soul. O son! Know that the ashramas and the fruits of all deeds are his face. The supreme and undecaying one is also the fruit of not performing deeds. The metres are his body hair and the syllables are his speech. The different kinds of modes and the various aspects of dharma are based in his heart. He is the brahman. He is supreme dharma. He is austerities. He is the truth. He is *shruti* and the sacred texts.[630] He constitutes the vessels used in sacrifices, sacrifices and the sixteen officiating priests.[631] He is the grandfather. He is Vishnu. He is the Ashvins. He is Purandara. He is Mitra. He is Varuna. He is Yama. He is the lord of riches.[632] Though he is seen as separate, he is known as one. Know that this entire universe is under the control of that single god. O Indra among the daityas! In all beings, he is spoken of as the single one. When a creature perceives this through his knowledge, truth is manifested before him. Between creation and destruction, beings exist for one thousand crore and this is also true of the others.[633] O daitya! The measure of the duration of the creation of beings is in terms of many thousands of lakes. Each lake is one *yojana* in width, one *krosha* in depth and five

[629]The five senses, the five organs of action and the mind.

[630]Shruti is sacred texts that are in the nature of revelation, but there are other sacred texts too.

[631]There were four categories of priests—*hotri*, *udhvaryu*, *udgatri* and brahmana. While each of these was associated with one of the Vedas, in this case, the number four is probably being multiplied by the four Vedas.

[632]Kubera.

[633]Meaning, years. The text uses the word *koti*, naturally translated as crore. But this may very well be a mistranslation. A kalpa or period of creation lasts for one thousand divine years. Koti also means highest point or eminent position. So perhaps one thousand divine years is meant.

hundred yojanas in length. The distance between one lake and another is one yojana. Let water be taken away from one of these lakes, using a single hair and not a second one, with this being done only once a day. Know that the time it takes for all the lakes to be dried up is the period of creation of beings, and destruction is of the same duration. There is supreme evidence that creatures have six complexions—dark, smoky, blue in the middle, red, which is easier to tolerate, yellow, which is extremely pleasant, and white.[634] White is supreme. O Indra among danavas! It is unblemished and without sorrow. It is bereft of exhaustion and brings success. O daitya! A creature goes through birth in thousands of wombs before it obtains success. Indra of the gods considered all the possible ends and also examined what the auspicious sacred texts had said about the ends. The gods then decided that the ends of creatures were determined by their colour and that their colour was determined by time. O daitya! A creature has to pass through fourteen hundred thousand existences[635] and the number isn't unlimited.[636] Know that depending on deeds, a creature can ascend, stay in the same place or descend. The end obtained by a dark complexion is the worst. Such a person is submerged in hell and is cooked there. It is said that the creature has to undergo hardships in that state for many thousands of kalpas. After having been there for hundreds and thousands of years, the creature obtains a smoky complexion. The creature dwells there helplessly, until the end of the yuga, with its atman enveloped in tamas. But when the creature is united with the qualities of sattva, it uses its own intelligence to dispel the darkness. It may then obtain a red complexion. However, if it is stuck with the blue, it circles around in the world of men.[637] Bound down by its own deeds, it is

[634]Implicitly, each succeeding colour is superior to the preceding one.

[635]Lives.

[636]This has complicated interpretations and one shouldn't interpret this in the straightforward sense of number of births. Five senses, five organs of action, mind, intelligence, ego and consciousness add up to fourteen. These have hundreds of thousands of variations and a creature rises or falls, depending on how these behave.

[637]The preceding colours signify birth as non-human species.

then afflicted by death and rebirth. However, when it attains a yellow complexion, though it is beyond immediate destruction, it still has to return.[638] With that yellow complexion, it roams around for thousands of kalpas. O daitya! But it has still not been emancipated and has to spend time in hell for a thousand and ten years. There are still ends determined by nineteen thousand cycles of deeds.[639] Know that one is freed from hell and every other form of birth only through emancipation. A creature may roam around in the world of the gods. But when the merits decay, it is dislodged and becomes human again. After having remained a mortal for one hundred and eight kalpas, it can become immortal again. However, if in that state,[640] it deviates because of destiny, it obtains the status of a dark complexion and suffers from every kind of hardship. O brave one among the asuras! I will now tell you about how a creature in the world of the living can obtain success, if it so desires. Through seven hundred different kinds of acts, a creature progresses from red to yellow and white.[641] Having finally united with white, it obtains and roams around in the supreme eight worlds.[642] These eight, or sixty, or hundreds, are extremely radiant. But they are created by the mind.[643] The white complexion is the supreme objective and its greatness is more than that of the other three.[644] Even if one

[638]The yellow colour signifies the status of a god. However, divinity isn't permanent either.

[639]To the earlier fourteen, the five breaths of life have been added to get nineteen. Gods are still subject to these nineteen and thousands of consequences resulting from deeds undertaken by these nineteen. Therefore, they are still in hell.

[640]Of a human.

[641]The five senses, the mind and the intelligence add up to seven. Each of these leads to hundreds of different kinds of acts.

[642]This probably means the worlds associated with the eight guardians of the worlds.

[643]That is, these regions of bliss are not permanent.

[644]These are sections that are extremely difficult to understand. The four states are of being awake (*jagrata)*, sleeping with dreams (*svapna*), deep sleep without dreams (sushupti) and the supreme state of consciousness (turiya). Turiya is superior to the other three. There are five elements, five senses, five attributes of the senses, five organs of action, mind, intelligence, ego, consciousness and

transcends the kalpas, one dwells cheerlessly in the eight worlds or in the other four.[645] The sixth complexion[646] attains the supreme objective. Such a distinguished person obtains success and is devoid of exhaustion. One can dwell cheerlessly in the seven superior worlds[647] for hundreds of kalpas. When this ends, one is born in the world of men, although one obtains greatness there. In due course of time, one transcends these and moves up in the hierarchy of creatures. For several kalpas, one dwells seven times in those superior worlds. If one can escape from destruction and misfortune there, it is possible that one might reach the world of success. Those regions without decay are infinite and belong to Shiva, Vishnu, Brahma, Shesha, Nara, unadulterated consciousness and Para-Brahma. At the time of destruction, though their bodies are burnt, such subjects approach the brahman. All the various categories of gods also endeavour to obtain immortality in Brahma's world. When it is time for creation after the period of destruction is over, all beings move to their designated regions. But once the fruits are over, those regions terminate. So do those ends and they become like men. However, for those who are progressively dislodged from the world of success,[648] their end remains what it used to be earlier. When there is creation after destruction, all superior beings obtain forms that are in conformity with their destinies. However, creatures who have obtained success retain their white complexion and both kinds of knowledge.[649] Their sentiments are pure and controlled and they see everything, as if with their own five senses.[650] Their ends are pure.

---

the gross body. When ignorance, desire, karma, the atman and the jagrata state are added, there is a number of thirty. For the svapna stage, one similarly has another thirty, adding up to sixty.

[645]Those other four worlds are those of *mahar, jana, tapas* and satya.

[646]White.

[647]*Bhu, bhuvar, svar,* mahar, jana, tapas and satya.

[648]That is, those who have been emancipated. Because of their knowledge, they do not regress.

[649]*Para vidya*, knowledge about the self, and *apara vidya*, knowledge about the material world.

[650]Supreme knowledge is as evident as if with one's own senses.

Their objectives are supreme. In their minds, they always think of what is auspicious. They obtain Brahma's world, which is without decay. It is eternal and is difficult to obtain. O spirited one! I have thus recounted to you everything about Narayana's powers.'

'"Vritra said, 'Since this is the case, there is nothing for me to grieve. I can clearly see the truth in your words. O one with a cheerful spirit! On hearing your words, I have become cleansed of all evil and sin. O illustrious one! O maharshi! O immensely radiant one! The immensely energetic wheel[651] is moving. The infinite and eternal Vishnu is the spot from which all creation originates. He is the great-souled Purushottama. Everything in the universe is established in him.'"

'Bhishma said, "O Kounteya! Having said this, Vritra gave up his life. He united his atman and obtained the supreme region."

'Yudhishthira asked, "O grandfather! In ancient times, Sanatkumara spoke to Vritra about an illustrious god. Is Janardana that same person?"

'Bhishma replied, "With his own infinite energy, the illustrious one is the foundation. From there, the immensely ascetic one creates many kinds of beings. Know that Keshava is not dislodged from his richness of turiya. The intelligent one creates the three worlds from his richness of turiya. Stationed at one end, at the end of a kalpa, he transforms himself. The immensely strong and illustrious lord lies down on the water. From there, the one with the cheerful soul roams around the eternal worlds. The great-souled one is not obstructed in his creation. Everything in this wonderful universe is established in him."

'Yudhishthira said, "O one who knows about the supreme truth! I think that Vritra himself knew his end was going to be auspicious. O grandfather! That is the reason he was happy and did not grieve. O unblemished one! A person who is white in complexion, a person who belongs to the white category and a person who is successful does not return.[652] O grandfather! Such a person is freed from hell

[651] Of time.

[652] There is no rebirth.

and from birth as inferior species. O king! But a person who has a yellow or red complexion has deeds that are enveloped by tamas and is seen to be born as inferior species. We are extremely afflicted. We are addicted to things that take us to the mouth of hardships and unhappiness. What ends will we obtain, blue or dark, the worst of them all?"

'Bhishma replied, "You are Pandavas and you have been born in a pure lineage. You are rigid in your vows. Having obtained pleasure in the world of gods, you will again be born as men. Having enjoyed happiness as long as creation lasts, you will return to the gods and enjoy bliss. In joy, you will be counted among the Siddhas. Do not entertain any fear on this account. All of you will be unblemished."'

Chapter 1600(272)

'Yudhishthira said, "O father![653] It is evident that the infinitely energetic Vritra was devoted to dharma. His knowledge was unequalled and so was his devotion to Vishnu. O father! Vishnu's infinite energy is difficult to comprehend. O tiger among kings! How was Vritra capable of understanding that state? O one without decay! You have spoken about him and I have heard faithfully. But there is something that I still do not understand. Hence, I am asking you again. O bull among the Bharata lineage! How could Vritra be slain by Shakra? He was devoted to dharma and faithful to Vishnu. He knew about the true state. O bull among the Bharata lineage! I have a doubt on this account and am asking you. O tiger among kings! How was Vritra vanquished by Shakra? O grandfather! Tell me how this extraordinary thing happened. O mighty-armed one! I have supreme curiosity. Tell me in detail."

'Bhishma replied, "In ancient times, Indra had left on a chariot, with large numbers of gods with him. He saw Vritra stationed

[653]The word used is tata.

before him, like a mountain. O scorcher of enemies! He was five hundred yojanas tall and three hundred yojanas in circumference. On seeing that form of Vritra's, which was difficult for the three worlds to vanquish, the gods were terrified and could not obtain any peace. O king! At that time, on suddenly seeing Vritra's supreme form, Shakra was frightened and his thighs were paralysed. Having presented themselves at that battle, the gods and the asuras roared and sounded musical instruments. O Kouravya! However, on seeing Shakra present himself, Vritra was not scared or terrified and made no efforts. An encounter, frightful for the three worlds, ensued between Shakra, Indra of the gods, and the great-souled Vritra. There was the great sound of swords, battleaxes, tridents, javelins, spikes, clubs, many kinds of stones, bows, diverse kinds of divine weapons, fire and flaming torches. All the soldiers of the gods and the asuras clashed against each other. With the grandfather at the forefront, all the numerous gods, and the immensely fortunate rishis came on their celestial vehicles to witness the battle. O great king! O bull among the Bharata lineage! There were the siddhas too. Gandharvas came on their celestial vehicles and so did the apsaras. Vritra, supreme among those who upheld dharma, covered the sky and showered down boulders, which were as large as mountains, on the Indra among the gods. The large numbers of gods were enraged at this. In that battle, in every direction, they used their weapons to counter the boulders that had been showered down by Vritra. O tiger among the Kurus! Vritra was gigantic in form and extremely strong. He resorted to fighting with maya,[654] and in every way, confounded the Indra among the gods. Shatakratu was overcome with confusion and afflicted by Vritra."

'"However, Vasishtha addressed him in a *rathantara*.[655] Vasishtha said, 'O Indra among the gods! You are chief among the gods. O destroyer of the enemies of the gods! O Shakra! You possess the strength of the three worlds. Why are you distressed? O Shakra! Brahma, Vishnu, Shiva, the lord of the universe, the illustrious

[654]Illusion.

[655]A kind of Sama hymn.

god, Soma, and all the supreme rishis are looking towards you. O Shakra! Do not fall prey to lassitude, like an inferior god. O noble one! Make up your mind to fight. O lord of the gods! Slay the enemy. The three-eyed one,[656] the preceptor of the worlds and worshipped by all the worlds, is looking at you. O illustrious one! O lord of the gods! Discard this confusion. O Shakra! These brahmarshis, with Brihaspati at the forefront, are using divine chants to praise you, so that you may be victorious.' The great-souled Vasishtha addressed Vasava in this way and ignited and extended his strength and energy. The illustrious chastiser of Paka used his intelligence to resort to great yoga and dispelled the maya.

'"The illustrious son of Angiras[657] and the other supreme rishis witnessed Vritra's valour and went to Maheshvara. They worshipped him for the welfare of the worlds and for Vritra's destruction. The illustrious lord of the universe then assumed the form of a fever and in this extremely terrible form, penetrated the body of Vritra, supreme among the daityas. The illustrious god Vishnu, revered by all the worlds, was engaged in the protection of the worlds and entered Indra's vajra. The intelligent Brihaspati, the immensely energetic Vasishtha and the other supreme rishis approached Shatakratu. They worshipped Vasava, the granter of boons and worshipped by the worlds, and said, 'O lord! Slay Vritra with single-minded attention.' Maheshavara said, 'O Shakra! This gigantic Vritra is surrounded by a great army. He is the soul of the universe. He can go everywhere. He possesses great powers of maya and is learned. Therefore, this best of asuras is incapable of being vanquished by the three worlds. O lord of the gods! Resort to a state of yoga and then slay him. O lord of the immortals! To obtain strength, he has tormented himself with austerities for sixty thousand years. Thus, Brahma gave him boons—the greatness that yogis possess, great powers of maya, immense strength and fierce energy. O lord of the gods! O Vasava! My energy has permeated into this danava.[658] You are capable of

[656]Shiva.

[657]Brihaspati.

[658]In the form of fever.

slaying Vritra with your vajra.' Shakra replied, 'O illustrious one! This son of Diti is extremely difficult to assail, but I will do it with your favours. O bull among the gods! While you look on, I will slay him with the vajra.' The daitya, the great asura, was permeated by that fever and the gods and the rishis uttered loud roars of delight. Thousands of drums, conch shells, kettledrums and tambourines were loudly sounded. All the asuras lost their memories and their great wisdom and strength disappeared in an instant. On realizing that tamas had penetrated them, the rishis and the gods praised Shakra and Ishana and urged them. At the time of the battle, the great-souled Shakra was stationed on his chariot and his form was extremely difficult to look at. He was praised by the rishis."'

Chapter 1601(273)

'Bhishma said, "O great king! In every way, that fever penetrated Vritra. Listen to the signs that then manifested themselves on his body. His mouth flamed and assumed a terrible form. He became extremely pale. His body trembled mightily and he began to breathe heavily. His body hair stood up and turned fierce. O great king! He sighed deeply. O descendant of the Bharata lineage! His memory assumed the form of an extremely terrible, fearful and inauspicious jackal, emerged from his mouth and fell down. Blazing and flaming meteors descended along his flanks. Vultures, herons and cranes emitted extremely hideous shrieks and happily circled around above Vritra. Stationed on his chariot in the battle, the god Shakra glanced towards Vritra and prepared to use the vajra. The great asura released a superhuman roar. O Indra among kings! Overwhelmed by that fierce fever, he yawned. While he was thus yawning, Shakra released the vajra. That extremely energetic vajra was like the fire of destruction. It swiftly brought down the giant form of the daitya Vritra. O bull among the Bharata lineage! On seeing that Vritra had been slain, the gods again roared in every direction. Having slain the danava, Vritra, the illustrious and immensely famous one[659] entered heaven with the vajra, which was permeated by Vishnu.

'"O Kouravya! At this, the sin of having killed a brahmana[660] emerged from Vritra's body. She was extremely terrible and horrible and caused fear to the worlds. Her teeth were fearsome. She was hideous and malformed, dark and tawny. Her hair stood up and her eyes were awful. O bull among the Bharata lineage! She was thin and wore a garland of skulls. O one who knows about dharma! She was attired in tattered rags and bark that were wet with blood. O Indra among kings! O supreme among the Bharata lineage! That terrible form emerged and searched for the wielder of the vajra. O descendant of the Kuru lineage! After some time, with the welfare of the worlds in mind, Vritra's slayer was headed in the direction of heaven. On seeing that the immensely energetic Shakra was advancing, she seized Indra of the gods by the throat and adhered to him. The sin of having killed a brahmana generated great fear in him. He therefore entered the stalk of a lotus and spent many years there. O Kouravya! But the sin of having killed a brahmana still sought to pursue him. Grasped by her, he lost all his enterprise. Though Shakra made great efforts to rid himself of the sin of having killed a brahmana, Indra of the gods wasn't able to shake her off. O bull among the Bharata lineage! Indra of the gods was seized by her. He went to the grandfather and bowed his head down before him. O supreme among the Bharata lineage! On knowing that Shakra had been seized by the sin of having killed a brahmana, Brahma began to think.

'"O mighty-armed one! O descendant of the Bharata lineage! In a reassuring and gentle voice, the grandfather spoke to the sin of having killed a brahmana. 'O beautiful one! Do what is agreeable to me and free this Indra of the thirty gods. Tell me what I can do for you now. What is your desire?'

'"The sin of having killed a brahmana replied, 'O god! You are worshipped by the three worlds. You are the creator of the three worlds and you are pleased with me. You have thus done everything

659Indra.

660In personified form. Vritra was the son of a brahmana.

that I wish for. But decree an abode for me. It was for the sake of protecting the worlds that you laid down this rule.[661] O god! This extremely great ordinance was laid down by you. O one who knows about dharma! O lord and master of all the worlds! Since you are pleased with me, I will leave Shakra. But decree an abode for me.'"

'Bhishma said, "At this, the grandfather spoke to the sin of having killed a brahmana. He thought of a means so that the sin of having killed a brahmana might be removed from Shakra. Svayambhu thought of the great-souled Agni. He presented himself before Brahma and spoke these words. 'O illustrious god! O scorcher of enemies! I have presented myself before you. O god! You should tell me about the task that I have to accomplish.'

'"Brahma said, 'I will divide the sin of having killed a brahmana into many parts. For the sake of saving Shakra, accept one-fourth of it from me.'

'"Agni replied, 'O Brahma! O lord! But think of a means whereby I shall also be saved. O one who is revered by the worlds! I wish to know the truth about how that will come about.'

'"Brahma said, 'There will be people who will be enveloped by tamas. When they approach your blazing form, they will not offer seeds, herbs and juices into the fire. O bearer of oblations! The sin of having killed a brahmana will then swiftly leave you and enter into them. Let your mental anxiety be dispelled.'"

'Bhishma said, "Having been thus addressed by the grandfather, the illustrious lord who was the devourer of oblations[662] accepted this. The grandfather summoned trees, herbs and grass. O great king! To accomplish the objective, he spoke to them along similar lines.[663] O king! But the trees, herbs and grass were just as distressed as Agni and spoke to Brahma along similar lines. 'O grandfather of

[661]That killing a brahmana would be a sin.

[662]The text uses *havya-kavya* for oblations. Havya is oblations offered to the gods. Kavya means offerings to the wise and represents oblations offered to the ancestors.

[663]Asking them to accept one-fourth of the sin.

the worlds! If we accept the sin of having killed a brahmana, what will become of us? We are naturally afflicted and you are oppressing us again. O god! We always have to endure heat, cold, rain and wind, not to speak of the cutting down and chopping that we are subjected to. On your command, we will accept the sin of having killed a brahmana. O lord of the three worlds! But while we accept it, please think of a means so that we may be saved.'

'"Brahma said, 'If there is a man who is confounded by tamas and indulges in cutting down and chopping on auspicious days, then it[664] shall penetrate him.'"

'Bhishma said, "Thus addressed by the great-souled Brahma, the trees, herbs and grass worshipped him. They quickly went to wherever they had come from. The god who was the grandfather of the worlds then summoned the apsaras. O descendant of the Bharata lineage! He reassured them and spoke to them in gentle words. 'O ones with supreme limbs! Indra has been overcome by the sin of having killed a brahmana. Instructed by me, accept one-fourth of that.'

'"The apsaras replied, 'O lord of the gods! On your instructions, we will make up our minds to accept it. O grandfather! But let us have an agreement. Think of a means to save us.'

'"Brahma said, 'Do not have any mental anxiety. If a person has intercourse with a woman who is menstruating, it will leave you and quickly go to him.'"

'Bhishma said, "The large numbers of apsaras became cheerful at these words. O bull among the Bharata lineage! They went to their respective regions and pleasured there. The immensely ascetic god who was the creators of the three worlds then thought of the waters. When he thought of them and summoned them, all the waters appeared before the infinitely energetic Brahma. O king! They bowed down before the grandfather and spoke these words. 'O god! O scorcher of enemies! On your instructions, we have thus arrived before you. O lord of the gods! O lord! Command us.'

[664]The sin.

'"Brahma said, 'Puruhuta[665] is suffering from this great fear on Vritra's account. Accept one-fourth of the disquiet that has come about because of killing a brahmana.'

'"The waters replied, 'O lord of the worlds! O master! It shall be as you say. But let us have an agreement that you will think of a means for saving us. You are the lord of the gods. You are the supreme preceptor of the entire universe. Who else can grant us favours? Therefore, free us of the hardship.'

'"Brahma said, 'There will be a man with limited intelligence and confused understanding. He will release phlegm, urine and excrement into the water. It[666] will then swiftly leave you and begin to reside in him. You will be freed in this way. I am telling you this truthfully.'"

'Bhishma said, "O Yudhishthira! Thus Indra of the gods was freed from the sin of having killed a brahmana. On the instructions of the god,[667] it left him and went to the designated spots. O lord of men! In this way, Shakra was afflicted with the sin of having killed a brahmana. With the grandfather's permission, he decided to perform a horse sacrifice. O great king! It has been heard that Vasava was tainted by the sin of having killed a brahmana, but obtained purification through performing the horse sacrifice. The god regained his prosperity and slew thousands of enemies. O lord of the earth! Vasava obtained a great deal of delight. O Partha! Khurvundas[668] were born from Vritra's blood. That is the reason brahmanas and ascetics who have consecrated themselves do not eat these. In every situation, you must act so as to bring pleasure to brahmanas. O descendant of the Kuru lineage! They are said to be gods on earth. O Kouravya! In this way, Shakra used his subtle intelligence to decide in advance about means so that the infinitely energetic and great asura, Vritra, might be killed. O Kouravya! You will also be unvanquished on earth and be like the god Shatakratu, the slayer of enemies. If a person reads this divine account

[665]Indra's name, meaning worshipped by many.

[666]The sin.

[667]Brahma.

[668]This is almost certainly a typo, though it is difficult to figure out what this should be. Probably some kind of cock that scratches the ground is meant.

about Shakra, in the midst of brahmanas and on auspicious occasions, he will never be tainted by sin. This is the great and extraordinary account about Vritra's encounter with Shakra. O son! I have recounted that deed to you. What else do you desire to hear now?"'

Chapter 1602(274)

'Yudhishthira said, "O grandfather! O immensely wise one! You are accomplished in all the sacred texts. From this account about the slaying of Vritra, a question has arisen in my mind. O lord of men! You have said that Vritra was confused by a fever. O unblemished one! He was then slain by Vasava with the vajra. O immensely wise one! Where did this fever manifest itself from? O lord! I wish to hear the details about the origin of this fever."

'Bhishma replied, "O king! Listen to the origins of this fever. It is an account that is famous in the worlds. O descendant of the Bharata lineage! I will tell you in detail about how this came about. O great king! In ancient times, there was a summit in Meru that was famous in the three worlds. It was named Savitra. It was resplendent and was decorated with every kind of jewel. O descendant of the Bharata lineage! It was immeasurable and no one in the worlds could approach it. There was a bed on the slope of that mountain, adorned with gold and minerals. The dazzling god[669] was seated there. The shining daughter of the king of the mountains[670] was always seated by his side. The great-souled and immensely energetic gods, the Vasus, were also there and so were the great-souled Ashvins, supreme among physicians. King Vaishravana[671] was also there, served by the *guhyakas*.[672] He was the prosperous master and lord of the yakshas

[669]Shiva.

[670]Uma or Parvati.

[671]Kubera.

[672]Guhyakas are semi-divine species, companions of Kubera.

and Kailasa was his abode. There were the devarshis, with Angiras as the foremost. The gandharva Vishvavasu was there and Narada and Parvata. A large number of apsaras gathered there. An auspicious, sacred and pleasant breeze blew there, with many kinds of scents. In every direction, there were giant and blossoming trees. There were *vidyadharas* and ascetics who were stores of austerities. O descendant of the Bharata lineage! All of them worshipped Mahadeva Pashupati. O great king! There were many kinds of creatures, with diverse forms. There were extremely terrible rakshasas and immensely powerful pishachas. They were cheerful, with many kinds of forms, and they wielded diverse kinds of weapons. There were the companions of the god there, like the fire in their forms. The illustrious Nandi was there, ready to follow the instructions of the god. He wielded a flaming and blazing spear, resplendent in its own energy. O descendant of the Kuru lineage! Ganga, supreme among rivers, was there, the source of all the waters in the tirthas. In that form, she worshipped the god. Thus worshipped by the gods and the rishis, the illustrious and extremely fortunate god, Mahadeva, was established there.

'"After some time passed, Prajapati Daksha[673] followed the ancient rites and decided to perform a sacrifice. All the gods, with Shakra at the forefront, made up their minds to go to the sacrifice. Those great-souled ones ascended blazing celestial vehicles that were like the fire in complexion. It has been heard that they took the god's permission and went to Gangadvara.[674] On seeing that the gods had left, the virtuous daughter of the Himalayas spoke these words to her husband, the god Pashupati. 'O illustrious one! Where are the gods, with Shakra at the forefront, going? O one who knows

[673]Sati was originally born as Daksha's daughter, married to Shiva. She self-immolated herself at Daksha's sacrifice and was reborn as Uma or Parvati, the daughter of the Himalayas.

[674]Thus, the gods took Shiva's permission before going to the sacrifice. Daksha's sacrifice is believed to have taken place in Kankhal in Haridwar. Gangadvara is literally the gate of the Ganga, that is, the point from which the Ganga emerges. This is usually understood as Gomukh or Gomukha, where the Ganga becomes visible. However, the Ganga actually emerges unseen, 20 km away, on the Gangotri glacier.

about the truth! Tell me the truth about this. I have a great doubt on this account.'

'"Maheshvara replied, 'O immensely fortunate one! Daksha is the supreme lord of beings. He is performing a horse sacrifice and the residents of heaven are going there.'

'"Uma asked, 'O immensely fortunate one! Why are you not going to the sacrifice? Is there any reason preventing you from going there?'

'"Maheshvara replied, 'O immensely fortunate one! All the gods determined that I should not have a share in any of the sacrifices. O supreme among beautiful ones! That is the method that they had decided on earlier. And following that dharma, the gods do not give me a share in sacrifices.'

'"Uma said, 'O illustrious one! Among all beings, you are the supreme in qualities. In your energy, fame and prosperity, you cannot be vanquished and cannot be assailed. O immensely fortunate one! I am extremely miserable at this obstruction to you obtaining a share. O unblemished one! I am trembling.'"

'Bhishma said, "Having been thus addressed by the goddess, the god Pashupati, her husband, was silent. O king! His senses began to burn. He realized what was in the mind of the goddess and the desire of her heart. He summoned Nandi and asked him to wait there. The lord of all the lords of yoga resorted to the strength of his yoga. The god of the gods, the wielder of Pinaka, went to the sacrifice with his extremely energetic and terrible followers and destroyed it. Some of them[675] roared, others laughed. O king! Others extinguished the fire with blood. Some, with malformed faces, uprooted the sacrificial stakes and whirled them around. There were others who devoured the attendants with their mouths. O king! In every direction, the sacrifice was destroyed. It assumed the form of a deer and fled through the sky. But realizing that the sacrifice was running away in that form, the lord seized a bow and arrow and pursued it. The infinitely energetic lord of the gods was overcome by rage and a terrible drop of sweat manifested itself on

[675]The followers.

his forehead and fell down on the ground. From that, an extremely large fire resulted and it was like the fire of destruction. O bull among men! A man was born from that. He was short and his eyes were extremely red. He was dreadful and his beard was green. His hair stood up. He was covered with hair, like a hawk or an owl. He was horrible and dark in complexion. He was attired in red garments. That greatly spirited being destroyed the sacrifice, like a fire consuming deadwood. All the gods were terrified and fled in the ten directions. O lord of the earth! That man began to roam around everywhere on earth. O king! O bull among the Bharata lineage! Woes of lamentation, frightful to the worlds, arose. The grandfather manifested himself before Mahadeva and said, 'O lord! From now on, all the gods will give you a share in the sacrifices. O lord of all the gods! Withdraw the destruction that you have wrought. O scorcher of enemies! O Mahadeva! Because of your rage, all the gods and the rishis are finding it impossible to obtain peace. O supreme among gods! There is this man who has been born from your sweat. O one who knows about dharma! In the form of fever, let him wander around the worlds. O lord! If all of this energy is concentrated, the entire earth will not be able to bear it. Let it be divided into fragments and let there be safety.' The god was thus addressed by Brahma, who also decreed shares for him. He agreed to what the illustrious and infinitely energetic Brahma had said. The wielder of Pinaka was filled with great delight and smiled. Bhava accepted the share that Brahma had spoken about.

'"For the sake of peace for all beings, the one who knew about all forms of dharma divided the fever into many parts. O son! Listen to how he did this. O one who knows about dharma! The heat that is in the heads of elephants, in the bitumen in mountains, in the hornwort plants that float around in the water, in the cast-off skins of snakes, in diseases in the hooves of cattle, in sterile spots on the surface of the earth, in the dullness of sight of animals, in diseases that are in the throats of horses, in the crests of peacocks and in the eye diseases of cuckoos—the great-souled one decreed all these to be fever. We have heard all this and about the diseases that goats have in their livers and the hiccups that parrots suffer from. All of these are said to be fever. O one who knows about dharma! The exhaustion in tigers is said to be fever. O one who knows about dharma! There is also something known as fever among men. It penetrates men at the time of birth, death, and in the middle. This is Maheshvara's energy, known as extremely terrible fever. The lord of all beings must be worshipped and revered. When Vritra yawned, it is he who penetrated that supreme among the upholders of dharma. It was thus that Shakra could release his vajra at him. O descendant of the Bharata lineage! The vajra penetrated Vritra and shattered him. The great asura and great yogi was splintered by the vajra. He went to the infinitely energetic Vishnu's supreme region. Earlier, it was because of his devotion to Vishnu that he obtained the entire universe. Having been slain in the battle, he obtained Vishnu's region. O son! I have told you in detail about the great fever that Vritra was overwhelmed by. What else do you wish me to tell you? A man who is extremely controlled and reads this account about the origin of the fever with a cheerful mind, is freed from all disease. He is happy and full of delight. He obtains all the desires that are there in his mind."'

Chapter 1603(275)

'Yudhishthira asked, "O grandfather! Creatures are always terrified of sorrow and misery and death. O grandfather! Tell me how both of these can be prevented."

'Bhishma replied, "O descendant of the Bharata lineage! In this connection, there is an ancient history about a conversation between Narada and Samanga.

'"Narada said, 'You bow down with your chest and cross with your arms.[676] You are always cheerful and are seen to be without

[676]Prostrate yourself down, with the chest touching the ground. Crossing has the image of crossing the river of life and 'with your arms' probably signifies self-dependence, as compared to relying on others.

sorrow. One cannot discern the slightest bit of anxiety in you. You are always content and satisfied and seem to be like a child in your endeavours.'

'"Samanga replied, 'O one who grants honours! I know the truth about the past, the present and the future. Since I know the truth about these, I am never distressed. I also know about how exertions result and their fruits. There are many different kinds of fruits. Therefore, I am never distressed. O Narada! Behold. Those who are unfathomable in destitution, those who are not healthy and those who are blind and dumb are also alive. They are seen to live. It has been ordained that the residents of heaven should have no disease in their limbs. The strong and the weak are also thus created.[677] A person who rules over thousands is alive. A person who rules over hundreds is also alive. There are others who sustain themselves only on vegetables. Behold. I am also alive. O Narada! I do not grieve. What use do I have for dharma or deeds? One comes under the control of happiness that results from deeds and it is only misery that grows. When a person realizes that wisdom is actually the foundation of all the gratification of the senses, such a man is said to be wise. The senses cause confusion and sorrow. If a person is confounded because of the senses, such a person cannot obtain wisdom. A foolish person also suffers from pride and delusion. There is no world here, or in the hereafter, for a foolish person. Misery does not last forever. Any happiness obtained is also not eternal. Since I know that everything created is always changeable, a person like me never suffers from fever. I do not care for objects of desire or the happiness that results from possessions. Nor do I think about any unhappiness that may befall. I am controlled and do not desire the possessions of others. I do not bother about what has not been obtained. Nor do I find delight in what has been obtained. I am not delighted at obtaining a great deal of riches. Nor am I distressed if riches are destroyed. Relatives, riches, noble birth, learning, mantras and valour are incapable of saving one from miseries and they have to be tolerated. Good conduct alone

[677]Because of earlier deeds.

can bring peace in the world hereafter. If a person does not possess intelligence or yoga, he cannot obtain happiness. There cannot be any happiness without both fortitude and the abandoning of misery. Anything that brings delight is pleasant. But delight also increases pride. Pride leads to hell. That is the reason I have discarded these. Sorrow and fear cause delusion and so do pleasure and pain. I may move around in my body. But I look upon all these as an indifferent witness. I have abandoned all desire for riches. I am bereft of sorrow and bereft of fever. I roam around the entire earth, having discarded thirst and confusion. There is no death. There is no adharma. Where will greed come from? I have drunk amrita. I have no fear in this world and in the next. Because of the great and undecaying austerities that I have performed, I have got to know the brahman. O Narada! Having obtained that, there is no grief that can constrain me.'"'

Chapter 1604(276)

'Yudhishthira asked, "O grandfather! There may be a person who does not know the truth about the sacred texts. He may always have doubts in his mind. He may not be accomplished in his conduct. What is best for him? Tell me."

'Bhishma replied, "The worship of seniors, serving the aged and listening to the learned and the superior—these are said to be the best. In this connection, an ancient history is recounted about a conversion between Galava and devarshi Narada. That brahmana was free from confusion and fatigue. He was content in his knowledge and had conquered his senses. Having conquered his atman, but desiring to know what was best for himself, Galava spoke to Narada. 'There are qualities that are revered among men. I can see all those qualities, in undecaying form, in you. There are several doubts in those like us. Therefore, you should sever them. We are foolish and will always remain stupid. We do not know the truth about the worlds. Should there be an inclination towards knowledge and the renunciation of acts? How does one know which acts to undertake? What are the tasks one should not undertake? You should speak about these to us. O illustrious one! All the ashramas indicate different kinds of conduct. Some say, this is superior. Others say, that is superior. We are driven in different directions. Therefore, it is seen that even those who resort to the sacred texts do not take delight in all the sacred texts. They are satisfied with their own sacred texts and do not necessarily realize what is superior. Had all the sacred texts been unified, the best would have manifested itself. But because there are many kinds of sacred texts, what is best is immersed in a mystery. That is the reason why the superior appears to me in a confused form. O illustrious one! I have resorted to you. You should instruct me.'

'"Narada replied, 'O son![678] There are four ashramas and they were thought of in separate ways.[679] O Galava! Examine all of them and then choose the one you wish to resort to. Those ashramas differ from each other. They speak of many different kinds of qualities and instructions. These are not only distinct, they are also contradictory. But if one considers them, free from doubt, one sees that all of them convey to what is appropriate. Behold. All the ashramas lead straight to the appropriate and supreme objective. There can be no doubt in one's mind about what is appropriate and beneficial—favour to friends, suppression of enemies and accumulation for pursuing the three objectives.[680] The learned ones have said that these are beneficial. One must always abstain from wicked deeds and be auspicious in conduct. One must exhibit good conduct towards those who are virtuous. There is no doubt that these are beneficial. Mildness towards all beings, uprightness in conduct and pleasantness in speech—there is no doubt that these

[678]The word used is tata.

[679]It is by no means obvious that this refers to the ashramas of brahmacharya, garhasthya, vanaprastha and sannyasa. It might also refer to different kinds of religious belief.

[680]Dharma, artha and kama.

have been said to be beneficial. Giving the appropriate shares to gods, ancestors, guests and not depriving servants—there is no doubt that these are beneficial. Truthfulness in speech is beneficial. But ascertaining true knowledge is extremely difficult. I am telling you the truth when I say that one must ensure welfare towards all beings. The renouncing of pride, the suppression of attachment, contentment and following one's own conduct—the wise say that these are beneficial. Following dharma and studying the Vedas and the Vedangas and inquisitiveness for the sake of knowledge—there is no doubt that these are beneficial. O scorcher of enemies! A person who seeks excellence must not enjoy sound, form, taste, touch and scent for their sake alone, without some other objective in mind. A person who seeks excellence must give up roaming around in the night, sleep during the day, idleness, calumny, pride, excessive indulgence and complete abstinence.[681] One must not seek to establish that one's own deeds and path are superior by deprecating others. Through one's own qualities, one will be able to establish that the path followed is superior and different from that followed by other people. There are many men who are devoid of qualities, but are full of self-pride. They find faults in those who possess qualities. They inflict their own undecaying qualities on others. When they are not restrained, they think of themselves as great people. Thinking their own qualities to be superior, they are full of insolence and pride. They are learned people who possess qualities and they obtain great fame, but without speaking censorious words about others, or describing the honour that is due to their own selves. Pure ones with excellent minds are like fragrant flowers. They do not have to speak about their own selves. The sparkling sun, with dispersing rays in the sky, is also like that. In this way, there are others who renounce, using their intelligence. Nevertheless, their fame blazes in the world and is not reduced. A foolish person cannot blaze in the world through his self-praise alone. However, a person who is accomplished in his learning manifests himself, even

[681]Indulgence and abstinence refer to the objects of the senses.

if he is hidden in a hole. Wicked words, even if spoken loudly, are soon pacified. But excellent words, even if spoken gently, illuminate the worlds. Foolish ones, who are full of their own insolence, speak many futile words. However, the sun in heaven displays its own inner self. That is the reason one searches for different kinds of wisdom. It seems to me that the obtaining of wisdom is the supreme objective for creatures. One should not speak until one is asked. Nor should one speak if asked improperly. In this world, a person who is learned and intelligent behaves like one who is dumb. One must scrutinize and dwell with virtuous people who are always devoted to dharma. They are generous men who are devoted to their own dharma. A person who desires benefit must never dwell with the four varnas when they act contrary to the dharma. In this world, one should abstain from embarking on any action, but should subsist on whatever has been obtained. Dwelling among the meritorious, one will obtain sparkling merits. But dwelling among the wicked, one will obtain sin. One can comprehend the touch of the water, the fire, or the rays of the moon. In that way, one can discern the touch of both the wicked and the virtuous. There may be those who do not look towards enjoying material objects and eat only leftovers. However, if a person is still concerned with the flavours of the food, know that he is still bound by material objects and deeds. A brahmana may be asked and may discourse about dharma, when asked. But if he has not been asked reverentially, one must abandon that spot. Instead, there may be a spot where there is a controlled discourse, following the sacred texts, between disciples and a preceptor. Who will abandon that spot? Without any foundation, there may be ignorant people who wish to earn respect for themselves, who speak about taints, though none exists. Which learned person will dwell there? There may often be greedy people, who try to agitate the boundaries of dharma, like setting fire at the extremities of a mountain. Who will not abandon such a spot? One should dwell and roam among virtuous people who are auspicious in their conduct. Dharma is followed there, without any doubt and without any malice. One should not dwell in places where men pursue dharma only for the sake of artha. Those are people who are wicked in their conduct. One must swiftly flee from places where wicked deeds are performed with a desire to ensuring sustenance, as if from a room where there is a snake. Right from the beginning, one must act with a desire to realize one's own atman. One must not engage in tasks that make one stretch out on a bed.[682] Where the king, royal officers and those who are in charge of the frontier regions eat before their relatives, a person who is in control of his atman must abandon that kingdom. One must dwell in a kingdom where learned brahmanas, who are always devoted to eternal dharma and are engaged in performing sacrifices and studying, are fed first. Without any reflection, one must dwell in a place where svaha, svadha and *vashatkara* are properly uttered numerous times. Where brahmanas are seen to be engaged in inauspicious acts, one must swiftly abandon that kingdom, as if it is a piece of poisoned meat. Where men cheerfully give before they have been asked, a person who has accomplished his tasks and is based on his own atman, must dwell there. One must roam and dwell among virtuous people, those who are righteous in their conduct, where there is punishment for those who are wicked and reverence for those who are cleansed in their souls. In those places, those who are not generous, those who are wicked and evil in conduct and those who are unruly and greedy are afflicted with extremely severe chastisement. Those are places where the king and the kingdom always serve dharma, desiring purity and without falling prey to desire. Without any reflection, those are places one should dwell in. When the king displays such conduct, everyone enjoys prosperity. Benefit is swiftly obtained and welfare presents itself. O son! You asked me and I have thus told you about what is beneficial. But I am incapable of enumerating what is most important, what brings benefit to the atman. There is conduct that has been ordained for the benefit of the atman. It is evident that there are many kinds of austerities that will bring about that benefit.'"'

[682]There is an image that requires interpretation. That image is one of deeds tying one down to the consequences, leading to death and rebirth, as if one is stretched out on a bed of thorns.

Chapter 1605(277)

'Yudhisthira asked, "How should a king who has been emancipated move around on earth? What qualities should he always possess, so that he is freed from the noose of attachment?"

'Bhishma replied, "In this connection, there is an ancient history about what Arishtanemi spoke when Sagara asked him."

'"Sagara asked, 'O brahmana! What is supremely beneficial? What action enables one to obtain happiness? How does one avoid grief and agitation? I wish to know about this.'"

'Bhishma said, "Tarkshya[683] was knowledgable about all the sacred texts. He also knew that the person who was before him deserved to hear virtuous words. Having been asked, he said, 'The real happiness in the world is the happiness that comes from emancipation. People do not understand this, because they are attached to sons and animals and anxious about riches and grain. If the intelligence is full of attachment and if the atman is not tranquil, treatment is impossible. A stupid person who is tied to the bonds of affection cannot be free. I will tell you about the bonds that result from affection. Listen to them. Using the ears and the head, one is capable of knowing and severing them. At the right time, one must have offspring. When they attain youth, after ascertaining that they are capable of earning a living, one should be cheerful and roam around free. When one's wife has had a son that she is devoted to, when she is aged and is affectionately attended to by that son, know that this is the time to depart and search for a superior objective. However, whether one has obtained offspring or one has not obtained offspring, the senses and the objects of the senses have been pursued in the proper way. Therefore, one should be cheerful and roam free. One has performed one's tasks. One should be inquisitive and cheerful, roaming freely. One must be equal vis-à-vis what has been gained and the reasons that do not lead to any gain. I have recounted this briefly to you. I will again tell you in detail about

[683]Arishtanemi was descended from Tarkshya.

the objective of emancipation. Listen. A free man roams around happily in this world, bereft of fear. There is no doubt that a man who has sentiments of attachment is destroyed, just like insects and ants engaged in the accumulation of food. Those who are detached are happy in this world. Those with attachments are destroyed. A person whose intelligence has turned towards emancipation has no business to think about his relatives, such as, "How will these people survive without me?" A creature is born on its own. A creature grows on its own. A creature advances towards happiness, unhappiness and death on its own. In this world, people do not obtain anything because of anything that they have done, or because of the food and garments that have been stored up by their mother and father. It is all because of what they have done earlier. On earth, the one who ordain has laid down food for all living beings. Though people run after it, this has actually been determined by their own acts. A man is himself like a lump of clay. He is always under someone else's control. What is the reason behind sustaining one's relatives? Instead, one should be firm in protecting one's atman. While you look on, your relatives will be slain by death, even if you make great efforts. Therefore, know your own atman. While they are still alive and you are engaged in sustaining and protecting them, you may have to give it up incomplete, since you end up dying. In that way, when your relatives die, you will never know whether they are happy or miserable. Therefore, you should know your own atman. While you are alive, these people die or are freed because of their own deeds. Therefore, one should turn one's intelligence towards ensuring welfare for the atman. In this world, since one knows this, how does one determine who belongs to whom? Therefore, fix your mind on emancipation. I am entreating you again. A man who has conquered hunger and thirst and similar sentiments, and also anger, greed and confusion, such a spirited person is indeed free. If a man is not distracted by gambling, drinking, women and hunting and is not confused, such a person is free. If a man is only anxious about what he will enjoy from one day to another day and from one night to another night, his intelligence is said to be tainted. A person who always realizes that his birth is due to nothing but attachment for women, such a person is free. In this world, a person who knows the truth about the birth, destruction and exertion of beings is indeed free. A person who sees no difference between a handful of corn and thousands of crores of carts loaded with it, or a person who sees no difference between a palace and a clump of bamboos is free. The world suffers from death and is afflicted by disease and oppressed by famine. A person who sees this is free. A person who sees it in this way is happy and content. A person who does not see this, is destroyed. If a person is satisfied with only a trifle, he is free in this world. A person who sees that everything is destroyed, as if by fire, and is not touched by sentiments on account of this, is free. If a person regards a bed and the bare earth, or *shali* rice and awful food, as equal, he is free. If a person regards linen and grass or rags, silk and bark, sheepskin and ordinary leather, as equal, such a person is free. A person who sees that everything in this world results from the five elements and having seen this, acts in accordance with this, is free. If a person regards happiness and unhappiness, gain and lack of gain, victory and defeat, like and dislike, fear and anxiety[684] as equal, he is always free. The body is full of many taints, it is a store of imperfections like blood, urine and excrement. A person who sees it in this way is free. It is subject to decay, wrinkles, emaciation, paleness, bending down and old age. One who sees it in this way is free. In the course of time, there is impotence, weakness of sight, deafness and a slowdown in the life force. One who sees it in this way is free. The rishis, the gods and the asuras have gone from this world to other superior worlds. One who sees it in this way is free. There are thousands of powerful lords of the earth who have had to leave the earth and depart. A person who knows this is free. In this world, the accumulation of riches is extremely difficult. Hardship is extremely easy. There is misery on account of relatives. A person who sees this is free. There are offspring without qualities. There are people without qualities. If a person repeatedly sees this in the world, why should he not hanker after emancipation? There may be a man who sees everything in the

[684]Lack of fear, or lack of anxiety, would have fit better.

world on the basis of the intelligence of the sacred texts. He sees that everything human is without substance. Such a person is free in every way. Having heard these words of mine, you should always roam around as if you are free. Whether you pursue garhasthya or whether you pursue emancipation, act so that your intelligence is not clouded.' On hearing these words attentively, the lord of the earth[685] protected the subjects, acquiring qualities that are conducive to emancipation."'

Chapter 1606(278)

'Yudhishthira asked, "O father! There has always been a curiosity in my heart. O grandfather of the Kuru lineage! I wish to hear the truth about this from you. Devarshi Ushanas[686] was always engaged in what was agreeable to the asuras and unpleasant for the gods. Why was he then called the immensely intelligent Kavya? Why did the infinitely energetic one always increase their energy?[687] Why were the danavas always engaged in enmity with the supreme among the gods? How did Ushanas, as radiant as an immortal, become Shukra? How did he obtain prosperity? Tell me everything about this. Though he possesses energy, why can he never go to the middle of the sky?[688] O grandfather! I wish to know everything about this."

'Bhishma replied, "O king! With undivided attention, listen to what exactly transpired. O unblemished one! I will tell you what I have heard earlier, as I have understood it. This sage, heir of the Bhargava lineage,[689] was truthful and firm in his vows. Because of

[685]Sagara.

[686]Shukracharya, the preceptor of the demons. Kavya was his name, meaning the wise one.

[687]Of the demons.

[688]Shukra is the planet Venus and this is a reference to that.

[689]Shukra was descended from Bhrigu.

the compassion in his soul, he became engaged in ensuring what was pleasant for the asuras. The lord of riches,[690] the king of the yakshas and the rakshasas, was entrused with superintendence of the treasure house of Indra, the lord of the universe. The great sage[691] was accomplished in yoga. He used yoga to enter the lord of riches and bind up that god. He robbed him of his riches. On seeing that his riches had been seized, the lord of riches could find no peace. Anxious and filled with rage, he approached the infinitely energetic Shiva, supreme among the gods, and told him everything. This was the foremost among the gods, who possessed many forms, terrible and amiable. Kubera said, 'Using his yoga, Ushanas bound me and stole my riches. The immensely ascetic one entered my body through yoga and has thereafter left.' On hearing this, the great yogi, Maheshvara, became angry. O king! His eyes were red and he stood there, with his spear. Having grasped that supreme weapon, he asked, 'Where is he? Where is he?' However, from a distance, Ushanas got to know what he[692] desired. The great-souled one got to know about the great yogi's rage. The lord did not know whether he should run away, advance,[693] or stay in the same spot. He used his fierce austerities to think about the great-souled Maheshvara. Ushanas was accomplished in the use of yoga. He next used this to place himself at the tip of the spear. The archer[694] comprehended that the one who had obtained success in austerities had assumed that form. The lord of the gods therefore bent the bow with his hand. The infinitely energetic lord used his hand to bend the spear down and the terrible weapon that was the spear came to be known as Pinaka.[695] Thus, Uma's consort saw that Bhargava had now been

[690]Kubera.

[691]Ushanas. Ushanas penetrated Kubera.

[692]Shiva.

[693]Towards Shiva.

[694]Shiva.

[695]Since Ushanas was on the tip, the spear could not be hurled. Pinaka is the name of both Shiva's bow and trident and the two are being equated here, with the spear bent into the form of a bow. The etymology of Pinaka is based on its being bent with the hand (*pani*).

brought into the palm of his hand. Kakudi[696] opened his mouth and used his hand to swiftly fling him inside. The lord Ushanas entered Maheshvara's stomach. The great-souled descendant of the Bhrigu lineage began to wander around there."

'Yudhishthira asked, "O king! How could the intelligent Ushanas roam around inside the stomach of the god of the gods? What did the immensely resplendent rishi do there?"

'Bhishma replied, "O king! In that ancient time, the one who was great in his vows[697] entered the water and remained there, immobile like a pillar, for a million years. He performed extremely difficult austerities in that great lake and then arose. Brahma, the first god among the gods, approached and asked him whether he was hale and well and whether his austerities had prospered. The one with the bull on the banner[698] replied that the austerities had proceeded well. Shankara was immensely intelligent and is impossible to fathom. He is always devoted to the dharma of truth. Through yoga, he saw the growth inside.[699] The great yogi[700] was prosperous because of austerities and riches. O great king! The one who was valiant in the three worlds was roaming around inside. At this, the wielder of Pinaka, with yoga in his atman, entered the yoga of meditation. The extremely anxious Ushanas continued to wander around inside the stomach. But though located there, the great yogi[701] tried to please the god from there. He desired to emerge and craved that the energy might be withdrawn. From inside the stomach, the great sage, Ushanas, said, 'Show me your favours.' O scorcher of enemies! He said this repeatedly. Mahadeva replied, 'Go. Free yourself through my penis.' Earlier, the bull among the thirty gods had closed all the other outlets. On seeing that the doors had been closed on every side, the sage roamed around here and there, being burnt by the

[696]Shiva's name, literally meaning the bull.

[697]Shiva.

[698]Shiva.

[699]Ushanas was growing inside the stomach.

[700]Ushanas.

[701]Ushanas.

energy. He finally emerged through the penis and came to be known as Shukra.[702] That is the reason he is never able to go to the middle of the firmament. On seeing him emerge, flaming in energy, Bhava was filled with rage and stood there, with the spear in his hand. However, the goddess restrained her angry husband, Pashupati. When Shankara was restrained by the goddess in this way, he came to be regarded as her son.[703]

'"The goddess said, 'You should not cause any injury to him. He has become your son and my son. O god! Someone who has emerged from your stomach does not deserve to be destroyed.'"

'Bhishma said, "Bhava was pleased by these words of the goddess. O king! He smiled and repeatedly spoke these words. 'Let him go wherever he wishes.' He bowed down before the god who is the granter of boons and also the goddess Uma. The intelligent and great sage, Ushanas, went to his desired destination. O son! O best among the Bharata lineage! I have thus spoken to you about the great-souled Bhargava and his conduct. That is what you had asked me about."'

Chapter 1607(279)

'Yudhishthira said, "O mighty-armed one! After this, tell me what is best for me. O grandfather! I am not satisfied with your words, which are like amrita. O supreme among men! What are the auspicious acts a man can perform, so that he obtains supreme benefit in this world and in the world after death? Tell me that."

'Bhishma replied, "In this connection, I will tell you what the immensely illustrious King Janaka asked the great-souled Parashara in ancient times. 'What is best for all beings here and in the hereafter, so that one can obtain prosperity? Tell me about this.' The sage

[702]Shukra means semen.

[703]Ushanas came to be regarded as Parvati's son.

was full of austerities and knew about the ordinances associated with all kinds of dharma. To show favours to the king, he spoke these words. 'Deeds of dharma bring benefit in this world and in the next. The learned ones have said that there is nothing that is superior to this. Through such dharma, a man obtains greatness in the world of heaven. O supreme among kings! For all beings, the rites and ordinances that have been laid down represent the essence of dharma. That is the reason virtuous people perform their respective acts in their respective ashramas. O son![704] Four kinds of modes have been laid down for progress in this world.[705] When mortals follow these, they obtain what they desire. They perform good and bad deeds and attain their respective ends. In different ways, creatures are divided into five elements. Just as a golden or silver vessel reflects the sheen of the metal, creatures are bound down by the acts that they have performed earlier. Nothing is generated without a seed. Without acting for it, happiness cannot be obtained. When the body is destroyed, a man obtains happiness because of the good deeds he has performed. O son! I do not see any destiny in this, nor any action on the part of the gods. Gods, gandharvas and danavas become what they are because of their natures. After death, people never remember what they have done in their earlier lives. But they obtain the consequences of the four kinds of acts that they have performed.[706] For progress in the world, the words of the Vedas have described the deeds that one must resort to. O son! That is what brings peace to the mind, not merely the instructions of the elders. There are four kinds of action one can perform with the eye, the mind, words and deeds. Whatever the nature of the action, the consequence is like that. O king! Often, one obtains mixed consequences as a result of a deed. However, whether it is good or bad, deeds are never destroyed. O son! Sometimes, the consequences of good deeds remain concealed and submerged in the cycle of life,

[704]The word used is tata.

[705]This refers to the four varnas.

[706]Acts are divided into *nitya* (daily), *naimittika* (occasional), *kamya* (desirable) and *nishiddha* (prohibited).

one is not freed from misery. However, once the misery has been exhausted, the results of good deeds will become evident. O lord of men! Know that when good deeds have been exhausted, the results of bad deeds will become evident. Self-control, forgiveness, fortitude, energy, contentment, truthfulness, modesty, lack of injury, not indulging in vices and skilfulness—these are the things that yield happiness. For no creature are the effects of good deeds and bad deeds eternal. That is the reason an accomplished person always tries to fix his mind. One does not face the consequences of the good or bad deeds performed by another person. The consequences one reaps are commensurate with the deeds that one has performed. Along one path,[707] a man can give up both happiness and unhappiness. O king! But there are many other people who are always prone to attachment. A man must never undertake an act that he censures in someone else. If he does something like this, he will be laughed at. A king who is a coward, a brahmana who eats everything, a vaishya without exertion, an inferior varna[708] who is lazy, a learned person who lacks good conduct, a noble person who is without a means of sustenance, a brahmana who has deviated from the truth, a wayward woman, a 'free' person who is still attached, a person who cooks only for himself, a foolish person who is eloquent, a kingdom without a king and a king who has no affection for his subjects—all these are reasons for grief.'""

Chapter 1608(280)

'"Parashara said, 'A person who drives the chariot[709] in accordance with his wishes, controlling the horses that are the objects of the senses with the reins of knowledge, is intelligent. A person who serves these with his mind, even if he does not possess

[707]The path of knowledge.

[708]Meaning a shudra.

[709]An image for the body.

a means of sustenance, is praised. A brahmana and a person who has refrained from action are not equal to each other.[710] O lord of the earth! Having obtained a designated span of life, one should not diminish it. A man must strive for auspicious deeds, so that he can improve himself. A person who has been dislodged from his varna deserves to be censured. A person who has obtained the consequences of good deeds must not perform deeds associated with rajas. A man obtains a superior varna through auspicious deeds. However, having obtained what is difficult to obtain, one destroys it because one is overcome with tamas and performs wicked deeds. Wicked deeds perpetrated due to ignorance can be destroyed through the practice of austerities. But a wicked deed that is perpetrated knowingly leads to evil consequences. Therefore, one must never perform wicked deeds. They lead to miserable consequences. An intelligent person will never be bound down by wicked deeds, even if they lead to great fruits, just as an auspicious person will not touch water that has been tainted. As the fruits of wicked deeds, I see great hardships. Though virtue and the atman are evident, one acts perversely and contrary to this. If a foolish person does not turn back, he is like a person who is dead and faces great wickedness. A garment that is not dyed can be cleaned, but not one that has been dyed black. O Indra among men! Listen to me. That is also the case with sinful efforts. If a man knowingly performs wicked deeds and then performs good ones in atonement, he will separately obtain the fruits of both.[711] Brahmanas who know about the brahman mention the instructions of the sacred texts. If an act of injury is committed in ignorance, an act of non-injury can correct it. However, if an act of violence is committed knowingly, brahmanas who are accomplished in the Vedas and versed in the sacred texts, say that this is an act of adharma. I see that all the acts that are performed, good or evil ones, lead to manifestations of their qualities. All deeds that are performed, using the intelligence and the mind, lead to corresponding fruits, gross or subtle. O one who knows about dharma! But acts that are done involuntarily lead

[710]The person who has refrained from action is superior.

[711]The good and the evil.

to smaller fruits. Fierce deeds performed knowingly always lead to strong consequences. There may be acts that are performed by gods and sages.[712] If a person with dharma in his soul hears about these, he should not censure them. But nor should he practise them. O king! One should use one's mind to reflect on one's own capacity. A person who performs auspicious deeds sees what is fortunate. If a vessel is new,[713] water placed into it gradually becomes less and less. But that is not the case if the vessel has been baked. One obtains happiness through such sentiments. When water is poured into a vessel that already has water, the quantity of the water is increased. Intelligence is also increased in that way. O lord of the earth! That is the way one should perform deeds on earth, using one's intelligence. One's store of merits is then not diminished, but added to. A king's proper duty is to protect the subjects, raising his weapons to subjugate those who are unruly. He must kindle many fires and perform sacrifices. Then, in middle or old ages, he must resort to the forest. Self-controlled and with dharma in conduct, a man must look upon all beings as one's own self. One must worship those who are superior and disabled. O Indra among men! Through truthfulness and good conduct, one obtains happiness.'"'

Chapter 1609(281)

'"Parashara said, 'No one does a favour to another. No one gives anything to another. In every way, all creatures only act for their own selves. When there is a lack of affection, one's own uterine brothers are proudly discarded. What should one say about unrelated people? Giving gifts to superior people and receiving gifts from superior people are equal. But among these, the gift given to a brahmana is more sacred. With the objectives of dharma and artha

[712]That is, inappropriate acts.

[713]An earthen vessel that has not been baked.

in mind, each of the varnas must endeavour to protect riches earned through fair means, and increase them. For the sake of dharma and artha, one should not undertake tasks that seek to obtain wealth through injurious means. One must remember the virtuous and perform all tasks according to one's capacity. According to one's capacity, if one gives cool water or that heated through a fire to a guest, one obtains fruits that are like those got by giving food to someone hungry. The great-souled Rantideva obtained success in the world. But all he did was to worship hermits with fruits, leaves and roots. Shaibya, lord of the earth, satisfied Mathara[714] with fruits and leaves and obtained a supreme region. Through being born, mortal people incur debts to gods, guests, servants, ancestors and their own selves and one must act so as to repay these debts. There is studying for maharshis, sacrifices and rites for gods, funeral sacrifices and donations for ancestors and honouring for men.[715] Debts to one's own self are repaid through words,[716] eating leftovers and protecting one's own self. If one is interested in following dharma, right from the beginning, one should discharge debts to the various categories of servants. Even if one is devoid of riches, one can make efforts to obtain success. Hermits offered oblations of clarified butter into the fire and obtained success. Vishvamitra's son went to Richika's son.[717] The mighty-armed one worshipped the gods who have shares in sacrifices with hymns from the Rig Veda. Through the favours of the god of the gods,[718] Ushanas became Shukra. Through praising the goddess, he was surrounded by energy and found pleasure in the sky.[719] Asita-Devala, Narada and Parvata, Kakshivat, Jamadagni's son Rama, Tandya, Anshuman, Vasishtha, Jamadagni, Vishvamitra,

[714]One of the attendants of the sun god, though this is a term also used for Vyasadeva.

[715]These are means of repaying those respective debts.

[716]Probably the words of the sacred texts.

[717]This is unclear. Richika's son was Jamadagni. Vishvamitra's son was Koushika. So Koushika must have gone to Jamadagni.

[718]Shiva.

[719]As the planet Venus.

Atri, Bharadvaja, Harishmashru, Kundadhara, Shrutashrava—these maharshis controlled themselves and praised Vishnu, using hymns from the Rig Veda. Through the favours of that intelligent one, they obtained success in their austerities. By praising him, even those who are undeserving have become deserving and virtuous. One should not desire to perform acts that increase one's prosperity in this world. Riches obtained through dharma are true riches. Shame on those obtained through adharma. Dharma is eternal in this world and must not be abandoned for the sake of riches. A person who has dharma in his soul and makes offerings to the fire is supreme among the performers of auspicious deeds. O Indra among kings! O lord! All the Vedas are established on the three fires.[720] If a brahmana possesses the sacred fire, his deeds are never diminished. However, if one does not perform the rites of agnihotra, it is better to give up the sacred fire. O tiger among men! The sacred fire, the mother, the father who has provided the seed and the preceptor must be served in the proper way. If a man abandons pride and serves the aged, if he is learned, if he behaves as if he is impotent,[721] if he looks upon everything with affection, if he is accomplished and if he is non-violent—even if he does not possess wealth, he is worshipped in this world as a virtuous and noble person.'"'

Chapter 1610(282)

'"Parashara said, 'It is appropriate that the inferior varna[722] should earn a living by serving the other three. If this designated service is rendered affectionately, that person always remains devoted to dharma. Even if the ancestors of the shudra were not engaged in such an occupation, it is certain that he should not

[720]Dakshina, garhapatya and ahavaniya.

[721]Gives up sexual desire.

[722]A shudra.

engage himself in any means of sustenance other than servitude. It is my view that under all circumstances, it is proper that they[723] should always associate with virtuous people who know about dharma, not with those who are wicked. When they are close to Mount Udaya,[724] objects blaze. Similarly, an inferior varna blazes when it is associated with the virtuous. A white garment assumes the colour with which it is dyed. They assume their appearances in the same way. Therefore, one should rejoice because of qualities and never because of taints. The lifespan of mortals, whether mobile or immobile, is temporary. If an accomplished person only acts in accordance with good policy, whether he faces joy or misery, he faces fortune in this world. An intelligent person does not deviate from virtue, even if that act of deviation from dharma yields great fruits. If a king steals thousands of unprotected cattle and then gives them away as a gift, he only obtains the fruits that the sound of that action makes. He is actually a thief. Right at the beginning, Svayambhu created Dhata, revered in the worlds. Dhata created a son who is engaged in sustaining beings.[725] It is through worshipping him that vaishyas earn wealth and prosperity. The kings must think of means to protect brahmanas. Shudras should, honestly, faithfully and without anger, clean the objects used to offer havya and kavya. Through such acts, dharma is not destroyed. If dharma is not destroyed, subjects are happy. O Indra among kings! Through their happiness, the gods in heaven are delighted. A king who follows dharma and protects is revered. So are brahmanas who study, vaishyas who are enaged in the welfare of people and shudras who serve, always in control of their senses. O Indra among men! If they act in any other way, they deviate from their own dharma. Not to speak of thousands, even if a few *kakinis*[726] are earned lawfully and donated, without causing grief to one's life, that leads to great fruits. If a lord of men honours brahmanas and always donates to

[723]This is specifically directed at shudras.

[724]The mountain behind which the sun rises.

[725]Dhata's son is regarded as the god of the clouds.

[726]Cowrie shells used as money.

them, he earns fruits that are commensurate. If one seeks out the donee and satisfies him, that is said to be the best. When one gives when asked, the learned say that this is medium. Sages who are truthful in speech say that gifts given indifferently and disrespectfully are the worst. Through transgressions, men are always submerged in different ways. Therefore, one should make efforts so that one is freed from one's doubts. A brahmana is always radiant through self-control, a kshatriya through victory, a vaishya through riches and a shudra through skill.'"'

Chapter 1611(283)

'"Parashara said, 'Whatever little riches a brahmana obtains through receiving gifts, a kshatriya through conquest by weapons, a vaishya through lawful means and a shudra through servitude, are praised. When spent for dharma, these yield great fruits. It is said that the shudra must always serve the three varnas. But if a brahmana doesn't have means of sustenance and follows the dharma of kshatriyas or the dharma of vaishyas, he suffers no downfall. But if a brahmana follows the dharma of shudras, then he does face a downfall. When a shudra does not possess a means of sustenance, then trade, animal husbandry and subsistence on the basis of artisanship are recommended for him. If a person has not engaged in such occupations earlier, then descending in an arena,[727] earning a living through one's beauty and earning a living through the sales of liquor, flesh, iron and leather are not recommended. These are censured in the world. It has been heard that if one has been engaged in such tasks and has then given them up, this leads to great dharma. In this world, it is said that if a successful man is overcome by arrogance in his mind and acts wickedly, that cannot be accepted. It has been heard in the ancient accounts that subjects used

[727]Probably actors.

to be self-controlled and placed dharma at the forefront, following the fair policy of dharma. Shaming them through words was sufficient chastisement. O king! At that time, dharma alone was praised among men. Men on earth served and extended the qualities of dharma. O son! O lord of men! But the asuras could not tolerate this. They increased themselves and gradually penetrated the subjects. Because of this, insolence was generated among subjects and this destroyed dharma. Resulting from insolence, anger was again generated within them. Having been overcome with anger, their conduct became shameful. O king! When they were overcome with lack of modesty, confusion was generated in them. Having become overcome with confusion, they no longer looked at things the way they had done earlier. They cheerfuly conducted themselves and crushed each other. Shaming them through words was no longer sufficient chastisement then. They served their senses and no longer showed respect towards gods and brahmanas. At this time, the gods sought refuge with Shiva, supreme among the gods, the brave one with many forms and the lord of the ganas. With the combined energy of the gods, with a single arrow, he brought down the three cities from the sky onto the ground.[728] Their lord was terrible and fearsome in valour, frightful to the gods. But he was slain by the wielder of the trident. When he was slain, men regained their own nature. As was the case earlier, the Vedas and the sacred texts were revived. The saptarshis instated Vasava in the kingdom of the gods in heaven and he was given the task of wielding the staff of chastisement over men. After the saptarshis, there were the king named Viprithu and several other kshatriyas who became kings over separate categories. However, even when they were born in great lineages, there were some who continued to follow the earlier conduct. Their hearts were full of sentiments like that of the asuras. Because of those sentiments, those kings, terrible in valour, continued to be attached to deeds that were like those of the asuras. Men who are exceedingly foolish continue

[728]This is the story of Tripura, the three cities of the asuras in the sky, destroyed by Shiva. However, this is sometimes interpreted in metaphorical fashion, the three cities standing for desire, anger and greed.

to be devoted to such acts, rever them and establish them. O king! That is the reason I am telling you that you must reflect about the sacred texts. You must discard all notions of violence within you and act so as to obtain success. An accomplished person does not think of obtaining riches by mixing up the means. For the sake of dharma or artha, he does not abandon what is proper. That is not said to be the way towards welfare. It is recommended that a kshatriya should be self-controlled, affectionate towards relatives and protect subjects, servants and sons in accordance with his own dharma. Because of prosperity and adversity, there can be enmity and affection. One is born and circles around in thousands of lives in many ways. Find delight in the qualities and never in sins. Even if a person is evil-minded and devoid of qualities, he realizes this internally. O great king! Dharma and adharma are prevalent among men. Other than men, these notions are not seen to exist in other creatures. Whether a man is concerned with this life or is not concerned with this life, he must be learned and must follow dharma in conduct. He must cause injury and must always regard everyone like his own self. When there is no longer any desire in the mind, there is no longer any falsehood and one desires what is beneficial.'"'

Chapter 1612(284)

'"Parashara said, 'O son! I have told you about the dharma that is recommended for householders. I will now tell you about the techniques for austerities. Listen attentively. O best among men! It is often seen that because of being overcome with tamas and rajas, householders suffer from attachment and have a sense of ownership. Since they resort to homes, men acquire cattle, fields, riches, wives, sons and servants. In their conduct, they are always seen to look towards these. Their attachment and aversion are always seen to increase. Overcome by attachment and aversion, a man comes under the control of material objects. O lord of men! When confusion has been generated, the object known as desire is generated. Seeking to obtain objects of pleasure, he becomes addicted to desire. He does not see anything beyond the gains from ordinary pleasure and desire. Having become overwhelmed by greed, attachment is increased in people. Men become interested in sustaining these objects. Even if he knows, a man performs acts that should not be undertaken, for the sake of objects. Because he is overcome with affection for the children, he is tormented at the prospect of these[729] being destroyed. He is full of pride and seeks to protect himself against all defeat. He acts so as to enjoy pleasure and is thereby destroyed. It is known that those who have seen the brahman are full of intelligence and engage in austerities. Such men seek auspicious deeds and give up happiness.[730] O king! They obtain indifference towards loss of affection and riches and physical and mental hardships. That indifference leads to knowledge of the atman and knowledge of what the sacred texts have said. O king! Having seen the purport of the sacred texts, they see the importance of austerities. O Indra among men! A man who realizes what is essential and what is damaging is extremely rare. Realizing that all beloved happiness decays, he resorts to austerities. O son! Austerities are everything. They are recommended even for those who are inferior. A person who has conquered his senses and is self-controlled is on the road to heaven. O king! Earlier, the lord Prajapati created subjects through austerities, sometimes resorting to different kinds of vows. O son! The Adityas, the Vasus, the Rudras, Agni, the Ashvins, the Maruts, the Vishvadevas, the Sadhyas, the ancestors, the large numbers of Maruts,[731] the yakshas, the rakshasas, the gandharvas, the siddhas, the other residents of heaven and all other celestial ones obtained success through austerities. In the beginning, Brahma created brahmanas. Earlier, through their austerities, they prospered the earth and also roamed around in heaven. In the world of mortals, kings and other householders who are seen to have been born in great lineages

[729]The objects.

[730]Happiness that results from desire.

[731]Maruts are mentioned twice.

have all obtained the fruits of their austerities.[732] The silken garments, the radiant ornaments, the mounts, the seats and the vehicles—all these are the fruits of austerities. Thousands of beautiful women who follow them and the dwelling in palaces—all these are the fruits of austerities. The best of beds, many kinds of objects of pleasure and all that is—these are the outcomes of past deeds. O scorcher of enemies! There is nothing in the three worlds that cannot be obtained through austerities. The renunciation of objects of pleasure also represents the fruits of earlier deeds. Whether he is happy or miserable, a man must abandon greed. O supreme among kings! He must use his mind and intelligence to look towards the sacred texts. Discontent leads to misery. Greed leads to confusion of the senses. Wisdom is then destroyed and knowledge is not accompanied by practice. When wisdom is destroyed, one does not see what is proper. Therefore, even when happiness has been destroyed, a man must resort to fierce austerities. Whatever is beneficial represents happiness. Whatever is hated is said to represent misery. Behold. These are the fruits of austerities that have been performed and have not been performed. If one performs unblemished austerities, one goes to what is best. One always faces the fortunate and enjoys the objects of pleasure. However, a person who gives up the virtuous path and goes after the fruits[733] obtains the unpleasant and faces many kinds of misery, despite obtaining objects of pleasure. Dharma, austerities and donations are desirable. But because desire is generated, one performs wicked deeds and obtains hell. O supreme among men! But whether he faces joy or misery, if a man does not deviate from his own conduct, he possesses the sight of the sacred texts. O lord of the earth! It is said that the pleasure from touch, taste, sight, scent and hearing only lasts for as long as it takes for an arrow to fall down on the ground. When these are over, a fierce pain again takes over. That is the reason the learned praise emancipation, productive of supreme bliss. Those who follow that obtain fruits with superior

[732]Austerities performed in earlier lives.

[733]That is, unblemished austerities are those that are performed without any desire for the fruits.

qualities. For those who always have a conduct in accordance with dharma, kama and artha do not diminish them. Householders must never make efforts to serve objects of pleasure. But it is my view that they must always make efforts to follow their own dharma. Those who are revered and are born in noble families always have the sight of the sacred texts. However, those who have separated themselves from acts of dharma are incapable of controlling their atmans. All other deeds that are performed by men are destroyed. These should be ignored in this world and nothing other than deeds of austerities followed. However, there may be householders who have made up their minds to perform deeds. O king! They should skilfully observe their own dharma and offer havya and kavya. All the male and female rivers flow to the ocean and find their refuge there. In that way, all the other ashramas are based on that of the householder.'"'

Chapter 1613(285)

'"Janaka asked, 'O maharshi! How were the different complexions generated among the varnas? O supreme among eloquent ones! I wish to hear about this. Tell me. The sacred texts say that one's offspring are nothing but one's own self. In particular, having been generated from brahmanas, how has there been decay?'

'"Parashara replied, 'O great king! It is indeed that way. The offspring are generated from one's own self. But because of the deviation from austerities, this decay into jatis has set in.[734] When the field is good and the seed is good, an auspicious crop results. However, if these are inferior, an inferior crop results. Those who are learned about dharma know that when Prajapati created the worlds, some were created from his mouth, some from his arms, some from his thighs and some from his feet. O son! The brahmanas were born from the

[734]The text uses the word jati or class, not the same as varna.

mouth and the kshatriyas and their relatives from the arms. O king! The rich ones[735] were born from the thighs. The attendants[736] were born from the feet. O bull among men! These were the only four varnas that were created. The sacred texts say that all the others that were created, over and above these, were the result of a mixture. Among those that resulted from the kshatriya jati were Atirathas, Ambashthas, Ugras, Vaidehakas, Shvapakas, Pulkasas, Stenas, Nishadas, Sutas and Magadhas. O lord of men! The Ayogas, Karanas, Vratyas and Chandalas were born from an intermingling between the four varnas.'

'"Janaka asked, 'How did brahmanas with different *gotras*[737] result? O supreme among sages! There are many gotras in the world. How can those born from different wombs, those born from shudra wombs and those born from inferior wombs become sages?'

'"Parashara replied, 'O king! Though these are not brahmanas by virtue of their inferior birth, these great-souled ones can resort to austerities and cleanse their souls. O king! Here and there, the sages had sons. However, because of their[738] own austerities, they again succeeded in becoming rishis. O king! O ruler of Videha! Earlier, my grandfather,[739] Rishyashringa, Kashyapa, Vata, Tandya, Kripa, Kakshivat, Kamatha and the others, Yavakrita, Drona, supreme among eloquent ones, Ayu, Matanga, Datta, Drupada and Matsya obtained their own natural states by resorting to austerities. They were knowledgable about the Vedas and were established in self-control and austerities. O king! Initially, only four gotras were born—Angiras, Kashyapa, Vasishtha and Bhrigu. O king! But because of their deeds, other gotras were generated. Their names resulted from the austerities that those virtuous ones resorted to.'

'"Janaka asked, 'O illustrious one! Tell me about the specific dharma of different varnas. What is the general template of dharma that leads to welfare everywhere?'

[735]The vaishyas.

[736]The shudras.

[737]Subdivisions.

[738]The offspring.

[739]Parashara's grandfather was Vasishtha.

'"Parashara replied, 'O king! Receiving gifts, officiating at sacrifices and studying represent the specific dharma for brahmanas. Kshatriyas are radiant when they protect. The vaishyas must engage in agriculture, animal husbandry and trade. O lord of men! The task of shudras is to serve the other three varnas.[740] O king! I have described to you the specific dharma of the varnas. O son! Now listen to the details about general dharma. O king! Non-violence, lack of injury, lack of distraction, giving proper shares, performing funeral rites, attending to guests, truthfulness, lack of anger, contentment with one's own wife, purity, constant lack of malice, knowledge of the atman and endurance—these represent general dharma. Brahmanas, kshatriyas and vaishyas are the three varnas that are *dvijas*.[741] O supreme among bipeds! These are the ones who have rights to such dharma. O king! If these three varnas resort to perverse deeds, then that leads to their downfall. They are elevated if they stick to their own deeds, just as the righteous ones do. No downfall has been determined for a shudra, nor is there any means of his cleansing himself from such a downfall. He cannot follow the conduct of dharma laid down in the sacred texts. However, he should not act against such dharma. O ruler of Videha! O great king! Learned ones say that shudras are like brahmanas. O Indra among men! I see such a person as the god Vishnu, the foremost one in the universe.[742] Even an inferior person can desire to uplift himself by resorting to the conduct of the virtuous. They are not censured if they perform any of the rites that lead to nourishment. But they must avoid mantras. Whenever inferior people resort to the conduct of the virtuous, they obtain happiness, both in this world and in the hereafter.'

[740]The word used is dvija. Here it clearly means the other three varnas, not brahmanas alone.

[741]They are born twice, the sacred thread ceremony representing the second birth.

[742]This is cryptic and requires interpretation. Brahma is equated with brahmanas and Vishnu with kshatriyas. The preceding sentence seems to say that shudras can become brahmanas in their next lives. But Parashara thinks that they can only become kshatriyas in their next lives.

'"Janaka asked, 'O great sage! What taints a person? Is it his deeds or his jati? A doubt has arisen in my mind. You should explain this to me.'

'"Parashara replied, 'O great king! There is no doubt that both can give rise to taints. But listen specifically to how both deeds and jati can be countered. Regardless of birth and deeds,[743] a person may perform wicked acts. However, even if the birth is tainted, if a person does not act wickedly, he is truly a man. If a man of superior birth performs wicked deeds, he is censured. Those acts taint him. Therefore, such deeds are not appropriate.'

'"Janaka asked, 'O supreme among brahmanas! In this world, which are the acts of dharma? Which are the acts that never lead to injury to beings?'

'"Parashara replied, 'O great king! Listen to what you have asked me. These are acts of non-injury that always save a man. Those who renounce and worship the fire can see that their anxiety is dispelled. They are the ones who resort to the beneficial path of dharma and ascend progressively. They are devoted and humble. They are always self-controlled and restrained. They abandon all kinds of action and go to the spot that is without decay. O king! All the varnas should perform the deeds of dharma properly and speak truthful words. In the world of the living, they must give up terrible adharma. They will go to heaven. There is no need to reflect on this.'"'

Chapter 1614(286)

'"Parashara said, 'Fathers, friends, preceptors and women belonging to those who are devoid of qualities bring them no status in the world. O king! Even if one is devoted to them, speaks pleasantly to them, ensures their welfare and is obedient, that brings no gains. For men, the father is the supreme god. The

[743]Presumably deeds in earlier lives.

father is said to be superior to the mother. Knowledge is said to be the supreme gain. By controlling the objects of the senses, one obtains the supreme. If the son of a king faces the flames of arrows in the field of battle and is consumed by them and killed, he goes to the immortal worlds that are extremely difficult to obtain. As he pleases, he obtains the fruits of heaven there. O king! One should not strike the exhausted, the terrified, those who have lost their weapons, the weeping, those who are not willing to fight, those who have been deprived of their mounts, those who are not exerting themselves, those who are ill, those who are seeking refuge, those who are very young and those who are aged. One should fight someone who is mounted, properly equipped, ready to fight and one's equal. In a battle, a king should engage against the son of a kshatriya. It is certain that it is best to be killed by someone who is an equal or superior. Kings who are slain by inferiors and cowards are censured. O lord of men! It is said that if one is slain by a wicked person who resorts to evil conduct, or is inferior, that is wicked and certainly leads to hell. O king! If a person's fortune is over and he has come under subjugation,[744] then no one can save him. But if the lifespan is left, no one can assail him. If a person has attained one hundred years of age or he is senior in age, one must gently restrain him from performing any injurious acts. O son! When a householder suspects that his end is near, it is appropriate that his death should occur near a river or at a sacred place. When the lifespan is over, one merges into the five elements. This can happen without reason and can also occur with reason.[745] Having obtained a body, if a person gives it up in a mishap, after losing the body, he follows the same kind of course.[746] This is like a man going from one house to another house. There is no second reason for a person to obtain a similar kind of body. That is the way he pursues the goal of emancipation. The body consists of a mass of arteries,

[744]Meaning, if one's life is over.

[745]Respectively, accidental and natural deaths.

[746]That is, obtains a similar kind of body. This seems to mean accidents and suicides.

sinews and bones. It is terrible and impure. It is a mixture of the elements, the senses and the qualities. This body is then covered by a skin. Learned ones who have thought about adhyatma say this. When the qualities decay, the body becomes mortal. The body is abandoned and becomes immobile and senseless. The elements return to their natural states and the body merges with the ground. Driven by the urge to act, the body is born, here and there. O ruler of Videha! Whatever be the state in which the body dies, driven by the deeds it has performed, its next birth is seen to be determined by that nature. O king! But the atman in the creature is not born again immediately. Like a giant cloud, it roams around in the sky. O king! It is born again only after it has obtained a new receptacle. O king! The atman is superior to the mind. The mind is superior to the senses. O king! Of the two kinds of creations, the mobile are superior.[747] It is held that bipeds are supreme among mobile ones. Among bipeds, dvijas are held to be superior. O Indra among kings! Among dvijas, the wise are held to be superior. Among the wise, those who know about the atman are superior and among those who know about the atman, the ones who are humble. It is certain that men who are born must die. Because of the qualities,[748] subjects undertake tasks that also come to an end. O king! A man who dies when the sun is in its northern solstice[749] and when the nakshatras and muhurtas are auspicious, is a person who performs auspicious deeds. A person must undertake tasks to the best of his capacity. He must cleanse himself of all wicked deeds and without causing hardship to people, face the natural course of death. Poison, hanging, burning, being slain by bandits and being bitten to death by animals are said to be inferior kinds of death. Those who are the performers of auspicious deeds do not confront these and many other inferior kinds of death. O king! The life forces of

[747]Compared to the immobile.

[748]Sattva, rajas and tamas. The fruits of deeds are not eternal.

[749]The text uses the word kashtha, which has more than one meaning. Solstice fits best, though it might also mean when the sun is in one of the northern cardinal directions.

virtuous ones ascend upwards, those who are middling in merit remain towards the middle and the perpetrators of wicked deeds head downwards. O king! For any man, there is only one foe and no second enemy, and that happens to be ignorance. It is because he is enveloped by this that he is goaded to perform extremely terrible and loathsome deeds. For the sake of realization, one must serve the aged and follow the dharma of the sacred texts. O prince! One must make efforts for success. That enemy can only be brought down through the arrow of wisdom. One must study the Vedas, perform austerities and be a brahmachari. To the best of one's capacity, one must perform the five sacrifices.[750] With a desire to obtain dharma, a man must then go to the forest. He must control himself and seek to obtain what is best. However, he must not emaciate himself by giving up all material objects. O son! Birth as a human is extremely difficult to obtain, even as a *chandala*.[751] O lord of the earth! This is the first kind of birth, because one can seek to save the atman by performing auspicious deeds. O lord! Who will destroy such a life once it has been obtained? Using the sacred texts as a yardstick, men perform acts of dharma. But though the status as a human may be very difficult to obtain in this world, there may be a man who ignores dharma. He is overcome by desire and thereby deceives himself. O son! A person who looks at all beings with eyes of affection is not destroyed, like the flames of a lamp that have been protected. He comforts everyone and speaks pleasantly to them. He is impartial towards delight and misery. He obtains greatness in the hereafter. Donations, renunciation, making the appearance pleasant and amiable, repeated purification of the body through bathing and austerities—these must be undertaken near the Sarasvati, in Naimisha, in Pushkara, or in other sacred spots on earth. For those who die in houses, it is recommended that their dead bodies should be taken out from there and taken to cremation grounds in vehicles. Cremation must be performed in accordance

[750] *Brahma yajna, deva yajna, pitri yajna, manushya yajna* and *bhuta yajna*.
[751] Therefore, that life must be preserved.

with the rites of purification. Rites, beneficial sacrifices, officiating at sacrifices, donations and efforts to undertake auspicious deeds according to one's capacity—these have been recommended for the sake of the departed ancestors. A man also undertakes these for his own self. O lord of men! The sacred texts, the Vedas and the six Vedangas have been laid down for the benefit of men who perform unblemished deeds.'"

'Bhishma said, "O lord of men! The extremely great-souled sage related all this and, in those ancient times, spoke to the king of Videha for his benefit."'

Chapter 1615(287)

'Bhishma said, "For the sake of determining supreme dharma, Janaka, the lord of Mithila, again asked the great-souled Parashara. 'O brahmana! What is the supreme objective? Which deeds are never destroyed? Which is the spot, from which, one does not have to return? O great sage! Tell me that.'

'"Parashara replied, 'Detachment is the best foundation of knowledge. Knowledge represents the best path. Austerities are never destroyed. Seeds sown in a field are not destroyed. If a person severs the noose of adharma and takes pleasure in dharma, if he grants the gift of fearlessness, then he obtains success. A person who gives away thousands of cattle and hundreds of horses and grants fearlessness to all beings, he is the one who truly gives. One may dwell in the midst of material objects. However, if one is intelligent, one does not really dwell amidst them. It is only the evil-minded person who dwells amidst trifling material objects. Like water on the leaf of a lotus, a wise person is not stained by adharma. Sin attaches more to an ignorant person, just as lac and wood attach to each other. Adharma can only be extinguished after the fruits have been felt and do not let go of the doer. At the right time, the doer will have to endure all of these. But they do not afflict those who have clean souls and have seen the atman. An ignorant person is distracted by his intelligence and the organs of action. Attached to good and bad deeds, he suffers from great fear. Even when he is in the midst of objects, a person who is devoid of attachment and has properly conquered his anger, is never united with sin. When there is a dam, the store of water swells up. In that way, someone with the dam of dharma does not suffer. The gem purifies itself by attracting the rays of the sun.[752] O tiger among kings! A person who practices yoga receives in that way. When sesamum seeds are separately mingled with flowers, they imbibe those pleasant qualities. By resorting to the quality of sattva, men on earth can improve themselves by associating with those who have clean souls. When a man makes up his mind about heaven, he abandons his wife, his riches, his excellent horses, his vehicles and all kinds of rites. His intelligence is then delinked from material objects. If a man's intelligence is addicted to material objects, he can never comprehend what brings welfare to his atman. O king! His consciousness is attracted by all these sentiments, like fish after a bait of meat. All mortal beings in this world encounter each other and depend on each other. But like a plantain tree, this lacks essence. They sink like a boat in the ocean. No time has been designated for a man to follow dharma. Death does not wait for any man. It is appropriate that one should always practise the rites of dharma, since a man is always headed towards the jaws of death. Through practice, a blind man can roam around in his own house. In that way, by concentrating the mind, a wise person can follow the desired path. It has been said that everything that is born must die. Birth is associated with death. A person who is ignorant about the dharma of emancipation is bound and is whirled around in that cycle. The stalk of a lotus can swiftly free itself from the mire. In that way, a man's atman can free itself of the mind. It is the mind that initially brings the atman to yoga. Engaged in one's own acts, one tends to ignore the

[752]This is the suryakanta jewel, the sun-stone.

supreme objective. By being addicted to the objects of the senses, one falls away from one's true acts. Though heaven is the supreme objective, one obtains birth as inferior species. Through his own deeds, a wise person's atman obtains the supreme benefit. When an earthen vessel has been baked, the liquid kept there does not escape and diminish. Even if one is in the midst of material objects, it is the same with a person who has tormented his body through austerities. There is no doubt that a person who discards material objects can obtain emancipation, delinking his atman from objects of pleasure. But there are others who base themselves on objects of pleasure. A person attached to his penis and stomach is shrouded in mist. His soul is enveloped, like a person who has been born blind and does not understand. Merchants who go out to sea obtain riches that are proportionate to the capital invested. Know that in the world of mortals, creatures obtain ends that are proportionate to their deeds. In this world, made up of days and nights, death roams around in the form of old age and devours creatures, like a snake devouring the air. A creature obtains a birth that is determined by the deeds that he has himself performed. There is nothing, pleasant or unpleasant, that is obtained but is not dependent on earlier acts. Whether he is lying down, moving around or is seated, or is in the midst of material objects, a man always obtains the fruits of good and bad deeds. But it is seen that someone who has obtained the furthest shore,[753] which is so difficult to reach in this great ocean, does not return again. When a burden is to be carried, boats are lowered into the great ocean through ropes.[754] That is the way the mind uses yoga to uplift the body. Rivers head towards the ocean and unite with it. In that way, yoga always makes one unite with prakriti. The minds of men are attached to many kinds of bonds of affection. Their nature is destroyed, like houses of sand by the water. The being must realize that the body is like a house and that it has to be purified through sacred waters. If one advances along

[753]Has been emancipated.

[754]If boats are not being used, they are not left in the water, for fear of damage. When they are needed, ropes are used to lower them into the water.

the path of intelligence, one obtains happiness in this world and in the next. There are many things that lead to hardship, but there are only a few that bring happiness. The learned say that among the many things that lead to benefit in the hereafter, renunciation is the best. There are large numbers of friends who have their own intentions. There are relatives who follow their own reasons. There are wives, servants and sons. All of them wish to enjoy one's riches for their own reasons. A mother or a father cannot bring about anything in the hereafter. Donations are the medication and a creature reaps the fruits of his own deeds. Mothers, sons, fathers, brothers, wives and friends are only like etchings of gold against the real stuff.[755] All the deeds that have been done earlier, good and bad, follow a creature's atman. Knowing that the fruits of deeds present themselves, one should turn one's intelligence towards the inner atman. One should resort to one's conduct, using others as aides. One who has begun his acts in this way, never suffers. One must have no doubt in one's mind. One must be brave, patient and learned. Prosperity will never abandon such a person, just as the rays don't leave the sun. If a person believes and uses means to engage in such conduct, without any wonder and without any doubt, and if he controls himself, then his atman does not suffer and he does not deviate from the objective. All the deeds that a creature himself performed, good and bad, control him from the moment he obtains a womb. Both types of earlier deeds restrain him. Death cannot be countered and time severs everything, like a saw scattering dust from wood. In the end, the fruits of deeds are obtained. Through the acts that he has himself performed earlier, good and bad, a man obtains everything—his appearance, birth, material objects, prosperity and other stores.'"

'Bhishma said, "O king! The learned one thus spoke about the truth to Janaka. Having heard, the best among those who were knowledgable about dharma, obtained great delight."'

[755]The text uses the word *ashtapada*, which is a measure of gold. Relatives are like etchings, they aren't the real gold.

Chapter 1616(288)

'Yudhishthira asked, "O grandfather! Learned men in this world praise truthfulness, forgiveness, self-control and wisdom. What is your view?"

'Bhishma replied, "O Yudhishthira! In this connection, there is an ancient history about a conversation between the Sadhyas and a swan. Once upon a time, the eternal Prajapati assumed the form of a golden swan. In this form, he travelled through the three worlds and came upon the Sadhyas.

'"The Sadhyas said, 'O bird! We are the gods who are known as the Sadhyas. You are the one who truly knows about moksha and we wish to ask you about the dharma of moksha. We have heard that you are learned, patient and eloquent. O bird! Virtuous words are heard from you. O bird! What do you think is the best? O great-souled one! Where does the mind find delight? O supreme among birds! It should be your task to instruct us. O Indra among birds! What do you think is the best among deeds, so that one can be swiftly emancipated?'

'"The swan replied, 'O ones who have fed on amrita! I have heard that one must resort to these tasks—austerities, self-control, truthfulness and the protection of the atman. All the strands of the heart must be loosened and the pleasant and the unpleasant must be brought under one's control. One must not hurt others and be harsh in speech. One must not receive anything good from those who are inferior. One must not excite others through speech. One must not speak words that make them go to wicked worlds. Spoken words descend like arrows. Struck by those, one grieves day and night. A learned person will not make these descend towards the vitals of others. He will not release these at other people. If one is severely struck with arrows of extreme words released by others, it is one's task to pacify them. If a person replies angrily, all his good merits from the hereafter are taken away. A person should control his blazing anger, pacify his pride and counter the futile humiliation. He should be cheerful and free from malice. He then takes away the good merits that the evil-minded person has earned in the hereafter. I do not speak anything when I am censured. Even when I am incessantly assailed, I ignore it. Noble ones say that forgiveness, truthfulness, uprightness and non-violence are the best. Truth is the foundation of the Vedas. Self-control is the foundation of truth. Emancipation is the foundation of self-control. These are all the various instructions. I think that a person who can control the force of words, the force of anger in the mind, the force of knowledge,[756] the forces of the stomach and the genitals and all the other forces that consume and destroy, is a brahmana and a sage. Lack of anger is superior to anger. Patience is superior to the lack of patience. A human is superior to those who are not human. In that way, knowledge is superior to ignorance. One who is not enraged is superior to one who is angered. One must be patient when one is raged against. In that event, the assailant is burnt[757] and one obtains all his good merits. In such a case, if a person does not say anything, harsh or pleasant, in reply, if when struck, a person is patient and does not strike back, if when assailed, he does not desire anything wicked in retaliation, such a person is always desired by the gods. A wicked person must be forgiven, as if he is equal to a superior person, even if one has been dishonoured, assailed and censured. That is the way to obtain success. I no longer possess any thirst. Nor is there any rage in me. In private, I always serve noble ones. I do not desire anything that belongs to others and I do not seek any of their possessions. When I am cursed, I do not curse back. I know that this is the door towards immortality. I am telling you the secret about the brahman. There is nothing superior for men. They will then be freed from sin, like the moon from the clouds. Such a patient person will obtain success through his patience and be radiant while he waits for the right time to come.[758] He deserves to

[756]Presumably, false knowledge.

[757]Through remorse.

[758]The right time for death.

be worshipped by everyone and is like a pillar that holds everything up. Words of great praise are spoken about him. Such a person has control over his atman and goes to the gods. Revilers who are full of anger do not wish to speak about his lack of qualities, because there is nothing like that. His words and mind have been protected and controlled in the appropriate way. Through the Vedas, austerities and renunciation, he has obtained everything. Such a learned person does not react to the censure and disrespect shown by ignorant people. Nor does he cause injury to his own self by extolling others.[759] Like one who is content with amrita, he ignores this. Such a person is a brahmana. He sleeps happily and disrespect does not destroy him. If there is rage when sacrifices are performed, gifts given, austerities performed or oblations offered, Vaivasvata[760] takes all these away. The efforts of a person who is enraged are futile. O supreme among the immortals! If a person protects the four gates—the genitals, the stomach, the hands and speech as the fourth—well, he knows about dharma. Truthfulness, self-control, modesty, uprightness, non-violence, fortitude, patience, renunciation, constant studying, lack of desire towards the possessions of others—if a person has the good conduct to practise these single-mindedly, he will rise upwards. Like a calf sucking at the four udders of the cow, these are all the things that one should follow. There is nothing that is purer than the truth. I have seen men and have travelled around among gods. Truth is the ladder to heaven, like a boat on an ocean. One becomes like the people one dwells and associates with. Whoever a person advances towards, he becomes like that. If one associates with the virtuous, one becomes virtuous. The same is the case with ascetics or thieves. This is like a garment being dyed with the colour it has been immersed in. In that way, one comes under their subjugation. The gods always converse with the virtuous. They are not seen to be interested in human objects. A person should know that material objects come and go, like the moon and the wind.[761] If the being

[759]Extolling those who praise him. He is beyond both praise and censure.

[760]Yama.

[761]The moon waxes and wanes and the wind comes and goes.

inside the heart has not been stained and walks along the path of the righteous, the gods are pleased with him. From a distance, the gods avoid those who are always addicted to their penis and stomach, men who are thieves and always harsh in speech, even if one knows that they have tried to atone for those sins. The gods are not satisfied with those who are inferior in spirit, those who eat everything and those who are the perpetrators of wicked deeds. They honour men who are truthful in their vows, grateful and devoted to dharma. It is said that silence is superior to speech. The second course is that of speaking the truth. The third course is to speak words of dharma. The fourth course is of speaking pleasant words.'[762]

'"The Sadhyas asked, 'What is the world covered by? Why does it not shine? Why are friends cast away? What are the reasons for not reaching heaven?'

'"The swan replied, 'The world is enveloped in ignorance. Malice leads to a lack of shining. Friends are abandoned because of greed. Because of attachment, one does not go to heaven.'

'"The Sadhyas asked, 'Among the brahmanas, who is the single one who is always happy? Who is the single one who is silent amidst the many? Who is the single one, who though weak, is strong? Who is the single one who does not quarrel?'

'"The swan replied, 'Among the brahmanas, the wise one is the single one who is always delighted. The wise one is the single one who is silent amidst many. The wise one is the single one who is strong, though weak. The wise one is the one who does not quarrel.'

'"The Sadhyas asked, 'What is divinity among brahmanas? What is said to be their virtue? What is wicked among them? What is held to constitute their humanity?'

'"The swan replied, 'Studying represents their divinity. Vows are said to be their virtue. Censuring others is their wickedness. Mortality constitutes their humanity.'"

'Bhishma said, "I have recounted the excellent conversation concerning the Sadhyas. The body is the womb for deeds and a virtuous existence is said to be the truth."'

[762]This is a hierarchy, in terms of desirability, of different kinds of speech.

Chapter 1617(289)

'Yudhishthira said, "O father! You should explain to me the difference between sankhya and yoga. O one who knows about everything! O supreme among the Kuru lineage! You know everything about this."

'Bhishma replied, "Brahmanas who follow sankhya praise sankhya and those who follow yoga praise yoga. Driven by reasons and sentiments, they proclaim the superiority of their own school. O afflicter of enemies! Learned ones who follow yoga have appropriately given reasons for their superiority. How can someone who does not believe in an Ishvara be emancipated? But those brahmanas who follow sankhya also speak about appropriate reasons. By knowing the progress of everything, one becomes detached from material objects. When one ascends upwards from the body, it is evident that this can be nothing other than emancipation. This is said by the immensely wise ones who are conversant with the emancipation set out in sankhya. Whichever school one follows, one should accept those reasons. One will then be capable of ensuring benefit with those words. The views of the virtuous must be accepted and there are virtuous and revered people on both sides. The reasons behind yoga can be experienced. Those for sankhya are determined on the basis of the sacred texts. O son! O Yudhishthira! It is my view that both sides represent the truth. O king! It is my view that both sides represent knowledge and are revered by the virtuous. If one follows the sacred texts and practises them, both will convey to the supreme objective. O unblemished one! Both are equal in recommending purification and compassion towards beings. Both are comparable in the vows that have been laid down. They are only unequal in their philosophy."

'Yudhishthira asked, "O grandfather! They are comparable in vows, purification and compassion. O grandfather! In that case, why is it that they are not equal in their philosophy? Tell me."

'Bhishma replied, "Attachment, confusion, affection, desire and anger—by resorting to yoga, one severs these five sins and obtains success. Large fish break through nets and regain the water. In that way, through yoga, one transcends sins and attains the objective. O king! Greed and other bonds are powerful. Having severed these, the yogi treads along the supreme path, sparkling and auspicious. O king! There is no doubt that weak animals are enmeshed in nets and later destroyed. This is also true of those who do not possess the strength of yoga. O Kounteya! Weak ones are like fish caught in a net. O Indra among kings! Those yogis who are extremely weak also meet their end in the same way. O destroyer of enemies! This is like birds caught in fine nets. They can free themselves from that hardship, but only if they are strong. O scorcher of enemies! There are yogis who are bound down by the bonds of action. They are weak and are destroyed, while the powerful ones escape. O king! A small and weak fire is pacified when a large quantity of kindling is placed atop it. O lord! It is the same with yogis who are weak. O king! However, if that fire obtains its strength back again, it can swiftly burn down the entire earth, fanned by the wind. When strength has been generated in him, a yogi blazes in his energy and is immensely strong. He is like the sun that has arisen at the time of destruction and can dry up the entire universe. O king! A weak man is borne away by the current. A weak yogi is helpless and is borne away by the objects of the senses. However, an elephant is capable of withstanding the same strong current. Having obtained the strength of yoga, one can discard many objects of the senses. O Partha! Through the strength of yoga, a yogi can bring under his control and penetrate Prajapatis, rishis, the great elements and the Ishvaras. O king! Yama, the enraged destroyer, and Death, terrible in valour, cannot afflict the yogi, who is infinite in his energy. O bull among the Bharata lineage! Through the power of yoga, he can create many thousand who are like him and wander around the entire earth in these forms. Through practising fierce austerities, he can also obtain the objects of desire. O Partha! He can then fling them away again, like the sun discarding its qualities of energy. O king! There is no doubt that with the strength of yoga, and having freed himself from the bonds, a person can obtain Vishnu's powers and free himself. O lord of the earth! I have spoken to you about the power of yoga. I will now again tell you about the subtle signs. O lord! O bull among the Bharata lineage! The indications of dharana and samadhi in the atman are subtle.[763] Listen to them. An archer who is controlled and not distracted can strike the target. There is no doubt that a yogi who is properly focused in this way can obtain emancipation. A man ascending a flight of stairs with a liquid in a vessel, concentrates his mind.[764] The mind has to be withdrawn and rendered immobile in that way. O king! Uniting it with the atman in yoga, he becomes completely immobile. He cleanses his atman and makes it as resplendent as the sun. O Kounteya! O king! When a boat is tossed around on the mighty ocean, it is like a boatman taking control and swiftly steering the boat. In that way, a yogi who knows the truth unites his atman in samadhi. O king! Having gone to a desolate spot, he then gives up the body. O bull among men! A charioteer can yoke well-trained horses, control them and swiftly take the archer to the designated region. O king! That is the way a yogi is concentrated in dharana. He swiftly reaches the supreme spot, like a released arrow hitting the target. A yogi makes his self penetrate the atman and remains motionless. He destroys his sins and obtains the spot that is without decay. O infinitely valorous one! O lord of the earth! In his navel, in his throat, in his head, in his heart, in his chest, along his flanks, in his eyes, in his touch and in his nose, and in the spot that he has resorted to, the yogi controls himself in that great vow and merges his self with the subtle atman. Cleansed in his wisdom, he quickly burns all his deeds, auspicious and inauspicious. Resorting to that excellent yoga, he frees himself as he wills."

'Yudhishthira asked, "O descendant of the Bharata lineage! How does a yogi obtain strength? What should he eat and what should he conquer? You should tell me this."

'Bhishma replied, "A yogi obtains strength by eating grain, by eating oilcakes and avoiding fatty products. O destroyer of enemies!

[763]Dharana and samadhi are the last two stages in the eightfold path of yoga. Dharana can loosely be translated as concentrated meditation and samadhi as liberation.

[764]So that the liquid does not spill.

A yogi obtains strength by being pure in soul and eating only once a day and subsisting for a long period of time on rough barley.[765] A yogi obtains strength by only drinking water mixed with milk once a fortnight, once a month, once in two months, and finally, once a year. O lord of men! A yogi obtains strength and purifies his soul properly by always avoiding meat. O king! O supreme among kings! He conquers desire, anger, cold, rain, fear, sleep, breath, the penis, material objects, hatred, which is so difficult to conquer, terrible thirst, touch and all the other senses and sleep, which is so difficult to defeat. The great-souled ones blaze and find their own subtle selves in their atmans. Those immensely wise ones are devoid of attachment. Their riches are meditation and studying. It is the view that the path followed by learned brahmanas is extremely difficult to traverse. O bull among the Bharata lineage! No one who is disturbed can walk along this. It is like a fearful forest full of terrible serpents and reptiles, covered with pits and without water, dense with many thorns and difficult to travel in. It is like a path frequented by bandits, with nothing to eat and no trees, as if the large trees have been burnt down in a forest conflagration. Young people do not find safety along it. Since the path of yoga is like this, very few brahmanas can travel along it. But it is said that the other paths, which have safety, have many taints. O lord of the earth! Those who can sustain yoga can safely walk along it, though it is as sharp as a razor's edge. But those who have not cleansed their souls find it difficult to remain there. O son! However, if dharana is disturbed, it takes one to an inauspicious end. O king! This is like a blind man steering a boat on the ocean. O Kounteya! But if one is based in dharana in the proper way, one can free oneself from death, birth, unhappiness and happiness. All this has been stated in different sacred texts on yoga. This entire and supreme yoga is certainly seen among brahmanas. The great brahman is supreme. Those great-souled ones can enter the lord Brahma, Vishnu, the granter of boons, Bhava, Dharma, the six-faced one,[766] the six great

[765]Rough in the sense of not being mixed with anything else.

[766]Kartikeya.

sons of Brahma,[767] tamas, which makes one face such a great deal of difficulty, the pure sattva, supreme prakriti, the goddess Siddhi, Varuna's wife, all energy, great patience, the sparkling lord of the stars and all the stars, the Vishvadevas and the ancestors, their followers, all the mountains and the terrible oceans, all the rivers, the forests, the clouds, serpents, mountains, the large numbers of yakshas, the directions and the groups of gandharvas, male and female. Those great-souled ones and these great ones attain each other. The yogi becomes perpetually free. O king! This auspicious account is about the immensely valorous god. The great-souled yogi has Narayana in his soul and overcomes everything that is mortal."'

Chapter 1618(290)

'Yudhishthira said, "O king! You have properly described to me the path of yoga, which is approved by the virtuous. You have explained it, as if to a disciple whose benefit you desire. I am now asking you about all the principles of sankhya. You know all the knowledge that is to be known in the three worlds."

'Bhishma replied, "Listen to the pure principles of sankhya. Intelligent ascetics who know about the atman have laid them down, Kapila and the other lords being the first. O bull among men! No errors can be seen in those doctrines. They have many qualities and no taints. O king! Through knowledge, one can enumerate that all objects have faults. Men and pishachas are associated with objects that are extremely difficult to conquer. The rakshasas and yakshas are associated with objects. The serpents and the gandharvas are associated with objects. O king! The ancestors, who roam diagonally above, are associated with objects. The Suparnas[768] and the Maruts

[767]Brahma had ten sons. Because of the number six, this probably refers to the Vedangas.

[768]In this context, large birds.

are associated with objects. The rajarshis and the *brahmarshis* are associated with objects. The asuras and the Vishvadevas are associated with objects. The devarshis and the lords of yoga are associated with objects. The lords of subjects and Brahma are associated with objects. O supreme among eloquent ones! Knowing about all these and knowing the truth about the ultimate lifespans and time in this world, they find happiness in the supreme truth. At the right time, those who search for objects descend into hardships. Some find misery as inferior species, others descend into hell. O descendant of the Bharata lineage! There are all the qualities and all the demerits of heaven. There are taints and qualities in the words of the Vedas and in those who speak about the Vedas. O king! There are taints and qualities in jnana yoga and in yoga itself. O king! There are also taints and qualities in the knowledge of sankhya. There are ten qualities in sattva, nine qualities in rajas, eight qualities in tamas, seven qualities in intelligence, six qualities in the sky, five qualities in the mind, four qualities in intelligence and yet again, three great qualities in tamas, two qualities in rajas and one single quality in sattva.[769] One gets to know all this. One gets to know and obtains insight about the path of destruction. Having become full of jnana and vijnana and learnt the auspicious reasons behind everything, one obtains sacred emancipation, as subtle as the ultimate parts of the sky. Sight is attached to form, just as the nose is attached to

[769]The ten qualities of sattva are delight, cheerfulness, enthusiasm, fame, virtue, contentment, faith, uprightness, generosity and power. The nine qualities of rajas are faith, generosity, enjoyment, enterprise, desire, anger, pride, malice and calumny. The eight qualities of tamas are lack of consciousness, confusion, delusion, lack of understanding, sleep, carelessness, procrastination and blindness towards consequences. The seven qualities of intelligence are Mahat, consciousness and the five elements. The six qualities of the sky are space, water, wind, light, earth and expanse. The five qualities in the mind are the five senses. The four qualities in intelligence are doubt, determination, pride and memory. The three qualities of tamas are inability to understand, partial understanding and wrong understanding. The two qualities of rajas are action and sorrow. The single quality of sattva is enlightenment. But this is only indicative and other listings also exist.

the quality of smell. Sound is attached to hearing, the tongue to the quality of taste and touch to the skin. The wind finds refuge in the sky. Confusion is attached to tamas and has greed for riches as its foundation. Vishnu is attached to motion, Shakra to strength and Agni to the stomach. Water is attached to the goddess[770] and water has the fire as its foundation. Fire is attached to the wind and the wind has space for its foundation. Space is attached to Mahat and Mahat has intelligence for its foundation. Intelligence is attached to tamas and tamas has rajas for its foundation. Rajas is attached to sattva and sattva is attached to the atman. The atman is attached to the lord and god, Narayana. That god is attached to emancipation and emancipation has no foundation. One knows that sattva is attached to this body, surrounded by the sixteen qualities[771] and that natural consciousness has the body as a foundation. O king! One knows that the single atman is in the middle and that sin cannot attach to it and that the second element is acts committed in pursuit of the objects of the senses. All the senses and the objects of the senses have their foundation in the atman. There is also the truth about prana, apana, samana, vyana and udana. One knows about the two breaths of life that flow upwards and downwards. These seven breaths of life also possess their determined roles. O scorcher of enemies! One knows about Prajapatis, the rishis, the many different supreme paths and the large number of saptarshis and rajarshis. There are the great celestial rishis and the maharshis, as resplendent as the sun. O king! One knows that in the great course of time, they are also dislodged from their prosperity. O king! One learns that the large number of great creatures are destroyed. O king! One knows the outcome of inauspicious acts and evildoers. When Yama brings about destruction, there are hardships undergone by those who fall into Vaitarani.[772] There are many kinds of inauspicious wombs in the cycle of life. There is residence in inauspicious wombs, feeding on blood, water, phlegm, urine and excrement, terrible in smell. Bodies result from

[770]The earth.

[771]The five elements, the five senses, the five organs of action and the mind.

[772]The river that flows in the nether regions.

the union of semen and blood and have marrow and sinews. In that inauspicious city with the nine gates,[773] there are hundreds of veins and arteries. O king! One learns about the many kinds of yoga that bring welfare to the atman and about tamas, which envelopes the beautiful atmans of creatures. O bull among the Bharata lineage! There is sattva among creatures, but also the abhorrent and censured one[774] from the perspective of greatness. Those who know about sankhya know about the atman. They see the terrible devouring of the energy of the moon,[775] the fall of the stars and the deviation of the nakshatras. O king! They see the piteous coming together and separation of creatures and the unholy ways in which they eat each other. They know the delusion of childhood and the inauspicious destruction of bodies and because of attachment and confusion, the rare resort to sattva. Among thousands of men, only one possesses intelligence that turns to moksha. They know what the sacred texts have said earlier, that emancipation is extremely difficult to obtain. O king! They know of the great importance that is given to things that have not been obtained and the limited importance to those that have been obtained, since the objects of the senses are overwhelming. O Kounteya! When life has departed, they see that the bodies are unholy. O descendant of the Bharata lineage! They know that in the midst of homes and families, creatures are in misery. They know of the extremely terrible ends faced by those who are the killers of brahmanas and evil-souled brahmanas who are addicted to drinking. O Yudhishthira! They know the unholy ends that come to those who have intercourse with the wives of their preceptors, to those who do not show proper respect to their mothers and men in this world who do not revere the gods. They have the knowledge to know what happens to the perpetrators of wicked deeds and they are also conversant with the different kinds of birth as inferior species that takes place. They know about the colourful words of the Vedas, the progress of the seasons and the fading of the years and the months.

[773]The body.

[774]Rajas.

[775]An eclipse.

They see the decay of the fortnights and the decay of the days. They can directly see the waxing and waning of the moon, the ebb and the flow in the oceans and the destruction of riches and their subsequent increase. In particular, they see the coming together and separation of the yugas, the destruction of mountains and the destruction of rivers. They see the decay and repeated destruction of varnas. They see old age, death, birth and hardships. They know the truth about the taints of bodies and their miseries. O descendant of the Bharata lineage! They are conversant with the frailties of bodies. They know about the faults in their own atmans and those that all atmans are prone to. They know about the inauspicious scents that arise from their own bodies."

'Yudhishthira asked, "O immensely valorous one! What are the faults that you see in your own body? I have a doubt about this. You should explain in detail the truth about this to me."

'Bhishma replied, "O lord! The learned have said that there are five faults in the body. Those who know about the paths propagated in Kapila's sankhya have spoken about this. O destroyer of enemies! Listen. There are desire, anger, fear, sleep and the fifth is said to be the breath. These faults are seen in all those who possess bodies. Anger can be severed through forgiveness and desire through the abandoning of resolution. In that way, sattva and good conduct can be used against sleep and lack of distraction against fear. O king! The fifth one of breath can be severed through a restrained diet. The qualities can be comprehended through hundreds of other qualities, the faults through hundreds of faults. One can understand the truth about colourful reasons through hundreds of diverse reasons. The world is surrounded by one hundred of Vishnu's maya and is like foam in the water. It has the appearance of something that has been painted and its essence is as futile as that of a reed. One sees that it is like a dark pit and the years are like bubbles. It is about to be destroyed and is without happiness, with the characteristics of inevitable destruction. It is submerged in rajas and tamas and is as immobile as an elephant stuck in mud. O king! The immensely wise ones who know about sankhya generate offspring and then discard their bodies. O king! They use the great and pervasive knowledge of sankhya. O king! As instructed, they use the auspicious scent of sattva to dispel all the inauspicious scents of rajas and tamas, all the sense of touch that resides in the body. O descendant of the Bharata lineage! They quickly sever these through the weapon of knowledge and the rod of austerities. The waters of the ocean[776] are terrible misery. Anxiety and sorrow are its large lakes. Disease and death are the giant crocodiles. The great fears are the giant serpents. Tamas is the tortoises and rajas is the fish. One can cross over with the use of wisdom. Affection is the mud. O scorcher of enemies! Old age represents the impenetrable fortifications and touch is like the islands. Deeds are the great depth, truth represents the banks. O king! One has to base oneself on one's vows. Injury represents the swift and strong current. The many kinds of tastes are like large mines. The different kinds of gratification are the gems. Grief and fever are the breeze. Sorrow and thirst are the giant whirlpools. Fierce diseases are the large elephants. O destroyer of enemies! Bones are like flights of stairs and phlegm is foam. Donations provide the pearls. Lakes of blood are the coral. Loud laughter constitutes the roar. The different kinds of knowledge[777] make it extremely difficult to cross. Tears are the salt. One should resort to the refuge of abandoning attachment. O king! Sons are the large number of leeches. Relatives are the inhabitations. Lack of injury and truthfulness set boundaries to this. The giving up of life is the giant wave. Vedanta is an island one advances towards and all creatures can use it as pots[778] for support. Emanicpation is an object that is extremely difficult to obtain, but that is the reason one is heading to the ocean, with subterranean fire that is like a mare's head. O descendant of the Bharata lineage! Through using the yoga of knowledge, sages can successfully cross it. Having been born and having crossed what is extremely difficult to cross, they enter into the sparkling sky. From there, the sun uses its rays to bear those who practise sankhya, the performers of virtuous deeds. O king! This is like the stalk of a lotus bearing the water.

[776]Of life.

[777]Because they confuse a person.

[778]Water pots used as buoys while swimming.

O descendant of the Bharata lineage! The breeze that blows there receives them. Those stores of austerities are devoid of attachment. They are full of valour and successful. O descendant of the Bharata lineage! The breeze is subtle, cool, fragrant and pleasant to the touch. Those best of the seven Maruts convey them to an auspicious world. O Kounteya! It takes them to the ultimate end of space. O lord of men! Space conveys them to the ultimate end of rajas. O Indra among kings! Rajas conveys them to the ultimate end of sattva. O one who is pure in soul! Sattva conveys them to the supreme lord, Narayana. The lord bears those pure-souled ones and makes them part of the paramatman. O lord! They attain immortality there and never return. O Partha! Those great-souled ones are beyond opposites and attain the supreme objective."

'Yudhishthira asked, "O illustrious one! Those who are firm in their vows obtain that supreme region. O unblemished one! Do they remember anything about their birth and death? You should tell me the truth about this. O Kourava! Other than you, there is no no man I should ask this. I find this taint in the description about the greatness of moksha. Having reached and obtained success there, do the rishis retain consciousness and continue to endeavour for something else? O king! In that case, I see that the dharma of pravritti[779] is supreme. Once one is immersed in supreme knowledge, what can be more miserable than that?"

'Bhishma replied, "O son! The question that you have asked is proper, but it is extremely difficult. O bull among the Bharata lineage! Such is this question that even the learned have been confounded. Listen properly to the supreme truth on this. The great-souled ones who follow Kapila have supreme intelligence. O king! Embodied beings have senses in their bodies so that they can perceive. But these are instruments and the subtle atman uses them to perceive. Without the atman, they are like lumps of wood. They will no doubt be destroyed, like foam in the giant ocean. O scorcher of enemies! When the senses sleep, the subtle atman roams around everywhere, like the wind in space. O lord! It sees what can be seen and touches what can

[779]Undertaking action.

be touched. O descendant of the Bharata lineage! It comprehends everything, just as in a state of being awake. All the senses continue to be there, in their respective places. But because they are without their lord,[780] they are extinguished and are like snakes with their poison missing. There is no doubt that the subtle atman roams around, goes to the respective places of the senses and performs their tasks then. O descendant of the Bharata lineage! O one with dharma in your soul! O Partha! O Yudhishthira! All the qualities of sattva, all the qualities of rajas, all the qualities of tamas, all the qualities of intelligence, all the qualities of the mind, all the qualities of space, all the qualities of wind, all the qualities of energy, all the qualities of water, all the qualities of earth and all the qualities of the atman are in the atman. It is the atman which makes the atman perform good and bad acts. O lord! The senses wait on the great atman, like disciples. The undecaying atman transcends prakriti and proceeds. It goes to the supreme atman, Narayana, who is beyond opposites and is beyond prakriti. Free from taint and emancipated from good deeds and evil ones, it[781] enters the paramatman and does not return from the qualities there. O son! O descendant of the Bharata lineage! But the mind and the senses remain. At the right time, on the instructions of the preceptor, they have to return.[782] If a person desires peace and the qualities, he is capable of obtaining it within a short period of time. O Kounteya! United with knowledge in this way, they can find emancipation. O king! The immensely wise ones, who know about sankhya, go to that supreme objective. O Kounteya! There is no knowledge that is equal to this knowledge. Do not have any doubt about this. The views of sankhya represent supreme knowledge. They are without decay and certain and were earlier revealed by eternal Brahma, who is the creator without a beginning, a middle and an end, beyond opposites and everlasting. Those who have tranquility in their souls say that he is deep and eternal. All the acts of creation and destruction flow from him. This has been praised in the sacred

780The atman.

781The jivatman.

782The body isn't dead, but is in a state of samadhi.

texts and spoken about by the supreme rishis. For all the brahmanas, gods and people who know about the sacred texts, the eternal and undecaying brahman is the supreme god and there is nothing superior to him. The brahmanas pray to him and the learned speak about his qualities. This is the view of the far-sighted ones who properly practise yoga and sankhya. O Kounteya! The sacred texts of sankhya are a manifestation of the one who is without form.[783] O bull among the Bharata lineage! That is the reason these views have been regarded as his signs. O lord of the earth! There are two kinds of creatures on earth, mobile and immobile, and the mobile are superior. O king! This knowledge, which is the greatest of the great, is in the Vedas, in sankhya and in yoga. O Indra among men! Whatever is seen in the various Puranas can be found in sankhya. O king! Whatever is seen in the great accounts of history, in the sacred texts about artha, as prescribed by the virtuous, and all the knowledge that exists in the world, can be found in sankhya. It is the greatest of the great. O king! Tranquility, supreme strength, the subtle knowledge that has been spoken about, subtle austerities and happiness can be found in sankhya. O Partha! Even when they suffer, the practitioners of sankhya always go to the gods and enjoy happiness there. Having followed it and having become successful in their objectives, in cases of a downfall,[784] they become brahmanas and ascetics. O Partha! Those who practise sankhya give up their bodies, join the residents of heaven in the firmament and find emancipation. O lord of the earth! The excellent knowledge of sankhya is the best and is revered by all virtuous brahmanas. O king! If a brahmana knows about this and is devoted to this knowledge, he is not seen to be born as inferior species, or reach the abodes that are meant for the perpetrators of wicked deeds. O king! Sankhya is large, supreme and ancient. It is like a giant, sparkling, infinite and generous ocean. A great-souled person who follows all of sankhya sustains the immeasurable Narayana. O god among men! I have now told you the truth about the ancient Narayana, who is everywhere in the universe. At the time of creation,

[783]Brahma.

[784]Because they fall short of emancipation and are dislodged from heaven.

he causes creation. He is the one who again withdraws at the time of destruction."'

Chapter 1619(291)

'Yudhishthira asked, "What is said to be without decay and something from which one does not return? What is said to be the one with decay and something from which one has to return? O slayer of enemies! I wish to know the difference between that which is without decay and that which is with decay. O mighty-armed one! O descendant of the Kuru lineage! I wish to realize the truth about this. Brahmanas who know about the Vedas speak of you as an ocean of knowledge. So do the immensely fortunate rishis and the great-souled ascetics. There are only a few days left for the sun in dakshinayana. When the illustrious sun turns, you will go to your supreme objective. When you have departed, where will we hear what is best for us? You have been like a lamp for the lineage of the Kurus and have always illuminated with your knowledge. O extender of the Kuru lineage! That is the reason I wish to hear the truth about this. O Indra among kings! I am not satisfied with hearing amrita like this."

'Bhishma replied, "In this connection, there is an ancient history, about a conversation between Vasishtha and Karala, of Janaka's lineage. Vasishtha, best among the rishis and with the resplendence of the sun, was seated. King Janaka asked him about the knowledge that was supremely beneficial. Maitravaruni[785] was seated. He was accomplished about the knowledge of supreme adhyatma and had determined the progress of adhyatma. In ancient times, King Karala, of Janaka's lineage, greeted him. Joining his hands in salutation, he asked the supreme of rishis in words that were articulated well, humble, sweet and devoid of arguments. 'O illustrious one! I wish to hear about the supreme and eternal brahman, on obtaining whom,

[785]Vasishtha's name.

learned ones do not return. What is that which decays, into which the universe is itself destroyed? What is said to be without decay, auspicious, beneficial and without any taint?'

'"Vasishtha said, 'O lord of the earth! Listen to how this universe is destroyed and about that which has not been destroyed earlier and will never be destroyed. Know that twelve thousand years constitute a yuga and four such, taken one thousand times, are said to make up a kalpa, one of Brahma's days.[786] O king! Understand that Brahma's night is of the same duration. When he is destroyed, Svayambhu Shambhu, the performer of infinite deeds, creates a great being, who is the first among creatures.[787] This has form, though he[788] is without form. This is Ishana and he is resplendent and without decay. *Anima* and *laghima* are in him.[789] The extremities of his hands and feet extend in all the directions. His eyes, head and mouth are everywhere. His ears are everywhere in the world and he is stationed, enveloping everything. This illustrious Hiranyagarbha[790] is said to be intelligence. In the texts of yoga, he is known as Mahat and Virincha. He is addressed by many different names in the sacred texts of sankhya. He has many different forms and he is the soul of the universe. He is known as Ekakshara.[791] The three worlds have been created by him and he pervades everything with his atman. He is also known as Bahurupa and Vishvarupa.[792] Through transformations,

[786]This isn't stated very clearly. A mahayuga consists of a cycle of satya yuga, treta yuga, dvapara yuga and kali yuga, made up of twelve thousand years of the gods. One thousand mahayugas make up one kalpa, one of Brahma's days.

[787]This is a description of the great destruction, not temporary cycles of creation and destruction. Therefore, Brahma is himself destroyed.

[788]Svayambhu Shambhu.

[789]Yoga leads to eight major siddhis or powers. These are anima (becoming as small as one desires), *mahima* (as large as one desires), laghima (as light as one wants), *garima* (as heavy as one wants), *prapti* (obtaining what one wants), *prakamya* (travelling where one wants), *vashitvam* (powers to control creatures) and *ishitvam* (obtaining divine powers).

[790]Equated with Ishana.

[791]Literallly, the single one and the one without decay.

[792]Respectively, the one with many forms and the one with the universe as his form.

he creates himself from his own atman. The immensely energetic one creates consciousness[793] and Prajapati is created from that consciousness. The manifest[794] is created from the unmanifest and this is said to be the creation of knowledge. Mahat and Ahamkara also represent the creation of ignorance. Those who have thought about, and know the purport of the sacred texts, have said that knowledge and ignorance came about through these contrivances.[795] O king! Know that the elements are created from consciousness as the third.[796] Know that transformations lead to a fourth kind, ego in creatures and wind, light, space, water and earth and their attributes of sound, touch, form, taste and scent. There is no doubt that the ten categories were created in this way. O Indra among kings! Know that there is a fifth kind of creation that resulted from the elements—the ears, the skin, the eyes, the tongue, the nose as the fifth, speech, the two hands, the two feet, the anus and the genitals. These are the senses of knowledge and the organs of action. O king! They were created at the same time as the mind. It is the truth that these twenty-four exist in all creatures.[797] A brahmana who knows and has seen the truth about this does not sorrow. These are said to be in the bodies of everything in the three worlds. O best among men! Know that they exist in gods, men, danavas, yakshas, demons, gandharvas, kinnaras, giant serpents, charanas, pishachas, devarshis, travellers in the night,[798] gnats, insects, mosquitoes, filthy worms, rats, dogs, *svapacha*s, *vaineya*s,[799] chandalas, *pulkasa*s, elephants,

[793]*Ahamkara.* This also means self-consciousness or ego.

[794]Hiranyagarbha.

[795]This is a terse shloka and the meaning isn't obvious. The sense seems to be something like the following. While there was knowledge initially, ego and consciousness cloud it and lead to ignorance.

[796]The first being Hiranyagarbha and the second being Ahamkara.

[797]The five senses, the five objects of the senses, the five organs of action, the five elements, mind, intelligence, ego and consciousness.

[798]Rakshasas.

[799]There is probably a typo here, which is difficult to figure out. As stated, vaineyas can only be interpreted as those who have been converted back to the true religion.

horses, mules, tigers, trees and cattle. These manifestations are seen in everything that has form, in the water, on earth and in the sky. We have heard that it has been determined that these are the only regions where those with bodies exist. O son![800] Everything that has the sign of manifestation is destroyed. It has been said that, from one day to another, all creatures are destroyed. It has been said there is Akshara and there is the universe, which is destroyed. The universe has signs of the manifest and the unmanifest, but is enveloped in illusion. Mahat, the one who was created first, is also always referred to as an example of one who is destroyed. O great king! I have told you what you asked me. However, there is also a twenty-fifth. This is Vishnu. He is the truth and his manifestations are the truth. The learned ones have said that it is true that he is the refuge of all truth. Everything that is manifest and has form is based on that which has no form. Those twenty-four are manifest. However, the twenty-fifth has no form. He is in the heart of all beings and his form is established in his own atman. Consciousness and lack of consciousness always exist in all bodies that have form. They follow the characteristics of creation and destruction, but he[801] is without creation and without destruction. Although he is without qualities, he can always be perceived and is the one who invests qualities. Those who know about creation and destruction have said that this is the way that the intelligent Mahat acts, having united with Prakriti. In that womb, he is united with tamas, sattva and rajas. He dwells in the atmans of creatures and does not think that there is anything else. Though he possesses knowledge, because of loss of memory, he is conveyed into ignorance. Restrained by the qualities, he says, "I am this," or "I am that." Having been enveloped by the darkness of tamas, he is overcome by sentiments of ignorance. In that way, rajas and sattva lead to the sentiments of rajas and sattva. There are the three complexions of white, red and black.[802] Know that prakriti gets associated with these three complexions. Tamas conveys to hell and

[800]The word used is tata.

[801]Vishnu.

[802]Respectively associated with sattva, rajas and tamas.

rajas to the status of humanity. With sattva, one enjoys happiness and goes to the world of the gods. If one is helpless and indulges in wicked deeds, one obtains birth as inferior species. Men have both good and wicked deeds, gods have good ones only. The learned ones have spoken about these objects as those that are destructible. But it is the twenty-fifth that those with knowledge follow.'"'

Chapter 1620(292)

'"Vasishtha said, 'Because of forgetfulness, he[803] follows ignorance and has to go through thousands of lives in bodies. Depending on the qualities and the strengths of those qualities, he is born thousands of times as inferior species, and sometimes, also as gods. From the status of humanity, he goes to heaven. From heaven, he obtains the status of humanity. From humanity, for an infinitely long time, he sinks into hell. This is like an insect weaving a sheath around itself,[804] using thread as strands. In that way, the qualities are always like threads woven around the atman. Though he should be beyond opposite sentiments, it is thus that creatures succumb to opposite sentiments. Because of this headaches, eye diseases, toothaches, throat problems, dropsy, haemorrhoid, diseases like enlargement of glands, cholera, white leprosy, leprosy, *agnidaha*,[805] *sidhma*,[806] epilepsy and many other kinds of opposites are naturally seen in bodies. He sees himself to be afflicted by these and other ailments. Because of arrogance, he thinks that he enjoys the fruits of good deeds. He attires himself in a single garment or in torn garments.[807] He always lies down

[803]The atman. The text is gender neutral.

[804]A cocoon.

[805]Disease treated by thermal cauterization.

[806]Spots. There were eighteen kinds of leprosy and this is one of those.

[807]Different kinds of austerities are being described.

in inferior places. He lies down like a frog, or seats himself in *virasana*.[808] He clothes himself in rags and lies down under the sky. Or he lies down on bricks and stones, or thorns and stones. He lies down on ashes or bare stones. Or he smears himself and lies down on the ground. He sleeps in places meant for heroes, in mud and on stakes. Searching for many kinds of fruits, he futilely uses these different kinds of beds. He attires himself in girdles of munja grass or is naked. Or he wears silk and the skin of black antelopes. He attires himself in hemp or hair, or is dressed in tiger skin, lion skin, woven silk, those woven by insects and torn rags. Dressed in many other kinds of attire, he thinks himself to be intelligent. There are many kinds of food and many kinds of ornaments. He sometimes wears a single piece of cloth and eats only once a day. Alternatively, he eats at every fourth hour or every sixth hour, or once every six days or eight days. He eats once every seven days, or once every twelve days. He fasts for a month, or eats only roots and fruits. He subsists on air or water, or only eats oilcakes. He drinks only cow's urine, or vegetables and flowers. He eats moss and only drinks water from the palm of the hand. He subsists on leaves that have fallen down, or fruit that has fallen down. In a desire for happiness, he undergoes many other kinds of hardship. There are many types and many kinds of *chandrayana*.[809] There are the modes of the four ashramas. One can follow those ashramas, or deviate from those ashramas. Resorting to mountainous caverns, the good and the wicked practise them. They are solitary under the shades of mountains, or near fountains. There are many different kinds of meditation and diverse kinds of vows. There are colourful rituals and many kinds of austerities. There are different kinds of sacrifices and diverse ordinances. There are many kinds of donations for merchants, brahmanas, kshatriyas, vaishyas and

[808]Literally, posture of a hero. A seated position used by ascetics.

[809]A chandrayana is fasting determined by the moon's progress. For example, during krishnapaksha, the food taken is diminished by one mouthful per day and during shuklapaksha, it is increased by one mouthful per day.

shudras, decreed for the miserable, the blind and the helpless. Instigated by the three qualities, he is full of ignorance. He pursues sattva, rajas and tamas and dharma, artha and kama. With Prakriti influencing the atman, he engages in all these. He performs rites, to the words of svadha, vashat and svaha. He officiates at sacrifices, teaches, gives donations, receives, performs sacrifices, studies and does many other things. For birth, death, disputes, causing death and everything connected with the good and the bad, it has been said that there is the path of rituals. But it is the goddess Prakriti who actually does everything. At the time of the great destruction, at the end of the day,[810] all those qualities are withdrawn, like the sun withdrawing its net of rays at the time of setting. In this way, she[811] can be thought of, as repeatedly sporting with everything. Depending on the atman, there are many kinds of qualities that bring pleasure to the heart. But this is the way, the originator of creation and destruction works. There are rituals along the path of rituals. Those who are attached to the three qualities follow those three qualities. Driven by those, a person follows rituals along a path of rituals. He[812] has a sense of ownership and it is that sense of ownership that binds him down. O lord of men! It is because of ignorance that he thinks that all these can be transcended through good deeds. "These objects of pleasure will be enjoyed by me. I will enjoy the fruits of good and bad deeds in the world and then go to the world of the gods. It is my task to ensure happiness and through these good deeds, happiness will be mine. I will obtain happiness till the end of this life and also ensure it when I am born and born again. But because of what I do, till the end of my life, I may also confront misery. There is great misery for humans and the prospect of submerging in hell. From hell, it will take a long period of time before I become human again. From humanity, I may obtain divinity. From divinity, I may again obtain humanity. From humanity, I may also progressively have to descend into hell."

[810]Brahma's day.

[811]Prakriti.

[812]The atman.

Those who always think in this way are those whose atmans are covered by the qualities and therefore, it is as if they are without an atman. From that state of divinity or humanity, they obtain hell. They are enveloped by a sense of ownership and always circle around there. At the end of death, they have to go through millions of births. If a person acts in this way, with a desire for good and bad fruits in mind, he obtains the fruit of having to assume a body in the three worlds. But it is actually Prakriti who enjoys that desire in the three worlds. Inferior species, humanity and the world of the gods—all those three regions should be known as belonging to Prakriti. Prakriti has no attributes. But she is said to possess attributes in this world. In that way, Purusha is also thought of as possessing attributes. Prakriti is without attributes or taints, but she enters inside something[813] that possesses attributes. Therefore, one thinks that she is established in those attributes and undertakes action. The ear and the other senses, the five organs of action and speech and the others unite with the qualities and become engaged. Because of the senses, he thinks, "I am the one who is acting." He[814] is actually devoid of the senses. He is without attributes. But he thinks that he is with attributes. He is beyond signs, but thinks himself to have signs. He is beyond time, but thinks himself to be subject to time. He is beyond understanding, but thinks himself to be understanding. He is beyond truth, but thinks himself to be truth. He is immortal, but thinks himself to be mortal. He is motionless, but thinks himself to possess motion. He is without a field,[815] but thinks himself to possess a field. He is beyond creation, but thinks himself to be created. He is beyond austerities, but thinks himself to be made up of austerities. He is beyond all objectives, but thinks himself to possess an objective. He is beyond sentiments, but thinks himself to possess sentiments. He is beyond fear, but finds himself to be touched by fear. He is beyond decay. But because of ignorance, he thinks himself to be subject to decay.'"'

[813]The body.

[814]The atman.

[815]The body.

Chapter 1621(293)

'"Vasishtha said, 'Thus, because of his ignorance and because of association with those who are ignorant, he faces downfall and goes through millions of births. He goes through thousands of abodes, but each of those ends in death. He is born as inferior species, as human, or in the world of the gods. Like the encasement of the moon, he waxes and wanes thousands of times. It is known that the moon always has kalas.[816] Fifteen of these increase and decrease, but the sixteenth is always there. That is the way with the atman too, with abodes increasing and decreasing. But like the moon, the sixteenth is always subtle and sustained.[817] It is not united with anything. Nor is it used up in the course of anything that happens. O supreme among kings! These[818] are the ones which are destroyed and take birth again. These are seen as Prakriti and their destruction is said to be emancipation. The sixteenth kala in the body is not manifest. But because of the sense of ownership, it circles around. One is ignorant about the twenty- fifth[819] that is there in the atman. It is sparkling and pure and is fanned by an auspicious breeze. O king! Though the atman is pure, because of the taint, it is rendered impure. Though one knows, one serves ignorance and roams around, like an ignorant person. O supreme among kings! That is the one who should be known. However, because of serving the three qualities of Prakriti, one is rendered ordinary.'

'"Karalajanaka said, 'O illustrious one! It is said that the relationship between that which is not destroyed and that which

[816]The moon's diameter is divided into sixteen kalas. The moon waxes and wanes by one kala each day and the sixteenth one is the one that remains on the night of the new moon.

[817]The five senses, the five organs of action, mind, intelligence, ego, ignorance and prakriti (or consciousness influenced by prakriti) are probably the fifteen which are modified. Pure consciousness (not influenced by prakriti) is the sixteenth.

[818]The fifteen.

[819]Vishnu.

is destroyed is like the relationship between a woman and a man. Without a man, a woman can never conceive. Without a woman, a man can also not create a form.[820] They have a relationship with each other and depend on the qualities of each other. That is the way forms are created among all kinds of beings. For the sake of desire, they have intercourse with each other at the right season and resort to each other's qualities. That is the way forms result. Let me tell you about these signs. There are qualities for a man and there are qualities for a mother. O brahmana! We know that bones, sinews and marrow come from the father. We have heard that skin, flesh and blood comes from the mother. O best among brahmanas! This is what has been laid down in the sacred texts of the Vedas. Since it has been laid down in the Vedas and in the sacred texts, it can be taken as proof. The proofs of the Vedas and the sacred texts represent eternal proof. This is the eternal relationship between Prakriti and Purusha. O illustrious one! But I cannot see any signs about the dharma of emancipation. I can see no signs of this inside me. Therefore, if there is anything evident about the truth, please tell me about it. I desire emancipation. I desire that which grants freedom from fear. It[821] is without a body. It is without decay. It is divine and is beyond the senses. It is the ultimate lord.'

'"Vasishtha replied, 'What you have said about the proofs of the Vedas and the sacred texts is indeed true and you have accepted them. O lord of men! O one who knows about the truth! But though you have accepted both those types of books, the Vedas and the sacred texts, you have not grasped the truth that is there in those two sets of books. If a person is eager to accept books like the Vedas and the sacred texts, but does not know the truth about the purport of those books, his acceptance is fruitless. A person who does not understand the purport of those books only bears a burden. If a person does not understand the truth about the purport of a book, his study of that book is fruitless. If a person is asked about the purport of a book, he should explain what he

[820]Have offspring.

[821]The atman.

has grasped by studying the truth carefully. If a person is gross in his intelligence and cannot explain the meaning of a book in an assembly, it is evident that his knowledge is limited and he cannot speak about its meaning. A person whose soul is imperfect cannot speak about the truth. He is laughed at. This is also true of those who know about the atman. O Indra among kings! Therefore, listen to what has been instructed by the great-souled ones who know about sankhya and yoga. What is seen by those who practise yoga is exactly that which is followed by those who practise sankhya. A person who sees that sankhya and yoga are identical is intelligent. O son! Skin, flesh, fat, bile, marrow and sinews—these belong to the senses and you have spoken to me about them. Objects result from objects and senses from the senses. Like seeds from seeds, bodies originate from bodies. The atman is beyond senses, without seed and without objects. How can that great-souled one, who possesses no qualities, give rise to qualities? Qualities result from qualities and are destroyed. They are born from Prakriti and do not exist otherwise. Skin, flesh, blood, fat, bile, marrow, bones and sinews—know that these eight are created from the seed and Prakriti. Male and non-male—these three[822] genders are said to result from Prakriti. Those that are not male are said to be non-male genders. Prakriti has no gender. But her offspring obtain gender and form. For example, flowers and fruit have form, though they result from what is formless. It is inferred that gender is obtained in this way. O son! It is the twenty-fifth one who determines the gender of the atman. He is without beginning and without end. He is infinite. He sees everything. He is without disease. It is because of ego that qualities are said to result from qualities. Qualities can result in qualities. How can qualities result from one who possesses no qualities? People who have insight about qualities know this. That is the reason all those qualities are seen to originate with Prakriti. A person who goes beyond the qualities, sees the supreme. All those who are intelligent in the schools of sankhya and yoga speak about the supreme. Those immensely wise ones are intelligent

[822]Non-male includes female and neuter.

and have abandoned ignorance. Those who are ignorant speak of a manifest Ishvara who possesses qualities. Ishvara is always established as someone who is devoid of qualities. Those who are accomplished in sankhya and yoga understand about the supreme. They know about a twenty-fifth who is beyond Prakriti's qualities. Those who know about the unmanifest can overcome the fear of birth. Those who know go there, just as the intelligent ones do.[823] O scorcher of enemies! These are the indications that have been properly instructed, though the paths of those who are intelligent and those who know are separate. They respectively speak about the signs of what is destroyed and what is not destroyed. There is a single one who is not destroyed and everything else is said to be subject to destruction. When a person has studied the twenty-five attributes properly, he realizes that all philosophy leads to the single one and many kinds of philosophy are irrelevant. There is a truth that is over and above individual indications. In the twenty-five categories that are created, the learned speak of this as the truth. The supreme truth is said to be what is beyond the twenty-five. There are categories and there is conduct according to the categories. While this is true, the eternal truth is above this.'"'

Chapter 1622(294)

'"Karalajanaka asked, 'O supreme among rishis! You have spoken about the characteristics of the many and the one.[824] But I still detect some doubt about the signs of the two. O

[823]This is expressed in a convoluted way. Intelligent ones know about Vishnu. Those who know are those who know about the unmanifest. But since Vishnu and the unmanifest one are identical, the two destinations are also identical. Intelligent is an expression being applied to the practitioners of sankhya, while those who know is a label that is being applied to the practitioners of yoga.

[824]The many is destructible and the one is indestructible.

unblemished one! This is comprehended by both those who are knowledgable and those who are ignorant.[825] However, because my intelligence is gross, I still have some doubt about the truth of this. You have spoken about the causes behind that which is destructible and that which is not destructible. O unblemished one! However, because my intelligence is fickle, I have forgotten about all of that. That is the reason I wish to know how one can be seen in many. How does a knowledgable or ignorant person comprehend the truth about this? O illustrious one! Tell me, completely and separately, what sankhya and yoga say on knowledge and ignorance and on the indestructible and the destructible?'

'"Vasishtha replied, 'I will tell you what you have asked me about. O great king! Hear separately from me about the practice of yoga. For yogis who practice yoga, meditation is the supreme strength. Those who know about the Vedas say that there are two kinds of meditation—concentration of the mind and pranayama. Pranayama possesses qualities, while concentration of the mind is without qualities.[826] O lord of men! With the exception of three times—passing urine, releasing excrement and eating—at all other times, the mind should be devoted to the supreme. A sage uses his mind to withdraw from the senses and the objects of the senses and should engage in the twenty-two and the supreme twenty-four.[827] The intelligent person uses these to direct the atman. Learned ones have said that this is the undecaying entity that resides in the body. It has been instructed that the atman must always be known. It has been determined that this is for someone whose mind has been delinked from objects and not for others. He must be free from all attachments. He must be restrained in diet and conquer the senses. During the early and later part of the night, the mind must be fixed

[825]That the atman is one.

[826]Pranayama is performed while chanting mantras, but concentration of the mind doesn't require mantras.

[827]The twenty-four have been mentioned earlier. In pranayama, there are different methods of breathing and controlling prana, with a list that runs into around fifty. Clearly, twenty-two of these are being singled out.

on the atman. O lord of Mithila! All the senses must be stilled by the mind. The mind must be stilled with intelligence. Having done this, one should be as motionless as stone. He must be as motionless as a pillar. Like a mountain, he must not move. When learned ones, who know about the techniques, are like this, they are said to be united in yoga. He does not hear. He does not inhale. He does not taste. He does not see. He does not know any touch and there is no resolution in his mind. He does not pay attention to anything, or understand anything. He is like a piece of wood. The learned say that such a person is then united with Prakriti. One is seen to blaze like a lamp in a place where there is no wind. He does not move and is immobile. Such a person ascends upwards and doesn't descend into inferior species. Then he sees what is to be seen. Having seen, he does not speak. People like us say that the heart of the knower and what is to be known, the atman, have become one. He is like a smokeless fire with the seven flames.[828] He is like the sun with its rays. He is like the fiery lightning in the sky. He sees the atman in his own self. Great-souled and intelligent and learned brahmanas see it in this way. This is the brahman, who has not been born. This is immortality that exists in the atman. It is said that this is more subtle than what is most subtle and greater than what is greatest. Though it is inside all beings, it is certain that it cannot be seen. The creator of the world can be seen through the wealth of intelligence and the lamp of the mind. It is the greatness that is beyond darkness. It is located beyond darkness. Those who know about the truth of the Vedas say that it is the dispeller of darkness. It is sparkling. It is beyond darkness. It is without attributes. It has the characteristic of being without traits. Yogis say that this is yoga. I think that these are the signs of yoga. This is the way they see the supreme and undecaying one in their own atmans. I have thus told you the truth about the philosophy of yoga.

""'I will now tell you about the knowledge of sankhya, where one progressively destroys the errors. Those who know about

[828] A fire has seven flames.

Prakriti say that the unmanifest Prakriti is the supreme. O supreme among kings! From this, the second entity, known as Mahat, is generated. We have heard that the third entity, consciousness, results from Mahat. Those who have the insight of sankhya say that the five elements are created from consciousness. These eight are Prakriti.[829] There are sixteen transformations of these. In particular, there are the five senses and the five organs of action.[830] Learned ones who know about sankhya say that this is the truth. They know about the ordinances of sankhya and are always established along the path of sankhya. Whatever is generated from the cause, is also destroyed within it. As they have been created from inside that atman, they are destroyed in reverse order. They are created in the proper order, but are destroyed in the reverse order.[831] O supreme among kings! The qualities are always like waves in an ocean. This is the way the creation and destruction of Prakriti also take place. When there is destruction, the single one[832] alone remains and many are subsequently created from it. O Indra among kings! This is what has been determined by those who have reflected on it. It is evident that the presider[833] is not manifest. It is both one and many and so is the case with Prakriti. There is a single one at the time of destruction and many at the time of creation. Prakriti generates from its womb and the atman makes it many.[834] The great-souled one is established over the twenty-five that constitute the field.[835] O Indra among kings! That is the reason the best among ascetics say that it[836] is the presider. We have heard that it is the presider and it presides

[829]The five elements, consciousness, Mahat and the original Prakriti.

[830]Added to the five elements, there are fifteen, and the mind is added to get sixteen.

[831]That is, consciousness is created after Mahat, but is destroyed before Mahat.

[832]In this context, the Purusha.

[833]Purusha.

[834]Purusha makes Prakriti many.

[835]Prakriti is the field and the great-souled one is the brahman.

[836]The brahman.

over the field.[837] Because it knows the kshetra, the umanifest one is known as kshetrajna. Since the unmanifest one lay down in earlier times, it is known as Purusha.[838] Those that are known as kshetra and kshetrajna are distinct. While kshetra is also not manifest, it becomes discernible because of the twenty-fifth. Knowledge and the object of knowledge are said to be distinct. Knowledge is not manifest, but becomes known because of the twenty-fifth. The kṣhetra is not manifest and neither are intelligence and Ishvara. The lack of Ishvara isn't truth. Truth is known because of the twenty-fifth. These are the principles of sankhya philosophy. Those who believe in the philosophy of sankhya say that, in accordance with sankhya, it is Prakriti that acts. They enumerate and ascertain the truth about the twenty-four elements. Those who believe in sankhya talk about Prakriti and the twenty-fifth, which is devoid of qualities. It is said that if a person has got to know the twenty-fifth, he is the one who knows. A person who knows this realizes that it is the atman alone that exists. I have properly spoken to you about the true nature of sankhya philosophy. A person who knows this obtains tranquility. Prakriti is manifest to such a person, as something that is directly seen. It is the one with qualities and there is also the entity without qualities. When they no longer exist,[839] they do not have to return again. They obtain sentiments that are without decay and also obtain the supreme and unmanifest one. But there are also those who do not see properly and do not see everything as one. O destroyer of enemies! They do not reach the unmanifest and have to return again and again. They have not understood everything and have not comprehended. They are born in manifest forms and are under the subjugation of the manifest. Everything that is manifest results from the unmanifest and the twenty-fifth. A person who knows this does not suffer from any fear.'"'

[837]The field or kshetra is Prakriti and the one who knows about the field, kshetrajna, is the brahman.

[838]The word *pura* means earlier, ancient, in the beginning. Hence, purusha means the original or primeval one.

[839]When they die.

Chapter 1623(295)

"'Vasishtha said, 'O supreme among kings! I have spoken to you about the philosophy of sankhya. Now listen to me as I describe knowledge and ignorance to you progressively. The manifest, which is subject to the rule of creation and destruction, is said to be ignorance. The twenty-fifth, freed from creation and destruction, is knowledge. Listen to what has, in due course, been described as knowledge. O son! Rishis who have the sight of sankhya have laid this down. Among the senses and the organs of action, the senses are said to represent knowledge. Among the senses, we have heard that intelligence is superior. The learned ones have said that the mind is superior to the senses and represents knowledge. Compared to the mind, the five elements are said to represent knowledge. There is no doubt that consciousness is superior to the five elements. O lord of men! Compared to consciousness, understanding represents knowledge. Compared to understanding, the unmanifest Prakriti, expressive of the truth about the supreme lord, is superior. O best among men! Among the different kinds of knowledge that are to be known, the ordinances are said to be the supreme. The unmanifest and twenty-fifth is said to be the supreme form of knowledge. O king! Among everything that can be known, this is said to be the supreme kind of knowledge. The twenty-fifth is the object of knowledge and knowledge about this is said to be unmanifest. A person who knows about the twenty-fifth knows about what is unmanifest. I have told you the difference between knowledge and ignorance. I will now tell you what has been said about the destructible and the indestructible. Listen. Both[840] have been said to be destructible and perishable. I will tell you truthfully the reasons that have been cited in support of this. There is the view that both are imperishable and both are without a beginning and without an end. Those who have thought about knowledge have said that both are truly nothing but principles. Though it leads to the principles of creation and

[840]The jivatman and Prakriti.

destruction, the unmanifest[841] is said to be indestructible. It is through its qualities that it repeatedly creates. Mahat and the other qualities are respectively generated. It is said to be the truth that the twenty-fifth presides over the field. The unmanifest that is the twenty-fifth withdraws the net of qualities and the qualities merge into it. The qualities merge into its quality and the single one that remains is Prakriti. O son! Kshetrajna then merges into kshetra.[842] Prakriti, characterized by its qualities, then goes towards destruction. O king of Videha! With the qualities withdrawn, it no longer possesses any qualities. In this way, kshetrajna's knowledge of kshetra is also destroyed. We have heard that Prakriti is then devoid of qualities. The one with qualities then becomes destructible. He[843] realizes that just like himself, Prakriti is devoid of qualities. Discarding Prakriti, he then becomes pure. The intelligent one realizes himself to be distinct.[844] O Indra among kings! When he gives up that combination, he exists separately and Prakriti is also seen to be distinct from that combination. When he no longer desires Prakriti and that net of qualities, he can behold the supreme.

"''Having seen the supreme, he is free from all anxiety. "What have I done? I have been like a person overtaken by destiny. Because of my ignorance, I have been like a fish entangled in a net. Because of my delusion, I have moved from one body to another body. My conduct has been like that of an ignorant fish, moving from one body of water to another body of water and thinking in its ignorance that the water is everything. In that fashion, because of my ignorance, I have not known my own atman. Shame on my ignorance that I have been repeatedly submerged thus. Because of my confusion, I have followed the course from one body to another body. This[845] is alone my friend and my emancipation is with it. I am capable of being

[841]Prakriti.

[842]Purusha into Prakriti.

[843]Purusha.

[844]Distinct from Prakriti. Succeeding shlokas suggest that this is a description of a yogi in meditation.

[845]The brahman.

united with it. I am just as it is. I see myself as equal to it. I am like it. It is without blemish. It is evident that I am just like it. I have been ignorant and deluded. Because of ignorance and delusion, I have been properly entangled. Though without attachments, I have spent a long period of time being attached. For a long period of time, I have been controlled by others, but did not realize it. There are different kinds of states—high, medium and low.[846] How can I be like that? How can I dwell with her[847] as an equal? Because of my ignorance, I went to her earlier. I will still myself now. I will not dwell with her and be deceived for a long period of time. I am without transformations. However, I have been deceived by the one who possesses transformations.[848] That is not her crime. It is my crime. It is because of my sentiments that I became attached and withdrew from what had presented itself.[849] That is the reason I assumed many forms and moved from one body to another body. Despite being one without a body, I have assumed the form of a body and have been assailed, because of that sense of ownership. Prakriti has accordingly conveyed me into those wombs. I am without a form. Thanks to the sense of ownership, what acts have I performed in those forms? She is in those wombs and destroys sense and consciousness. I do not possess any sense of ownership. But goaded by ego, I have performed acts. She divided my atman into many parts and repeatedly engaged me. However, now. I have no sense of ownership and no ego. I have acted so as to discard the sense of ownership and have always removed a sense of ego from myself. Having escaped from all that, I have resorted to what is beneficial. I will go to that tranquility and not unite with what is without consciousness. That kind of union is beneficial. I have no similarity with her." He thus realizes the supreme relationship with the twenty-fifth. He abandons what is destructible and not beneficial and is conveyed to the indestructible. This is unmanifest. But because

[846]Referring to states of birth—high being gods, medium being humans and low being inferior species.

[847]Prakriti.

[848]Prakriti.

[849]The brahman.

of the nature of becoming manifest, one without qualities is vested with qualities. O one from Mithila! Having seen the original one who is without qualities, he becomes like it. I have spoken to you about the indications of what is indestructible and destructible, according to the knowledge that I have obtained and according to what the sacred texts have instructed. I will now again tell you about what I have heard. This is knowledge that is sparkling, without any doubt, and subtle. I have told you what the sacred texts of sankhya and yoga instruct. This has been stated in the sacred texts of sankhya and the philosophy of yoga. O lord of the forests! The knowledge of sankhya can awake people and for the welfare of disciples, this has been clearly enunciated. Accomplished people say that those sacred texts are extensive. The yogis also accept these sacred texts. O lord of men! Those who follow sankhya do not see the truth about a supreme twenty-fifth. What they regard as supreme has already been described.[850] Those who cite indications from yoga talk about the truth of awakening, knowledge, that which is to be known and the one who knows.'"'[851]

Chapter 1624(296)

'"Vasishtha said, 'Hear about awakening and the unmanifest one, from whom all qualities are created. He sustains these qualities and creates and withdraws them. O lord of men! For the sake of sport, he[852] divides his own self into many parts and collects them again. The one who can understand this action[853] does not

[850]Sankhya philosophy does not believe in a personal god and this simply states that.

[851]The one who knows is the jivatman and the one who is to be known is the paramatman or brahman. Yoga talks of both.

[852]The brahman. Throughout this chapter, the shlokas are very difficult to understand and several liberties have been taken.

[853]The jivatman.

understand. Because he is capable of understanding the one who is not manifest, he is spoken of as *budhyamana*.[854] Nevertheless, he cannot understand the one who is not manifest, whether it is with qualities or without qualities. Therefore, rare is the case when he is awakened. The learned texts have said that whenever budhyamana gets to know the unmanifest and twenty-fifth one, he becomes united with it. That is the reason the one who is not manifest is spoken of as ignorant.[855] Budhyamana is spoken of as being both unmanifest and ignorant. Nothing with life can comprehend the great-souled and twenty-fifth. The twenty-sixth is sparkling, immeasurable and eternal and it can understand.[856] It can always understand the twenty-fourth and the twenty-fifth. The immensely radiant one[857] follows her nature, vis-à-vis both what is seen and is not seen. O son! Those who truly understand can not only see the twenty-fourth and the twenty-fifth, but also the unmanifest brahman. When a person knows the atman, he thinks himself to be it.[858] He uses that sight to look at prakriti and the unmanifest. With that pure and unsullied knowledge, he comprehends the supreme. O tiger among kings! He is then established in knowledge about the twenty-sixth. He then casts aside the unmanifest,[859] which is subject to the rules of creation and destruction. Though because of consciousness, prakriti is invested with qualities, he knows the one without qualities. Having seen the unmanifest, he is only full of dharma. Having approached the whole, he is freed and obtains the atman. This is said to have form and also not have form.[860] It is immortal and without decay. O one who grants honours! Though it resorts to what has form, it has no form. The learned ones talk about twenty five principles. O son! But

[854]Budhyamana means the one who comprehends and is being used for the jivatman, which can understand the nature of the paramatman.

[855]This seems to be a reference to the jivatman, but can mean prakriti too.

[856]The jivatman seems to be the twenty-fourth, prakriti the twenty-fifth and the paramatman the twenty-sixth.

[857]Prakriti.

[858]Thinks that the jivatman is no different from the paramatman.

[859]Prakriti.

[860]Because of ignorance, the brahman is perceived to have form.

the intelligent one[861] has no form and is beyond these principles. The swift freeing from principles is a sign of intelligence. A wise person knows himself to be the twenty-sixth and accepts himself to be the immortal one, without decay. Through the strength of the absolute, he has no doubt that he is identical to it.[862] However, though awakened by the intelligent twenty-sixth, there is still ignorance. The sacred texts of sankhya have spoken about the signs of this. When one is united with consciousness and the twenty-fifth,[863] because of that consciousness, one does not comprehend the sense of unity. O lord of Mithila! O lord of men! Because of the rules of attachment, one is not awakened. However, when one is awakened and loses attachment, one realizes unity. Without any sense of attachment, a learned person approaches the twenty-sixth. Abandoning the unmanifest,[864] he obtains powers and comprehends the truth. With knowledge about the twenty-sixth awakened, he realizes that the twenty four are valueless. As indicated in the sacred texts of sankhya, I have spoken to you about the true nature of knowledge. It is with the sight of the sacred texts that one must consider the many and the one. One must understand the difference between the gnat and the fig,[865] the fish and the water and this and that.[866] That is the one one must approach the one and the many. When one has knowledge about ignorance and the unmanifest, that is said to be emancipation. This twenty-fifth resides in bodies and is said to be freed through comprehension about the unmanifest. It has been determined that this is the only method for emancipation and there is no other. Because it[867] dwells in the body, it conveys the impression of being different. By uniting with purity, one becomes pure. By uniting with intelligence, one becomes intelligent. O bull among men! By uniting with the dharma of emancipation, one becomes emancipated. By

[861]The atman.

[862]The jivatman being equated with the paramatman.

[863]Prakriti.

[864]Prakriti.

[865]Gnats are found inside ripe figs.

[866]The jivatman and the paramatman.

[867]The jivatman.

following the dharma of becoming engaged in this way, the atman becomes engaged. By striving for emancipation, one unites with emancipation. By peforming pure deeds, one becomes pure and resplendent. By uniting with the unblemished atman, one's own atman becomes unblemished.[868] By uniting with the absolute, one obtains the absolute in one's atman. By uniting with the one who is free, one uses that freedom to obtain freedom.

'"'O great king! I have told you the truth. I have accurately described the exact truth to you. This is about the eternal, pure and original brahman, and accept the purport of this. O king! You can pass on this supreme knowledge to a person who does not follow the Vedas, as long as that person is free of malice. But he must seek this knowledge, which leads to an awakening. As long as he bows down and follows instructions, you can pass this on, for the sake of his awakening. However, it should not be passed on to a person who has falsehood in his soul, or is deceitful, impotent or fraudulent in his intelligence. Nor must the knowledge be given to learned men who are jealous. Listen to the ones to whom it can be given. A person who is faithful, possesses qualities, one who always abstains from censuring others, one who performs pure yoga for the sake of knowledge, a forgiving person who performs rites for the sake of welfare, one who can discriminate about good conduct, a person who loves the rituals, one who is extremely learned and does not engage in quarrels, one who is knowledgable and forgives those who cause injury, one who possesses strength and self-control—these are the people to whom it can be given. It is said that this pure and supreme knowledge of the brahman should not be given to those who are devoid of these qualities. Those who know about dharma have said that no benefits or fruits accrue from giving it to undeserving people. If a person does not observe the vows, it should not be given to him, even if one obtains the earth, full of riches, in exchange. O Indra among men! But there is no doubt that this supreme knowledge can be communicated to a person who has conquered his senses. O Karala! Having heard

[868]Respectively, the paramatman and the jivatman.

about the supreme brahman now, you should not have the slightest reason for fear. I have spoken about the pure and the supreme, the dispeller of sorrow, and without a beginning, a middle and an end. O king! This is deep and without birth and death. It is auspicious and free from disease and fear. Having seen it, abandon all your delusion now. Know that this is the true nature of knowledge. O lord of men! In ancient times, I gratified the eternal Hiranyagarbha and obtained it from him. I made efforts to please the one who is fierce in his energy. Having obtained knowledge about the supreme brahman, I have now passed it on to you. O Indra among men! Asked by you, I have now told you exactly what I learned. O Indra among men! This is what I obtained from Brahma. This is great knowledge, the ancient wisdom about emancipation.'"

'Bhishma said, "O great king! I have told you about the instructions of the supreme rishi. I have spoken to you about the twenty-fifth, the supreme brahman from whom one does not return. If one does not comprehend this supreme knowledge, one has to return again. But if one knows the truth, there is no decay and no death. O son! O king! I heard about this supreme and beneficial knowledge from the devarshi[869] and have recounted it to you. The great-souled Vasishtha obtained it from Hiranyagarbha. Narada obtained it from Vasishtha, tiger among rishis. I got to know about the great and eternal brahman from Narada. O Indra among Kouravas! Do not grieve. You have heard about this supreme objective. A person who knows about the destructible and the indestructible has no reason to fear. O lord of the earth! A person who does not know about it has reason to fear. Because of ignorance and being foolish in the soul, a person has to repeatedly return. After death, he is born thousands of times and dies again. He is sometimes born in the world of the gods, but is also born as inferior species. However, if he is purified over time, he can cross that ocean of ignorance. That ocean of ignorance is terrible. It is said to be unmanifest and fathomless. O descendant of the Bharata lineage! Day after day, beings are submerged in it. O lord of the earth! But you have crossed that eternal, unmanifest

[869]Narada.

and fathomless ocean of ignorance. Therefore, you have been freed from rajas and from tamas."'

Chapter 1625(297)

'Bhishma said, "Once, Janaka's son was roaming around in a desolate forest. In the course of the hunt, he saw a brahmana rishi who was Bhrigu's descendant. Vasuman bowed his head down before the seated sage and also sat down. Having taken his permission, he then asked him a question. 'O illustrious one! What brings the greatest benefit, in this world and in the next, to a man who possesses a temporary body, but is overcome by desire?' Having been honoured and asked, the great-souled and great ascetic was gratified and spoke these beneficial words. 'If your mind desires what is positive in this world and in the next, then you must control your senses and restrain yourself from causing injury to beings. Dharma brings benefit to those who are virtuous. Dharma is the refuge of those who are virtuous. O son! It is from dharma that the three worlds, with their mobile and immobile objects, are generated. You wish for the taste of desire. Why have you not become satiated with these? O evil-minded one! You see the honey, but not the downfall.[870] A person who seeks the fruits of knowledge must pursue it. Like that, a person who seeks the fruits of dharma must pursue it. If a wicked person desires dharma, it will be extremely difficult for him to perform pure deeds. However, if a virtuous person desires dharma, it is extremely easy for him to perform those difficult deeds. If one dwells in the forest but pursues what would bring happiness in a village, then one is just like a villager. Similarly, if one dwells in a village but pursues what would bring happiness in the forest, then one is just like a forest dweller. Controlling yourself faithfully,

[870]The image is of a man who climbs a tree in search of honey, but falls down and dies.

observe dharma in thoughts, words and deeds. Examine the good and the bad aspects of attachment and detachment. Without any malice, always donate a lot to virtuous people who ask for it, but bearing the time and the place in mind and honouring them with vows and purification. One should earn through auspicious means and then give it away. When giving, one must discard anger and not be tormented at having given. Nor should one boast about it. Non-violent, pure, self-controlled, truthful in words, upright, pure in birth and deeds and learned in the Vedas—such a brahmana is a worthy recipient. He must have been born from a virtuous mother who has had only one husband. He must know about Rig, Sama and Yajur and must perform the six tasks.[871] Such a recipient is said to be a deserving one. If one does not consider the time and the place and performs the act of giving to an undeserving person, a man acts in a contrary way and dharma becomes adharma. A man can clean a little dirt on the body easily. More requires greater effort. In that way, much effort needs to be made to dispel great sin. After easing oneself, clarified butter is a good medication. In that way, once one has cleansed the sins and follows dharma, this brings happiness in the hereafter. There is good and evil in the minds of all beings. One must withdraw from the evil and use the good to cross. One must be attached to one's own dharma and desire that dharma. You do not possess patience. Cultivate patience. You do not possess intelligence. Cultivate intelligence. You do not possess tranquility. Cultivate tranquility. You do not possess wisdom. Cultivate wisdom. If one associates with the right people, one is capable of using one's energy to obtain what is beneficial in this world and in the next. Fortitude is the foundation for this. Because of lack of fortitude, rajarshi Mahabhisha fell down from heaven. Yayati obtained the worlds through his fortitude, but fell down when his merits were exhausted. Serve ascetics who are devoted to dharma and are learned. You will then obtain great intelligence and the welfare that you desire.' His[872]

[871]Recommended for brahmanas—performing sacrifices, officiating at the sacrifices of others, studying, teaching, receiving and giving.

[872]Vasuman's.

natural disposition was good and he heard the words spoken by the sage. He withdrew his mind from desire and turned his intelligence towards dharma."'

Chapter 1626(298)

'Yudhishthira said, "There is adharma. There is dharma, which brings emancipation and freedom from all foundations. It frees from birth and death and also frees from good and evil deeds. It is always auspicious and grants freedom from fear. It is always eternal and without decay. It is pure and always brings comfort. You should speak to me about this."

'Bhishma replied, "O descendant of the Bharata lineage! In this connection, there is the ancient history of a conversation between Yajnavalkya and Janaka. Yajnavalkya was the best among rishis and was supreme among those who knew the answers to all questions. The immensely illustrious King Daivarati, from Janaka's lineage, asked him this question. 'O brahmana rishi! How many senses are there? How many kinds of prakriti are there said to be? What is the unmanifest and supreme brahman? What is superior to even that? What is creation and destruction? What is the measurement of time? O Indra among brahmanas! You should tell me about this. I desire to obtain your favours. You are a store of knowledge. I am ignorant and am asking you. On all these doubts, I wish to hear from you.' Yajnavalkya replied, 'O protector of the earth! Listen to what you have asked. This is the supreme knowledge of yoga and in particular, that of sankhya. None of this is unknown to you. Nevertheless, you have asked me. It is eternal dharma that one must answer when one has been asked. It is said that there are eight kinds of prakriti and sixteen kinds of transformations. Those who have thought about adhyatma have said that there are seven kinds of the manifest. There are the unmanifest, Mahat, ego, earth, wind, space, water and light as the eight.[873] These eight are known as prakriti. Listen to the transformations. These are the ear, the skin, the eye, the tongue, the nose as the fifth, sound, touch, form, taste, scent, speech, the two hands, the two feet, the anus and the penis.[874] O Indra among kings! O one from Mithila! Those that originate in the five great elements[875] are known as Vishesha and the senses of knowledge are known as Savishesha. Those who have thought about adhyatma say that the mind is the sixteenth. You, and other intelligent ones who know the truth, also hold the same view. O king! The Mahat atman is generated from the unmanifest. The learned say that this is the first and most important creation. O lord of men! Ego[876] is created from Mahat. Those who know about adhyatma say that this second creation is that of intelligence. The mind is generated from consciousness and this creates qualities in beings. This is said to be third creation, which results from consciousness. O lord of men! The five great elements are generated from the mind. I say that this fourth creation is from the mind. Those who know about the elements say that sound, touch, form, taste and scent are the fifth creation and concern the elements. The ear, the skin, the eye, the tongue and the nose as the fifth, are said to be sixth creation by those who have thought a lot about the atman. O lord of men! Those that are created after the ear and the other senses are said to be the seventh creation, concerning the senses.[877] O lord of men! There are the flows that rise upwards and move diagonally and the learned know these as the eighth and straight creation.[878] O lord of men! There are also flows that move directly and diagonally downwards. The learned call these the ninth and straight creation. O lord of

[873]Here, the unmanifest means prakriti. The other seven are manifest.

[874]The two hands are counted as one and the two feet are also counted as one. When one adds the mind, which has not been mentioned, one gets the sixteen transformations.

[875]The organs of action and the objects of the senses.

[876]That is, consciousness.

[877]This isn't very clear, but probably refers to the organs of action.

[878]This refers to the various breaths of life, some of which rise upwards, while there are others that move diagonally.

men! This is the truth about the nine different kinds of creation. The learned texts speak of these as possessing twenty-four signs. O great king! After this truth about the qualities, the great-souled ones have spoken about the measurement of time. Listen to this.'"'

Chapter 1627(299)

'"Yajnavalkya said, 'O best among men! I will tell you about the measurement of time for the unmanifest. Ten thousand kalpas make up a single day for him. O lord of men! His night is said to be of the same duration. When night is over, he awakes and first creates the herbs, which provide sustenance to all living beings. He then creates Brahma, who arises from the golden egg. It has been heard by us that his form is there in all[879] living beings. Having dwelt for one year inside the egg, the great sage Prajapati emerged and created the entire earth, heaven above it, and all that is below. O king! Those who have studied the Vedas know that the sky is between earth and heaven. The lord created the sky to lie between them. Those who are learned about the Vedas and the Vedangas say that the duration of his day is seven thousand and five hundred kalpas. Those who have thought about adhyatma say that his night is of an equal duration. From his divine self, he creates Mahat and consciousness. Before creating any other beings, the great rishi created four sons.[880] O supreme among kings! We have heard that these were the ancestors of the fathers. O best among men! We have heard that the gods, the ancestors, all those who surround the world of the gods and mobile and immobile objects were their sons. Parameshthi, the consciousness, then created the five elements—the earth, the wind, the sky, the water and the light, as the fifth. This consciousness, which led to the third creation, is said to

[879]Brahma.

[880]Through his mental powers, Brahma created four sons—Sanaka, Sanatana, Sananda and Sanatkumara. However, this is also interpreted as mind, intelligence, consciousness and superconsciousness.

have five thousand kalpas as his night and his day is said to possess an equal duration. O lord of the earth! Sound, touch, form, taste and scent, as the fifth, are known as Vishesha and adhere to the five great elements. Because they are enveloped by these, beings kill each other. They respect each other, but also rival each other. Overcome by those undecaying qualities, they slaughter each other. They whirl around in this world and are born as inferior species. O lord of men! Their[881] day is said to last for three thousand kalpas. Their night is of the same duration and this is also the case with the mind. O Indra among kings! Instigated by the senses, the mind circulates among all of them. The senses do not see anything. It is the mind that sees. The eye perceives form only when it is driven by the mind. The eye doesn't do this alone. When the mind is distracted, the eye may seem to see, but does not actually see. It is said that all the senses perceive. O king! But this is incorrect. When the mind does not act, the senses do not act either. The mind does not cease to act because the senses cease to act. The mind is the foremost and influences the senses. The mind is said to be the lord of all the senses. O immensely illustrious one! These penetrate all creatures.'"'

Chapter 1628(300)

'"Yajnavalkya said, 'I have enumerated the truth about the different types of creation and about the measurement of time. I have progressively described them. Now hear about destruction. Beings are repeatedly created and destroyed. The eternal and undecaying Brahma, without a beginning and without an end, does this. When his day is over and he realizes that it is night, he makes up his mind to sleep. The illustrious and unmanifest one urges the creation of a being from his consciousness and this manifests itself as a sun with a hundred thousand rays. It then divides itself into twelve suns that blaze like fire. O lord of men! With this energy, the four kinds

[881]Of the great elements.

of beings are swiftly consumed—those born from wombs, those born from eggs, those born from sweat[882] and herbs. In a short instant, all mobile and immobile objects are destroyed and, in every direction, the earth becomes as plain as the back of a tortoise. When everything in the universe has been destroyed with this great force, in every direction, it is filled up with the great force of water. At this, the fire of destruction dries up the water. O Indra among kings! When the water has been destroyed, a great fire begins to rage. An immeasurable and extremely powerful fire continues to blaze. The energy of those seven flames is infused with the heat from all creatures. But it is devoured by an extremely powerful wind that has its own inner strength. This courses upwards, downwards and diagonally. However, that extremely strong and terrible wind is devoured by space. But mind cheerfully and swiftly swallows up space. Consciousness, the Prajapati and the atman of everything, devours mind. Consciousness is devoured by the soul of Mahat, who knows about the past, the present and the future. The soul of the universe, Shambhu Prajapati, swallows up Mahat. This is the radiant and undecaying Ishana, with the properties of anima, laghima and prapti. His hands and feet extend in every direction. His eyes, head and face are everywhere. His ears are everywhere. He is established, enveloping all the worlds. He is in the heart of all creatures and his size is only that of a thumb. The infinite and great-souled lord of the universe devours everything. With everything swallowed, what is left is the immutable and the undecaying. This is the unblemished one, the creator of the past and the future of humans. O Indra among kings! I have thus described all this to you accurately. Now I will make you hear about adhyatma, *adhibhuta* and *adhidaiva*.'""

Chapter 1629(301)

'"Yajnavalkya said, 'Brahmanas who have seen the truth speak of the two feet as adhyatma, the act of motion as

[882]Worms and insects.

adhibhuta and Vishnu as adhidaiva. Those who have seen the truth exactly say that the anus is adhyatma, the releasing is adhibhuta and Mitra is adhidaiva.[883] Those who know the indications of yoga say that the penis is adhyatma, its pleasure is adhibhuta and Prajapati is adhidaiva. Those who know the indications of sankhya say that the hands are adhyatma, tasks are adhibhuta and Indra is adhidaiva there. Those who know the indications of the sacred texts say that speech is adhyatma, what is spoken is adhibhuta and Agni is adhidaiva there. Those who know the indications of the sacred texts correctly say that the eyes are adhyatma, form is adhibhuta and Surya is adhidaiva there. Those who know the indications of the sacred texts correctly say that the ears are adhyatma, sound is adhibhuta and the directions are adhidaiva there. Those who know the truth correctly say that the tongue is adhyatma, taste is adhibhuta and water is adhidaiva there. Those who know the indications of the sacred texts correctly say that the nose is adhyatma, smell is adhibhuta and the earth is adhidaiva there. Those who are accomplished in their learning say that the skin is adhyatma, touch is adhibhuta and the wind is adhidaiva. Those who know the indications of the sacred texts say that the mind is adhyatma, the object of the mind is adhibhuta and the moon is adhidaiva. Those who know the true indications say that consciousness is adhyatma, pride is adhibhuta and Bhava is adhidaiva there. Those who know the indications of the Vedas correctly say that intelligence is adhyatma, what is understood is adhibhuta and the kshetrajna is adhidaiva. O king! O one who knows about the truth! I have thus described to you the power of the manifest and the truth about the beginning, the middle and the end. O great king! As if in sport and easily according to her desire, Prakriti brings about hundreds and thousands of transformations in her qualities. It is like a man lighting thousands of lamps from a single lamp. In that way, Prakriti creates many qualities in Purusha. Spirit, joy, prosperity, contentment, radiance, happiness, purity, lack of disease, satisfaction, devotion, generosity, lack of hatred, forgiveness, fortitude, lack

[883]Mitra is sometimes equated with Surya and Mitra is adhidaiva for this organ.

of injury, equanimity, truthfulness, repayment of debts, mildness, humility, lack of fickleness, cleanliness, uprightness, observance of conduct, lack of passion, lack of fear in the heart, indifference at separation from good and bad things, lack of boasting about acts performed, receiving when given, lack of desire for riches, the welfare of others and compassion towards all beings—these are said to be the qualities of sattva. The qualities of rajas are manifested in quarrels over beauty and prosperity, lack of generosity, lack of compassion, the enjoyment of happiness and unhappiness, attachment towards speaking ill of others, fondness for disputes, insolence, thoughts that show no respect, the practice of enmity, repentance, seizing the property of others, lack of humility, lack of uprightness, strife, harshness, desire, anger, intoxication, pride, hatred and excessive speech. These are said to be the qualities of rajas. I will now tell you about the accumulations that tamas leads to—delusion, lack of radiance, darkness and darkness that makes one blind. Darkness is said to be anger and darkness that makes one blind is death. The signs of tamas are gluttony in eating, lack of satisfaction even though one has enough to eat and drink, attachment towards fragrances, garments, sporting, beds, seats, sleeping during the day, quarrels and distraction, taking pleasure in singing, music and dancing, ignorance, lack of faith and hatred of dharma. In particular, these are the qualities of tamas.'"'

Chapter 1630(302)

'"Yajnavalkya said, 'O supreme among men! These are the foremost signs of the three qualities. They always attach themselves to everything in the universe and are established there. He[884] divides himself into hundreds, thousands, hundreds of thousands and crores of different selves. Those who have thought

[884]Purusha.

about adhyatma say that sattva has a superior spot, rajas a medium one and tamas an inferior one. Through auspicious deeds alone, one heads towards an upwards destination. As a result of both good and wicked deeds, one becomes human. Through adharma, one obtains a destination that is downwards.[885] There is also the truth about what happens if two or three of the qualities are mixed. Sattva may exist with rajas or tamas. Listen to me. Sattva can be seen with rajas and rajas with tamas. Sattva can exist with tamas and sattva may exist with the unmanifest.[886] When sattva is united with the unmanifest, one obtains the world of the gods. When rajas is united with sattva, one becomes human. When rajas is united with tamas, one is born as inferior species. When rajas, tamas and sattva are united, one becomes human. It is said that learned ones obtain a region that is separated from both good deeds and wicked ones. It is eternal and immutable. It is without decay and there is no fear there. Learned ones obtain births in that best of places, without faults and without decay. They go beyond the senses. That does not lead to any generation and is beyond birth and death. O lord of men! You asked me about the supreme and the unmanifest.[887] He is established in his own nature. O lord of the earth! It is the view that he resides in Prakriti, without any consciousness. She can create and destroy only when she is presided over by him.'

'"Janaka replied, 'O great sage! Both of them are without beginning and without end. They are without form and without change. They are without blemish and without decay. O tiger among rishis! They cannot be comprehended. How can one of them be without consciousness? How can one have consciousness? Why is one called kshetrajna? O Indra among brahmanas! You are the one who has practised everything about the dharma of emancipation. It is my resolution that I wish to hear the truth about the dharma of emancipation, about the existence of the absolute and about non-existence, about the regions that creatures progressively go to

[885]Tamas leads to birth as inferior species, rajas as humans and sattva as gods.

[886]Prakriti.

[887]Purusha.

and about their separation from those. With the progress of time, what regions do they obtain? O brahmana! Tell me this. Tell me the truth about the knowledge of sankhya and separately about yoga. O supreme one! You should also tell me the truth about misfortune. You know everything about these, like a myrobalan that is held in your hand.'"'

Chapter 1631(303)[888]

'"Yajnavalkya said, 'O son! O lord of the earth! One cannot describe something without qualities by ascribing qualities to it. I will tell you the truth about what possesses qualities and what doesn't have qualities. Listen to me. The great-souled sages who have seen the truth have spoken about the qualities obtained by the one with qualities and the qualities not obtained by the one without qualities. The unmanifest one[889] naturally has qualities and cannot surpass those qualities. Because she is united with those, she naturally lacks knowledge. The unmanifest Purusha is naturally the one who knows and always thinks, "There is nothing superior to me." It is because of this reason that this unmanifest one is without consciousness. He is always spoken of as indestructible. But it is also true that he combines with the destructible.[890] It is because of the repeated association with various categories of qualities that one becomes ignorant. When he does not know his own atman, he is spoken of as the manifest. When he assumes lordship over those principles,[891] he is said to follow the dharma of those attributes. Because he has lordship over wombs, he is said to follow the dharma of wombs. Because he has lordship

[888]Some of the shlokas in this chapter are extremely difficult to understand and liberties have been taken.

[889]Prakriti.

[890]Prakriti.

[891]Prakriti.

over Prakriti, he is said to follow the dharma of Prakriti. Because he has lordship over seeds, he is said to follow the dharma of seeds. Because he is associated with birth, he observes the dharma of birth.[892] Because he has lordship over destruction, he follows the dharma of destruction. Because of association with Prakriti, he follows creation and destruction. This is despite the absolute knowing that he is indifferent and distinct. Ascetics who are pure, devoid of anxiety and knowledgeable about adhyatma, think of him in this way. We have heard of him as permanent and unmanifest, but also as unstable.[893] However, those who depend only on knowledge and are compassionate towards all beings say that the unmanifest is one and Purusha is many.[894] There are others who hold that the unmanifest Purusha, even though apparently unstable, has all the signs of stability. He is distinct, just as a blade of grass is different from its sheath. The gnat that is inside a fig should be known of as distinct. Despite being associated with the fig, the gnat doesn't get attached to it. The fish is said to be different from the water it is in. Though the fish is touched by the water, it isn't in any way attached to it. The fire in a boiler is always known to be distinct. Though the fire touches the boiler, it isn't attached to it. A lotus is said to be different from the water. Though it touches the water, the lotus isn't attached to it. In this way, there is always separation, even when one dwells together. This can never be understood by people who are always ordinary. Those who cannot see it in this way, do not see properly. It is evident that they will repeatedly be submerged in a terrible hell. I have enumerated the supreme philosophy of sankhya. Enumerating it in this way, those who follow sankhya obtain the absolute. I have also told you about the others who are accomplished and know the truth about the manifestations. I will now tell you about the philosophy of yoga.'"'

[892]Here, birth is used in the sense of creation.

[893]Because of the association with Prakriti.

[894]Prakriti is one and Purusha is many. But clearly, the suggestion is that this is not a valid view.

Chapter 1632(304)

'"Yajnavalkya said, 'I have already spoken to you about the knowledge of sankhya. Now hear about the knowledge of yoga. O supreme among kings! This is the truth about what I have learnt and what I have seen. There is no knowledge that is equal to sankhya. There is no strength that is equal to yoga. They prescribe similar practices and both are said to lead to prosperity. However, men who possess limited intelligence perceive them as distinct. O king! We see them as identical and have arrived at this determination. Whatever is seen through yoga is exactly the same as whatever is seen through sankhya. A person who sees yoga and sankhya as identical actually sees the truth. O scorcher of enemies! Know that restraining the breath[895] is the foremost and supreme aspect of yoga. Through this, they wander around in the ten directions in their bodies.[896] O son! O unblemished one! When the body is destroyed, one cheerfully abandons it and, in subtle form, uses the eight qualities of yoga[897] to roam around in the worlds. Those who are learned about yoga speak of these eight qualities. O supreme among kings! They also speak about the eight other subtle qualities.[898] The practice of yoga has been said to be excellent and these are the two kinds of qualities that are practised in yoga. The sacred texts have given indications about how this is to be done, with qualities and without qualities.[899] O lord of

[895]The text uses the word Rudra, a rare term for prana.

[896]Yogis roam around in their subtle bodies.

[897]There are eight steps in yoga. But this probably refers to eight major *siddhis* or powers. These are anima (becoming as small as one desires), mahima (as large as one desires), laghima (as light as one wants), garima (as heavy as one wants), prapti (obtaining what one wants), prakamya (travelling where one wants), vashitvam (powers to control creatures) and ishitvam (obtaining divine powers).

[898]This probably means the eight steps of *asana*, pranayama, yama, niyama, *pratyahara*, *dhyana*, dharana and samadhi.

[899]Pranayama with qualities is when a mantra is simultaneously chanted, recommended for early stages. When a mantra is no longer necessary, that is pranayama without qualities.

the earth! Together with pranayama, there has to be dharana in the mind. Pranayama can be with qualities. Without qualities, dharana occurs in the mind. O supreme among those from Mithila! The breath of life is seen to be released. However, one should not act so as to have an excess of the breath.[900] In the first quarter of the night, twelve principles of breathing have been prescribed. Having slept in the middle, in the last quarter of the night, there are another twelve principles of breathing. One must practise these, self-controlled and satisfied with one's own self. One must turn one's intelligence towards finding pleasure in one's own atman. There is no doubt that one must join oneself with the atman.[901] The five taints associated with the five senses—sound, touch, form, taste and scent—must be flung away. O lord of Mithila! One must withdraw from thoughts of what can be obtained through action. All the objects of the senses must be immersed in the mind. O lord of men! The mind must be established in the consciousness, consciousness in intelligence and intelligence in prakriti. Having merged in this way, one must meditate on the absolute. He is radiant and without blemish. He is eternal and infinite. He is pure and without decay. He is the purusha of sattva, beyond mortality and destruction. He is eternal and unmanifest. He is Ishana and the unmanifest Brahma. O great king! Listen to the signs of someone who has been united in this fashion. The signs are of satisfaction, contentment and cheerful sleep. He is like a lamp ignited with oil, but burning in a place where there is no wind, with straight flames rising upwards. The learned speak of him in this way. He is like a rock that does not move, even when it has been struck by the rain. He is incapable of being moved in any way. Those are the signs of a person who is united. The sounds of conch shells, drums and many kinds of singing and the playing of musical instruments do not make him tremble. These are the signs of a person who is united. It is like a man who climbs a flight of steps with a full vessel of oil in his hand, not spilling any, even if he is frightened. A person

[900]The inhalation, holding and exhalation is for a prescribed period of time. This duration is gradually increased. The purport seems to be that in the initial stages, this duration should not be excessively great.

[901]Paramatman.

who has controlled his atman is like that, not spilling a drop from the vessel, though scared. He ascends, single-minded. He calms his senses and is immobile. These are the signs of a sage who has been united in this way. Having been united in this way, he sees the supreme and unmanifest Brahma, blazing, as if located in the midst of a great darkness. O great king! The eternal sacred texts say that, after a long period of time, he is like a witness and abandons this body, advancing to the absolute. This is the yoga of yogis. What other signs can there be of yoga? Knowing this, the learned ones think themselves to have been successful.'"'

Chapter 1633(305)

'"Yajnavalkya said, 'O king! Now listen attentively to the places that they go to. If it[902] emerges through the feet, the person is said to go to Vishnu's region. If it emerges through the calves, we have heard that he obtains the gods known as the Vasus. If it emerges through the knees, he obtains the immensely fortunate gods known as the Sadhyas. If it emerges through the anus, he obtains Mitra's region. If it emerges through the loins, it is the earth's region.[903] If it is through the thighs, it is Prajapati's. Through the flanks, it is the gods Maruts. Through the nose, it is the region of the moon. Through the arms, it is Indra's. Through the chest, it is Rudra's. Through the neck, he obtains the supreme region of the best of rishis, Nara. Through the mouth, he obtains the Vishvadevas and through the ears, the directions. Through the nose, he obtains the wind god and through the eyes, Surya. Through the brows, it is the region of the gods, the Ashvins. Through the forehead, it is the ancestors. Through the crown of the head, it is the region of

[902]This is after death. The reference is to that part of the anatomy, from where the jivatman emerges at the time of death.

[903]This is probably not meant to signify being born on earth, but is a reference to Prithivi's region.

the lord Brahma, the foremost among the gods. O lord of Mithila! I have thus told you about the different places that can be obtained through emerging. I will now tell you about the signs described by learned ones, signifying that an embodied being only has one year of lifespan left. If a person fails to see Arundhati, although he has seen it earlier, or if it is the same with Dhruva, or if the moon appears like a lamp, with the radiance broken towards the south, it is said that he only has one year of lifespan left.[904] O lord of the earth! Those who can no longer see their own selves reflected in the eyes of others only have one year of lifespan left. If a person has been extremely radiant, but loses that radiance, or if a person has been extremely wise, but loses that wisdom, or if there are changes in his inner or outer nature, those are signs that he will die within six months. If a person disrespects the gods, if he acts against brahmanas, if his dark complexion turns pale—those are signs that he will die within six months. If the lunar disc is seen to have holes, like a spider's web, or if this is the case with the one with one thousand rays[905]—such a person will confront death within seven nights. If the fragrant scents in temples of the gods appear to a man to be like the putrid scent from corpses, he will confront death within six nights. A depression in the ears or the nose, a discolouring of the teeth or the eye, the loss of consciousness and the loss of heat from the body—these are the signs of imminent death. O lord of men! If there is a sudden flow of tears from the left eye, or if vapour rises from the crown of the head—these are the signs of imminent death. Knowing these signs, a man with a cleansed atman should spend day and night in uniting the atman with the paramatman. That is the way he should spend his time, until the time for setting arrives. Even if he doesn't wish to die, he should establish himself in all the rites. He should control himself and discard all fragrances and tastes. By fixing his atman on the supreme, he can conquer death. O bull among men! He knows the practice of those who follow sankhya. By using yoga to fix his atman

[904]Arundhati is the wife of the sage Vasishtha. She is also the fainter of the two stars in the double star in Ursa Major. Mizar is Vasishtha and Arundhati is Alcor. Dhruva is the Pole Star.

[905]The sun.

on the supreme, he can conquer death. He goes to the place that is completely indestructible, without birth and death. It is auspicious and without decay. It is the eternal and immutable region, difficult for those with unclean souls to obtain.'"'

Chapter 1634(306)

"'Yajnavalkya said, 'O lord of men! You asked me about the supreme, established in the unmanifest. This question is about a great secret. O king! Listen attentively. O lord of Mithila! Having conducted myself in accordance with the precepts of the rishis, I obtained the *yajus* from Aditya.[906] I gratified the god of heat through great austerities. O unblemished one! Pleased with me, the lord Surya said, "O brahmana rishi! Ask for the boon you desire, even if it is very difficult to obtain. I am pleased and will give it to you. It is extremely difficult to obtain my favours." I bowed my head down before that supreme of heat-givers and said, "I do not know the yajus. I wish to know them quickly." The illustrious one replied, "O brahmana! I will give it to you. Sarasvati, speech personified, will enter your body." The illustrious one then asked me to open my mouth. When I opened my mouth, Sarasvati entered through the mouth. O unblemished one! When she entered, I began to burn and plunged into the water. Not understanding what the great-souled Bhaskara[907] intended, I became angry. However, while I was burning, the illustrious Ravi told me, "Tolerate this burning for an instant. You will be cooled down." When he saw that I had cooled down, the illustrious Bhaskara said, "O brahmana! All the Vedas and Vedanta will be established in you. O bull among brahmanas!

[906]We have deliberately retained this as yajus, meaning sacrificial formulae. The mantras were compiled into the Yajur Veda Samhita. There are two versions of the Yajur Veda Samhita, Shukla and Krishna. Yajnavalkya compiled the Shukla Yajur Veda.

[907]Bhaskara, Ravi and Vibhavasu are also names for the sun god.

You will compile all the Shatapathas.[908] When that has been done, your intelligence will turn towards the question of rebirth. You will obtain the objective desired by those who practise sankhya and yoga." Having said this, the illustrious one disappeared. On hearing these words and on seeing that the god Vibhavasu had departed, I happily returned home and thought of Sarasvati. The auspicious goddess Sarasvati instantly appeared. She was adorned with the vowels and the consonants and she gave me the syllable "Om". As is prescribed, I offered Sarasvati an arghya and another to the best of heat-givers,[909] the refuge of the distressed. To my great delight, all the Shatapathas, with their mysteries, compilations and appendices, appeared before me. I taught them to one hundred supreme disciples and caused displeasure to my maternal uncle and his disciples.[910] O great king! With my disciples, like the sun with its rays, I was engaged in performing a sacrifice for your great-souled father. There was a dispute about who should get the dakshina. In Devala's presence, I took half of the dakshina and gave the other half to my maternal uncle. Sumantu, Paila, Jaimini, your father and the other sages agreed to this. O unblemished one! I thus obtained fifty yajus. I then studied the Puranas from Lomaharshana.[911]

"'O lord of men! Placing the original mantra[912] and the goddess Sarasvati at the forefront, and with the resolution obtained from Surya, I comprehended and compiled the Shatapatha, not done by anyone earlier. I thus accomplished the path I wished to follow. I instructed that entire and complete compilation to my disciples.

[908]The Shatapatha Brahmana is associated with the Shukla Yajur Veda.

[909]The sun god.

[910]Vaishampayana was Vyasadeva's disciple and used to teach the Krishna Yajur Veda. He was also Yajnavalkya's maternal uncle and teacher. There is a story of a dispute between Vaishampayana and Yajnavalkya. When Yajnavalkya subsequently began to teach the Shukla Yajur Veda, Vaishampayana was understandably unhappy.

[911]Lomaharshana (alternatively Romaharshana) was Vedavyasa's disciple and Vedavyasa taught him the Puranas.

[912]The text uses the word *bija* (seed), which is not quite 'original'. Bija is the mystical syllable that exists in any mantra.

All those disciples were purified and became supremely delighted. The knowledge instructed by Bhaskara had fifty branches[913] and I established it. As I desired, I then began to think about knowledge. O king! The gandharva Vishvavasu was accomplished in the knowledge of Vedanta. While I was contemplating, he came there and asked me, "What is the immortal brahman? What is supreme knowledge?" O lord of the earth! He thus asked me twenty-four questions about knowledge. He then asked me a twenty-fifth question about metaphysics. What is the universe? What is the negation of the universe? What is Ashva and what is the negation of Ashva?[914] What is Mitra? What is Varuna? What is knowledge? What is the object of knowledge? Who is ignorant? Who is not ignorant? Who possesses heat? Who is without heat? Who devours Surya? Who is Surya? What is knowledge? What is ignorance? O king! What exists? What does not exist? What is mobile? What is immobile? What has no beginning? What is without destruction? What can be destroyed? O king! These were the excellent questions that the supreme king of the gandharvas asked me. One after another, he asked me these questions, which were full of meaning. I told him to wait for an instant, while I thought about it. When I had restrained him in this way, the gandharva was silent and remained there. In my mind, I thought again about the goddess Sarasvati and the answers to the questions arose, like clarified butter from curds. O lord of the earth! O son! I churned the Upanishads and their annexures in my mind and saw the supreme objective of metaphysics. O tiger among kings! This is the fourth kind of knowledge, concerning the next world.[915] I have already spoken to you about this, which is based on the twenty-fifth. O king! I spoke about it to King Vishvavasu then. I told him, "O illustrious one! I have heard the questions that

[913]The word *shakha* means branch, but is usually applied to reascension. Two shakhas of the Shukla Yajur Veda are known now.

[914]*Ashva* usually (not always) means horse, or something related to a horse. The answer that follows suggests that there might be a typo here. Perhaps it should read *asva*, meaning, without properties.

[915]Fourth because it is about moksha, not about dharma, artha and kama.

you asked me. O gandharva! You asked me, 'What is the universe and what is the negation of the universe?' Know that the supreme and unmanifest one[916] is the universe. She has the terrible aspects of creation and destruction. She possesses the three qualities[917] and invests everything with these. The one without these is said to be the negation of the universe.[918] In that way, Ashva and the negation of Ashva are said to be the couple.[919] The unmanifest is said to be prakriti and the one without qualities is purusha. Mitra is purusha and Varuna is prakriti. Knowledge is said to be prakriti and the object of knowledge is purusha. The ignorant and the not ignorant are said to be purusha, since both are without qualities. The one with heat is prakriti and the one without heat is said to be purusha. In that way, ignorance is the unmanifest one[920] and knowledge is said to be purusha. You asked me about the mobile and the immobile. Listen to me. Prakriti is said to be mobile. It undertakes transformations and is the reason behind creation and destruction. The immobile one, who has lordship, but does not undertake transformations for creation and destruction, is said to be purusha. Those who have determined the nature of adhyatma speak of both of them as without beginning, without sentiments, without offspring, without destruction, without decay, without creation and eternal.[921] Though it[922] leads to creation, it is said to be without decay, without beginning and without change. Purusha is said to be without destruction. There is no decay in it. The learned say that the qualities created by prakriti are destructible, but not she herself. This is the fourth knowledge of metaphysics, that concerning the next world. O Vishvavasu! It has been said that one's

[916]Prakriti.

[917]Sattva, rajas and tamas.

[918]Purusha.

[919]If this is asva, without qualities, asva will mean purusha and the negation of asva will be prakriti.

[920]Prakriti.

[921]There seems to be an inconsistency with what has been said about prakriti earlier. That's probably because there were different schools and types of belief.

[922]Prakriti.

duty is to obtain riches through knowledge and always perform the ordained tasks, studying all the Vedas attentively. O supreme among gandharvas! This[923] is not dislodged. Everything is born from it and merges into it after death. Those who do not understand this purport of the Vedas know nothing. Even if they study the five Vedas,[924] with the Vedangas and the subsequent branches, they do not understand the knowledge of the Vedas. The Vedas are like a burden to such a person. O supreme among gandharvas! This is like a person who desires clarified butter by churning the milk of a she-ass. He only sees the excrement there. There is no cream from the milk, nor any clarified butter. In that way, despite studying the Vedas, one does not obtain the knowledge in the Vedas. Such a person is said to be foolish in his intelligence and only bears a burden. In one's atman, one must always single-mindedly think about the supreme objective, so that one does not have to repeatedly go through birth and death. One must abandon what is indestructible in this world and resort to the dharma of the indestructible. O Kashyapa![925] Day and night, if one only contemplates the absolute, then one sees oneself as devoid of qualities, united with the absolute. Those virtuous ones see the two as one.[926] They get to know the undecaying nature of the twenty-fifth. Desiring the supreme, those practitioners of sankhya are beyond birth, death, fear and enterprise."

'"Vishvavasu replied, 'O supreme among brahmanas! O illustrious one! You have spoken about the twenty-fifth. But this is not easy to comprehend and you should explain it. I have heard about this earlier from Jaigishavya, Asita, Devala, the brahmana rishi Parashara, the intelligent Varshaganya, Bhikshu, Panchashikha, Kapila, Shuka, Goutama, Arshtishena, the great-souled Garga, Narada, Asuri, the intelligent Pulastya, Sanatkumara, the great-souled Shukra and my father, Kashyapa. Later, I heard about this from Rudra and the intelligent Vishvarupa, and also the gods, the ancestors and the

[923]The brahman.

[924]The epics and the Puranas are known as the fifth Veda.

[925]The gandharvas were also descended from the sage Kashyapa.

[926]The paramatman and the jivatman.

daityas. I have obtained the knowledge that they always speak about. O brahmana! However, using my intelligence, I wish to hear about this from you. O illustrious one! You are foremost among those who know the sacred texts. You are eloquent and extremely intelligent. There is nothing that is not known to you. O brahmana! In the world of the gods and in the world of the ancestors, you are said to be an ocean of learning. The great rishis who dwell in Brahma's abode say that Aditya, the eternal lord of all those who give heat, taught you about this. O brahmana! O Yajnavalkya! You have obtained the entire knowledge of sankhya and in particular, the knowledge of yoga. There is no doubt that you are learned and know about the mobile and the immobile. I wish to hear about that knowledge, which is like clarified butter inside cream.'

'"Yajnvalkya said, 'O supreme among gandharvas! I think that you are capable of bearing all of it. O king! You have asked me. Listen to what I have learned. Prakriti cannot be comprehended, but can be realized by the twenty-fifth.[927] O gandharva! But the twenty-fifth cannot be comprehended by prakriti. Because it cannot be realized in this way, those who know the truth about sankhya and yoga and about the instructions of the sacred texts refer to it as Pradhana.[928] But though it cannot be seen, it can see itself. It can see the twenty-fourth, the twenty-fifth and the twenty-sixth.[929] Even when it does not see,[930] it is capable of seeing. The twenty-fifth thinks that there is nothing superior to itself. The twenty-fourth is incapable of being grasped by those who do not possess the sight of knowledge. The fish dwells in water. But though they are together, they are distinct. Like the fish, those who are learned know that it is different.[931] There is always consciousness from the attachment that results from dwelling

[927]The twenty-fifth is the jivatman.

[928]The chief or foremost one.

[929]The twenty-fourth is prakriti, the twenty-fifth is the jivatman and the twenty-sixth is the paramatman. In a state of knowledge, the jivatman can comprehend the paramatman.

[930]In a state of ignorance.

[931]Prakriti is different from the jivatman.

together. However, those who do not understand the unity[932] are submerged in time. Enveloped by a sense of ego, they are submerged in time. A person who thinks that he is no different from the other one is a true brahmana. He becomes one with the absolute and sees the twenty-sixth. O king! The other one and the twenty-fifth are perceived to be different. But those who see them as one are virtuous. They do not find delight in the indestructible twenty-fifth alone. O Kashyapa! Those practitioners of sankhya and yoga are terrified because of their fear of birth and death. They are devoted to purity and see the twenty-sixth. They are learned in every way and do not enjoy rebirth. O unblemished one! I have thus told you about what is to be known. Following the indications of the sacred texts, I have told you about true knowledge. O Kashyapa! I have told you about what is seen and what is not seen, about seeing what is indestructible, about what is absolute and what is not absolute and about what is superior to the twenty-fifth.'

'"Vishvavasu replied, 'O lord! You have spoken auspicious words to me and told me properly about what is indestructible and is the origin of divinity. May you always be fortunate and without decay. I bow down before you. May you always be vested with intelligence.'

'"Yajnavalkya said,[933] 'Having said this, he left for heaven, radiant in his handsome appearance. Having been satisfied, the great-souled one circumambulated me first and I was exceedingly pleased with him. O Indra among men! He passed on the knowledge that he obtained from me to those who live in Brahma's world and those who dwell in the sky and on earth and they appropriately chose the path that leads to the indestructible. Those who follow sankhya are devoted to the dharma of sankhya. Those who follow yoga are devoted to the dharma of yoga. There are other men who desire emancipation. To all those who desire insight, this brings knowledge. Among men, emancipation results from knowledge.

[932]Between the jivatman and the paramatman.

[933]Yajnavalkya is now speaking to Janaka.

O Indra among men! It is said that it cannot be obtained through ignorance. Therefore, one must search for the truth about knowledge, so that one can free oneself from birth and death. With faith and devotion, one must always obtain knowledge from a brahmana, a kshatriya, a vaishya or even a shudra who is of low birth. A person who has faith is not assailed by birth and death. Since they are born from Brahma, all the varnas are brahmanas. All of them always speak about Brahma. I have spoken to you the truth about the sacred texts and about knowledge of Brahma. The entire universe is completely pervaded by Brahma. Brahmanas were generated from Brahma's mouth. Kshatriyas were generated from his arms. Vaishyas were generated from his navel and shudras from his feet. All the varnas should not be thought of in any other way. O king! It is because of ignorance that one suffers from birth and deeds and the pangs of existence. Devoid of knowledge, all the varnas fall down in this way. They are immersed in terrible ignorance and enveloped in prakriti's net of birth. Therefore, one must seek every means to stick to the path of knowledge. I have spoken to you about this. A person who is established in the supreme brahman is always said to obtain emancipation and is an Indra among brahmanas. I have instructed you about what you had asked me. I have told you the truth. Be bereft of grief. O king! Cross over to the other side. You have spoken properly. May you always be fortunate.'"

'Bhishma said, "Having been thus instructed by the intelligent Yajnavalkya, the king, the lord of Mithila, was delighted. He circumambulated the supreme of sages and departed. Daivarati, the lord of men, obtained knowledge about emancipation. He seated himself and touching one crore cattle, gold and an accumulation of jewels, gave them away to brahmanas. He instated his son in the kingdom of Videha. The lord of Mithila then resorted to the dharma of mendicants. He studied the entire knowledge of sankhya and the sacred texts of yoga. O Indra among kings! He abandoned the ordinary practices of dharma and adharma. He always thought of himself as the infinite and the absolute. O Indra among kings! O lord of men! He no longer thought of ordinary things like birth and death, but always devoted himself to tasks associated with the unmanifest brahman. The practitioners of yoga and sankhya, accomplished about the indications of their own sacred texts, see that the brahman is supreme and is superior to good and evil. Those learned ones always speak of it as pure. You should also become pure. O best among men! The giver, the receiver, what is intended as a gift, what is given, what is received, what is instructed to be given, what is instructed to be received—all these are aspects of the unmanifest. The atman is the only thing that belongs to the atman and there is nothing that is superior to this. Always regard it in this way and do not think otherwise. A person who does not know the unmanifest, with qualities and without qualities,[934] always goes to places of pilgrimage and performs sacrifices. He is ignorant. O descendant of the Kuru lineage! One cannot realize the state of the unmanifest through studying, austerities or sacrifices. The unmanifest must be comprehended. It is the same with the state of Mahat and consciousness. One must obtain the state that is superior to that of consciousness. Those who are devoted to the sacred texts always know about the supreme and the unmanifest. They are disassociated from birth and death and are disassociated from the qualities. O king! In ancient times, I obtained this knowledge from Janaka and he from Yajnavalkya. This special knowledge is superior to sacrifices. It is through knowledge that one can traverse what is difficult to cross, not through sacrifices. O king! Those who are learned say that birth, death and hardships are difficult to traverse through sacrifices, austerities, rituals and vows. Even if one obtains heaven, one falls down on the ground. You should worship the supreme, great and pure one, auspicious, without blemish and sacred, the path to emancipation. O king! As the kshetrajna, perform the sacrifice of knowledge. That is the truth that the rishi spoke about. It has been spoken about in the Upanishads and in ancient times, Yajnavalkya told King Janaka about this. It is the eternal and the undecaying and he enumerated the auspicious and the immortal. He[935] then obtained the one who is beyond sorrow."'

[934]Prakriti and purusha respectively.

[935]Janaka.

Chapter 1635(307)

'Yudhishthira asked, "O bull among the Bharata lineage! Having obtained prosperity, great riches and a long lifespan, how can one overcome death? Can one overcome old age and death through extremely great austerities, deeds, learning and the application of medicines?"

'Bhishma replied, "In this connection, an ancient history is recounted about the conversation between the mendicant Panchashikha and Janaka. To dispel his doubt about dharma, King Janaka of Videha progressively asked the great rishi Panchashikha, who was supreme among those who knew about the Vedas. 'O illustrious one! What is the conduct through which one can overcome old age and death? Is it through austerities, intelligence, deeds or learning?' Having been thus addressed by the ruler of Videha, the one who knew about the supreme replied, 'These two cannot be overcome. But it is not true that they can never be overcome. Days, nights and months pass. Though a person is temporary, he can obtain what is permanent and certain. All creatures are destroyed. Without a raft, they are continuously borne along on a flow and submerged in the ocean of time. Old age and death are the giant crocodiles and there is no escape from them. There is no one who can aid a person. Nor can he help anyone else. Along that path, one gets to know wives, relatives and others. There is no one with whom one has spent a great deal of time earlier. Because of time, they are repeatedly brought together and repeatedly thrust apart. They are like accumulations of clouds, moved around by the wind. Like wolves, old age and death devour all creatures, regardless of whether they are strong or weak, short or tall. Though creatures are impermanent, in those creatures, there is a being[936] who is eternal. Why should one take delight at birth? Why should one suffer anxiety on account of death? Where have I come from? Who am I? Where will I go? To whom do I belong? Where am I established? Where will I be? Therefore, why are you

[936]The atman.

grieving? Even if you see heaven or hell, you will not remain there. This cannot be overcome through sacred texts, gifts or sacrifices.'"'

Chapter 1636(308)

'Yudhishthira asked, "O supreme among rajarshis of the Kuru lineage! Without abandoning garhasthya, has anyone obtained emancipation and been conveyed to wisdom? Tell me the truth about this. How can the atman be discarded? How can the atman be discarded?[937] What is supreme emancipation? O grandfather! Tell me about this."

'Bhishma replied, "O descendant of the Bharata lineage! In this connection, an ancient history is recounted about a conversation between Janaka and Sulabha. It has been heard that in ancient times, there was a king of Mithila who was descended from Janaka and was named Dharmadhvaja. He determined to obtain success through renunciation. He was learned about the sacred texts on emancipation. He was also accomplished in his own sacred texts.[938] He restrained his senses and ruled the earth. O lord of men! He was knowledgable about the Vedas. He was wise and learned. His conduct was virtuous and other men in this world wished to emulate him. In that yuga when dharma prevailed, there was a mendicant[939] named Sulabha. She followed the dharma of yoga and wandered around the earth. As she roamed around the entire earth, she heard from various *tridandis*[940] about the lord of Mithila, who was pursuing emancipation. On hearing these accounts, she had doubts about the truth of these

[937]This is repeated twice, because the reference is to both the subtle and the gross forms of the atman.

[938]Presumably, those meant for kshatriyas.

[939]A female mendicant.

[940]A tridandi carries three staffs (*tridanda*) tied together. This is the sign of a mendicant.

and wished to ascertain the subtleties. Therefore, she formed a resolution that she should see Janaka. Through the powers of yoga, she discarded her earlier form and assumed a supremely beautiful appearance, flawless in her limbs. Her eyebrows were excellent and her eyes were like the petals of lotuses. In the twinkling of an eye and with great speed, she went to the city of Videha.[941] She reached the beautiful city of Mithila, inhabited by a large number of people. Assuming the form of a mendicant, she presented herself before the lord of Mithila. The king saw her supremely delicate form. He was astounded and asked her who she was, who did she belong to, and where she had come from. Having welcomed her, he instructed that an excellent seat should be given to her. He honoured her by offering her water to clean her feet and satisfied her with wonderful food. Having eaten this, she was gratified. The king was surrounded by his advisers and was in the midst of an assortment of learned people. But the mendicant Sulabha still had her doubts about whether he had understood the dharma of emancipation and wished to test him. She used her powers of yoga to penetrate the king's spirit with her own spirit. She restrained the rays that emanated from his eyes with the rays that emanated from her eyes. Wishing to test him, she tied him up in the bonds of yoga, determined to make him dumb. But King Janaka, supreme among kings, prided himself on his own invincibility. He countered her resolution with his own. They were both situated thus. He was without his umbrella and she was without her three staffs.[942] Listen to the conversation that took place between them.

'"The lord of the earth asked, 'O illustrious one! What conduct do you follow? Who are you? Having accomplished your purpose, where will you go? Whom do you belong to? Where have you come from? Learning, age, birth and good conduct cannot be ascertained without asking. Therefore, having arrived here, you should answer me truthfully. In particular, know that I have rid myself of my umbrella

[941]The capital of Videha, Mithila.

[942]The king and Sulabha were in their subtle forms and the conversation took place between the subtle forms.

and other signs. I wish to know who you truly are. I think that you are deserving of my respect. In earlier times, I have obtained knowledge about *vaisheshika*.[943] There is no one else who can speak to you about emancipation. Listen to me. There was an aged and extremely great-souled mendicant named Panchashikha, from the Parashara gotra. As a pupil, he regarded me greatly. All my doubts have been severed about the three kinds of moksha dharma—knowledge of sankhya, yoga and the rites that are followed by kings. When he[944] roamed around as a mendicant, as instructed in the sacred texts, in ancient times, he happily dwelt in my city for four months during the monsoon. He instructed me well and told me the truth about the three modes of emancipation, with sankhya as the foremost. But he didn't ask me to give up the kingdom. I completely follow the three kinds of conduct that lead to emancipation. I am without attachment. In solitude, I have based myself on the supreme. Renunciation is the foremost conduct for emancipation. Renunciation results from knowledge and that leads to liberation. One must endeavour for knowledge. It is through endeavour that one can obtain Mahat. Mahat frees one from opposite sentiments. That is the success that transcends death. I am devoid of opposite sentiments and have obtained that supreme intelligence. I am free from attachment and roam around in this world, bereft of delusion. When a field is flooded with water and softened, it leads to seeds sprouting. In that way, the deeds of men lead to rebirth. If a seed is heated in a dish, though the inherent strength for sprouting remains in it, the seed no longer sprouts. The illustrious mendicant Panchashikha spoke to me about knowledge and I no longer have the seed that creates attachment towards material objects. I do not hate anyone. Nor do I love my wife. Since both kinds of attachment are futile sins, I do not find pleasure in either. If a person smears my right hand with sandalwood paste and if another person wounds my left hand, I regard both

[943]This may refer to the school of philosophy known as vaisheshika, or to some special aspects of sankhya.

[944]Panchashikha.

equally. I am happy at having accomplished my objectives and a lump of earth, a stone and gold are the same for me. I am established in my kingdom, but am free from attachments. Therefore, I am superior to tridandis. Maharshis have earlier instructed that there are three kinds of devotion that lead to emancipation.[945] Some hold knowledge to be the best, others the renunciation of all acts. There are people who know about the sacred texts of moksha and say that knowledge is the best. However, there are other ascetics, subtle in their sight, who hold that acts are the best. The great-souled one held that knowledge or deeds alone would not suffice and that the third mode was best.[946] A householder can be the equal of a tridandi in yama, niyama, hatred, desire, receiving, pride, insolence and affection. If emancipation results from knowledge, then there is nothing to prevent the possessor of an umbrella[947] from obtaining it either. Because of different objectives and reasons, one becomes associated with different objects and receives them. One may perceive taints in garhasthya and advance towards a subsequent ashrama. But despite giving up the objects, one may not be freed from attachment. Lordship means that one must chastise and reward. However, rajarshis and mendicants are equal in this and why should they alone be liberated? Irrespective of lordship, one is freed through knowledge alone. If one establishes oneself in the supreme objective, why should one not be freed? The wearing of ochre robes, shaving the head, carrying the three sticks and the *kamandalu*[948]— these are only signs. It is my view that these do not lead to emancipation. Whether these signs exist or not, knowledge alone is the cause for emancipation and freedom from sorrow. The signs alone are futile. Therefore, despite the umbrella, why should it not be found? Freedom is not found in possessing nothing. Nor does possessing something lead to bondage. Irrespective of whether a creature possesses or does not, knowledge results in emancipation. One receives a kingdom for the sake of dharma, artha

[945]This probably means knowledge, yoga and rites.

[946]Panchashikha held yoga to be superior.

[947]A king, an umbrella being part of royal insignia.

[948]Water pot used by ascetics.

and kama and if one is not careful, this can lead to bondage. But though I am in that state, I am without bondage. There is a noose from the kingdom's prosperity. There are the bonds of affection. But I have used the sword of renunciation, severed on the stone of emancipation, to sever those. O female mendicant! I have thus been freed. However, I have a liking for you. Therefore, let me tell you that your conduct does not befit your vocation. Your form is delicate. Your body possesses beauty. You are extremely young. I have doubts that you follow niyama. The signs do not suggest it. To test whether I am emancipated, you have assailed and seized me, rendering me immobile. A tridandi wishing to be emancipated should not fall prey to desire. If you cannot protect yourself from this, you will not be able to preserve the liberation you have obtained. You have entered my body. Listen to the transgression you have committed. I have been married earlier. Why have you used your nature to enter me? Why have you entered my kingdom and my city? Have there been any signs suggesting that you are entitled to enter my heart? You are a brahmana, chief and foremost among all varnas. I am a kshatriya. There can be no union between us. Do not cause a mixture of varnas. You follow the dharma of moksha. I am in the ashrama of a householder. This will lead to a second evil, a mixture of ashramas. I do not know whether we have the same gotra or different gotras, and neither do you.[949] If I belong to the same gotra, by entering me, you have confused gotras and caused a third evil. If your husband is alive and lives in a distant place, you are someone else's wife and cannot be approached. Therefore, by causing a confusion of dharma, there has been a fourth evil. Have you committed these evil acts with some specific objective in mind? Has it been caused by ignorance or false knowledge? Perhaps it is your own evil nature that leads to such independence. If you possess any learning, you should know that all these acts have been wicked. There is a third sin that comes from the touch of an unchaste woman.[950] This sign of sin is evident in what you have expounded. In your desire for victory, it is not me alone

[949]Union within the same gotra is prohibited.

[950]Ignorance/false knowledge and evil nature are probably the first two.

that you wish to defeat. You also desire to defeat all my advisers. You are repeatedly glancing towards them and then towards your own self, as if you wish to defeat those on my side and establish the superiority of your own side. You have been confused by the delusion of your powers and intolerance. Therefore, you have invoked the weapon of yoga and have mixed poison with amrita. The mutual desire between a man and a woman, when they seek to obtain each other, is like amrita. However, when one doesn't obtain the person one desires, that is a sin that is like poison. Do not touch me. Know that I am virtuous. Follow the instructions of your own sacred texts. You wished to know whether I am emancipated or not, and that enquiry has been accomplished. You should not have concealed all your secret motives. Perhaps you are doing this at the instigation of some other king.[951] The truth about those secret motives shouldn't have been hidden from me. One must never be deceitful before a king or a brahmana. Nor must one approach a wife with deceit, as long as that wife possesses all the qualities. Prosperity is a king's strength. Knowledge of the brahman is a brahmana's strength. Beauty, youth and good fortune are the greatest strength for a woman. Those who are strong in this way can accomplish their objectives and must be approached with sincerity.[952] Deceit leads to destruction. You should tell me the truth about your birth, learning, conduct, character, natural inclination and the reason why you have come here.'

'"She was addressed in these unpleasant and inappropriate words by that Indra among men.[953] However, Sulabha did not tremble. When the king had spoken those words, the beautiful Sulabha replied in words that were more beautiful than her person. 'There are nine taints associated with speech and nine taints associated with intelligence. Meaningful words must possess eighteen qualities. O king! It has been said that meaningful words must possess five characteristics—subtlety, judging the pros, judging the cons, final determination and ascertaining necessity. I will progressively explain

[951]A hostile king.

[952]A strong king must be approached with sincerity.

[953]This is Bhishma speaking.

the meaning and characteristics of each of these, beginning with subtlety. Listen to how meanings of words and words should be combined to form sentences. There are differences between knowledge and the object of knowledge. Subtlety consists of using great intelligence to bring out these differences. Before using intended words, one must enumerate and think about their meanings and the various good and bad qualities these words possess. Having examined this progressively, one must then use them in speech. People who are accomplished in framing sentences say that words must thus be progressively used in a sentence. One must specially examine the ends of dharma, artha, kama and moksha and having determined this, then use the instructions to formulate a sentence. O king! When desire and hatred are intense, hardships multiply. O king! Therefore, conduct[954] must be in accordance with necessity. O lord of men! When subtlety and the other mentioned characteristics are combined together, the sentence is perceived to be intelligible. The words I speak to you will be full of meaning, consistent in meaning, restrained, to the point, smooth, without any doubt and excellent. They will not have long syllables. They will not be unkind and harsh. They will not be false. They will be refined and will not be against the three objectives.[955] There will not be words that are difficult to understand, ones that go in different directions. There will be nothing with alternative meanings, nor anything without a reason or an objective. I will not tell you anything because of desire, anger, fear, avarice, misery, destitution, lack of nobility, shame, compassion or pride. O king! When the speaker, the listener and the words are in harmony, the meaning of what is spoken becomes clear. When the speaker disrespects the listener, irrespective of whether it is for his own or someone else's objective, the words spoken have no impact. Even if a man gives up his own objective and accepts the objective of someone else, those words are sinful, because they are capable of giving rise to doubt. O king! If a person speaks words that are incapable of double meaning and are comprehensible to the listener, then he is an

[954]In the choice of words.

[955]Dharma, artha and kama.

excellent speaker, not anyone else. I will speak words that are full of meaning and rich in purport. O king! You should listen to them with single-minded attention. Who am I? Whom do I belong to? Where have I come from? This is what you asked me. I will speak words in reply. O king! Listen attentively. O king! All beings created are combinations, like lac and wood, dust and drops of water.[956] Sound, touch, taste, form and scent are the five senses. They may seem to be different, but are actually together, like lac and wood. It has thus been determined that no one should ask who someone else is. No one knows about his own self, not to speak of someone else. The eye cannot see itself. The ear cannot hear itself. Nor can they undertake each other's tasks. Like dust and water, even when they combine, they cannot know their own selves. Listen to me. Even for the sake of obtaining their qualities, they have to resort to external objects. Form, eye and light—these three are required for seeing. This is also the case with the other senses of knowledge and the objects of the senses. Between a sense of knowledge and the object of that sense, there is the quality of what is known as the mind. It reflects and arrives at its own determination about what exists and what does not exist. It has been said that the quality known as intelligence is the twelfth.[957] When the others have a doubt, it is intelligence that settles matters. The thirteenth quality that is beyond this is known as sattva.[958] It is inferred that creatures may possess a lot of sattva or a limited quantity of sattva. There is yet another attribute, the fourteenth, known as kshetrajna. This helps one think—"I am this. I am not that." O king! There is yet another quality, said to be the fifteenth.[959] O king! There is said to be a sixteenth that is attached to this collection.[960] There is

[956]Everything is made out of the elements. So is Sulabha. There is no point in asking who she is.

[957]The five senses of knowledge, the five organs of action and the mind are the other eleven.

[958]We have deliberately not translated this. It means the spirit or essence of life.

[959]This has not been named in the text, but is interpreted as desire.

[960]The text uses the word kala. In this context, this means the sixteenth. The sixteenth has also not been named in the text, but is interpreted as ignorance. Ignorance adheres to the collection of the other fifteen.

an interaction between these sixteen qualities. The qualities of *akriti* and *vyakti* are attached to these.[961] Happiness and unhappiness, old age and death, gain and loss, pleasant and unpleasant—the union of these opposite sentiments are said to constitute the nineteenth. Beyond these, there is the twentieth characteristic, known as time. Know that the creation and destruction of all beings is because of this twentieth. There is interaction between these twenty characteristics and the five great elements. Existence and non-existence are the other characteristics of manifestation.[962] It is thus said that there are twenty-seven characteristics. Know that there are three characteristics beyond these—Vidhi, Shukra and Bala.[963] It has been said that the number of characteristics is thirty-one.[964] It has been said that all of them circle around in the body. There are those who hold that the unmanifest prakriti is the cause behind all the characertistics.[965] There are others who are gross in their vision and think that the manifest is the cause.[966] Whether it is the unmanifest, the manifest, the combination of the two[967] or all four taken together,[968] those who have thought about adhyatma hold that prakriti creates all beings. Prakriti is unmanifest, but becomes manifest in the form of these characteristics. O Indra among kings! I, you and everything that possesses a body are the outcome of this. There is a point at which creation results from the mixture of semen with blood. Because of this union, a *kalala*[969] is generated. A *budbuda*[970] results from the

[961]These are the seventeenth and the eighteenth. Akriti means form. It is possible that there is a typo in the Critical edition, since some non-critical versions say prakriti. Vyakti means manifestation.

[962]With the addition of the five great elements, the list numbers twenty-seven.

[963]Respectively, destiny, seed and exertion. By seed, one probably means the consequences of past deeds.

[964]Including prakriti.

[965]They do not believe that there is anything higher than prakriti.

[966]They do not even believe in prakriti.

[967]Purusha and prakriti.

[968]Purusha, prakriti, the jivatman and ignorance.

[969]Embryo, just after conception.

[970]Embryo that is five days old.

kalala and a *peshi*[971] results from the budbuda. The limbs manifest themselves in the peshi, and nails and hair are attached to the limbs. O lord of Mithila! When nine months are over, the creature is born. When it has been born, on ascertaining whether it is a boy or a girl, a name is given. Immediately after birth, the nails and fingers are seen to have the complexion of copper. When that person becomes an infant, that earlier form is no longer discerned. Infancy becomes youth and youth becomes old age. In this way, from one stage to another, the earlier form is no longer seen. The separate characteristics change from one instant to another. These transformations occur in all creatures, but are so subtle that they are not noticed. O king! The beginning and the end of these minute changes cannot be seen, just as one cannot discern the movement in the flame of a lamp. This is the state of all creation, rushing along like a well-trained horse. Among these numerous people, is it possible to answer who has come from where and who has not come from where? Whom does someone belong to? Whom does someone not belong to? How does one know where someone has come from, or where someone has not come from? What is the connection between beings and their physical forms? Just as fire results when sticks are rubbed together, all creatures are generated from the characteristics mentioned earlier. You see your atman in your own self. In that fashion, why don't you see your atman in other people? But perhaps you do regard yourself and others as identical. In that event, why did you ask me who I am and whom I belong to? O lord of Mithila! If it is true that you have been freed from opposite sentiments, what was the need for expressions like "Who are you?" and "Whom do you belong to?"—At times of peace and war, if a king's action towards enemies, friends and neutrals are no different from that of others, where are the signs that he has become free? The three objectives exist in seven combinations.[972] If one does not know this and does not show it in his deeds and if one is attached

[971]Embryo that has flesh and muscles.

[972]Dharma, artha, kama, taken singly; then dharma and artha, dharma and kama, artha and kama, taken two at a time; and finally, dharma, artha and kama, all three taken together.

to the three objectives, where are the signs of emancipation in him? If one does not cast an impartial sight towards the pleasant and the unpleasant and the weak and the strong, where are the signs of emancipation in him? O king! You pride yourself on having become emancipated. This is without basis. Your well-wishers should restrain you and treat you with medication. O scorcher of enemies! You should think of other similar things that you are attached to. Glance towards the atman inside your own self. That is a sign of emancipation. There are other subtle signs of having resorted to liberation, such as not being attached to the four pursuits.[973] Listen to me. A person who brings the entire earth under a single umbrella[974] is praised. That king then lives in a single city. In that city, he lives in a single house. In that house, there is a single bed, on which, he lies down at night. Half of that bed has earlier been occupied by his wife. In this context, this is the kind of fruits he enjoys.[975] This is true of all objects of pleasure, food and garments. The qualities he enjoys are limited. He also has to apportion out reward and chastisement. The king is always engaged in the tasks of others. There is little that he directly enjoys. Whether there is peace or whether there is war, how is the king independent? In sporting with women and other kinds of pleasure, the king's independence is always circumscribed. With all those ministers and advisers, where does he have independence? When he instructs others, he is said to be independent. However, he is incapable of personally checking whether they undertake those tasks. He cannot sleep when he wishes. People who have work with him prevent his sleep. He can only lie down after taking their permission. When he is asleep, he is unable to prevent his being awakened. Bathing, obtaining, drinking, eating, offering oblations into the fire, performing sacrifices, speaking, hearing—in all of these, he is helpless and is driven by the objectives of others. Groups of men always come to him and solicit things. However, because he is also the supervisor of the treasury, he is incapable of giving, even if he wishes to. If he gives, the treasury is

[973]Excessive addiction for sleep, desire, food and clothes.

[974]Becomes a universal emperor.

[975]Very little of what the king ostensibly owns is actually enjoyed by him.

exhausted. If he does not give, there is enmity. These kinds of taints swiftly generate detachment in him. If wise, brave and rich men gather together in one place, he is suspicious. Even when there is no reason for fear, the king is always frightened of those who serve him. The ones I have mentioned also blame the king. Behold. A similar kind of fear is also generated in them. In their own houses, all men are kings. In their own houses, all men are householders. O Janaka! Like kings, they too chastise and reward. They also possess sons, wives, their own selves, stores, friends and treasuries. Because of these reasons, he[976] is not really different from other people. The country has been destroyed, the city has been burnt down, the best of elephants is dead—in all of these, he is tormented like others. He has a false sense of knowledge. The king is not freed from mental grief that results from desire, hatred, love and fear. He is also afflicted by headaches and other diseases. Opposite sentiments prey on him and he is always alarmed. There are many kinds of hardships in the kingdom and he counts the nights.[977] There is only a little bit of happiness and there is a great deal of misery. How can there be peace if one has obtained a kingdom? You think that this capital and kingdom are yours. O king! But these soldiers, this treasury and these advisers aren't really yours. Whom do they belong to? O king! Allies, advisers, the capital, the country, the staff, the treasury and the king—these seven limbs of the kingdom depend on one another. These seven limbs hold up the kingdom, like three staffs tied together. They depend on each other's qualities. There is none that is superior to the others in qualities. At particular points in time, when a specific task has to be accomplished by it, one of these limbs may be thought to be superior to the rest. O supreme among kings! However, those seven limbs and three others[978] come together. These ten categories enjoy the kingdom, as if they are the king himself. If a king has great enterprise and is devoted to the dharma of kshatriyas, then he should be satisfied with one-tenth

[976]The king.

[977]He cannot sleep.

[978]Extending the kingdom, decay and maintenance of the status quo.

share.[979] There are others who are satisfied with less than one-tenth. There is no extraordinary king and there is no kingdom without a king. If there is no kingdom, how can there be dharma? If there is no dharma, how can the supreme objective be attained? The supreme and sacred dharma depends on a king and a kingdom. O lord of Mithila! The earth can be offered as dakshina, but there are those who do not even perform a horse sacrifice. There are many who act so as to cause hardships to their kingdoms, though they are capable. I can mention hundreds and thousands. I am not even attached to my own body. How can I then seize someone else's? You should not therefore say that I have caused an obstruction in your emancipation in this way. From Panchashikha, there is no doubt that you have heard a complete account of what is known as moksha, with techniques, modes, practices and conclusions. O king! However, if you have been freed from all attachment and have overcome all your bonds, specifically, why are you still attached to the umbrella and other objects? I think that you have not heard the sacred texts. Or perhaps you have heard some false sacred texts. Perhaps you came close to the sacred texts, but heard some other texts instead. It is only the consciousness of the material world that is established in you. Therefore, like an ordinary person, you are tied down by these excellent possessions. If you are emancipated in every way, how have I harmed you by penetrating your spirit? It is the ritual and dharma of ascetics to dwell alone. Had you tried to dwell alone, how could I have caused any harm to you? O unblemished one! I have not touched you with my hands, my arms, my feet or my thighs. O lord of men! Nor have I touched your body in any other way. You have been born in a great lineage. You are humble. You are far-sighted. Whether my entering you was good or bad, surely it was bad and futile to speak about it.[980] These brahmanas are superior. They are the foremost among advisers. They are your seniors. You treat each other with reverence. That being the case, you should have thought about what should be said and what should not be said. In an

[979] As share obtained through taxes.

[980] And thus reveal a private affair before the court.

assembly, you should not have spoken about the union between a woman and a man. The water rests on the leaf of a lotus without really touching the leaf of the lotus. O lord of Mithila! I am dwelling with you in that way, without touching you. You have felt my touch, even though I have not touched you. What is the seed of knowledge that you then obtained from the mendicant? You have not been able to give up garhasthya. Nor have you obtained moksha, which is so difficult to understand. Though you desire moksha, you are stuck in between the two. If an emancipated person mingles with another emancipated person, that union does not lead to a mixing of varnas, like the mingling between the existent and the non-existent.[981] Those who regard the varnas and the ashramas to be distinct are those who do not perceive that this is different from that.[982] Because they do not know that this is different from that, they think that this acts differently from that. There is a pot in the hand. There is milk in the pot. There is a fly in the milk. Though they mingle and coexist with each other, they are distinct from each other. The pot does not assume the characteristics of milk. Nor does the milk assume the characteristics of a fly. They each possess their own characteristics and not those of something else. The different varnas and ashramas are just like that. Since they are different from each other, how can there be a mixture of varnas? I have not been born in a varna that is superior to yours. Nor am I a vaishya or something worse than that. O king! I belong to the same varna as you and have been born in a pure lineage. There was a rajarshi named Pradhana and it is evident that you have heard of him. Know that I was born in his lineage and my name is Sulabha. In the sacrifices performed by my ancestors, Drona,[983] Shatashringa and Mount Vakradvara came to the altars, accompanied by Maghavan. Since I had been born in such a lineage, a husband could not be found for me. Humbly, I adopted

[981]Respectively, prakriti and purusha.

[982]This is cryptic. They suffer from an error in judgement because they think this (the body) is the same as that (the atman).

[983]This Drona is not to be confused with the Drona who taught the Kouravas and the Pandavas. These are the names of mountains.

the vow of a sage and roamed around alone, observing the dharma of moksha. There is no deceit in my rites. Nor do I desire the possessions of others. I will not cause confusion in dharma. I am firm in my vows and follow my own dharma. I will not be dislodged from my own resolve. Nor do I speak without thinking about it first. O lord of men! I have not come to you and approached you without having thought about it first. I had heard that your intelligence had turned towards moksha and had thought that coming here would be beneficial. I came here, wishing to ask you about moksha. I am not saying this to boast about my side and denigrate another side. A person is not liberated and freed until he is peaceful and tranquil. A mendicant spends only a single night in an empty house. In that way, I will not dwell in your body for more than one night.[984] You have honoured me by treating me like a guest and giving me a seat and speaking pleasant words. O lord of Mithila! I will happily sleep inside you tonight and leave tomorrow.' These sentences were full of reason and purport. On hearing these, the king could not say anything after that."'

Chapter 1637(309)

'Yudhishthira asked, "In ancient times, how did Shuka, Vyasa's son, obtain knowledge? O Kouravya! I am curious and wish to hear about it."

'Bhishma said, "The father saw that the son was engaged in the ordinary norms of good conduct and was roaming around fearlessly. He saw that he was capable of studying and taught him everything that there was to be studied. He said, 'O son! Serve dharma. Conquer extreme cold, heat, hunger, thirst and the wind. Having vanquished these, always subjugate your senses. Always preserve the ordinances

[984]There is a suggestion that the king's body is also empty, because there is no knowledge there.

of truth, uprightness, lack of anger, lack of malice, self-control, austerities, non-violence and lack of injury. Always base yourself on the truth. Be attached to dharma. In every way, discard deceit. Eat what is left after serving gods and guests. In this journey, life in the body is like foam in a vessel. The jivatman is like a bird.[985] O son! Living with beloved ones is temporary. Why dream about it? Even if you are distracted, the enemies are always awake.[986] They are searching for a weakness. Do not be so foolish as to ignore this. As one counts the years passing, your lifespan becomes less and less. As long as you are alive, why are you not rushing, to be instructed like a disciple? There are extreme non-believers who desire objects in this world and seek to increase their flesh and blood. Regarding tasks for the world hereafter, they are asleep. The intelligence of these men has been deluded and they censure dharma. They advance along wrong paths and those who follow them are also afflicted. However, there are also those who are content and extremely controlled. They are devoted to truth and the sacred texts. They tread along the path of dharma. Worship them and seek instruction from them. Accept the instructions of those aged ones, who have the insight of dharma. Use supreme intelligence to exercise restraint and prevent the consciousness from treading along wrong paths. There are those whose intelligence is fixed only on today. They are fearless and think that tomorrow is far away. They eat everything. Devoid of consciousness, they do not see that this is an arena for action.[987] You are like a silkworm inside a cocoon now, but do not know that you are tied down. There are non-believers who disregard the restraints. They are like bamboos standing up with pride, when the river's bank is being broken down by a current. Avoid these mean men and keep them to your left.[988] Desire, anger, death and the five senses are the water in the river that flows from birth. It is difficult to cross.

[985]Perched unattached on a tree and a witness to what is going on.

[986]These are vices as metaphorical enemies, not literal ones.

[987]The text uses the word *karmabhumi*, field for action, implying good deeds and the resultant fruits.

[988]Keeping to the left is a metaphor for treating them with disfavour.

However, using the boat of resolution, cross it. People are afflicted by death and assailed by old age. The progress of dharma cannot be repulsed and descends on them. Whether you are seated or lying down, death will seek you out. How will you obtain salvation? How will you escape being devoured by death? Despite acquisitions, desire is not satisfied. Like a she-wolf grasping a young ram, death seizes and departs, while one is still engaged in acquiring. The great intelligence of dharma is like the flame of a lamp. Hold it carefully and enter the darkness. Descending through a maze of various bodies, a creature rarely becomes a man and becoming a brahmana is rarer still. O son! Therefore, protect it. You have not been born in this body of a brahmana for the sake of satisfying desire. In this world, it is meant to be tormented through austerities, so that one obtains supreme happiness in the hereafter. The status of a brahmana is obtained after austerities. Having obtained it, it must not be carelessly frittered away. Always be engaged in studying, austerities and self-control. Always endeavour to obtain what is best and beneficial for you. The life of a man is like a horse and it is continuously running. The sixteen parts of the unmanifest Prakriti constitute the body. Its essence is subtle. Kshana, *truti* and nimesha[989] are the body hair. The seasons are the mouth. Shuklapaksha and krishnapaksha, equal in strength, are the eyes. The months are the limbs. If you possess the sight, look at it. It is extended in front, always advancing with great speed. Hear what others have to say about the hereafter and turn your mind towards dharma. There are those who are overcome by desire and are dislodged from dharma. They are always enraged, and engaged in causing harm. Their bodies will be afflicted by pain. Since they do not wish for dharma, they will be burnt by flames.[990] A king who is devoted to dharma and always protects the auspicious can look forward to worlds meant for those with righteous deeds. If he performs many kinds of good deeds, he obtains an unblemished felicity that cannot be obtained in thousands of births. If a man transgresses the words of his preceptor, he goes to hell after death.

[989]All three are small measurements of time.

[990]In Yama's world.

Fierce dogs, crows with iron beaks, large numbers of wild crows, vultures and other birds and blood-sucking worms attack him. In his mind, Svayambhu fixed ten ordinances that must be followed in this world.[991] If one does not follow these, such a wicked person confronts terrible misery and has to dwell in the desolate dominion of the ancestors.[992] If a man is extremely avaricious, loves falsehood, is always addicted to deception and fraud and causes hardship by appropriating what has been left to him in trust, is the performer of wicked deeds. He goes to the worst of hells and suffers great misery there. He is submerged in the boiling waters of the great river Vaitarani. His body is mangled in a forest where the leaves are like swords. He is flung down and made to lie on a bed made out battle axes. He has to dwell in that great hell and is severely afflicted. You speak about great worlds, but do not see what is supreme. You have never understood that death will always follow. Why don't you go there?[993] A great fear has arisen in front of you. It is terrible and you should arrange for your happiness. Death is ahead of you. On Yama's instructions, death will convey you to him. Yama is terrible. Make efforts to be upright. Earlier, regardless of your misery, the lord has uprooted your relatives. Though you are still alive, there is nothing that can stand in Yama's way. The winds that advance ahead of Yama will begin to blow in front. Since you will be conveyed before him, act for the sake of the hereafter. Like a hiccup, Yama's winds will blow soon. When that great fear arrives, the directions will whirl around in front of you. O son! Soon, the learned texts will disappear. You will head towards agitation. Therefore, act so as to obtain supreme samadhi. Search for the only store of riches. Remembering the past, may you not be tormented by the good and bad deeds that you have done, or have not done. On account of those deeds, may you not be overcome by confusion. Soon, old age will destroy your body and take away your strength, limbs and beauty. Search for the

[991]Purity, contentment, austerities, studying, meditation, lack of cruelty, truth, abstaining from theft, observance of vows and acquisition of wealth.

[992]This means Yama's world.

[993]To the supreme objective.

only store of riches. In front of you, Yama will mangle your body with diseases that are like arrows. You will have to tolerate the destruction of your life. Therefore, perform great austerities. Soon, the terrible wolves that are within the human body will attack you in every way.[994] Therefore, try to perform auspicious acts. Soon, you will be alone and will perceive a great darkness. Soon, you will see golden trees atop a mountain.[995] Soon, you will have evil companions and enemies disguised as well-wishers. They will make you deviate from your insight. O son! Therefore, strive for the supreme. Obtain the radiant riches that suffer no fear on account of theft. Even when one dies, those riches are not taken away. That is earned through one's own deeds and does not have to be shared with anyone else. One enjoys whatever one has earned. O son! Give, so that one is able to live in the hereafter. On your own, accumulate the riches that are indestructible and permanent. Do not think that greater riches can be obtained after material objects have been cooked and enjoyed.[996] Even before those material desires have been satisfied, you may soon be taken away. When there is the hardship,[997] one has to traverse alone. Mothers, fathers, relatives, praised and beloved people and companions do not follow one there. When one goes there, one only carries the riches that one has earned through one's own acts, good or bad. Stores of gold and jewels, accumulated through fair means or foul, accomplish no objective when the body is destroyed. When one goes to the hereafter, there are deeds that have been performed and deeds that have not been performed. For all these, a man has no witness other than his atman. When one goes there, the human body amounts to nothing. However, through the intelligence of insight, it[998] can see everything that there is to see. In this world, there are three things that exist in the body—the fire,

[994]Vices are being compared to wolves.

[995]These golden trees are believed to be a premonition of death.

[996]*Yavaka* is a dish made out of barley. The cooking and eating of this is used as a metaphor for material objects.

[997]Death.

[998]The jivatman.

the sun and the wind. They possess the insight of dharma and are witnesses to everything. When it is night, one desires all the other wives.[999] One thinks that this conduct remains secret, but it is revealed. Therefore, follow your own dharma. There are many obstructions along the path, which is guarded by terrible and malformed creatures. But protect your own deeds. Perform your own deeds and go there. One's own deeds do not have to be shared with anyone else. One enjoys the fruits, depending on the acts that one has oneself performed. Large numbers of apsaras and maharshis obtain the fruits of bliss. They obtain the fruits of their deeds and go where they will, on celestial vehicles. In a similar way, pure people with cleansed souls, men who have been born in pure wombs, also obtain the fruits of their good deeds. In the hereafter, those who follow the ordinances of the dharma of garhasthya roam around in the worlds of Prajapati, Brihaspati or Shatakratu. I can speak to you about many thousands of methods. However, there is lack of intelligence and delusion and the perception that there is nothing other than material objects.[1000] Twenty-four years have certainly passed and you are twenty-five years old now. Your life is thus passing. Act so as to build a store of dharma. Soon, Yama will be there and he will smear your self-control with delusion. Before he arises and seizes you, swiftly act in accordance with dharma. On the road that you have to follow, you alone will lead the way and you alone will follow. You[1001] and others do not matter. Without any companions, one has to go there alone. There is fear in the hereafter. Therefore, accumulate the great treasure. Even if one tries to restrain him,[1002] the lord takes away the relatives one is attached to, with the foundations of the family. Thus, act to build up the store of dharma. O son! The instructions I have given you are the ones I honour. I have described them. Use your own insight to

[999]Of other men.

[1000]If one transcends this, methods are irrelevant.

[1001]In the sense of the physical body.

[1002]Yama.

examine them and act accordingly. If a person gives away whatever riches he has earned through his own deeds, he is freed from a hundred qualities that are associated with ignorance and delusion.[1003] One must perform the auspicious rites that are in conformity with the sacred texts. The insight that is given there is beneficial and full of purport. The attachment to dwelling in a village[1004] is like a bond made out of ropes. Having severed it, one can perform good deeds. If one does not sever it, one performs bad deeds. O son! What will you do with riches? What will you do with relatives? What will you do with sons? They will die. Enter a cave and search for your atman. Where have all your ancestors gone? Do today a task meant for tomorrow. Do in the forenoon a task meant for the afternoon. Who knows what is today. The soldiers of death do not wait to see. The relatives follow you to the end of the cremation ground and return. Kin and well-wishers hurl a man into the fire. Non-believers are hateful. They are established in their wicked ways. Ignore them and keep them on the left. With undivided attention, seek the supreme. The world is thus afflicted and is oppressed by time. Therefore, resort to dharma with all your soul and resort to the great riches. A man who knows the methods for obtaining this insight well, acts appropriately, in accordance with dharma, and obtains felicity in the hereafter. Know that resorting to another body does not mean death. There is no destruction for a person who himself sticks to the indicated path. A person who enhances dharma is learned. A person who deviates from dharma is deluded. If a person is engaged in his own deeds along the path of action, in due course, he obtains the fruits that have been spoken about. A performer of inferior deeds goes to hell. A person who is devoted to dharma goes to heaven. In general, it is extremely difficult for a man to obtain the staircase to heaven. Therefore, having obtained it, one should

[1003]The text uses the word *yujyate*, meaning united. This does not fit. Why should one be united with ignorance and delusion? It should probably read *muchyate*, meaning freed. We have thus treated this as a typo.

[1004]Meaning, a habitation in general.

concentrate one's atman, so that one does not fall away again. If a person's intelligence is such that he follows the path to heaven, he is spoken of as a performer of auspicious deeds and his friends and relatives grieve at his death. If a person's intelligence is determined and does not waver, he obtains heaven and does not suffer from great fear. Even if a person has been born in a hermitage and dies there, despite not having experienced desire and objects of pleasure, he obtains only a little bit of dharma. I think that if a person forsakes objects of pleasure and torments his body through austerities, he doesn't obtain only a little, but obtains great fruits. Thousands of mothers and fathers and hundreds of sons and wives have come and will come again.[1005] Whom do they belong to? Whom do we belong to? Their tasks have nothing to do with you. Your tasks have nothing to do with them. People are born because of their own deeds and depart from here. In this world, others act as relatives when one is rich. If a person is poor, even when he is alive, relatives are destroyed. For the sake of a wife, a man willingly commits inauspicious acts. Because of those, he suffers hardships in this world and in the next. Behold. In the world of the living, the weaknesses of creatures result from their own deeds. O son! Therefore, act entirely in accordance with the instructions I have imparted to you. Look on this as a field of action and enter it. If you desire worlds in the hereafter, your conduct should be auspicious. Time is the witness of all deeds committed by creatures and forcibly cooks them. It uses the months and the seasons to whirl them around. The sun is the fire and the nights and days are the kindling. What can be gained through riches that are not given away? If strength is not used to restrain enemies, what is its use? If dharma is not followed, what is the use of sacred texts? If the senses are not subjugated, what purpose can the atman have?' These were the beneficial words that Dvaipayana spoke. Shuka took his father's leave and went in search of someone who could instruct him about moksha."'

[1005]In successive births.

Chapter 1638(310)

'Yudhishthira asked, "O grandfather! How did Shuka, the great ascetic with dharma in his soul, obtain birth as Vyasa's son? How did he obtain supreme success? Tell me that. Through which woman did Vyasa, the store of austerities, generate Shuka? We do not know anything about his mother, or about the birth of that fierce and great-souled one. When he was a child, how did his intelligence turn towards the pursuit of subtle knowledge? There is no second person in the world in whom such signs can be seen. O immensely radiant one! I wish to hear about all this in detail. Your words are the equal of amrita and I am never satisfied with hearing them. O grandfather! In due course, tell me about Shuka's greatness, the yoga in his atman and about his knowledge."

'Bhishma replied, "The rishis did not make dharma dependent on grey hair, riches or relatives. A person who is devoted to learning is great. O Pandava! Everything that you have asked me about has austerities as a foundation. Austerities can be resorted to by controlling the senses and not in any other way. There is no doubt that addiction to the senses is associated with sin. It is through controlling them that a man obtains success. O son! One thousand horse sacrifices and one hundred *vajapeya* sacrifices are not equal to one-sixteenth of the fruits that one can obtain through these means. I will tell you how the fierce Shuka's birth came about, the fruits of his yoga and the end that he attained. It is difficult for a person with an unclean soul to understand this. In ancient times, Mahadeva was sporting on the summit of Mount Meru, which was decorated with *karnikara* flowers.[1006] He was surrounded by a large number of terrible spirits. In those ancient times, the goddess[1007] who was the daughter of the king of the mountains, was also there. The lord, Krishna Dvaipayana, tormented himself through divine austerities

[1006]The Indian laburnum.

[1007]Parvati.

there. He was devoted to the dharma of yoga and using yoga, penetrated his atman. O supreme among the Kuru lineage! For the sake of a son, he tormented himself through austerities, meditating in dharana. He repeatedly said, 'O lord![1008] Give me an energetic son who will have the power of the fire, the earth, the water, the wind and space.' Driven by this resolution, he prayed to the lord of the gods, one whom those with unclean souls find difficult to obtain. He worshipped him through supreme austerities. Subsisting only on air, the lord was there for one hundred years. He worshipped the many forms of Mahadeva, Uma's consort. The brahmana rishis, all the devarshis, the guardians of the worlds, the lords of the worlds, the Sadhyas, accompanied by the Vasus, the Adityas, the Rudras, the sun, the moon, the wind, the Maruts, the oceans, the rivers, the Ashvins, the gods, the gandharvas, Narada, Parvata, the gandharva Vishvavasu, the Siddhas and large numbers of apsaras were also there. Rudra Mahadeva was decorated with beautiful karnikara flowers. He blazed in his radiance, like moonlight from the moon. That beautiful and divine forest was full of gods and devarshis. For the sake of a son, the rishi[1009] was engaged in supreme yoga there. His complexion did not fade and there was no decay in his beauty. The three worlds thought that this was extraordinary. In his matted hair, his energy was like the flames of a fire. United in that infinite energy, he was seen to be blazing. The illustrious Markandeya told me about this. He always talked about the conduct of the gods. O son! Because, Krishna's[1010] matted hair blazed through those austerities, even today, it is seen to possess the complexion of the fire. O descendant of the Bharata lineage! In this way, he faithfully performed austerities. Maheshvara was gratified and decided to grant him his wish. The illustrious Tryambaka seemed to smile and said, 'O Dvaipayana! You will get the kind of son you desire. You will have a pure and great son and he will be like the fire, the wind, the earth, the water and space. His sentiments and his intelligence will be like

[1008]He was praying to Shiva.

[1009]Vedavyasa.

[1010]Krishna Dvaipayana.

that and he will seek refuge in the atman. He will be enveloped in energy and he will obtain fame in the three worlds.'"'

Chapter 1639(311)

'Bhishma said, "Satyavati's son obtained this supreme boon from the god. One day, in a desire to create a fire, he collected two sticks and was rubbing them together. O king! At that time, the illustrious rishi saw the apsara named Ghritachi. She blazed in her energy and her beauty was supreme. O Yudhishthira! In that forest, on seeing the apsara, the rishi, the illustrious Vyasa, was suddenly overcome by desire. O great king! On seeing that Vyasa's mind was overwhelmed by desire, Ghritachi assumed the form of a she-parrot and appeared before him. Seeing the apsara assume a different form, the desire in his body did not vanish, but spread all over his body. The sage summoned his great fortitude and tried to suppress it. However, Vyasa was unable to control it and his mind was agitated. What was going to happen was certain to happen. Thus, Ghritachi's body seized him. Wishing to control it, the sage tried to create a fire. However, his semen suddenly fell down on those sticks. However, without any anxiety in his mind, the supreme among brahmanas continued to rub those sticks. O king! Through her, the brahmana rishi had a son named Shuka.[1011] When the semen fell down, the great ascetic, Shuka, was born. The supreme rishi and great yogi was born from the womb of those two sticks. At a sacrifice, when oblations are poured on the kindling, a blazing fire results. Shuka was born in such a form, flaming in his energy. O Kouravya! His radiance and supreme beauty and complexion were like that of his father. The one with the clean soul was as resplendent as a fire blazing without any smoke. O lord of men! In her own personified form, Ganga, best among rivers, came to the slopes of Meru and bathed him with her water. O Kouravya!

[1011]Shuka means parrot.

O Indra among kings! From the sky, a staff and a black antelope skin fell down on the ground, for the sake of the great-souled Shuka. Gandharvas sang and large numbers of apsaras danced. The drums of the gods were sounded with a loud roar. The gandharvas Vishvavasu, Tumburu and Narada, and the gandharvas Haha and Huhu, praised Shuka's birth. With Shakra at the forefront, the guardians of the worlds arrived. So did the gods, the devarshis and the brahmana rishis. The wind god showered down all kinds of divine flowers. Everything in the universe, mobile and immobile, was delighted. The great-souled and immensely radiant one[1012] was delighted. With the goddess,[1013] he himself arrived and when the sage's son was born, performed the sacred thread ceremony, following the proper rites. Shakra, the lord of the gods, was delighted and gave him a divine and extraordinary kamandalu[1014]and celestial garments. O descendant of the Bharata lineage! Swans, *shatapatra*s,[1015] thousands of cranes and blue jays circled around Shuka. The immensely radiant one obtained a divine birth from those sticks. He dwelt there, intelligent, controlled and a brahmachari. O great king! As soon as he was born, all the Vedas, with their mysteries and their collections, presented themselves before him, just as they had before his father. O great king! Thinking about dharma, he[1016] chose Brihaspati, learned about the Vedas, the Vedangas and their commentaries, as his preceptor. He studied all the Vedas, with their mysteries and their collections. The lord also studied all the histories and the sacred texts about royal policy. Having given a dakshina to his preceptor, the great sage returned. Controlled and a brahmachari, he started fierce austerities. Even when he was a child, the gods and the rishis revered him, because of his knowledge and his austerities. O lord of men! His intelligence found no delight in the three ashramas, with garhasthya as their foundation. He sought insight about the dharma of moksha."'

[1012]Mahadeva.

[1013]Parvati.

[1014]Water pot.

[1015]Bird with one hundred feathers, can be peacock, parrot, crane or woodpecker.

[1016]Shuka. Dharma requires one to have a preceptor.

Chapter 1640(312)

'Bhishma said, "Thinking about emancipation, Shuka went to his father. Humbly and desiring what was beneficial, he saluted the preceptor and said, 'O illustrious one! You are accomplished in the dharma of moksha. Tell me about it. O lord! Let supreme tranquility be generated in my mind.' On hearing his son's words, the supreme rishi replied, 'O son! Study the different texts on moksha and dharma.' O descendant of the Bharata lineage! Shuka, supreme among those who know about the brahman, accepted the instructions of his father and studied the sacred texts of yoga and everything propounded by Kapila.[1017] He was united with the prosperity of the brahman and became like Brahma in his valour. Vyasa thought that his son had become accomplished in knowledge about moksha. He said, 'Go to Janaka, the lord of Mithila. In particular, he will tell you everything about the objective of emancipation.' Instructed by his father, he decided to go to Janaka, the king of Mithila, to ask him about the benefit of dharma and devotion to moksha. He was told,[1018] 'Follow the path that humans take. Do not proceed so as to cause wonder. Do not use your powers to travel through the sky. Be upright in your path. Do not seek happiness along the way. In particular, do not get attached. And in particular, do not seek out companions. You must not show any insolence when you perform sacrifices for that lord of men. If you are obedient to him, he will dispel your doubts. The king is skilled about dharma and is accomplished in the sacred texts of moksha. I am the officiating priest at his sacrifices. Without any doubt, you should do whatever he asks you to.' Having been thus addressed, the sage, with dharma in his soul, left for Mithila.

'"He proceeded on foot, though he was capable of traversing the earth, with all its oceans, through the sky. He passed mountains and traversed rivers and lakes. There were many kinds of forests, full

[1017]That is, sankhya.

[1018]By his father. Vyasa told him not to use the powers of yoga.

of predators and diverse other animals. He passed through the two *varsha*s, Meru and Hari, and went through the varsha Himavat.[1019] In due course, he arrived in Bharatavarsha. Having seen many countries, inhabited by the Chins and the Hunas, the great sage arrived in the country known as Aryavarta. Thinking about the words of instruction given by his father, he travelled, like a bird travelling through the sky. Despite many beautiful habitations, prosperous cities and wonderful gems, Shuka saw them, without quite seeing them.[1020] There were beautiful groves and plains and sacred places of pilgrimage. The traveller passed through them. In a short while, he reached Videha, protected by the great-souled Dharmaraja[1021] Janaka. He saw many villages there and many men with food. There were prosperous habitations of cowherds, full of large numbers of cattle. There were fields rich with rice and barley and hundreds of lakes full of lotuses, inhabited by swans and cranes. They were beautiful and adorned. Videha was rich and densely populated. Passing through it, he arrived in the beautiful and expensive groves of Mithila. It was full of elephants, horses and chariots and populated with men and women. The undecaying one passed through them, seeing, but not quite seeing. His mind bore a burden and he kept thinking about this. He found pleasure in his atman. He took delight in his atman and arrived in Mithila. When he arrived at the gate, he was restrained by the gatekeepers. He waited there, free and devoted to meditation.

'"Having obtained permission, he entered. He advanced along the royal road, frequented by prosperous people. Without any hesitation, he entered, desirous of meeting the king. But there too, the gatekeepers used harsh words to bar his entry. Like earlier, without any anger, Shuka waited. The heat and the travel had not distressed

[1019]A varsha is a division of the earth, a bit like a continent. Varshas are separated by mountain ranges. While geographical descriptions vary a bit, Meru, Hari and Himavat varshas are to the north of Bharatavarsha.

[1020]He did not stop there. Like a bird, he did not alight.

[1021]A title used for kings who follow dharma, not to be confused with Yudhishthira, to whom, the term is also applied.

him, despite his suffering from hunger, thirst and exhaustion. He did not suffer from any misery, nor did the heat trouble him. Shuka waited there, like the midday sun. On seeing him there, one of the gatekeepers was filled with grief. He honoured him in the proper way, greeting him with hands joined in salutation. He escorted him to the second chamber in the king's palace.[1022] O son! Seated there, Shuka began to think about moksha. The immensely radiant one was indifferent as to whether a place was in the sun or in the shade. In a short while, the king's minister arrived. Joining his hands in salutation, he escorted him to the third chamber in the king's palace. The great inner quarters were there, the equal of Chaitraratha.[1023] It was excellently divided into waterbodies used for pleasure. There were beautiful and flowering trees. The minister showed Shuka that supreme grove. He instructed that a seat should be given to him and departed. There were young and beautiful women there, attired in handsome garments. Their hips were excellent and their attire was wispy. They were adorned in ornaments made out of molten gold. They were skilled in conversation and accomplished in dancing and singing. They smiled before they spoke and their beauty was like that of apsaras. They were accomplished in all aspects of kama. They could discern signs and were skilled in everything. Fifty such excellent women, foremost among courtesans, surrounded him. One after another, they seized his feet and washed them, worshipping him. They satisfied him with excellent objects that were appropriate to the time and the place. O son! O descendant of the Bharata lineage! Once he had eaten, one after another, they led him and showed him the beautiful groves in the inner quarters. They sported, laughed and sang before Shuka. He was generous in his spirit and knew about the truth. However, all of them entertained him in this way. The one with the pure soul had been born from two sticks. His senses were under subjugation and his anger had been conquered. The performer

[1022]This explains the earlier sets of gatekeepers. The first set stopped him at the gate of the city. The second set stopped him at the entry to the palace, the first chamber, so to speak.

[1023]The name of Kubera's garden.

of the three kinds of karma did not have the three kinds of doubt concerning these.[1024] He was neither delighted, nor enraged. Those supreme women gave him a bed and a seat, decorated with jewels, excellent and supreme. They were strewn with spreads and cushions. Having washed his feet, Shuka performed his evening prayers. He sat down on the seat and began to think about his auspicious objective. In the first part of the night, he engaged in meditation there. As is proper, in the middle of the night, the lord ate and went to sleep. In a short while, he arose and performed the rites of ablution. Surrounded by those women, the intelligent one meditated. O descendant of the Bharata lineage! Following the rites, in this way, Krishna's undecaying son spent the day and the night in the king's household."'

Chapter 1641(313)

'Bhishma said, "O descendant of the Bharata lineage! Later, King Janaka, with all his ministers and with his priest at the forefront, came to the inner quarters. He brought an expensive seat and many kinds of jewels. Bearing those offerings on his head, he approached his preceptor's son.[1025] He gave him the expensive seat. It was decorated with many gems, was covered with spreads and cushions and was fortunate in every way.[1026] With his own hands, the king received the seat from the priest. He gave it to Shuka, his preceptor's son, and worshipped him. Krishna's son was seated there and honoured, in accordance with the sacred texts. Water to wash the feet was offered first. A gift and a cow were given next. Following

[1024]The number three is difficult to understand. It can conceivably refer to *sanchita* (accumulated) karma, *prarabdha* karma (karma that has ripened or matured) and *kriyamana* karma (that undertaken in the current life).

[1025]Vedavyasa was Janaka's preceptor and officiating priest.

[1026]The seat is described as *sarvatobhadra*. This means fortunate in every way, or in every direction. However, this can also be interpreted as a square or circular seat.

the prescribed rites and reciting the mantras, he accepted the honour. Having received the honours, the supreme among brahmanas worshipped Janaka. Taking the king's permission, he accepted the cow. The immensely energetic one asked the king whether he was well and in good health. Shuka next asked about the welfare of the followers. Having taken his permission, the Indra among kings and his followers seated themselves. The generous king joined his hands in salutation and sat down on the ground. The king asked whether Vyasa's son was well and healthy. The king then asked why he had come.

'"Shuka said, 'O fortunate one! My father said that you are accomplished in the meaning of the dharma of moksha. He said that he is the officiating priest to the famous King Janaka of Videha. If I had any doubts in my heart, he asked me to quickly go there. He said that you would sever my doubts about pravritti and nivritti. Instructed by my father, I have come here to ask you. You are the foremost among the upholders of dharma. Therefore, you should tell me. If a brahmana desires the objective of emancipation for himself, what are the tasks that he should undertake? What are the tasks required for emancipation? Is it knowledge or austerities?'

'"Janaka replied, 'From the time of birth, hear about the tasks a brahmana must undertake. O son! When the sacred thread ceremony is over, he must devote himself to the Vedas. O lord! He must devote himself to austerities, tending to his preceptor and brahmacharya. Without any malice, he must repay the debts to the gods and the ancestors. Having controlled himself, he must study the Vedas. Once this is over, he must take the preceptor's permission, offer a dakshina, and return. Having returned, with his wife, he must dwell in the state of a householder. He must not go to anyone else.[1027] He must be free from malice and must possess the household fire. Having obtained sons and grandsons, he must dwell in the ashrama of vanaprastha. Following the sacred texts, he must establish a fire there and affectionately attend to the guests. In the forest, a person who knows about dharma ignites another fire in his

[1027]Any other woman.

atman.[1028] He is without the opposite pairs of sentiments. There is no attachment in his soul and he dwells in the ashrama that is devoted to the brahman.'

'"Shuka asked, 'If jnana and vijnana have been generated and if one can see the eternal in one's heart, is it necessary to reside in the ashrama of the forest? I am asking you about this and you should tell me. O lord of men! Tell me the truth about the purport of the Vedas.'

'"Janaka replied, 'One cannot advance towards emancipation without jnana and vijnana. It has been said that one cannot obtain jnana without association with a preceptor. It has been said that jnana is the boat and the preceptor is the one who steers the boat. After having obtained knowledge, one has accomplished one's objective. After having reached the shore, one can abandon both.[1029] It has been said that the four ashramas of dharma and their codes of conduct were thought of earlier, to prevent the destruction of the worlds and the destruction of rites. In the course of progress, one performs many kinds of tasks. However, emancipation cannot be obtained in this world by performing good or bad deeds. By thinking about the reasons through many births in this cycle of existence, one can obtain a pure soul and attain emancipation even in the first ashrama. When one has obtained liberation in this way, the learned person can see the purpose behind everything. For someone who desires the supreme in this way, what is the purpose behind the other three ashramas? One must always discard the taints associated with rajas and tamas. Perceiving the atman in one's atman,[1030] one must adhere to the path of sattva. One must see one's atman in all beings and all beings in one's atman. However, one will not be attached, like an aquatic creature in the water. If one is free from the body in this way, one is liberated and beyond opposites. One obtains tranquility. Like a bird, one soars above the flood and obtains the infinite in this world. In ancient times, King Yayati sung a chant about this. Listen. O son! This is upheld by brahmanas who are accomplished in the

[1028]This is a reference to the ashrama of sannyasa.

[1029]Jnana and the preceptor.

[1030]Respectively, the paramatman and the jivatman.

sacred texts of moksha. "The radiance exists in the atman and not anywhere else.[1031] Be attached to it. If one is extremely controlled in one's consciousness, one is capable of seeing it oneself. Such a person is not frightened of others and others are not frightened of him. He does not desire or hate. He then obtains the brahman. In deeds, thoughts or words, he does not entertain wicked sentiments towards any creature. He then obtains the brahman. He engages himself in austerities. He discards the enticement of jealousy. He abandons desire and avarice. He then obtains the brahman. In words and sight, he does not cause injury to any creature. He is impartial and beyond opposites. He then obtains the brahman. He looks upon praise and censure equally. He is indifferent to gold and iron, joy and misery, cold and heat, good and evil, pleasant and unpleasant, birth and death. He then obtains the brahman." A tortoise extends its limbs and then draws them back again. That is the way a mendicant restrains his senses and his mind. When a house is enveloped in darkness, one can see with the light of a lamp. In that way, using the lamp of intelligence, one is capable of seeing the atman. O supreme among intelligent ones! I can see that you are already aware of all of this. You also know the truth about everything else that there is to be known. O brahmana rishi! Through the favours of your preceptor and because of his teachings, you already know about all these subjects. O great sage! It is also because of his favours that this divine knowledge has manifested itself before me and I know all this. Your vijnana is superior to mine and your destination is superior to mine. Even if you do not realize it, your prosperity is superior to mine. Though that vijana has been generated in you, you are not aware of its existence, perhaps because of doubts associated with a young age, perhaps because of fear that you might not obtain emancipation. Through my pure conduct, I may have been able to sever the doubts. With the bonds of the heart loosened, you will obtain the objective. The vijnana has already been generated in you. You are firm in your intelligence and without avarice. O brahmana! However, without

[1031]The text does not clearly indicate the Yayati quote and our choice is subjective.

the appropriate conduct, one cannot obtain the supreme. There is no joy or misery in you. In particular, there is no greed. You are not interested in dancing and singing. No attachment was generated in you. You are not bound down by relatives. You are not terrified of things that lead to fear. O immensely fortunate one! I can see that you regard a lump of earth or iron and gold as the same. I and other learned ones can see that you are established on the supreme path, which is without decay and eternal. O brahmana! All the fruits of the objective of moksha exist in you. O brahmana! What else do you wish to ask me?'"'

Chapter 1642(314)

'Bhisma said, "Hearing these words, the one with the cleansed soul became firm in his resolution. He based his atman on the atman and saw the atman in his atman. He was happy and tranquil at having accomplished his objective. Silently, with the speed of the wind, he headed towards the northern direction, towards the cold mountains. At this time, devarshi Narada wished to see the Himalayas, inhabited by siddhas and charanas. It was populated by a large number of apsaras and reverberated with the sound of singing. There were large numbers of kinnaras and bees. There were diver-birds, wagtails and wonderful pheasants. There were colourful peacocks, calling in hundreds of tones. There were collections of swans and cheerful cuckoos. Garuda, the king of birds, always went there. To ensure the welfare of the worlds, the four guardians of the worlds, the gods and large numbers of rishis always gathered there. For the sake of a son, the great-souled Vishnu tormented himself with austerities there.

"'In his childhood, it was there that Kumara hurled his spear down on the ground, disrespecting the three worlds and the residents of heaven. Having flung it down, Skanda spoke these words to the universe. 'Is there anyone superior to me? Is there anyone who loves brahmanas more? Is there a second valiant Brahmanya[1032] in the three worlds? If there is any such person, let him raise this spear, or make it tremble.' On hearing this, the worlds were distressed and wondered who would be the saviour. The large number of gods were frightened that he wished to become Indra. The illustrious Vishnu saw that the asuras and the rakshasas were also agitated. He began to think, 'What is the best thing to be done under the circumstances?' He could not afford to tolerate and ignore the act of flinging down by Pavaki.[1033] The one with the pure soul laughed at the blazing spear. Purushottama grasped it in his left hand and it began to tremble. The powerful Vishnu made the spear tremble in this way. The earth, will all its mountains, forests and groves, began to shake. Although he could have uprooted the spear, he only made it tremble a little. In this way, the lord Vishnu preserved Skandaraja's pride. Having made it tremble, the illustrious one spoke to Prahlada. 'Behold Kumara's valour. No one else is capable of acting in this way.' Unable to tolerate these words, he[1034] determined to uproot the spear. He grasped it, but could not make it tremble. Uttering a loud roar, he fell down on the summit of the mountain, unconscious. Hiranyakashipu's son was numbed and fell down on the ground.

'"O son! The one with the bull on his banner[1035] always goes to the northern slopes of that king among mountains and torments himself with austerities there. The hermitage there is surrounded by a blazing fire and is extremely difficult to approach. It is known as Adityabandhana and a person with an unclean soul cannot approach it. It is surrounded by a blazing fire that extends for ten yojanas.[1036] The valiant and illustrious Pavaka is himself established there. He

[1032]Subrahmanya (Brahmanya) is Kartikeya's name and means someone who is kind to brahmanas.

[1033]Pavaki is Kartikeya's name, Kartikeya being described as the son of the fire god (Pavaka).

[1034]Prahlada.

[1035]Shiva.

[1036]Measure of distance, between two and three miles. Originally, a yojana was a distance that could be travelled by one yoking of horses to a chariot.

removes all impediments for the intelligent Mahadeva. Mahadeva was firm in his vows. There, he stood on a single foot for one thousand divine years, thereby tormenting the gods.

'"On the slopes of those mountains, Vyasa, Parashara's immensely ascetic son, taught the Vedas. The great ascetic instructed his disciples—the immensely fortunate Sumantu, Vaishampayana, the immensely wise Jaimini and the ascetic Paila. The great ascetic, Vyasa, was surrounded by these disciples. At that sacred hermitage, the supreme father saw that the one who had been born from the sticks[1037] was approaching, pure in his soul and like the sun in the sky. Vyasa saw that his son was approaching, like a fire scattering flames on every side. He was like the sun in his resplendence. The great-souled one was united with yoga and did not seem to touch the trees, the mountains, or the uneven terrain. He was like an arrow that had been released from a bow. The son of the two sticks approached his father and grasped his feet. Following the rites, the great sage welcomed him. Cheerful in his mind, Shuka informed his father about his conversation with King Janaka. He told him everything. With his son, the great sage, Parashara's son, Vyasa, continued to dwell on the slopes of the Himalayas, instructing his disciples. They were accomplished in studying the Vedas and tranquil in their souls, having conquered their senses. Those ascetics had obtained the benefits from the Vedas and the Vedangas.

'"On one occasion, Vyasa was surrounded by them. The disciples joined their hands in salutation and spoke to their preceptor. 'We have obtained great benefits and our fame has increased. However, through the favours of our preceptor, there is one thing that we still desire.' On hearing their words, the brahmana rishi replied, 'Tell me what you wish for. I will act so as to bring you pleasure.' On hearing their preceptor's words, the disciples were cheerful in their minds. They joined their hands in salutation and again bowed their heads down before their preceptor. O king! Together, they spoke these supreme words. 'O supreme among sages! If our preceptor is pleased,

[1037]Shuka.

we have been blessed. O maharshi! All of us desire that you should grant us a boon. Through your favours, other than us, let no sixth person become famous.[1038] The four of us are your disciples and the preceptor's son is the fifth. We desire the boon that the Vedas may only be established in us.' Vyasa knew about the true purport of the Vedas. On hearing the words of his disciples, Parashara's intelligent son thought about welfare in the world hereafter. The one with dharma in his soul spoke these words, which were full of beneficial dharma, to his disciples. 'They must always be given to a brahmana who is devoted to the brahman, one who certainly wishes to dwell in Brahma's world. May you multiply and spread the undecaying words of the Vedas. They should not be given to someone who has not become a disciple, nor to a person who is without vows and has not cleansed his soul. These should be known as the true qualities of someone who becomes a disciple. Without testing for character, the knowledge should never be given. Pure gold is tested by heating, cutting and rubbing. In that way, a disciple's birth and qualities must be tested. Do not employ a disciple in a task that should not be undertaken, or where there is great danger. The fruits of knowledge are proportional to intelligence and studying. Let all the difficulties be overcome. Let everyone see what is fortunate. You are accomplished to teach the four varnas, with brahmanas at the forefront. In studying the Vedas, these are said to be the great tasks that must be observed. To praise the gods, Svayambhu created the Vedas. If a person is ignorant and deluded and is jealous of brahmanas, disrespecting a brahmana who is accomplished in the Vedas, there is no doubt that he will be overcome. If a person speaks about this without following dharma, or if a person asks about this without following dharma, there will be no affection between them.[1039] Instead, there will be hatred. I have thus told you everything about the rites to be followed in the course of studying. Bear these in your hearts and bring welfare to your disciples.'"'

[1038]Sumantu, Vaishampayana, Jaimini, Paila and Shuka being the five.

[1039]Implicitly, this refers to a preceptor and a disciple.

Chapter 1643(315)

'Bhishma said, "On hearing these words of their preceptor, the immensely energetic disciples of Vyasa were delighted in their minds and embraced each other. They said, 'The illustrious one spoke beneficial words. We will firmly bear these in our minds and act in accordance with them.' Cheerful in their minds, they again embraced each other. Accomplished in the use of words, they again addressed their preceptor. 'O great sage! We wish to descend from this great mountain and depart. O lord! If it pleases you, we wish to divide the Vedas into many parts.' On hearing the words of his disciples, the lord who was Parashara's son replied in beneficial words that were full of dharma and artha. 'Go wherever you wish, to earth, or to the world of the gods. However, always be attentive. Brahma has a lot of deceit.'[1040] They obtained the permission of their preceptor, who was truthful in his speech. Circumambulating Vyasa and bowing their heads down before him, they departed. They descended to earth and performed four sacrifices. They began to officiate at the sacrifices of brahmanas, kings and vaishyas. They were cheerful and devoted themselves to the householder mode of life, honoured by brahmanas. They were prosperous and famous in the worlds, engaged in studying and officiating at sacrifices.

'"When his disciples had descended, Vyasa was only accompanied by his son. The intelligent one was silent and seated alone, engaged in meditation. Narada saw the extremely ascetic one in that hermitage. At that time, he spoke to him in these sweet words and syllables. 'O maharshi! O one who is descended from Vasishtha's lineage![1041] The chants of the brahman can no longer be heard. You are silent and seated alone in meditation. What are you thinking about? Without chants of the brahman, the mountain is no longer beautiful. It is like the moon, when it is invaded by

[1040]This requires interpretation. Unless carefully studied, the Vedas (the words of Brahma) are capable of being misunderstood.

[1041]Parashara was Vasishtha's grandson.

Upaplava[1042] and enveloped in dust and darkness. It is no longer as radiant as it was earlier and looks like a habitation of the *nishadas*. Though there are a large number of devarshis here, the sounds of the Vedas can no longer be heard. The rishis, the gods and the infinitely energetic gandharvas have been deprived of the sounds of the brahman. It is no longer as resplendent as it used to be.' On hearing Narada's words, Krishna Dvaipayana replied, 'O maharshi! You are accomplished in the words of the Vedas and I am in agreement with what you have said. You have indeed said what is appropriate. You know everything. You see everything. You are curious about everything. Everything that happens in the three worlds is known to you. O brahmana rishi! Therefore, tell me what I can do for you. O brahmana rishi! Instruct me about what I should do now. Separated from my disciples, my mind has become cheerless.'

'"Narada said, 'The stain of the Vedas is in their not being chanted. The stain of brahmanas is in the non-observance of vows. Carriers[1043] are the stain of the earth. Curiosity is the stain of women. With your intelligent son, study the Vedas. Let the chants of the brahman protect us from the fear of darkness.'"

'Bhishma continued, "Vyasa was supremely devoted to dharma. On hearing Narada's words, he agreed with those words. Firm in his vows, he cheerfully began to practise the Vedas. With his son Shuka, he began to chant the Vedas. Those syllables were accomplished and seemed to fill the worlds. Both of them were learned about all kinds of dharma. One day, as they were chanting, a turbulent wind arose. That wind seemed to have arisen from the depths of the ocean. Vyasa instructed his son to refrain from chanting. Having been restrained, Shuka was filled with curiosity. He asked his father, 'O brahmana! Where has this wind originated? You should tell me everything about the progress of the wind.' Hearing Shuka's words, Vyasa was greatly astounded. He spoke these words, explaining why this portent meant

[1042]Upaplava is Rahu's name, when Rahu is in the ascendant. The reference is to a lunar eclipse.

[1043]Those who carry or bear burdens. It is not obvious what is meant.

that the chanting should cease. 'You possess divine sight. Your pure mind has also been cleansed. You have discarded tamas and rajas and have resorted to sattva. Just as a person sees a reflection in the mirror, you see the atman in your atman. Basing yourself on your atman, you use your intelligence to think about the Vedas. Vishnu walks along *devayana*. There is darkness along *pitriyana*.[1044] After death, there are two paths. One goes to heaven, or one heads downwards. The wind blows on earth and in the firmament. There are seven courses that the wind follows. In due progression, listen to them. O son! The large numbers of gods and the immensely strong Sadhyas gave birth to a son named Samana. He was invincible. Udana was his son. Vyana was his son. Vyana's son was Apana. Know that Apana's son, Prana, came after that.[1045] Prana was invincible and the scorcher of enemies. However, he didn't have any offspring. I will now tell you accurately about their separate deeds. In all living bodies, these winds have their separate courses. Prana is said to be the breath of life in creatures. The first wind, which follows the first course, is known by the name of Pravaha.[1046] It whirls along the large masses of clouds that are full of smoke and heat. It is attached to clouds in the sky and manifests itself in the form of flashes of lightning. The second wind is known as Avaha[1047] and it blows with a loud roar. This is the one that causes Soma and the other stellar bodies to rise and set. Inside bodies, maharshis speak of it as Udana. There is a wind that sucks up water from the four oceans. Having sucked it up, this wind gives it to the clouds in the sky. Having given it to the clouds, it then gives it to Parjanya.[1048] This is the third wind, which always blows and gives rise to rain. This has the name of Udvaha.[1049] There is a wind that causes confusion in the sky and creates separate clouds for the sake of releasing rain. It roars in the clouds. It brings them together and separates them again. It is the roar

[1044]Devayana is the path of the gods and pitriyana is the path of the ancestors.

[1045]These five are also the breaths of life in the body.

[1046]Equated with Samana.

[1047]Equated with Udana.

[1048]The god of rain.

[1049]Equated with Vyana.

in the rivers. For the sake of preserving creatures, it appears in the form of clouds. In the sky, it bears the celestial vehicles of the gods. This fourth wind is named Samvaha[1050] and it shatters mountains. There is a fifth and immensely forceful wind named Vivaha.[1051] It is powerful and dry and shatters the trees that yield juice. When they are attached to it, clouds are known as Balahaka. When this wind moves, it creates terrible calamities. It roars in the firmament. The sixth wind is supreme among upright ones and is named Parivaha. It bears the celestial waters in the firmament and prevents them from overflowing. It supports the sacred waters of the Ganga in the sky and prevents them from being dislodged. The sun possesses one thousand rays and lights up the earth. However, because it is restrained from afar by this wind, the sun seems to possess a single ray. It is because of this wind that Soma becomes the store of divine amrita. There is another wind by the name of Paravaha. When the time of death arrives, this takes away the breath of life from all creatures. Death and Vaivasvata[1052] follow its trail. However, there are also those who use their intelligence to properly see. They are tranquil and always devoted to adhyatma. They are cheerful in their practice of meditation. They can think of themselves as immortal. Daksha's ten sons and the thousands of sons of Prajapati encountered its force at the place where the directions end.[1053] Though it is created, those who can subjugate it don't have to return.[1054] O son! These Maruts are the extremely wonderful sons of Aditi.[1055] They blow and go everywhere. They sustain everything, but do not get attached to anything. It is a great wonder that this supreme among mountains should suddenly be made to tremble because of the blowing of the wind. Since this blows with great force, it is the wind that results from

[1050]Equated with Apana.

[1051]Equated with Prana.

[1052]Yama.

[1053]Here, Prajapati probably means Daksha and thousands probably means offspring generated through the ten sons.

[1054]Paravaha is also responsible for emancipation.

[1055]All the gods were descended from Aditi and the sage Kashyapa.

Vishnu's breath. O son! When it blows suddenly, the entire universe is distressed. Hence, as long as it is blowing, those who know about the brahman do not chant the name of the brahman. They are also a form of the wind.[1056] It is said that when the brahman is chanted, the other wind that blows suffers from a fear and a difficulty.' Having spoken these words, the lord who was Parashara's son instructed his son to chant again, so that the firmament should again be full of the Ganga."'[1057]

Chapter 1644(316)

'Bhishma said, "At that time, Narada came to the spot where Shuka was alone,[1058] engaged in studying. He wished to ask him about the purport of the Vedas. On seeing that devarshi Narada had presented himself, Shuka first offered him arghya and then honoured him, following the rites laid down in the Vedas. Narada was delighted and spoke these words. 'O supreme among those who know about the brahman! O son! How can I ensure what is best for you? Cheerfully, instruct me.' O descendant of the Bharata lineage! Hearing Narada's words, Shuka replied, 'What is beneficial in this world? You should instruct me about the truth of this.'

'"Narada answered, 'Earlier, rishis with cleansed souls desired to find out about the truth. The illustrious Sanatkumara spoke these words to them. "There is no sight that is like that of knowledge. There are no austerities that are equal to learning. There is no misery that is equal to attachment. There is no bliss that is equal to renunciation. Abstention from wicked deeds, constant engagement in auspicious conduct, virtuous conduct and virtuous behaviour constitute supreme benefit. Having obtained the miserable status of

[1056]The chants of the brahman are also a form of the wind.

[1057]Clearly, the wind had stopped blowing.

[1058]Vedavyasa had left.

being born as a man, if a person becomes attached, he is confused. Such a person will not be freed from misery. Attachment is the sign of misery. The intelligence of someone who is attached is fickle. The net of delusion is only widened. If one is enmeshed in the net of delusion, one obtains misery in this world and in the next. Every means must be used to restrain desire and anger. These two arise to destroy what is beneficial and prevent observance of beneficial tasks. Austerities must always be protected against anger, and prosperity must be protected against jealousy. Knowledge must be protected against honour and dishonour and the atman against distraction. Non-violence is supreme dharma. Forgiveness is supreme strength. Knowledge of the atman is supreme knowledge. There is nothing that is superior to the truth. Truthful words are the best. However, beneficial words are preferable to the truth. It is my view that whatever brings great benefit to creatures is the truth. A person who has renounced the fruits of all enterprise, is without desires, delinked from possessions and has renounced everything, is knowledgable and learned. If a person enjoys the senses and the objects of the senses without his self being subjugated by them and if he is not attached, he is tranquil in his soul. He is indifferent and controlled. If a person is immersed in his atman and if he is not attached to anything he is associated with, he has been freed. He will soon obtain the supreme benefit. O sage! If a person does not really see, touch or converse with other creatures, he will obtain the supreme benefit. One should not act violently towards any being. One should always be affectionate. Having obtained birth, one should never exhibit enmity. A person who is content with a trifle, a person who is without hopes and not fickle—such a person is said to have conquered himself. He knows his atman and will obtain the supreme benefit. O son![1059] Discard all possessions and conquer your senses. Be established in the place that has no sorrow and be without fear, in this world and in the next. Those who have no desires do not grieve. Cast aside all desire from your self. Cast aside all desire and be tranquil. You will thus free yourself from misery and calamity. A

[1059]Since the rishis are being addressed, this should really be in the plural.

sage must control his self, be restrained and always engage in austerities. He must conquer desire, which is difficult to vanquish. In the midst of attachments, he must not be attached. If a brahmana is not attached to an association with any of the qualities and if he always dwells alone, he will soon obtain supreme bliss. Creatures are addicted to the pleasure that comes from sexual congress. In the midst of this, a sage takes pleasure in himself alone. Know him to be a person for whom wisdom has brought contentment. A person who is content with his knowledge does not sorrow. Through auspicious deeds, one obtains divinity in the firmament. Through mixed deeds, one obtains birth as a human. Through inauspicious deeds, one obtains an inferior birth. One is powerless against what has been obtained through deeds. Creatures are cooked in the cycle of life. One is always assailed by death, old age and misery. Why do you not understand this? Something that is not beneficial is regarded by you as beneficial. Something that is transitory is regarded by you as permanent. Something that is undesirable is regarded by you as desirable. Why do you not understand this? Like a silkworm, you are enmeshing yourself in these multiple strands. You are entangling yourself in this cocoon. But you do not comprehend. There has been enough of possessions. Possessions are associated with sins. The worm encased in a cocoon is destroyed by what it has itself done. Beings who are attached to sons, wives and families have to suffer. They are like an aged and wild elephant that has got stuck to the mud in a pond. They have been captured in a large net, like fish that have been dragged to the land. Behold. Creatures are entangled in the net of affection and undergo great misery. Families, sons, wives, bodies and accumulations of objects are all transitory and serve no purpose in the hereafter. There is nothing except one's good and bad deeds. One must certainly abandon everything and go there. Why should one then be attached to the undesirable and not be engaged in what brings one benefit? There is no place for resting along that path, no refuge and no provisions. That region is desolate, unknown and enveloped in darkness. How will you go there alone? When you advance there, there is nothing that will follow you from the rear.

Your good and bad deeds are the only things that will follow you. One searches for one's objectives through learning, deeds, valour and extremely great wisdom. Once one is successful in accomplishing that objective, one is freed. The attachment towards dwelling in a village[1060] is like a noose made out of ropes. When one has severed it, the ones with good deeds move forward. Without severing it, the ones with bad deeds find it difficult to make progress. Beauty constitutes the banks.[1061] The mind is the current. Touch constitutes the islands and taste is the flow. Scent is the mud. Sound is the water. The flow along the road to heaven is extremely difficult. Forgiveness constitutes the oars. Truth, patience and dharma are the ropes. Renunciation is the wind that swiftly drives it. Using one's intelligence as a boat, one must cross that river. Abandon both dharma and adharma.[1062] Cast aside truth and falsehood. Having cast aside both truth and falsehood, cast aside everything that must be abandoned. Abandon all resolution about dharma. Abandon adharma and violence. Having cast aside both truth and falsehood, use your intelligence to form a resolution about what is supreme. The bones[1063] are the pillars. The sinews are like strings. Flesh and blood are the external plaster. The skin is a sheath. It emits a foul smell and is full of urine and excrement. It is pervaded by the sorrow of old age. It is an abode for disease and affliction. Abandon this residence of creatures, full of passion and impermanent. Everything in the universe is in this universe. This universe has originated in the five great elements. Everything results from the atoms[1064] of Mahat. There are the five senses and tamas, sattva and rajas. The collection of the seventeen[1065] is said to be indicative of the manifest. With the objects of the senses, the manifest and the unmanifest, there are said

[1060]Interpreted as any habitation.

[1061]There is an image of a river of life.

[1062]Interpreted in the narrow sense.

[1063]In the body.

[1064]The word used is *paramanu*.

[1065]The five senses, the five organs of action, the five breaths of life, mind and intelligence.

to be twenty-five,[1066] with the qualities of the manifest and the unmanifest. When all of these are united together, one is always described as a being.[1067] If a person knows the nature of the three objectives,[1068] life and death, he knows the truth. He knows about creation and destruction. A person who has the slightest bit of knowledge knows that prosperity exists in the hereafter. Anything that can be grasped by the senses is established in the realm of the manifest. One must know the unmanifest and attentively comprehend it through the signs. The senses always satisfy a creature, like a shower. However, a person who sees the atman sees that the atman is extended everywhere in the world. Through the strength of knowledge, a person can see the supreme and he does not perceive the lack of a shore. In every way and in every circumstance, he sees it in all beings. Even if he is associated with other creatures, he does not suffer anything undesirable on this account. Through knowledge, one can overcome many kinds of hardship that are due to delusion. When a person's knowledge has become manifest, he does not suffer any injury on account of the ways of the world. An illustrious person who knows about the sacred says that in its atman, a creature is without beginning and without end. It is without decay. It is not the doer and it is without form. Because of its own deeds, a creature is always engaged in tasks and confronts misery. In an attempt to counter this misery, it kills many other creatures. Having performed such an act, it goes through many other births. It is tormented, and suffers like a diseased person without any medication. There are many who are afflicted by such delusion, thinking that unhappiness is actually happiness. Slain and crushed, it is always churned in these deeds. That is the reason one must refrain from the bonds that are caused by deeds. One is wheeled around in this cycle of life and suffers many kinds of pain. However, you have withdrawn from those bonds. You have restrained yourself from deeds. You know

[1066]The five objects of the senses, ego, ignorance and prakriti added to the earlier list of seventeen.

[1067]That is, the jivatman.

[1068]Dharma, artha and kama.

everything. You have conquered everything. Be successful and free from all sentiments. Through restraint, abstaining from new bonds and resorting to the strength of austerities, many people have become successful. They have obtained unrestrained bliss.”’”’

Chapter 1645(317)

‘“Narada said, ‘There are sacred texts that dispel sorrow and destroy all grief. They lead to tranquility and are auspicious. If one listens to them, one obtains intelligence and attains happiness. From one day to another, there are thousands of reasons for sorrow and hundreds of reasons for fear. They pervade a foolish person, but not one who is learned. Therefore, for the sake of destroying the undesirable, listen to the history. If one follows their instructions, one obtains the intelligence that destroys sorrow. Through association with the disagreeable and lack of association with the agreeable, men of limited intelligence suffer from mental grief. When things belong to the past, one should not think about their qualities. By not having bonds of attachment with what is in the past, one can be emancipated. Whenever there is attachment, one should look for evils in it. If one sees the undesirable in such bonds, one is quickly separated from them. If a person sorrows over the past, he has no artha, dharma or fame. Thinking about their absence does not make them return. Creatures obtain some qualities and are also separated from them. All of these, and not just one, are reasons for grief. If a person grieves over the past, over something that is dead or destroyed, he piles misery on misery and doubles the grief. On seeing the progress of the worlds, intelligent people do not shed tears. Those who do not shed tears are the ones who see everything properly. A calamity may lead to physical or mental grief and even if one makes the best of efforts, one may be incapable of doing anything about it. Then, one should not think about it. Not thinking about it is the medicine for grief. Thoughts do not dispel it, but make it increase. Mental grief is destroyed through wisdom, physical through medication. Such is the capacity of learning and one must not behave like a child. Youth, beauty, life, stores of possessions, health and dwelling with loved ones are temporary. A learned person does not desire them. One should not sorrow alone over a calamity that has affected the entire country. Instead of grieving, if one perceives a way, one should act so as to counter it. In life, there is no doubt that there are many more reasons for misery than for joy. There is delusion over the fondness for satisfying the objects of the senses. Death is regarded as unpleasant. A man who casts aside both unhappiness and happiness obtains the brahman, and learned people do not sorrow over the end that he has obtained. There is misery in abandoning riches. But there is no happiness in protecting it. There is misery in obtaining it. Therefore, if there are no riches left, one should not think about it. Specific kinds of men obtain different types of riches. However, they are discontented and meet destruction. Learned people are content. All stores are destroyed. Anything that goes up, falls down. Association ends in disassociation. Life ends in death. There is no end to thirst. Contentment is supreme happiness. Therefore, learned people look upon contentment as the greatest prosperity. One's lifespan passes in an instant. It does not tarry. When one's own body is transitory, there is nothing that one can think of as permanent. Those who think about the nature of beings realize that everything is covered in darkness. They do not sorrow over those who have departed, but look towards the supreme objective. If a person is not satisfied with objects of desire and thinks that they are insufficient, death seizes him and departs, like a tiger grasping an animal. Therefore, one should seek means to be freed from misery. Even if one confronts a hardship, one should not sorrow. Even if one possesses a little riches, once one has enjoyed sound, touch, form, scent and taste, there is nothing further to tie one down.[1069] Before a creature was united with these, there was no misery and all was well. Consequently, a separation from these results in the natural state and there is nothing

[1069]Sensual pleasures are temporary.

to grieve about. Fortitude must be used to control the penis and the stomach, the eyes to control the hands and feet. The mind should be used to control the eyes and the ears and knowledge used to control the mind and speech. If a person controls affection towards those who are superior and inferior and conducts himself in accordance with humility, such a person is learned and happy. A person who is devoted to adhyatma, is seated,[1070] is indifferent, without desire and depends only on the atman, is happy.'"'

Chapter 1646(318)[1071]

'"Narada said, 'When happiness and misery appear and disappear, they cannot be countered through wisdom, good policy or enterprise. Established in one's own nature, one must make efforts not to suffer from lassitude. A person who loves his atman saves himself from old age, death and disease. Physical and mental diseases afflict the body, like sharp-pointed arrows that have been released from the bows of firm archers. A person who is frightened and desires to remain alive, wishing to be free from the afflictions, is rendered incapable. His body is afflicted and he is destroyed. Through nights and days, the lifespan of a mortal creature is continuously running, like the flowing current in a river, which does not retreat. Shuklapaksha and krishnapaksha incessantly progress. Without tarrying for an instant, they decay mortal creatures who have been born. The sun is without decay, but continuously rises and sets. The happiness and unhappiness of creatures is like that and is subject to decay. While he is concerned with what he has not seen earlier and what he has not obtained earlier, the desirable and undesirable aspects of a man set and depart like the night. Had

[1070]In yoga.

[1071]There is a certain abruptness and lack of continuity in the shlokas in this chapter.

a man not been dependent on the consequences of his earlier deeds, he would have obtained whatever he wished for and all his desires would have been satisfied. There are men who are controlled, accomplished and intelligent. However, if such virtuous people have not performed their own tasks,[1072] they are seen to be unsuccessful. There are others who are foolish, devoid of qualities and the worst among men. But because they possess the benedictions, they are seen to obtain everything that they desire.[1073] There are other creatures who are always ready to indulge in violence. Though they deceive the worlds, they age in happiness. There is someone who doesn't exert at all, but obtains prosperity. There is another one who undertakes all the tasks, but does not get what he should. Do you think that this is due to a transgression in a man's nature? The semen that is generated somewhere, goes somewhere else. Even when it has been placed inside a vagina, there may or may not be conception. It is then like the flower of a mango and it is as if there was abstinence. There are some who desire a son and wish for offspring. They are potent and make efforts, but no embryo results. There may be another brahmana who wishes to avoid embryos, like a venomous serpent. But he has a son with a long lifespan. Without a life after death, how could he have become a father? There are those who are miserable and desire sons. They satisfy the gods and perform austerities. After being borne for ten months, a son who is the worst of the lineage is born. There are others who obtain auspicious and extensive stores of riches and grain stored by their fathers and only enjoy them. When two people approach each other in an act of sexual intercourse, the vagina is invaded and an embryo results. When the body decays, the wind of life leaves and enters another body. When a creature's life is destroyed, the flesh and phlegm are rendered immobile. When the next body is burnt, movement and lack of movement pass on to a further body. This ends in destruction. And there is an end in a further destruction. This is like boats moving back and forth.[1074] Through

[1072]In an earlier life.

[1073]Again, because of deeds performed in an earlier life.

[1074]Ferrying passengers back and forth across a river.

sexual intercourse, an unconscious drop of semen is deposited in the womb. What do you see? Through whose efforts does that embryo become alive? Inside the stomach, why is that embryo not digested? Inside the womb, there is a natural progression of urine and excrement. It[1075] cannot do anything about whether it is retained or discharged. It is not independent. Some foetuses suffer a miscarriage, others are born. There are some that are destroyed as soon as they are born. When there is union with the vagina, semen is released. Sometimes, an offspring results. In due course, that offspring is also submerged in intercourse. Among the hundreds who are born, some survive till seven or ten years of age. Some die and do not survive to be one hundred years old. There is no doubt that when men are assailed by disease, they are unable to get up. They are crushed, like small animals by predatory beasts. They are devoured by disease and spend a great deal of riches. But even then, despite the best efforts of physicians, the pain is not reduced. The physicians may be skilled. They may be accomplished in the use of large numbers of herbs. However, they are themselves afflicted by disease, like animals by hunters. They may drink astringent concoctions and diverse kinds of clarified butter. But they are seen to be crushed by old age, like serpents by stronger serpents. When animals and birds suffer from disease, who on earth treats them? In general, among predatory beasts and poor people, there are rarely those who are afflicted. There may be fiercely energetic kings. Even they are attacked by terrible diseases that are extremely difficult to withstand, like animals by stronger animals. Overcome by confusion and sorrow, people shriek. They are suddenly flung into a current and borne away by something that is stronger. Those with bodies can't counter what is natural—through riches, kingdoms or fierce austerities. Otherwise, no one would have died or become old. Everyone would have obtained everything that he desired. No one would have seen anything unpleasant and all and the fruits would have been obtained. Every person wishes to rise upwards. They try their utmost. But it doesn't work out that way. Even people who are not distracted by deceit and are brave without

[1075]The embryo.

being cruel, become insolent and intoxicated because of riches and drunk and maddened with liquor. For some, hardships disappear even before they have seen them. There are others who are searching, but do not obtain anything. A great difference is seen between fruits and the undertaking of acts. There are some who bear palanquins. Others ride on those palanquins. Everyone desires prosperity. But only some have chariots advancing in front of them. There are men with hundreds of wives and there are hundreds of widowed women. There is conflict and pleasure in creatures and hundreds of men face these. Therefore, look only towards the hereafter and do not get confused. Cast aside both dharma and adharma. Abandon both truth and falsehood. Having abandoned both truth and falsehood, cast aside everything that must be cast aside. O supreme among rishis! I have told you about a supreme secret. Using this, the gods abandoned the mortal world and went to heaven.'"

'Bhishma said, "Hearing Narada's words, the extremely intelligent Shuka patiently thought about this in his mind, but could not arrive at a conclusion. 'Sons and wives lead to great hardship. Knowledge requires great effort. What is the eternal spot that is free from hardship and leads to greatness?' Having thought about this for some time, he made up his mind to follow the atman. He knew about supreme dharma and the supreme and beneficial end. 'How can I be unattached and go to that supreme objective? From there, there will no return and birth in this ocean of life. I desire that supreme state, so that I do not have to return again. I have determined in my mind that I will cast aside all attachment and strive towards that end. I will go to the place where the atman will find peace. I will establish myself in the eternal there and there will be no decay and destruction. Without yoga, I cannot obtain that supreme objective. Deeds cannot lead to that unattached state of liberation. Therefore, I will resort to yoga and cast aside this body, which is like a house. I will become a wind and enter the mass of energy in the rays of the sun. Having gone there, there is no decay, unlike the moon and the large number of gods, who tremble and fall down on the ground, ascending again when they have acquired merit. The moon always wanes and waxes again. The sun heats the world with its rays. It receives all the energy and the solar disc never decays. Therefore, going to the sun's blazing energy appeals to me. I will dwell there, without being assailed, without attachment and based on my inner atman. I will cast my body into the sun's residence. With the rishis, I will go to the sun's energy, which is extremely difficult to withstand. I am seeking the permission of the trees, the elephants, the mountains, the earth, the directions, the firmament, gods, danavas, gandharvas, pishachas, serpents and all the creatures in the world. There is no doubt that I will enter there. Let all the gods and the rishis behold the power of my yoga.' Narada, the rishi who was famous in the worlds, gave him permission. Having obtained his permission, he went to his father. Having greeted the great-souled sage and rishi, Dvaipayana, Shuka circumambulated him. He then asked the sage Krishna's permission. On hearing the words of the rishi Shuka, the great-souled one was delighted and said, 'O son! Stay here today, so that my eyes are gratified at the sight of you.' Shuka had become indifferent, without affection and free from all attachment. Having thought about moksha, he had made up his mind to go. Leaving his father, the supreme among brahmanas went away."'[1076]

Chapter 1647(319)

'Bhishma said, "O descendant of the Bharata lineage! Vyasa's son ascended the slope of the mountain. He sought out a flat spot that was devoid of grass and sat down there. Following the sacred texts, the great sage, accomplished in yoga, progressively held his atman in different parts of the body, beginning with the feet.[1077] A short time after the sun had risen, the learned one sat facing the east, humbly drawing in his hands and feet. There weren't any flocks of birds there, nothing to see and nothing to hear. Vyasa's intelligent son

[1076]One thus deduces that Shuka did not listen to his father's request.

[1077]In practising yoga, one goes upwards through the body.

embarked on yoga there. Delinked from all attachments, he saw his atman there. On seeing the sun, Shuka laughed. To realize the path of moksha, he again resorted to yoga. The great lord of yoga overcame all limits of the sky.[1078] He circumambulated devarshi Narada and told the supreme rishi that he had resorted to yoga. 'O one rich in austerities! May you be fortunate. I have seen the path that I should resort to. O immensely radiant one! With your favours, I will go to that beneficial objective.' Having obtained Narada's permission, Dvaipayana's son saluted him.

'"He again resorted to yoga and entered the sky. He arose from the slopes of Kailasa and ascended into the sky. Vyasa's handsome son had made up his mind and travelled through the firmament. As he arose, the best among brahmanas looked like Vinata's resplendent son.[1079] He possessed the speed of the thought and the wind and all the creatures saw him. Along that divine path, the lord's complexion was like that of the fire or the sun. He thought about the progress of all the three worlds. He proceeded without any fear, single-minded in his attention. All the creatures, mobile and immobile, saw him. As is proper, they worshipped him, according to their capacity. The residents of heaven showered down celestial flowers. All the gandharvas and the large number of apsaras were astounded on seeing him. The rishis and the Siddhas were also extremely surprised. 'Who is this who has obtained success through his austerities and is travelling through the sky? His body is downwards and his face is upwards. He is looking at everything with tranquility.' The supremely patient one, famous in the three worlds, turned his face towards the east and looked at the sun. He seemed to fill the entire sky with his sound. On seeing him swiftly advance, all the large numbers of apsaras were frightened in their minds. O king! They were filled with great wonder. There were Panchachuda[1080] and the others and their eyes dilated widely. 'Who is this divinity who has attained such a

[1078]This means that space no longer held any meaning for him.

[1079]Garuda.

[1080]Panchachuda is an apsara, the word means one with five tufts (or crests) of hair.

supreme end? There is no doubt that he has been emancipated and is without desire. That is the reason he has been able to come here.' Passing beyond them, he went to Mount Malaya, always frequented by Urvashi and Purvachitti.[1081] At the sight of the brahmana rishi's son, they too were filled with great wonder. 'Behold. This brahmana has used his intelligence and has studied the Vedas. Like the moon, in a short while, he will traverse through the sky. It is through serving his father that he has obtained this supreme success. He is devoted to his father. He is firm in his austerities. He is a son who is loved by his father. Why has his father not paid attention? Why has he allowed him to go?' Shuka was supremely devoted to dharma. When he heard Urvashi's words and the purport of those words penetrated his mind, he looked towards all the directions. He glanced at the firmament, the earth, with its mountains, forests and groves, and the lakes and rivers. All the gods also looked towards him. They joined their hands in salutation and showed great reverence towards Dvaipayana's son. Shuka, supremely knowledgable about dharma, spoke these words. 'My father may follow me and call out my name. In that event, all of you control yourselves and reply to him. Since all of you bear affection towards me, please speak those words for my sake.' On hearing Shuka's words, all the directions, the forests, the groves, the oceans, the rivers and the mountains answered in every direction, 'O brahmana! It shall be as you instruct. When the rishi speaks words to us, we will loudly reply in that way.'"'

Chapter 1648(320)

'Bhishma said, "Having spoken these words, the greatly ascetic brahmana rishi, Shuka, established himself in that success and cast away the four kinds of creatures.[1082] He cast aside the eight kinds

[1081]Names of two other apsaras.

[1082]Born from wombs, born from eggs, born from sweat and from plants and trees.

of tamas and discarded the five kinds of rajas.[1083] The intelligent one also abandoned sattva and this was extraordinary. In that state, he was always without any qualities and was divested of all signs. He was like a blazing fire without any smoke and established himself in the brahman. Meteors showered down. The directions were aflame. The earth trembled. At that time, all these manifestations were extraordinary. Trees released their branches and mountains their summits. There were loud sounds, as if the Himalaya mountains were being shattered. The one with the thousand rays[1084] was no longer radiant. The fire did not blaze. The ponds, rivers and oceans were agitated. Vasava showered down water that was tasty and fragrant. Winds began to blow, with auspicious and divine scents. He saw two divine and unmatched peaks, rising from the Himalayas and Meru. They were sacred and close to each other. One was white, the other was yellow. One was made of silver, the other was made of gold. O descendant of the Bharata lineage! Each was one hundred yojanas in expanse, both in height and in breadth. As he headed towards the northern direction, he saw these beautiful peaks. Without any fear in his mind, Shuka descended on them. At this, the two mountain peaks were cleft into two. O great king! That sight was extraordinary. The mountain peaks suddenly withdrew. Those supreme among mountains were unable to impede his progress. All the residents of heaven created a great roar in heaven. And so did the gandharvas and the rishis who resided in the mountains. O descendant of the Bharata lineage! At the sight of Shuka dividing the peaks and proceeding, roars of 'Wonderful! Wonderful!' arose everywhere. He was worshipped by the gods, the gandharvas, the rishis, the large numbers of yakshas and rakshasas and innumerable vidyadharas. In every direction, the firmament was strewn with celestial flowers.

[1083]This means the qualities. The eight qualities of tamas are lack of consciousness, confusion, delusion, lack of understanding, sleep, carelessness, procrastination and blindness towards consequences. There are actually nine qualities of rajas and these are faith, generosity, enjoyment, enterprise, desire, anger, pride, malice and calumny.

[1084]The sun.

O great king! This is what happened when Shuka descended. As Shuka, with dharma in his soul, travelled above, he saw groves with flowering tree, and the beautiful Mandakini flowed through that region. Large numbers of apsaras were engaged in bathing there. Their bodies were naked and without garments. Because Shuka was without a form, they were not ashamed of their nudity.

'"In due course, his father learnt about the excellent route that he had taken. Overcome with affection, he followed him from the rear. Shuka had ascended up into the sky, beyond the region traversed by the wind. Displaying his own powers, he had identified himself with all creatures.[1085] The immensely ascetic Vyasa resorted to the same fierce mode of great yoga. In a short while, he reached the spot where Shuka had descended. He saw the two mountain peaks that Shuka had shattered as he had proceeded. The rishis praised the deeds of his son. Using his learning, for a long time, he called out Shuka's name. The sounds of his own father's voice resounded in the three worlds. By then, Shuka had become one with everything. He was in the soul of everything and faced every direction. The one with dharma in his soul replied in an echo, with the sound of '*Bho*'.[1086] All the worlds, with their mobile and immobile objects, replied loudly, resounding with the single syllable of 'Bho'. Even today, when separate sounds are uttered in mountains, caves and slopes, that echo of 'Bho' is heard, as if replying to Shuka. Having exhibited his powers, Shuka disappeared. He abandoned all the qualities, the attributes of sound and the others. He attained the supreme end. On witnessing the greatness of his infinitely energetic son, he[1087] sat down on the slopes of the mountain and began to think about his son. Large numbers of apsaras were sporting on the banks of the Mandakini. On seeing that the rishi had come there, they were frightened and came to their senses. Some of them immersed themselves in the water. Some others tried to cover themselves with creepers. On seeing that supreme among sages, some others tried to clutch at their garments. The sage

[1085]That is, he had identified himself with the brahman.

[1086]It is impossible to translate 'Bho'. A loose translation would be 'Hello'.

[1087]Vyasa.

realized that though they were naked, they had not been ashamed of his son. He understood that though he still had attachment, his son had been freed. He was both pleased and ashamed.

'"Surrounded by gods and gandharvas and worshipped by large numbers of maharshis, the illustrious Shankara arrived there, with the Pinaka in his hand. Mahadeva spoke these words of comfort to Krishna Dvaipayana, who was tormented by grief on account of his son. 'In earlier times, from me, you sought a son whose valour and conduct would be like that of the fire, the earth, the water, the wind and space. Because of your austerities, a son with such traits was born from you. He was pure and full of the energy of the brahman. This happened because of my powers. He has attained the supreme objective, one that is extremely difficult for someone who has not conquered his senses to obtain, even if that person is a god. O brahmana rishi! Why are you grieving? As long as the mountains are established and as long as the oceans exist, your son's undecaying deeds will endure. A shadow that is like your son will always be with you. O great sage! Through my favours, you will be able to see it in this world.' O descendant of the Bharata lineage! Thereafter, through the favours of the illustrious Rudra himself, the sage was enveloped by a shadow and he could see it follow him. He was supremely delighted. O bull among the Bharata lineage! This is Shuka's birth and progress. You asked me about it and I recounted it to you in detail. O king! In ancient times, I was told about this by devarshi Narada, and the great yogi, Vyasa, also told me about it on several occasions. This is an auspicious history, full of purport about the dharma of moksha. A person who bears this in mind obtains supreme tranquility and goes to the supreme destination."'

Chapter 1649(321)

'Yudhishthira asked, "If a person is in the status of garhasthya, brahmacharya, vanaprastha or a mendicant, and wishes to establish himself in success, which god should be worshipped? How can he certainly go to heaven? How can one obtain supreme benefit? What rites should one observe in offering oblations to the gods and the ancestors? Where does one go when one is emancipated? What is the essence of moksha? Having obtained heaven, how should one act, so as not to be dislodged from heaven? Who is the god of the gods? Who is the ancestor of the ancestors? What is superior to him?[1088] O grandfather! Tell me this."

'Bhishma replied, "O unblemished one! O one who knows how to ask! The question you have asked me is about a mystery. Even if one speaks for one hundred years, one is incapable of answering this through arguments. O king! Without the favour of the gods or without resorting to the sacred texts, this fathomless mystery cannot be recounted. O slayer of enemies! I will recount it to you. In this connection, an ancient history is cited. This concerns a conversation between Narada and the rishi Narayana. My father told me that the eternal Narayana, the soul of the universe, was born in four forms as Dharma's son. O great king! This happened in ancient times, during krita yuga, during Svayambhuva.[1089] These were Nara, Narayana, Hari and Krishna. Out of these, Nara and Narayana travelled to the hermitage of Badari in their golden wagons and engaged in fierce austerities there.[1090] These were beautiful, yoked to the elements and possessed eight wheels.[1091] Those protectors of the worlds went there and because of the exertions that they undertook, became

[1088]Superior to the god of the gods and the ancestor of the ancestors.

[1089]Each era (manvantara) is presided over by a Manu. After fourteen manvantaras, the cycle of destruction and creation starts again. In the present cycle of fourteen manvantaras, Svayambhuva Manu was the first and we are now in the seventh manvantara, presided over by Vaivasvata Manu. Each manvantara has seventy-one mahayugas and the reference to Svayambhuva probably means one of the krita yugas out of the seventy-one in Svayambhuva manvantara.

[1090]Badrinath or Badarikashrama is in Uttarakhand.

[1091]This refers to the wagons. The interpretation is that these wagons are to be taken as metaphors, not literally. That is, they are the bodies, consisting of the five elements. The eight wheels represent the five objects of the senses, ego, ignorance and prakriti.

emaciated. The energy of their austerities was such that even the gods were unable to look at them. Only a god to whom they showed their favours was capable of seeing them. Narada was devoted to them in his heart and was goaded by a desire to see them. From the summit of the great mountain Meru, he descended on Gandhamadana and this was extremely wonderful. O king! Roaming through the worlds, he quickly went to the spot where the hermitage of Badari was. He was overcome by curiosity and went to the region where those two, the foundations of all the worlds, with the gods, the asuras, the gandharvas, the rishis, the kinnaras and the serpents, were based. Earlier, they were in one single form. However, they had been born in four different forms as Dharma's offspring and had been reared by that great one. It was wonderful that Dharma had thus been honoured by those gods, Nara, Narayana, Hari and Krishna. For some reason, Krishna and Hari were elsewhere then. However, those two[1092] wished to enhance dharma and were engaged in austerities there. This was the time for daily rites.[1093] However, these two are the supreme refuge. What daily rites should they engage in? They are illustrious gods and the ancestors of all creatures. Which god or ancestor will those extremely intelligent ones worship? Thinking this in his mind and full of devotion towards Narayana, Narada suddenly appeared before those two gods. When they finished their prayers to the gods and the ancestors, they glanced towards him and honoured him, in accordance with the rites that are laid down in the sacred texts. Seeing that they followed the rites and prayed, Narada was filled with great wonder. The illustrious rishi was pleased and sat down. Delighted in his mind, he looked towards Narayana. Worshipping the great god, he spoke these words. 'You have been praised in the Vedas, the Puranas, the Vedangas and the additional Vedangas. You are without birth and eternal. You are held to be the creator and the supreme amrita. You are the foundation of everything in the universe, what has happened and what will happen. O god! All the four ashramas, with garhasthya as their foundation, incessantly worship you in the

[1092]Nara and Narayana.

[1093]Narada arrived at the time for daily rites.

many forms in which you are established. You are the father and mother of the entire universe. You are the eternal preceptor. Which god and ancestor are you worshipping? We do not understand this.'

'"The illustrious one replied, 'This is an eternal mystery and nothing should be said about this. O brahmana! However, because of your devotion, I will tell you the truth about this. It is subtle, impossible to comprehend, unmanifest, without mutation and eternal. It is disassociated from the senses, the objects of the senses and all the elements. It is in the atman of beings and is known as kshetrajna. It is beyond the three qualities[1094] and has been thought of as Purusha. O supreme among brahmanas! The manifest one,[1095] with the three qualities, has been generated from him. Though unmanifest, she has a manifest form and is the undecaying Prakriti. Know that she is the womb from which we have been generated. We worship that pervading atman, thinking of him as gods or ancestors. There is nothing that is superior to him. There is no other ancestor, god or brahmana. He should be known as our atman and we worship him. O brahmana! Thinking of the worlds, he is the one who has formulated the ordinances. The rites for gods and ancestors are based on his instructions. Brahma, Sthanu, Manu, Daksha, Bhrigu, Dharma, Tapa, Dama, Marichi, Angiras, Atri, Pulastya, Pulaha, Kratu, Vasishtha, Parameshthi, Vivasvat, Soma, the one known as Kardama, Krodha and Vikrita—these twenty-one Prajapatis are said to have been generated from him. They worshipped the god's eternal ordinances. They always knew the truth about what had been laid down for the gods and the ancestors. Those supreme among brahmanas knew, and obtained, their atmans. Through his favours, embodied beings and those in heaven who worship him, obtain all the fruits and ends that they desire. It has been determined that those who are devoid of deeds and the seventeen qualities[1096] and have cast aside the fifteen,[1097]

[1094]Sattva, rajas and tamas.

[1095]Prakriti.

[1096]Five senses, five organs of action, five breaths of life, mind and intelligence.

[1097]This is a reference to the physical body, consisting of the five senses, five organs of action and five breaths of life.

are liberated. Those who are liberated attain an end that has been thought of as the brahman or the kshetrajna. That is the destination of everything and has been spoken about as being devoid of qualities. We have been generated from there and he can be seen through the yoga of knowledge. Knowing this, we worship that eternal atman. The Vedas and the ashramas resort to many different kinds of forms. However, he is the one who is worshipped with devotion and he is the one who grants the objective. If a person in this world thinks of him alone and is controlled, he obtains a superior end and penetrates into him. O Narada! O brahmana rishi! Because of your devotion and because of our affection towards you, I have recounted this mystery. It is because of your faith that you have been able to listen to it.'"'

Chapter 1650(322)

'Bhishma said, "Having been thus addressed by Narayana, the supreme being and best among men, for the welfare of the worlds, the best among men[1098] spoke these words to Narayana. 'In four forms, you have obtained this excellent birth in Dharma's house for a reason. For the welfare of the worlds, let that objective be accomplished. I will now see Prakriti. O protector of the worlds! I have studied the Vedas. I have tormented myself through austerities. I have never uttered a falsehood. I have always worshipped my seniors. I have never revealed the secrets of others. Following the secret texts, I have protected the four.[1099] I have always treated enemies and friends equally. I have always single-mindedly worshipped the original god and not several. Having purified myself in these special ways, why should I not be able to see the eternal lord?' Hearing the words of

[1098] Narada.

[1099] The hands, the feet, the stomach and the penis, the hands and the feet being counted in the singular. Protection means that they have not been improperly used.

Parameshthi's son,[1100] Narayana, the protector of the dharma of the Satvatas,[1101] honoured him with many kinds of rites and said, 'O Narada! Go.' Having been given permission to leave, Parameshthi's son also worshipped the ancient rishi.[1102]

'"Having ascended into the sky with great force, he suddenly descended on Meru's peak. For a short while, the sage remained in a solitary spot on the peak of that mountain. He then glanced towards the north-western direction and beheld an extraordinary sight. There is an extensive region named Shvetadvipa to the north of the ocean of milk. The wise ones have said that it is thirty-two thousand yojanas to the north of Meru. Those who dwell there are beyond any senses and do not eat. Their eyes do not blink and their bodies possess fragrances. The men in Shveta have been cleansed of all sins. They uproot the eyes of men who perform wicked deeds. Their bones and bodies are as firm as the vajra and they are impartial towards respect and disrespect. They are divine in form and are marked with auspicious signs. Their heads are like umbrellas and their voices rumble like the clouds. Their feet bear the marks of four *pushkaras* and one hundred *rajivas*.[1103] They possess sixty white teeth and eight smaller ones. They have many tongues and with these, they seem to lick the bright rays of the sun. They are devoted to the god from whom all the people in the universe, the Vedas, dharma, the sages, the tranquil gods and all their offspring have been generated."

'Yudhishthira asked, "They do not possess senses. They do not eat. Their eyes do not blink and they emit fragrances. How were these men born? What is the supreme end that they attain? O supreme among the Bharata lineage! What are the signs of emancipation exhibited by the men who are the residents of Shvetadvipa? I have great curiosity. Sever my doubt about this. You are the repository of all the accounts and we depend on you."

[1100]While there are different stories about Narada's birth, here he is being described as Brahma's son.

[1101]The Satvatas are the Yadavas.

[1102]Narayana.

[1103]Pushkara and rajiva are different types of blue lotuses.

'Bhishma replied, "O king! This is an extensive account that I heard from my father. What I will tell you is regarded as the essence of all accounts. There used to be a king on earth, by the name of Uparichara. He was famous as Akhandala's[1104] friend and was devoted to Hari Narayana. He was always devoted to dharma and always attentive towards his father. In ancient times, he obtained his kingdom as a boon from Narayana. Earlier, the *satvata* rituals had emerged from Surya's mouth.[1105] He first used these to worship the lord of the gods and then used the remnants to worship the grandfather.[1106] With what remained, he first worshipped the ancestors and then divided up the rest among brahmanas. He was truthful and only ate what remained thereafter. He did not cause injury to any creature. In every kind of way, he was faithful to Janardana, the god of the gods. O destroyer of enemies! His devotion to Narayana was great. Because of this, Shakra, the king of the gods, shared his own bed and his own seat with him. He[1107] regarded his own self, his kingdom, his riches, his wives and his mounts as having been obtained from the illustrious one[1108] and offered all these to him. He desired to perform many sacrifices and excellent rites. Following the satvata rituals, he observed all of these. In the great-souled one's household, there were many foremost ones who knew about the *pancharatra* rites and instructed by the illustrious one, they generally ate before all the others.[1109] Thus, the slayer of enemies followed dharma and ruled his kingdom. He did not speak any falsehood and there were no wicked thoughts in his mind. Nor did he perform any exceedingly wicked deeds.

'"Marichi, Atri, Angiras, Pulastya, Pulaha, Kratu and Vasishtha—these seven extremely energetic sages were known as

[1104]Akhandala is Indra's name.

[1105]The satvata rituals are the pancharatra vows, observed over five nights.

[1106]He first worshipped Narayana. With the leftovers, he worshipped Brahma.

[1107]Uparichara.

[1108]Narayana.

[1109]Uparichara instructed that these brahmanas should be fed first.

the Chitrashikhandins.[1110] The Chitrashikhandins came together and prepared an excellent sacred text. They were like seven Prakritis and Svayambhu was the eighth. The sacred text that emerged from their mouths is studied by all the worlds. Those sages were single-minded in their attention, devoted to restraint and self-control. 'This is the best. This is the brahman. This constitutes the greatest welfare.' Thinking about the worlds in this way, they created the sacred text. This speaks about dharma, artha and kama. Later, it also speaks about moksha. It prescribes the many kinds of ordinances that heaven and earth should resort to. Together, all those rishis performed austerities and worshipped the lord god, Hari Narayana, for one thousand celestial years. For the welfare of the worlds, instructed by Narayana, the goddess Sarasvati entered all those rishis. That is the reason those brahmanas could engage so well in the composition of that first creation—full of words, meanings and reasons. Right at the beginning, the sacred text was ornamented with the syllable 'Om'. The rishis first recited it at the spot where the compassionate one[1111] was. The illustrious Purushottama was pleased. Unseen by the rishis and in an invisible voice, he instructed them, 'You have composed one hundred thousand excellent shlokas. So that dharma is observed, everything in the worlds will flow from this. Notions of pravritti and nivritti will be generated from this, so will Rig, Sama, Yajur and Atharva of Angiras.[1112] As proof of this, I have created Brahma through my favours, Rudra from my anger, all of you brahmanas from my nature, the sun, the moon, the wind, the earth, the water, the fire, the large number of nakshatras and everything that is known as a creature. Those who speak about the brahman are regarded as authorities. In that fashion, all proof will be found in this excellent sacred text. It is my instruction that this will be taken to be proof. Based on this, Svayambhuva Manu will himself promulgate dharma. When Ushanas[1113] and Brihaspati are

[1110]Saptarshis, Chitrashikhandin are names used for Ursa Major.

[1111]Narayana.

[1112]The Atharva Veda is believed to have been compiled by Angiras.

[1113]Shukracharya.

born in the future, they will also base their instructions on this sacred text. The worlds will think of this as the sacred texts on dharma prepared by Svayambhuva, Ushanas and the intelligent Brihaspati. O supreme among brahmanas! King Vasu[1114] will obtain the sacred text prepared by you from Brihaspati. That king will think about me and be devoted to me. All the rites in the worlds will be performed in accordance with that sacred text. Among all the sacred texts, this sacred text will be known as the best. Artha, dharma and supreme fame will be based on this. Having propounded it, you will have offspring. The great King Vasu will also be prosperous. This eternal sacred text will exist as long as that king is there, but will disappear after that. I am telling you this truthfully.' Having said this in that invisible voice, Purushottama left the rishis. As they wished, they too left for the different directions. Thus, those ancestors of the worlds[1115] thought about the welfare of the worlds and compiled that sacred text. It is the eternal source of all dharma. When Brihaspati was born in the lineage of Angiras in the first yuga, he established that sacred text, with the Vedangas and the Upanishads. The upholders of all the worlds,[1116] the propounders of all kinds of dharma, left for their desired destinations, having determined to perform austerities."'

Chapter 1651(323)

'Bhishma said, "When that great kalpa was over, the descendant of Angiras was born and all the gods were delighted that a priest had been born for the gods.[1117] O king! The words Brihat, Brahma and Mahat progressively convey the same meaning and he came to

[1114]Uparichara.

[1115]The rishis.

[1116]The original rishis.

[1117]A kalpa or period of creation lasts for one thousand divine years. Brihaspati is the priest of the gods.

be known as Brihaspati because he possessed all these qualities.[1118] The foremost king, Uparichara Vasu, became his disciple. He properly studied the sacred texts of the Chitrashikhandins. The gods had earlier thought of the birth of King Vasu and he protected the earth, like Akhandala in heaven. The great-souled one performed a gigantic horse sacrifice. His preceptor, Brihaspati, was the officiating priest there. Prajapati's three sons, the maharshis Ekata, Dvita and Trita, acted as assistant priests at the sacrifice. Dhanushaksha; Raibhya; Arvavasu; Paravasu; the rishi Medhatithi; the great rishi Tandya; the immensely fortunate rishi Shakti, also known as Vedashira; Kapila, the foremost rishi who was the grandfather of Shalihotra; the first Katha; Taittira, the elder brother of Vaishampayana; Kanva; and Devahotra—all these sixteen were famous.[1119] O king! The great sacrifice had all the ingredients. On the instructions of the king, no animals were slain. He was not violent, pure, not inferior, without desire and devoted to the rites. The shares offered in the sacrifice were all products of the forest. The ancient and illustrious god of the gods[1120] was delighted at this. Though he was incapable of being seen by anyone else, he manifested himself. Though he was not seen by anyone, the god Hari himself seized and took away his share of the sacrificial cake. At this, Brihaspati was enraged. He forcefully picked up the ladle and flung it up into the sky. Shedding tears of rage, he told Uparichara, 'I have placed a share[1121] in front. While I see, there is no doubt that the god will accept it himself. The other gods are seen to have appeared in person and have accepted the shares offered to them. Why should the lord Hari not manifest himself?' When he arose in this way, the great King Vasu and all the assistant priests sought to satisfy the sage. Without displaying any fright, they told him, 'You should not be enraged. In krita yuga, it is not dharma for anyone to display wrath. The god who accepted the share does not also yield to anger. O Brihaspati! He is incapable

[1118]Literally, Brihaspati means the protector or lord of Brihat.
[1119]It becomes sixteen after including Brihaspati, Ekata, Dvita and Trita.
[1120]Narayana.
[1121]For Narayana.

of being seen by you or us. He can only be seen by those towards whom he exhibits his favours.'

'"Ekata, Dvita and Trita said, 'We are named as Brahma's sons, those who have been born through his mental powers. To ensure our benefit, we once went to the northern direction. For four thousand years, we tormented ourselves through excellent austerities. We controlled ourselves and stood on one foot, like wooden pillars. This was to the north of Meru and on the shores of the ocean of milk. That is the spot where we tormented ourselves through extremely terrible austerities. "How can we see the god Narayana?" This is the vow that we resorted to. When we bathed ourselves at the end, we heard an invisible voice. "O brahmanas! Cheerful in your souls, you have tormented yourselves through austerities. With devotion, you have asked how you can see the lord. To the north of the ocean of milk, there is the immensely radiant Shvetadvipa. The men there are as radiant as the moon and are devoted to Narayana. They worship Purushottama with single-minded devotion. They enter the eternal god, who possesses one thousand rays. They are devoid of senses. They do not eat. Their eyes do not blink and they emit fragrant scents. Those men, who live in Shvetadvipa, worship one person alone. O sages! Go there. That is the place where I have revealed myself." On hearing these invisible words, all of us followed the path that had been indicated and went to that country. Our hearts were full of the desire to see him and went to the great Shvetadvipa. However, when we went there, our sight was blinded by his energy and we could not see that being. At this, we decided that we had not undertaken enough yoga to see the god. Without further austerities, we wouldn't be able to see the energetic being. At that time, we again performed great austerities for another one hundred years. When we bathed at the end of the vow, we saw some extremely auspicious men. They were as fair as the moon and they possessed all the auspicious signs. Facing the northern and the eastern direction, with hands joined in salutation, they were silently meditating on Brahma. Those great-souled ones were thus engaged in mental chanting. Hari was pleased because of their single-minded devotion. O tiger among men! The radiance and resplendence of each of those men was like that of the sun that arises at the end of a yuga. We thought that energy alone resided in that region. No one was superior or inferior. All of them were equal in energy. O Brihaspati! We suddenly saw another mass of blazing energy, as if one thousand suns had simultaneously arisen. Together, those men quickly ran towards this. Cheerfully, they joined their hands in salutation and said, "We bow down." A great collective shout arose from them, as if those men were offering a sacrifice to the god. Suddenly, that energy robbed us of our senses. Bereft of sight, strength and senses, we could not see anything. We only heard a single sound, uttered incessantly. "O Pundarikaksha! O creator of the universe! We bow down to you. Victory is yours. O Hrishikesha! We bow down before you. You are the great being and you are the one who was born first." We heard these sounds, the syllables articulated properly. At that time, an auspicious wind began to blow and it bore all the fragrant scents. There were the fragrances of celestial flowers and herbs that had been used in the rites. Those men knew about the beneficial rituals of pancharatra. They single-mindedly worshipped Hari. There is no doubt that, invoked by those words, the god arrived there. However, because we were confounded by his maya, we could not see him. O supreme among those of the Angiras lineage! When the wind retreated and the sacrifice was over, our minds became full of anxious thoughts. Those thousands of men were born in pure lineages. But they did not honour us with their thoughts or their sight. Those large numbers of sages were single-minded in their vows. They were based on the brahman and paid no attention to us. We were exhausted and afflicted by the austerities. An invisible voice addressed us. "Are you well? These men from Shveta are bereft of all the senses and are capable of seeing the being. Only those who are given sight by these best among brahmanas are capable of seeing him. O sages! All of you should quickly leave this place and go where you have come from. Those without devotion are incapable of ever seeing the god. The illustrious one's circle of radiance is difficult to see. It can only be witnessed by those who desire to, and have single-mindedly spent a long period of time in worshipping him. O supreme among brahmanas! You have a great task to perform. There will be a catastrophe at the end of this krita yuga. O brahmanas! At the time of Vaivasvat Manu, there will be a treta yuga. You will then become aides in performing a task for the gods." O drinker of soma! We heard these wonderful words. Having obtained this favour, we returned from that radiant region. In this way, despite austerities and offering of havya and kavya, we could not see that god. How can you see him? Narayana is extremely wonderful. He is the unmanifest creator of the universe. He is the devourer of oblations.'"

'Bhishma said, "The intelligent Brihaspati was entreated by these words of Ekata, Dvita and Trita and also by the assistant priests. He honoured the gods and completed the sacrifice. When the sacrifice was over, King Vasu protected the subjects. Because of the curse of brahmanas, he was dislodged and submerged in the ground.[1122] He was always devoted to dharma, but was submerged inside the earth. He was devoted to Narayana and attained the objective of Narayana. It is through his favours that he arose again from the nether regions of the earth and obtained the abode of the brahman. Because of this devotion to the highest one, he attained a supreme end."'

Chapter 1652(324)

'Yudhishthira asked, "Since the great king Vasu was devoted to the illustrious one, why was he dislodged? Why did he have to sink into a hole in the ground?"

'Bhishma replied, "O descendant of the Bharata lineage! In this connection, there is the history of a conversation between the rishis and the residents of heaven. The gods told the supreme among brahmanas that *ajas* should be killed in sacrifices.[1123] However, by aja, one should understand a goat and no other animal.

'"The rishis said, 'The shruti texts of the Vedas aver that only seeds should be offered at sacrifices. The word aja signifies seeds.

[1122]King Uparichara Vasu ascended to heaven, but was dislodged from there.

[1123]As a noun, the word aja means goat. As an adjective, the word aja means something that has not been born.

You should not slaughter goats. O gods! The slaughter of animals cannot constitute virtuous dharma. This is the best yuga of krita. How can one slaughter animals?'"

'Bhishma continued, "This conversation was going on between the rishis and the gods. At that time, travelling along a path, Vasu, best among kings, arrived at the spot. He could travel through the sky. He was prosperous and all the soldiers and mounts were ahead of him. On seeing Vasu suddenly arrive through the sky, the brahmanas told the gods, 'He will dispel our doubts. He performs sacrifices. He is foremost among those who donate. He is affectionate towards all creatures and is devoted to their welfare. How can the great Vasu speak contrary words?' Thus conversing, the gods and the rishis approached King Vasu, who had suddenly arrived, and asked him. 'O king! How should one sacrifice? Should one use goats or herbs? Sever our doubt about this. We will accept your view as the proof.' Thus asked, Vasu joined his hands in salutation and said, 'What are your views? Let both sides tell me the truth.' The rishis responded, 'O lord of men! The view of our side is that grain should be offered at sacrifices. The gods are of the view that animals should be offered. O king! Tell us your opinion.' Ascertaining the views of the gods, Vasu opted for their side. He said that goats should be offered at sacrifices. All the sages were as radiant as the sun and were enraged at this. Vasu was on his celestial vehicle and had spoken on the side of the gods. They told him, 'You have opted for the side of the gods. Therefore, you will fall down from heaven. O king! From today, you will no longer be able to travel through the sky. Because of our curse, you will shatter the earth and penetrate there.' As soon as they said this, King Uparichara quickly fell down. The king penetrated a hole in the ground. However, because of Narayana's instructions, he did not lose his memory.

'"All the gods began to think of a means to free Vasu from his curse. The gods anxiously reflected on the king's good deeds. 'The great-souled king has obtained this curse on our account. The residents of heaven must unite and do what is agreeable for him.' Having determined this, the lords swiftly went to where King Uparichara was. They cheerfully spoke to him. 'You are devoted to the god of the brahmanas, Hari, the preceptor of the gods and the asuras. You should desire to please him. He will then act, so as to free you from this curse. However, the great-souled brahmanas also deserve respect. O supreme among kings! Their austerities must yield fruits.[1124] That is the reason you have suddenly been dislodged from heaven and have fallen down on the surface of the earth. O supreme among kings! However, we will show you a favour. O unblemished one! Because of the taint of the curse, there will be a period when you will be in this hole in the ground. The great-souled brahmanas offer excellent oblations at sacrifices, in the name of "Vasudhara".[1125] Through our favours, as long as you are here, you will obtain those and hardships and despair will not touch you. O Indra among kings! As long as you are in this hole in this ground, you will not be afflicted by hunger or thirst. You will drink Vasudhara and your energy will not be diminished. Because of our boon, that god[1126] will be pleased with you and will convey you to Brahma's world.' This is the boon that all the residents of heaven granted to the king. The gods and the rishis, rich in austerities, returned to their own abodes.

'"O descendant of the Bharata lineage! He always worshipped Vishvaksena.[1127] He always worshipped him through mantras that had emerged from Narayana's mouth. O scorcher of enemies! Though he was in the hole in the ground, at five times of the day, he worshipped Hari, the lord of all gods, through the five sacrifices.[1128] The illustrious Narayana Hari was satisfied at his devotion. He was entirely devoted to him. He conquered his soul and was always faithful to him. In the presence of the best among brahmanas, the illustrious Vishnu, the granter of boons, smiled and spoke to the immensely swift Garuda, who was near him. 'O supreme among

[1124]Hence, the curse cannot be completely nullified.

[1125]This means a stream of gifts or a stream of wealth and there is an obvious pun on the word Vasu. In sacrifices, clarified butter offered through some mantras is known as Vasudhara.

[1126]Narayana.

[1127]Vishnu's name, also the name of one of Vishnu's attendants.

[1128]Studying, sacrificing to gods, sacrificing to ancestors, sacrificing to other humans (guests) and sacrificing to other creatures.

birds! O greatly fortunate one! Listen to my words and go there. There is an emperor named Vasu. He has dharma in his soul and is devoted to me. Because of the wrath of the brahmanas, he has penetrated into the ground. The Indras among brahmanas have already been shown due respect. O supreme among birds! O Garuda! On my instruction, go to that hole in the ground. The best among kings can no longer travel up. Without any delay, bring him up into the sky.' The bird, Garuda, left, with a speed that was like that of the wind. He entered the hole in the ground and saved Vasu, as he had been asked to. Vinata's son violently rose up into the sky and quickly released him there. In a short instant, King Uparichara regained his senses. In his own body, the supreme among kings went to Brahma's world. O Kounteya! In this way, in his ignorance, he committed a fault in speech. Because of the curse of the great-souled brahmanas, the performer of sacrifices obtained that end. However, he only worshipped the lord Hari, the great being. He was thus quickly freed from the curse and went to Brahma's world. I have told you everything about the origin of men. I will now tell you everything about how the rishi Narada went to Shvetadvipa. O king! Listen with single-minded attention."'

Chapter 1653(325)

'Bhishma said, "Having arrived at the great Shvetadvipa, the illustrious rishi, Narada, saw those men, who were fair in complexion and were like the rays of the moon. He was honoured by them and he worshipped them in his mind, bowing his head down. Desiring to see the supreme one, he remained there, suffering all the hardships. The brahmana and great sage was single-minded and remained there, with his arms upraised. He chanted this *stotra*[1129] to the great-souled one, who is without qualities and is the universe."

[1129]Hymn.

'"Narada said, 'I bow down before you. (1) O god of the gods![1130] (2) You are without acts. (3) You are without qualities. (4) You are the witness of the worlds. (5) You are kshetrajna. (6) You are infinite. (7) You are Purusha. (8) You are Mahapurusha.[1131] (9) You are the one with the three qualities. (10) You are Prathana.[1132] (11) You are amrita. (12) You are space. (13) You are eternal. (14) You are the existent and the non-existent, the manifest and the unmanifest. (15) You are the abode of truth. (16) You are the first among the gods. (17) You are the granter of riches. (18) You are Prajapati. (19) You are Suprajapati.[1133] (20) You are the trees. (21) You are the great Prajapati. (22) You are the lord of energy. (23) You are the lord of speech. (24) You are the lord of the mind. (25) You are the lord of the universe. (26) You are the lord of heaven. (27) You are the lord of wind. (28) You are the lord of the water. (29) You are the lord of the earth. (30) You are the lord of the directions. (31) You are the original abode.[1134] (32) You are Brahmapurohita.[1135] (33) You are Brahmakayika.[1136] (34) You are the one with the gigantic body. (35) You are Maharajika.[1137] (36) You are Chaturmaharajika.[1138] (37) You are Abhasura.[1139] (38) You are Mahabhasura.[1140] (39) You are Saptamahabhasura.[1141] (40) You are Yamya.[1142] (41) You are Mahayamya.[1143] (42) You are with a

[1130]The numbering exists in the text.

[1131]The great Purusha.

[1132]The one who is spread out.

[1133]The excellent Prajapati.

[1134]Before the universe was created.

[1135]The priest for the brahman.

[1136]One with the body of the brahman.

[1137]The great king.

[1138]The four great kings. Chaturmaharajika is one of Vishnu's names and refers to the four worlds of the gods. This concept probably had a Buddhist influence.

[1139]The shining one.

[1140]The greatly shining one.

[1141]A reference to the seven flames of the fire.

[1142]The one in the southern direction.

[1143]The great Yamya.

name and you are wihout a name. (43) You are Tushita.[1144] (44) You are Mahatushita.[1145] (45) You are Pratardana.[1146] (46) You are Parinirmita.[1147] (47) You are the one who possesses power. (48) You are Aparinirmita.[1148] (49) You are the sacrifice. (50) You are the great sacrifice. (51) You are the origin of sacrifices. (52) You are generated from sacrifices. (53) You are the womb of sacrifices. (54) You are the heart of sacrifices. (55) You are praised in sacrifices. (56) You are the one who takes shares in sacrifices. (57) You are the one who holds up the five sacrifices. (58) You are the one who creates the five measurements of time.[1149] (59) You are Pancharatra. (60) You are Vaikuntha. (61) You are the unvanquished one. (62) You are the one who is in the mind. (63) You are the supreme lord. (64) You are the one who has been bathed well.[1150] (65) You are Hamsa.[1151] (66) You are Paramahamsa.[1152] (67) You are supreme among those who sacrifice. (68) You are sankhya yoga. (69) You are the one who lies down on amrita. (70) You are the one who lies down on gold. (71) You are the one who lies down on the Vedas. (72) You are the one who lies down on kusha. (73) You are the one who lies down on the brahman. (74) You are the one who lies down on the lotus. (75) You are the lord of the universe. (76) You are the one whom the universe follows. (77) You are prakriti in the universe. (78) There is fire in your mouth. (79) You are the fire that is in the form of a mare's head.[1153] (80) You are the oblations. (81) You are the charioteer. (82) You are vashatkara. (83) You are the sound of "Om".[1154] (84) You are the

[1144]Tushita is one of the worlds of the gods and the names of divinities who reside there. This too seems to have a Buddhist influence.

[1145]The great Tushita.

[1146]The destroyer.

[1147]The one who has been formed.

[1148]The one who has not been formed.

[1149]Days, nights, months, seasons, years.

[1150]After a ritual or a sacrifice.

[1151]A goose or a swan, but a term used for a great spirit.

[1152]The supreme spirit.

[1153]The subterranean fire.

[1154]*Omkara.*

mind. (85) You are the moon. (86) You are the original eyes. (87) You are the sun. (88) You are the elephants in the directions. (89) You illuminate the directions. (90) You are Hayashira.[1155] (91) You are the first among those who know the hymns. (92) You are the five fires.[1156] (93) You are Trinachiketa.[1157] (94) You are the one who has laid down the six Vedangas.[1158] (95) You are Pragjyotisha.[1159] (96) You are first among those who chant the Sama hymns. (97) You are the one who upholds the vows of the Sama Veda. (98) You are Atharvashira.[1160] (99) You are Panchamahakalpa.[1161] (100) You are Phenapacharya.[1162] (101) You are Valakhilya. (102) You are Vaikhanasa.[1163] (103) You do not deviate from yoga. (104) You do not deviate from enumerating. (105) You are the beginning of a yuga. (106) You are the middle of a yuga. (107) You are the end of a yuga. (108) You are Akhandala. (109) You are the ancient womb. (110) You are Koushika. (111) You are Purushtuta.[1164] (112) You are Puruhuta.[1165] (113) The universe is your form. (114) You are infinite in your progress. (115) You are infinite in your pleasure. (116) You are infinite. (117) You are without beginning. (118) You are without

[1155]Hayashira (head of a horse) or Hayagriva (neck of a horse) is one of Vishnu's incarnations. There are different stories associated with Hayashira, some connected with killing a demon named Hayagriva, others connected with the demons Madhu and Kaitabha.

[1156]The five fires of austerities, with four fires on four sides and the sun overhead.

[1157]A reference to the three fires of garhapatya, ahavaniya and dakshinagni, the word *nachiketa* means a fire.

[1158]*Shiksha* (phonetics), kalpa (rituals), *vyakarana* (grammar), *nirukta* (etymology), chhanda (metre) and jyotisha (astronomy).

[1159]The one who is lit from the east.

[1160]The *Ganapati Atharvashirsha* (or *Atharvashira*) *Upanishad*.

[1161]Five great kalpas or five mahakalpas. While kalpa is a measurement of time, the term mahakalpa is more common in Buddhism. The number five is difficult to pin down.

[1162]Literally, the preceptor who feeds on foam.

[1163]Both Valakhilya and Vaikhanasa are kinds of ascetics.

[1164]Praised by many.

[1165]Invoked by many.

a middle. (119) You are without a middle that is manifest. (120) You are without an end that is manifest. (121) You are the refuge of vows. (122) You dwell in the ocean. (123) You dwell in fame. (124) You dwell in austerities. (125) You dwell in prosperity. (126) You dwell in learning. (127) You dwell in fame. (128) You dwell in beauty. (129) You dwell in everything. (130) You are Vasudeva. (131) You are charming in every way. (132) You are Harihaya.[1166] (133) You are Harimedha.[1167] (134) You are the one who accepts shares in great sacrifices. (135) You are the granter of boons. (136) You are the one who upholds the rules of yama, niyama, great niyamas, austerities, extreme austerities, great austerities and all kinds of austerities. (137) You are the one who can be reached through the words spoken about the dharma of nivritti. (138) You are engaged in the rites of the Vedas. (139) You are without birth. (140) You go everywhere. (141) You can see everything. (142) You cannot be grasped. (143) You do not move. (144) You are immensely powerful. (145) Your body is formed out of greatness. (146) You are pure. (147) You are immensely pure. (148) You are golden. (149) You are large. (150) You cannot be countered. (151) You cannot be comprehended. (152) You are foremost among brahmanas. (153) You are the creator of beings. (154) You are the destroyer of beings. (155) You are the one who displays great maya. (156) You are Chitrashikhandin. (157) You are the granter of boons. (158) You are the one who accepts a share of the sacrificial cakes. (159) You are the one who has travelled. (160) You are without thirst. (161) You are without doubt. (162) You have withdrawn from everything. (163) You are in the form of a brahmana. (164) You are affectionate towards brahmanas. (165) The universe is your form. (166) Your form is great. (167) You are the friend. (168) You are affectionate towards your devotees. (169) You are the god of brahmanas. (170) I am your devotee and wish to see you. (171) I wish to see you with single-minded devotion. I worship you. I bow down before you.'"'

[1166]The one with the tawny horses.

[1167]In one of the manvantaras (during Tamasa Manu), Vishnu was born as Hari, the son of Harimedha.

Chapter 1654(326)

'Bhishma said, "The illustrious one was thus praised with secret names. The one who upholds the universe in his form showed himself to the sage Narada. His pure soul was somewhat like the moon, but it was also somewhat different from the moon. The lord's complexion was somewhat like that of the fire and his form was somewhat like that of a meteor. His complexion was somewhat like that of a parrot's feathers and his radiance was somewhat like that of a crystal. His radiance was seen to be somewhat like that of a mass of black antimony and somewhat like that of gold. His complexion was a bit like that of young coral and somewhat white. Some of the complexion was like that of gold and some of it was like lapis lazuli. The hue was a bit like blue lapis lazuli and a bit like sapphire. The complexion was somewhat like that of a peacock's neck and somewhat like that of a necklace of pearls. The eternal one was thus radiant in many diffierent kinds of complexions and diverse forms. He possessed a thousand eyes, one hundred beautiful heads and a thousand feet. There were one thousand stomachs and one thousand arms and some of those could not be seen. With one of his mouths, he chanted 'Om'. With another mouth, he chanted 'Savitri'.[1168] When this was over, with other mouths, he chanted the beneficial four Vedas. The *Aranayaka*s were also under the god, Hari Narayana's, control. In his hands, he held a sacrificial altar, a kamandalu, some *darbha* grass, some gems, a pair of sandals, a deerskin, a wooden staff and a blazing fire. The lord of gods and the lord of sacrifices held these in his hands and was cheerful. Narada, supreme among brahmanas, was delighted at this. Restrained in speech, he bowed down before the supreme lord. While his head was still bowed down, the first and undecaying god said, 'Wishing to see me, the maharshis Ekata, Dvita and Trita came to this spot. However, they could not see me. With the exception of someone who is single-minded in devotion towards me, no one can see me. O brahmana! It is my view that

[1168] The *gayatri* mantra.

you are thus single-minded. These are the best of my forms, born in Dharma's house. You must always endeavour to worship these, who have appeared before you. O brahmana! Ask for whatever boon you desire from me. I am pleased with you today and have appeared in my universal form, which is without decay.'

'"Narada replied, 'O god! My austerities, yama and niyama have instantly received their fruits now, since your illustrious self has been seen by me. That I have seen your eternal self is the ultimate boon. O illustrious one! O immensely great lord! In your different forms, you see the entire universe.'"

'Bhishma continued, "Having thus shown himself to Narada, the one generated from Parameshthi again spoke these words. 'O Narada! Without any delay, leave this spot. These devotees of mine are like the moon in their complexions. They are devoid of senses and do not eat. They single-mindedly think of me. Let there not be any obstructions in their pursuits. They are successful and immensely fortunate. In ancient times, they were single-mindedly devoted to me. They have been freed from tamas and rajas. There is no doubt that they will merge into me. There is one who cannot be seen with the eyes. He cannot be touched with touch. He cannot be smelt through smell. He is beyond taste. He is beyond the qualities of sattva, rajas and tamas. He is a witness to everything and people speak of him as the atman. He is in the body of all creatures and is never destroyed. He is without birth. He is everlasting. He is eternal. He is without qualities. He cannot be divided into components. He is beyond the twenty-four principles and is known as the twenty-fifth. He is the passive Purusha and is said to be comprehended through knowledge. O supreme among brahmanas! A person who merges into him is emancipated. He is known as Vasudeva. He is the eternal paramatman. O Narada! Behold the greatness and power of that god. He is never touched by good and bad deeds. Sattva, rajas and tamas are said to be the qualities. These exist in all bodies and roam around there. Though these qualities are enjoyed, kshetrajna does not enjoy them. He is without qualities. He is free from the qualities. He is the creator of qualities. He is superior to the qualities. O devarshi! When the universe is destroyed, the earth merges into water. Water merges into light. Light merges into the wind. The wind merges into space. Space merges into the mind. The mind is a supreme element and it merges into the unmanifest.[1169] O brahmana! The unmanifest merges into the inactive Purusha. There is nothing that is superior to the eternal Purusha. There is no creation in the universe, mobile or immobile, that is eternal. The only single exception is the eternal Purusha Vasudeva. The immensely powerful Vasudeva is in the atmans of all creatures. The great-souled one exists in bodies, known as the accumulation of the earth, the wind, space, water and light as the fifth. O brahmana! Though he cannot be seen, he uses his great valour to enter. That is how birth occurs, through the efforts of the lord. Without a combination of the elements, there cannot be a body. O brahmana! Without the jivatman, that combination of elements wouldn't have moved. That jivatman is also known as the lord Shesha or Samkarshana. Using his own deeds, the one who arises from this is known as Sanatkumara. When all creatures are destroyed, it is into him that they merge. The mind of all creatures is known as Pradyumna. It is from him[1170] that the the doer and cause and effect arise. Everything in the universe, mobile and immobile, is generated from Aniruddha. He is also known as Ishana and he manifests himself through all his deeds. The illustrious Vasudeva is kshetrajna and possesses no qualities in his soul. When that illustrious one is born in any creature, he is known as the lord Samkarshana. Pradyumna is said to be generated from the mind and is born from Samkarshana. Aniruddha is generated from Pradyumna and is consciousness, or Maheshvara. Everything in the universe, mobile and immobile, is generated from me. O Narada! This is true of the destructible and the indestructible, the existent and the non-existent. Those who are devoted to me, enter me and are emancipated. Know that I am the inactive Purusha, the twenty-fifth. I am without qualities. I am without separate constituents. I am without opposite sentiments and I am without possessions. You will not understand this, since you are seeing me

[1169]Prakriti.

[1170]Pradyumna.

in a form. However, if I so desire, I can make this form disappear instantly. I am the preceptor of the universe. O Narada! That you can see me is only because of a maya that has been created by me. I seem to possess the qualities of all creatures, but that's because you cannot comprehend me. I have appropriately told you about my four forms. O sage! There are successful and immensely fortunate men who are single-minded in their devotion to me. They are freed from both tamas and rajas and they enter me. O Narada! I am the doer. I am the cause. I am the effect. The consciousness of creatures is because of me. All creatures find a refuge in me. All creatures are pervaded by me and do not think that you have seen me. O brahmana! I go everywhere. I am in the atmans of all categories of creatures. When the bodies of creatures are destroyed, I am not destroyed. I am Hiranyagarbha, the origin of the worlds. I have four faces and can be understood through nirukta. The eternal god Brahma thinks of me in many ways. Behold! The eleven Rudras are established on my right. The twelve Adityas are established on my left. Behold! The eight Vasus, supreme among gods, are established to my front. Behold! Nasatya and Dasra, the physicians,[1171] are to my rear. Look at all the Prajapatis. Look at the seven rishis. Look at the Vedas, hundreds of sacrifices, amrita, the herbs, the austerities, the niyamas, the separate yamas and the eight kinds of prosperity.[1172] Look at them in their embodied form. Look at Shri, Lakshmi,[1173] Kirti,[1174] the earth, the mountains and the goddess Sarasvati, the mother of the Vedas. Behold! They are all established in me. O Narada! Look at Dhruva[1175] and the best of the stellar bodies in the firmament and also at the oceans full of water, the lakes and the rivers. Behold the embodied forms of the best among the four classes

[1171]The two Ashvins.

[1172]Yoga leads to eight major siddhis or powers and this is probably a reference to that.

[1173]Since Shri and Lakshmi are listed separately, the first can be interpreted as beauty and the second as wealth.

[1174]Deeds, fame.

[1175]The Pole Star.

of ancestors.[1176] Behold the three qualities. Abandoning their embodied forms, they are vested in me. O sage! Tasks undertaken for ancestors are held to be superior to tasks undertaken for gods. I alone am the original father of the gods and the ancestors. Along the northern and the western ocean, I became Hayashira. I drank the havya and the kavya, offered faithfully, to the accompaniment of mantras. Earlier, I created Brahma and he himself honoured me through sacrifices. Thus pleased with him, I granted him many excellent boons. At the beginning of the kalpa, I told him, "You will be born as my son and will be the supervisor of the worlds. Once there is consciousness, you will progressively be addressed by different names. No one will transgress the ordinances you lay down. O Brahma! For those who desire boons, you will also be the granter of boons. O one rich in austerities! O immensely fortunate one! Large numbers of gods and asuras, the rishis, ancestors who are rigid in their vows and many kinds of creatures will worship you. To accomplish the tasks of the gods, I will always manifest myself. O Brahma! For such purposes, you can always instruct me, like a father instructs his son." Since I was pleased with him, I granted the infinitely energetic Brahma these and many other excellent boons. Thereafter, I again resorted to nivritti. Among all the kinds of dharma that lead to emancipation, nivritti is said to be the supreme. That is the reason one should follow nivritti and act so as to withdraw all one's limbs. Preceptors like Kapila have set out their firm conclusions in the knowledge of sankhya. That is an aid in advancing towards my eternal self, with the resplendence of the sun. Metrical compositions have praised me as the illustrious Hiranyagarbha. O brahmana! In the sacred texts of yoga, I have been spoken about as the objective of yoga. I am established in the eternal firmament and am thus manifest in the sacred texts. At the end of one thousand yugas, I will destroy the universe again. I will

[1176]There are seven categories of ancestors, four embodied and three disembodied. This is thus a reference to the four embodied categories. While names differ in different lists, these are usually known as Sukala, Angirasa, Susvadha and Somapa.

withdraw all mobile and immobile objects into myself. O supreme among brahmanas! I will then exist alone, with nothing except knowledge. Using that knowledge, I will again create everything in the universe. My fourth form creates the undecaying Shesha. This is also spoken of as Samkarshana, and Pradyumna is created from this. From Pradyumna, I repeatedly create myself as Aniruddha. Brahma, the one who is born from the lotus, results from Aniruddha. All mobile and immobile creatures are created by Brahma. Know that this repeatedly happens in several kalpas. It is I who make the sun rise and set in the sky. When it has disappeared, at the right time, I use my force to bring back the extremely radiant one. For the sake of the welfare of creatures, it is I who will bring the earth forcefully back and restore her to her proper state.[1177] When all her limbs are destroyed in the girdle of the ocean, I will assume the form of a boar and bring her back to her right place. I will slay the daitya Hiranyaksha, intoxicated of his valour.[1178] To accomplish the tasks of the gods, I again will slay Diti's son, Hiranyakashipu, the destroyer of sacrifices, in the form of *narasimha*.[1179] The great asura Bali will be the powerful Virochana's son. He will dislodge Shakra from his own kingdom. Defeating Shachi's consort, he will deprive him of the three worlds. I will be born as the twelfth son of Aditi and Kashyapa.[1180] I will give the kingdom back to the infinitely energetic Shakra. O Narada! I will establish the gods in their own places. I will act so that Bali becomes a resident of the nether regions. In treta yuga, in the lineage of Bhrigu, I will be born as Rama.[1181] I will exterminate the kshatriyas, powerful with their soldiers and

[1177]The tense used is the future, suggesting that such incidents occur again and again.

[1178]Hiranyaksha stole the earth and took her down to the bottom of the ocean. Vishnu killed Hiranyaksha in his boar (varaha) incarnation.

[1179]Hiranyakashipu was Hiranyaksha's elder brother and was killed by Vishnu in his man-lion (narasimha) incarnation.

[1180]This is a reference to Vishnu's dwarf (vamana) incarnation, Vishnu being born as the son of Aditi and Kashyapa. The dwarf robbed the generous Bali of the three worlds.

[1181]Parashurama.

mounts. At the conjunction of treta and dvapara, I will be born as King Rama, the son of Dasharatha. Because of the injury that they caused to Trita, the two rishis who are the sons of Prajapati, Ekata and Dvita, will become malformed and will be born as monkeys.[1182] Born in those forms, those noble ones will be residents of the forest. O brahmana! They will become my allies in accomplishing the tasks of the gods. The terrible lord of the rakshasas will be the worst among those born in the Pulastya lineage. He will be like a thorn to the worlds. In a battle, I will kill Ravana and all his companions. When the intervening period between dvapara and kali is about to end, for Kamsa's sake, I will again manifest myself in Mathura. There, I will slay many danavas, who will be like thorns to the gods. I will dwell in Kushasthali, in the city of Dvaraka. While residing there, I will slay Naraka, the son of the earth, who will cause an injury to Aditi,[1183] and also the danavas Mura and Pitha. The beautiful city of Pragjyotishapura[1184] will be full of many kinds of riches. Having slain that supreme danava, I will bring those to Kushasthali. Shankara and Mahasena will be revered in the world of the gods, but they will be engaged in ensuring the welfare of Bana.[1185] Though they will exert themselves on his side, I will defeat the thousand-armed Bana and win back my son through force. I will also destroy all the residents of Soubha.[1186] There will be the famous Kalayavana, born from Garga's energy. I will slay him.[1187] The powerful Jarasandha will act against all other kings. That

[1182]The story of the injury has been recounted in Section 76 (Volume 7).

[1183]He stole Aditi's earrings.

[1184]Narakasura's capital.

[1185]Mahasena is Kartikeya. Krishna's son was Aniruddha. Banasura's daughter, Usha, was in love with Aniruddha. When the thousand-armed Banasura abducted Aniruddha, Krishna killed him in the battle. The standard stories mention Banasura's devotion to Shiva, but not usually to Kartikeya.

[1186]Described in Section 31 (Volume 2).

[1187]Kalayavana was Garga's son and invaded Mathura. The powerful King Muchukunda was sleeping inside a cave. Krishna lured his enemy, Kalayavana, into the cave and Kalayavana was killed by Muchukunda's fiery sight, when that king awoke.

powerful asura will be born as the king of Girivraja. It is through my intelligence that someone else will kill him. When the armies of all the kings on earth come together, I alone will be the excellent aide to Vasava's son.[1188] The worlds will speak of us as the rishis Nara and Narayana. To accomplish the objectives of the world, these two lords will consume the kshatriyas. As is desired, we will reduce the burden of the world. O excellent one! I will create a terrible destruction that will devastate my own kin and absorb the foremost among the Satvatas and Dvaraka into my own self. With the four forms, I will thus perform immeasurable deeds. Honoured by Brahma, I will then go to the worlds that I have myself created. O supreme among brahmanas! It is I who will manifest himself as Hamsa and Hayashira. When the sacred texts of the Vedas were lost, I retrieved them.[1189] Earlier, in krita yuga, it is I who had composed the sacred texts of the Vedas. Whenever the Puranas and the sacred texts have suffered, from my excellent self, I have resurrected them several times. Having performed the tasks of the worlds, I have myself entered Prakriti. Single-minded in your devotion, you have been able to see me now and even Brahma has been unable to see me in this kind of form. O brahmana! O excellent one! Because you are faithful to me, I have told you everything, about the mysteries of the past and the future.' The illustrious and undecaying god, with the universe as his form, spoke these words and immediately vanished. The extremely energetic Narada obtained the desired favour. He went and saw Nara and Narayana in the hermitage of Badari. This great Upanishad[1190] is in conformity with the four Vedas and sankhya and yoga, and is referred to by this name in the pancharatra rituals. O son! This song arose from Narayana's mouth and was heard by Narada, in exactly the same way that it is uttered and heard in Brahma's abode."

'Yudhishthira asked, "The greatness of the intelligent one is extraordinary. Did Brahma not know what Narada had heard?

[1188]Arjuna.

[1189]The demons Madhu and Kaitabha stole the Vedas.

[1190]A reference to what Narayana spoke.

What is the difference between the grandfather and that illustrious god? Why should he not know about the power of that infinitely energetic one?"

'Bhishma answered, "O Indra among kings! There have been thousands of mahakalpas and hundreds of mahakalpas and cycles of creation and destruction. At the beginning of every cycle of creation, Brahma is thought of as the lord who creates creatures. O king! He knows that the supreme among gods[1191] is superior to him. He is the paramatman. He is the powerful lord of the atmans. There were large numbers of siddhas who assembled in Brahma's abode and they wished to hear about the ancient accounts that were in conformity with the Vedas. He recited it to them.[1192] There, Surya heard it from the brahmana with the cleansed soul. O descendant of the Bharata lineage! He repeated it to the sixty-six thousand rishis, with cleansed souls, who follow him.[1193] Surya had earlier been created to heat the worlds. Surya repeated the account to all those with cleansed souls. O son! Those great-souled rishis were Surya's followers. They repeated this excellent account to the gods who assembled on Meru. The brahmana Asita first heard it from the gods. O Indra among kings! That supreme among sages recounted it to the ancestors. O son! My father, Shantanu, told me about it. O descendant of the Bharata lineage! I have recounted to you what I had heard. All the gods and sages who have heard this Purana repeatedly worship the paramatman. O king! This account has progressively been handed down by the rishis. It should never be recounted to someone who is not Vasudeva's devotee. O king! You have heard many other hundreds of accounts from me, but this represents the essence of the dharma described in those. O king! In ancient times, the gods and the asuras churned the ocean for amrita. In that fashion, the brahmanas churned the accounts for this amrita. If a man continuously reads it or hears it, alone, controlled and single-minded in his devotion, he obtains the great Shvetadvipa and becomes a man with the complexion of the

[1191]Narayana.

[1192]Narada recited it to them.

[1193]These are the *valakhilya* rishis.

moon. There is no doubt that he merges into the god with the one thousand rays. If a diseased person listens to this account, he is freed from his affliction. A curious person obtains the objects of his desire. A devoted person obtains the object of faith. O king! You should also always worship Purushottama. He is the mother and the father. He is the preceptor of the entire world. The illustrious and eternal one is the god of the brahmanas. O mighty-armed Yudhishthira! Let the mighty-armed Janardana be pleased with you."'

Vaishampayana said, 'O Janamejaya! On listening to this excellent account, Dharmaraja and all his brothers became devoted to Narayana. O descendant of the Bharata lineage! They spoke the words, "Let us be victorious because of the illustrious one. Let him always be victorious." Our supreme preceptor is the sage Krishna Dvaipayana. He uttered great words of chanting in Narayana's name. He went to the oceans of milk and amrita that are near the firmament and honoured the lord of the gods there. Then, he returned to his hermitage.'

Chapter 1655(327)

Janamejaya asked, 'The illustrious god and lord is the one who receives the shares at sacrifices. He upholds the sacrifices and knows the Vedas and the Vedangas. He comforts those who are devoted to the illustrious one, established in the dharma of nivritti. Why has the illustrious one created the dharma of pravritti? Why has he arranged for the gods to share in the dharma of pravritti? Why has he created such ordinances for the intelligent ones who wish to engage in the dharma of nivritti? O brahmana! We have a doubt about this eternal mystery. Dispel it. You have heard the accounts about Narayana that are consistent with dharma. The worlds, Brahma, the gods, the asuras and men are always seen to be addicted to rites and engage in them. O brahmana! You have said that emancipation through moksha is supreme bliss. In this world, those who are freed from good and bad deeds merge into the auspicious god with the one thousand rays. The eternal dharma of moksha seems to be exceedingly difficult to follow. Therefore, all the gods abandon it and enjoy havya and kavya. Brahma, Rudra, Shakra, the lord who killed Bala, Surya, the lord of the stars,[1194] Vayu, Agni, Varuna, the sky, the universe and the remaining residents of heaven don't seem to know about the knowledge of the atman that ensures destruction.[1195] That is the reason they do not resort to the certain, indestructible and undecaying path. It has been said that the existence of those who resort to pravritti is circumscribed by time. This is the great taint associated with deeds, being circumscribed by time. O brahmana! That is the reason I have this doubt in my heart, as if a stake has been impaled there. Dispel it by recounting the histories. My curiousity is great. O brahmana! Why are the gods spoken of as ones who accept shares in sacrifices? O brahmana! Why are the residents of heaven worshipped through sacrifices? O supreme among brahmanas! They receive shares in sacrifices. Why do they themselves perform great sacrifices and give away shares there?'

Vaishampayana replied, 'O lord of men! The question that you have asked me is an extremely great mystery. A person who has not tormented himself through austerities, a person who does not know the Vedas and a person who is not acquainted with the Puranas is incapable of explaining this in its entirety. However, I will tell you what you have asked me. In ancient times, our preceptor was Krishna Dvaipayana Vyasa, the great rishi Vedavyasa. Sumantu, Jaimini, Paila, extremely firm in his vows, I as the fourth, and Shuka as the fifth are known as his disciples. All five of us were together and these disciples were controlled. We were pure in our conduct. We had conquered anger and had won victory over our senses. On the beautiful slopes of Mount Meru, frequented by the Siddhas and the charanas, we studied the Vedas, and the Mahabharata as the fifth.[1196] There, on one occasion, we had a doubt about the Vedas. This

[1194]The moon.

[1195]Of the self.

[1196]The other four being the four Vedas.

concerns the question that you have asked and we asked him.[1197] O descendant of the Bharata lineage! I will now tell you what I heard then. Parashara's son was the dispeller of the darkness of ignorance. On hearing the words of his disciples, the prosperous Vyasa spoke these words. "O excellent ones! I have tormented myself through extremely great and extremely terrible austerities. I thus know the past, the present and the future. I tormented myself through austerities and restrained my senses. Hence, because of the favours of Narayana, I dwelt on the shores of the ocean of milk. All the knowledge in the three worlds, everything that I desired, manifested itself before me. Based on that knowledge, I will tell you about this great doubt. Listen. Through the sight of knowledge, I got to know about everything that happened at the beginning of the kalpa. People who know about sankhya and yoga speak of him as the paramatman. Because of his own deeds, he has obtained the name of Mahapurusha. From him was generated the unmanifest being, whom the learned know as Pradhana. For the sake of creating the worlds, the manifest lord was generated from the unmanifest. In the worlds, this is known as Aniruddha and the great atman. The one who was generated from this manifest is the grandfather. He is spoken of as consciousness and he is full of every kind of energy. O descendant of the Bharata lineage! Earth, wind, space, water and light as the fifth—these great elements resulted from consciousness. After creating the great elements, he again created their qualities.[1198] On the basis of the elements, the embodied beings were derived. Listen to them. Marichi, Angiras, Atri, Pulastya, Pulaha, Kratu, the great-souled Vasishtha and Svayambhuva Manu—these should be known as the eight Prakritis. The worlds are established on them. For the success of the worlds, Brahma, the grandfather of the worlds, then created the Vedas, the Vedangas, combined with sacrifices and other elements of sacrifices. The entire universe was generated from the eight Prakritis. Rudra was generated from anger. Having been generated, he created ten others that were like himself. These eleven Rudras are

[1197]Vedavyasa.

[1198]Respectively, smell, touch, sound, taste and sight.

known as Vikara-Purushas.[1199] Having been generated, for the success of the worlds, the Rudras and the prakritis who were the divine rishis approached Brahma. 'We have been created by your illustrious self, through the powers of Vishnu. O grandfather! What are the rights that will be vested in us? Having thought about the objectives, you must have determined rights for us. What powers will we have to protect and supervise those rights? Having thought about our rights, you must also instruct us about our strengths.' On being thus addressed, the great god spoke to those gods. 'O gods! O fortunate ones! It is good that you have brought this to my notice. This was also a thought that had arisen in my mind. How should the worlds be upheld and preserved? How should your strength and mine not be diminished in the process? Therefore, let us all go and seek the refuge of the witness of the worlds. He is the unmanifest Mahapurusha.[1200] He will tell us what is beneficial.' With the welfare of the worlds in mind, Brahma, the rishis and the gods went to the shores of the ocean of milk. They resorted to the austerities that Brahma had laid down in the Vedas. Those are the extremely terrible austerities that are known by the name of the great niyamas. They fixed their minds and raised their eyes and arms upwards. They stood on a single foot. They were controlled and were like pillars of wood. For one thousand celestial years, they tormented themselves through those wonderful austerities. Pleasant words, ornamented with the Vedas and the Vedangas, were then heard. 'O Brahma! O gods! O rishis who are rich in austerities! Welcome. All of you should listen to these excellent words. I know the reason why you have come, for the great welfare of the worlds. I will increase your strength of life so that you are engaged in tasks of pravritti. O gods! Desiring to worship me, you have tormented yourselves through excellent austerities. O great spirits! Now enjoy the excellent fruits of your austerities. This Brahma is the preceptor of the worlds. He is the grandfather of all the worlds. You are the best among the gods. Worship me with controlled minds. Always give me a share in the

[1199] *Vikara* means transformation, malady, passion, agitation.

[1200] Vishnu.

sacrifices that you perform. O lords! I will then ensure your benefit and lay down rights for you.' Hearing the words of the god of the gods, all the gods, Brahma and the maharshis were increasingly delighted. Following the rites laid down in the Vedas, they performed a sacrifice to Vishnu. Brahma determined the share that he would give to him.[1201] Similarly, all the gods and the devarshis also thought of the shares that they would give. They honoured him greatly and following the dharma of krita yuga, offered him a share. He is the Purusha who has the complexion of the sun and is beyond darkness. He is large and goes everywhere. He is the god Ishana, the lord who is the granter of boons. The god granted boons to all the immortals who were assembled there. The great lord was invisible, stationed in the sky, and spoke these words. 'The shares that you have given me have reached me. I am pleased with you. However, I will give you fruits that will be characterized by the cycle of rebirth. O gods! This is the certain fruit that you will obtain through my favours. In every yuga, you will perform sacrifices for the sake of boons and give away dakshina when the sacrifice is over. You will enjoy the fruits of those who follow pravritti. O gods! Following the ordinances of the Vedas, men will also perform sacrifices and give you shares at these. In the *sutras*[1202] of the Vedas, I will lay down that whatever share someone has given me at this great sacrifice will be proportionate to the share that he receives at those sacrifices.[1203] Based on the shares obtained at the sacrifices, you will hold up the worlds. Those are your rights and you will think of the welfare of the worlds on that basis. You will be greatly honoured and obtain fruits from rites performed from pravritti. That will give you the strength to hold up the worlds. In the world, men will think of you at all these sacrifices. When you are gratified in this way, you will also gratify me. This is what I have thought of. That is the reason I have created the Vedas, sacrifices and herbs. If these are properly

[1201]Vishnu.

[1202]Formula, rule.

[1203]The share a god has given to Vishnu at the great sacrifice will be proportional to the share he receives from sacrifices performed by humans.

used on earth, the gods will be pleased. O best among the gods! As long as this kalpa is not destroyed, I have created you with the attributes of pravritti. O lords! Therefore, based on your rights, think of the welfare of the worlds. Marichi, Angiras, Atri, Pulastya, Pulaha, Kratu and Vasishtha—these seven were created from the powers of the mind. They will be foremost among those who know the Vedas. They have been thought of as the preceptors of the Vedas. However, because they will give birth to offspring, they will also follow the dharma of pravritti. This is eternal path of rites for manifest creatures. Aniruddha is spoken about as the lord who created the worlds. Sana, Sanatsujata, Sanaka, Sanandana, Sanatkumara, Kapila and Sanatana as the seventh—these seven will be spoken of as the rishis who were born through Brahma's mental powers as his sons. They obtained vijnana on their own and will resort to the dharma of nivritti. They are foremost among those who know about yoga. They also know about the dharma of sankhya. They are the teachers of the sacred texts of emancipation. They are the ones who will expound the dharma of moksha. It is from me that the unmanifest has flowed earlier, as have the three great qualities.[1204] The one who is beyond these is thought of as kshetrajna and I am he. Along the path of rites, it is extremely difficult to obtain the spot from where there is no return. Different creatures have been created for different tasks. Helplessly, a creature obtains the fruits of pravritti or nivritti. This Brahma is the preceptor of the worlds. He is the original creator of the worlds. He is the father and the mother and your grandfather. It is on my instructions that he has become one who grants boons to all creatures. Rudra is junior to him and was created from his forehead. It is on Brahma's instructions that he became one who grants boons everywhere. Go and exercise your own rights. Think of the appropriate rights. Without any delay, let all the rites be observed in all the worlds. O supreme among gods! Depending on the acts undertaken and conduct followed by creatures, determine their spans of life. This period of krita yuga will be the best. In this yuga, at sacrifices, no violence will be exhibited towards animals and

[1204]Respectively, prakriti and sattva, rajas and tamas.

there will be no violation of this. O gods! Dharma will possess all its four parts. Thereafer, there will be treta yuga. Animals will be slaughtered then, but only at sacrifices. One part of dharma will no longer exist and only three quarters will remain. After that, there will be the mixed period known as dvapara. Two parts of dharma will decay in that yuga. When that is over, kali yuga will present itself and only one quarter of dharma will remain.'

'"The gods asked, 'When only one quarter of dharma remains, where will we go? What will our tasks be then? O illustrious one! Tell us that.'

'"The illustrious one answered, 'O supreme among gods! You should frequent countries where the Vedas, sacrifices, austerities, truth, self-control, non-violence and the practice of dharma continue to be followed. Adharma will then not touch you with its feet.'"

'Vyasa continued, "Thus instructed by the illustrious one, the gods and the large numbers of rishis worshipped the illustrious one and went away to the regions they wished to go to. When the residents of heaven had gone, Brahma remained there. He remained there, wishing to see the illustrious Aniruddha. The god showed himself in the form of the great Hayashira. He held a kamandalu and tridanda and chanted the Vedas and the Vedangas. On seeing the infinitely energetic god, Hayashira, the lord Brahma, the creator of the worlds, desired the welfare of the worlds and bowed his head down in obeisance. He joined his hands in salutation and stood before the one who was the granter of boons. The god embraced him and spoke these words. 'Think of appropriate means so that all the worlds can progress. You are the creator of all beings and you are the lord and preceptor of the universe. I will impose this burden on you and be completely free from all anxiety. However, whenever the tasks of the gods becomes very difficult to undertake, using my knowledge, I will go to that place and manifest myself.' Having said this, Hayashira disappeared from the spot. Receiving the instructions, Brahma also went to his own world. He[1205] is the immensely fortunate one. He is the eternal Padmanabha. He is said

1205Vishnu.

to be the first one who receives shares in sacrifices. He is the one who always upholds sacrifices. He resorts to the dharma of nivritti, the dharma that leads to an indestructible end. However, for the welfare of the worlds, he has created the colourful dharma of pravritti. He is the beginning, he is the middle and he is the end of all creatures. He is the creator and he is the object of meditation. He is the doer and he is the task. At the end of a yuga, he withdraws the worlds and sleeps. At the beginning of another yuga, he awakes and creates the universe. Bow down to that god. He is without qualities, but has the qualities in his atman. He is without birth. The universe is his form. He is the refuge of all the residents of heaven. He is the lord of the great elements. He is the lord of the Rudras. He is the lord of the Adityas. He is the lord of the Vasus. He is the lord of the Ashvins. He is the lord of the Maruts. He is the lord of the Vedas and the sacrifices. He is the lord of the Vedangas. He always dwells in the ocean. He is Hari. He is Munjakeshi.[1206] He is tranquility for all creatures who are in search of the dharma of moksha. He is the lord of austerities, energy and fame. He is always the lord of speech and the lord of the rivers. He is the intelligent Kapardin, Varaha and Ekashringa.[1207] He is Vivasvat. He is Ashvashira.[1208] He is the one who always bears the four forms. He is mysterious, but can be seen through knowledge. He is both indestructible and destructible. This is the undecaying god who pervades everything and goes everywhere. In ancient times, this is the one I beheld with my sight of knowledge. I have told you the truth about everything that you had asked me. O disciples! Act in accordance with my words and serve the lord Hari. Sing of him in the words of the Vedas and worship him, following the proper rites."'

Vaishampayana continued, 'The intelligent Vedavyasa told us this. He told all the disciples, including his son, Shuka, supremely devoted to dharma. O lord of the earth! We and our preceptor worshipped him, using hymns from the four Vedas. I have told you everything

[1206]One whose hair is like munja grass.

[1207]Literally, with one horn or peak. Used for a person with singular eminence.

[1208]Same as Hayashira.

that you asked me about. O king! This is what my preceptor, Dvaipayana, said in earlier times. If a man is controlled in his mind, says, "I bow down before the illustrious one" and always listens to this account, or recites it, he is then free of disease, radiant, strong and handsome. An afflicted person is freed from ill health. A person who has been tied down is freed from his bondage. A person who desires something obtains the objects that he desires. A long lifespan is obtained. A brahmana gets to know all the Vedas. A kshatriya becomes victorious. A vaishya obtains great gain. A shudra obtains happiness. A person without a son obtains a son. A maiden obtains the desired husband. A *lagnagarbha* is freed.[1209] A woman who is expecting gives birth to a son. A barren woman gives birth and has many sons and grandsons. A traveller who reads this reaches his destination without facing any hardships. There is no doubt that everyone obtains the object that he desires. These are the words of the maharshi, after due deliberation. They speak about the great-souled Purusha and about the assembly of the rishis and the residents of heaven. Having heard, those devotees obtained great felicity.'

Chapter 1656(328)

Janamejaya said, 'O illustrious one! Vyasa and his disciples praised Madhusudana with many kinds of names that they uttered. You should tell me about those. I wish to hear about Hari, the lord of all Prajapatis. On hearing them, I will become purified and will be like the bright moon in the autumn.'

Vaishampayana replied, 'O king! Listen to what the lord Hari told Phalguna.[1210] Cheerfully, the great-souled Keshava recounted

[1209] A lagnagarbha is an expectant mother, who, at the time of delivery, faces a difficulty because either the baby or the placenta adheres to the uterus and does not emerge.

[1210] Arjuna.

these names. O king! Phalguna, the destroyer of enemy heroes, had asked Keshava about these names and the qualities and deeds that led to their being used.

'Arjuna said, "O illustrious one! O lord of the past and the future! O creator of all beings! O immutable one! O refuge of the worlds! O protector of the universe! O one who grants the worlds freedom from fear! O god! There are names that the maharshis have used to praise you in the Vedas and the Puranas, because of your mysterious deeds. O Keshava! I wish to hear the true explanations about these. O lord! With the exception of you, there is no one else who is capable of explaining these names."

'The illustrious one replied, "O Arjuna! In the Rig Veda, the Yajur Veda, the Atharva Veda, the Sama Veda, the Puranas, the Upanishads, the sacred texts of sankhya, yoga and ayurveda, the maharshis have recounted many of my names. Some of those names are based on qualities, others are based on deeds. O unblemished one! Listen attentively. I will explain the ones that are based on deeds. O son! I will tell you. It has been said that in earlier times, you were half of me. I bow down to the extremely famous one, the paramatman who exists in all bodies. He is Narayana. He is the universe. He is without qualities. He possesses all the qualities in his atman. It is through his favours that Rudra was generated from Brahma's rage. He is the womb of everything, mobile and immobile. O supreme among those who possess sattva! He possesses the eighteen qualities of sattva.[1211] After me, there is Prakriti, who holds up heaven and earth through her yoga. She is truth. She is immortal. She is invincible. She is the consciousness in the worlds. Everything, the transformations of creation and destruction, flow from her. The ancient and great Purusha is the sacrifice and the person who performs the sacrifice. He is known as Aniruddha and he is the reason behind the creation and the destruction of the worlds. O one whose eyes are like lotus petals! When Brahma's night is over, it is through the favours of the infinitely

[1211]Amiability, lustre, superiority, dexterity, happiness, generosity, lack of fear, contentment, devotion, forgiveness, fortitude, non-violence, lack of sorrow, uprightness, equanimity, truthfulness, lack of anger and lack of malice.

energetic one that a lotus manifests itself. It is through his favours that Brahma is generated from this. When the day is over, it is because of that god that a son is born from the forehead, as the outcome of rage. This is Rudra, the destroyer.[1212] These two, the best among the gods, are said to be the result of favour and rage. They follow his indicated paths in becoming agents of creation and destruction. Though they are capable of granting boons to all creatures, they are actually nothing but instruments. Rudra is Kapardi, Jatila and Munda.[1213] His house is the cremation ground. He is a yogi who engages in fierce vows. He was terrible for Tripura.[1214] He destroyed Daksha's sacrifice and uprooted Bhaga's eyes. O Pandaveya! From one yuga to another yuga, know that Narayana is always present in his atman. O Partha! Therefore, if Maheshvara, the god of the gods, is worshipped, that is the same thing as the lord god, Narayana, being worshipped. O descendant of the Pandu lineage! I am the atman of all the worlds. Therefore, I single-mindedly worship Rudra as my own self. If Ishana Shiva, the granter of boons, is not worshipped, then I think of that as my own self not being worshipped. The worlds follow my ordinances. Those ordinances must be honoured and I also honour them. A person who knows him,[1215] knows me. A person who knows me, knows him. O Kounteya! Rudra and Narayana possess a single essence, although they divide themselves into two, pervade people and make them engage in all the acts. O descendant of the Pandava lineage! There is no one else who is capable of granting me a boon. In ancient times, I mentally thought this and worshipped the great-souled lord of the universe,[1216] for the sake of obtaining a son. There is no other god that Vishnu bows down before, with the exception of Rudra, who is my own self. Therefore, I worship him. Brahma, the Rudras, Indra and the rishis worship the god who is foremost among the gods, Narayana

[1212]Rudra is born from Aniruddha's forehead, not Brahma's. That seems to be the suggestion.

[1213]Respectively, holding a skull, with matted hair and with a shaved head. Obviously, not simultaneously.

[1214]Shiva destroyed Tripura.

[1215]Rudra.

[1216]Meaning Rudra.

Hari. O descendant of the Bharata lineage! Among creatures of the past, the present and the future, Vishnu is the foremost and he must always be served and worshipped. Bow down before Vishnu, the one to whom havya is offered. Bow down before the one who is the refuge. O Kounteya! Bow down before the one who is the granter of boons. Bow down before the one who eats havya and kavya. You have heard that four kinds of people are my devotees.[1217] Among these, the best are the ones who single-mindedly seek me, and not any other god, as the objective. They are without desire and do not pursue rites. Though virtuous, it is the view that the three other categories of devotees desire the fruits. They follow a dharma that leads to rebirth. The enlightened obtain the best outcome. It is said that enlightened ones may serve Brahma, Shitikantha[1218] or any of the other gods, but they obtain me, who is beyond them. O Partha! I have recounted the differences among my devotees. O Kounteya! You and I are known as Nara and Narayana. O Partha! We have entered these human forms to reduce the burden.[1219] O descendant of the Bharata lineage! I know adhyatma yoga, who I am and where I have come from. I know the attributes of nivritti and the means whereby dharma is awakened. I alone am known as the eternal refuge of men. The water is known as Nara[1220] and Nara obtained birth from the waters.[1221] Since, in earlier times, the water was my road, I am known as Narayana.[1222] Assuming the form of Surya, I envelop the world and the universe with my rays. Since I am the dwelling of all creatures, I am Vasudeva.[1223] O descendant of the Bharata lineage! I am the destination of all creatures and subjects.

[1217]This probably means the pursuit of the fruits of dharma, artha and kama and the fruitless pursuit of moksha.

[1218]Shiva.

[1219]Of the earth.

[1220]Actually, *naara*.

[1221]*Nara* means human or man and an etymological derivation is being given for this name.

[1222]Ayana means road or progress. Earlier, before creation, Narayana slept on the water.

[1223]*Adhivasa* is dwelling or habitation and the Vasu part of Vasudeva is being linked to this.

O Partha! My extreme splendour pervades heaven and earth. O descendant of the Bharata lineage! At the end, all perishable creatures desire to merge into me. O Partha! Since I make everything progressively flow, I am known by the name of Vishnu.[1224] People who desire success in self-control wish for me and I am in between heaven and earth. That is the reason I am Damodara.[1225] Food, the Vedas, water and amrita are known as *prishni*.[1226] Since I always bear these in my womb, I am known as Prishnigarbha. The rishis have said that when Trita was flung into a well and hurled there by Ekata and Dvita, he called out, 'O Prishnigarbha! Save Trita.' The rishi Trita, who was Brahma's original son, was thus raised from the well, after calling out the name of Prishnigarbha. The sun fiercely heats the worlds and there are the rays of the moon too. Know these to be my hair. The best among brahmanas, who know everything, therefore call me Keshava.[1227] When the great-souled Utathya's wife had conceived, through a maya worked by the gods, Utathya disappeared.[1228] Brihaspati, best among rishis, approached Utathya's wife for the sake of intercourse. O Kounteya! The fetus had already been formed, constituted of the five elements. It said, 'O one who is the granter of boons! I am already here. You should not oppress my mother.' Hearing this, Brihaspati was angered and cursed him. 'Since you have prevented me when I was about to engage in intercourse, there is no doubt that, because of my curse, you will be born blind.' In ancient times, thanks to the curse imposed by that foremost rishi, the rishi named Dirghatama was born and remained blind for a long time.[1229] He studied the eternal Vedas, the Vedangas and the subsidiary branches. Using this secret name, he invoked me. Following the prescribed ordinances,

[1224]From the verb *visho*, which means to flow or cause to flow.

[1225]This is a slightly contrived explanation based on self-control (*dama*) and stomach (*udara*), a stomach being in between.

[1226]Prishni means water and these are all derived from water.

[1227]*Kesha* means hair.

[1228]This story has been recounted in Section 7 (Volume 1). Brihaspati was Utathya's younger brother.

[1229]Dirghatama means darkness/blindness for a long time.

he repeatedly called out to Keshava. Because of this, he obtained his eyesight and later came to be known as Goutama. O Arjuna! This is the boon that the name Keshava grants to all the gods and great-souled rishis who invoke it. Agni and Soma come together and unite in the mouth.[1230] Everything in the universe, mobile and immobile, is based on the essence of Agni and Soma. This is what is said in the Puranas. Agni and Soma are spoken of as having united together. Agni is spoken of as the mouth of the gods. These two great ones come together and hold up the worlds."'[1231]

Chapter 1657(329)

'Arjuna asked, "In ancient times, how did it happen that Agni and Soma came together? O Madhusudana! I have a doubt about this. Dispel it."

'The illustrious one replied, "O descendant of the Pandu lineage! In this connection, there is an ancient account. O Partha! This concerns what was generated from my own energy. Listen with single-minded attention. When four thousand yugas are over, the time for cleansing arrives. All creatures, mobile and immobile, are destroyed and merge into the unmanifest. Light, earth and wind vanish. There is blind darkness everywhere and the world is covered in water. When everything is enveloped in this fashion, nothing other than the unmanifest exists. There is no night, nor day. There is no existence, or non-existence. There is no manifest, or unmanifest. In this state,

[1230]Agni is the digestive fire and Soma is food.

[1231]This seems to have nothing to do with the rest of the chapter. That's because the suggestion is left implicit. Agni (the sun) and Soma (the moon) have earlier been described as Narayana's hair (kesha). *Hrishika* is an organ of the senses. Since *kasha* exists in hrishika, we have the name Hrishikesha. This is a convoluted explanation for the name Hrishikesha, usually taken to mean the lord of the senses.

Narayana is the refuge of qualities. He is without destruction. He is without old age. He is incapable of being grasped by the senses. He is without birth. He is truth. He is beyond the attributes of injury and gain. He is indestructible, immutable and immortal. He is without form, but pervades everything. In that darkness, he is the eternal Purusha who undertakes everything. The undecaying Hari then manifests himself. These are the signs then. There is no day. Nor is there night. There is no existence. Nor is there non-existence. In the beginning, there was only darkness everywhere in the universe. This darkness is spoken of as the mother of the universe. Purusha was born from that darkness. Brahma, born from the lotus, was generated from Purusha. Having been created, this being wished to create subjects and created Agni and Soma from his eyes. After this, the various categories of creatures were generated, progressively subjects like brahmanas and kshatriyas. Soma is the same as Brahma and Brahma is the same as brahmanas. Agni is nothing but the kshatriyas and the brahmanas were more powerful than the kshatriyas. Why did this happen? This is an evident attribute of the worlds. Everything was created after the brahmanas, not before them. Oblations are offered into the blazing Agni. After having created the various categories of beings, Brahma established these creatures, so that the three worlds might be held up. The mantras speak about this. 'O Agni! For the benefit of the universe, you are the one who receives the oblations at sacrifices. You are the one who is engaged in the welfare of gods, men and the worlds. There are signs for this. O Agni! In the universe, you are the one who receives the oblations at sacrifices. You are the one who is engaged in the welfare of gods, men and the universe. O Agni! You are truly the one who offers oblations and performs sacrifices.' Agni is Brahma. No oblations can be offered without mantras. There can be no austerities without someone to undertake them. Oblations are offered with mantras and worship. 'O Agni! The gods and men have appointed you as the receiver of oblations.' There are men who have been given the right to offer oblations. For kshatriyas, vaishyas and all the twice-born categories, it is only brahmanas who can officiate at sacrifices. That is the reason brahmanas are like Agni. They uphold sacrifices. The gods are satisfied through sacrifices. The gods sustain the earth. There are hundreds of ways to be a brahmana. If a learned person gives food to the mouth of a brahmana, that is like offering kindling and oblations into a fire. The learned have thus come to think of brahmanas as Agni. Since it penetrates all creatures and sustains life, Agni is also Vishnu. There is a shloka that Sanatkumara sung about this. 'In creating the universe, Brahma created them first. Through chanting about the brahman, those who are born as brahmanas become immortal and are established in the firmament and in heaven. The intelligence, speech, acts, faith and austerities of brahmanas hold up the earth and the sky, like great amrita sustaining one during the cold season. There is no dharma superior to the truth. There is no preceptor equal to the mother. In this world and in the next, there is nothing superior to a brahmana.' In a kingdom where brahmanas are without a means of subsistence, bulls do not grow or bear burdens, milk does not produce anything when it is churned and property comes under the possession of bandits. The Vedas, the Puranas and the histories state that brahmanas emerged from Narayana's mouth. They are in the atmans of everything. They are in all doers. They are in all creatures. It is said that when the god who is the granter of boons had restrained his speech, the brahmanas emerged first and all the other varnas were born later. That is the reason the brahmanas are superior to gods and asuras. In ancient times, I myself created gods, asuras and maharshis and established brahmanas as superior, so that they could restrain other creatures.

'"Because he oppressed Ahalya, Indra was cursed by Goutama and got a tawny beard. Through Koushika's curse, Indra lost his testicles and obtained a ram's testicles.[1232] When Chyavana wished to give

[1232]Ahalya was the sage Goutama's wife. There are different versions about the way Indra seduced her. Both Indra and Ahalya were cursed. In different versions of the curse, Indra got a tawny beard, lost his testicles and got one thousand vaginas all over his body (later changed to eyes). Koushika does not fit with Goutama. Koushika probably refers to Vishvamitra, who told Rama and Lakshmana the Ahalya story. But Vishvamitra didn't curse Indra.

shares to the Ashvins, Purandara, the wielder of the vajra, tried to prevent this and his arms were paralysed.[1233] When his sacrifice was destroyed, Daksha was overcome by great rage. He performed austerities again and obtained another eye on his forehead, to replace the one that had been uprooted by Rudra. When Rudra consecrated himself and advanced for the destruction of Tripura, Ushanas[1234] uprooted a strand from his matted hair and hurled it down. Serpents were generated from this. Oppressed by these serpents, his neck turned blue.[1235] Earlier, in Svyambhuva manvantara, Narayana had seized his throat with his hand and that is how it had turned blue. To obtain amrita, Brihaspati, born in the Angiras lineage, wished to perform *purashcharana*.[1236] However, when he tried to touch the water, it turned dirty. Brihaspati was enraged and cursed the water. 'When I tried to touch you, you did not show me your favours and your water turned filthy. Therefore, from now on, you will be dirty and will be populated by fish, makaras, other fish, turtles and aquatic creatures.' Since then, the waters of the ocean have been thus infested.

'"Vishvarupa, Tvashtri's son, was the priest of the gods. But his mother was related to the asuras.[1237] Outwardly, he offered shares to the gods. However, secretly, he offered shares to the asuras. With Hiranyakashipu at the forefront, the asuras went to their sister, Vishvarupa's mother, and asked for a boon. 'O sister! Your son, Vishvarupa, also known as Trishira, is Tvashtri's son. As a priest of the gods, he outwardly gives them their shares and only gives us a

[1233]This incident has been described in Section 33 (Volume 3). The Ashvins restored Chyavana's youth and at King Sharyati's sacrifice, Chyavana wished to ensure that they were given a share in the sacrificial offerings. When Indra resisted, Chyavana paralysed Indra's arms.

[1234]Shukracharya, the preceptor of the demons.

[1235]There are other stories, like the churning of the ocean, for Shiva's throat turning blue.

[1236]Preparatory rites. This incident occurred at the time of the churning of the ocean and Brihaspati cursed the ocean.

[1237]His mother was the asura lady Rachana. Trishira means one with three heads.

share privately. Because of this, the gods are prospering and we are suffering. You should restrain him, so that he also serves us.' At that time, Vishvarupa was in the forest of Nandana. His mother went to him and said, 'O son! Why are you making the side of the enemy prosper and why are you destroying your maternal side? You should not act in this way.' Unable to ignore his mother's words, Vishvarupa honoured her and went over to Hiranyakashipu. At this, Hiranyakashipu was cursed by Vasishtha, Hiranygarbha's son.[1238] 'Since you have appointed someone else to offer the oblations, this sacrifice will not be completed. A being, the like of whom has never been born before, will slay you.' Hiranyakashipu was slain because of this curse. To make his mother's side prosper, Vishvarupa engaged in austerities. To make him desist from his vows, Indra and Agni sent beautiful apsaras. On seeing them, his mind was agitated and within a short period of time, he became attached to those apsaras. Realizing that he had become attached to them, the apsaras said, 'We will not remain here any more. We will return to the place we have come from.' Tvashtri's son replied, 'Where will you go? Stay here with me and I will do what brings you benefit.' They answered, 'We are celestial women, the apsaras. In earlier times, we obtained boons from Indra and the powerful Vishnu.' At this, Vishvarupa replied, 'Indra and the gods will no longer exist.' He chanted a mantra and meditated. Because of the mantra, Trishira began to grow. In all the worlds, the brahmanas offered oblations and soma at sacrifices. With one mouth, he drank the soma. With a second mouth, he ate the oblations. With a third mouth, he sapped the energy of Indra and the gods. Indra saw that because he was drinking the soma, every limb of his body was growing. He began to worry. Indra and the gods went to Brahma and said, 'Vishvarupa is drinking all the soma offered as oblations at sacrifices. We no longer obtain our shares. The side of the asuras is prospering and we are decaying. O creator! You should arrange for our welfare.' Brahma replied, 'The rishi Dadhicha of the Bhargava

[1238]Vasishtha was Brahma's (Hiranyagarbha's) son. Earlier, Vasishtha used to be Hiranyakashipu's priest. When Vishvarupa arrived, Hiranyakashipu dismissed Vasishtha.

lineage is tormenting himself through austerities. Go and seek a boon from him, so that he gives up his body. Use his bones to construct a vajra.' The gods went to the place where the illustrious rishi Dadhicha was tormenting himself through austerities. Indra and the gods went to him and said, 'O illustrious one! We hope your austerities are proceeding well, without any hindrances.' Dadhicha replied, 'Welcome. What can I do for you? I will do what you ask me to.' They answered, 'O illustrious one! For the welfare of the worlds, you should cast aside your body.' Dadhicha was a great yogi. Joy and misery were the same to him and he was not distressed at this. He controlled his atman and gave up his body. When he had merged into the paramatman, Dhatri[1239] collected his bones and constructed the vajra. The invincible vajra was created with the bones of a brahmana and Vishnu penetrated it. Using this, Indra slew Vishvarupa and severed his head. Thereafter, when the body of Vishvarupa, Tvashtri's son, was churned, the energy gave birth to Vritra and Indra also killed Vritra. However, Indra was frightened because he had killed two brahmanas.[1240] He gave up the kingdom of heaven. He entered a lotus stalk that grew in the cool waters of Lake Manasa. Using the powers of anima obtained through yoga, he became minute and penetrated the fibres of the lotus. Shachi's consort, the protector of the three worlds, disappeared, terrified at having killed brahmanas. When the lord of the universe vanished, the gods were enveloped in rajas and tamas. Mantras were no longer chanted. Maharshis were attacked by rakshasas. The sons of the brahman disappeared. The worlds were without an Indra. Weakened, they were easily attacked. At this, the gods and the rishis instated Nahusha, the son of Ayusha, in the kingdom of heaven. There were five hundred blazing stars on Nahusha's forehead and they robbed everyone of energy. He began to rule in heaven. The worlds regained their natural state of comfort. Nahusha said, 'Everything that Shakra used to enjoy has presented itself before me. Shachi is the only exception.' Having said this, he went to Shachi and said, 'O extremely beautiful one! I am the Indra

[1239]The architect of the gods, Vishvakarma.

[1240]Both Vishvarupa and Vritra were descended from brahmanas.

of the gods now and you should serve me.' Shachi replied, 'You are naturally devoted to dharma and you have also been born in the lunar dynasty. You should not oppress someone else's wife.' Nahusha said, 'I have obtained the title of Indra. I have obtained his kingdom and there is no adharma in enjoying anything that Indra used to enjoy.' She replied, 'There is a vow that I am observing now. Within a few days, after the vow has been completed, I will come to you.' When he was thus addressed by Shachi, Nahusha departed. Shachi was afflicted by grief. She wished to see her husband and was frightened of being seized by Nahusha. She went to Brihaspati. On seeing her approach, Brihaspati discerned through his meditations that she wished to ensure her husband's objectives. Brihaspati said, 'Because of the vow and austerities you have observed, you should summon the goddess Upashruti, the granter of boons. She will show Indra to you.' She engaged in those great rituals and using mantras, summoned the goddess Upashruti, the granter of boons. Upashruti arrived before Shachi and said, 'Since you have summoned me, I have come here. What can I do to please you?' Bowing her head down, Shachi replied, 'O illustrious one! You should show me my husband. It is my view that you are the truth.' He took her to Lake Manasa and showed her Indra, hidden in the fibres of the lotus. Seeing that his wife was pale and distressed, he began to think. 'This is a great misery that has presented itself before me. My possessions have been destroyed and I confront this calamity.' Indra asked her, 'How are you?' She replied, 'Nahusha has summoned me and I have only obtained the pledge of some time.' Indra said, 'Go. Speak these words to Nahusha. Tell him that he should come to you on a vehicle that has not been used before. Let him ascend a vehicle to which rishis have been yoked. Tell him that this is the desire in your mind, that there should be a vehicle that is superior to those possessed by Indra and that he should act so as to please you.' Thus addressed, she left cheerfully. Indra again entered the fibres of the lotus. On seeing that Indrani[1241] had returned, Nahusha told her that the time period was over. Shachi repeated what Shakra had asked her to. He

[1241]Shachi.

ascended a vehicle yoked to maharshis and came to Shachi. Agastya, born in a jar and the son of Maitravaruna, saw Nahusha being dragged by those maharshis. When he was touched by him with the foot,[1242] he told Nahusha, 'You have performed a wicked act and will fall down on earth. As long as the earth and the mountains exist, you will be a snake.' As soon as the maharshi spoke these words, he fell down. The three worlds were again without an Indra. For the sake of an Indra, the gods and the rishis went to the illustrious Vishnu. They said 'O illustrious one! You should save Indra from the sin of having killed brahmanas.' The granter of boons replied, 'Let Shakra perform a horse sacrifice in Vishnu's honour. He will then regain his status.' The gods and the rishis searched for Indra, but could not find him. They went to Shachi and said, 'O beautiful one! Bring Indra here.' She again went to the lake. Indra arose from the lake and went before Brihaspati. For Shakra's sake, Brihaspati arranged for a great horse sacrifice. Instead of a horse, a black antelope was used and Indra, the lord of the Maruts, was made to ride this. In this way, Brihaspati got his old state back for him. The king of the gods was cleansed of sin. Praised by the gods and the rishis, he was established in heaven. The sin of killing a brahmana was divided into four parts and vested in women, fire, trees and cattle. Indra's energy was thus extended through a brahmana. He could slay his enemies and also regain his own status.

'"In ancient times, maharshi Bharadvaja was on the banks of the Ganga that courses through the sky. At that time, he was touched by one of Vishnu's three feet.[1243] Bharadvaja picked up some water in his hand and struck him in the chest with this. This left a mark.[1244] Maharshi Bhrigu cursed Agni that he would devour everything. Aditi cooked some food for the gods, so that on eating it, they would be

[1242]There is a slight error in the sense that Agastya was also one of the maharshis bearing the vehicle. Hence, it is obvious that Agastya would have seen this. While Agastya was bearing the vehicle, Nahusha inadvertently touched him with his foot.

[1243]In his vamana (dwarf) incarnation, Vishnu covered the three worlds in three steps. What is meant is that one of those steps was placed there.

[1244]The *srivatsa* mark on Vishnu's chest.

able to kill the asuras. Having completed a vow, Budha appeared before Aditi and asked for some alms. Aditi thought that no one should be given alms before the gods had eaten. At being refused alms, Budha, who possessed the brahman inside him, was enraged. He cursed her that when Vivasvat would have the second birth in Aditi's womb in the form of an egg, he would cause her pain.[1245] This form of Vivasvat, Martanda, is the god of funeral ceremonies.

'"Daksha had sixty daughters. He gave thirteen to Kashyapa, ten to Dharma, ten to Manu and twenty-seven to the moon. These twenty-seven, known as nakshatras, were equal. But Soma loved Rohini the most. The other wives were jealous. They went to their father and censured Soma. 'O illustrious one! All of us are equal in beauty. But he loves Rohini more.' They informed Daksha about this disrespect. Daksha cursed King Soma that tuberculosis would penetrate him. Thus struck by tuberculosis he went to Daksha. Daksha told him, 'Treat them all equally.' The rishis saw that Soma was afflicted by tuberculosis and said, 'Towards the western directions of the ocean, there is the tirtha known as Hiranyasara. Go and bathe there.' Soma went to the tirtha known as Hiranyasara. He went and bathed there. Having bathed, he was cleansed from his sin. Since that tirtha was illuminated by Soma, the tirtha has come to be famous by the name of Prabhasa.[1246] However, because of the curse, Soma still suffers from the inner trait of waning. On the night of the full moon, his complete form can be seen and is then gradually covered by lines of darkness. Even when he is sparkling, a dark sign can be seen on him, with the mark of a hare.[1247]

'"Maharshi Sthulashira went to the northern directions of Meru and tormented himself through austerities there. While he tormented himself through austerities there, an auspicious breeze began to blow.

[1245]There are twelve Adityas who are the sons of Aditi. The list varies. In earlier lists, Aditi only had seven sons who were born first. Martanda, the eighth son, was born later. Martanda also means a dead or lifeless egg.

[1246]*Prabhasa* means something that is bright and has been lit up. Prabhasa is near Dvaraka.

[1247]Because of the taint that was left. A hare is *shasha* and the moon is known as Shashi or Shashanka.

That breeze bore all kinds of fragrant scents and touched his body. His body was tormented because of those austerities. It was lean. Fanned by the breeze, his heart was satisfied. While he was fanned in this way, to satisfy him and show their beautiful selves, the trees blossomed out in flowers. He cursed them, 'You will not be able to bear flowers all the time.'[1248] In ancient times, for the welfare of the worlds, Narayana became a maharshi named Vadavamukha. He tormented himself through austerities in Meru and summoned the ocean there. Since it did not arrive when it had been summoned, through the heat of his body, the rishi stilled the waters of the ocean. He cursed them and said, 'Your water will be salty, like the sweat from a body. Your water will be sweet only when Vadavamukha drinks it.'[1249] Since that day, the waters of the ocean cannot be drunk, except by the one known as Vadavamukha.

'"Uma, the daughter of the Himalaya mountains, desired Rudra. Maharshi Bhrigu appeared before the Himalayas and said, 'Give your daughter, Uma, to me.' The Himalayas replied, 'I have already chosen Rudra as a groom.' Bhrigu said, 'You have refused me your beautiful daughter. Therefore, you will no longer be full of jewels.' Even today, the words of the rishi remain true. These are the different kinds of greatness of brahmanas. It is through the benedictions of brahmanas that kshatriyas are able to look upon this eternal and undecaying earth as their wife and are able to enjoy her. It is they who hold up the universe."'

Chapter 1658(330)

'The illustrious one said, "Surya and Chandra and their eternal rays are said to be my hair. They are known to separately exist and heat up the universe. Since they heat up the universe in

[1248]The trees were cursed because they were jealous of the wind.

[1249]Vadavamukha is the horse-headed subterranean fire.

this way, they cause delight. O descendant of the Pandu lineage! It is because of these deeds of Agni and Soma that I am known as Hrishikesha.[1250] I am Ishana, the granter of boons and the creator of the worlds. When I am invoked through prayers at a sacrifice, I accept the share. Since my complexion is the best one of tawny, I am known as Hari.[1251] Those who have thought about it regard me as amrita and the refuge of all the worlds. Since I am the truth, brahmanas praise me as Ritadhama.[1252] In earlier times, the earth had disappeared and was hidden. Since I found her out and raised her, the gods praise me as Govinda.[1253] I am known as Shipivishta, since I am devoid of body hair.[1254] Someone who is only covered in skin is known as Shipivishta. This is the only name in which the rishi Yaska anxiously chanted my name in sacrifices. Thus, I came to hold the secret name of Shipivishta. Having praised me through the name of Shipivishta, the intelligent rishi, Yaska, could use my favours to recover the nirukta, which had got submerged.[1255] I was not born earlier. I have not been born now. I will never be born. I am kshetrajna in all creatures. That is the reason I am known as Aja.[1256] I have never spoken anything that is inferior or obscene. The goddess, Sarasvati, Brahma's daughter, is the truth and is always with me. O Kounteya! The existent and the non-existent are immersed in my atman. In Pushkara, in Brahma's abode, the learned rishis addressed me as Satya.[1257] I have never deviated from sattva. Know that sattva has been created by me. O Dhananjaya! In this life too, as earlier, I have resorted to sattva. Those who act, but without any desires, think of me as Satvata. I can be seen by those who have the knowledge of sattva. I am Satvata, the lord of the Satvatas. O Partha! Assuming the

[1250]There is a play on *harsha* (delight) and kesha (hair), to provide another convoluted explanation for the name Hrishikesha.

[1251]*Hari* means tawny, or reddish-brown.

[1252]The abode of truth.

[1253]*Vinda* means finding or getting and *go* means the earth.

[1254]*Shipi* means skin, so Shipivishta is someone who is only covered in skin.

[1255]Yaska is a grammarian who is regarded as the author of nirukta.

[1256]Aja means without birth.

[1257]Meaning truth.

form of a plough made up of black iron, I till the earth. O Arjuna! It is because of my dark complexion that I am known as Krishna.[1258] I have united the earth with space, the space with wind and wind with energy. The quality of Vaikuntha[1259] is in me. Emancipation is supreme felicity and dharma is said to be superior to both of these. Since I have never deviated from these in my deeds, I am known as Achyuta.[1260] People on earth know that the earth and the firmament extend in all directions. Since I hold all of them up, I am known as Adhokshaja.[1261] Those who are learned about nirukta and the Vedas and have thought about the purport of words have sung my praises, giving me the first share, and addressing me as Adhokshaja. The supreme rishis have invoked me by that single name too. With the exception of the lord Narayana, there is no one else in the world who can be addressed as Adhokshaja. Clarified butter, which sustains the life of creatures in this world, represents my rays. That is the reason concentrated ones who know about the Vedas address me as Ghritarchi.[1262] There are said to be three elements—bile, phlegm and the wind. Their union is said to constitute all deeds. It is said that when these are weak, creatures are also weakened. In Ayurveda, I am therefore spoken of as Tridhatu.[1263] O descendant of the Bharata lineage! In the world, the illustrious Dharma is known by the name of Vrisha. Thus, in the words of Nighantuka, I am known as the supreme Vrisha.[1264] Kapi is said to be the best among boars and Vrisha is said to be the best among dharma. Therefore, Prajapati Kashyapa has addressed me as Vrishakapi.[1265] I am without beginning, without middle and without end. The gods and the asuras have never been able to comprehend my beginning, my middle, or my end. I have been praised as the lord, the lord who is a witness to the worlds. O

[1258]*Krishna* means dark.

[1259]Without hesitation.

[1260]Someone who has not deviated or been dislodged.

[1261]Someone who prevents things from falling down.

[1262]Someone for whom, clarified butter represents the rays or radiance.

[1263]The three elements.

[1264]*Nighantu* or *Nighantuka* was a glossary of obscure terms used in the Vedas.

[1265]The word means man-ape and is a term used for both Agni and Surya.

Dhananjaya! I do not hear, or cause to be heard, anything that is inauspicious. I do not accept anything that is wicked. Hence, I am Shuchishrava.[1266] In earlier times, I assumed the form of a boar and it possessed a divine form, with a single horn. In that form, I raised up the earth. That is the reason I am Ekashringa.[1267] When I assumed that form of a boar, I had three humps. As a measure of my body, I became famous as Trikakud.[1268] Those who have thought about the knowledge propounded by Kapila speak of me as Virincha.[1269] I am Prajapati, the consciousness that created all the worlds. With knowledge as a companion, I am established in the eternal Aditya. Those who have arrived at conclusions about sankhya also refer to me as the preceptor, Kapila. I am praised in the chants as the radiant Hiranyagarbha. I am always worshipped by yogis and I am known as Vibhu.[1270] I have been spoken about in the twenty-one recensions of the Rig Veda.[1271] Those learned in the Vedas have spoken about me in one thousand branches of the Sama Veda. Devoted brahmanas who sing about me in the *Aranyaka*s are extremely rare. The *adhvaryu* priests have spoken about me in one hundred and one branches of the Yajur Veda. The brahmanas who know about the Atharva Veda have thought of me as the five kalpas and the rituals of the Atharva Veda.[1272] Know that all the recensions, divisions, knowledge, branches, songs, vowels and pronunciation have been fashioned by me. O Partha! Hayashira, the granter of boons, arose. I am he and all the subsequent sections, divisions and syllables are based on me. It is through the instructions of Rama and my favours that the great-souled Panchala progressively obtained that eternal being.[1273]

[1266]One who hears auspicious things.

[1267]One with a single horn.

[1268]One with three humps.

[1269]Virincha is Brahma's name.

[1270]The powerful, excellent and omnipresent one.

[1271]Only one major one survives now.

[1272]In this context, it is not obvious what kalpa means. Period is logical, but part makes better sense.

[1273]Panchala is a reference to the rishi Galava. It is not clear who the Rama in question is.

He was born in the Babhravya gotra and progressively became accomplished. Through Narayana's boon, he attained supreme yoga. Thus, Galava was progressively led on to set out rules on shiksha.[1274] Kandarika and King Brahmadatta repeatedly kept thinking about the misery that comes through birth and death.[1275] Through their efforts, they obtained supreme prosperity for seven births. O Partha! In earlier times, for a certain reason, I was born as Dharma's son. O tiger among the Kuru lineage! I was therefore known as Dharmaja. Earlier, I performed undecaying austerities as Nara-Narayana. On the slopes of Mount Gandhamadana, I ascended on that vehicle that leads to dharma. There was a time when Daksha performed a sacrifice. O descendant of the Bharata lineage! He refused to earmark a share for Rudra. Following Dadhicha's instructions, he repeatedly hurled his blazing spear and uprooted Daksha's sacrifice. The spear reduced Daksha's entire sacrifice to ashes and violently advanced towards us in the hermitage of Badari. O Partha! It descended with great force on Narayana's chest. Narayana's hair became suffused with energy and assumed the complexion of munja grass. That is the reason I am known as Munjakesha. The great-souled Narayana repulsed the whirling spear with the sound of '*Hum*' and it returned to Shankara's hand. At this, Rudra attacked the rishis who were engaged in austerities. When he attacked in this way, Narayana, the soul of the universe, seized his throat with his hand, and he became Shitikantha. To destroy Rudra, Nara picked up a blade of grass. He swiftly invoked mantras and it became a giant battle axe. He hurled it violently, but Rudra shattered it into fragments before it reached him. Since the battleaxe was shattered, I came to be known as Khandaparashu."[1276]

[1274]As in the Vedanga of phonetics and phonology.

[1275]Brahmadatta was a king of Panchala. Brahmadatta is believed to have rearranged some parts of the Rig Veda and the Atharva Veda. His minister Kandarika did the same for the Sama Veda.

[1276]Literally meaning shattered battleaxe. Nara and Narayana are often regarded as the same person.

'Arjuna said, "O Varshneya! That encounter was capable of devastating the three worlds. O Janardana! Who was victorious? Tell me."

'The illustrious one replied, "An encounter started between the souls of Rudra and Narayana. All the worlds suddenly became anxious. The fire god no longer accepted the auspicious oblations offered at sacrifices. The Vedas no longer manifested themselves before the rishis who possessed cleansed souls. Rajas and tamas penetrated the gods. The earth trembled and the firmament started to waver. All the energy diminished and Brahma was dislodged from his seat. The oceans dried up and the Himalayas were shattered. O descendant of the Pandu lineage! Ominous portents manifested themselves. Brahma, surrounded by large numbers of gods and the great-souled rishis, swiftly went to the spot where the battle had commenced. The four-faced one[1277] can only be comprehended through nirukta. Because of those portents, he joined his hands in salutation and spoke to Rudra. 'Let everything in the worlds be auspicious. O lord of the universe! For the welfare of the universe, you should thrown down your weapon. He is indestructible. He is unmanifest. He is the lord who has created the worlds. He is subtle. He is the doer. He is beyond opposites. He is the learned one. He has assumed this manifest form. Nara and Narayana have been born in Dharma's lineage and actually have a single and auspicious form. These best of gods are engaged in great austerities and major vows. For a different reason, I have also been generated from them. O son! Though you are eternal, in an earlier cycle of creation, you have been born from his rage. O one who is the granter of boons! With the gods and the maharshis, I am soliciting your favours. Let there quickly be peace in the worlds.' Thus addressed by Brahma, Rudra withdrew the fire of his anger and sought to please the lord god Narayana. He sought the refuge of the one who should be worshipped, the granter of boons, Hari. The god, the granter of boons, was in control of his rage and had vanquished his senses. He cheerfully met Rudra. He was worshipped by the rishis, Brahma and the gods. Hari, the

[1277]Brahma.

lord of the universe, spoke to the god Ishana. 'He who knows you, knows me. He who follows you, follows me. There is no difference between you and me. Do not think otherwise. Your spear will leave the srivatsa mark on my chest. My hand will leave a beautiful mark on your throat, to be known as *shrikantha*.'[1278] They thus left marks on each other. Rudra and the rishis exhibited a great deal of friendliness towards each other. Giving permission to the residents of heaven to go, they[1279] engaged in austerities again. O Partha! I have told you how Narayana was victorious in that encounter. O descendant of the Bharata lineage! I have also told you about the secret names and their meanings. The rishis speak about these and recount them. O Kounteya! In this way, I roam around the earth in many forms and also in the world of Brahma and eternal Goloka.[1280] You were protected by me in the great battle and obtained victory. O Kounteya! When the battle presented itselft, there was a being who advanced in front of you. Know him to be Rudra Kapardin, the god of the gods. He is also known as Kala[1281] and he was born out of my rage. He had already slain all your enemies. Uma's consort, the god of the gods, is immeasurable in his power. Bow down before that god. He is the lord of the universe and he is the undecaying Hara."'[1282]

Chapter 1659(331)

Janamejaya said, 'O brahmana! You have narrated a great account. On hearing this, all these sages are overcome by great wonder. This has been churned from the excellent and extensive ocean of knowledge known as the Mahabharata, consisting of one hundred

[1278]Literally, beautiful throat.

[1279]Nara and Narayana.

[1280]Vishnu's world.

[1281]Death, destruction, destiny, in addition to meaning time.

[1282]Hara is Shiva's name.

thousand,[1283] like getting butter from curds, sandalwood from Mount Malaya, the *Aranyaka*s from the Vedas and amrita from herbs. O brahmana! O store of austerities! You have raised it like excellent amrita and stated it, based on accounts about Narayana. The illustrious lord and god has created the atmans of all creatures. O supreme among brahmanas! Narayana's energy is impossible to look at. Brahma and all the other gods, the rishis, the gandharvas and everything mobile and immobile merge into him at the end of a kalpa. I do not think that there is anything in heaven that is more sacred than him. Visiting all the hermitages and bathing in all the tirthas do not yield as many fruits as listening to Narayana's account does. Hari is the lord of the universe and is the one who destroys all sins. There is nothing colourful that was done by the noble Dhananjaya. Nor is there any excellent victory that was accomplished by him. After all, he had Vasudeva as his aide. I think that someone who has Vishnu, the protector of the three worlds, as his friend, is capable of obtaining anything in the three worlds. O brahmana! All these ancestors of mine were blessed. Janardana was engaged in their welfare and prosperity. The illustrious one is revered in the worlds and cannot be seen through austerities. However, they directly saw the one adorned with the shrivatsa mark on his chest. Narada, Parameshthi's son, was even more fortunate. Narada is known as the undecaying rishi whose energy is significant. He went to Shvetadvipa and saw Hari himself. It is through that god's favours that he obtained that vision. There, he saw the god in the form of Aniruddha. Thereafter, he again went to the hermitage of Badari to see Nara and Narayana. Why did the sage do that? Having returned from Shvetadvipa, the rishi Narada, Parameshthi's son, again went to the hermitage of Badari. After returning from Shvetadvipa, the extremely great-souled one went there. How long did he dwell there and what did he ask them? What did the great-souled rishis, Nara and Narayana, say? Tell me the truth about this. You should tell me everything.'

Vaishampayana replied, 'I bow down to the illustrious and immensely energetic Vyasa. I will narrate this account about

[1283]Shlokas.

Narayana through his favours. Having reached the great Shvetadvipa, he saw the immutable Hari. O king! Narada then swiftly returned to Meru. The brahmana bore in his heart the words spoken by the paramatman. O king! Thereafter, he thought to himself that he had achieved great success. He had travelled a long distance and had returned safe. From Meru, he went to Mount Gandhamadana. He travelled through the sky and quickly descended on the extensive region of Badari. There, he saw the ancient gods, the supreme rishis. They were engaged in extremely great austerities and were following wonderful vows, basing themselves on their own atmans. Their energy illuminated all the worlds and was greater than that of the sun. Those revered ones bore the srivatsa mark and their hair was matted. They had the marks of a *jalapada* on their palms.[1284] Their feet bore the auspicious marks of a chakra. Their chests were broad. Their arms were long. They possessed four arms each. They possessed sixty teeth each and their voices rumbled like the clouds. Their faces were beautiful and their foreheads were broad. Their jaws were beautiful and their eyebrows and noses were excellent. Their heads were like umbrellas. These were the signs that those two great beings were marked with. On seeing them, Narada was delighted. He worshipped them and was honoured back in return. They welcomed him and asked him whether he was well. On seeing them, Narada thought within himself, "These two Purushottamas, revered by all creatures, are just like the supreme rishis I saw in Shvetadvipa." Thinking this in his mind, he circumambulated them and sat down on an auspicious seat that was made out of kusha grass. They were the abodes of austerities. They were illustrious and full of energy. Those rishis were tranquil and self-controlled. Having performed their ablutions, they calmly honoured Narada with water for washing the feet and a gift. O king! After observing the rites to welcome a guest, they sat down on two wooden seats. When they sat down there, the entire area was illuminated. It was just like a sacrificial altar, blazing with large flames of the fire, when oblations have been offered. Narada was happily seated. He was rested and

[1284]A jalapada is a web-footed bird, like a swan. This is an auspicious sign.

having been received with hospitality, was cheerful. Narayana spoke to him. "The original and eternal paramatman is illustrious. He is the supreme form of our Prakriti and you have seen him in Shvetadvipa."

'Narada replied, "I have seen that illustrious and immutable Purusha. The universe is his form. All the worlds and the gods and the rishis are in him. Having seen the two of you now, I see that eternal one in you. The unmanifest Hari did not possess a form. But the signs he possessed are the signs that exist in you, in manifest and embodied forms. There, I saw you on both sides of the god. Having taken the permission of the paramatman, I have come here. With the exception of you two, born as Dharma's sons, who in the three worlds can possess energy, fame and prosperity like his? Earlier, he has told me the signs of the kshetrajna. He has also told me how he will manifest himself in the future. In Shveta, there were men who were devoid of their five senses. Their knowledge has been awakened and they are Purushottama's devotees. They always worship the god and he finds pleasure in them. The illustrious paramatman is affectionate towards his devotees and loves brahmanas. He always finds pleasure in those who are devoted to the illustrious one. The god enjoys everything in the universe and is friendly and affectionate towards his devotees. He is the doer. He is the cause and the effect. He is immensely powerful and radiant. That supreme one in Shvetadvipa represents austerities and sacrifices for those who are united with their atmans. He is famous for his energy. He is illuminated through his own radiance. For successful ones in the three worlds, who have cleansed their souls, he is tranquility. There, the devoted ones have resorted to vows, using their auspicious intelligence. The lord of the gods performs very difficult austerities in a spot where the sun does not heat, the moon does not shine and the wind does not blow. The enjoyer of the universe has constructed an altar on the ground and it measures the length of eight palms. The god is stationed there, standing on a single foot and with his arms raised. He faces the eastern direction. He performs those extremely difficult austerities, chanting from the Vedas and the Vedangas. Brahma, the rishis, Pashupati himself, the other best among gods, daityas, danavas, rakshasas, serpents, birds, gandharvas, siddhas and rajarshis always offer havya and kavya, following the ordinances. All of these present themselves at that god's feet. Intelligent ones perform rites with single-minded attention. That god himself receives all these on his head. There is no one he loves more in the three worlds than learned and great-souled ones who are single-minded in their devotion to him. Having been given permission to leave by the paramatman, I have come here. The illustrious god, Hari, himself told me that I should always reside with you, obtaining supreme benedictions."'

Chapter 1660(332)

'Nara and Narayana said, "You are blessed, since you have seen and have been favoured by the lord himself. The one who has been born from the lotus[1285] has himself been unable to see him. The illustrious Purushottama has an unmanifest origin and is extremely difficult to see. O Narada! The words we are speaking to you are entirely true. O best among the brahmanas! There is no one in the worlds that he loves as much as a devotee. That is the reason he has shown himself to you. The paramatman torments himself through austerities in a region. O supreme among brahmanas! With our exception, no one is capable of going there. Because of his radiance, that place seems to be illuminated by one thousand suns together. That place shines through his own resplendence. O brahmana! He is the lord behind the creation of the universe. The quality of forgiveness, and the best among those who forgive, the earth, arose from him. For the welfare of all creatures, the quality of taste also arose from that god and the attribute of fluidity that is associated with the water. It is from that god that light, and the quality of form with which it is associated, arose. United with this, the sun radiates the worlds. It is from the supreme god Purushottama that touch has arisen. United with the wind, this makes the worlds

[1285]Brahma.

feel. Sound arose from the god who is the lord of the universe. This is attached to space, which extends unconstrained in all the directions. Mind arose from that god and is inside all beings. This becomes attached to the moon and assumes the quality of showing things. That place, associated with the Vedas, is known as the region where the six elements arose.[1286] The illustrious one, the devourer of havya and kavya, resides there, accompanied by knowledge. O supreme among brahmanas! There are people who have been cleansed from sin and are disassociated from good and bad deeds. They are capable of going to that sacred region. That is a region which frees the worlds from delusion and Aditya is said to be the door to that. On entering Aditya, the bodies of such people are consumed. Others are rendered invisible. Becoming like atoms,[1287] such people merge into the god. They are thus emancipated and are established in Aniruddha. After that, they only retain the attributes of the mind and merge into Pradyumna. Freed from Pradyumna, the being next enters Samkarshana. The best among brahmanas, those who know about sankhya and are devoted, merge there. O best among brahmanas! When the three qualities[1288] are completely extinguished, they merge into the paramatman, the kshetrajna who is devoid of qualities. Truly know that Vasudeva, the refuge of everything, is kshetrajna. There are those who have controlled their minds, are restrained and have checked their senses. Single-minded in devotion, they enter into Vasudeva. O supreme among brahmanas! We have been born in Dharma's house. Dwelling in this beautiful spot, we have practised fierce austerities. O brahmana! We have done this for the welfare of the three worlds, so that the supreme one, beloved by the gods, can manifest himself. O supreme among brahmanas! We have observed rites that have not been witnessed earlier. We have properly observed all the wonderful vows of hardship. O store of austerities! In Shvetadvipa, you saw us too. Having met the illustrious one, you formed a resolution and we know about it. We know everything in

[1286]The five elements and mind.

[1287]Paramanu.

[1288]Sattva, rajas and tamas.

the three worlds of mobile and immobile objects, everything that has happened, is happening and will happen, good or bad."'

Vaishampayana said, 'They were engaged in fierce austerities. Having heard their words, Narada, devoted to Narayana, joined his hands in salutation. He meditated on many kinds of mantras, all of which had originated with Narayana. He spent one thousand divine years in the hermitage of Nara and Narayana. The immensely energetic and illustrious rishi, Narada, dwelt there. He worshipped the gods, Nara and Narayana.'

Chapter 1661(333)

Vaishampayana said, 'There was a time when Narada, Parameshthi's son, resided there. Having performed rites in honour of the gods, he thereafter got ready to perform rites in honour of the ancestors. At that time, the lord who was Dharma's elder son spoke these words. "O best among brahmanas! What are these rites you are performing in honour of the gods and the ancestors? You are the best among intelligent ones. Tell us about these rites from the sacred texts. Why are you undertaking these rites? What are the fruits you desire?"

'Narada replied, "Earlier, you yourself said that rites in the honour of the gods must be performed. You said that sacrifices to gods are supreme, from the point of view of obtaining the eternal paramatman. It is because of what you have determined that I perform sacrifices to the undecaying Vaikuntha. Brahma, the grandfather of the worlds, was formerly generated from him. Parameshthi cheerfully gave birth to my father, though I was the first son that he mentally thought of.[1289] I am performing this sacrifice for my virtuous ancestors and observing the rites in honour of Narayana. The illustrious one is my

[1289]This sounds confusing because of the conflicting accounts about Narada's birth. In some, he is Brahma's son, created through Brahma's mental powers. In others, Daksha is Brahma's son and Narada is Daksha's son.

father, my mother and my grandfather. I always perform these rites and sacrifices in honour of the ancestors, to worship the lord of the universe. The gods instructed the various sacred texts to their sons and the latter offered sacrifices to their ancestors. However, when the Vedas and sacred texts were destroyed, they again had to study them from their sons.[1290] Using the mantras, the sons therefore became like fathers. In this way, fathers and sons came to worship each other and these ancient accounts are certainly known to both of you. Having first spread kusha grass on the ground, I have offered three *pinda*s to the ancestors.[1291] In ancient times, why did the ancestors come to acquire the name of pindas?"

'Nara and Narayana replied, "In ancient times, the earth was destroyed and disappeared inside the girdle of the ocean. Assuming the form of a boar, Govinda swiftly raised it up. Purushottama established the earth in its proper place. He raised it to accomplish the objective of the worlds and his limbs were covered in water and mud. The sun was at its midday position then and it was time to perform the afternoon ablutions. The lord violently shook his tusks and three balls of mud fell down from there. O Narada! He laid these out on a bed of kusha grass on the ground. Following the proper rites, he offered these to the ancestors, that is, to himself. Following the ordinances, the lord thought of these as three pindas. The heat generated from his own body became the oil obtained from sesamum seeds. The lord of the gods faced the eastern direction and himself declared these special rules. So as to establish the ordinances, he spoke these words. 'I am the ancestor. I have readied myself to create the worlds.' Having thought this, he immediately began to think of

[1290]The gods taught the sacred texts to their sons, the sages. But the gods went to fight the demons and forgot the sacred texts. On return, they had to relearn the sacred texts from the sages.

[1291]A pinda is a ball of rice offered to the ancestors. The offering of three pindas is known as *tripindi* and there are two equally valid explanations for the number three. The first is that these offerings are made for three successive years. The second is that these offerings are made in the months of Kartika, Chaitra and Shravana. The text gives a different interpretation, with all three pindas offered simultaneously.

rites in honour of the ancestors. There were those three lumps of mud that fallen down from his tusk on the ground, in the southern direction. He declared that these balls on the ground should thereafter be known as pindas offered to the ancestors. 'These three have no from. Let these pindas on the ground be assumed to have form. I have thus created the eternal ancestors for the worlds. I am the father, the grandfather and the great grandfather. It is I who will be regarded as being established in these three pindas. There is no one who is superior to me. Whom can I myself worship? Who is my father in this world? Who is my grandfather? I am the grandfather, the father and the cause.' These were the words that Vrishakapi, the god of the gods, spoke. O brahmana! On the slope of a mountain, the boar spread out and offered those pindas. Having worshipped himself, he disappeared at that spot. Through this auspicious intelligence, the pindas came to be known as the ancestors. Following Vrishakapi's words, they always obtain the worship. If a person worships the ancestors, the gods, the preceptors, the guests, cattle, the foremost among brahmanas, the earth and the mother, in deeds, mind and thoughts, then it is as if that person worships Vishnu. That illustrious one is inside all bodies. The lord is impartial towards all creatures and towards happiness and unhappiness. He is the large and great-souled one. He is inside all atmans. He is known as Narayana."'

Chapter 1662(334)

Vaishampayana said, 'Hearing these words of Nara and Narayana, Narada became extremely devoted towards that single god. He spent one thousand years in Nara and Narayana's hermitage. He heard accounts about the illustrious one and saw the undecaying Hari. Then he quickly went to his own hermitage, on the slopes of the Himalayas. The famous rishis, Nara and Narayana, continued to dwell in their own beautiful hermitage, tormenting themselves through supreme austerities. You are extremely valiant.

You are the extender of the lineage of the Pandavas. Having heard about these accounts, right from the beginning, you have been completely purified. O supreme among kings! A person who hates the immutable Vishnu in deeds, thoughts and words, possesses neither this world, nor the next. For an eternal number of years, his ancestors are submerged in hell. This is what happens to someone who hates the best among the gods, the god Narayana Hari. How can one hate someone whose atman is in all the worlds? O tiger among men! Know that Vishnu is established in all atmans. Our preceptor is the rishi who is Gandhavati's son.[1292] O son! He is the one who told us about the paramatman's greatness. O unblemished one! I have told you what I heard from him. Know that Krishna Dvaipayana is the lord Narayana. O tiger among men! Who else could have composed the Mahabharata? Other than that lord, who could have spoken about the many kinds of dharma? The great sacrifice that you thought of, is going on.[1293] Having listened to the truth about what the sacred texts say about dharma, think of a horse sacrifice.

'Souti said, "The king who was Parikshit's son heard this great account.[1294] He started all the rites that were necessary for the completion of the sacrifice."'

Vaishampayana said, 'I have recounted to you the stories about Narayana. O king! In earlier times, Narada told my preceptor about these, in the hearing of the rishis, the Pandavas, Krishna and Bhishma. He[1295] is the supreme preceptor and the lord of the universe. He is the one who holds up the earth. He is the store of tranquility and rituals. He is the store of the sacred texts and humility. He is engaged in the supreme welfare of brahmanas. The beneficial Hari should be your destination. He is the great store of extremely great austerities. He is famous. He is worshipped by the ones who do not cause injury. He is the single refuge. He is the end that grants freedom from fear.

[1292]Gandhavati is another name for Satyavati.

[1293]The story is being told by Vaishampayana to Janamejaya, at the latter's snake sacrifice. It was later retold by Souti to the sages.

[1294]The text does not clearly say this. But it is now Souti speaking.

[1295]Narayana.

He is the one who accepts shares at sacrifices. He is beyond the three qualities. He has four and five sacred forms.[1296] He accepts a share in the fruits of sacrifices. He is always worshipped. He cannot be vanquished. He is extremely strong. He is the destination for the atmans. He constitutes the good deeds of the rishis. He is a witness to the worlds. He is without birth. He is the Purusha. He is like the sun in complexion. He is the lord who progresses along many paths. He is the single one to whom one should bow down. He emerged from the waters. It is before him that the rishis bow down. He is the origin of the worlds. He is the immortal destination. He is subtle, ancient, immobile and supreme. He is the one who is always upheld by intelligent ones who know about sankhya and yoga, those who are controlled in their souls and know about him.'

Chapter 1663(335)

Janamejaya said, 'I have heard about the greatness of the illustrious paramatman, about how he was born in Dharma's house in the form of Nara and Narayana and about the ancient origin and creation of pinda by the great boar. O brahmana! O unblemished one! I have heard how the modes of pravritti and nivritti were thought of. Earlier, you have also spoken about Hayashira, the devourer of havya and kavya, Vishnu's form that arose from the north-eastern part of the great ocean. That was seen by the illustrious Brahma Parameshthi. O supreme among intelligent ones! When Hari, the upholder of the worlds, adopted that form in earlier times, what were the aspects of power and greatness that had not been witnessed earlier? O sage! On seeing that sacred and infinitely energetic form of Hayashira, foremost among the gods and never witnessed earlier, what did Brahma do? O brahmana! Based on that ancient account,

[1296]The four forms have already been mentioned. The fifth form is seen when one has been completely emancipated and one is in Vaikuntha.

such a doubt has arisen. Why did the great being create this excellent form? O brahmana! You have purified us by telling us about these sacred accounts.'

Vaishampayana replied,[1297] 'I will tell you everything about that ancient account, which is in conformity with the Vedas. This was told to the king who was Dharma's son by the illustrious Vyasa. On hearing about the god Harimedha[1298] adopting the form of Hayashira, there was a doubt in the king's mind and he went and asked him.[1299] Yudhishthira asked, "Brahma saw the god in the form of Hayashira. Why did this happen and why did the god appear in such a form?"

'Vyasa said, "O lord of the earth! Everything in the world that possesses a body is made out of the five elements. This creation results from the lord's intelligence. The great god and lord, Narayana, is the creator of the universe. He is in the atmans of all beings. He is the granter of boons. He is with qualities and without qualities. O supreme among kings! It is the unmanifest one who brings about the destruction of beings. Listen. First, the earth was submerged in water and everything was one large ocean. Water merged into light and light merged into the wind. The wind merged into space and space merged into the mind. Mind merged into the manifest[1300] and the manifest merged into the unmanifest.[1301] The unmanifest merged into Purusha and Purusha merged into the one who pervaded everything.[1302] There was darkness everywhere and nothing could be seen. The brahman arose from the darkness. He created himself from that foundation of darkness. With the desire to create the

[1297]This is what the text says. Since Janamejaya has asked the question, this should be Souti replying, not Vaishampayana.

[1298]In this context, Harimedha can be taken as Vishnu's name, though strictly speaking, in one of the manvantaras, Vishnu was born as Hari, and he was then the son of Harimedha.

[1299]Vyasa.

[1300]Meaning consciousness.

[1301]Meaning Prakriti.

[1302]The paramatman.

universe, he assumed the form of Purusha. This form is known as Aniruddha and is also known as Pradhana. O supreme among kings! He is also known as the manifest and as a combination of the three qualities. With knowledge as his companion, the lord is also known as Vishvaksena or Hari. Immersed in yoga, he slept on the waters. He thought of creating the universe, with wonderful and diverse attributes. While thinking of creation, he remembered his own great qualities. Consciousness was generated then and this was the auspicious and four-faced Brahma. The illustrious Hiranyagarbha is the grandfather of all the worlds. He possessed eyes that are like a lotus and he emerged from a lotus that was in Aniruddha.[1303] The eternal and radiant one was seated on the flower with the one thousand petals. Wishing to create the worlds, the lord looked at the water that was on all sides. Basing himself on sattva, Parameshthi created the different categories of beings. Before this, Narayana had placed two drops of water, invested with excellent qualities, into the petals of the lotus, which were as bright as the rays of the sun. The illustrious Achyuta is without beginning and without end. He looked at those two drops of water. One of these was beautiful and radiant and looked like honey. On Narayana's instructions, Madhu, based on tamas qualities, was generated from this.[1304] The other drop was hard, and Kaitabha, based on rajas qualities, was generated from this. With the qualities of tamas and rajas, these two superior ones advanced. They were powerful and held clubs in their hands. They roamed around inside the stalk of the lotus. Inside the lotus, they saw the infinitely radiant Brahma. He was engaged in creating the first forms of the four beautiful Vedas. The supreme asuras saw the forms of the Vedas. While Brahma looked on, they violently seized the Vedas. Having seized the eternal Vedas, the best among the danavas quickly entered the nether regions, inside the waters of the great ocean.

'"When the Vedas were stolen, Brahma was immersed in grief. Deprived of the Vedas, he spoke these words to the lord. 'The Vedas

[1303]A lotus that blooms from Aniruddha's navel.

[1304]Madhu means honey, as well as sweet and pleasant.

are my supreme sight. The Vedas are my supreme strength. The Vedas are my supreme refuge. The Vedas are the supreme brahman. All my Vedas have been stolen by the powerful danavas. With the Vedas having been stolen, the world is enveloped in darkness. Without the Vedas, how will I engage in the task of creating the worlds? I am suffering from a great grief because my Vedas have been stolen. My heart is afflicted and I am consumed by a great misery. Who will raise me from this ocean of grief into which I have been submerged? Who will save the destroyed Vedas and do something agreeable for me?' O supreme among kings! These were the words that Brahma spoke. O supreme among intelligent ones! The intelligent one thought of some hymns in praise of Hari. Joining his hands in salutation, the lord bowed down and approached the supreme one. He chanted, 'I bow down before you. You are Brahma's heart. I bow down before you. You were created before me. You are the origin of the worlds. You are the best in the universe. You are the lord who is the store of sankhya and yoga. You are the creator of the manifest and the unmanifest. You are established on the path of tranquility. You are the enjoyer of the universe. You are inside all creatures. You are without birth. I have been generated through your favours. O Svayambhu! You are the abode of the worlds. My first birth, honoured by all the brahmanas, was from your mind. My ancient and second birth was from your eyes. It is through your favours that my great and third birth occurred from your speech. O lord! It is the truth that my fourth birth was from your ears. O one without decay! It is the truth that my fifth birth was from your nose. It is true that you thought of my sixth birth from an egg. O infinitely powerful lord! This, my seventh birth, has happened from a lotus. O one who is devoid of the three qualities! From one cycle of creation to another cycle of creation, I have been your son. You are famous as Pundarikaksha. You are Pradhana, who has thought of the qualities. You are the natural lord. You are Svayambhu and Purushottama. I have been created by you and the Vedas are my eyes. The Vedas, which are my eyes, have been stolen. Though I have been born, I am blind. Please awake. Give my eyes back to me. I am dear to you. You are dear to me.' The illustrious Purusha, who faces every direction, was thus praised.

'"To accomplish the task of recovering the Vedas, he raised himself from his sleep. Using his powers, he assumed a second form. He assumed a form with an excellent nose and it was as radiant as the moon. The lord who is the abode of all the Vedas assumed the auspicious form of Hayashira. The firmament, with its nakshatras and stars, became his head. His long and flowing hair was as radiant as the rays of the sun. The sky and the nether regions constituted his ears. The earth was his forehead. The sacred and great rivers, Ganga and Sarasvati, were his eyebrows. The sun and the moon were his eyes. The evening was said to be his nose. The syllable 'Om' was his mind and the lightning was his tongue. O king! The ancestors, who drink soma, were known as his teeth. Goloka and Brahmaloka[1305] became the great-souled one's lips. O king! The terrible night of universal destruction, which is beyond the three qualities, became his neck. He created this form of Hayashira and it was covered with many kinds of other forms. The god who was the lord of the universe disappeared and penetrated the nether regions. Having entered the water, he resorted to supreme yoga. Using accomplished techniques of pronunciation, he uttered the syllable 'Om'. This sound was pleasant in every way and echoed everywhere. It possessed all the beneficial qualities and reverberated in the nether regions. Having decided to come back for the Vedas, the asuras flung them down into the nether regions and swiftly proceeded to the spot where the sound was coming from. O king! Meanwhile, Hari, the god who was in the form of Hayashira, picked up all the Vedas from the nether regions. He gave them back to Brahma and assumed his natural form again. Hayashira was the abode of the Vedas and he established this form of Hayashira in the north-eastern parts of the great ocean. O king! The danavas, Madhu and Kaitabha, could not find anyone and quickly returned to the spot. However, they found that the place where they had flung the Vedas was empty. Those two supremely powerful ones resorted to great speed. They quickly raised themselves from the nether regions and saw the lord Purusha, who had originally created them. He was based in the form of Aniruddha and he was as pure

[1305]The worlds of Vishnu and Brahma respectively.

in complexion as the fair moon. The valiant one had again resorted to yoga and was sleeping on the waters. He had manifested himself in this form and was sleeping on the waters. He was sleeping on the hood of a serpent[1306] and seemed to be enveloped in a covering of flames. The beautiful lord was full of sattva and without any blemish. On seeing him, the Indras among the danavas laughed loudly. Full of rajas and tamas, they said, 'This Purusha is fair and he is lying down, immersed in sleep. There is no doubt that he is the one who has stolen the Vedas from the nether regions. Whom does he belong to? Who is he? Who belongs to him? Why is he sleeping on a snake?' While they were speaking in this way, Hari was awakened. The god Purushottama realized that they wished to fight with him. He saw that the two Indras among rakshasas had made up their minds to fight. A battle commenced between them on one side and Narayana on the other. Madhu and Kaitabha were full of rajas and tamas. To please Brahma, Madhusudana slew them.[1307] Purushottama quickly killed the ones who had stolen the Vedas and dispelled Brahma's grief. Brahma was again revered and surrounded by the Vedas that had been stolen. Without any sense of ownership, he created the worlds, with their mobile and immobile objects. He[1308] gave the grandfather the powerful intelligence required for the creation of the worlds. Having given this to the god, Hari went away. It is thus that Hari assumed the form of Hayashira and killed the two danavas. He assumed that form so that the dharma of pravritti could be propagated again. Thus did the immensely fortunate Hari assume the form of Hayashira. This form of the lord who grants boons is regarded as the most ancient. If a brahmana always hears it, or recites it, his studies will never be destroyed. Using fierce austerities, the rishi Panchala worshipped the god who assumed the form of Hayashira and learnt shiksha, following the path instructed by Rama. O king! I have recounted the story of Hayashira to you. This is an ancient account that is in conformity with the Vedas and you had asked me

[1306]Shesha or Ananta.

[1307]Madhusudana means the destroyer of Madhu.

[1308]Narayana.

about it. To accomplish different kinds of tasks, the god assumes different kinds of forms. Using his atman, the god creates himself and performs those different tasks.

'"He is the store of the Vedas. He is prosperous. He is the store of austerities. The powerful lord Hari is yoga, sankhya and the brahman. Narayana is the supreme Vedas. The sacrifices constitute Narayana's atman. Narayana represents supreme austerities. Narayana is the supreme objective. Narayana is the supreme truth. Amrita is Narayana's atman. Naryana is the supreme dharma and from this, it is extremely rare to return.[1309] Dharma with the characteristics of pravritti has Narayana as its soul. Scent, said to be the best attribute of the earth, has Narayana as its soul. O king! Taste, the quality of water, has Narayana as its soul. Form, the quality of light, is said to have Narayana as its soul. Touch, the quality of the wind, is said to have Narayana as its soul. Sound, resulting from space, also has Narayana as its soul. Mind, with the quality of the unmanifest,[1310] has Narayana as its soul. Time, computed through the measurement of the stellar bodies, is nothing but the supreme Narayana. The supreme Narayana is the deities of Kirti, Shri and Lakshmi.[1311] Sankhya and yoga are the supreme Narayana and they have Narayana as their soul. He is the cause as Purusha. He is also the cause as Pradhana. All deeds are in his nature. He is the cause behind the gods. He is enumerated as the five kinds of causes.[1312] Hari is there in all devotion. He is the truth that the curious ones seek. He is the reason that faces all the directions. He is the single truth. He is the great yogi. He is the lord Hari Narayana. He is the one Brahma, the worlds, the great-souled rishis, the practitioners of sankhya and yoga and the ascetics seek to know. The learned ones know of him as Keshava. Everything that is done in all the worlds

[1309]If one has obtained Narayana, rebirth is rare. This is a reference to nivritti.

[1310]Prakriti.

[1311]Respectively, deeds, beauty and prosperity.

[1312]This proably refers to the five sheaths that cover the atman. These are annamaya (related to food), pranamaya (related to energy), manomaya (related to the mind), vijnanamaya (related to knowledge) and anandamaya (related to bliss).

for the sake of gods and ancestors, the donations that are given, the great austerities that are observed—all these have the lord Vishnu as their refuge. He has determined the ordinances for these. He resides in all creatures and is said to be Vasudeva.[1313] He is eternal. He is the supreme maharshi. He possesses the greatest power. He is beyond qualities. He is without the three qualities. When the occasion arises, he acts so as to quickly bring about a union of the qualities. The great-souled ones cannot comprehend his progress. No one can see his movements. Maharshis who are restrained and possess knowledge in their atmans always see the Purusha, who is beyond the qualities."'

Chapter 1664(336)

Janamejaya said, 'The illustrious Hari is affectionate towards all beings who are single-minded in their devotion to him. The illustrious one himself accepts offerings made according to the ordinances. There are people who have burnt up the kindling,[1314] are free of good and bad deeds and have followed the instructions that have progressively been passed down.[1315] They advance towards the fourth objective of Purushottama.[1316] Those single-minded ones go to the supreme objective. There is no doubt that the dharma of being single-minded is the best and is loved by Narayana. They do not have to pass through the other three, but directly go to the undecaying Hari. There are brahmanas who study the Vedas and the Upanishads properly, following the strictures and observing

[1313]Based on the root *vas*, meaning, reside or dwell.

[1314]Extinguished their desire.

[1315]Through the chain of succession from preceptor to disciple.

[1316]Vasudeva or Purshuttoma is the fourth, higher than Aniruddha, Pradyumna and Samkarshana. The sense is that through knowledge, one goes to Vasudeva, but progressively, through the the other three. However, with faith or devotion, one directly goes to Vasudeva, bypassing the others.

the dharma of ascetics. I know that men who are single-minded in their devotion are superior to them. Was it a god or a rishi who first propounded this kind of dharma? O lord! When did this single-minded mode of worship develop? Please dispel my doubt about this. My curiosity is great.'

Vaishampayana replied, 'The armies of the Kurus and the Pandavas were arrayed in the battle. When Arjuna was distracted, the illustrious one himself sung about this, about the ends that are obtained and the ends that are not obtained.[1317] I have told you about this earlier. This dharma is deep and is difficult for those who have not cleansed their souls to comprehend. This is in conformity with the Sama Veda and was thought of in the first yuga.[1318] O king! It was sustained by the lord Narayana himself. O great king! Partha asked the immensely fortunate Narada about the purport of this, in the midst of the rishis and in the hearing of Krishna and Bhishma. O supreme among kings! My preceptor heard what was said.[1319] He heard what Narada said. O lord of the earth! Brahma was born through Narayana's mental powers and heard what emerged from Narayana's mouth. O descendant of the Bharata lineage! Following dharma, Narayana himself performed the divine rites that any father should. The rishis who subsist on foam then obtained the dharma. The Vaikhanasas obtained the dharma from those who lived on foam. Soma obtained it from the Vaikhanasas. But it then disappeared again. O king! Brahma had a second birth from the eyes.[1320] Then, the grandfather obtained and learned this dharma from Soma. O king! He gave this, which has Narayana as its soul, to Rudra. O king! In that ancient krita yuga, Rudra immersed himself in yoga and taught this dharma to all the Valakhilya rishis. However, because of the god's[1321] maya, it disappeared again. Brahma had a third birth

[1317]In the Bhagavadgita, in Section 63 (Volume 5).

[1318]Krita yuga.

[1319]Making it clear that the Krishna in the previous sentence is Krishna Dvaipayana Vedavyasa.

[1320]Narayana's eyes.

[1321]Narayana's.

from his[1322] great speech. O king! The dharma was again generated from Narayana himself. A rishi named Suparna obtained it from Purushottama and tormented himself with austerities, following self-restraint and rituals. Suparna followed this supreme dharma thrice a day. Because of this, on earth, he came to be known as Trisouparna.[1323] These are read when one studies the Rig Veda and the vows to be followed are extremely difficult. O best among men! From Suparna, this eternal dharma was obtained by the wind god, who is known as the one who sustains life in the universe. Vayu gave it to the rishis who only subsist on leftovers. The great ocean obtained the supreme dharma from them. However, it disappeared again and merged into Narayana. The great-souled one, Brahma, was again born from his ear.[1324] O tiger among men! I will tell you what happened. Listen. The god, Hari Narayana, himself thought of creating the universe. The lord, who is the creator of everything in the universe, thought of a being. When he thought of this, the being, his son, emerged from his ears. The lord of the universe spoke to Brahma, the creator of different categories of subjects. "O son! Create. Create everyone from your mouths and feet. O one who is excellent in vows! I will do what is beneficial for you. I will give you the strength and the energy. Also receive this dharma from me. It is known as satvata. Use it to create and establish all the rites of krita yuga." At this, Brahma bowed down before the god Harimedha. He eagerly accepted the dharma, with its mysteries and collections and groups of *Aranyaka*s. These arose from Narayana's mouth. With infinite energy, he instructed this dharma to Brahma and said, "You know about the dharma of krita yuga, which has the traits of being without desire and without deeds." Having said this, he[1325] departed to beyond tamas, to the place where the unmanifest is established. Then, Brahma, the god who grants boons and is the grandfather of

[1322]Narayana's.

[1323]Trisouparna is the same as Trisuparna. The Yajur Veda has three mantras that are recited together and these are known as *trisuparna*.

[1324]Brahma was born from Narayana's ears.

[1325]Narayana.

the worlds, created all the worlds, with their mobile and immobile objects. That is how the first sacred krita yuga commenced. The dharma of satvata pervaded everything in the world. Brahma, the creator of the various worlds, used that original dharma to worship the lord Hari Narayana, the lord of the gods. For the welfare of the worlds and for the sake of establishing this dharma, he then taught it to Svarochisha Manu.[1326] O king! In ancient times, Svarochisha, the lord and protector of all the worlds, himself carefully taught it to his son, Shankhapada. O descendant of the Bharata lineage! Shankhapada taught it to his son Sudharma, the protector of the directions. When treta yuga commenced, it[1327] disappeared again. O supreme among kings! Then, in ancient times, Brahma was born from the nose. In Brahma's presence, the lord and god, the lotus-eyed Hari Narayana, himself chanted this dharma. O king! The illustrious Sanatkumara studied it. O tiger among the Kuru lineage! From Sanatkumara, at the beginning of krita yuga, Prajapati Virana obtained this dharma and studied it. Having studied it, Virana gave it to the intelligent Rouchya and Rouchya gave it to his son Shudra, who was excellent in his vows and great in his intelligence. He gave it to Kukshi, who protected the directions.[1328] However, the dharma that arose from Narayana's mouth vanished again. Brahma was again born as Hari's son, from an egg and this dharma arose again, from Narayana's mouth. O king! Brahma received it, and following the instructions, applied it. O king! He taught it to the sages named Barhishada.[1329] A brahmana who knew about the Sama Veda obtained it from the Barhishadas. His name was Jyeshtha and because of this, he came to be known as Jyeshtha Hari, the follower of the Sama vows. King Avikampana obtained it from Jyeshtha. O king! Then the dharma that had been received from the lord Hari

[1326]There are fourteen manvantaras in every kalpa. In the present kalpa, we are in the seventh manvantara of Vaivasvat Manu. The six earlier Manus were Svayambhuva, Svarochisha, Uttama, Tamasa, Raivata and Chakshusha.

[1327]The dharma.

[1328]The suggestion seems to be that Kukshi was Shudra's son.

[1329]Literally, sages who seated themselves on sacrificial grass.

disappeared again. O king! Brahma had a seventh birth from the lotus and Narayana himself spoke to him about this dharma. At the beginning of the yuga, the sacred grandfather was the upholder of the worlds. In those ancient times, the grandfather gave this dharma to Daksha. O supreme among kings! Daksha gave it to Aditya, who was the eldest of his grandsons through his daughters and was also older than Savitri. Vivasvat obtained it from him.[1330] At the beginning of treta yuga, Vivasvat gave it to Manu. For the prosperity of the worlds, Manu gave it to his son, Ikshvaku. When Ikshvaku spoke about it, it spread in all the worlds. O king! At the end of the destruction, it will again merge into Narayana. O supreme among kings! This is the dharma that is practised by the mendicants. With the collection of the ordinances, it has been recounted in *Hari Gita*.[1331] O king! Narada obtained this dharma, with its mysteries and its collections, from the protector of the worlds himself. O king! These are the origins of this great and eternal dharma. It is difficult to comprehend and it is difficult to practise. It is always sustained by those with sattva. Those who know about dharma appropriately apply it in their deeds. This dharma is without violence and it pleases the lord Hari. Some worship him in one form and some in two forms.[1332] He is sometimes enumerated in three forms.[1333] He is sometimes seen in four forms.[1334] Hari is kshetrajna. He is without a sense of ownership and he is without parts. He is the atman in all beings and is beyond the five elements. O king! He is spoken of as the mind that controls the five senses. He is the intelligent one who ordains the worlds. He is the creator of the worlds. He is not the doer. But he is also the doer. He is the cause and the effect. O king! He is the immutable Purusha, who sports as he wills. O supreme among kings! I have spoken to you about the dharma of single-minded devotion. It is difficult for those with unclean souls to

[1330]From Aditya.

[1331]The Bhagavadgita.

[1332]Aniruddha and Aniruddha and Pradyumna respectively.

[1333]With Samkarshana added.

[1334]With Vasudeva added.

understand. I have obtained it through my preceptor's favours. O king! Men who are single-minded in their devotion are difficult to find. O descendant of the Kuru lineage! Had the worlds been full of many such people, who are non-violent and devoted to their atmans, engaged in the welfare of beings, then it would have been krita yuga. People would have been free of desire and freed from rites. O lord of the earth! This is what the illustrious Vyasa, my preceptor, the one who knows about dharma, and supreme among brahmanas, told Dharmaraja. O king! This was in the hearing of the rishis and of Krishna and Bhishma. He had earlier been told this by Narada, the immensely ascetic one. Narayana is the god who is the supreme brahman. He is immutable and fair in complexion, with the radiance of the moon. Those who are single-minded go to him.'

Janamejaya asked, 'Those who have been awakened practise many different kinds of dharma. Why don't other brahmanas follow this too, instead of devoting themselves to diverse vows?'

Vaishampayana replied, 'O king! Those who are bound in bodies possess three kinds of nature. O descendant of the Bharata lineage! They follow sattva, rajas and tamas. O extender of the Kuru lineage! Among those who are bound in bodies, the best man is one who follows sattva. O tiger among men! It is certain that he will be emancipated. A man who is devoted to the brahman and is attached to Narayana is known and spoken of as a *sattvika* person. Such a person thinks of Purushottama and obtains learning. He is always devoted to Narayana and is single-minded in his faith. There are some learned people who desire emancipation. Hari, who looks after yoga and *kshema*,[1335] eliminates their thirst.[1336] Know that if a man is born and Madhusudana looks favourably at him, he is sattvika and his emancipation is certain. The dharma of those who are single-minded is equal to sankhya and yoga. A person who has Narayana in his soul obtains liberation and goes to the supreme destination. Such a person cheerfully comprehends Narayana. O

[1335]Yoga means getting what has not been obtained. Kshema means protecting what has been obtained.

[1336]That is, desire.

king! However, unless he so desires,[1337] knowledge is not awakened. It is said that a nature that has rajas and tamas is confused. O lord of the earth! A person with these traits in his soul is born again. If a person possesses these attributes of attachment, Hari does not look at him himself. If a man is immersed in rajas and tamas, he is born again and it is Brahma, the grandfather of the worlds, who looks at him. O supreme among kings! The gods and the rishis desire sattva. However, sattva is subtle and those who deviate from it are said to undergo transformations.'[1338]

Janamejaya asked, 'How can a man with transformations advance towards Purushottama?'

Vaishampayana replied, 'Purusha is united with the subtlety of sattva. It is united with the three syllables.[1339] Abstaining from acts, a man goes to the one who is the twenty-fifth. He is the single one who has been spoken about in sankhya, in yoga, in the Vedas, in the *Aranyaka*s, in the other limbs and in the doctrines of pancharatra. Those who are single-minded in their dharma go to Narayana, the paramatman. O king! The waves of the ocean seem to retreat from it, only to return to it again. In that way, the great waves of knowledge again merge into Narayana. O relative of the Yadus![1340] I have spoken to you about satvata dharma. O descendant of the Bharata lineage! If you can, follow it properly. This is what the extremely fortunate Narada told my preceptor, about the single-minded mendicants of Shvetadvipa, who followed the immutable one. Vyasa affectionately recounted it to Dharma's intelligent son.[1341] Passed down from my preceptor, I have also told you about it. O supreme among kings! This dharma is extremely difficult to follow. There are others who are so confused that they do not follow it. It is Krishna, the creator of the worlds, who confuses them in this way. O lord of the universe! That is because he is also the reason behind destruction.'

[1337]Unless Narayana desires.

[1338]Even gods and rishis can deviate and undergo transformations of growth and destruction.

[1339]Om, written as AUM.

[1340]Through Subhadra, Janamejaya was descended from the Yadavas.

[1341]Yudhishthira.

Chapter 1665(337)

Janamejaya asked, 'O brahmana rishi! Sankhya, yoga, pancharatra, the Vedas and the *Aranyakas*—these kinds of knowledge are prevalent in the worlds. O sage! Do they speak about the same thing, or different things? Tell me what I have asked and in due order, describe the rites that they prescribe.'

Vaishampayana replied, 'A son was born to maharshi Parashara and Gandhavati in the midst of an island.[1342] He is infinite and knows a lot. He is the knowledge that dispels darkness. I bow down before him. Learned ones speak about his power and say that he is the sixth one, even before the grandfather.[1343] Dvaipayana was the single son[1344] who was born as part of Narayana. He is the great store of the Vedas. He is immensely powerful and was born at that time of darkness.[1345] Narayana, the great store of the brahman, created the generous and energetic one as his son. Thus, the great-souled Vyasa is actually ancient and without birth.'

Janamejaya said, 'O best among brahmanas! It has been said that, earlier, Vasishtha had a son named Shakti and that Shakti's son was Parashara. Parashara's son was the sage Krishna Dvaipayana. However, you have also spoken about him as Narayana's son. Did the infinitely energetic Vyasa have an earlier birth? Tell me about that excellent birth, when he was born from Narayana.'

Vaishampayana replied, 'My preceptor desired to know about the purport of the Vedas. He was devoted to dharma and was the store of austerities. Devoted to knowledge, he spent some time on the slopes of the Himalayas. Having composed the account of the Mahabharata, the intelligent one was exhausted and performed austerities. O king! At that time, we tended to him—Sumantu,

[1342]Vedavyasa.

[1343]The preceding five probably mean Purusha, Vasudeva, Aniruddha, Pradyumna and Samkarshana.

[1344]His parents had no other son.

[1345]The sage Parashara created mist and darkness when Parashara and Satyavati were together.

Jaimini, Paila, extremely firm in his vows, I as the fourth disciple, and Shuka, Vyasa's son. Vyasa was thus surrounded by five excellent disciples. He was resplendent on the slope of the Himalayas, like the lord of the demons,[1346] surrounded by the demons. After having been instructed about the Vedas, the Vedangas, the Mahabharata and all their meanings, we worshipped the generous one, when he was reflecting in his mind. In the course of the conversation, we asked that supreme among brahmanas to tell us about the meanings of the Vedas, the meanings of the Mahabharata and about Narayana's birth. The one who knew the truth first told us about the meanings of the Vedas and the meanings of the Mahabharata. He next told us about his birth from Narayana. "Listen to this excellent account about the birth of a supreme rishi. O brahmanas! Through my austerities, I got to know about my ancient birth. This was the seventh cycle of creation[1347] that resulted from the lotus. The great yogi, Narayana, is free from good and bad deeds. From his navel, he created the infinitely radiant Brahma, his son. When he manifested himself, he spoke these words. 'You have been born from my navel. You are the lord who will create different categories of subjects. O Brahma! Create many kinds of subjects, those who are learned and those who are dumb.' Having been thus addressed, he was reluctant and anxiously thought about this in his mind. He bowed down before Hari, the lord and god who is the granter of boons, and said, 'O lord of the gods! I bow down before you. But where do I possess the strength to create subjects? O god! I do not possess the requisite wisdom. You decide what is to be done next.' Having been thus addressed, the illustrious one who is the creator of beings,[1348] disappeared. The intelligent one, the lord of the gods and supreme among intelligent ones, began to think. The lord Hari resorted to yoga and used this yoga to make the goddess of intelligence present herself before him. Using the power of yoga, the undecaying lord then addressed the virtuous and powerful goddess of intelligence. 'O goddess of intelligence! Enter Brahma, so

[1346]Shiva.

[1347]The seventh manvantara.

[1348]This means Narayana.

that the objective of creating the worlds become successful.' Having been thus instructed by the lord, the goddess of intelligence swiftly entered him. Hari saw that he was united with intelligence and again spoke to him. 'Create different categories of subjects.' Saying this, the illustrious one vanished from there and in an instant, returned to his one state of divinity. He entered Prakriti and remained united with her. However, the intelligent one again began to think along the following lines. 'Brahma Parameshthi will create all the subjects—daityas, danavas, gandharvas and large numbers of rakshasas. The ascetic, the earth, will become burdened with those who have been born. The earth will be full of many strong daityas, danavas and rakshasas. They will engage in austerities and obtain excellent boons. Insolent at having obtained these different kinds of boons, they will obstruct the large numbers of gods and the rishis, stores of austerities. It is proper that I should devise a method for removing this burden. Therefore, in different forms, I will progressively be born on earth. I will chastise the wicked and protect the virtuous. The virtuous and ascetic earth will then be able to bear the burden. In the form of a serpent,[1349] I will hold her up from below. Thus held up by me, she will hold up the universe, with its mobile and immobile objects. So that I can save the earth, I will have incarnations.' The illustrious Madhusudana thought in this way. 'I will create and manifest in different kinds of forms—boar, man-lion, dwarf and human. I will slay the insolent enemies of the gods.' After this, the creator of the universe uttered the sound of '*Bho*'.[1350] This sound echoed and Sarasvat manifested himself. This son, who manifested himself from the lord's speech, came to be known as Apantaratama.[1351] He was truthful, firm in his vows and knew about the past, the present and the future. He bowed his head down before the original and immutable god, who told him, 'O supreme among intelligent ones! Your task is the recounting of the Vedas and the sacred texts. O sage! You should act in accordance with these instructions of mine.' In the

[1349]As Shesha.

[1350]Loosely translated as 'Hello'.

[1351]This means someone whose darkness (ignorance) has been destroyed.

manvantara known as Svayambhuva, he[1352] collated the Vedas. The illustrious Hari was pleased with his deeds, his tormenting himself with austerities, his self-restraint and rituals.

'"The illustrious one said, 'O son! In each manvantara, you will thus establish the way of the worlds. O brahmana! You will not deviate and you will always be unassailable. The Kurus, known as the Bharatas, will be descended from you. They will be great-souled kings who are famous on earth. They will be born from you. But there will be a dissension within the lineage. O supreme among brahmanas! Barring you, all the others will destroy themselves. Then too, engaged in austerities, you will classify the Vedas. In that dark age, you will have a dark complexion. You will know about different kinds of dharma and the diverse tasks that have to be performed. However, despite engaging in austerities, you will not be freed from attachment. Your son will be free from attachment and will be like the paramatman. This will happen through the grace of Maheshvara and my words will not be falsified. Vasishtha is spoken of as the intelligent son who has been born from the grandfather's mental powers. He is a store of austerities and his radiance transcends that of the sun. A maharshi named Parashara will be descended from him and he will be extremely powerful. He will be supreme among those who are storehouses of the Vedas. He will be a great ascetic and will immerse himself in austerities. He will be your father. There will be a maiden who will dwell in her father's house. While still a virgin, she will have you as her son, through that rishi.[1353] You will know about the past, the present and the future, and all your doubts will be dispelled. The progress of thousands of yugas will pass before you. Through my instructions, you will witness all of them and be engaged in austerities. O sage! I am without beginning and without end. When thousands of yugas have passed, you will again see me, with the chakra in my hand. O sage! All this will happen to you because of your meditations and my words will not be falsified. Shanaishchara[1354]

[1352]Apantaratama.

[1353]The sage Parashara restored Satyavati's virginity.

[1354]Literally, the one who moves slowly, Shani or Saturn.

will be Surya's son and will be a great Manu. In that manvantara, because of my grace, you will be superior to the saptarshis. O son! There is no doubt about this.'"

'Vyasa said, "The virtuous rishi, Sarasvata Apantaratama, heard these words spoken by the lord. Through the favours of the god Harimedha, I am the one who was born as Apantaratama. I was born through Hari's commands. I was again born as the famous one who is a descendant of the lineage of Vasishtha.[1355] I have thus told you about my earlier birth, whereby I was born through Narayana's favours and as Narayana's part. I performed extremely great austerities. I performed terrible austerities. O best among intelligent ones! In ancient times, I performed excellent meditation. O sons! I have told you everything that you asked me about, about my earlier birth and my future. You are devoted to me and I am affectionate towards you."'

Vaishampayana continued, 'O king! I have thus told you how my preceptor was born earlier. Vyasa was cheerful in his mind and when he was asked, this is what he said. Listen. O rajarshi! Know that there are many kinds of knowledge—sankhya, yoga, pancharatra and *pashupata*. The great rishi, Kapila, is said to be the exponent of sankhya. The ancient Hiranyagarba, and no one else, is known as the exponent of yoga. Apantaratama is said to be the teacher of the Vedas. Some speak of him as the rishi Prachinagarbha. Brahma's son, Shiva Shrikantha, the lord of the demons and Uma's consort, is said to be the attentive exponent of the knowledge known as pashupata. The illustrious one[1356] himself is the exponent of all of pancharatra. O best among kings! All of these are considered as the exponents of knowledge. O lord of the earth! All the sacred texts and all knowledge speaks of devotion to the lord Narayana. Those who are enveloped in darkness do not comprehend this. There are learned ones who have propounded the sacred texts. They said that there is nothing other than faith in the rishi Narayana. There is no doubt that Hari always resides in everything. However, Madhava

[1355]That is, Krishna Dvaipayana Vedavyasa himself.

[1356]Narayana.

does not reside in those in whom doubt is strong and who dispute. O king! There are those who know about pancharatra and follow it properly. They are single-minded in their devotion and merge into Hari. O king! Sankhya and yoga are eternal and so are all the Vedas. All the rishis have said that the ancient Narayana pervades everything in the universe. Everything that is done in all the worlds, good or bad, depends on him. All forms of knowledge flow from him. He is in the firmament, the sky, the earth and the water.'

Chapter 1666(338)

Janamejaya asked, 'O brahmana! Are there many Purushas or is there only one? Which is the best Purusha and what is said to be the origin of everything?'

Vaishampayana replied, 'In the reflections of sankhya and yoga, people have spoken about many Purushas. O extender of the Kuru lineage! They do not wish to accept that there is a single Purusha. All these many Purushas are held to have a single origin. That is explained as the single Purusha in the universe, possessing superior qualities. I will first bow down before my preceptor, the infinitely energetic Vyasa. He is a supreme rishi, controlled and united with austerities, deserving to be worshipped. O king! This *purushasukta* exists in all the Vedas.[1357] It is famous as both *rita* and satya.[1358] The lion among rishis[1359] thought about this. O descendant of the Bharata lineage! Kapila and the other rishis thought about adhyatma and devoted themselves to the contradictions spoken about in the sacred texts. Vyasa brought all this together and spoke

[1357]The famous purushasukta is 10.90 in the Rig Veda and also occurs in the other three Vedas.

[1358]Rita and satya both mean truth, but there is a subtle difference. Satya means truth vis-à-vis the external world and rita means truth vis-à-vis what is internal.

[1359]Vyasa.

about a single Purusha. Through the favours of that infinitely energetic one, I will tell you about the truth. O lord of the earth! In this connection, there is an ancient history about a conversation between Brahma and Tryambaka. O king! In the midst of the ocean of milk, there is a supreme mountain, known by the name of Vaijayanta. Its hue is like that of gold. Thinking about the progress of adhyatma, the god[1360] used to go there alone. He always went there from his resplendent abode and spent time on Vaijayanta. The intelligent one with the four faces was seated there. His son, Shiva, born from his forehead, arrived there. Travelling as he willed through the sky, the three-eyed lord of yoga saw him seated there. From the sky, the lord quickly dropped down on the summit of the mountain. He cheerfully presented himself before his superior and worshipped his feet. On seeing him prostrate at his feet, Prajapati, the single lord, raised him with his left hand. Having met his son after a long time, the illustrious one welcomed him and said, "O mighty-armed one! Welcome. It is through good fortune that you have come before me. O son! Is everything well? You are always engaged in studying and austerities. You are always engaged in fierce austerities. That is the reason I am asking you about those."

'Rudra answered, "O illustrious one! Through your favours, all is well with my studies and austerities. The entire universe is also without decay. O illustrious one! It has been a long time since I saw you in your radiant abode. That is the reason I have come to this mountain, where your feet are resting now. Since you have decided to come here alone, I am curious. O grandfather! There must be a grave reason why you have done that. Your excellent abode is free from hunger and thirst. It is always inhabited by gods, asuras, the infinitely radiant rishis and gandharvas and apsaras. Why have you given that up and come alone to this supreme mountain?"

'Brahma said, "Vaijayanta, this supreme mountain, is always frequented by me. Here, with concentration in my mind, I think of the great Purusha."

[1360]Brahma.

'Rudra replied, "O Brahma! You are Svayambhu and you have created many Purushas. O Brahma! You are creating others too. But there is only a single great Purusha. O Brahma! Whom are you thinking about? Who is that Purushottama?[1361] I have great curiosity and a doubt about this. Tell me."

'Brahma said, "O son! As has been stated by you, there are many Purushas. But this one cannot be seen and transcends all the others. I am telling you that this single Purusha is alone the foundation. That single one is said to be the origin of the many Purushas. That Purusha is the universe. He is supreme and extremely great. He is devoid of qualities. Devoid of qualities, they[1362] enter the eternal one."'

Chapter 1667(339)

'Brahma said, "O son! Hear about the eternal and undecaying Purusha. He is said to be without destruction and immeasurable. He goes everywhere. O virtuous one! I, you, nor anyone else, can see him. He is this universe, with qualities and without qualities. It is said that he can be seen through wisdom. He is without a body. But he also dwells in every body. Though he dwells in bodies, he is not touched by any of the acts committed by them. He is in my atman, in yours and in that of others, conscious of the bodies. He is a witness to everything, but cannot be grasped by anyone. The universe is his head. The universe is his arms. The universe is his feed, his eyes and his nose. As he wills, he alone cheerfully wanders among all the kshetras.[1363] The kshetras are the bodies, the seeds of everything, good or bad.[1364] Since he knows them through the yoga of his atman, he is known as kshetrajna. No creature can discern his

[1361]Literally, the supreme Purusha.

[1362]The other Purushas.

[1363]Bodies.

[1364]Acts are seeds.

coming and going, though this progress is indicated in the ordinances of sankhya and yoga. Even if I think about his progress, I will be unable to comprehend that supreme progress. According to my knowledge, I will tell you about that eternal Purusha. His alone is the greatness. There is said to be only one Purusha. That single and eternal one should be praised by the words of Mahapurusha.[1365] There is one fire, but it blazes in different kinds of kindling. There is one sun. There are many austerities, but their origins are the same. There is one wind, but it blows in many ways in the world. There is one great ocean, though there are many sources of water. There is one Purusha, devoid of qualities. The universe is his form and it also enters Purusha, devoid of qualities. One should abandon all the qualities. One should discard all acts, good and bad. One should give up both truth and falsehood. In this way, one should be divested of qualities. One can then know the one who is unthinkable. He has four subtle forms.[1366] An ascetic who roams around in this way can advance towards the lord, Purusha. There are some learned ones who desire him as the paramatman. There are others who have thought about adhyatma and think of him as the single atman within their own selves. The paramatman is always spoken of as one who is devoid of qualities. He is known as Narayana. He is the Purusha who is inside all atmans. Like water on the leaf of a lotus, he is not touched by any acts. He is sometimes engaged in acts.[1367] He is sometimes freed from bonds and united with moksha. He is sometimes united with the accumulation of the seventeen.[1368] In this way, in due order, Purusha is spoken of in many ways. Everything in the worlds has a refuge in him. He is the supreme object of knowledge. He is the one who knows and he is also what is to be known. He is the thinker and the object of thought. He is the eater and the object that is eaten. He is the one who smells and the object that is smelt. He is the one

[1365]The great Purusha.

[1366]Aniruddha, Pradyumna, Samkarshana and Vasudeva.

[1367]In bodies.

[1368]In bodies. The seventeen are the five senses, the five organs of action, five kinds of breaths of life, mind and intelligence.

who touches and the object that is touched. He is the seer and the object that is seen. He is the hearer and the object that is heard. He is the one who learns and he is the object of learning. He is with qualities and without qualities. He has been spoken of as Pradhana, the accumulation of qualities. He is always eternal and immutable. He is the foundation and the prime cause behind Dhatri.[1369] Brahmanas speak of him as Aniruddha.[1370] There are virtuous and beneficial acts in the world, sanctioned by the Vedas. All these flow from him. All the gods and sages, righteous and controlled, take their places on the altar and offer him a share in the sacrifices. I am Brahma. I am the first lord of subjects. I have been generated from him and all of you have been generated from me. O son! I am the origin of all mobile and immobile objects in the universe, and all the Vedas and their mysteries. Purusha is divided into four parts and sports as he wishes. The illustrious one is awakened through his own knowledge. O son! I have thus told you exactly what you have asked. I have described to you the knowledge of sankhya and yoga."'

Chapter 1668(340)

'Yudhishthira said, "O grandfather! You have spoken about dharma and the sacred dharma of moksha that one must seek refuge with. Among the different ashramas, you should now tell me what is the best kind of dharma."

'Bhishma replied, "If followed, all kinds of dharma lead to heaven and yield the fruits of truth. There are many doors to dharma and no rites in the world are fruitless. O supreme among the Bharata lineage! Whoever determines that he should follow one particular mode, decides that all the others are not worth knowing. O tiger among men! In this connection, you should listen to an account. In

[1369]In the sense of the creator.

[1370]Literally, the one who is without obstruction or restraint.

ancient times, Narada, the rishi of the gods, and Shakra spoke about this. O king! Narada, the rishi of the gods, had obtained success and was revered by the three worlds. He progressively roamed around the worlds, like a wind that is not restrained. O great archer! On one occasion, he went to the abode of the king of the gods. The great Indra honoured him well and welcomed him. After some time, when he was seated, Shachi's lord[1371] asked him, 'O brahmana rishi! O unblemished one! Have you seen anything wonderful? O brahmana rishi! You wander amidst the mobile and immobile objects of the three worlds, always curious. You have obtained success and are like a witness to what transpires. O devarshi! There is nothing in the worlds that is unknown to you. Tell me about anything that you might have heard, felt or seen.' O king! Narada, supreme among eloquent ones, was seated. At this, he told Indra of the gods about an extensive account. I will tell it to you as that supreme among brahmanas described it. He recounted this account when he was asked. You too should listen to this."'

Chapter 1669(341)

'Bhishma said, "O best among the Kuru lineage! In an excellent city named Mahapadma, on the southern banks of the Ganga, there lived a brahmana who was controlled. He was amiable and was born in the lineage of the moon. All his doubts had been dispelled and he knew the path he should pursue. He was always devoted to dharma and had conquered anger. He was always content and had conquered his senses. He was always engaged in non-violence. He was truthful and was revered by the virtuous. He obtained riches through proper means and through his own efforts. His conduct was good. He possessed many relatives and kin. There were honoured friends who

[1371]Shachi is Indra's wife.

sought refuge with him. He was born in a noble and great family and resorted to the best of conduct. O king! On seeing that he had many sons, who were engaged in the extensive tasks of dharma that the family required, he thought about a dharma that would be superior to this. He thought there were three kinds of dharma—that spoken about in the Vedas, that laid down in the sacred texts[1372] and the dharma practised by virtuous people. Which are the auspicious tasks that I should perform? What will bring benefit? What should I resort to? He always thought about such things and could never arrive at a conclusion. While he thus reflected on dharma, a guest arrived at his house. He was also an extremely controlled brahmana and was devoted to the supreme. He honoured him well, in accordance with the proper rites that have been laid down. When he was rested and seated, he spoke these words."'[1373]

Chapter 1670(342)

'"The brahmana said, 'O unblemished one! Because of the weight of your words, I have become attached to you.[1374] You have become my friend. Listen to me. I will tell you something. O Indra among brahmanas! I have handed over the dharma of garhasthya to my son. O brahmana! I now want to be established on the path of supreme dharma. What should I do? I have based my atman on the atman[1375] and wish to be established in the atman. I do not wish to do anything that leads to bondage to the ordinary qualities. So far, all of my life has been spent on acquiring the fruit of a son. Therefore, I desire provisions for the world hereafter. The

[1372]Other than the Vedas. A distinction is presumably being drawn between shruti and *smriti*.

[1373]That is, the host addressed the guest.

[1374]There is a break in continuity, because the guest hasn't said anything, beyond the expected words of salutation.

[1375]The jivatman and the paramatman respectively.

virtuous ones in this world desire the supreme that will enable them to cross the hereafter. That resolution has been awakened in me. Where will I obtain the raft of dharma? I have heard that people are confused in this world and even those with sattva in their souls find it difficult to emerge. Above the heads of all subjects, I have seen the garlands, flags and standards of dharma held aloft. My mind no longer finds delight in time spent on pleasure. I have seen that mendicants desire the hereafter. O guest! You possess the strength of intelligence and know the truth about the purport of dharma. Engage me in that.'"

'Bhishma continued, "The guest heard the words of the one who desired to pursue dharma. The wise one replied in gentle and sweet words. 'I am also confused and that is my wish too. I cannot make up my mind. There are many doors to heaven. Some praise moksha, other brahmanas the fruits of sacrifices. Some resort to the dharma of vanaprastha, others resort to garhasthya. Some resort to the dharma of kings, others to the fruits of the atman. Some resort to serving preceptors, others speak words in favour of yama. Some have gone to heaven by serving their mothers and fathers. Others have gone to heaven through non-violence, and still others through truth. Some have advanced towards battle, were slain and have gone to heaven. Others became successful through the practice of the vow of *unchha*[1376] and have advanced along the path that leads to heaven. Some have been engaged in studying and have been devoted to the auspicious vows of the Vedas. Intelligent ones have gone to heaven by being content and conquering their senses. There are others who were upright, but were killed by people who were deceitful. There are upright ones, pure in their souls, who have been established in the vault of the sky.[1377] In this way, in this world, there are many doors to heaven that have been opened. Thus, my mind is also anxious, like a light cloud that is driven by the wind.'"'

[1376]There are grains left after a crop has been harvested, or after grain has been milled. If one subsists on these leftovers, that is known as unchhavritti.

[1377]Meaning heaven.

Chapter 1671(343)

'"The guest said, 'O brahmana! I will instruct you in accordance with the sacred texts. I will tell you the purport of what I have learned from my preceptor. Listen. In an earlier cycle of creation, the wheel of dharma was set in motion in Naimisha, on the banks of the Gomati. There is a city of the serpents there. O bull among brahmanas! All the residents of heaven had assembled there and had performed a sacrifice. There, the supreme king, Mandhata, had surpassed Indra. The great Padmanabha dwells there. He has dharma in his soul and follows it in deeds, sight and words. The immensely fortunate resident is famous by the name of Padma. O bull among brahmanas! He pleases creatures in three different ways—words, deeds and thoughts. He protects everything through his insight and controls wicked people through the four techniques of conciliation, gifts, dissension and chastisement. You should go and ask him about the desired techniques. When you bow down before him, he will show you what supreme dharma is. The intelligent serpent is accomplished in all the sacred texts and is attentive towards guests. He possesses the rare and desired nine qualities.[1378] His nature is such that he is always immersed in water.[1379] He is always engaged in studying. His conduct is excellent and he practises austerities and self-control. His inclinations are towards performing sacrifices and donations. He is forgiving and his conduct is supreme. He is truthful in speech and without malice. He always resorts to good conduct. He eats what is left.[1380] He is pleasant in speech. He has discarded deceit. He does what is best and is grateful. He is without enmity and is engaged in the welfare of beings. He has been born in a lineage that is as noble as the waters in a lake in the midst of the Ganga.'"'

[1378]The nine qualities of rajas are faith, generosity, enjoyment, enterprise, desire, anger, pride, malice and calumny. It is not obvious what the nine qualities mentioned in the text are. But it could be a reference to the nine qualities of rajas, some of which exist and some of which are absent in the serpent.

[1379]This is also difficult to understand. Perhaps it means that he performs rites in the water. Perhaps it is a reference to serpents dwelling in the water.

[1380]After gods, ancestors, guests and servants have eaten.

Chapter 1672(344)

'"The brahmana said, 'I have heard your words of reassurance. It is as if a load has been taken off the back of someone who is bearing a great load. Your words have delighted me—like a tired person when he lies down, like an exhausted person when he finds a seat, like a thirsty person when he finds a drink, like a hungry person when he finds food, like a guest who is given the desired food at the right time, like an aged person who obtains a beloved son after a long time and like the sight of a beloved one has been thinking about. I have been like a hesitant person, casting his eye towards the sky. Your words of wisdom have served to instruct me. I will certainly do what you have asked me to. O virtuous one! Spend this night with me. In the morning, happily go wherever you wish to. The illustrious Surya is gradually withdrawing his rays.'"

'Bhishma continued, "O destroyer of enemies! At this, the guest accepted his hospitality. He spent the night with the brahmana. They had a conversation that was full of words of dharma. They spent the night in this way and it was almost as if it was day. When it was morning, the brahmana honoured the guest, according to his capacity, and desired to accomplish his own objective. The brahmana made up his mind to accomplish dharma. The one who knew about dharma took the permission of his relatives. As instructed, at the right time, resolving to perform good deeds, he set out for the residence of the Indra among serpents."'

Chapter 1673(345)

'Bhishma said, "Progressively, he passed through many wonderful groves, places of pilgrimage and lakes and arrived before a sage. The brahmana asked him about the serpent the other brahmana had spoken about. Having been duly instructed, he proceeded again. He was clear about his intention and went to the residence of the famous serpent. Having reached, he exclaimed, 'I am here. Is there anyone here?' The serpent's wife was devoted to her husband. She was beautiful and devoted to dharma. She came and showed herself to the brahmana. She was devoted to dharma and following the prescribed rites, honoured him. She said, 'Welcome. What can I do for you?'

'"The brahmana replied, 'I was exhausted. But your gentle words of reverence have swept that away. I wish to see your lord, the supreme serpent. This is my supreme task. This is the fruit that I desire. That is the reason I have come here now, to the serpent's abode.'

'"The serpent's wife said, 'O honourable one! He has gone for a month, to bear Surya's chariot. O brahmana! There is no doubt that he will return in fifteen days and show himself to you. I have told you the reason why the noble one is not here. That being the case, what else can I do for you? Tell me that.'

'"The brahmana replied, 'O virtuous one! That is the reason why I decided to come here. O goddess! I will wait for him to return and dwell in that great forest. When he returns, tell him I have come here, anxious to see him. You should also tell me when he returns. O beautiful one! Till then, I will reside on the banks of the Gomati. I will spend the time, following the practice of living on a restrained diet.'"

'Bhishma said, "The brahmana repeatedly entreated the serpent's wife in this way. The bull among brahmanas then went to the banks of the river."'

Chapter 1674(346)

'Bhishma said, "O best among men! The serpents were distressed when the ascetic brahmana began to dwell there, without any food. All the serpent's relatives, including his brother, son and wife, assembled and went to where the brahmana was. They saw him in a lonely spot along the riverbank, controlled in his vows. Without any food, the brahmana was seated, devoted to meditation. All of them approached the brahmana and worshipped him properly. The relatives wished to extend hospitality and spoke these words. 'O one rich in austerities! Since you arrived here, this is the sixth day. O one who is devoted to dharma! But you do not desire any food. We have come and have presented ourselves before you. All of us belong to the household and it is our duty to extend hospitality to a guest. O supreme among brahmanas! O brahmana! You should take whatever food you wish to have—roots, fruits, leaves or water. As a virtuous person, you are dwelling in the forest, without any food. All of us, old and young, are afflicted and face a conflict of dharma. None of us has killed a foetus. None of us is one from whom food cannot be received. None of us utters a falsehood. There is no one in our family who eats before serving to gods, guests and relatives.'

'"The brahmana replied, 'Because of your entreaty, it is almost as if I have eaten. Eight nights are still left for the serpent to return. If the serpent does not return after eight nights are over, then I will indeed eat. But until then, I have this vow, for the serpent's sake. You should not be tormented on this account. Go wherever you have come from. My vow is for him and you should not do anything that causes it to be violated.'"

'Bhishma said, "The serpents then took leave of the brahmana. O bull among men! Having accomplished their objective, they returned to their own houses."'

Chapter 1675(347)

'Bhishma said, "When those many lunar days were over,[1381] the serpent completed his task. He took Vivasvat's[1382] permission and returned to his own house. On seeing that he had arrived, his wife gave him water to clean his feet and performed other similar

[1381]When the fortnight was over.

[1382]The sun's.

tasks. The virtuous one approached him and the serpent asked, 'O fortunate one! I hope you have been attentive in tending to the gods and the guests, as used to be the case when I was here. I hope you followed the ordinances I told you about. The intelligence of women is not straightforward and is often false towards accomplishing an objective. O one with the excellent hips! I hope you have not violated the norms of dharma in my absence.'

'"The serpent's wife replied, 'The duty of disciples is to serve the preceptor, that of brahmanas to be devoted to the Vedas, that of servants to follow the words of their master and that of kings to protect people. It is said that the dharma of kshatriyas is to protect all creatures and that of vaishyas is to support sacrifices and attend to guests. The task of shudras is to serve brahmanas, kshatriyas and vaishyas. O Indra among serpents! The dharma of householders is to be engaged in the welfare of all beings. Restrained diet and the constant observance of vows, in the proper order, are dharma. In particular, there is an association between dharma and the senses.[1383] Whom do I belong to? Where have I come from? Who am I? Who belongs to me? If a person is devoted to the state of pursuing moksha, it is necessary that he should always ask these questions. It is said that being devoted to the husband is the supreme dharma for a wife. O Indra among the serpents! I have learnt the truth about this through your instructions. You are always devoted to dharma and I also know about dharma. Why will I abandon the path of virtue and advance along an uneven road? O immensely fortunate one! There has been no decrease in the dharma with which I have worshipped the gods. I have always been attentively engaged in tending to the guests. Fifteen days ago, a brahmana arrived here. He desired to meet you and has not divulged his objective to me. He is waiting on the banks of the Gomati, anxious to meet you. The brahmana is rigid in his vows and is seated there, concentrated on the brahman. O Indra among serpents! O supreme among serpents! I pacified him and told him that when you arrived before me, I would sent you to him. O immensely wise one! Having heard this, you

[1383]Dharma requires control over the senses.

should go there. O one who hears with the eyes![1384] You should show yourself to him.'"'

Chapter 1676(348)

'"The serpent asked, 'O one with the beautiful smiles! In the form of a brahmana, whom did you see? Was that brahmana only a human, or was he a god? O illustrious one! Among men, who is capable of seeing me, or would desire that? Would anyone like that speak and leave words of instruction that I should go and see him? O beautiful one! Among the number of gods, asuras and devarshis, the serpents are certainly immensely valorous. They are the descendants of Surasa and are swift.[1385] They deserve to be honoured and are the granters of boons. We deserve to be followed by others. In particular, it has been heard that men follow us for riches.'

'"The serpent's wife replied, 'O one who subsists on air! From his uprightness, I know that he is not a god. O one who is extremely wrathful! I know that he is devoted to you alone. He desires to accomplish some task through you and is waiting, like the chataka bird for water.[1386] Like the bird which loves the monsoon, he desires to meet you. He should be protected against any misfortune and anxiety. A person like you, with noble birth, should not disregard someone who has come before you. You should cast aside your natural anger and go and see him. You should not cause torment to yourself by destroying his hopes. If a king or a prince does not wipe away the tears of someone who has come with hope, he commits the sin of having killed a foetus. Knowledge is the fruit of silence. Great fame results from giving. Through eloquence and truthful words,

[1384]*Naga*s were believed to hear with their eyes.

[1385]Daksha's daughters, Kadru and Surasa, were married to the sage Kashyapa. While accounts vary, usually Kadru is described as the mother of serpents (nagas) and Surasa as the mother of snakes (*sarpa*s).

[1386]The chataka bird waits for rain.

one obtains greatness in the hereafter. Through donating land, one obtains an end that is lauded by all the ashramas. Even if the riches obtained have been destroyed in this way, one gets fruits. If one desires benefit, one must perform all the desirable acts. One will then never go to hell. Those who are learned about dharma say this.'

'"The serpent said, 'O virtuous one! Because of the great pride associated with the sinful species that I have been born into, I possessed insolence and resolved to yield to anger. But that has been burnt down by the fire of your words. O virtuous one! I do not see any darkness that is greater than being consumed by anger. Serpents are said to be especially prone to this. This is the sin that the powerful Dashagriva[1387] fell prey to. He rivalled Shakra and was slain by Rama in the battle. On hearing that Rama had entered the inner quarters of the palace to seize the calf, the sons of Kartavirya were also afflicted by this sin and were slain.[1388] The immensely strong Kartavirya was like the thousand-eyed one.[1389] However, he was slain in a battle by Rama, Jamadagni's son. Because of your words, I have controlled my anger, which is the enemy of austerities and destroys all benefit. You are large-eyed and possess all the qualities. I am indeed praiseworthy, since I have someone like you as my wife. I will therefore go where that brahmana is waiting. In every way, I will speak appropriate words to him. He will not depart as one unsuccessful.'"'

Chapter 1677(349)

'Bhishma said, "The lord of the serpents advanced towards the brahmana, mentally thinking about the task that might have

[1387]Ravana.

[1388]Kartavirya Arjuna was a king of the Haihaya kingdom. Parashurama's father was Jamadagni. In one version of the story, Kartavirya Arjuna visited Jamadagni's hermitage and stole a calf. He and his sons were then killed by Parashurama.

[1389]Indra.

brought him there. O lord of men! The Indra among serpents was intelligent and devoted to dharma. Having arrived there, he addressed him in naturally pleasant words. 'I am addressing you peacefully. You should not be enraged with me. What is the task that has brought you here? What is your purpose? O brahmana! I have arrived before you and am asking you affectionately. On the banks of the Gomati, whom do you desire to worship?'

'"The brahmana replied, 'Know me to be Dharmaranya, foremost among brahmanas. I have come here to see the serpent Padmanabha. I have some work with him. I have heard that he has gone away, so I am waiting nearby for him, like a person waiting for a relative, or a farmer waiting for the rain. I wish to dispel his hardships and do what is beneficial for him. Therefore, without any difficulty, I am engaged in yoga here, united with the brahman.'

'"The serpent said, 'O virtuous one! Your conduct is beneficial and you are devoted to righteous people. O immensely fortunate one! I have heard that you bear supreme affection towards him. O brahmana rishi! I am that serpent and you have now met me. What is your command? Tell me what I can do to bring you pleasure. I have heard from my relatives that you had come here. O brahmana! That is the reason I have myself come here to meet you. Now that you have come here, you will be successful in your pursuits. O foremost among brahmanas! You can instruct me to be engaged in whatever pursuit you wish. In particular, all of us have been won over by your qualities. You have abandoned your own welfare and are engaged in seeking ours.'

'"The brahmana replied, 'O immensely fortunate one! I have come here with a desire to meet you. O serpent! I do not know the truth and have a desire to ask you about the truth. With my atman based on the atman,[1390] I wish to embark on a path that brings benefit to the atman. O immensely wise one! I am not attached to anything and wish to worship that which is powerful. You are radiant and famous through your qualities, as if you are

[1390]The jivatman and the paramatman respectively.

the origin of the sun's rays. The radiant touch of your inner self now seems to be like the touch of the moon's beams. O one who survives on air! Answer the question that has arisen. Later, I will tell you about the task that has brought me here. I should hear about this from you.'"'

Chapter 1678(350)

'"The brahmana said, 'Vivasvat's[1391] chariot has a single wheel and in due course, you firmly draw it. If you have seen anything wonderful and praiseworthy, you should tell me about it.'

'"The serpent replied, 'Successful sages and the gods reside in his thousand rays, like birds perched on branches during the spring. The great wind emerges from Surya's rays and yawns in the sky. O brahmana! What can be more wonderful than that? The one named Shukra is at his feet.[1392] At the time of the monsoon, he showers down rain from the clouds in the sky. What can be more wonderful than that? For eight months, he sucks up the water through his pure rays and at the right time, showers them down again. What can be more wonderful than that? The atman is always established in specific parts of his energy. That is the seed of the earth and sustains mobile and immobile objects. The mighty-armed god is eternal. He is supreme and without decay.[1393] O brahmana! He is without beginning and without end. What can be more wonderful than that? There is something that is even more extraordinary than all these wonders. Hear about it from me. Residing with Surya, I have seen this in the sparkling sky. In ancient times, at midday, the sun used to scorch the worlds. At that time, an entity was seen to advance towards the sun. It illuminated all the worlds with its own natural

[1391]The sun's.

[1392]Shukra is Venus. This should probably read Shakra, that is, Indra.

[1393]This seems to be a reference to the brahman or paramatman.

radiance. It advanced towards the sun and seemed to splinter the sky in the process. The rays of that energy blazed like oblations poured into the fire. That form was like that of a second sun and could not be looked at. As it advanced, Vivasvat stretched out his hand. As if honouring back in return, the entity also stretched out its right hand. Splintering the firmament, it then entered the solar disc. It mingled with Aditya's energy and in an instant, merged inside it. A doubt arose, because we could no longer distinguish between the two different masses of energy. Of these two, which one was Surya on his chariot? And which was the one that had arrived? Since a doubt arose in us, we asked Ravi,[1394] "O Surya! Who is the one who has advanced through the firmament and has merged into you, like a second self?"'"'

Chapter 1679(351)

'"Surya said, 'O friend! This is not the wind god, an asura or a serpent. This is a sage who has gone to heaven because he has become successful through the vow and conduct of unchha. This brahmana controlled himself and subsisted on roots and fruits. He ate dry leaves. He did not eat, or subsisted only on air. The brahmana obtained favours by reciting hymns from the Rig Veda Samhita. His acts opened the doors to heaven and he went to heaven. O serpent! He was restless in his desire, but he possessed fortitude. He always subsisted only on unchha. This brahmana was always engaged in the welfare of all beings. He was not a god, a gandharva, an asura, or a serpent. But because he was powerful among beings, he obtained the supreme objective.'

'"The serpent said, 'O brahmana! Such was the wonder that I witnessed. He obtained success in his human form and obtained the

[1394]Surya's name.

destination meant for those who are successful. O brahmana! With Surya, he circles around the earth.'"'

Chapter 1680(352)

'"The brahmana said, 'O supreme among serpents! There is no doubt that this is extraordinary. I am extremely delighted. Your sentences are full of meaning and have shown me my path. O virtuous one! O supreme among serpents! May you be fortunate. I will depart. Remember me and send your messengers to find out how I am.'

'"The serpent replied, 'You have not told me about the task that you are attached to. How can you then go? O brahmana! Tell me what is to be done and the reason why you have come here. O bull among brahmanas! Whether you state it or don't state it, take my permission and leave only after you have accomplished your purpose. O brahmana! You should only go after you have honoured me and received my permission. I have become attached to you. You should not go only after having seen me, seated near the root of this tree. O brahmana rishi! This is not how you should depart. O foremost among brahmanas! There is no doubt that you have also become attached to me. O unblemished one! All these people belong to you. In staying with me, what is there to think about?'

'"The brahmana said, 'O immensely wise one! O serpent! It is exactly as you have understood it. The gods are not superior to you in any way. O serpent! I am you and you are me. I, you, and all the creatures can always go everywhere.[1395] O lord of Bhoga![1396] There was a doubt in my mind about the way to accumulate merit. O virtuous one! I have now seen the truth and will follow the vow of unchha. O virtuous one! I have now made up my mind to follow

[1395]Everyone is part of the universal brahman.

[1396]Bhogavati is the capital city of the serpents.

the best method. O fortunate one! O serpent! I have obtained success and I seek your leave.'"'

Chapter 1681(353)

'Bhishma said, "O king! The brahmana honoured the foremost among serpents. He made up his mind to be initiated and desiring this, resorted to Chyavana, of the Bhargava lineage. O king! He[1397] performed the sacraments for him to be initiated into the way of dharma. O king! O Indra among kings! Bhargava also recounted this story in Janaka's abode. He[1398] described this sacred account to the great-souled Narada. O Indra among kings! O foremost among the Bharata lineage! When he was asked, Narada, unblemished in his deeds, recounted this account in the abode of the gods. O lord of the earth! In ancient times, the king of the gods recounted this sacred account to an assembly of the praiseworthy Vasus. O king! When I fought that extremely terrible battle with Rama,[1399] the Vasus recounted this story to me. O lord of the earth! O supreme among those who uphold dharma! Having been asked by you, I have told you the truth about this sacred account, which is full of dharma. O descendant of the Bharata lineage! You asked me about supreme dharma. O king! This account is about a patient person who acted in accordance with dharma and artha. That foremost among brahmanas was firm in his resolution and to accomplish his objective, was instructed by the lord of the serpents. At the extremities of the forest, he practised yama and niyama. He engaged in practices that were sanctioned by those who eat in accordance with unchha."'

This concludes Moksha Dharma Parva and also concludes Shanti Parva.

[1397]Chyavana.

[1398]Janaka.

[1399]Parashurama. The story of the battle between Bhishma and Parashurama has been recounted in Section 60 (Volume 5).

Anushasana Parva

Anushasana means instruction or advice and Anushasana Parva continues with Bhishma's instructions. In the 18-parva classification, Anushasana Parva is the thirteenth. In the 100-parva classification, Anushasana Parva constitutes Sections 87 and 88. Anushasana Parva has 154 chapters. In the numbering of the chapters in Anushasana Parva, the first number is a consecutive one, starting with the beginning of the Mahabharata. And the second number, within brackets, is the numbering of the chapter within Anushasana Parva.

SECTION EIGHTY-SEVEN

Dana Dharma Parva

This parva has 6409 shlokas and 152 chapters.

Chapter 1682(1): 76 shlokas
Chapter 1683(2): 95 shlokas
Chapter 1684(3): 18 shlokas
Chapter 1685(4): 61 shlokas
Chapter 1686(5): 31 shlokas
Chapter 1687(6): 49 shlokas
Chapter 1688(7): 29 shlokas
Chapter 1689(8): 28 shlokas
Chapter 1690(9): 24 shlokas
Chapter 1691(10): 70 shlokas
Chapter 1692(11): 20 shlokas
Chapter 1693(12): 49 shlokas
Chapter 1694(13): 6 shlokas
Chapter 1695(14): 199 shlokas
Chapter 1696(15): 51 shlokas
Chapter 1697(16): 75 shlokas
Chapter 1698(17): 171 shlokas
Chapter 1699(18): 59 shlokas
Chapter 1700(19): 25 shlokas
Chapter 1701(20): 76 shlokas
Chapter 1702(21): 24 shlokas
Chapter 1703(22): 19 shlokas
Chapter 1704(23): 41 shlokas
Chapter 1705(24): 101 shlokas
Chapter 1706(25): 12 shlokas
Chapter 1707(26): 66 shlokas
Chapter 1708(27): 104 shlokas
Chapter 1709(28): 28 shlokas
Chapter 1710(29): 16 shlokas
Chapter 1711(30): 16 shlokas
Chapter 1712(31): 64 shlokas
Chapter 1713(32): 33 shlokas
Chapter 1714(33): 25 shlokas
Chapter 1715(34): 29 shlokas
Chapter 1716(35): 23 shlokas
Chapter 1717(36): 19 shlokas
Chapter 1718(37): 19 shlokas
Chapter 1719(38): 30 shlokas
Chapter 1720(39): 12 shlokas
Chapter 1721(40): 59 shlokas
Chapter 1722(41): 35 shlokas
Chapter 1723(42): 33 shlokas
Chapter 1724(43): 26 shlokas
Chapter 1725(44): 54 shlokas

Chapter 1726(45): 24 shlokas
Chapter 1727(46): 14 shlokas
Chapter 1728(47): 61 shlokas
Chapter 1729(48): 49 shlokas
Chapter 1730(49): 28 shlokas
Chapter 1731(50): 26 shlokas
Chapter 1732(51): 48 shlokas
Chapter 1733(52): 39 shlokas
Chapter 1734(53): 69 shlokas
Chapter 1735(54): 40 shlokas
Chapter 1736(55): 35 shlokas
Chapter 1737(56): 20 shlokas

Dana *means gifts, donations, giving things away in charity. So this section is about the dharma to be followed in dana.*

Chapter 1682(1)

'Yudhishthira said, "O grandfather! It has been said that tranquility is subtle and of many different types. But having acted in this way, there is no peace in my mind. O unblemished one! In this connection, you have spoken in many different ways about peace. Because of what I myself have done, these diverse kinds of peace are not available to me. I can see the terrible wounds left by the arrows on your body. O brave one! Thinking of the wicked deeds I have done, I can find no peace. Blood is flowing from your limbs, like streams from a mountain. O tiger among men! On seeing this, I am suffering, like a lotus during the rains. O grandfather! Could I have done anything more painful than this? Having confronted your enemies in the field of battle, you have now been reduced to this state. This is also what has happened to other kings, with their sons and relatives. Under the subjugation of destiny, we, and the sons of Dhritarashtra, were overcome by anger. We have perpetrated this reprehensible act. O king! What end will we obtain? I am the one who has caused your death. I am the one who has killed the well-wishers. On seeing you in this miserable state, lying down on the ground, I cannot find any peace."

'Bhishma replied, "When something else is responsible, why do you see yourself as the cause? O immensely fortunate one! The course of action is subtle and beyond the grasp of the senses. In this connection, an ancient history is cited, about a conversation between Mrityu,[1] Goutami, Kala,[2] a hunter and a serpent. O Kounteya! There was an aged lady named Goutami and she was full of tranquility. She saw that her son had been bitten by a snake and was unconscious. A hunter named Arjunaka was enraged with the snake. He tied it up with some rope and brought it to Goutami. He said, 'This worst of snakes has killed your son. O illustrious one! Quickly tell me how I should kill it. Should I fling it into the fire, or should I chop it up into bits? This slayer of a child does not deserve to remain alive for much longer.'

'"Goutami said, 'O Arjunaka! You have limited intelligence. Release it. Do not kill it. Virtuous ones who have thought about it do not act so as to impose such a heavy burden on their own selves. They use the boat of dharma to tide over this world, like crossing the waters with a boat. Those who have made themselves heavy with sin sink, like a weapon sinks in the water. By killing it, the one who is dead will not come back to life. What purpose will be achieved by killing this creature? By letting it go, this creature will have life. Why should it be dispatched to the eternal world of death?'

'"The hunter responded, 'I know that you know the difference between good and bad. Everyone bears a great burden. But those words of instruction are for a balanced person only. Therefore, I will kill this inferior snake. For the sake of something immediate, something far away in time must be abandoned. Those who know about objectives realize that it is the immediate that is good and not incessant grieving about what is good and what is bad.[3] That is the reason why it must not be released. Once it has been killed, conquer your sorrow.'

[1]Death.

[2]Time or destiny.

[3]Good or bad behaviour leads to distant fruits in the future. In contrast, killing the snake is an immediately good objective.

'"Goutami said, 'Those who know are not afflicted in this way. The virtuous always seek delight in dharma. The death of this child was predetermined. I cannot go against the power of dharma. Brahmanas are not enraged.[4] Why should I face the pain from anger? O virtuous one! Be mild and forgiving. Let the serpent go.'

'"The hunter replied, 'Killing it will bring inexhaustible gain. An immediate gain and increase in strength is praised. There is an immediate gain. And by killing such a wicked creature, there may even be long-lasting gain.'

'"Goutami asked, 'Why should one kill an enemy who has been captured, when one can obtain peace by releasing that enemy? O amiable one! Why don't you wish to forgive the serpent? What is the reason why you don't want to release it?'

'"The hunter replied, 'O Goutami! There are many who can be protected from this one. A single one should not be protected at the expense of many. Those who know about dharma abandon the vicious. This reptile is wicked and you should allow it to be killed.'

'"Goutami said, 'O hunter! My dead son will not come back to life if this serpent is killed and I will not get him back. Nor do I see any other good from killing it. O hunter! Therefore, save the life of this creature.'

'"The hunter replied, 'After killing Vritra, the king of the gods obtained the best share. By destroying a sacrifice, the god with the trident obtained a share.[5] Therefore, follow the conduct of the gods. Do not entertain any doubts about quickly killing this snake.'"

'Bhishma continued, "The hunter asked the immensely fortunate Goutami to act in this wicked way towards the serpent, but she had no intention of perpetrating that evil act. Meanwhile, tied up in the rope and afflicted, it was facing difficulties. It sighed a little and spoke slowly, in a human voice. 'O foolish Arjunaka! What is the crime that I have committed? I am not independent. I am powerless and Mrityu sent me here. I bit him because of his instructions, not

[4]Obviously, Goutami was a brahmana.

[5]Shiva and Daksha's sacrifice.

because of any anger or desire. O hunter! If there has been any sin, that sin therefore vests with him.'

'"The hunter said, 'O serpent! Even if you have committed an inauspicious act because you have been under someone else's subjugation, since you have been the instrument, the sin also vests in you. When an earthen pot is fashioned, the rod and the wheel are thought of as instruments. O serpent! You are also like that. Anyone who has committed a crime deserves to be slain by me. O serpent! You have committed a crime. O serpent! Indeed, you have described yourself as an instrument.'

'"The snake replied, 'The rod and the wheel are helpless in every way. I am just like that. Therefore, I am not the cause that you have mentioned. If you hold a contrary view, realize that these objects are being used by someone else. When something is urged by something else, there is a doubt about which one is the cause and which one is the effect. Thus, I am not guilty. I do not deserve to be killed. I have not committed a crime. Even if you think that there has been a crime, the crime is due to multiple reasons.'

'"The hunter said, 'Even if you are not the prime cause, you have been the agent responsible for his death. Therefore, you deserve to be killed. That is my view. O serpent! Even if you think that if you perform a wicked act and you will not be touched by it, you are the cause whereby that act was undertaken. That is sufficient for you to be killed. Why do you want to speak more?'

'"The snake replied, 'Regardless of whether there has been some other cause or not, an act is driven by its motive. The intention behind my words was to draw particular attention to the motive. O hunter! Even if you truly think that I was the cause, the motive behind that use was someone else's. The sin of killing a living being then also vests with someone else.'

'"The hunter said, 'O one who is extremely evil-minded! You deserve to be slain by me. You have committed the cruel deed of killing a child. Why do you keep speaking? O worst among serpents! You deserve to be killed.'

'"The snake replied, 'O hunter! In this world and in the next, officiating priests who offer oblations into a sacrifice do not obtain any fruits.[6] I am like that.'"

'Bhishma continued, "Having been goaded by Mrityu, the serpent spoke in this way. Mrityu then arrived before the serpent and spoke these words. 'O serpent! I was goaded by Kala and I goaded you in turn. I or you are not the causes behind this child's destruction. The clouds are moved here and there by the wind. O snake! Just like the clouds, you and I are under Kala's subjugation. All the attributes of sattva, rajas and tamas exist in Kala's essence and thus exist among beings. Mobile and immobile objects, in heaven and on earth, are all controlled by Kala. O snake! The entire universe is influenced by Kala. Inclinations of people towards pravritti and nivritti and all their various transformations are all said to be dependent on Kala. O serpent! Aditya, the moon, Vishnu, water, wind, Shatakratu, Agni, the sky, the earth, Mitra, the herbs, the Vasus, the rivers, the oceans, existence and non-existence—all these are created by Kala and destroyed again. O snake! Since you know this, why do you think that I am guilty? Had I been a sinner, you would also have been a sinner.'

'"The snake replied, 'O Mrityu! I am not saying that you are absolved, nor am I saying that you are guilty. I have only said that I have been goaded by you. Nor do I say anything about Kala being blamed, or not being blamed. You or I do not possess the right to examine that crime. It is my duty to ensure that I am absolved of the sin. It may also be necessary for me to show that Mrityu is innocent.'"

'Bhishma continued, "The snake then spoke to Arjunaka. 'You have heard what Mrityu said. I am innocent. You should not torment me in these bonds.'

'"The hunter said, 'O serpent! I have heard your words, as well as those of Mrityu. O serpent! But that does not make you innocent. You and Mrityu are both responsible for this creature's destruction. I think that both of you are causes. Something that is a cause should not be regarded as not being a cause. Shame on the evil-souled

[6]The fruits are obtained by the performer of the sacrifice.

Mrityu. He cruelly afflicts the virtuous. I will kill you too.[7] You are the sinful cause behind a sinner.'

'"Mrityu replied, 'We are helpless. We are under the subjugation of Kala. We do what he instructs us. If you look at this objectively, there should not be anything to blame us.'

'"The hunter said, 'O Mrityu! O serpent! If both of you are under the subjugation of Kala, how are joy and anger generated?[8] I desire to know this.'

'"Mrityu responded, 'Everything that all of us have endeavoured to do is because of us being goaded by Kala. O hunter! I have already told you that all of this is because of Kala. If the two of us have caused any injury, that is because we have been under Kala's subjugation. O hunter! There is no way that we can be held to be guilty.'"

'Bhishma continued, "At that time, while there was this confusion about dharma, Kala arrived at the spot. He spoke to the serpent, Mrityu and the hunter Arjunaka.

'"Kala said, 'O hunter! Mrityu or the serpent or I am not guilty of any sin, on account of having caused the death of any creature. O Arjunaka! These outcomes are caused by the deeds a creature commits. Nothing other than one's own deeds is responsible for destruction and death. It was because of his deeds that he faced death. All of us are under the subjugation of our deeds and those deeds are the reason for destruction. People reap the fruits of their deeds. Being bound by one's deeds is the manifestation. One deed leads to another, just as we urge each other. A doer fashions whatever he wants with a piece of clay. In that fashion, a man confronts the consequences of his deeds. Light and shadow are always connected to each other. In that fashion, a deed and a doer are connected because of past deeds. You, Mrityu, the snake, you and the aged brahmana lady are not the reasons for the child's death.'"

[7]Meaning Mrityu.

[8]The implication is that joy results from doing good and anger results from doing bad. Stated differently, if everything is driven by Kala, how can anything be 'good' or 'bad'?

'Bhishma continued, "O king! When he spoke in this way, Goutami, the brahmana lady, realized that people suffered the consequences of their own deeds. She told Arjunaka, 'Kala, the serpent or Mrityu aren't the cause of the death. This child has died because of his own deeds. And it is because of my earlier deeds that my son has died. O Arjunaka! Let Kala and Mrityu go and release this serpent.' Mrityu, Kala and the serpent went away to wherever they had come from. Arjunaka was freed of his anger and Goutami of her sorrow. O king! Hearing this, be tranquil and do not think a lot. O bull among men! Know that people obtain the three worlds because of their own deeds.[9] O Partha! You did not do anything, nor did Duryodhana. Know that the kings died because of what Kala did."'

Vaishampayana said, 'On hearing these words, the immensely energetic Yudhishthira lost all his anxiety. The one who followed dharma had more questions.'

Chapter 1683(2)

'Yudhishthira said, "O grandfather! O immensely wise one! One who knows about all the sacred texts! O supreme among intelligent ones! I have heard this great account. O king! However, I again to hear about things connected with dharma and artha. You should tell me about some such account. Has any householder been able to conquer death by resorting to garhasthya dharma? O king! Tell me the truth about all of this."

'Bhishma replied, "In this connection, there is an ancient history, about a householder who conquered death by resorting to dharma. O king! Prajapati Manu had a son named Ikshvaku. That king had one hundred sons who were as radiant as the sun. O descendant of

[9]Good deeds take them to heaven, bad deeds take them to hell and average deeds lead to rebirth on earth.

the Bharata lineage! The tenth son was named Dashashva. He had dharma in his soul, was truthful in his valour and became the king of Mahishmati. Dashashva's son was a king who was extremely devoted to dharma. His mind was always devoted to truth, austerities and donations. Throughout the earth, that lord of the earth was known by the name of Madirashva. He was always engaged in studying the Vedas and in Dhanurveda. Madirashva's son was the king named Dyutimat. He was immensely fortunate, immensely energetic, immensely spirited and immensely strong. Dyutimat's son was the king named Suvira. He possessed dharma in his soul and his treasury was like that of the king of the gods. Suvira had a son who was invincible in battle. He was known by the name of Durjaya and he was accomplished in all the sacred texts. Durjaya's body was like that of Indra's. He had a son who was resplendent as the fire. O supreme among kings! He was a great king and his name was Duryodhana. His valour was like that of Indra and so were his possessions and power. He never retreated from the field of battle. His city and kingdom were full of separate stores of jewels, riches, animals and grain. There was no one in the kingdom who was weak or afflicted. No man there was diseased or lean. He[10] was accomplished and pleasant in speech. He was without jealousy and had conquered his senses. He had dharma in his soul and was non-violent. He was valiant, but did not boast. He performed sacrifices and was restrained in speech. He was intelligent, devoted to brahmanas and devoted to the truth. He did not disrespect others. He was generous and knowledgable about the Vedas and the Vedangas. The celestial river, Narmada, is sacred and auspicious, with cool waters. O descendant of the Bharata lineage! In a natural state, she served that best among men![11] O king! Through the river, he had a daughter named Sudarshana. Her eyes were like a lotus. Her form was beautiful to look at.[12] O Yudhishthira! No woman with such beauty had been born earlier. Duryodhana's daughter, Sudarshana, was supremely beautiful.

[10]Duryodhana.

[11]Natural state means personified form.

[12]Sudarshana means a lady who is beautiful to look at.

'"Agni wished to marry the princess Sudarshana. Adopting the disguise of a brahmana, he appeared before the king and sought her hand in marriage. The king was unwilling to bestow his daughter, Sudarshana, on the brahmana. After all, he was poor and did not belong to the same varna. At this, Agni disappeared and his sacrifice was destroyed. King Duryodhana spoke these words to the priests who offered oblations. 'O bulls among brahmanas! What wicked act have I committed, to make Agni disappear? That is the way he should behave towards wicked people. I must have committed an extremely wicked deed to make Agni vanish thus. You must have done something, or I must have done something. Ascertain the truth about this.' O bull among the Bharata lineage! On hearing the king's words, the brahmanas controlled themselves and using eloquent words, sought Agni's refuge. The illustrious bearer of oblations showed himself to them. The firmament blazed with his radiance. He was as resplendent as the autumn sun. The great-souled one scorched those bulls among brahmanas and said, 'I seek the hand of Duryodhana's daughter.' All the brahmanas were astounded at what Chitrabhanu[13] had said. They immediately arose and went and reported this to the king. The king heard the words of the ones who knew about the brahman and was supremely delighted. However, the intelligent king sought a bride price from the illustrious fire god and this was that Chitrabhanu should always dwell near him. The illustrious Agni agreed to the king's condition. That is the reason why, even today, the fire god is in Mahishmati and in the course of his conquest, Sahadeva saw him in that direction. The maiden was attired in new garments and ornamented. King Duryodhana gave her to the great-souled Pavaka. Following the ordinances laid down in the Vedas, Agni accepted the princess Sudarshana, just as he accepts offerings of clarified butter. Agni was delighted with her beauty, good conduct, noble lineage, form and grace and resolved to have offspring through her. Agni thus had a son named Sudarshana.[14] Even as a child, he knew everything about the eternal brahman.

[13]Agni's name.

[14]The mother is Sudarshanaa, while the son is Sudarshana.

'"There was a king named Oghavat and he was Nriga's grandfather. He had a daughter named Oghavati and a son named Ogharatha. Oghavat gave his daughter, Oghavati, who was as beautiful as a goddess, to the learned Sudarshana as a wife. O king! In the ashrama of garhasthya, Sudarshana dwelt with Oghavati in Kurukshetra. O lord of the earth! The intelligent lord, blazing in his energy, took a pledge that he would conquer death in the state of garhasthya. O king! Pavaka's son told Oghavati, 'Always act so as to satisfy the guests. One should offer one's own self, without even thinking about it. This vow is always circulating in my mind. O one with the beautiful hips! For householders, there is nothing that is superior to guests. O one with the beautiful thighs! O beautiful one! If you set any store by my words, always bear these words in your heart, without doubting them. O fortunate one! O unblemished one! This is irrespective of whether I am here, or have gone out. If you set any store by my words, never disrespect a guest.' Oghavati joined her hands in salutation and raised them up above her head. She said, 'It is my duty to never disregard your words.' O king! Mrityu sought to test this and followed Sudarshana around in the house, searching for a weakness. Agni's son, Sudarshana, went out for some firewood and a handsome brahmana arrived as a guest before Oghavati. He said, 'O beautiful one! I seek your hospitality today. Please grant it to me. Prove to me that you are following the dharma of the garhasthya ashrama.' O lord of the earth! Thus addressed by the brahmana, the illustrious princess welcomed him, following the rites that are spoken about in the Vedas. She gave the brahmana a seat and water to wash his feet. Oghavati then asked the brahmana, 'Why have you come here? What should I give you?' The brahmana told the princess who belonged to Sudarshana, 'O fortunate one! I have come here for you. Without any hesitation, you should act for that objective. O queen! If you wish to prove that you are following the dharma of garhasthya ashrama, you should give yourself to me. Do what I find to be agreeable.' The king's daughter tried to dissuade him by offering many other desirable objects. However, the only boon that the brahmana sought was that she should offer herself. The daughter of the king remembered the words that her husband had spoken. Though she was ashamed, she agreed to what the bull among brahmanas had proposed. She rememberd her husband's words and desired to follow the ashrama of garhasthya. Therefore, she went to the brahmana rishi and lay down with him.

'"Having collected the firewood, Pavaka's son returned. Like a friend who follows, the terrible Mrityu was constantly at his side. Having arrived at the hermitage, Pavaka's son called out to Oghavati. Since there was no reply, he wondered where she could have gone. She was in no position to reply to her husband then. The virtuous one, devoted to her husband, was locked in an embrace in the arms of the brahmana. She thought that she had been defiled and was ashamed of facing her husband. Therefore, the virtuous one remained silent and did not say anything. At this, Sudarshana addressed her again. 'Where can the virtuous one be? Where could she have gone? Nothing is more important to me than her. She is devoted to her husband. She is truthful in her conduct. She is always upright. As she used to earlier, why is she not smiling and answering?' The brahmana who was inside the cottage replied to Sudarshana. 'O Pavaka's son! Know me to be a brahmana guest who has arrived. O excellent one! This upright one is firm in her mind about tending to guests. She offered me other things, but I was only interested in her. Following the prescribed rites, the fair-faced one is now serving me. Whatever you say should be appropriate to the occasion.' Mrityu raised the heavy club in his hand, thinking that he would slay a person who deviated from his pledge. However, Sudarshana had discarded all anger in his mind, deeds, sight and speech. He smiled and replied, 'O foremost among brahmanas! Enjoy the intercourse well. This brings great pleasure to me. The prime dharma for a householder is to honour a guest who has arrived. The learned have said that there is no dharma superior to a householder than the departure of a guest after being honoured. My life, my wife and all the riches I possess are to be given to a guest. That is the vow I have taken. There should be no doubt about the words that I have spoken. O brahmana! I speak the truth when I say that it is through this means that I will get to know my own atman. O supreme among those who uphold dharma! The earth, wind, space, water, light as the fifth, intelligence, the atman, the mind, time, the directions and the ten qualities[15] are always a witness to good and bad deeds. Depending on the truth or falsehood of the words I have spoken today, let the gods protect me or consume me.' O descendant of the Bharata lineage! At this, a great roar arose in all the directions. 'This is true in every way. This is not false.' The brahmana also emerged from the hut. He arose like the wind and his form covered the sky and the earth. The brahmana spoke in accomplished tones and his voice resounded in the three worlds. 'O one who knows about dharma! In the mantras, you have earlier invoked me as Dharma. O unblemished one! I arrived here to test you. On knowing that you are devoted to the truth, I am greatly delighted with you. You have conquered Mrityu, who has been following you around. He has always been searching for your weaknesses. But your fortitude has subjugated him. O supreme among men! This virtuous one is devoted to her husband and no one in the three worlds is capable of even looking at her. She is protected by your qualities and by her qualities of being devoted to her husband. She has not been touched. The words that I have spoken are not false. This one knows about the brahman and is united with austerities. To purify the worlds, she will become the best of rivers.[16] This immensely fortunate one will control her body through yoga. While half of her self will remain in her body, the other half will become the River Oghavati. With her, you will go to the worlds you have earned through your austerities. There is no return from those eternal and everlasing worlds and you will obtain those worlds in your physical body. You have conquered Mrityu and have obtained the greatest prosperity. Through the valour of your mind, you have transcended the five elements. You have resorted to the dharma of garhasthya and have conquered desire and anger. O king! You have conquered affection, attachment, lassitude, delusion and hatred through your service and have also obtained this princess.' An excellent chariot arrived, yoked to one thousand white horses. It arrived and bore the illustrious one away. Mrityu, the atman, the worlds, the five elements, intelligence, time, mind, space, desire, anger—all these were conquered through the

[15]Five senses and five organs of action.

[16]Oghavati is that part of the River Sarasvati that flows through Kurukshetra.

garhasthya ashrama. O tiger among men! There should be no doubt in one's mind that there is no god who is greater than a guest. The learned ones have said that in one's mind, one must always remember the auspicious fact that even one hundred sacrifices are not equal to honouring a guest. If there is a deserving guest who is not honoured in accordance with good conduct, when he goes away, he takes the good deeds earned and leaves the bad deeds earned.[17] O son! I have thus recounted this excellent account to you, wherein, in ancient times, a householder conquered death. This account[18] brings renown, fame and a long life. A person, who desires prosperity and wants his evil conduct to be dispelled, should listen to it. O descendant of the Bharata lineage! If a person recites this account of Sudarshana's conduct every day, he obtains the sacred worlds."'

Chapter 1684(3)

'Yudhishthira asked, "O lord of men! O great king! If the other three varnas find it extremely difficult to become a brahmana, how did the great-souled kshatriya, Vishvamitra, with dharma in his soul, become a brahmana? O grandfather! I wish to hear the truth about this. Please tell me. O great grandfather! Through his austerities and infinite valour, the great-souled one instantly killed one hundred of Vasishtha's sons. When anger entered his body, he created many *yatudhanas*[19] and rakshasas who were fierce in their energy. They were like the Destroyer himself. There were hundreds of brahmana rishis in the great lineage of Kushika.[20] Having

[17]The guest leaves his bad deeds with the host and takes away the host's good deeds.

[18]Listening to the account.

[19]Evil spirits or demons.

[20]Vishvamitra was born as a kshatriya and was the great-grandson of a king named Kusha. Thus, Vishvamitra is also known as Kushika or Koushika. His father was Gadhi.

established this lineage in the world of men, he was praised by the learned brahmanas. The great ascetic, Shunahshepa, was Richika's son. He was treated like an animal at a great sacrifice and was freed by him.[21] The energetic Harishchandra performed a sacrifice and pleased the gods, thus becoming the intelligent Vishvamitra's son. O lord of men! Because they did not honour their eldest, Devarata, fifty of his sons were cursed and became shvapakas .[22] Trishanku, the son of Ikshvaku, was abandoned by his relatives. However, he[23] affectionately conveyed him to heaven, with his head hanging downwards. Vishvamitra created a large, pure and sacred river named Koushiki and this was frequented by the rajarshis and also frequented by the brahmana rishis. There was the apsara named Rambha, who had five tufts of hair and was extremely beautiful. However, because she disturbed his austerities, she was cursed and turned into stone. In ancient times, because he was scared of him, Vasishtha submerged himself in the water and rose after he had been freed from his bonds. That is the reason the sacred and large river came to be known as Vipasha.[24] This was a famous deed the great-souled one performed for Vasishtha's sake. The lord praised and pleased the eloquent and illustrious one who was at the forefront of the army of the gods and thus freed himself from the curse.[25] He always blazes in the northern direction in the midst of the brahmana rishis and Uttanpada's son, Dhruva.[26] O Kourava! These and many others are his deeds. This is despite his being born as a kshatriya and I am curious about this.

[21]Freed by Vishvamitra.

[22]The offspring of *mritapas*, and chandalas, are shvapakas, and they are extremely vile. Mritapas are also outcastes.

[23]Vishvamitra.

[24]Vipasha means something that releases from bonds (*pasha*). This is the river Beas.

[25]This is left unclear. It probably refers to Vishvamitra eventually becoming a brahmana. When this happens, Brahma (presumably the eloquent and illustrious one) arrives, with all the gods following him. Brahma declares that Vishvamitra will henceforth be a brahmana rishi and gives him the name of Vishvamitra.

[26]Dhruva was Uttanpada's son and became the Pole Star. The saptarshis constitute the constellation Ursa Major (Great Bear).

O bull among the Bharata lineage! How did this happen? Tell me the truth about this. Without taking birth in another body, how did he become a brahmana? O king! You should tell me the entire truth about this. Tell me the truth about Matanga too. O bull among the Bharata lineage! Having been born in the womb of a chandala, Matanga did not obtain the status of a brahmana. How did he[27] then become a brahmana?"'

Chapter 1685(4)

'Bhishma replied, "O Partha! O son! Listen to the ancient and truthful account about Vishvamitra, about how be obtained the status of a brahmana and became a brahmana rishi. In the lineage of the Bharatas, there was a king named Ajamidha.[28] O best among the Bharata lineage! He performed sacrifices and was supreme among those who upheld dharma. His son was the great king named Jahnu. The great-souled one obtained Ganga as his daughter.[29] His son was the immensely illustrious Sindhudvipa, who was his equal in qualities. The immensely strong rajarshi, Balakashva, was born from Sindhudvipa. His son was Vallabha, who was like Dharma himself. His son was Kushika, whose radiance was like that of the thousand-eyed one.[30] Kushika's son was the prosperous King Gadhi. The mighty-armed one was without a son and began to dwell in the forest. While he dwelt in the forest, a daughter was born to him. Her name was Satyavati and her beauty was unmatched on earth. The illustrious Chyavana's son was the lord Richika, born in the Bhargava

[27]Vishvamitra.

[28]Descended from this king, Yudhishthira and Dhritarashtra are also occasionally referred to as Ajamidha.

[29]In the usual stories, Jahnu is described as a sage, who drank up Ganga and later released the water through his ear. Ganga thus became his daughter and is known as Jahnavi.

[30]Indra.

lineage. Because of his great austerities, he was famous. He sought her hand. However, Gadhi, the destroyer of enemies, thought that the great-souled Richika was poor and did not give her to him. When he was refused and about to go away, the supreme among kings again said, 'If you give me a price, I will then give you my daughter.'

'"Richika asked, 'O Indra among kings! What will I give you as a price? O king! Without hesitating about it, tell me what I should give you for your daughter.'

'"Gadhi replied, 'O Bhargava! Give me one thousand horses that are as swift as the wind, as white as the beams of the moon, but with each one possessing one black ear.'"

'Bhishma continued, "The lord who was Chyavana's son and was a tiger of the Bhrigu lineage went to Varuna, Aditi's son and the lord of the waters, and said, 'O supreme among gods! I seek alms from you—one thousand horses that are as swift as the wind, as white as the beams of the moon, but with each possessing one black ear.' Varuna, the god Aditya, agreed to what the supreme one of the Bhrigu lineage had asked. 'As soon as you think of them, the horses will be there.' Richika thought of horses that were as radiant as the moon and one thousand of them arose from the waters of the Ganga, great in their energy. Not far from Kanyakubja, there are the excellent banks of the Ganga. Even today, men still refer to the spot as Ashvatirtha.[31] O son! Richika, foremost among those who meditate, cheerfully gave those one thousand fair horses to Gadhi, as a price. King Gadhi was astounded, but was also terrified of a curse. He therefore gave his ornamented daughter to Bhrigu's descendant. Following the recommended rites, the supreme among brahmana rishis accepted her hand. She was also extremely delighted at having obtained such a husband. O descendant of the Bharata lineage! The brahmana rishi was pleased at her conduct and desired to grant a boon to the beautiful one. O supreme among kings! The maiden reported this to her mother. As the daughter stood before her, with

[31]The tirtha of the horses. Kanyakubja is Kannauj. Ganga means the Goutami Ganga or the Southern Ganga, that is, Godavari. There is an Ashvatirtha on the banks of the Godavari.

downcast eyes, the mother said, 'O daughter! You should ask your husband to show me his favours too. That great ascetic is capable of granting me a son too.' O king! She swiftly went to Richika and told him everything about what her mother desired. He said, 'O fortunate one! Because of my love for you, she will give birth to a son who possesses all the qualities. There will be no violation of this. O fortunate one! You will also have a son who will be proud of his qualities. This prosperous one will extend our lineage. Your brother will also extend his lineage. When you have bathed at the end of your seasons, let her embrace an ashvattha tree and you should embrace a fig tree. O fortunate one! Thereby, both of you will obtain what you wish for. O one with the beautiful smiles! Here are two vessels of *charu*,[32] sanctified with the pronouncement of mantras. When you consume these, you will obtain the desired sons.' Satyavati happily told her mother what Richika had said. She also told her about the two vessels of charu. The mother inhaled the fragrance of her daughter Satyavati's head and told her, 'O daughter! Act in accordance with my words. Your husband first gave you a vessel of charu, sanctified with mantras. Give that to me. Accept the one he gave me instead. O one with the sweet smiles! We should also exchange the trees. O unblemished one! If you honour your mother, this is what you should do. It is evident what the illustrious one wants to do.[33] O slender-waisted one! Therefore, I desire your charu and your tree. You should also think about obtaining a superior brother for yourself.' O Yudhishthira! Satyavati and her mother acted in this way and both of them conceived.

'"When the great rishi, the supreme one of the Bhrigu lineage, saw that his wife, Satyavati, had conceived, he was distressed in his mind and said, 'It will soon be apparent that you have not done well in exchanging the charu. O beautiful one! It is clear that you have exchanged the trees too. I had placed all the brahmana energy in the universe in your charu. I had placed all the kshatriya valour in

[32]Charu is a mixture of rice, barley and pulses, cooked in butter and milk and offered as an oblation.

[33]Obtain the better son for himself.

her charu. You would have given birth to a brahmana who would have been famous in the three worlds because of his qualities. She would have given birth to an excellent kshatriya. That is what I had arranged for. However, you and your mother have effected an exchange. Therefore, your mother will give birth to the best among brahmanas. O fortunate one! You will give birth to a kshatriya who will be terrible in his deeds. O beautiful one! Thanks to your affection for your mother, you have not done a good deed.' O king! On hearing this, the beautiful Satyavati was overcome by grief and fell down on the ground, like a creeper that has been severed. When she regained her senses, she bowed her head down on the ground. The wife, Gadhi's daughter, spoke, to her husband, the bull among brahmanas. 'O supreme among those who know about the brahman! Show mercy towards your miserable wife. O brahmana rishi! Show me your favours, so that I do not have a son who is a kshatriya. If you so desire, let my grandson be the performer of terrible deeds. O brahmana! Grant me the boon that my son should not be like that.' The greatly ascetic agreed to what his wife had said.

'"She gave birth to an auspicious son named Jamadagni. O Indra among kings! Through the rishi's powers, Gadhi's illustrious wife gave birth to the brahmana rishi, Vishvamitra, knowledgable about the brahman. The immensely ascetic Vishvamitra obtained the status of a brahmana. Though he was born as a kshatriya, he became the originator of a lineage of brahmanas. His sons were great-souled and the extenders of the lineages of brahmanas. They were ascetics who knew about the brahman. They were the creators of gotras. The illustrious Madhuchanda, the valiant Devarata, Akshina, Shakunta, Babhru, Kalapatha, the famous Yajnavalkya, Sthuna, great in his vows, Uluka, Yamaduta, the rishi Saindhavayana, the illustrious Karnajangha, the great rishi Galava, the rishi Vajra, the famous Shalankayana, Lalatya, Narada, the one known as Kurchamukha, Vaduli, Musala, Rakshagriva, Anghnika, Naikabhricha, Shilayupa, Sita, Shuchi, Chakraka, Marutantavya, Vataghna, Ashvalayana, Shyamayana, Gargya, Jabali, Sushruta, Karishiratha, Samshrutya, Parapourava, Tantu, the great rishi Kapila, the rishi Tarakayana, Upagahana, the rishi Arjunayana, Margamitri, Hiranyaksha,

Janghari, Babhruvahana, Suti, Vibhuti, Suta, Suranga, Aradvina, Amaya, Champeya, Ujjayana, Navatantu, Bakanakha, Shayana, Yati, Shayaruha, Arumatsya, Shirishi, Gardhabhi, Ujjayani, Adapekshi, the great rishi Naradi—all these sages were knowledgable about the brahman and were descended from Vishvamitra. O king! The great ascetic, Vishvamitra, was born as a kshatriya. O Yudhishthira! But Richika had brought the supreme brahman to him. O bull among the Bharata lineage! I have truthfully told you the entire account about Vishvamitra's birth. His energy was like that of the moon, the sun and the fire. O supreme among kings! Tell me about everything that you have a doubt over. I will sever your doubts."'

Chapter 1686(5)

'Yudhishthira said, "I wish to hear everything about the dharma of non-violence and about the qualities of those who are devoted. O grandfather! Tell me this."

'Bhishma replied, "In the kingdom of Kashi, a hunter left his village to hunt for deer. He had poisoned arrows with him. Searching for flesh, the hunter entered a large forest. He saw some deer at a distance and carefully shot an arrow at them. The weapon was difficult to repulse. However, in that large forest, though it has been released in order to kill a deer, it missed the target and struck a tree. The powerful poison in the arrow burnt it down. Having dried up, the tree shed its fruits and leaves. A parrot lived in a hollow in that withered tree. Because of its affection for the tree, it did not leave its abode. It did not emerge in search of food and starved. It suffered and became feeble. Because it was grateful to the tree, the one with dharma in its soul dried up with it. The chastiser of Paka[34] was astounded on learning that it looked upon happiness and unhappiness equally. Shakra wondered, 'This bird has been born as an inferior

[34]Indra.

species. How did it come to resort to non-violence? Or perhaps there is nothing wonderful in this, since all creatures are everywhere seen to be kindly disposed towards each other.' Thus did Vasava think.

'"Shakra assumed a human form, in the attire of a brahmana. He descended on earth and addressed the bird. 'O parrot! O best among the birds! Daksha's daughter has indeed had excellent offspring.[35] I wish to ask you a question. Why are you not abandoning this withered tree?' Having been thus asked, the parrot bowed its head down in obeisance and replied, 'O king of the gods! Welcome. Through my austerities, I know who you are.' The one with the one thousand eyes exclaimed words of praise. 'The austerities through which it has discerned this deserve to be honoured.' The destroyer of Bala[36] knew that the parrot was extremely devoted to dharma and that it was the performer of auspicious deeds. However, he still wanted to know why the parrot wouldn't leave. 'This tree is without leaves and without fruit. It is withered and can no longer be a refuge for birds. Why are you still on this tree? There are many other trees in this great forest and they have leaves and are full of hollows. In this great forest, there are many other places where you will find a fortunate spot. This one has lost its lifespan and its capacity. Its essence has been destroyed. It has lost its prosperity. O wise and patient one! Why are you not abandoning a tree that has been destroyed and is now fragile?' The parrot, with dharma in its soul, heard the words that Shakra had spoken. It sighed deeply and spoke these words of distress. 'O Shachi's consort! Destiny cannot be overcome. O lord of the gods! Listen to the reason why I am still here. I have been born in this tree. All my virtuous qualities result from it. It protected me well in my infancy and I was not assaulted by my enemies. O unblemished one! Why are you asking questions about the fruits I seek—non-violence, affection and attachment towards those who are devoted? Lack of anger is a great trait of

[35]Daksha's daughters were married to the sage Kashyapa and all creatures were born from these unions. The names sometimes differ. Usually, the mother of the birds is said to be Daksha's daughter, Tamra or Patangi.

[36]Indra killed a demon named Bala.

those who are virtuous. Lack of anger always grants cheer to the virtuous. When there is a doubt about dharma, it is you whom the gods ask. O god! That is the reason you have been established as a lord of the gods. O thousand-eyed one! You should not ask me to abandon someone who is devoted to me. When it was capable, it sustained my life. How can I abandon it now?' At these amiable words, Paka's chastiser was delighted. He was satisfied with the parrot's non-violence and knowledge of dharma and said, 'O parrot! Ask for a boon.' The parrot, always devoted to non-violence, asked for the boon that the tree might be revived. Shakra had got to know about the parrot's firmness and richness of good conduct. Delighted, he quickly sprinkled amrita on the tree. Beautiful fruits, leaves and branches sprouted. Because of the parrot's firm devotion, the tree regained its beauty again. O great king! Because of its deeds and acts of non-violence, when its lifespan was over, the parrot obtained Shakra's world. O Indra among men! In this way, those who are devoted become successful in everything, just as the tree did, through the parrot."'

Chapter 1687(6)

'Yudhishthira asked, "O grandfather! O immensely wise one! O one who is accomplished in all the sacred texts! Which is stronger, destiny or human endeavour?"

'Bhishma replied, "O Yudhishthira! In this connection, an ancient history is recounted about a conversation between Vasishtha and Brahma. In ancient times, Vasishtha asked the illustrious grandfather, 'Which is superior, destiny or the deeds of men?' O king! At this, the grandfather, born from the lotus and the god of the gods, replied in pleasant words that were full of purport and reason. 'Nothing is born without a seed. There are no fruits without a seed. It is said that seeds result from seeds and fruits result from seeds. The tiller of a field may sow good or bad seeds. The fruits obtained are in accordance with that. Without seeds, a ploughed field does not yield fruits. But in that way, without human enterprise, destiny doesn't become successful. The field is said to be like human enterprise, the seed is like destiny. Crops are harvested from a union of the field and the seed. The fruits of deeds are not destroyed. The doer reaps them himself. The consequences of good and evil deeds are evident in the world. There is happiness through good deeds and misery through wicked deeds. What is done is enjoyed. What is not done is never enjoyed. A person who does deeds[37] obtains prosperity in every way and his good fortune is not destroyed. A person who does not do deeds is destroyed, like caustic matter being poured into a wound. Austerities, beauty, good fortune and many kinds of jewels—all these are obtained through deeds, not through deeds coupled with individual inaction. In a similar way, heaven, objects of enjoyment and everything that one wishes for—all these are obtained through human endeavour, not through lack of action. The stellar bodies, the gods, the serpents, the yakshas, the moon, the sun, the Maruts—all these have been elevated from humanity to divinity through enterprise. Riches, categories of friends, prosperity, good lineage, beauty and objects of pleasure are extremely difficult to obtain, unless one has embarked on action. A brahmana obtains prosperity through purity, a kshatriya through valour, a vaishya through exertion and a shudra through servitude. It is not obtained by someone who is not generous and not brave, someone who is impotent and does not act, someone who does not engage in good deeds, someone who is not valiant and someone who does not resort to austerities. The illustrious Vishnu created the three worlds, the daityas and all the gods. But even he tormented himself through austerities in the ocean. Had there not been fruits from deeds, all these fruits would not have materialized. The worlds would only have looked towards destiny and become indifferent. If a man does not undertake deeds and only follows destiny, all his exertions will be futile, like a woman with an impotent husband. In the world of men, one should not be that frightened of good

[37]Good deeds.

and bad deeds. More important is the slightest bit of fear in the world of the gods.[38] Deeds and human enterprise follow destiny. However, when there is inaction, destiny cannot provide anything. The status of the gods is also seen to be temporary. Without deeds, how can the gods remain established in their states? The gods never approved of good conduct in this world, since they fear that such fierce deeds might lead to their being dislodged. That is the reason there is always conflict between the rishis and the gods. Therefore, if the gods have themselves determined it, how can one speak of destiny? How is destiny itself supposed to have arisen? There are many kinds of deceit that are practised in the world of the thirty gods.[39] One's own atman is one's friend. One's own atman is also one's enemy. The atman is a witness to one's own self and to the deeds that have been performed and the ones that have not been performed. Between good deeds and perverse deeds, it is the good deeds that lead to success. Sometimes, good and bad deeds do not lead to consequences.[40] Divinity has the auspicious as a foundation. Everything is based on what is auspicious. A man with auspicious deeds will obtain everything. What can the gods do? In ancient times, Yayati was dislodged from heaven and fell down on the ground.[41] He was again restored to heaven through the auspicious deeds of his grandsons. In ancient times, the rajarshi, King Pururava, descended from Ila's lineage, obtained heaven, but was restrained by the brahmanas.[42] Soudasa, the lord of Kosala, performed a horse sacrifice and other sacrifices. However, cursed by a maharshi, he became a maneater.[43] Ashvatthama and Rama[44] were the sons of

[38]This shloka isn't very clear. It probably means that good and bad deeds lead to greater fear in the world hereafter than in the present world.

[39]The gods don't want people to perform deeds and dislodge them. Therefore, they practise deceit and speak of destiny.

[40]Immediate consequences in this world.

[41]Yayati's story has been recounted in Section 7 (Volume 1).

[42]Pururava's story has been recounted in Section 7 (Volume 1).

[43]Soudasa's story has been recounted in Section 7 (Volume 1).

[44]Parashurama.

sages and great archers. However, despite their good deeds in this world, they could not go to heaven. Like a second Vasava, Vasu[45] performed one hundred sacrifices. However, because of a single act of falsehood, he was dispatched to the nether regions. Destiny bound down Bali, Virochana's son, in the noose of dharma. But it was Vishnu's enterprise that made him lie down in the nether regions. Janamejaya followed in the footsteps of Shakra. He killed brahmana women.[46] Could destiny prevent this? The brahmana rishi, Vaishampayana, killed a brahmana child in his ignorance and was tainted by this.[47] Could destiny prevent this? In ancient times, in a great sacrifice, rajarshi Nriga made the false promise of giving cattle to a brahmana. Because of this, he became a lizard.[48] While performing a sacrifice, rajarshi Dhundumara was overcome by old age.[49] Abandoning all these delights, he fell asleep in Girivraja. The immensely strong sons of Dhritarashtra seized the kingdom of the Pandavas. They obtained it back by resorting to their arms, not

[45]Uparichara Vasu. The story has been recounted in Section 6 (Volume 1).

[46]Which Janamejaya is this? Is this Janamejaya, the son of Parikshit? There is a story about this Janamejaya. When he wanted to perform a sacrifice, his queen arrived, wearing transparent clothes. When the brahmanas laughed at this, Janamejaya killed them. Cursed, he became a leper. However, according to this story, he killed the brahmanas, not brahmana women. Assuming this is the right Janamejaya, since Bhishma is recounting this to Yudhishthira, the story doesn't belong. A speculative and symbolic interpretation has also been applied to this. Parikshit had a brahmana wife too and she was bypassed. In that symbolic sense, Janamejaya killed his brahmana stepmother.

[47]Vaishampayana didn't actually kill a brahmana. The sages had decided to assemble on Mount Meru. There was an agreement that any sage who absented himself would incur the sin of killing a brahmana. Engaged in the funeral ceremonies of his father, Vaishampayana absented himself and thus incurred the sin of killing a brahmana.

[48]The generous King Nriga had promised to give a brahmana a herd of cattle. But when a beggar turned up, Nriga gave the cattle to the beggar and was cursed by the brahmana that he would become a lizard in a well. The lizard was subsequently saved by Krishna.

[49]Dhundumara's story has been recounted in Section 37 (Volume 2).

through destiny. The sages are devoted to their vows and are engaged in austerities and rituals. Are they able to levy curses because of their deeds or because of destiny? If one abandons wickedness in this world, one can obtain everything that is difficult to get. If a man is overcome by avarice and delusion, destiny cannot save him. Even if a fire is small, when it is fanned by the wind, it becomes large. When united with deeds, a virtuous person thus prospers, aided by destiny. When the oil in a lamp is exhausted, it is extinguished. In that way, if deeds are exhausted, a person is also extinguished. Even if a man obtains a great store of riches and women to be enjoyed, devoid of acts, he will not be able to enjoy them in this world. If a person resorts to the qualities of virtuous deeds, protected by destiny, he will find riches, even if those are well hidden. The world of men is superior to the world of the gods, because the houses of men are full of many riches. In contrast, that of the immortals is seen to be like that of the dead. Devoid of deed, destiny cannot bring success in the world of the living. Destiny can exert no power over someone who has deviated from the path. The performance of great deeds is superior. It drives destiny. The uninterrupted and generous desire to perform deeds conveys enterprise towards the store of destiny. O supreme among sages! I have told you everything about this. It is true that the fruits of enterprise are always seen. Destiny arises because of being engaged in action. By performing the prescribed tasks, one obtains the road to heaven."'

Chapter 1688(7)

'Yudhishthira said, "O bull among the Bharata lineage! O best among the great ones! I wish to ask you about all the fruits of auspicious deeds. Tell me."

'Bhishma replied, "O Yudhishthira! Listen to this secret of the rishis, about the ends that they obtain and the ends that they desire after death. Whatever are the deeds performed in these bodies, the proportionate fruits are reaped in similar bodies. Whatever is the state in which one performs good deeds or evil deeds, from one birth to another, the fruits are enjoyed in a similar state. Deeds that are performed with the five senses are never destroyed. As a sixth, the atman always remains as a witness. A sacrifice must be performed by honouring with the five dakshinas—by giving one's eyes,[50] by giving one's mind, by giving one's words and by giving one's devotions.[51] If one cheerfully gives to an exhausted traveller, even if one has never seen him before, one obtains great and auspicious merits. If one lies down on the bare ground, one obtains houses and beds.[52] If one wears rags and barks, one obtains garments and ornaments. A person who is a store of austerities and immerses himself in yoga obtains mounts and vehicles. A king who lies down alongside a fire is said to obtain manliness. A person who refrains from tasty food obtains good fortune. A person who refrains from flesh obtains animals and sons. A person who hangs, with his head downwards, lives in the water, or always sleeps alone,[53] obtains the desired objective. If a person honours a guest and gives him water to wash the feet, a seat, a lamp, food and refuge, it is as if he has performed a sacrifice with the five kinds of dakshinas. If a person sits on a seat meant for heroes, lies down on a bed meant for heroes and frequents the places meant for heroes,[54] he obtains the eternal worlds where all the objects of desire are available. O lord of the earth! Riches are obtained by making gifts. Silence leads to others being obedient. Objects of pleasure are obtained through austerities. A long life is obtained through brahmacharya. Beauty, prosperity and lack of disease are the fruits obtained through non-violence. A person who eats fruits and roots obtains a kingdom. A person

[50]Metaphorically.

[51]Implicitly, for a guest.

[52]In a subsequent life.

[53]An indirect reference to brahmacharya.

[54]All of these are references to the field of battle.

who eats leaves obtains heaven. If a person fasts, there is happiness everywhere in the kingdom. Heaven is obtained through truth, an excellent lineage is obtained by being consecrated for a sacrifice. Through subsisting only on vegetables, cattle are obtained. Those who desire to go to heaven should subsist on grass. If one bathes thrice after intercourse with one's wife and inhales air, one obtains the fruits of a sacrifice. A person who only subsists on water is like a cleansed brahmana who always tends to the fire. A desert-like penance[55] ensures a kingdom and indestructible residence in the vault of heaven. O king! If a person consecrates himself in a sacrifice that involves fasting and performs this for twelve years, he obtains a region that is better than the one meant for heroes. If one studies all the Vedas, one is instantly freed from all misery. If one follows dharma in one's mind, one obtains the world of heaven. Evil intentions are extremely difficult to conquer. They are not destroyed, even when the body ages. They are like a disease that causes loss of life. If one can discard this thirst, one obtains happiness. A calf is able to identify its mother even among one thousand cows. In that way, earlier deeds always follow the doer. When the time arrives, flowers and fruits develop. So it is with deeds that have been performed earlier. When the body ages, the hair also ages. When the body ages, the teeth age. The eyes and ears also age. However, thirst is not destroyed. When the father is pleased, Prajapati is pleased. When the mother is pleased, it is as if the earth is worshipped. When the preceptor is pleased, it is as if Brahma is worshipped. When these three are respected, all kinds of dharma are respected. When they are disrespected, all rites are fruitless."'

Vaishampayana said, 'On hearing Bhishma's words, the bulls among the Kurus were astounded. Their minds became cheerful and they were delighted. Mantras are futile without sacrifices. Soma is futile unless it is rendered as an offering. A fire without oblations is futile. In that way, without studying, everything is futile. O lord! I have told you what the rishis said about the fruits of good and bad deeds. What else do you wish to hear?'

[55]That is, abstinence from drinking.

Chapter 1689(8)

'Yudhishthira asked, "O descendant of the Bharata lineage! Who should be worshipped? Whom should one bow down to? Whom do you bow down before? O king! Tell me everything about the ones you like. When you confront a hardship, what excellent things does your mind turn towards? Amidst everything in the world of men, and in the next world, what is most beneficial?"

'Bhishma replied, "I like brahmanas for whom the brahman represents supreme wealth and who have themselves determined that austerities and careful studying constitute heaven. I like those who bear the burden of the aged, the young and fathers and grandfathers, without suffering from this. There are virtuous ones who are learned, humble, self-controlled, mild in speech, full of knowledge and good conduct and always knowledgable about the brahman. When they speak in an assembly, they are like flocks of swans.[56] Their words are beautiful and auspicious in form, like the rumblings of celestial clouds. O Yudhishthira! When they are heard, their words are pronounced well. Their words are heard by kings, for happiness in this world and in the next. They are always honoured by those who hear them in assemblies. They are accomplished with the qualities of vijnana. I like them. O king! O Yudhishthira! There are those who always give and try to satisfy brahmanas who are extremely polished and auspicious, possessing the qualities. I like them. It is easy to fight in a battle. But it is not easy to give, without a sense of malice. O Yudhishthira! In this world, there are hundreds of brave and valiant people. Among all those numbers, those who are brave in giving are superior. I would have regarded myself as fortunate had I been an ordinary and amiable brahmana, not to speak of one born in a noble lineage, devoted to austerities and learning and knowledgable about the progress of dharma. O descendant of the

[56]If milk is mixed with water, swans have a reputation for drinking the milk, leaving out the water. Learned people can thus distinguish between the good and the bad.

Pandu lineage! In this world, there is nothing that is dearer to me than you. O bull among the Bharata lineage! However, brahmanas are dearer to me than you. O extender of the Kuru lineage! Since brahmanas are dearer to me than you, through that truth, I will go to the world where Shantanu has gone. However, my father is not dearer to me than brahmanas. Nor is this true of my father's father, or other well-wishers. There is nothing that I desire from brahmanas, small or large, though I am known as a performer of virtuous deeds.[57] O scorcher of enemies! In deeds, thoughts and words, I have done good to brahmanas. That is the reason I am not tormented now.[58] I am content that I am referred to as one who is devoted to brahmanas. It is said that they are supremely sacred among all those who are sacred. Since I have followed brahmanas, I see many pure and auspicious worlds. O son! In a short while, those are the regions I will go to. O Yudhishthira! In this world, the dharma for women is to be devoted to their husbands. They are like gods. Like that, other than brahmanas, there is no other destination for kshatriyas. If a kshatriya is one hundred years old and a brahmana is ten years old, know that in deciding who is a father and who is a son, it is the brahmana who will be regarded as the father. In the absence of her husband, a woman accepts her husband's younger brother as her husband. In that way, in the absence of brahmanas, the earth made kshatriyas her lord. O supreme among the Kuru lineage! Like the fire, brahmanas must be worshipped. They must be protected like a son and revered like a father. They are upright and virtuous. They are truthful and good in conduct. They are engaged in the welfare of all beings. They must always be honoured. When brahmanas are enraged, they are like venomous serpents. Their energy and austerities can always cause fright. Therefore, one must avoid their energy and their austerities. If they are unleashed, both can swiftly lead to fear. O great king! The wrath of an ascetic brahmana can kill. If either is released against a brahmana who has conquered anger, both are extinguished. But though extinguished, one is not

[57]The reverence is without a desire for fruits.

[58]Despite lying down on the bed of arrows.

entirely extinguished.[59] With a staff in his hand, a herdsman is always engaged in protecting the herd. Similarly, kshatriyas must always protect brahmanas and the brahman. They must protect brahmanas, who possess the energy of the brahman, like a father protects his son, and must look towards their houses, so that they have a means of sustenance."'

Chapter 1690(9)

'Yudhishthira asked, "O grandfather! O immensely wise one! There may be people who have promised things to brahmanas, but because of confusion, they do not subsequently give these. What happens to them? O supreme among those who uphold dharma! Tell me about this kind of dharma. What happens to the evil-minded men who do not give, despite having promised to?"

'Bhishma replied, "There may be a person who has promised to give a little or a lot, but does not give according to that promise. All his hopes are destroyed, like an impotent person trying to get offspring. O descendant of the Bharata lineage! Whatever good deeds he has performed between the night of his birth and the night of his death and all the oblations that he has offered are destroyed. People who are learned about the sacred texts of dharma have a saying about this. O best among the Bharata lineage! Using their supreme intelligence, they have spoken about this. People who are learned about the sacred texts of dharma cite an example, about being freed if one gives away one thousand horses with black ears.[60] O descendant

[59]This requires explanation. Kshatriyas possess energy, brahmanas possess both energy and austerities. Applied against a brahmana who has conquered anger, both are powerless. In general, if energy (the domain of kshatriyas) and austerities (the domain of brahmanas) are released against each other, energy is extinguished, but is unable to completely extinguish the power of austerities.

[60]Freed from the sin of having gone back on the promise. But this statement about giving away one thousand horses is left dangling.

of the Bharata lineage! In this connection, an ancient history is recounted, about a conversation between a jackal and a monkey. O scorcher of enemies! When they were humans, they used to be friends. They were subsequently born in the wombs of a she-jackal and a she-monkey. The monkey saw the jackal feeding off a corpse in the midst of a cremation ground. Remembering its earlier life, it asked, 'What wicked and extremely terrible deed did you perform earlier? Why are you in this cremation ground, feeding off vile and putrid carcasses?' Thus addressed by the monkey, the jackal replied, 'O monkey! I promised a brahmana something, but committed the injury of not giving it. Because of that sin, I have been born in this species. That is the reason, when I am hungry, I have to eat this kind of food.' O king! Earlier, I heard this spoken about, in connection with brahmanas.[61] The one who knows about dharma[62] recounted this ancient and auspicious story. O lord of the earth! O Pandava! I heard this again, when Krishna related accounts about brahmanas earlier.[63] This is the reason there is the perennial instruction. If one has promised to give something to a brahmana, one must always give it. One must not bring about one's destruction through brahmanas.[64] O lord of the earth! It has been said that if a brahmana's hopes have earlier been raised, this is like a blazing fire into which kindling has been offered. O king! If the hopes have been raised and he glances at anything angrily, he will burn everything down, like dead wood being consumed by a fire. O descendant of the Bharata lineage! If he resides in the kingdom, he must be rendered affectionate and satisfied, honoured with words. Then sons, grandsons, animals, relatives and stores in the city and the countryside will be nurtured with peace and benefit. The supreme energy of brahmanas can be seen, like the sun with the thousand rays shining down on the surface of the earth. O

[61]The Critical edition abruptly excises some shlokas that figure in non-critical versions. In those, the jackal asks a counter-question to the monkey. The monkey replies that it has been born as a monkey because it (in the earlier life) stole the fruits of brahmanas.

[62]Because of the abruptness, we do not know who this is.

[63]This Krishna is probably Vedavyasa.

[64]Through their curses.

Yudhishthira! O supreme among the Bharata lineage! Therefore, if one has promised something and desires a good birth in the next life, one must always give it. It is certain that one is capable of obtaining supreme heaven by giving to brahmanas. This is the greatest rite and the best of gifts. Know that such donations to brahmanas are gifts that keep the gods and the ancestors alive. O best among the Bharata lineage! Brahmanas are said to be like a great tirtha. There is no time of the day when one should not honour a brahmana who has arrived."'

Chapter 1691(10)

'Yudhishthira asked, "O rajarshi! O grandfather! If because of friendship or affection, a person imparts instructions to someone of inferior birth, is any sin incurred because of this? I wish to hear the truth about this. Please explain it. The progress of dharma is subtle. That is the reason men are confused."

'Bhishma replied, "O king! In this connection, following the sacred texts, rishis spoke about this earlier and I heard them. Listen. Instructions must never be given to someone who is of inferior birth. It is said that a teacher who imparts such instruction incurs a great sin. O king! O descendant of the Bharata lineage! There is an example about this. Listen. O king! O Yudhishthira! The evil that occurs has earlier been spoken about. There was a hermitage of brahmanas on the sacred slopes of the Himalayas. That sacred hermitage was full of a large number of trees. It was full of many creepers and plants and was inhabited by animals and birds. Siddhas and charanas frequented it. It was beautiful because of its flowering groves. There were many mendicants there and many handsome ascetics. The immensely fortunate brahmanas were like the sun or the fire in their splendour. It was full of ascetics who were accomplished in rituals and vows. O best among the Bharata lineage! They had consecrated themselves, were restrained in diet and had cleansed their souls. O bull among the

Bharata lineage! There were the sounds of the Vedas being studied. It was full of many valakhilya mendicants. There was a shudra who was driven by compassion. He arrived at that hermitage and was honoured by those ascetics. Those large numbers of sages were greatly energetic and were like the gods, having been consecrated in many kinds of ways. O descendant of the Bharata lineage! On seeing them, he was delighted. O bull among the Bharata lineage! His mind turned towards the idea of becoming an ascetic. O descendant of the Bharata lineage! He grasped the feet of the *kulapati*[65] and said, 'O bull among brahmanas! Through your favours, I wish to follow the path of dharma. O illustrious one! You should initiate me into a path of renunciation. O illustrious one! I belong to an inferior varna. O excellent one! I have been born as a shudra. I wish to serve you and have sought refuge with you. Show me your favours.'

'"The kulapati replied, 'It is not possible for a shudra to accept those indications. If your mind turns towards that, you should always engage in servitude.'"

'Bhishma continued, "O king! Having been thus addressed by the sage, the shudra began to think. 'What should I do now? I have great devotion towards the supreme dharma. Let it be known that I will do whatever brings me the greatest benefit.' Going some distance from the hermitage, he constructed a hut. O best among the Bharata lineage! He created a sacrificial altar and a spot for the gods on the ground. He cheerfully began to practise the rituals. He offered sacrifices and oblations and worshipped the gods. He controlled desire and followed the rituals. He lived on fruits and controlled his senses. He always collected herbs and fruits, so that he could worship the guests who arrived. In this way, he spent a long period of time. One day, to meet him, a sage came to that hermitage. He honoured the rishi who had come and following all the rites, satisfied him. He spoke pleasant words and as is proper, asked him about his welfare. The rishi was extremely energetic, with dharma in his soul and with

[65]Literally, kulapati means the head of a family or lineage. In this context, chancellor is more appropriate. More specifically, a kulapati is a teacher who has ten thousand students.

his senses in restraint. O bull among the Bharata lineage! O bull among men! In this way, desiring to see the shudra, the rishi came to the shudra's hermitage on several occasions. O bull among the Bharata lineage! On one such occasion, the shudra told the ascetic, 'I wish to perform rites for the ancestors. Please show me your favours.' O bull among the Bharata lineage! The brahmana agreed that he would certainly do so. The shudra purified himself and brought water for the rishi to wash his feet. O bull among the Bharata lineage! He brought darbha grass, wild herbs and the sacred seat known as a *brisi*.[66] However, the excellent head of the brisi was spread out in the southern direction. This was against the ordinances.[67] Seeing this, the rishi said, 'Place the head towards the east. Purify yourself and sit with your head facing the north.' The shudra acted in accordance with everything that the rishi had said. He was intelligent and spread out the darbha grass, following the instructions. As instructed by the ascetic, he followed all the rites of havya and kavya. He stayed on the path of dharma in observing rites for the ancestors. The rishi instructed him and when the rites for the ancestors were over, took his leave and departed. Subsequently, for a long period of time, the shudra ascetic tormented himself through austerities. O great king! Following these good practices, he died in the forest and thanks to these, the immensely radiant one was born in a lineage of kings. O son! O bull among the Bharata lineage! Following the progress of time, the rishi was also born as a brahmana, in a family of priests. The shudra and the sage were born in this way. They gradually grew up and became accomplished in learning. The rishi became extremely learned in the Atharva Veda, the Vedas,[68] and the application of kalpa[69] and also obtained excellence in astronomy. His delight in the study of the great sankhya increased. O descendant of the Bharata lineage! O king! When his father died, the prince performed the funeral rites and was instated by the subjects as a king. In turn, he

[66]Seat made of twisted grass and meant for an ascetic.

[67]The southern direction is inauspicious.

[68]The other three Vedas.

[69]The Vedanga that deals with rituals.

instated the rishi as his priest and placed him at the forefront. O bull among the Bharata lineage! He followed dharma and happily ruled the kingdom, protecting the subjects. However, whenever there was an occasion for sacred oblations to be offered or rites of dharma to be practised, the king glanced towards the priest and laughed loudly. O king! Thus, there were numerous occasions when he laughed at the priest. The priest noticed that the king always smiled or laughed at him. On seeing this, he was enraged. The priest came and met the king who was alone. He spoke pleasantly to him and put him at ease. O bull among the Bharata lineage! The priest then told that lord of men, 'O immensely wise one! I desire only a single boon from you.'

'"The king replied, 'O supreme among brahmanas! I will grant you one hundred boons, why only a single one? I like you and revere you greatly. There is nothing that I cannot give you.'

'"The priest said, 'O king! If you are satisfied with me, I desire only one single boon. O great king! If you wish to give me something, let it be such that you will always speak the truth to me, and never utter a falsehood.'"

'Bhishma said, "O Yudhishthira! Thus addressed, the king agreed and replied, 'I accept. If I know the answer, I will tell you. If I do not know, I will not speak.'

'"The priest asked, 'Whenever sacred oblations are being offered, the rites of dharma performed and chants of peace recited, why do you glance towards me and laugh? Since you laugh at me, my mind is ashamed. O king! You have pledged to tell me the truth. If you do not, you will be cursed. There must be some reason behind such sentiments. The laughter cannot be without reason. I am extremely curious. You should tell me the truth.'

'"The king replied, 'O brahmana! If you ask me in this way, I must certainly tell you the truth, even though this is not something that you should hear. O brahmana! Listen attentively. O supreme among brahmanas! Listen to what happened in our earlier births. O brahmana! I remember that. Listen with single-minded attention. I used to be a shudra earlier and practised terrible austerities. O supreme among brahmanas! You were a rishi who was fierce in his austerities. O brahmana! Your mind was favourably inclined towards me then. O unblemished one! Following your instructions, I had performed the funeral rites for my ancestors. O supreme among sages! I used brisi, darbha, havya and kavya. O Indra among brahmanas! Because of this transgression in deeds, you have been born as a priest.[70] I have been born as a king. Behold the progress of time. You imparted instructions for my sake and have reaped this fruit. O brahmana! O supreme among brahmanas! That is the reason I laugh at you. O brahmana! I do not laugh at you out of any disrespect. You are my superior. Indeed, I am enraged at this course of events and my mind is tormented. However, I remember our earlier births and laugh at you. Your fierce austerities have been destroyed by those instructions. Give up this priesthood and endeavour to be born again. O brahmana! Otherwise, you may obtain a birth that is inferior to the present one. O brahmana! Take whatever riches you want. O excellent one! Purify your self.'"

'Bhishma continued, "The king gave the brahmana many gifts and gave him permission to leave. He gave all the brahmanas riches, land and villages. As asked, that supreme among brahmanas observed many hardships. He went to places of pilgrimage and gave away diverse gifts. The brahmana donated cattle to brahmanas and cleansed his soul. He went to that hermitage[71] and performed a large number of austerities. O supreme among kings! In this way, the brahmana obtained supreme success. In that hermitage, he was revered by all those who dwelt in that hermitage. O supreme among kings! Thus, that rishi had faced this great hardship. A brahmana must not reveal things to someone of an inferior varna. O king! A brahmana must always refrain from parting with such instructions. A brahmana who parts with such instructions faces hardships. A king can always receive such instructions from a brahmana. But they should not be revealed to a person who belongs to an inferior varna. O king! Brahmanas, kshatriyas and vaishyas—these three

[70]A brahmana must not perform a sacrifice for a shudra. In this case, the brahmana hadn't actually performed the sacrifice, but had instructed the shudra on how to conduct it. Even that was a transgression.

[71]The hermitage of the earlier life.

are known as the twice-born varnas. A brahmana is not tainted if he tells them anything. Virtuous people do reveal things to those who are advanced in this way. The course of dharma is subtle and is difficult for those with unclean souls to comprehend. That is the reason sages remain silent and perform *diksha*[72] without speaking. O king! They are scared of saying something that should not have been said. There are those who follow dharma, possess all the qualities, are truthful and upright. Even they can perform the wicked act of speaking what should not be said. Therefore, one must never impart instructions to anyone. Through imparting instructions, a brahmana can incur a sin. Thus, a wise person who desires dharma should act wisely. Instruction bartered in exchange for something is evil. If one is asked about something, one must answer only after determining the consequences. An instruction must only be given when it leads to the accumulation of dharma. I have told you everything about imparting instructions. There can be great hardships as a result of imparting instructions."'

Chapter 1692(11)

'Yudhishthira said, "O bull among the Bharata lineage! O grandfather! In what kind of man or woman does Shri,[73] the one who resides in the lotus, always dwell? Tell me that."

'Bhishma replied, "I will tell you what transpired, as I have seen it and heard it. Rukmini asked this in the presence of Devaki's son.[74] She saw the blazing Shri seated on Narayana's lap, with a face like that of a lotus. The one with the beautiful eyes, the mother of the one

[72]Rite of initiating a disciple.

[73]Lakshmi, the goddess of prosperity and wealth.

[74]Devaki's son was Krishna. Rukmini was Krishna's wife and is regarded as Lakshmi's incarnation. Krishna and Rukmini's son was Pradyumna. The one with the makara on the banner is Kama, the god of love, and Pradyumna was his incarnation.

with a makara on his banner, was surprised and curious and asked this question. 'Who are the beings who worship you? Who are the ones you reside with? Who are the ones to whom you do not show favours? You are loved by the one who is the lord of the three worlds and is the destroyer of beings. O daughter of a maharshi![75] Tell me the truth about this.' Having been thus asked, in the presence of the one who has Garuda on his banner,[76] the goddess, whose face was as beautiful as the moon, was pleased and replied in sweet words. 'O beautiful one! O eloquent one! I dwell in men who are truthful and accomplished, who are engaged in deeds. I do not dwell in men who are not good in their deeds, or in those who are non-believers, cause a mixture of varnas and are ungrateful. I do not reside in those who are violent in conduct or indulge in perverse conduct. Nor do I reside in those who are thieves or malicious towards seniors. There are those who are limited in energy, strength, spirit and essence, who are incessantly delighted and enraged. I do not reside with them. O goddess! Nor do I reside with men who hide their true intentions. O goddess! If a man does not desire anything, has no natural enterprise and is always content with whatever little he possesses, I do not reside with him either. I dwell with those who follow dharma in their conduct, great-souled ones who know about dharma, those who serve their seniors, are great-souled and restrained and spirited. I dwell with women who are forgiving, generous, devoted to gods and brahmanas, truthful in their conduct and naturally restrained. I avoid women who do not look towards the broken vessels in their homes, who always speak against their husbands, who prefer the houses of others and are shameless. I avoid women who are fickle and unclean, who lick the corners of their mouths, who have no patience and are quarrelsome, who are addicted to sleep and are always lying down. I always reside with women who are truthful, beautiful to see, united with good fortune and qualities, devoted to their husbands, good in conduct and well-attired. I dwell in vehicles, maidens, ornaments,

[75]There are different stories about Lakshmi's origin. This is a reference to her being born as the daughter of the sage Bhrigu.

[76]Narayana.

sacrifices, clouds, rain, blooming lotuses, nakshatras in the autumn sky, mountains, pens of cattle, forests, lakes, blossoming lotuses,[77] rivers that resound with the calling of swans and the beautiful cries of cranes, with extensive banks and beautiful lakes, frequented by ascetics, siddhas and brahmanas. I always reside in large waterbodies where the water is agitated by lions and elephants. I am always there in mad elephants, bulls, kings, thrones and virtuous people. I always dwell in houses where oblations are offered to the fire, where cattle, brahmanas and gods are worshipped and in houses where, at the right time, flowers are offered as sacrifices in rites.[78] I reside in brahmanas who are always engaged in studying, in kshatriyas who are always devoted to dharma, in vaishyas who are engaged in agriculture and in shudras who are engaged in servitude. Single-mindedly, I dwell in Narayana. In every way, I am part of his body. It is in him that great dharma, the brahman and all delight exist. O goddess! I am incapable of saying that my embodied form resides in anything other than these. When I dwell in a man in the form of my attributes, his dharma, fame, artha and kama are enhanced.'"'

Chapter 1693(12)

'Yudhishthira said, "O king! When there is intercourse between a woman and a man, who feels the greater pleasure from this? I have a doubt about this and you should tell me."

'Bhishma replied, "In this connection, the ancient history of a conversation between Bhangashvana and Shakra is recounted, as if there was an old enmity between them. In ancient times, there was a rajarshi named Bhangashvana and he was extremely devoted to dharma. O tiger among men! He was without a son and performed

[77]The text mentions three words for lotus—*padma*, *utpala* (also a water-lily) and *pankaja*.

[78]The suggestion is that flowers are offered as sacrifices, instead of animal sacrifices.

a sacrifice for the sake of obtaining a son. The immensely strong one performed a sacrifice named Agnishtu,[79] one that is hated by Indra. Mortal beings who desire sons perform this, as atonement for their sins. The immensely fortunate Indra, lord of the gods, got to know about this sacrifice. Though the rajarshi was controlled in his soul, he began to search for an internal weakness. After some time, the king went out on a hunt. Taking this to be an opportunity, Shakra confused the king. Confused by Indra, the rajarshi wandered around, alone on his horse. The king could not determine any of the directions and was afflicted by hunger and thirst. Afflicted by thirst and exhaustion, the king wandered around, here and there. He then saw a beautiful lake and it was full of excellent water. O son! Having alighted from the horse, he made it drink from the lake. When the horse had drunk, the best among kings tied it to a tree. Descending into the lake, the king bathed and assumed the form of a woman. On seeing that he had turned into a woman, the best among kings was ashamed. He was anxious in his senses and consciousness. His entire self was immersed in thoughts. 'How will I climb onto the horse? How will I return to the city? Because of the sacrifice named Agnishtu, one hundred sons have been born from my loins. They have been born as immensely strong ones. What will I tell them, or my wives, well-wishers and the inhabitants of the city and the country? Rishis who have seen the truth about dharma have said that mildness, gentleness and timidity are the qualities of women. The attributes of men are exertion, harshness and valour. Why has my manliness been destroyed and why have I obtained womanhood? Because of these traits of having become a woman, I am no longer interested in climbing onto the horse again.' With a great deal of effort, the lord of men managed to climb onto the horse. O son! O supreme among kings! Having assumed the form of a woman, he returned to the city.

'"His sons, wives, servants and the inhabitants of the city and the countryside were extremely surprised on seeing him and wanted to know what had happened. The rajarshi, supreme among eloquent ones, had assumed the form of a woman and spoke to them. 'I went

[79]A sacrifice that invokes Agni.

out on a hunt, surrounded by a strong army. Confounded by destiny, I was confused and entered a terrible forest. That forest was extremely fearful. I was afflicted by thirst and had lost my senses. I then saw a beautiful lake that was populated by birds. Having bathed there, I assumed the form of a woman. There is no doubt that this is nothing but destiny. This must be because I am not content with my sons, my wives and my riches.' The best among kings, who had assumed the form of a woman, then spoke to his sons. 'O sons! Happily enjoy this kingdom. I will leave for the forest.' Consecrating those one hundred sons, the king left for the forest.

'"O son! That woman arrived in an ascetic's hermitage. Through that ascetic and in that hermitage, she gave birth to one hundred sons. Collecting these sons, she returned to her house and told her earlier sons, 'You are my sons when I was a man. I have obtained these one hundred sons as a woman. O sons! With fraternal sentiments, enjoy this kingdom together.' Together, they began to enjoy the kingdom, like brothers. Seeing that they were enjoying that excellent kingdom with brotherly affection, Indra of the gods began to think. He was overcome with anger. 'I seem to have done a good turn to this rajarshi, instead of injuring him.'[80] Assuming the form of a brahmana, Shatakratu, the king of the gods, went to the city, hoping to spread dissension among the princes. He said, 'There is no fraternal affection among brothers, even if they happen to be sons of the same father. On account of the kingdom, there was conflict between the gods and the asuras, though both were Kashyapa's sons. You are the sons of Bhangashvana. The others are the sons of the ascetic. The gods and the asuras were the sons of Kashyapa. This paternal kingdom is yours. It should not be enjoyed by the sons of the ascetic.' With Indra having spread dissension, they fought against each other and killed each other.

'"Hearing this, the ascetic lady[81] was tormented and started to lament. In the disguise of a brahmana, Indra arrived there and asked her, 'O one with the beautiful face! Why are you tormented by

[80]Indra had turned the king into a woman.

[81]Bhangashvana in the form of a woman.

grief and why are you weeping?' Seeing the brahmana, the woman piteously replied, 'O brahmana! Two hundred of my sons have been brought down by destiny. O brahmana! I used to be a king and had one hundred sons. O supreme among brahmanas! They were born from me and were handsome and valiant. On one occasion, I went out for a hunt and was confused in the desolate forest. O supreme among brahmanas! Having bathed in a lake, I assumed the form of a woman. Having established my sons in the kingdom, I departed for the forest. In the form of a woman, through a great-souled ascetic, I obtained one hundred sons. O brahmana! They were born in the hermitage and were conveyed by me to the city. O brahmana! Because of destiny, enmity was generated between them. O Indra among brahmanas! I have been overwhelmed by destiny and that is the reason I am grieving.' Seeing that she was afflicted, Indra spoke these harsh words. 'O fortunate one! Earlier, you caused me great hardship and your pain has been caused by me. O evil-minded one! You did not invoke Indra through a sacrifice and you showed me disrespect. I am Indra. O evil-minded one! That is the reason you have caused an enmity between us.' Seeing Indra, the rajarshi fell at his feet and bowed her head down. She said, 'O best among the gods! Be pacified. That sacrifice was performed for the sake of a son. O tiger among the gods! There was no intention to injure you and therefore, you should pardon me.' Seeing that she had prostrated herself, Indra was satisfied and granted her a boon. 'O king! Tell me. Which of your sons do you wish to bring back to life, those born while you were a woman, or those born while you were a man?' The ascetic lady joined her hands in salutation and replied to Indra, 'O Vasava! Let the ones born while I was a woman come back to life.' Surprised and pleased at this, Indra again asked the woman, 'Why do you dislike the sons you obtained while you were a man? Why is it that you entertain greater affection for those who were born while you were a woman? I wish to hear the reason behind this. You should tell me.'

'"The woman replied, 'The affection borne by a woman is much greater than that borne by a man. O Shakra! Therefore, the ones born while I was a woman should come back to life.'"

'Bhishma said, "Addressed thus, Indra was delighted and spoke these words. 'O one who speaks the truth! All of your sons will come back to life. O Indra among kings! O one excellent in vows! Ask for another boon that you desire. Ask for whatever you wish, the state of a man, or the state of a woman.'

'"The women replied, 'O Shakra! O Vasava! If it pleases you, I wish to remain as a woman.'"

'Bhishma continued, "Hearing this, Indra of the gods replied to the woman, 'O lord! Why do you wish to give up your manhood? Why does remaining a woman please you?' Thus addressed, the supreme among kings, who was in the form of a woman, replied, 'In an act of intercourse, the pleasure obtained by a woman is greater than that obtained by a man. O Shakra! That is the reason why I desire to remain as a woman. O supreme among gods! Truthfully, there is greater pleasure in being a woman. O lord of the thirty gods! I am content with this state of being a woman. Let me go.' Hearing this response to what he had asked, he agreed and returned to heaven. O great king! Thus, it is said that women obtain the greater pleasure."'

Chapter 1694(13)

'Yudhishthira asked, "If a man desires benefit in this progress through the world, what should he do? In this journey through the world, what kind of conduct should he follow?"

'Bhishma replied, "Three kinds of deeds done with the body, four kinds done with speech and three types done with the mind—these ten kinds of deeds should be avoided. Destruction of life, theft and intercourse with someone else's wife—these three kinds of wicked deeds done with the body should be avoided. O Indra among kings! Evil conversation, harsh words, calumny and falsehood—one should not think of committing these four kinds of sin with speech. Not desiring the possessions of others, affection towards all creatures and belief that deeds lead to fruits—these are the three that must be followed with the mind. With words, body or the mind, a man must not perform any sinful deeds. Depending on whether one performs good or bad deeds, one obtains the fruits."'

Chapter 1695(14)

'Yudhishthira said, "O grandfather! Tell me the truth about the different names of the lord Isha Shambhu, the tawny one who represents great fortune, the one who withdraws the universe."

'Bhishma replied, "O Yudhishthira! You have asked me about Shiva, whose form is the universe. The god Vishnu, the preceptor of the gods and the asuras, can tell you about him. In ancient times, Tandi[82] was born from Brahma. In Brahma's world, in front of Brahma, he recited one thousand names of that god. Dvaipayana and other rishis, controlled, rich in austerities and extremely good in their vows, heard these devotedly. He is Dhruva,[83] Nandi,[84] Hotri,[85] Goptri,[86] the creator of the universe, Agni, the immensely fortunate one, the lord, Mundin[87] and Kapardin.[88]

'"Vasudeva said, 'The gods, Indra and the maharshis, with Hiranyagarbha at the forefront, are incapable of understanding the truth about the progress of his deeds. Even those who possess the subtle sight of knowledge do not know the one who is the beginning and the end. How can an ordinary man comprehend the virtuous one? I will properly recount to you some of the qualities of the illustrious one who is the slayer of asuras and is the lord of vows.'"'

[82]A rishi.

[83]The fixed and immovable one.

[84]Shiva's name, meaning the cheerful one.

[85]The one who sacrifices.

[86]The guardian or protector.

[87]The one with the shaved head.

[88]The one with the matted hair.

Vaishampayana continued, 'Saying this, the illustrious, great-souled and intelligent one[89] purified himself by touching water and recounted the qualities.

'Vasudeva said, "O Indras among brahmanas! O Yudhishthira! O father![90] O son of the river![91] Listen to the names of the lord of the universe. For the sake of Samba, I meditated earlier and could see the illustrious one, something that is very difficult to accomplish.[92] Twelve years passed after Rukmini's intelligent son killed Shambara.[93] Jambavati spoke to me. She saw Pradyumna, Charudeshna and the other sons who had been born from Rukmini. O Yudhishthira! Desiring a son, she spoke these words to me. 'O one without decay! Quickly grant me a brave son who is the best among strong ones and is beautiful and without sin, one who is like you. There is nothing in the three worlds that you cannot obtain. O extender of the Yadu lineage! If you so desire, you can create supreme worlds. For twelve years, you dried yourself by subsisting only on air. You worshipped the lord of creatures[94] and obtained sons through Rukmini—Charudeshna, Sucharu, Charuvesha, Yasodhara, Charushrava, Charuyasha, Pradyumna and Shambhu. Through Rukmini, you obtained sons who are excellent in their valour. In that way, also grant me a son who is powerful.' Thus addressed by that goddess, I spoke to the one with the excellent waist. 'O queen! Grant me leave. I will act in accordance with your words.' She told me, 'Go. May you be victorious and obtain what is auspicious. May Brahma, Shiva, Kashyapa, the rivers, the gods who follow the mind, the fields, the herbs, the hymns that convey sacrificial offerings, the large numbers of rishis, the earth,

[89]Vasudeva.

[90]The word used is tata, which means father, but is used for anyone who is older or senior. Yudhishthira was older to Krishna.

[91]Meaning Bhishma.

[92]Samba was the son of Krishna and Jambavati. Krishna obtained Samba as a son, after praying to Shiva in the hermitage of the sage Upamanyu.

[93]Pradyumna was the son of Krishna and Rukmini. Pradyumna killed the demon Shambara.

[94]Shiva.

the oceans, the dakshinas, the chants, the bears, the ancestors, the planets, the wives of the gods, the daughters of the gods, the mothers of the gods, the manvantaras, the cattle, the moon, the son, Hari, Savitri, the knowledge of the brahman, the seasons, the years, the *kshapas*,[95] the kshanas, the lavas, the muhurtas, the nimeshas and the progress of the yugas always protect you. O Yadava! Wherever you go, may they bring you cheer. O unblemished one! May you be safe and undistracted along your path.' When she had pronounced her benedictions in this way, I took my leave of that daughter of the Indra of the apes.[96] I then went to my father, supreme among men, my mother, the king and Ahuka.[97] I told them the purport of what the daughter of the Indra among the vidyadharas had told me, in great affliction.[98] Miserably, I took their leave and then went to Gada and the immensely strong Rama.[99] Having taken the permission of the seniors, I thought of Tarkshya.[100] He bore me to the Himalayas and I let him go. It was on that supreme of mountains that I saw the one who is the creator of beings. I saw an excellent hermitage, the best place for performing austerities. This divine spot belonged to the great-souled Upamanyu, the descendant of Vyaghrapada. It was revered by the gods and the gandharvas and possessed all the signs of the brahman. There were *dhavas*,[101] *kakubhas*,[102] *kadambas*,[103]

[95]Kshapa means night and also means a day of twenty-four hours. Kshana is a measurement of time, with differing interpretations. A second or an instant is accurate enough. Lava is a small fraction of a second. Muhurta is forty-eight minutes. Nimesha is the twinkling of an eye, a minute.

[96]Jambavati was the daughter of Jambavan or Jambavat. Jambavat is sometimes described as a king of the bears and sometimes as a king of the apes.

[97]The king means Ugrasena and Ahuka was Ugrasena's father.

[98]A vidyadhara is a supernatural being. Here, the expression is being used for Jambavati.

[99]Rama means Balarama. Gada was Krishna's brother.

[100]Garuda.

[101]The axlewood tree.

[102]The Arjuna tree.

[103]Kind of tree, *Nauclea cadamba*.

coconut trees, *kurabakas*,[104] *ketakas*,[105] *jambus*,[106] *patalas*,[107] *vatas*,[108] *varunakas*,[109] *vatsanabhas*,[110] *bilvas*,[111] *saralas*,[112] *kapitthas*,[113] *priyalas*,[114] *salas*,[115] *talas*,[116] *badaris*, *kundas*,[117] *punnagas*,[118] *ashokas*,[119] mango trees, *atimuktakas*,[120] *bhallatakas*,[121] *madhukas*,[122] *champakas*,[123] *panasas*[124] and many other kinds of wild trees that were full of fruits and flowers. The place was covered with flowers, creepers and lantanas and was adorned with the roots of plantain trees. The trees were full of fruit and many kinds of birds fed on them. These[125] were flung around here and there, decorating the forest and making it beautiful. The place was inhabited by ruru antelopes, elephants, tigers, lions and leopards. There were deer and peacocks, wild cats and snakes. There were herds of animals and buffaloes and bears. Pleasant winds blew, bearing pollen from many flowers and the scent of *gajapushpa* flowers. Many songs were sung be celestial women. O brave one! There were sounds from streams,

[104]Red amaranth.

[105]The crew pine.

[106]Rose apple.

[107]*Bignonia suaveolens.*

[108]Banyan, Indian fig tree.

[109]Garlic pear tree.

[110]Kind of tree.

[111]Wood-apple tree.

[112]Kind of pine.

[113]Wood-apple tree.

[114]The Chironji tree.

[115]Kind of tree.

[116]Palm tree.

[117]Jasmine.

[118]This can mean either nutmeg or a white lotus. Here, white lotus fits better.

[119]Kind of tree, *Saraca indica.*

[120]The Harimantha tree.

[121]Cashew nut tree.

[122]The honey tree, *Madhuca longifolia.*

[123]*Magnolia champaca.*

[124]Jackfruit.

[125]The fruits.

the singing of birds, the auspicious trumpeting of elephants, the songs sung by kinnaras and the sacred chants of Sama hymns. The mind cannot think of those ornamented lakes. There were large altars for the sacrificial fire, covered in kusha grass. O king! That place was always decorated and swept by the pure and auspicious waters of Jahnu's daughter.[126] The best among maharshis, great-souled ones who were the upholders of dharma, were always there and they were like the fire. Some of them only subsisted on air and others only subsisted on water. Those ascetics were always engaged in meditating and cleansing themselves. Some subsisted on smoke, others on fire and still others on milk. In every direction, it was full of Indras among the brahmanas. There were some who followed the conduct of cattle.[127] Some used stones to grind grain.[128] Some used their teeth to grind.[129] Some fed on rays.[130] Some fed on foam. There were others who conducted themselves like deer.[131] They followed great hardships and rituals and observed excellent austerities. My eyes grew wide and I wished to enter that place. O descendant of the Bharata lineage! O king! That circle of hermitages was as radiant as the solar disc in the firmament. It was revered by the large number of gods and all great-souled ones, even the likes of Shiva. Snakes and mongooses played there. Deer and tiger were like friends. This was because of the power of those ascetics, who possessed all the qualities. That best of hermitages was pleasant to all creatures. It was inhabited by tigers among brahmanas, accomplished in the Vedas and the Vedangas. There were great-souled rishis, renowned because they practised many rituals. Entering there, I saw the lord,[132] who was attired in tattered rags and bark. Because of the energy of his austerities, he blazed like a fire. That bull among brahmanas was tranquil and young and was in the midst of his disciples.

[126]That is, Ganga.

[127]They ate what they found and did not store food.

[128]Known as *ashmakuttas*.

[129]Known as *dantolukhalinas*.

[130]Of the sun and the moon.

[131]Like the cattle.

[132]Upamanyu.

'"When I bowed my head down and greeted him, Upamanyu said, 'O Pundarikaksha! Welcome. Our austerities have now become successful. You should be honoured, but you are honouring me. You should be seen, but you wish to see me.' I joined my hands in salutation and asked him about his welfare and dharma, that of his disciples and that of the animals, the birds and the sacrificial fire. The illustrious one addressed me in amiable and extremely sweet words. 'O Krishna! There is no doubt that you will obtain a son who is just like your own self. Perform extremely great austerities and satisfy the lord Ishana. O Adhokshaja! With his wife, he sports here. O Janardana! In ancient times, it was here that the gods and the large numbers of rishis satisfied that best of gods with thier austerities, brahmacharya, truth and self-control and obtained their sacred wishes. The illustrious one is the store of energy and austerities here. He creates everything that is good and bad and withdraws them back again. O destroyer of enemies! He is the unthinkable god you wish to meet. He is here, with the goddess. A great danava named Hiranyakashipu was born. He could make Mount Meru tremble. From Sharva,[133] he obtained a boon that he would obtain the prosperity of the immortals for one billion years. His eldest son was the famous Mandara. Because of a boon from Mahadeva, he could fight with Shakra for one billion years. O son![134] O Keshava! In those ancient times, Vishnu's terrible chakra and Akhandala's[135] vajra were shattered on the evil one's body. Like an evil planet, that extremely powerful one afflicted the gods. O king! Because of the boon obtained from Shiva, that asura was a severe burden on Indra of the gods. Vidyutprabha[136] satisfied him and intoxicated at this, roamed around the three worlds. He was the lord of all the worlds for one hundred thousand years. He[137] said, "Always be my companion." The lord gave him the boon that he would have one million sons. The illustrious one, who has no birth, gave him the

[133]Shiva.

[134]The word used is tata.

[135]Indra's.

[136]Another demon.

[137]Shiva.

kingdom known as Kushadvipa. Dhatri[138] created another great asura named Shatamukha. For one hundred years, he offered flesh from his own body as oblations into the fire. Satisfied with this, the illustrious Shankara asked him, "What can I do for you?" Shatamukha replied, "O best among the gods! Please grant me extraordinary yoga, so that I can possess eternal strength." He[139] agreed. In ancient times, for the sake of sons, Svayambhu[140] performed a sacrifice. He entered his atman for three hundred years and resorted to yoga. Honoured by this sacrifice, the god[141] gave him one thousand sons. O Krishna! Know that there is no doubt about him being the lord of yoga, referred to in the songs of the gods. In ancient times, the Valakhilyas were disrespected by Maghavan.[142] They were enraged and satisfied the illustrious Rudra through their austerities. The best of the gods and the lord of the universe was pleased and told them, "Through your austerities, you will create Suparna and he will steal the soma."[143] In ancient times, the waters were destroyed because of Mahadeva's wrath. The other gods satisfied him with the sacrifice known as *saptakapala*[144] and made them flow again. Atri's wife was knowledgable about the brahman and abandoned her husband.[145] She said, "I will never again subjugate myself to this sage." Having said this, she sought refuge with Mahadeva. Terrified of Atri, she fasted for three hundred years, lying down on a bed of clubs and trying to please Bhava.[146] The god appeared before her, smiled and said, "You will obtain a son, as you desire. He will be famous in a lineage that is named after him."[147] O Keshava!

[138]Brahma.

[139]Shiva.

[140]Brahma.

[141]Shiva.

[142]Indra.

[143]As an act of revenge, the Valakhilyas created Garuda/Suparna, who stole the soma from Indra.

[144]Sacrifice performed in seven vessels.

[145]Atri's wife was Anasuya. She left Atri because he was too dominating.

[146]Shiva.

[147]This son was Dattatreya.

Shakalya[148] restrained his soul for nine hundred years and worshipped Bhava through mental sacrifices. The illustrious one was satisfied and told him, "You will be the composer of books. O son! Your deeds will be famous in the three worlds and will never decay. Your lineage will not decay and will be adorned by many maharshis." In krita yuga, there was a famous rishi by the name of Savarni.[149] For six thousand years, he tormented himself through austerities here. The illustrious Rudra was pleased. He showed himself to him and said, "O unblemished one! I am satisfied with you. You will be without old age and without death. You will be a composer of books and will be famous in the worlds." O son![150] O Madhava! In ancient times, I have also seen the lord, the god of the gods. I saw Pashupati himself. Listen to this. O immensely energetic one! In ancient times, I made endeavours to worship Mahadeva. Listen to the details. Earlier, I learnt this from Mahadeva, the god of the gods, himself. O unblemished one! I will tell you everything about that now. O son! In ancient times, in krita yuga, there was an immensely illustrious rishi. He was known as Vyaghrapada and he was accomplished in the Vedas and the Vedangas. I was his son and Dhoumya was born as my younger brother. O Madhava! On one occasion, while playing with Dhoumya, I went to a hermitage where there were sages who had cleansed their souls. I saw a cow being milked there. I saw the milk and it seemed to me to be as tasty as amrita. O Madhava! There were also cakes being boiled in water. We were given milk to drink. O son! I had never tasted the milk of cows earlier. O son! I was no longer happy with cakes boiled in water. In my childishness, I told my mother, "Please give me some food cooked in milk." My mother was overcome with grief. O Madhava! Out of affection for her son, she embraced me and inhaled the fragrance of my head. She said, "O son! How can sages who have cleansed their souls have food with milk? We always reside in forests and eat bulbs, roots and fruits.

[148]Famous sage. The major recension of the Rig Veda that still survives is the Shakalya version.

[149]This is probably a reference to the Manu of the eighth manvantara.

[150]The word used is tata.

O son! Without the favours of the undecaying Sthanu Virupaksha, how can one obtain food cooked with milk, objects of pleasure or garments? O son! In every possible way, always seek refuge with Shankara. O son! It is through his favours that you will obtain all the fruits that you desire." O slayer of enemies! Since that day, on hearing my mother's words, my faith and devotion in Mahadeva were aroused. I resorted to austerities to satisfy Shankara. I stood on the tips of my toes for one thousand celestial years. For one hundred years, I subsisted only on fruit. For a second one hundred, I subsisted on dried leaves. For a third one hundred, I subsisted on water. Then, for seven hundred years, I only lived on air. The lord Mahadeva, the lord of all the worlds, was pleased. He assumed Shakra's form and was surrounded by large numbers of all the gods. The immensely illustrious one was in the form of the thousand-eyed one and held the vajra in his hand. He was astride a gigantic elephant that was extremely white and red-eyed. Its ears were folded back and it was crazy with musth. The trunk was rolled back. It was terrible and had four tusks. The illustrious one was seated astride this, radiant in his own energy. He advanced, with a diadem on his head and adorned with necklaces and bracelets. A white umbrella was held aloft his head. He was served by apsaras and celestial gandharvas sung his praises. He said, "O supreme among brahmanas! I am Indra of the gods and I am pleased with you. Ask a boon from me, whatever it is that your mind cherishes." I wasn't pleased on hearing Shakra's words. O Krishna! Hearing the words of the king of the gods, I replied, "O amiable one! I desire no boon from you nor from any of the other gods, with the exception of Mahadeva. I am telling you this truthfully. On Pashupati's words, I am ready to become a worm, or a tree with many branches. Without Pashupati's favours, the prosperous kingdom of the three worlds will not bring me any benefit. On Shankara's instructions, I will become a worm or an insect. O Shakra! However, if they are granted by you, I do not desire the three worlds. He wears the sparkling crescent of the moon on his crest. As long as the illustrious lord, Pashupati, is not pleased with me, I will bear these hundreds of hardships of old age, death and birth. I will bear these miseries in bodies. He blazes like the sun, the moon and the fire. He is the single one who conveys across the impermanence of the three worlds. It is through Rudra's favours that one overcomes old age and becomes immortal. In this universe, where is the man who can obtain tranquility without him?" Shakra asked, "What is the reason why you regard him as the cause behind all causes? Why don't you desire the favours of any god other than him?"'

'"Upamanyu answered, 'Why does one have to think of reasons as to why Isha is the cause behind all causes? We have not heard of the gods worshipping anyone else's signs. If we leave aside Maheshvara, who is the other one whom the gods worship in all his signs? Has any such person been worshipped earlier? If you have heard this, tell me. You, Brahma, Vishnu and the other gods always worship his signs. Therefore, he is the supreme one. O Koushika![151] Therefore, I desire a boon from him and am ready to be destroyed otherwise. O Shakra! O slayer of Bala! Stay or go, as you wish. I desire to have a boon, or a curse, from none other than Maheshvara. I do not desire it from any other god, even if it brings all the fruits of desire.'

'"Upamanyu continued,[152] 'Once I had said this to Indra of the gods, my senses were overcome with grief. Why has Rudra not been pleased with me? That is what I thought. In a short instant, I again saw Airavata.[153] It transformed itself into a bull that was as white as a swan or jasmine, as radiant as the stalk of a white lily and like the ocean of milk itself. It was huge in size and its tail was black. Its eyes were reddish brown, like honey. Throughout, the horns were ornamented with molten gold. Its eyes were red and it had large nostrils. Its ears and waist were excellent. Its flanks were excellent and it possessed a huge neck. It was handsome and beautiful to behold. The dazzling hump covered the entire shoulder. It was like the snow-clad summit of a mountain, or the crest of a white cloud. With Uma,

[151]Koushika is one of Indra's names.

[152]Upamanyu has just finished speaking to Indra. Now he continues speaking to Krishna.

[153]Indra's elephant.

the illustrious god of the gods was seated on it. Mahadeva was as resplendent as the lord of the stars[154] on a full-moon night. The flames of his energy were like lightning tinging the clouds. It was as if one thousand suns had enveloped everything. The immensely energetic Ishvara was like the fire of destruction that arises at the end of a yuga and consumes all creatures. Since that energy pervaded everything, it was difficult to see anything. My heart again became anxious. I thought "what is this?" In a short while, that energy pervaded the ten directions. However, through the maya of the god of the gods, it also became pacified in an instant. I then saw the illustrious Sthanu Maheshvara stationed there. He was astride Surabhi's descendant[155] and was as peaceful as a fire without smoke. Parvati, beautiful in every limb, was with Parameshvara. The great-souled Nilakantha is the store of the energy of detachment. Sthanu possessed eighteen arms, adorned with all the ornaments. The god was attired in white garments. He had white garlands and unguents. The unassailable standard was white. His sacred thread was also white. His divine companions were like him in valour. They surrounded him, singing, dancing and playing on musical instruments. A white crescent moon was his diadem, arising like the moon in the autumn. The three eyes blazed and looked like three suns that had arisen. The god dazzled, wearing a garland that was white in complexion. It was made out of molten gold and strung with lotuses and decorated with gems. O Govinda! On the infinitely energetic Bhava's person, I also saw the embodied forms of weapons, all of them radiating energy. The great-souled one's bow possessed a thousand colours, like that of the rainbow. This is famous as Pinaka, but is actually a giant serpent. It is giant in form and has seven heads. Its fangs are sharp and its poison is virulent. With a giant neck, it was stationed in a man's embodied form, with the bowstring wound around it. The arrow was like the sun and was as resplendent as the fire of destruction. This was the great and extremely terrible divine weapon, the Pashupata. It was unmatched, impossible to describe and fearful to all creatures. It

[154]The moon.

[155]Surabhi is the mother of all cattle and is also the divine cow.

was gigantic in size, with sparks, and seemed to spout out fire. It possessed a single foot and giant teeth.[156] It had one thousand heads and one thousand stomachs. There were one thousand arms and one thousand eyes, and these seemed to spout out fire. O mighty-armed one! It is superior to Brahma, Narayana, Aindra, Agneya and Varuna weapons and is capable of countering all weapons. O Govinda! In ancient times, Mahadeva sported around and with this single arrow, in an instant, consumed and reduced Tripura to ashes. There is no doubt that if it is released from Maheshvara's arms, in an instant, it can consume the entire universe and the three worlds, with their mobile and immobile objects. There is nothing in the worlds that cannot be slain with it, even Brahma, Vishnu and the gods. O son! I saw that extraordinary, wonderful and supreme weapon there. There was another mysterious and supreme weapon, equal or superior.[157] This is famous in all the worlds as the spear of the one who wields the trident. It is capable of shattering the entire earth and drying up the giant ocean. When it is released from the hand of the one who wields the trident, it can destroy the entire universe. Yuvanashva's son, Mandhata, was an immensely energetic king who became an emperor by conquering the three worlds. In ancient times, Mandhata and all his soldiers were struck down by this.[158] O Govinda! He was immensely strong and immensely valorous and was like Shakra in his prowess. However, the rakshasa Lavana released it from his hand and struck him down. That trident is sharp at the points. It is extremely terrible and makes the body hair stand up. It seems to be stationed, ready to strike, as if its forehead is creased into three furrows. It is dark and is like a fire without smoke, like sun when it arises at the time of destruction. That trident is impossible to describe. Its handle is a snake. It is like the Destroyer with his noose. O Govinda! Near Rudra, I saw that weapon. In ancient times,

[156]The embodied form of the weapon.

[157]To Pashupata.

[158]Mandhata and his soldiers were defeated by a demon named Lavanasura. Lavanasura had inherited Shiva's trident from his father, Madhu, and he used this against Mandhata.

Mahadeva was gratified and gave Rama[159] a battleaxe that was sharp at the edges. This was used to destroy the kshatriyas. It was also used to slay Emperor Kartavirya in a great battle. Using this, there were twenty-one occasions when kshatriyas were exterminated from the earth. O Govinda! Jamadagni's son, Rama of the unblemished deeds, accomplished this. It flamed at the edges and was extremely terrible. This was also near the wielder of the trident, who had a snake strung around his neck. It looked like the blazing flames of a fire. The intelligent one also possessed numerous other divine weapons. O unblemished one! I have only recounted the main ones. Brahma, the grandfather of the worlds, was stationed on the god's left flank. He was astride a celestial vimana, yoked to swans that possessed the speed of thought. Narayana was also stationed on the left flank. He held a conch shell, chakra and club and was astride Vinata's descendant.[160] Astride a peacock, Skanda was near the goddess. Grasping a spear and a bell, he looked like a second fire.[161] Nandi could be seen, stationed in front of the god. Stationed with a spear in his hand, he looked like a second Shankara. The rishis, with Bhrigu at the forefront, born from Svayambhu's mental powers, were there and so were all the gods, with Shakra at the forefront. In every direction, they surrounded the great-souled one and worshipped him. The gods praised Mahadeva with many kinds of hymns. Brahma praised Bhava by uttering the rathantara. Narayana praised the lord of the gods with the *jyeshtha* Sama hymn. Shakra praised him with the excellent *shatarudriya*, which is about the supreme brahman.[162] Those three, Brahma, Narayana and Koushika, the king of the gods, were radiant around the great-souled one, like three fires. In their midst, the resplendent god Shiva was resplendent. He was like the rays of the autumn sun, freed from the clouds.

[159]Parashurama.

[160]That is, Garuda.

[161]Among other things, Skanda holds a spear and a bell (*ghanta*). The Critical edition's text says *kantha* (throat), which makes no sense and we have therefore corrected what seems to be a clear typo.

[162]Rathantara and jyeshtha are Sama hymns. Literally, shatarudriya means one hundred Rudras and is a mantra to Rudra, from the Yajur Veda.

'"'I followed excellent vows and worshipped the god through chants. "I bow down before the one who is the god of everything. I bow down before Mahadeva. You are Shakra. You are in Shakra's form. You are in Shakra's attire. I bow down before the one with the vajra in his hand. You are tawny. You are red. You always hold the Pinaka in your hand. You hold the sword and the trident. I bow down before the one with the dark garments, the one who has dark and curly hair. A black antelope skin forms your upper garment. You are the one who is worshipped on *krishnashtami.*[163] You are white in complexion. You are white. You are attired in white garments. You are smeared in white ashes. You are engaged in white deeds. Among all the gods, you are Brahma. Among all the Rudras, you are Nilalohita. You are the soul of all creatures. In sankhya, you have been spoken of as Purusha. You are the bull[164] among all things that are sacred. Among yogis, you are the Shiva who is indivisible. You are garhasthya among the ashramas. You are the lord Maheshvara. Among all the yakshas, you are Kubera. You are Vishnu among sacrifices.[165] Among mountains, you are the great Meru. Among nakshatras, you are the moon. You are Vasishtha among the rishis. You are said to be the sun among planets. Among forest animals, you are the lion. You are Parameshvara. Among domesticated animals, you are the bull. You are the illustrious one who is worshipped in the worlds. You are Vishnu among the Adityas. You are Agni among the Vasus. You are Vinata's descendant among the birds. You are Ananta among the serpents. Among the Vedas, you are Sama Veda. In the hymns of Yajur Veda, you are shatarudriya. You are Sanatkumara among the yogis. Among the exponents of sankhya, you are Kapila. O god! You are Shakra among the Maruts. Among the ancestors, you are the king of dharma.[166] Among the worlds, you are Brahma's

[163]This means the eighth (*ashtami*) day of krishnapaksha. There is no obvious connection between this day and Shiva. However, Krishna was born on krishnashtami. This probably means that Shiva is worshipped in the form of Krishna.

[164]In the sense of the best.

[165]The word Vishnu is also used to mean the foremost sacrifice.

[166]Yama.

world. Among all destinations, you are said to be moksha. Among oceans, you are the ocean of milk. Among mountains, you are the Himalaya mountains. You are brahmanas among varnas. Among brahmanas, you are brahmanas who have been initiated. You are the origin of the worlds. You are the destroyer who destroys everything. You are everything that is said to constitute superior energy in the worlds. You are the illustrious one who is everything. That is my firm view. O illustrious one! O god! I bow down before you. O one who is affectionate towards devotees! I bow down before you. O lord of yoga! I bow down before you. O origin of the universe! I bow down before you. Show your favours towards one who is devoted towards you. I am miserable. I am distressed. I am without prosperity. O Bhava! You are the eternal destination. O Parameshvara! O lord of the gods! I may have committed crimes in my ignorance. Since I am your devotee, you should pardon all these. O lord of the gods! I was confused because of the form you assumed. O lord of the gods! I did not offer you arghya and padya."[167] Thus, with devotion, I worshipped Ishana and offered him padya and arghya. I joined my hands in salutation and offered everything to him. O son! A shower of auspicious flowers descended on my head. They were sprinkled with cool water and possessed divine fragrances. The servants of the gods sounded celestial drums. An auspicious breeze started to blow. It was pleasant and bore sacred scents.

'"'With his wife, Mahadeva, the one with the bull on his banner, was pleased with me. Delighted with me, he spoke to the gods who were present. "O all the gods! Look at the great-souled Upamanyu. His single-minded devotion towards me is divine and supreme and he has no other sentiment." O Krishna! The one with the trident in his hand spoke in this way to the gods. All of them joined their hands in salutation. They bowed down before the one with the bull on his banner and said, "O illustrious one! O god! O lord of the gods! O protector of the worlds! O lord of the universe! Thanks to you, this excellent brahmana will obtain all the fruits that he desires." All the gods, with Brahma at the forefront, spoke in this

[167]Respectively, a gift and water to wash the feet, offered to a guest.

way to Sharva. The illustrious lord Shankara seemed to smile at me. He said, "O Upamanyu! O child! I am pleased with you. O bull among the sages! Look at me. Your devotion towards me is firm. O brahmana rishi! I wished to test you.[168] I am extremely delighted at your great devotion. Therefore, I will now give you everything that you wish for." This is what the lord Mahadeva told me there. My eyes filled with tears of joy and my body hair stood up. In a voice that was full of joy and devotion, I spoke these words to the god. I sank down on my knees and repeatedly prostrated myself before him. "O god! It seems to me as if I have been born today. My austerities have become successful today. O Mahadeva! I have seen you in person. You are stationed in front of me, pleased with me. I have seen the one who is worshipped, the infinitely valorous one whom even the gods cannot see. Having seen that god, who is more fortunate than me? Learned ones meditate on him as the supreme and eternal truth. He is famous as the lord of attachment. He is supreme of the supreme. He is the one without decay. He is the illustrious god who represents all that is true. He is without beginning and without destruction. He is the one who knows about all truth and ordinances. He is the lord who is the foremost Purusha. He is the one who created Brahma, the creator of the worlds, from his right flank. He is the lord who created Vishnu, for the protection of the worlds, from his left flank. When the end of a yuga arrives, he is the lord who creates Rudra from his limbs. Rudra destroys everything in the universe, mobile and immobile. He is the immensely energetic Destroyer, the fire of destruction. This god, Mahadeva, is the creator of everything in the universe, mobile and immobile. At the end of a kalpa, it has been said that everything is withdrawn into him. You go everywhere. You are the soul of all creatures. You are Bhava, the creator who creates the creator of beings. You always go everywhere, but are incapable of being seen by all the gods. O lord! O Shankara! If you are gratified with me and wish to grant me a boon, let me have eternal devotion towards you. O lord! O supreme among the gods! Through your

[168]By appearing before Upamanyu in the form of Indra.

favours, let me possess the intelligence so that I know everything about the past, the present and the future. Let me and my relatives be able to enjoy an inexhaustible supply of food cooked with milk. May your supreme self always reside near me, in my hermitage." The illustrious one, revered by the worlds, agreed to this.

'"'The lord Maheshvara, the immensely energetic preceptor of everything mobile and immobile, said, "Be without old age and without death. Be free from misery. Be full of good qualities. Know everything and be handsome. May you possess eternal youth. May you possess an energy that is like that of the fire. O sage! Wherever you desire, there will be an ocean of milk. As you desire, that store of milk will always be near you. Enjoy that ocean of milk, with amrita mixed in it. With your relatives, always think of worshipping me. O supreme among brahmanas! I will always be with you, in your hermitage. O child! Reside wherever you wish. You should have no anxiety. O brahmana! Whenever you remember me, I will always show myself to you." The illustrious one was as resplendent as one crore suns. Having granted me the boon, Ishana disappeared from that spot. O Krishna! Thus, through my meditations, I saw the god of the gods. I obtained everything that the intelligent one had mentioned. O Krishna! Behold. You can directly see the siddhas who reside here. There are the rishis, the vidyadharas, the yakshas, the gandharvas and the apsaras. Look at the trees that are always beautiful and full of flowers and fruit. There are flowers everywhere. There are pleasant leaves and excellent branches. O mighty-armed one! Everything has a celestial ring to it.'"'

Chapter 1696(15)

'"Upamanyu said, 'The great Hara has favoured many thousand others. O Madhava! Why will the illustrious one not show you his favours? Such an assembly of the gods is to be praised, especially by someone like you, who is faithful, devoted to brahmanas and non-violent. I will grant you the *japa*,[169] through which, you will be able to see Shankara'"

Krishna said,[170] "I told him, 'O brahmana! O great sage! Through your favours, I will see the lord of the gods, the one who crushed the large numbers of Diti's sons.'[171] On the eighth day, following the rites, I was initiated by the brahmana. I received the staff and shaved my head. I held the kusha grass and dressed myself in rags. I sprinkled myself with clarified butter and wore a girdle made out of grass. For one month, I lived on fruits. For a second month, I subsisted on water. For the third, fourth and fifth months, I only subsisted on air. I single-mindedly stood on one foot, raising my arms upwards. O descendant of the Bharata lineage! I saw the energy of one thousand suns in the firmament. O descendant of the Pandu lineage! In the midst of that energy, I saw a cloud that was decorated by an array of cranes. It looked like a blue mountain and there were rainbows all over it. Garlands of lightning seemed to form a window inside it. The illustrious and extremely radiant one was seated there, together with the goddess. With his wife, he blazed because of his austerities, energy and beauty. There, with the goddess, the illustrious Maheshvara looked resplendent. It was as if the sun was located inside that cloud, together with the moon. O Kounteya! My body hair stood up in delight. My eyes dilated in wonder. He is the refuge of the large numbers of gods. He is the dispeller of all affliction. I saw Hara. He wore a crown. He held a club and a trident in his hands. He was attired in tiger skin. His hair was matted and he held a staff in his hand. He held the Pinaka and the vajra. His teeth were sharp. He wore sparkling bracelets and his sacred thread was a snake. A celestial garland, with many colours, adorned his chest. It was so large that it hung down, right up to his ankles. I saw him and he looked like the moon in the evening, when the rains are over. Large numbers of demons[172]

[169]The mantra for silent meditation.

[170]This is Krishna speaking to Yudhishthira.

[171]The daityas.

[172]*Pramatha*s, spirits and ghosts.

surrounded him on every side. He was difficult to see, as dazzling as the autumn sun. He was seated on a bull and there were eleven Rudras around him. They sought to praise the deeds of the one who is the performer of auspicious deeds. The Adityas, the Vasus, the Sadhyas, the Vishvadevas, the Ashvins praised the god who is the lord of the universe. Everything in the universe chanted his praise. Shatakratu and the illustrious Vishnu, both sons of Aditi, and Brahma were near Bhava, praising him with the rathantara Sama hymn. O Yudhishthira! There were many lords of yoga, ancestors and preceptors who knew about yoga, brahmana rishis and their sons, devarshis, the earth, the firmament, the nakshatras, the planets, the fortnights, the months, the seasons, the nights, the years, the kshanas, the muhurtas, the nimeshas, the yugas in due order, the divine branches of knowledge, all the directions, Sanatkumara, the Vedas, *itihasa*, Marichi, Angiras, Atri, Pulastya, Pulaha, Kratu, the seven Manus, soma, the Atharvans, Brihaspati, Bhrigu, Daksha, Kashyapa, Vasishtha, *kashya*,[173] the metres, diksha, sacrifices, dakshina, the fire, oblations, the embodied forms of all the articles required at sacrifices, all the guardians of the worlds, the rivers, the serpents, the mountains, all the mothers of the gods, the wives and the daughters of the gods and thousands, tens of thousands and billons of sages. They, and the mountains, the oceans and the directions, bowed down before the lord of tranquility. There were gandharvas and apsaras, accomplished in singing and the playing of musical instruments. They sung divine and wonderful praises to Bhava. O great king! The vidyadharas, the danavas, the guhyakas, the rakshasas and all the beings, mobile and immobile, bowed down before the lord, in speech, thoughts and deeds. Sharva, the lord of the gods, manifested himself before me. O descendant of the Bharata lineage! On seeing that Ishana was in front of me, the universe, with Prajapati and Shakra, glanced towards me. However, I did not possess the strength to look towards Mahadeva.

[173]This is probably the liquor known as kashya.

'"At this, the god spoke to me. 'O Krishna! Look at me and speak to me.' Delighted, I bowed my head down before the god and the goddess, Uma. I praised Sthanu in words that are used by Brahma and the other gods to praise him. 'I bow down before the eternal one who is the womb of everything. The rishis speak of you as Brahma's lord. Virtuous ones speak of you as austerities, sattva, rajas, tamas and truth. You are Brahma. You are Rudra. You are Varuna. You are Agni. You are Manu. You are Bhava. You are Dhatri. You are Tvashtri. You are Vidhatri. You are the lord who faces all the directions. All creatures, mobile and immobile, originate in you. You are the origin of all beings and you are the one who destroys them. The rishis speak of you as being superior to all the objects of the sense, the mind, the wind, the seven kinds of fire and all the male gods who are in heaven. O illustrious one! There is no doubt that you are the Vedas, the sacrifices, soma, dakshina, the fire, the oblations and everything else required for a sacrifice. Sacrifices, gifts, studies, vows, rituals, modesty, fame, prosperity, radiance, contentment and success are offered to you. O illustrious one! Desire, anger, fear, avarice, insolence, confusion, malice, pain and disease are your offspring. You are deeds. You are the outcome of those deeds. You are destruction. You are the foremost one. You are power. You are immutable. You are the supreme origin of the mind. Your nature is eternal. You are the unmanifest. You are the purifying lord. You are golden and possess a thousand rays. You are the origin of all the qualities. All life is dependent on you. The great atman, Mati,[174] Brahma, the universe, Shambhu, Svayambhu, Buddhi,[175] Prajna,[176] realization, consciousness, fame and fortitude are all words that the great-souled ones have progressively used in the sacred texts to express your greatness. It is through comprehending you that learned brahmanas overcome the confusion that is in the hearts of all beings. The rishis have praised you as kshetrajna. Your arms and feet are in all

[174]Understanding.
[175]Intelligence.
[176]Wisdom.

the directions. Your eyes, heads and faces are in all the directions. You hear everything in the worlds. You are established, pervading everything. You are the fruits of everything that the one with the sharp rays[177] performs in a nimesha. As Purusha, the rays of your power are in all hearts. You are the obtaining of anima and laghima. You are Ishana, the resplendent and undecaying one. The worlds resort to your understanding and intelligence and seek you out as a refuge. Those who have conquered their senses and are devoted to the truth always use yoga to meditate on you. There are those who know you as the eternal one, the lord who is the deep refuge, the Purusha who is everywhere in the universe, the one who is golden in complexion, the one who is supremely intelligent and is the greatest destination. These intelligent ones based themselves on what transcends intelligence. Those intelligent ones know the seven subtle forms,[178] the six of your attributes[179] and the main techniques of yoga and penetrate into you.' O Partha! I spoke in this way to Bhava, the destroyer of all afflictions. At this, the entire universe and all mobile and immobile objects roared like lions. The large numbers of brahmanas, the gods, the asuras, the serpents, the pishachas, the ancestors, the birds, the large numbers of rakshasas, the large numbers of spirits[180] and all the maharshis bowed down before him. Fragrant and celestial flowers showered down on my head in large numbers. A pleasant breeze began to blow. For the welfare of the universe, the illustrious Shankara glanced towards the goddess Uma, Shatakratu and me and said, 'O Krishna! O slayer of enemies! We know of your great devotion towards us. I am extremely pleased with you and I will do what brings you benefit. O Krishna! O supreme one! Ask for eight boons and I will give them to you. O tiger among Yadavas! Tell me what you desire, even if it is something that is extremely difficult to get.'"'

[177]The sun.

[178]Mahat, consciousness and the five primal elements.

[179]Omniscience, completeness, contentment, independence, power and lack of finiteness.

[180]*Bhutas*.

Chapter 1697(16)

'Krishna said, "I bowed my head down before that great mass of energy. Filled with great delight, I told the illustrious one, 'Firmness in dharma, the ability to destroy enemies in battle, fame, ferocity, supreme strength, devotion to yoga, your proximity and hundreds and hundreds of sons—these are the boons I seek.' On hearing my words, Shankara agreed that it would be this way. Thereafter, the mother of the universe, the one who holds up everything, the one who cleanses everything, the store of austerities, Sharvani Uma, spoke to me. 'O unblemished one! The illustrious one has granted you a son named Samba. Ask for eight boons from me too and I will grant them to you.' O descendant of the Pandu lineage! Addressed thus, I bowed my head down before her and said, 'Lack of anger towards brahmanas, the favours of my father, hundreds of sons, supreme objects of pleasure, affection towards my family, the favours of my mother, the attainment of tranquility and skill—these are the boons I seek.' The goddess replied, 'It shall be that way. You will possess the power of an immortal. I never speak anything that is false. You will have sixteen thousand wives. Your love for them, and their love for you, will never decay. You will obtain great affection from your relatives. I also grant you a handsome body. Seven thousand guests will always feed in your house.'"

'Vasudeva continued, "O descendant of the Bharata lineage! The god and the goddess granted me these boons. O Bhima's elder brother! Then, with those companions,[181] they instantly disappeared. O supreme among the Kourava lineage! I recounted all these wonderful incidents to Upamanyu, the extremely energetic brahmana. The one who was excellent in his vows bowed down before the god of the gods and said, 'There is no one who is Sharva's equal in giving. There is no one who is Sharva's equal in battle. There is no god who is Sharva's equal. There is no refuge that is equal to Sharva. O son! In krita yuga, there was a famous rishi named Tandi. For ten thousand years, he meditated on that god. He worshipped him with devotion.

[181]*Ganas*.

Listen to what he obtained as a consequence. Having satisfied Mahadeva with his praises, he saw the lord. He said, "You are the most sacred of the sacred. You are the supreme destination among all destinations. You are the fiercest energy among all kinds of energy. You are the supreme austerity among all austerities. You are the wealth of the universe. You are the golden-eyed one. You are the one who is invoked by many. I bow down before you. O lord! You are the one who grants a lot of fortune. You are the supreme truth. I bow down before you. O lord! You are the one whom ascetics, scared of birth and death, strive to obtain. You are the one who grants emancipation. You are the one with the one thousand rays. I bow down before you. You are the abode of bliss. Brahma, Shatakratu, Vishnu, the Vishvadevas and the maharshis are incapable of comprehending your truth. How can those like us comprehend you? You are the one who gets time going. You are the one into whom time merges. You are spoken of as Kala.[182] You are spoken of as Purusha. You are also spoken of as Brahma. The celestial rishis who know about the Puranas speak of you as possessing three forms.[183] You are Adhipourusha, Adhyatma, Adhibhuta, Adhidaiva, Adhiloka, Adhivijnana and Adhiyajna.[184] Even the gods find it difficult to know you. But when learned people know you in the body, they are emancipated and obtain the supreme state of welfare. O lord! Those who do not wish to know you, undergo many births and deaths. You are the gate to heaven and emancipation. You grant and you take away. You are emancipation and heaven. You are desire and anger. You are sattva, rajas and tamas. You are the lower regions. You are the upper regions. You are Brahma, Vishnu, Rudra, Skanda, Indra, Savitri, Yama, Varuna, the moon, Dhatri, Vidhatri and the lord of riches.[185] You are earth, wind, water,

[182]Time.

[183]Brahma, Vishnu and Rudra.

[184]*Adhipourusha* is the supreme spirit, adhyatma is the atman inside the body, adhibhuta represents the gross or material elements, adhidaiva is the divine element operating in material objects, *adhiloka* is the principle in the various worlds, *adhivijnana* is the highest plane of consciousness or knowledge and *adhiyajna* exists in sacrifices.

[185]Kubera.

fire, water, speech, intelligence, understanding and mind. You are deeds. You are both truth and falsehood. You are the existent. You are the non-existent. You are the senses. You are the objects of the senses. You are beyond Prakriti. You are permanent. You are superior to the universe and superior to everything that exists in the universe. You can be thought of. You cannot be thought of. You are the supreme brahman. You are the supreme destination. There is no doubt that you are the objective of those who follow sankhya and yoga. There is no doubt that I have become successful today.[186] There is no doubt that I have obtained the destination of the virtuous. This is the destination obtained on earth by those whose knowledge and intelligence are unblemished. Alas! I was foolish. For a long period of time, I did not possess the consciousness. I did not know the supreme god, the eternal one who is known by the learned. It is through the devotion of many births that the god has shown me his favours and I have been able to directly see him. Knowing you is like obtaining amrita. You are the eternal mystery to gods, asuras and men. He is the illustrious god who does everything. His face is in every direction. He is inside all atmans. He sees everything and goes everywhere. He knows everything. He creates life and is the one who upholds life. He is the creator of beings and is the destination of all creatures. He is embodied and is the refuge of all those who are embodied. He is the one who enjoys a body. He is the destination of all those with bodies. He is adhyatma, the destination of all those who are virtuous, those who meditate and know about the atman. He is also the lord who is the immortal objective. He is the one who grants good and bad ends to all creatures. He is the one who ordains birth and death for all creatures. He is the lord who grants success to the rishis who desire success. He is the lord who grants emancipation to the brahmanas who desire emancipation. Beginning with the earth, he is the creator of all the worlds, including the residents of heaven. He maintains the gods and grants them welfare in his eight forms.[187]

[186]By obtaining your sight.

[187]Shiva's eight forms are as Bhava in water, Rudra in fire, Pashupati in officiating priests, Ishana in the sun, Mahadeva in the moon, Bhima in space, Sharva in the earth and Ugra in the wind.

Everything flows from him and he is established in everything. It is into him that everything is destroyed. He is alone the one who is eternal. He is the world of truth, desired by the supremely righteous ones who desire truth. He is the emancipation and freedom from hardships, sought by those who know about the atman. He is the lord whom Brahma and the Siddhas have kept secret and do not reveal to gods, asuras and humans.[188] That is the reason that gods, asuras and men do not know about Bhava. Though he resides in their hearts, they are confused. O descendant of the Bharata lineage! He resides in all atmans and shows himself to those who resort to the yoga of devotion. Knowing him, one is not born and does not have to face death. If one knows that supreme one, there is nothing else that remains to be known. Having obtained that supreme gain, there is nothing else that remains to be obtained. By obtaining that supreme and subtle being, one obtains a state that is without decay. There are those who know the truth about the qualities of sankhya, they are accomplished in the sacred texts of sankhya. Having got to know about that supreme knowledge, they are freed from bonds. He is the one known by those who are learned in the Vedas. He is the one who is established in Vedanta. Those who are devoted to pranayama and immerse themselves in it, meditate on him. He is devayana and is said to the gate to the sun. He is pitriyana and is said to be the gate to the moon.[189] He is the colourful progress of time, the years and the yugas. He is existence and non-existence. He is uttarayana and dakshinayana.[190] Earlier, Prajapati praised him in many chants. He accepted you as a son, under the name of Nilalohita. In their rites, officiating priests praise you with many hymns from the Rig Veda. Officiating priests know you in three different ways[191] and offer oblations with hymns from the Yajur

[188]This probably means secret references in sacred texts.

[189]Devayana is the path of the gods and leads to the sun. Pitriyana is the path of the ancestors and leads to the moon.

[190]Respectively, the sun's progress to the north of the equator and the sun's progress to the south of the equator.

[191]These three different ways are interpreted as the shruti texts, the smriti texts and meditation.

Veda. Those who are pure in their intelligence and know about the Sama Veda chant Sama hymns to you. You are the supreme origin of sacrifices. You are said to be the supreme lord. Night and day are his hearing and sight. Fortnights and months are his heads and arms. The seasons are his energy. Austerities are his patience. The year constitutes his anus, thighs and feet. He is Mrityu and Yama. He is the fire of destruction. He is time. He is the force of destruction. He is the supreme origin of time. He is eternal time. He is the moon, the sun, the nakshatras, the planets, the winds, Dhruva, the saptarshis and the seven worlds.[192] He is Pradhana and Mahat. He is not manifest. He is the specific destination of all deeds. He is all creatures, beginning with Brahma and ending with the lowest. He is the eight Prakritis.[193] He is beyond Prakriti. He is the state of lack of anxiety. He is the eternal brahman. He is the supreme objective that those who know about the sacred texts and Vedangas meditate on. He is the supreme kashtha. He is the supreme kala. He is supreme success. He is the supreme objective. He is supreme tranquility. He is supreme detachment. Having obtained him, learned ones think that they have obtained everything. He is contentment. He is success. He is said to be shruti and smriti. He is the objective of adhyatma, sought by the faithful. Learned ones obtain the one who is without decay. Those who desire to perform sacrifices, with a great deal of donations given away, seek him. He is the destination of the divine gods. He is the eternal destination. There are those who meditate, offer oblations and observe vows, subjecting their bodies to hardships and rituals. Their torments are with that god as an objective. Bhava is the objective. There are those who are detached and cast aside all rites. They desire Brahma's world, but you are actually that eternal objective. There are others who seek to overcome death and abandon all detachment, seeking an end to transformations and destructions. He is that eternal end

[192]Bhurloka, kharloka, svarloka, maharloka, janarloka, taparloka and satyaloka (brahmaloka).

[193]Earth, air, space, fire, water, mind, intelligence and ego.

too. He is the refuge of jnana and vijnana. He is said to be without form and without blemish. That god is the objective of emancipation. Bhava is the supreme goal. He has been spoken about in the Vedas, the sacred texts and the Puranas. He has been spoken of as the end after death. It is through the favours of the lord that one obtains, or does not obtain." Thus did Tandi satisfy the undecaying Ishana through his austerities and yoga. He spoke these words, which Brahma, the creator of the worlds, had said in ancient times. "Brahma, Shatakratu, Vishnu, the Vishvadevas and the maharshis are incapable of knowing him." Shiva was pleased at this and replied, "You will be without destruction and without transformation. You will be free from all misery. You will be famous and full of energy. You will possess divine knowledge. The rishis will come to you. Your son will be the composer of sutras.[194] O best among brahmanas! There is no doubt that this will happen through my favours. What will I give you or someone else? What do you desire? Tell me what you wish for." Joining his hands in salutation, he[195] replied, "Let my devotion towards you be firm." The god granted this boon. Praised and worshipped by the gods, the rishis and the residents of heaven, he then disappeared. O lord of the Yadavas! With her companions, the goddess also disappeared. The rishi came to my hermitage and told me everything that had happened. O best among men! For my success, Tandi recounted to me all those famous names.[196] Listen to those. The grandfather knew ten thousand names. The sacred texts have one thousand of Sharva's names. O Achyuta! Tandi mentioned some names of the illustrious one, but those are secret. Through the favours of the god,[197] in ancient times, the great-souled lord of the gods[198] uttered those names.'"'

[194]A sutra is an aphorism and also a collection of such aphorisms.

[195]Tandi.

[196]Mahadeva's names.

[197]Shiva.

[198]Brahma.

Chapter 1698(17)

'Vasudeva said, "O father![199] O Yudhishthira! The brahmana rishi[200] controlled himself. He joined his hands in salutation and told me those names, starting at the beginning.

'"Upamanyu said, 'I will satisfy Sthanu through these names, famous in all the worlds. Some were spoken of by Brahma and the rishis. Others are in the Vedas and the Vedangas. These are great names and uttered by those who are truthful, ensure success in every kind of endeavour. Having cleansed his soul, the rishi Tandi devotedly used these names for the god. These names, famous in the worlds, have been uttered by sages who know about the truth. He is supreme. He is the foremost. He is heaven. He is the one who is engaged in the welfare of all beings. These names have been heard everywhere in the universe and open up entry into Brahma's world. This is the supreme and eternal mystery that Brahma spoke about earlier. O best among the Yadu lineage! I will tell you. Listen with single-minded attention. You are devoted to the supreme god Bhava, Parameshvara. Therefore, listen to what the eternal Brahma said. Even if one tried for one hundred years, one is incapable of speaking about Sharva's powers in entirety and detail. Even the gods are incapable of comprehending his beginning, middle and end. O Madhava! Therefore, who is capable of speaking about all his qualities? Who is capable of speaking about that god's greatness of conduct? Through his favours, I will use phrases and syllables to touch on it briefly. Without his blessings, one can neither obtain nor praise the lord. Since I have been granted permission by him, I always praise Bhava. The great-souled one is without beginning and without end. He is the origin of everything. His own origin is unmanifest. I will tell you about some names that have been used for him. He is the granter of boons. He is the one to be revered. The intelligent one's form is the universe. Listen to the names

[199]The word used is tata.

[200]Upamanyu.

that were used for him by the one who was born from the lotus.[201] The great grandfather spoke of ten thousand names. Like clarified butter being churned out of curds, I will use my mind to churn names from those. Gold represents the essence of the mountains. Honey represents the essence of flowers. Cream represents the essence of clarified butter. This essence has been extracted like that. It cleanses all kinds of sins and is in conformity with the four Vedas. They need to be studied carefully and remembered with clean souls. They grant tranquility and benefit. They are great and auspicious and destroy rakshasas.[202] They should be told to devotees, those who are faithful and believers. They should not be told to those who are not devoted, have not cleansed their souls and are non-believers. The god who is the wielder of Pinaka is in all atmans. O Krishna! If a person hates him, he will go to hell, with his ancestors and his descendants. This[203] represents meditation. This represents knowledge. This is the supreme mystery. If one gets to know them at the time of death, one goes to the supreme destination. This is sacred, auspicious, pure and supremely beneficial. O mighty-armed one! Recite these names. This is the best chant among all chants of praise. In ancient times, Brahma, the grandfather of all the worlds, composed these. He thought of it as the divine king of all chants. Since that time, this praise to the great-souled lord has been famous in the universe and has been revered by the immortals. This king of hymns descended from Brahma's world. In ancient times, he recited it to Tandi and it is therefore thought of as something composed by Tandi. It was Tandi who brought it down from heaven to earth. It is the most auspicious among all things that are auspicious. It is destructive of all sins. O mighty-armed one! I will recite this hymn, which is supreme among all hymns. It is about the one who is the brahmana among all brahmanas, supreme among all things supreme, energy among all kinds of energy and austerity among

[201]Brahma.

[202]These rakshasas may also be metaphorical, as in vices.

[203]The list of names.

all types of austerities. He is peace among all kinds of peace, resplendence among all kinds of resplendence, restraint among all kinds of restraint, intelligence among all kinds of intelligence, god among all kinds of gods, sage among all kinds of sages, sacrifice among all kinds of sacrifice, auspicious among all things auspicious, Rudra among all the Rudras, the lord among all lords, the yogi among all yogis and the cause among all causes. All the worlds originate from him and merge into him when they no longer have existence. He is in the atman of all beings. He is the infinitely energetic Hara. Hear Sharva's one thousand and eight names. O best among men! If you listen to them, you will be successful in all your desires.

'"'(1) Sthira;[204] (2) Sthanu;[205] (3) Prabhu;[206] (4) Bhanu;[207] (5) Pravara;[208] (6) Varada;[209] (7) Vara;[210] (8) Sarvatma;[211] (9) Sarvavikhyata;[212] (10) Sarva;[213] (11) Sarvakara;[214] (12) Bhava;[215] (13) Jati;[216] (14) Charmi;[217] (15) Shikhandi;[218] (16) Sarvanga;[219] (17)

[204] Immobile. The numbering is not given in the text. We have introduced it, to make the count easier. Though we have introduced a numbering, there is a problem, since the names are often repeated. There is also another problem, since the names are capable of multiple meanings and interpretations. Consequently, the English renderings we have given are not the only ones that are possible.

[205] Fixed.

[206] Powerful.

[207] Lustrous.

[208] Foremost.

[209] Granter of boons.

[210] Supreme.

[211] Soul of everything.

[212] Famous among everything.

[213] Everything.

[214] Creator of everything.

[215] Existence, also interpreted as the origin and end of all existence.

[216] Matted one.

[217] One who wears hides.

[218] One with a crest.

[219] One with limbs everywhere.

Sarva-bhavana;[220] (18) Hari;[221] (19) Harinaksha;[222] (20) Sarvabhutahara; [223] (.) Prabhu;[224] (21) Pravritti; (22) Nivritti; (23) Niyata;[225] (24) Shashvata;[226] (25) Dhruva;[227] (26) Shmashanachari;[228] (27) Bhagavan;[229] (28) Khachara;[230] (29) Gochara;[231] (30) Ardana;[232] (31) Abhivadya;[233] (32) Mahakarma;[234] (33) Tapasvi;[235] (34) Bhuta-bhavana;[236] (35) Unmatta-vesha-prachchhanna;[237] (36) Sarva-loka-prajapati;[238] (37) Maharupa;[239] (38) Mahakaya;[240] (39) Sarvarupa;[241] (40) Mahayasha;[242] (41) Mahatma;[243] (42) Sarvabhuta;[244] (43) Virupa;[245] (44) Vamana;[246] (45) Manu;[247]

[220]Creator of everything.

[221]Tawny.

[222]With eyes like a deer.

[223]Destroyer of all creatures.

[224]Since this is duplication, we are not numbering this.

[225]Someone who has controlled himself.

[226]Eternal.

[227]Without change.

[228]One who resides in cremation grounds.

[229]The illustrious one, alternatively, Bhagavat.

[230]One who roams around in the air, also, wind or sun.

[231]Perceptible one.

[232]Destroyer.

[233]One saluted respectfully.

[234]Performer of great deeds.

[235]Ascetic.

[236]Creator of beings.

[237]One who hides himself in the attire of a lunatic.

[238]Lord/protector of all the worlds.

[239]Gigantic in form.

[240]Gigantic in body.

[241]One with a form everywhere.

[242]Immensely illustrious.

[243]Great soul.

[244]Present in all creatures.

[245]Multi-formed. Though the word also means deformed, the meaning of multi-formed is better.

[246]Short.

[247]The thinking one.

(46) Lokapala;[248] (47) Antarhitatma;[249] (48) Prasada;[250] (49) Hayagardabhi;[251] (50) Pavitra;[252] (51) Mahat; (52) Niyama;[253] (53) Niyamashraya;[254] (54) Sarvakarma;[255] (55) Svayambhu; (56) Adiradikara;[256] (57) Nidhi;[257] (58) Sahasraksha;[258] (59) Virupaksha;[259] (60) Soma; (61) Nakshatra-sadhaka;[260] (62) Chandra-surya-gati;[261] (63) Ketu-graha;[262] (64) Graha-pati-vara;[263] (65) Adriradyalaya;[264] (66) Karta;[265] (67) Mriga-banarpana;[266] (68) Anagha;[267] (69) Mahatapa;[268] (70) Ghoratapa;[269] (71) Adina;[270] (72) Dina-sadhaka;[271] (73) Samvatsara-kara;[272] (74) Mantra; (75) Pramana;[273] (76) Parama;[274] (77)

[248]Protector of the world.

[249]Residing inside atmans.

[250]Serenity.

[251]Someone whose vehicle is yoked to horses and donkeys.

[252]Pure.

[253]Rituals.

[254]Refuge of rituals.

[255]Performer of all deeds.

[256]Creator of everything at the beginning.

[257]Store.

[258]Thousand-eyed one.

[259]One with deformed eyes.

[260]Energizer of nakshatras.

[261]Progress of the moon and the sun.

[262]The planet Ketu.

[263]Supreme lord of the planets, alternatively, the supreme moon, or even, the supreme Mars.

[264]Probably, one whose primary abode is in the mountains.

[265]Doer.

[266]One who shoots an arrow at the deer.

[267]Unblemished one.

[268]Great ascetic.

[269]Terrible ascetic.

[270]One who is not distressed.

[271]Energizer of the distressed.

[272]Creator of years.

[273]Proof.

[274]Supreme.

Tapa;[275] (78) Yogi; (79) Yojya;[276] (80) Mahabija;[277] (81) Mahareta;[278] (.) Mahatapa;[279] (82) Suvarna-reta;[280] (83) Sarvajna;[281] (84) Subija;[282] (85) Vrisha-vahana;[283] (86) Dasha-bahu;[284] (87) Animisha;[285] (88) Nilakantha;[286] (89) Umapati;[287] (90) Vishvarupa;[288] (91) Svayam-shreshtha;[289] (92) Balavira;[290] (93) Bala;[291] (94) Gana;[292] (95) Ganakarta;[293] (96) Ganapati;[294] (97) Digvasa;[295] (98) Kamya;[296] (.) Pavitra;[297] (.) Parama;[298] (.) Mantra;[299] (99) Sarva-bhava-kara;[300] (100) Hara;[301] (101) Kamandalu-dhara;[302] (102) Dhanvi;[303] (103)

[275]Austerities.

[276]One who is yoked, such as to yoga.

[277]Great seed.

[278]Great semen.

[279]We have not numbered this, since it has already been listed.

[280]Golden semen.

[281]One who knows everything.

[282]Good seed.

[283]One with a bull as a mount.

[284]Ten-armed.

[285]One who doesn't blink.

[286]Blue-throated.

[287]Uma's consort.

[288]With the universe as a form.

[289]One who creates one's own superiority.

[290]Strong in valour.

[291]Strength.

[292]Ganas are companions of Shiva. However, since Shiva is himself being addressed as gana, this is best understood as deity.

[293]Creator of ganas.

[294]Lord of the ganas.

[295]With the directions as attire.

[296]Desired.

[297]Since this has already been mentioned, we are not numbering this.

[298]Since this has already been mentioned, we are not numbering this.

[299]Since this has already been mentioned, we are not numbering this.

[300]Creator of everything.

[301]One who takes away.

[302]One who holds a water pot.

[303]One who holds a bow.

Banahasta;[304] (104) Kapalavan;[305] (105) Ashani;[306] (106) Shataghni;[307] (107) Pattishi;[308] (108) Ayudhi-mahan;[309] (109) Sruvahasta;[310] (110) Surupa;[311] (112) Tejas;[312] (113) Tejaskara;[313] (.) Nidhi;[314] (114) Ushnishi;[315] (115) Suvaktra;[316] (116) Udagra;[317] (117) Vinata;[318] (118) Dirgha;[319] (119) Harikesha;[320] (120) Sutirtha;[321] (121) Krishna;[322] (122) Srigala-rupa;[323] (123) Sarvartha;[324] (124) Munda;[325] (125) Kundi;[326] (126) Kamandalu;[327] (127) Aja;[328] (128) Mrigarupa;[329] (129) Gandha-dhari;[330] (130) Kaparda;[331] (131)

[304]One with an arrow in one's hand.

[305]One who holds a skull.

[306]One with the vajra.

[307]One who has the weapon *shataghni*.

[308]One who has a spear.

[309]One who wields great weapons.

[310]With the sacrificial ladle in one's hand.

[311]Beautiful in form.

[312]Energy.

[313]Creator of energy.

[314]Since this has already been mentioned, we are not numbering this.

[315]One with a headdress.

[316]One with a beautiful face.

[317]The intense one.

[318]Modest one.

[319]Tall one.

[320]Tawny-haired.

[321]Excellent place of pilgrimage.

[322]Dark one.

[323]With the form of a jackal. Shiva had assumed the form of a jackal to console a brahmana.

[324]One who represents all objectives.

[325]With a shaved head.

[326]Pitcher.

[327]Water pot.

[328]Without birth.

[329]With the form of animals.

[330]The bearer of fragrances.

[331]With braided hair.

Urdhvareta;[332] (132) Urdhva-linga;[333] (133) Urdhva-shayi;[334] (134) Nabhastala;[335] (136) Trijata;[336] (137) Chiravasa;[337] (138) Rudra; (139) Senapati;[338] (140) Vibhu;[339] (141) Ahachara;[340] (142) Nakta;[341] (143) Tigma-manyu;[342] (144) Suvarchasa;[343] (145) Gajaha;[344] (146) Daityaha;[345] (147) Loka;[346] (148) Lokadhata;[347] (149) Gunakara;[348] (150) Simha-shardula-rupa;[349] (151) Ardra-charmambara-vrita;[350] (152) Kalayogi;[351] (153) Mahanada;[352] (154) Sarva-vasa-chatushpatha;[353] (155) Nishachara;[354] (156) Pretachari;[355] (157) Bhutachari;[356] (158) Maheshvara;[357] (159)

[332]One who holds up the seed, that is, practices brahmacharya.

[333]One whose linga faces upwards.

[334]One who lies on one's back.

[335]With an abode in the firmament.

[336]With three matted locks.

[337]Attired in rags.

[338]Commander, general.

[339]Powerful one.

[340]One who moves during the day.

[341]Night, one who moves during the night.

[342]Fierce in wrath.

[343]Extremely radiant.

[344]Destroyer of an elephant. An asura had attacked Varanasi in the form on an elephant and Shiva destroyed it.

[345]Destroyer of daityas.

[346]The world.

[347]Ordainer of the worlds.

[348]Creator of the qualities.

[349]With the form of a lion and a tiger.

[350]Clad in a garment that is made out of wet hide. Shiva killed the elephant and attired himself in its hide.

[351]Yogi who conquers time.

[352]With the giant roar.

[353]One who resides in all the crossroads.

[354]One who roams around during the night.

[355]One who roams around with spirits.

[356]One who roams around with demons.

[357]Great lord.

Bahubhuta;[358] (160) Bahudhana;[359] (161) Sarvadhara;[360] (162) Amitagati;[361] (163) Nrityapriya;[362] (164) Nityanarta;[363] (165) Nartaka;[364] (166) Sarvalasaka;[365] (167) Ghora;[366] (.) Mahatapa;[367] (168) Pasha;[368] (169) Nitya;[369] (170) Girichara;[370] (171) Nabha;[371] (172) Sahasra-hasta;[372] (173) Vijaya;[373] (174) Vyavasaya;[374] (175) Anindita;[375] (176) Amarshana;[376] (177) Marshanatma;[377] (178) Yajnaha;[378] (179) Kama-nashana;[379] (180) Daksha-yajnapahari;[380] (181) Susaha;[381] (182) Madhyama;[382] (183) Tejopahari;[383] (184) Balaha;[384] (185) Mudita;[385] (186) Artha;[386]

[358]One who is manifested in many ways.

[359]With a lot of riches.

[360]Refuge of everything.

[361]Unlimited in speed.

[362]One who loves dancing.

[363]One who is always dancing.

[364]Dancer.

[365]One who makes everyone dance.

[366]Terrible one.

[367]We have not numbered this because it has already been listed.

[368]One with a noose.

[369]One who is always there.

[370]One who roams around on a mountain.

[371]The sky.

[372]Thousand-armed.

[373]Victory.

[374]Exertion.

[375]Irreproachable.

[376]Intolerant.

[377]Tolerant in soul.

[378]Destroyer of a sacrifice, that is, Daksha's sacrifice.

[379]Destroyer of Kama. Shiva burnt down Kama, the god of love.

[380]Destroyer of Daksha's sacrifice.

[381]One who easily withstands.

[382]One who is moderate.

[383]Remover of energy.

[384]Destroyer of Bala, an asura.

[385]One who is delighted.

[386]Wealth.

(187) Jita;[387] (188) Vara;[388] (189) Gambhira-ghosha;[389] (190) Gambhira;[390] (191) Gambhira-bala-vahana;[391] (192) Nyagrodharupa;[392] (193) Nyagrodha;[393] (194) Vriksha-karna-sthithi-vibhu;[394] (195) Tikshnatapa;[395] (196) Haryashva;[396] (197) Sahaya;[397] (198) Karma-kala-vit;[398] (199) Vishnuprasadita;[399] (200) Yajna;[400] (201) Samudra;[401] (202) Vadavamukha;[402] (203) Hutashana-sahaya;[403] (204) Prashantatma;[404] (205) Hutashana;[405] (206) Ugrateja;[406] (207) Mahateja;[407] (208) Jaya;[408] (209) Vijaya-kala-vit;[409] (210) Jyotishamayana;[410] (211) Siddhi;[411] (212) Sandhi-vigraha;[412] (213) Shikhi;[413] (214)

[387]Someone who can be conquered, presumably through devotion. Alternatively, this is a typo and should read someone who cannot be conquered.

[388]Supreme.

[389]One whose roar is deep.

[390]Deep.

[391]One whose mount is deep and strong.

[392]With the form of a banyan tree.

[393]Banyan tree.

[394]Lord who is there in trees and plants.

[395]Fierce in heat.

[396]With tawny horses.

[397]Aide.

[398]One who knows about karma and time.

[399]Favoured by Vishnu.

[400]Sacrifice.

[401]Ocean.

[402]Subterranean mare-head fire.

[403]Aide to the fire.

[404]Tranquil in soul.

[405]Fire.

[406]Fierce in energy.

[407]Great in energy.

[408]Victory.

[409]One who knows about the time of victory.

[410]Progress of stellar bodies.

[411]Success.

[412]War and peace.

[413]One with a crest.

Dandi;[414] (215) Jvali;[415] (216) Murtija;[416] (217) Murdhaga;[417] (218) Bali;[418] (219) Vainavi;[419] (220) Panavi;[420] (221) Tali;[421] (222) Kala;[422] (223) Kala-katam-kata;[423] (224) Nakshatra-vigraha-vidhi-guna-vriddhi-laya-agama;[424] (225) Prajapati-disha-bahu-vibhaga;[425] (226) Sarvatomukha;[426] (227) Vimochana;[427] (228) Suragana;[428] (229) Hiranya-kavachodbhava;[429] (230) Medhraja;[430] (231) Balachari;[431] (232) Mahachari;[432] (233) Stuta;[433] (234) Sarvya-turya-ninadi;[434] (235) Sarva-vadya-parigraha;[435] (236) Vyalarupa;[436] (237) Bilavasi;[437] (238) Hemamali;[438] (239) Taranga-vit;[439] (240) Tridasha-trikala-dhrik;[440] (241) Karma-sarva-bandha-

[414]One with a staff.

[415]Blazing one.

[416]One with a form.

[417]One seated in the head of every creature.

[418]Strong one.

[419]One with a flute.

[420]One with a tambourine.

[421]One with the musical instrument known as *tali*.

[422]Time, destiny.

[423]One who stretches out the mat of time.

[424]One who cannot be reached by knowing about the waxing and waning and the qualities of the nakshatras.

[425]The directions, arms and divisions of Prajapati.

[426]Facing every direction.

[427]Liberation.

[428]Large number of gods.

[429]One born from golden armour.

[430]One generated from the penis.

[431]Powerful in movement.

[432]Great in movement.

[433]Praised.

[434]One present in the blare of all trumpets.

[435]One who accepts all musical instruments.

[436]One with the form of a snake.

[437]One who dwells in a cave.

[438]One with a golden garland.

[439]One who knows about the waves.

[440]One who holds up the gods and the past, the present and the future.

vimochana;[441] (242) Bandhana-asurendranam;[442] (243) Yudhi-shatru-vinashana;[443] (244) Sankhya-prasada;[444] (245) Durvasa; (246) Sarva-sadhu-nishevita;[445] (247) Praskandana;[446] (248) Vibhaga;[447] (249) Atulya;[448] (250) Yajna-bhaga-vit;[449] (251) Sarvavasa;[450] (252) Sarvachari;[451] (.) Durvasa;[452] (253) Vasava; (254) Amara;[453] (255) Hema;[454] (256) Hemakara;[455] (.) Yajna;[456] (257) Sarvadhari;[457] (258) Dharottama;[458] (259) Lohitaksha;[459] (260) Mahaksha;[460] (261) Vijayaksha;[461] (262) Visharada;[462] (263 Samgraha;[463] (264) Nigraha;[464] (.) Karta;[465] (265) Sarpa-chira-nivasana;[466] (266) Mukhya;[467] (267) Amukhya;[468] (268)

[441] One who frees from all the bonds of action.

[442] One who binds down the Indras among the asuras.

[443] One who destroys enemies in battle.

[444] The gift of sankhya.

[445] Served by all those who are virtuous.

[446] The daring one.

[447] Divisions.

[448] Unmatched.

[449] One who knows about the shares in sacrifices.

[450] One who resides everywhere.

[451] One who is in all conduct.

[452] Since this has been listed earlier, we have not numbered it.

[453] Immortal.

[454] Gold.

[455] Maker of gold.

[456] Since this has been listed earlier, we have not numbered it.

[457] One who holds up everything.

[458] Supreme among those who hold up.

[459] Red-eyed.

[460] Great-eyed.

[461] One with victorious eyes.

[462] Skilled.

[463] Collection.

[464] Suppression.

[465] Since this has been listed earlier, we have not numbered it.

[466] One whose garments are made out of rags and snake skin.

[467] Best.

[468] Worst. The sense is that Shiva is everything, the best and the worst.

Deha;[469] (269) Dehardhi;[470] (270) Sarvakamada;[471] (271) Sarva-kala-prasada;[472] (272) Subala;[473] (273) Bala-rupa-dhrik;[474] (274) Akasha-nidhi-rupa;[475] (275) Nipati;[476] (276) Uraga;[477] (277)Khaga;[478] (278) Roudra-rupa;[479] (279) Ashura-aditya;[480] (280) Vasurashmi;[481] (281) Suvarchasi;[482] (282) Vasuvega;[483] (283) Mahavega;[484] (284) Manovega;[485] (.) Nishachara;[486] (285) Sarvavasi;[487] (286) Shriyavasi;[488] (287) Upadeshakara;[489] (.) Hara;[490] (288) Muniratma;[491] (289) Pati-loke;[492] (290) Sambhojya;[493] (291) Sahasrada;[494] (292)

[469]Body.

[470]Intelligence in the body.

[471]Granter of all desire.

[472]Favours of all kinds of destiny.

[473]Extremely strong.

[474]One who holds up the form of strength.

[475]One whose form is like the storehouse of the sky.

[476]Guardian.

[477]Serpent.

[478]Bird.

[479]Terrible in form.

[480]God who is not brave. Unless there is a typo, in which case it would mean god who is brave, this probably means that Shiva covers all gods, from those who are brave to those who are not brave.

[481]Rich in rays.

[482]Extremely radiant. We have numbered this, though Suvarchasa has earlier been mentioned. Suvarchasa is masculine, while Suvarchasi is feminine.

[483]With the speed of the Vasus.

[484]With great speed.

[485]With the speed of thought.

[486]Since this has already been listed, we have not numbered it.

[487]Residing everywhere. This is in the feminine. Earlier, the masculine, Sarvavasa, has been listed.

[488]Residing in prosperity.

[489]One who imparts instruction.

[490]Since this has already been listed, we have not numbered it.

[491]In the atmans of sages.

[492]Lord of the worlds.

[493]One who is worshipped well.

[494]Giver of thousands.

Pakshi;[495] (293) Pakshirupi;[496] (294) Atidipta;[497] (295) Vishampati;[498] (296) Unmada;[499] (297) Madanakara;[500] (298) Arthathakara;[501] (299) Romasha;[502] (300) Vamadeva; (301) Vama;[503] (302) Prak;[504] (303) Dakshina;[505] (304) Vamana;[506] (305) Siddhayogapahari;[507] (306) Sarvarthasadhaka;[508] (307) Bhikshu;[509] (308) Bhikshurupa;[510] (309) Vishani;[511] (310) Mridu;[512] (311)Avyaya;[513] (312) Mahasena;[514] (313) Vishakha;[515] (314) Shashthi-bhaga;[516] (315) Gavampati;[517] (316) Vajrahasta;[518] (317) Vishkambhi;[519] (318) Chamustambha;[520] (319) Kratu;[521] (320) Kratukara;[522] (321)

[495]Bird.

[496]With the form of a bird.

[497]Extremely resplendent.

[498]Lord of the universe.

[499]Crazy.

[500]With the form of Madana (the god of love).

[501]One who acts so as to accomplish the objective.

[502]Hairy one.

[503]Left.

[504]East.

[505]South.

[506]Dwarf.

[507]One who takes away the success obtained through yoga.

[508]One who brings success in all pursuits.

[509]Mendicant.

[510]In the form of a mendicant.

[511]One with a tuft on the head.

[512]Gentle.

[513]Imperishable.

[514]Great commander, also Kartikeya's name.

[515]Without branches, also Kartikeya's name.

[516]One who knows about the sixty divisions. This is a reference to the sixty principles enunciated in elaborations of sankhya.

[517]Lord of cattle. Alternatively, lord of speech.

[518]With the vajra in the hand.

[519]One who obstructs.

[520]Stupefier of armies.

[521]Sacrifice.

[522]Performer of sacrifices.

Kala;[523] (322) Madhu;[524] (323) Madhukara;[525] (324) Achala;[526] (325) Vanaspatya;[527] (326) Vajasena;[528] (327) Nityam-ashrama-pujita;[529] (328) Brahmachari;[530] (329) Lokachari;[531] (330) Sarvachari;[532] (331) Sucharvit;[533] (332) Ishana;[534] (333) Ishvara;[535] (.) Kala;[536] (.) Nishachara;[537] (334) Pinakadhrik;[538] (335) Nandishvara;[539] (336) Nandi; (337) Nandana;[540] (338) Nandivardhana;[541] (339) Bhagasyakshi-nihanta;[542] (.) Kala;[543] (340) Brahma-vidam-vara;[544] (341) Chaturmukha;[545] (342) Mahalinga;[546] (343) Charulinga;[547] (344) Lingadhyaksha;[548] (345) Suradhyaksha;[549]

[523]Time, destiny.

[524]Honey.

[525]Creator of honey.

[526]Immobile.

[527]Dwelling in trees.

[528]One invoked in hymns of the Yajur Veda.

[529]Always worshipped in all the ashramas.

[530]One who follows brahmacharya.

[531]One who roams around in the worlds.

[532]One who roams around everywhere.

[533]One who knows about good conduct.

[534]The lustrous lord.

[535]Supreme lord.

[536]Since this has already been listed, we have not numbered it.

[537]Since this has already been listed, we have not numbered it.

[538]One who holds Pinaka.

[539]Nandi's lord. Nandi means happiness and Nandi is also of one of Shiva's companions.

[540]One who gladdens.

[541]One who increases joy.

[542]One who destroyed Bhaga's mouth and eyes.

[543]Since this has already been listed, we have not numbered it.

[544]Supreme among those who know about the brahman.

[545]One with four faces.

[546]The great linga.

[547]The beautiful linga.

[548]One who presides over signs.

[549]One who presides over gods.

(346) Lokadhyaksha;[550] (347) Yugavaha;[551] (348) Bijadhyaksha;[552] (349) Bijakarta;[553] (350) Adhyatmanugata-bala;[554] (351) Itihasa-kara;[555] (352) Kalpa; (353) Goutama; (354) Jaleshvara;[556] (355) Dambha;[557] (356) Adambha;[558] (357) Vaidambha;[559] (358) Vashya;[560] (359) Vashyakara;[561] (360) Kavi;[562] (361) Lokakarta;[563] (362) Pashupati;[564] (363) Mahakarta;[565] (364) Mahoushadhi;[566] (365) Akshara;[567] (.) Parama;[568] (366) Brahma; (367) Balavan;[569] (368) Shakra; (369) Niti;[570] (370) Aniti;[571] (371) Shuddhatma;[572] (372) Shuddha;[573] (373) Manya;[574] (374) Manogati;[575] (375) Bahuprasada;[576] (376)

550 One who presides over the worlds.

551 One who brings about the yugas.

552 One who presides over the seed.

553 One who creates the seed.

554 One whose strength follows adhyatma.

555 The maker of history (itihasa).

556 Lord of the water.

557 Deceit.

558 Lack of deceit.

559 Specific kinds of deceit.

560 One who is submissive.

561 One who causes submission.

562 The wise one.

563 Creator of the worlds.

564 Lord of animals.

565 The great creator.

566 The great herb.

567 Immutable.

568 Since this has already been listed, we have not numbered it.

569 The strong one.

570 Policy.

571 Lack of policy.

572 Pure in soul.

573 Pure.

574 Respected one.

575 The progress of the mind.

576 One with many favours.

Svapana;[577] (377) Darpana;[578] (378) Amitrajit;[579] (379) Vedakara;[580] (380) Sutrakara;[581] (381) Vidvana;[582] (382) Amara-darshana;[583] (383) Maha-meghanivashi;[584] (384) Maha-ghora;[585] (385) Vashikara;[586] (386) Agnijvala;[587] (387) Atidhumra;[588] (388) Huta;[589] (389) Havi;[590] (390) Vrishana;[591] (391) Shankara;[592] (.) Nitya;[593] (392) Varchasvi;[594] (393) Dhuma-ketana;[595] (394) Nilastathangalubdha;[596] (395) Shobhana;[597] (396) Niravagraha;[598] (397) Svastida;[599] (398) Svastibhava;[600] (399) Bhagi;[601] (400) Bhagakara;[602] (401) Laghu;[603] (402) Utsanga;[604] (403) Mahanga;[605]

[577]Sleep, dreams.

[578]Mirror.

[579]Vanquisher of enemies.

[580]Creator of the Vedas.

[581]Creator of the sutras.

[582]Learned.

[583]With a sight like that of the immortals.

[584]One who dwells in the giant clouds.

[585]Extremely terrible.

[586]One who subjugates.

[587]One who blazes like the fire.

[588]One who is extremely smoky.

[589]One who is invoked.

[590]Oblations.

[591]One who fertilizes.

[592]One who provides prosperity.

[593]Since this has been listed earlier, we have not numbered it.

[594]The vigorous one.

[595]One with smoke as the standard.

[596]One who likes blue in his limbs.

[597]Splendid one.

[598]One who cannot be perceived with the senses.

[599]One who grants sanctuary.

[600]One whose nature provides blessings.

[601]One who receives a share (at sacrifices).

[602]One who determines the share (at sacrifices).

[603]Light one.

[604]One who is like a lap.

[605]One with great limbs.

(404) Maha-garbha;[606] (405) Para;[607] (406) Yuva;[608] (407) Krishna-varna;[609] (408) Suvarna;[610] (409) Indriya-sarva-dehinam;[611] (410) Maha-pada;[612] (412) Maha-hasta;[613] (413) Maha-kaya;[614] (414) Maha-yasha;[615] (415) Maha-murdha;[616] (416) Maha-matra;[617] (417) Maha-netra;[618] (418) Digalaya;[619] (419) Maha-danta;[620] (420) Maha-karna;[621] (421) Maha-medhra;[622] (422) Maha-hanu;[623] (423) Maha-nasa;[624] (424) Maha-kambu;[625] (425) Maha-griva;[626] (426) Shmashana-dhrik;[627] (427) Maha-vaksha;[628] (428) Mahoraska;[629] (429) Antaratma;[630] (430) Mrigalaya;[631] (431) Lambana;[632] (432) Lambitoshtha;[633] (433) Maha-

[606]One who is the great origin.

[607]Supreme.

[608]Young one.

[609]Dark in complexion.

[610]Golden.

[611]The senses in every body.

[612]With giant feet.

[613]With large hands.

[614]With a gigantic body.

[615]With great fame.

[616]With a large head.

[617]Large in measurements.

[618]With large eyes.

[619]One who resides in the directions.

[620]With large teeth.

[621]With large ears.

[622]With a large penis.

[623]With a large jaw.

[624]With a large nose.

[625]With a large neck.

[626]With a large neck. *Kambu* is the front part of the neck, while *griva* is the rear part.

[627]One who holds up cremation grounds.

[628]With a broad chest.

[629]With a large breast.

[630]The inner soul.

[631]The abode of animals.

[632]One who hangs down.

[633]One whose lips hang down.

maya;[634] (434) Payonidhi;[635] (.) Maha-danta;[636] (435) Maha-damshtra;[637] (436) Maha-jihva;[638] (437) Maha-mukha;[639] (438) Maha-nakha;[640] (439) Maha-roma;[641] (440) Maha-kesha;[642] (441) Maha-jata;[643] (442) Asapatna;[644] (.) Prasada;[645] (443) Pratyaya;[646] (444) Giri-sadhana;[647] (445) Snehana;[648] (446) Asnehana;[649] (447) Ajita;[650] (448) Maha-muni;[651] (449) Vrikshakara;[652] (450) Vriksha-ketu;[653] (451) Anala;[654] (452) Vayu-vahana;[655] (453) Mandali;[656] (454) Meru-dhama;[657] (455) Deva-danava-darpaha;[658] (456) Atharva-shirsha;[659] (457) Samasya;[660] (458) Rig-sahasra-amitekshana;[661] (459)

[634]Great in use of maya.

[635]Store of milk.

[636]Since this has already been listed, we have not numbered it.

[637]With large teeth.

[638]With a large tongue.

[639]With a large face.

[640]With large nails.

[641]With large body hair.

[642]With long hair.

[643]With matted hair that is long.

[644]Without any rivals.

[645]Since this has already been listed, we have not numbered it.

[646]Conviction.

[647]One who creates the mountains.

[648]One with affection.

[649]One without affection.

[650]One who is not defeated.

[651]The great sage.

[652]With the form of a tree.

[653]One with a tree on the banner.

[654]Fire.

[655]One whose mount is the wind.

[656]One who possesses a halo.

[657]One with an abode on Mount Meru.

[658]One who destroys the insolence of gods and danavas.

[659]One whose head consists of the Atharva Veda.

[660]One whose mouth consists of the Sama Veda.

[661]One whose infinite eyes consist of the one thousand hymns of the Rig Veda.

Yaju-pada-bhujou;[662] (460) Guhya-prakasha;[663] (461) Jangama;[664] (462) Amoghartha;[665] (.) Prasada;[666] (463) Abhigamya;[667] (464) Sudarshana;[668] (465) Upahara-priya;[669] (466) Sharva; (467) Kanaka;[670] (468) Kanchana;[671] (469) Sthira;[672] (470) Nabhi;[673] (471) Nandi-kara;[674] (472) Bhavya;[675] (473) Pushkara; (474) Sthapati;[676] (.) Sthira;[677] (475) Dvadasha;[678] (476) Trasana;[679] (477) Adya;[680] (.) Yajna;[681] (478) Yajna-samahita;[682] (.) Nakta;[683] (479) Kali;[684] (.) Kala;[685] (480) Makara; (481) Kala-pujita;[686] (482) Sagana;[687] (483)Ganakara;[688]

[662]One whose arms and feet consist of the Yajur Veda.

[663]One who is all the revealed and hidden knowledge.

[664]One who is all the mobile objects.

[665]One whose objectives are always accomplished.

[666]Since this has already been listed, we have not numbered it.

[667]One who can be approached.

[668]The handsome one.

[669]One who loves gifts.

[670]Golden.

[671]Golden.

[672]Immobile.

[673]Navel (of the universe).

[674]One who causes delight.

[675]One who can be imagined.

[676]Architect.

[677]Since this has already been mentioned, we have not numbered it.

[678]Twelve. This can mean anything, such as the twelve Adityas or the twelve months. However, it has been interpreted as the twelve stages of life, from birth to death, that a person passes through.

[679]The one who terrifies.

[680]The original one.

[681]Since this has already been listed, we have not numbered it.

[682]One who is established in sacrifices.

[683]Since this has already been listed, we have not numbered it.

[684]Kali yuga or evil.

[685]Since this has already been listed, we have not numbered it.

[686]Worshipped by destiny.

[687]One with companions.

[688]One who creates ganas (Shiva's companions).

(.) Bhuta-bhavana;[689] (484) Sarathi;[690] (485) Bhasma-shayi;[691] (486) Bhasmagopta;[692] (487) Bhasmabhuta;[693] (488) Taru-gana;[694] (489) Agana;[695] (490) Lopa;[696] (.) Mahatma;[697] (491) Sarva-pujita;[698] (492) Shanku;[699] (493) Trishanku; (494) Sampanna;[700] (495) Shuchi;[701] (496) Bhuta-nishevita;[702] (497) Ashramastha;[703] (498) Kapotastha;[704] (499) Vishvakarma;[705] (500) Patirvara;[706] (501) Shakha;[707] (.) Vishakha;[708] (502) Tamroshtha;[709] (503) Ambujala;[710] (504) Sunishchaya;[711] (505) Kapila;[712] (506) Akapila;[713] (507) Shura;[714] (508) Ayu;[715] (.) Para;[716] (509) Apara;[717] (510) Gandharva; (511)

[689]Since this has already been listed, we have not numbered it.
[690]Charioteer.
[691]One who lies down on ashes.
[692]One who protects the ashes.
[693]One who is created from ashes.
[694]One who has trees as companions.
[695]One without companions.
[696]Destruction.
[697]Since this has been listed earlier, we have not numbered it.
[698]Worshipped by everyone.
[699]Pillar. The word *shanku* has multiple meanings, but pillar seems to fit best.
[700]Accomplished one.
[701]Pure.
[702]Attended by the bhutas.
[703]Dwelling in hermitages.
[704]One who is in pigeons.
[705]The creator of the universe.
[706]The supreme lord.
[707]With branches, because of the comparison with a tree.
[708]Since this has been listed earlier, we have not numbered it.
[709]One whose lips have the colour of copper.
[710]One who is in the net of waters.
[711]One with a firm resolve.
[712]One who is tawny.
[713]One who is not tawny.
[714]The brave one.
[715]Lifespan.
[716]Since this has already been listed, we have not numbered it.
[717]The ultimate one.

Aditi; (512) Tarkshya; (513) Suvijneya;[718] (514) Susarathi;[719] (515) Parashvadhayudha;[720] (516) Deva; (517) Arthakari;[721] (518) Subandhava;[722] (519) Tumbavini;[723] (520) Mahakopa;[724] (.) Urdhva-reta;[725] (521) Jaleshaya;[726] (522) Ugra;[727] (523) Vamshakara;[728] (524) Vamsha;[729] (525) Vamsha-nada;[730] (.) Anindita;[731] (526) Sarvanga-rupa;[732] (527) Mayavi;[733] (528) Suhrida;[734] (529) Anila;[735] (530) Anala;[736] (531) Bandhana;[737] (532) Bandha-karta;[738] (533) Subandhana-vimochana;[739] (534) Yajnari;[740] (535) Kamari;[741] (.) Maha-damshtra;[742] (536) Mahayudha;[743] (537) Bahustva-anindita;[744] (.) Sharva;[745] (.)

[718]One who can be comprehended well.

[719]One who is an excellent charioteer.

[720]One whose weapon is a battleaxe.

[721]One who accomplishes objectives.

[722]One who is an excellent friend.

[723]One who has a veena made out of a gourd.

[724]One whose rage is great.

[725]Since this has already been listed, we have not numbered it.

[726]One who lies down on the water.

[727]The fierce one.

[728]One who creates lineages.

[729]Lineages.

[730]One who is the sound of the bamboo.

[731]Since this has already been listed, we have not numbered it.

[732]One who is present in all the limbs.

[733]One who uses maya.

[734]Well-wisher.

[735]Wind.

[736]Fire.

[737]Bonds.

[738]Creator of bonds.

[739]One who frees from the excellent bonds.

[740]The enemy of sacrifices.

[741]The enemy of Kama (the god of love).

[742]Since this has been listed earlier, we have not numbered it.

[743]One with great weapons.

[744]Not censured by many.

[745]Since this has already been listed, we have not numbered it.

Shankara;[746] (538) Shankara-adhana;[747] (539) Amaresha;[748] (540) Mahadeva;[749] (541) Vishvadeva;[750] (542) Surariha;[751] (543) Ahirbudhna;[752] (544) Nirriti;[753] (545) Chekitana;[754] (.) Hari;[755] (546) Ajaikapada;[756] (547) Kapali;[757] (548) Trishankurjit;[758] (549) Shiva;[759] (550) Dhanvantari;[760] (551) Dhumaketu;[761] (552) Skanda; (553) Vaishravana;[762] (554) Dhatri; (555) Shakra; (556) Vishnu; (557) Mitra; (558) Tvashtri; (559) Dhruva; (560) Dhara;[763] (561) Prabhava;[764] (562) Sarvaga;[765] (563) Vayu; (564) Aryama; (565) Savitri; (566) Ravi; (.) Udagra;[766] (567) Vidhatri; (568) Mandhata; (.) Bhuta-bhavana;[767] (569) Rati-tirtha;[768] (570) Vagmi;[769] (571) Sarva-kama-gunavaha;[770] (572)

[746]Since this has already been listed, we have not numbered it.

[747]The Shankara who possesses no wealth.

[748]Lord of the immortals.

[749]Great god.

[750]God of the universe.

[751]Slayer of the enemies of the gods.

[752]One who is in the form of a serpent in the nether regions. This is Shiva being identified with the serpent Shesha.

[753]Destruction, death.

[754]The intelligent one.

[755]Since this has already been listed, we are not numbering it.

[756]The one-footed one. This is Shiva in his one-footed form, the Aja linking this to Aja-Ekapada, the Vedic deity.

[757]One with a beggar's bowl in the form of a skull.

[758]One who has conquered the three darts (sattva, rajas, tamas).

[759]Gracious one.

[760]One who is the physician of the gods.

[761]One who is like a comet.

[762]Kubera.

[763]One who holds things up.

[764]Power.

[765]One who goes everywhere.

[766]Since this has already been listed, we have not numbered it.

[767]Since this has already been listed, we have not numbered it.

[768]The place for all desire. It is also possible to translate this as a vagina.

[769]Eloquent one.

[770]One who makes all the qualities of desire flow.

Padma-garbha;[771] (573) Maha-garbha;[772] (574) Chandra-vaktra;[773] (575) Manorama;[774] (.) Balavan;[775] (576) Upashanta;[776] (577) Purana;[777] (578) Punya-chanchuri;[778] (579) Kuru-karta;[779] (580) Kala-rupa;[780] (581) Kurubhuta;[781] (.) Maheshvara;[782] (582) Sarvashaya;[783] (583) Darbhashayi;[784] (584) Sarvesham-praninam-pati;[785] (585) Deva-deva-mukha;[786] (586) Asakta;[787] (587) Sat;[788] (588) Asat;[789] (589) Sarva-ratna-vit;[790] (590) Kailasa-shikharavasi;[791] (591) Himavat-giri-samshraya;[792] (592) Kula-hari;[793] (593) Kula-karta;[794] (594) Bahu-vidya;[795] (595) Bahu-prada;[796] (596) Vanija;[797]

[771]One generated from a lotus.

[772]The great womb.

[773]One with a face like the moon.

[774]Beautiful one.

[775]Since this has already been listed, we have not numbered it.

[776]The pacified one.

[777]Ancient one.

[778]One who is searched out by the virtuous. The word *chanchuri* means a bee. One thus searches out, the way a bee searches out honey.

[779]One who gets action done.

[780]One with the form of time/destiny.

[781]One who creates the field of action.

[782]Since this has already been listed, we have not numbered it.

[783]One who resides in everything.

[784]One who resides in darbha grass.

[785]Lord of all creatures.

[786]Foremost god among the gods.

[787]Unattached.

[788]Existence.

[789]Non-existence.

[790]One who knows about all the jewels.

[791]One who resides on the summit of Kailasa.

[792]One who resorts to the Himalaya mountains.

[793]One who destroys the banks (with the imagery of a river).

[794]One who creates banks (with the image of a river).

[795]One who possesses many kinds of knowledge.

[796]One who gives in many ways.

[797]Merchant.

(597) Vardhana;[798] (598) Vriksha;[799] (599) Nakula-chandana-chhada;[800] (600) Sara-griva;[801] (601) Maha-jatru;[802] (602) Alola;[803] (603) Mahoushada;[804] (604) Siddhartha-kari;[805] (605) Siddhartha-chhanda-vyakaranottara;[806] (606) Simha-nada;[807] (607) Simha-damshtra;[808] (608) Simhaga;[809] (609) Simhavahana;[810] (610) Prabhavatma;[811] (611) Jagat-kala-tala;[812] (612) Lokahita-taru;[813] (613) Saranga;[814] (614) Nava-chakranga;[815] (615) Ketumali;[816] (616) Sabhavana;[817] (617) Bhutalaya;[818] (618) Sarva-bhutanam-nilaya;[819] (.) Vibhu;[820] (.) Bhava;[821] (619) Amogha;[822] (620) Samyata;[823] (621)

[798]One who creates prosperity.

[799]Tree.

[800]*Nakula* and *chada* are the names of plants, while *chandana* is the sandalwood tree. It is possible that instead of nakula, it should read *bakula* (a tree).

[801]One with a sturdy neck.

[802]One with a large collarbone.

[803]One who is steady.

[804]Great herb. The earlier name was Mahoushadhi, in the feminine. Mahoushadha is in the masculine.

[805]One who ensures success in objectives.

[806]One who provides firm conclusions about prosody and grammar.

[807]With the roar of a lion.

[808]With the teeth of a lion.

[809]One who moves around on a lion.

[810]One with a lion as a mount.

[811]The power in the soul.

[812]One whose rhythm is that of destroying the universe.

[813]The tree that brings benefit to the worlds.

[814]Multicoloured.

[815]One who is like a young swan.

[816]One who wears a garland of flags.

[817]One who provides instruction.

[818]Abode of creatures.

[819]Refuge of all creatures.

[820]Since this has already been listed, we have not numbered it.

[821]Since this has already been listed, we have not numbered it.

[822]Infallible.

[823]Restrained.

Ashva;[824] (622) Bhojana;[825] (623) Prana-dharana;[826] (624) Dhritiman;[827] (625) Matiman;[828] (626) Satkrita;[829] (627) Yugadhipa;[830] (628) Gopali;[831] (629) Gopati;[832] (630) Grama;[833] (631) Go-charma-vasana;[834] (.) Hara;[835] (632) Hiranya-bahu;[836] (633) Guha-pala-praveshinam;[837] (634) Pratishthayi;[838] (635) Maha-harsha;[839] (636) Jitakama;[840] (637) Jitendriya;[841] (638) Gandhara;[842] (639) Surala;[843] (640) Tapah-karma-rati;[844] (641) Dhanu;[845] (642) Maha-gita;[846] (643) Mahan-ritta;[847] (644) Apsara-gana-sevita;[848] (645) Maha-ketu-dhanu;[849] (646) Dhatunaika-sanu-chara;[850] (.) Achala;[851] (647)

[824]Horse.

[825]Food.

[826]One who upholds life.

[827]One with fortitude.

[828]One with intelligence.

[829]One who is worshipped.

[830]Lord of the yugas.

[831]Protector of the earth.

[832]Lord of the earth.

[833]Inhabited places.

[834]One with garments made out of cowhide.

[835]Since this has already been listed, we have not numbered it.

[836]One with golden arms.

[837]Protector of those who wish to enter their own selves (with the image of a cave being used).

[838]One who establishes.

[839]Great delight.

[840]One who has conquered desire, or conquered Kama, the god of love.

[841]One who has conquered the senses.

[842]The third (*ga*) of the seven primary notes.

[843]This should probably read Suralaya, meaning, the abode of the gods.

[844]One who is devoted to austere rites.

[845]Bow.

[846]One who is sung of as great.

[847]One worshipped with great hymns.

[848]Served by large number of apsaras.

[849]With a large standard and bow.

[850]One who roams around on summits with many minerals.

[851]Since this has been listed earlier, we have not numbered it.

Avedaniya;[852] (648) Avesha;[853] (649) Sarva-gandha-sukhavaha;[854] (650) Torana;[855] (651) Astarana;[856] (.) Vayu;[857] (652) Paridhavati;[858] (653) Ekata;[859] (654) Samyoga;[860] (.) Vardhana;[861] (655) Vriddha;[862] (656) Maha-vriddha;[863] (657) Ganadhipa;[864] (.) Nitya;[865] (658) Atma-sahaya;[866] (659) Devasura-pati;[867] (660) Pati;[868] (661) Yukta;[869] (662) Yukta-bahu;[870] (663) Dvivida;[871] (664) Suparvana;[872] (665) Ashada;[873] (666) Sushada;[874] (.) Dhruva;[875] (667) Harihana;[876] (.) Hara;[877] (668) Vapuravarta;[878] (669) Manebhya;[879] (670) Vasu-shreshtha;[880] (671)

[852]One who can be addressed.

[853]Frenzy.

[854]One who conveys all kinds of pleasant fragrances.

[855]Gate.

[856]Cover.

[857]Since this has already been listed, we have not numbered it.

[858]One who drives things around.

[859]Union.

[860]Combination.

[861]Since this has already been listed, we have not numbered it.

[862]Ancient one.

[863]Immensely ancient one.

[864]Lord of the ganas.

[865]Since this has already been listed, we have not numbered it.

[866]One who only depends on one's own self.

[867]Lord of the gods and the asuras.

[868]Lord.

[869]One who is united (in yoga).

[870]One whose arms are united (in yoga).

[871]One who is of two kinds, the two kinds are a matter of interpretation.

[872]Highly extolled.

[873]One who is a staff.

[874]One who is capable of bearing things.

[875]Since this has already been listed, we have not numbered it.

[876]One who destroyed Hari (Brahma).

[877]Since this has already been listed, we have not numbered it.

[878]One who makes bodies whirl around.

[879]One who deserves respect.

[880]Best among riches.

Maha-patha;[881] (672) Shirohari;[882] (673) Vimarsha;[883] (674) Sarva-lakshana-bhushita;[884] (675) Aksha;[885] (676) Ratha-yogi;[886] (677) Sarva-yogi;[887] (678) Maha-bala;[888] (679) Samannaya;[889] (680) Asamannaya;[890] (681) Tirtha-deva;[891] (682) Maharatha;[892] (683) Nirjiva;[893] (684) Jivana;[894] (.) Mantra;[895] (685) Shubhaksha;[896] (686) Bahu-karkasha;[897] (687) Ratna-prabhuta;[898] (688) Raktanga;[899] (689) Maharnava-nipan-vit;[900] (690) Mula;[901] (691) Vishala;[902] (692) Amrita; (693) Vyakta; (694) Avyakta; (695) Tapo-nidhi;[903] (696) Arohana;[904] (697) Niroha;[905] (698) Shailahari;[906] (.) Maha-tapa;[907] (699) Sena-kalpa;[908] (700) Maha-

[881]Great path.

[882]Severer of the head, a reference to Shiva severing Brahma's head.

[883]Impatience.

[884]One who is adorned with all the auspicious marks.

[885]Axle.

[886]One who drives a chariot (with an imagery of the body).

[887]One who is a yogi in every way.

[888]Extremely strong.

[889]One who is the sacred texts.

[890]One who is not the sacred texts.

[891]The god of the tirthas.

[892]Great charioteer.

[893]Without life (meaning, the inert element in every creature).

[894]Life (in every creature).

[895]Since this has already been listed, we have not numbered it.

[896]One with the auspicious eyes.

[897]One who is harsh in many ways.

[898]One with many jewels.

[899]Red-limbed.

[900]One who knows about drinking from the great oceans.

[901]Root.

[902]Large.

[903]Store of austerities.

[904]Ascent.

[905]One who is without ascent.

[906]One who eats from the mountains.

[907]Since this has already been listed, we have not numbered it.

[908]One who is like an army.

kalpa;[909] (701) Yugayuga-kara;[910] (.) Hari;[911] (702) Yuga-rupa;[912] (703) Maha-rupa;[913] (704) Pavana;[914] (705) Gahana;[915] (706) Naga;[916] (707) Nyaya-nirvapana;[917] (708) Pada;[918] (709) Pandita;[919] (710) Achalopama;[920] (711) Bahu-mala;[921] (712) Maha-mala;[922] (713) Sumala;[923] (714) Bahu-lochana;[924] (715) Vistara-lavana;[925] (716) Kupa;[926] (717) Kusuma;[927] (718) Safalodaya;[928] (719) Vrishabha;[929] (720) Vrishabhankanga;[930] (721) Mani-bilva;[931] (722) Jatadhara;[932] (723) Indu-visarga;[933] (724) Sumukha;[934] (725) Sura; (726) Sarvayudha;[935] (727) Saha;[936] (728) Nivedana;[937] (729) Sudha-

[909]The great kalpa.

[910]One who causes progression from one yuga to another yuga.

[911]Since this has already been listed, we have not numbered it.

[912]With the form of a yuga.

[913]Great in form.

[914]The purifier.

[915]Inaccessible, hard to understand.

[916]Mountain.

[917]One who determines good policy.

[918]Foot, root, foundation.

[919]Learned one.

[920]One who is like a mountain.

[921]With many garlands.

[922]With a great garland.

[923]With an excellent garland.

[924]With many eyes.

[925]The extensive ocean.

[926]Probably best interpreted as the mast of a ship, though the word also means cave or well.

[927]Flower.

[928]One whose appearance ensures success.

[929]Bull.

[930]One whose limbs are marked by the signs of a bull.

[931]Jewel of the wood-apple (bilva) tree.

[932]With matted hair.

[933]One who lets go of the moon.

[934]One with an excellent face.

[935]One who possesses all the weapons.

[936]One who can endure.

[937]Dedication.

jata;[938] (730) Sugandhara;[939] (731) Maha-dhanu;[940] (732) Gandhamali;[941] (733) Bhagavanutthana-sarva-karmanam;[942] (734) Manthana;[943] (735) Bahula;[944] (736) Bahu;[945] (737) Sakala;[946] (738) Sarva-lochana;[947] (739) Tarastali;[948] (740) Karastali;[949] (741) Urdhva-samhanana;[950] (742) Vaha;[951] (743) Chhatra;[952] (744) Suchattra;[953] (745) Vikhyata;[954] (746) Sarva-lokashraya;[955] (.) Mahat;[956] (.) Munda;[957] (.) Virupa;[958] (747) Vikrita;[959] (748) Dandi-munda;[960] (749) Vikurvana;[961] (750) Haryaksha;[962] (751) Kakubha;[963] (752) Vajri;[964] (753) Dipta-jihva;[965] (754) Sahasra-pat;[966] (755) Sahasra-

[938]Born from honey or nectar.

[939]The excellent third primary note (*gandhara* or ga) of music.

[940]With a giant bow.

[941]With fragrant garlands.

[942]The illustrious one who arises among all deeds.

[943]Churner.

[944]Abundant.

[945]Arm. But this may also have been used with an imagery of the staff in the pole of a chariot.

[946]Everything.

[947]With eyes everywhere.

[948]The sound of a palm slapping against a club.

[949]The sound of a palm slapping against another palm.

[950]A destroyer who strikes upwards.

[951]One who bears.

[952]Umbrella.

[953]One with an excellent umbrella.

[954]Famous.

[955]Refuge of all the worlds.

[956]Since this has already been listed, we have not numbered it.

[957]Since this has already been listed, we have not numbered it.

[958]Since this has already been listed, we have not numbered it.

[959]The transformed one.

[960]With a staff and shaved head.

[961]One who can assume different forms.

[962]Tawny-eyed.

[963]Distinguished one.

[964]Wielding the vajra.

[965]With a flaming tongue.

[966]With a thousand feet.

murdha;[967] (756) Devendra;[968] (757) Sarva-deva-maya;[969] (758) Guru;[970] (759) Sahasra-bahu;[971] (.) Sarvanga;[972] (760) Sharanya;[973] (761) Sarva-loka-krit;[974] (.) Pavitra;[975] (762) Tri-madhurmantra;[976] (763) Kanishtha;[977] (764) Krishna-pingala;[978] (765) Brahma-danda-vinirmita;[979] (.) Shataghni;[980] (766) Shata-pasha-dhrik;[981] (.) Padma-garbha;[982] (.) Maha-garbha;[983] (767) Jalodbhava;[984] (768) Gabhasti;[985] (769) Brahma-krit;[986] (770) Brahma; (771) Brahma-vid;[987] (772) Brahmana-gati;[988] (773) Ananta-rupa;[989] (774) Naikatma;[990] (775) Tigma-teja;[991] (.) Svayambhu;[992] (776) Urdhvagatma;[993] (.) Pashupati;[994] (777) Vatamraha;[995] (778)

[967]With a thousand heads.

[968]Lord of the gods.

[969]One with all the gods in him.

[970]Preceptor.

[971]With a thousand arms.

[972]Since this has already been listed, we have not numbered it.

[973]One with whom refuge is sought.

[974]Creator of all the worlds.

[975]Since this has already been listed, we have not numbered it.

[976]One with three (Rig, Sama and Yajur Vedas) sweet mantras.

[977]Youngest one, in the sense of being younger to Vishnu and Brahma.

[978]One who is dark and tawny.

[979]One who fashioned the staff of chastisement.

[980]Since this has already been listed, we have not numbered it.

[981]One who wields one hundred nooses.

[982]Since this has already been listed, we have not numbered it.

[983]Since this has already been listed, we have not numbered it.

[984]One who originated in the water.

[985]Shining one.

[986]Creator of Brahma.

[987]One who knows about the brahman.

[988]The objective of brahmanas.

[989]Infinite in form.

[990]With more than one atman.

[991]Fierce in energy.

[992]Since this has already been listed, we have not numbered it.

[993]One whose atman heads upwards.

[994]Since this has already been listed, we have not numbered it.

[995]With the speed of the wind.

Manojava;[996] (779) Chandani;[997] (780) Padmalagrya;[998] (781) Surabhyuttarana;[999] (782) Nara; (783) Karnikara-mahasragvi;[1000] (784) Nila-mouli;[1001] (785) Pinaka-dhrik;[1002] (786) Uma-pati;[1003] (787) Uma-kanta;[1004] (788) Jahnavi-dhrik;[1005] (789) Uma-dhava;[1006] (.) Vara;[1007] (790) Varaha;[1008] (791) Varesha;[1009] (792) Su-mahasvana;[1010] (793) Maha-prasada;[1011] (794) Damana;[1012] (795) Shatruha;[1013] (796) Shveta-pingala;[1014] (797) Pritatma;[1015] (798) Prayatatma;[1016] (799) Samyatatma;[1017] (800) Pradhana-dhrik;[1018] (801) Sarva-parshva-suta;[1019] (.) Tarkshya;[1020] (802) Dharma-sadharana;[1021] (.)

[996]With the speed of thought.

[997]Smeared with sandalwood paste.

[998]The tip of the stamen of a lotus.

[999]One who brought Surabhi down. Surabhi is the divine cow. Because Surabhi lied, alternatively, forced Brahma to lie, Surabhi was cursed by Shiva and brought down to earth.

[1000]One who is adorned with a giant garland of karnikara (Indian laburnum) flowers.

[1001]With a blue crest.

[1002]Wielder of Pinaka.

[1003]Uma's consort.

[1004]Uma's beloved.

[1005]One who holds up Jahnavi (Ganga).

[1006]Uma's husband.

[1007]Since this has already been listed, we have not numbered it.

[1008]Boar.

[1009]Supreme lord.

[1010]One with the extremely loud roar.

[1011]One who is great in his favours.

[1012]One who subdues.

[1013]Slayer of enemies.

[1014]One who is white and tawny.

[1015]One whose atman is cheerful.

[1016]One to whom all atmans go.

[1017]One whose atman is restrained.

[1018]One who holds up everything that is important.

[1019]One whose sons are on every side.

[1020]Since this has already been listed, we have not numbered it.

[1021]One who is general dharma.

Vara;[1022] (803) Characharatma;[1023] (804) Sukshmatma;[1024] (805) Suvrisha;[1025] (806) Go-vrisheshvara;[1026] (807) Sadhyarshi-vasuraditya-vivasvansavita-mrida;[1027] (808) Vyasa-sarvasya-samkshepa-vistara;[1028] (809) Paryaya;[1029] (810) Naya;[1030] (811) Ritu;[1031] (812) Samvatsara;[1032] (813) Masa;[1033] (814) Paksha;[1034] (815) Samkhya-samapana;[1035] (816) Kala; (817) Kashtha; (818) Lava; (819) Matra;[1036] (820) Muhurta; (821) Aha;[1037] (822) Kshapa;[1038] (823) Kshana; (824) Vishva-kshetra;[1039] (825) Praja-bija;[1040] (826) Lingamadya;[1041] (.) Anindita;[1042] (827) Sadas;[1043] (.) Vyakta;[1044] (.) Avyakta;[1045] (828) Pita;[1046] (829) Mata;[1047] (830) Pitamaha;[1048] (831) Svarga-dvara;[1049]

[1022]Since this has already been listed, we have not numbered it.

[1023]One who is the soul of everything mobile and immobile.

[1024]One whose soul is subtle.

[1025]Excellent bull.

[1026]Lord of cows and bulls.

[1027]One who delights sadhyas, rishis, Vasus, Adityas, Vivasvan and Savitri.

[1028]Everything composed by Vyasa, in brief and in detail.

[1029]Change, progression.

[1030]Guidance.

[1031]Season.

[1032]Year.

[1033]Month.

[1034]Fortnight.

[1035]Numbers that indicate the end (of those measures of time).

[1036]Musical unit of time.

[1037]Day.

[1038]Night.

[1039]With the universe as a field.

[1040]Seed of beings.

[1041]Original linga.

[1042]Since this has already been listed, we have not numbered it.

[1043]Heaven and earth.

[1044]Since this has already been listed, we have not numbered it.

[1045]Since this has already been listed, we have not numbered it.

[1046]Father.

[1047]Mother.

[1048]Grandfather.

[1049]Gate to heaven.

(832) Praja-dvara;[1050] (833) Moksha-dvara;[1051] (834) Trivishtapa;[1052] (835) Nirvana;[1053] (836) Hladana;[1054] (837) Brahma-loka;[1055] (838) Para-gati;[1056] (839) Devasura-vinirmata;[1057] (840) Devasura-parayana;[1058] (841) Devasura-guru-deva;[1059] (842) Devasura-namaskrita;[1060] (843) Devasura-mahamatra;[1061] (844) Devasura-ganashraya;[1062] (845) Devasura-ganadhyaksha;[1063] (846) Devasura-ganagrani;[1064] (847) Devatideva;[1065] (848) Devarshi-devasura-varaprada;[1066] (849) Devasureshvara;[1067] (.) Deva;[1068] (850) Devasura-maheshvara;[1069] (.) Sarva-deva-maya;[1070] (851) Achintya;[1071] (852) Devatatma;[1072] (853) Asambhava;[1073] (854) Udbhida;[1074] (855) Trivikrama;[1075] (856) Vaidya;[1076] (857)

[1050]Gate to offspring.

[1051]Gate to emancipation.

[1052]Resident of heaven.

[1053]Liberation.

[1054]Refreshment.

[1055]Brahma's world.

[1056]Supreme objective.

[1057]Creator of gods and asuras.

[1058]Devoted to gods and asuras.

[1059]The god who is the preceptor of gods and asuras.

[1060]Worshipped by gods and asuras.

[1061]Best among gods and asuras.

[1062]The refuge of large numbers of gods and asuras.

[1063]Supervisor of large numbers of gods and asuras.

[1064]Foremost among large numbers of gods and asuras.

[1065]God of the gods.

[1066]One who grants boons to devarshis, gods and asuras.

[1067]Lord of the gods and the asuras.

[1068]Since this has already been listed, we have not numbered it.

[1069]The great lord of the gods and the asuras.

[1070]Since this has already been listed, we have not numbered it.

[1071]One who cannot be thought of.

[1072]One who is the atman of the gods.

[1073]One who has not been generated.

[1074]Fountain.

[1075]One with three steps, an allusion to Vishnu's vamana (dwarf) incarnation.

[1076]Learned one, physician.

Viraja;[1077] (858) Virajombara;[1078] (859) Idya;[1079] (860) Hasti;[1080] (861) Sura-vyaghra;[1081] (862) Deva-simha;[1082] (863) Nararshabha;[1083] (864) Vibudhagra-vara;[1084] (865) Shreshtha;[1085] (866) Sarva-devottomottama;[1086] (867) Prayukta;[1087] (.) Shobhana;[1088] (868) Vajra; (.) Ishana;[1089] (.) Prabhu;[1090] (.) Avyaya;[1091] (.) Guru;[1092] (869) Kanta;[1093] (870) Nija;[1094] (871) Sarga;[1095] (.) Pavitra;[1096] (872) Sarva-vahana;[1097] (873) Shringi;[1098] (874) Shringa-priya;[1099] (875) Babhru;[1100] (876) Rajaraja;[1101] (877) Niramaya;[1102] (878) Abhirama;[1103] (879) Sura-gana;[1104] (880) Virama;[1105] (881) Sarva-

[1077]Shining one.
[1078]One with shining garments.
[1079]One who is praiseworthy.
[1080]Elephant.
[1081]God of tigers.
[1082]God of lions.
[1083]Bull among men.
[1084]Supreme among the foremost of gods.
[1085]The best.
[1086]Supreme among all the supreme among gods.
[1087]One who is yoked (to yoga).
[1088]Since this has already been listed, we have not numbered it.
[1089]Since this has already been listed, we have not numbered it.
[1090]Since this has already been listed, we have not numbered it.
[1091]Since this has already been listed, we have not numbered it.
[1092]Since this has already been listed, we have not numbered it.
[1093]Desired one.
[1094]One's own.
[1095]Creation.
[1096]Since this has already been listed, we have not numbered it.
[1097]One who conveys everything.
[1098]Horned one.
[1099]One who loves horns.
[1100]Tawny, reddish brown.
[1101]King of kings.
[1102]Lack of disease.
[1103]Pleasant.
[1104]All the gods together.
[1105]Pause, the end.

sadhana;[1106] (882) Lalataksha;[1107] (883) Vishva-deha;[1108] (884) Harina;[1109] (885) Brahma-varchasa;[1110] (886) Sthavaranam-pati;[1111] (887) Niyamendriya-bardhana;[1112] (888) Siddhartha;[1113] (889) Sarva-bhutartha;[1114] (.) Achintya;[1115] (890) Satya-vrata;[1116] (.) Shuchi;[1117] (891) Vratadhipa;[1118] (.) Parama;[1119] (.) Brahma;[1120] (892) Muktanam-parama-gati;[1121] (893) Vimukta;[1122] (894) Mukta-teja;[1123] (895) Shriman;[1124] (896) Shri-vardhana;[1125] and (897) Jagat.[1126]

"""Since you are the foremost and illustrious one, I have praised you with devotion. Brahma and the other gods and learned maharshis praise, worship and honour you. Who can satisfy the lord of the universe? However, because of my devotion, I have placed that prosperous lord of sacrifices at the forefront. Having obtained his permission, I have praised that supreme among intelligent ones. These names of Shiva enhance prosperity. If one is always pure and uses these to praise the god, one obtains the atman inside one's own atman.[1127]

[1106]One who accomplishes everything.

[1107]One with an eye on the forehead.

[1108]One whose body is the universe.

[1109]Deer.

[1110]With the radiance of Brahma.

[1111]Lord of immobile objects.

[1112]One who enhances control over the senses.

[1113]One whose objectives have been accomplished.

[1114]The objective of all creatures.

[1115]Since this has already been listed, we have not numbered it.

[1116]One who is truthful in vows.

[1117]Since this has already been listed, we have not numbered it.

[1118]Lord of vows.

[1119]Since this has already been listed, we have not numbered it.

[1120]Since this has already been listed, we have not numbered it.

[1121]The supreme objective of those who are liberated.

[1122]Freed.

[1123]Free in energy.

[1124]Prosperous one.

[1125]Enhancer of prosperity.

[1126]Universe.

[1127]Obtains the brahman inside one's own atman.

Svayambhu himself chanted these as a means towards the supreme brahman. The rishis and the gods subsequently chanted these. When he is thus praised, Mahadeva is himself pleased. Compassionate towards his devotees, the illustrious one comforts them. The foremost among men are believers and faithful and praise him across several births. Whether they are asleep, awake or wandering along different paths, they praise the one who should be praised and are content and delighted. They do this in thousands of crores of births and in many wombs of the cycle of life. When all the sins have been cleansed in a creature, devotion towards Bhava is created. That devotion towards Bhava is also created by him and by no one else. He is the reason behind the emancipation of everyone. This god is extremely difficult to obtain. It is rare to find single-minded, unobstructed and unwavering devotion towards Rudra among men. It is only through his favours that men obtain such faith. When their consciousness is overcome by such sentiments, they advance towards the supreme end. When men are overcome by such supreme sentiments in every way, the god becomes gracious towards them and saves them from this cycle of life. I think that other gods, with the exception of Mahadeva, do not wish that men should use the strength of their austerities to be freed from the cycle of life.[1128]

'"'O Krishna![1129] Tandi was pure in his intelligence and was Indra's equal. Thus did he praise the illustrious Krittivasa, the lord of officiating priests. Illustrious Brahma himself chanted this praise. Brahma recounted it to Shakra and Shakra recounted it to Mrityu. Mrityu recounted it to the Rudras and the Rudras presented it to Tandi. Through great austerities, Tandi obtained it in Brahma's abode. Tandi recounted it to Shukra and Bhargava[1130] recounted it to Goutama. O Madhava! Goutama told Vaivasvata Manu about it. The intelligent Manu instructed Narayana and the Sadhyas. Achyuta Narayana and the illustrious Sadhyas told

[1128]Other gods do not desire that men should become like gods, using the power of their austerities.

[1129]This is Upamanyu speaking now.

[1130]Descended from Bhrigu's lineage, meaning Shukra.

Yama about it. The illustrious Vaivasvata Yama told Nachiketa. O Varshneya! Nachiketa told Markandeya about it. O Janardana! Following the proper rituals, I obtained it from Markandeya. O slayer of enemies! I have now given this famous chant to you, and heaven, freedom from disease, a long life, riches and strength can be obtained through it. The danavas, yakshas, rakshasas, pishachas, yatudhanas, guhyakas and serpents cause no obstructions for such a person. If a person is pure, follows brahmacharya, is in control of his senses and reads this continuously for an entire year, he obtains the fruits of a horse sacrifice.'"'

Chapter 1699(18)

Vaishampayana said, 'After this, the great yogi, the sage Krishna Dvaipayana, spoke. "O son![1131] Read this.[1132] May you be fortunate and let Maheshvara be pleased with you. O son! In ancient times, I tormented myself through supreme austerities on the slopes of Meru. O great king! That was for the sake of a son and I praised him through this chant. O descendant of the Pandu lineage! Thus did I obtain my desires. In that way, you will also obtain all your wishes from Sharva." Then, Shakra's beloved friend, Chatushirsha, also known as Alambayana,[1133] spoke, driven by a feeling of compassion. "I went to Gokarna and performed austerities for one hundred years, thus obtaining one hundred sons who were not born from any woman's womb. They were self-restrained, learned about dharma and extremely radiant. Without facing old age and misery, they lived for one hundred thousand years. O son of King Pandu! In ancient times, I obtained them through Sharva." Next, the illustrious Valmiki spoke to Yudhishthira. "O descendant of the Bharata lineage! Once, in the

[1131]Vedavyasa was speaking to Yudhishthira.

[1132]Shiva's names.

[1133]The name of a sage.

course of a dispute, sages who were learned in the Sama Veda accused me of having killed a brahmana.[1134] As soon as they said this, in an instant, that adharma overcame me. To cleanse myself, I sought to satisfy the unblemished Ishana. I was incapacitated. But that dispeller of grief freed me. The destroyer of Tripura told me that I would obtain great fame." O son! Jamadagni's son,[1135] supreme among the upholders of dharma, spoke to Kounteya. Stationed amidst the rishis, he was like the sun radiating heat. "O eldest among the Pandavas! I was afflicted because I had killed brahmanas who were like my father.[1136] O king! To purify myself, I sought Mahadeva's refuge. I chanted the god's names and praised him. Bhava was satisfied and gave me a battleaxe. The god also gave me divine weapons. He said, 'From now on, no sin will attach to you and you will be invincible. Death will have no power over you and you will be famous.' The illustrious Shikhandi, auspicious in form, spoke to me in this way and I obtained everything through the favours of that intelligent one." Next, Asita-Devala spoke to the king who was Pandu's son. "Earlier, because of Shakra's curse, all my dharma was destroyed. I obtained my dharma, great fame and a long life because of Bhava." There was a rishi named Gritsamada and he was Shakra's beloved friend. This illustrious one was like Brihaspati in his radiance. He told Ajamidha,[1137] "The illustrious Vasishtha was Chakshusha Manu's son. Shatakratu performed the inconceivable task of a sacrifice that lasted for one thousand years. While that was going on, I was given the task of reciting Sama hymns and he[1138] told me, 'O foremost among brahmanas! The rathantara is not being chanted properly. O supreme among brahmanas! Cast aside your delight and use your

[1134]This was a metaphorical and not literal killing of a brahmana and concerned a dispute over Sama rituals.

[1135]Parashurama.

[1136]On his father's instructions, Parashurama had killed his mother. There are no stories about his having killed brahmanas. His elder brothers (brahmanas) were actually killed by his father, Jamadagni, and Parashurama revived them.

[1137]Yudhishthira's name.

[1138]Vasishtha.

intelligence to consider what you are doing again. O extremely evil-minded one! Why are you acting so that the sacrificial offerings will not be conveyed?' Having said this, he was overcome by great rage. Wrathfully, he again spoke these words. 'You will become a forest dweller. You will be miserable and bereft of wisdom. You will always be terrified and you will remain in that state for ten thousand, eight hundred and ten years. You will have neither food nor water and you will be abandoned by other animals.[1139] That spot will not have any trees that can be used for sacrifices and will be populated by ruru deer and lions. You will become a cruel animal and will face great hardships.' O Partha! Because of his words, when I died, I was born as an animal. I sought refuge with Maheshvara and the yogi told me, 'You will be without old age. You will be immortal. You will be free from misery. Your friendship[1140] will be ensured and both your sacrifices will prosper.' The illustrious lord exhibits his favours in this way. In matters of happiness and unhappiness, he is always superior to the creator and the ordainer. In deeds, thoughts and words, the illustrious one is incomprehensible. O son! I know of no warrior who is superior to him, nor anyone who is his equal in learning."'

'Jaigishavya added, "O Yudhishthira! In ancient times, in Varanasi, the illustrious and powerful one carefully protected me and gave me the eight kinds of powers."[1141]

'Gargya continued, "O Pandava! On the banks of the Sarasvati, I satisfied him through a mental sacrifice and he conferred on me the sixty-four different branches associated with the knowledge of time.[1142] He also gave me one thousand sons who were my equal in knowledge of the brahman. I and my sons obtained life-spans of one million years each."

'Parashara said, "O king! In earlier times, I thought of Sharva in

[1139]Gritsamada was cursed that he would become an animal.

[1140]With Indra.

[1141]The eight powers associated with yoga.

[1142]There was more than one Gargya. This is clearly the one who contributed to astronomy (jyotisha). There is no obvious way to pin down the number sixty-four.

my mind and gratified him. I desired a son from Maheshvara, one who would be great in asceticism, great in energy, immensely famous and a great yogi. He should be one who would classify the Vedas, be the abode of prosperity and be driven by compassion towards the brahmanas. Knowing that this was the desire in my heart, the supreme among gods spoke to me. 'The fruit that you desire from me will be obtained and you will have a son named Krishna.[1143] This will happen in the creation associated with Savarni Manu[1144] and he will be one of the saptarshis. He will classify the Vedas and extend the Kuru lineage. That son will compose itihasa[1145] and be engaged in the welfare of the universe. That great sage will be loved by the great Indra. O Parashara! Your son will be without old age and will be immortal.' Having said this, the illustrious one vanished from the spot. O Yudhishthira! The great yogi is full of energy. He is without decay and without transformation.

'"Mandavya added, 'I was no thief. But suspected of being one, I was impaled on a stake.[1146] While I was in that state, I praised the god. Maheshvara told me, "You will be freed from the stake and will live for one billion years. O brahmana! But you will not suffer any pain from being impaled on the stake. You will be free from all kinds of affliction and disease. O sage! Your atman has been generated from the fourth foot.[1147] Your birth is unrivalled. Make it successful. Without any obstructions, you will be able to bathe in all the tirthas. O brahmana! When you die, I ordain that you will obtain eternal heaven." The illustrious one, with the bull as his mount, spoke in this way. O great king! Maheshvara deserves worship. The immensely radiant one is clad in hides. With his companions, the best among gods then disappeared.'

'"Galava continued, 'Having obtained Vishvamitra's permission,

[1143]Parashara was the father of Krishna Dvaipayana Vedavyasa.

[1144]The manvantara that will follow the current one.

[1145]Itihasa is history and is used to mean the Ramayana and the Mahabharata, Vedavyasa being the composer of the Mahabharata.

[1146]Animandavya's story has been recounted in Section 6 (Volume 1).

[1147]Dharma has four feet. The sage was born from dharma's fourth foot, regarded as truth.

I went to my father.[1148] My mother was miserable and wept piteously. She said, "O son! Through Koushika's[1149] favours, you have been adorned with knowledge of the Vedas. O unblemished one! O son! You are young and self-controlled. But your father is unable to see you." On hearing my mother's words, I despaired, because I wouldn't be able to see my senior. I controlled my atman and devoted myself to Mahadeva. He showed himself and spoke to me. "O son! Your father and mother will not suffer from death. Swiftly enter your house and you will be able to see your father there." O Yudhishthira! Having obtained the illustrious one's permission, I went home. O son! I saw my father there, emerging after having completed a sacrifice. He held some offerings, kusha and other grass. With tears in his eyes, my father flung these away. O Pandava! I had bowed down before him. He raised me, embraced me and inhaled the fragrance of my head. He said, "I have seen you through good fortune. O son! You have returned after completing your learning."'"'

Vaishampayana continued, 'The sages spoke about these and other extraordinary deeds of the great-souled one. On hearing this, Pandava was astounded. Then Krishna,[1150] supreme among extremely intelligent ones, again spoke to Yudhishthira, who was always devoted to dharma, like Ishvara speaking to Puruhuta.[1151] "O Ajamidha! Aditya, Chandra, wind, fire, heaven, the earth, the water, the Vasus, the Vishvadevas, Dhatri, Aryama, Shukra, Brihaspati, the Rudras, the Sadhyas, Varuna, the protector of riches,[1152] Brahma, Shakra, the Maruts, the truth about the brahman, the Vedas, sacrifices, dakshina, those who chant the Vedas, soma, the one who sacrifices, all the offerings and oblations, protection, consecration, rituals, svaha, vashatkara, the brahmanas,

[1148]Galava had studied under Vishvamitra. After completing his studies, he obtained Vishvamitra's permission and returned home. By that time, Galava's father was dead.

[1149]Vishvamitra's.

[1150]This is Krishna Vasudeva and not Krishna Dvaipayana Vedavyasa.

[1151]Puruhuta is Indra. It is not clear who is meant by Ishvara.

[1152]Kubera.

the descendants of Surabhi, the wheel of dharma, the wheel of time, movement, fame, self-control, the steadfastness of intelligent and wise people, good and bad, the seven sages, the best of intelligence, thoughts, sight and touch, success in deeds, success itself, the large number of gods who drink heat and soma, the horizon, *suyamas*,[1153] *tushitas*,[1154] everything with a form of the brahman, the shining bodies, those who survive on scent, those who survive on sight, those who restrain their speech, those who restrain their thoughts, the pure, those who are devoted to emancipation, the gods who survive on touch, the gods who survive on sight, the gods who survive on clarified butter, the foremost among gods that one can think of, all the other gods, birds, gandharvas, pishachas, danavas, yakshas, serpents, charanas, the subtle, the gross, the mild, the extremely subtle, happiness, unhappiness, all that is intermediate between joy and misery, sankhya, yoga, everything that is superior to the most supreme and everything that I have recounted—know that all these originate with Sharva. All creatures have originated from him. He is the one who deserves to be revered. In ancient times, all the gods who are the protectors of the universe and all the rakshasas who have penetrated into the earth were created by him. I think of him in my mind and please him. He is the reason behind this breath of life and I bow down before him. When he is praised and pleased, that god, the lord without decay, grants boons. If a man purifies himself and reads this praise after having controlled his senses, restrained and not deviating from yoga for one year, then he obtains the fruits of a horse sacrifice. A brahmana obtains all the Vedas, a king conquers the entire earth, a vaishya obtains gains and dexterity and a shudra obtains a good destination and happiness after death. This is the king of chants. If one fixes one's mind on Rudra and chants it, one is freed from all sins and becomes pure, sacred and famous. O descendant of the Bharata lineage! Such a man dwells in heaven for thousands of years, for as many years as there are hairs on his body."'

[1153]A class of gods.

[1154]A class of gods.

Chapter 1700(19)

'Yudhishthira said, "O bull among the Bharata lineage! Why is it that at the time of accepting a woman's hand in marriage, it is stated in the learned texts that one must follow dharma together? This *sahadharma*[1155] has been spoken about by the great rishis earlier. Does this dharma result from *arsha*, *prajapatya* or asura?[1156] I have a grave doubt on this account and my mind refuses to accept this. Why has sahadharma been recommended, if there is death? O grandfather! When one dies, one goes to heaven. What does sahadharma mean then? If one of the couple dies first, what happens to the other one then? Tell me this. There are diverse fruits that result from deeds. There are diverse means of subsistence. Depending on what they do, there are diverse and many kinds of hells that men go to. Those who have laid down the sutras have said that women are false in their behaviour. O father![1157] If women are prone to falsehood, why have the sacred texts spoken about sahadharma? Even in the Vedas, one can read that women are prone to falsehood. The signs of dharma are said to be the observance of rituals and rites on auspicious occasions. I have thought about this incessantly, but it seems to be a great mystery to me.[1158] O grandfather! As has been instructed in the sacred texts, as it is practised and as it has come down, dispel all

[1155]We have deliberately used the Sanskrit. Sahadharma means that husband and wife follow dharma together.

[1156]There were eight kinds of marriage. Three of these were arsha, prajapatya and asura. In arsha, the father gives away his daughter after receiving a bride price. In prajapatya, husband and wife are instructed to follow dharma together. In asura, the bridegroom pays whatever he can afford to the bride's family. Yudhishthira evidently is asking which of these forms of marriage develop the concept of sahadharma.

[1157]The word used is tata.

[1158]If women are wicked, how can there be dharma with them? If dharma is interpreted as rituals, what happens when one of the couple dies? If dharma is not interpreted as rituals, it is individual. In that case, what is the concept of practising dharma together? Since the couple may not be married to each other in their next lives, how can the fruits of dharma be carried over?

my doubts about this. O immensely wise one? You should explain this to me in its entirety."

'Bhishma replied, "O descendant of the Bharata lineage! In this connection, there is an ancient history about a conversation between Ashtavakra and Disha. In ancient times, the great ascetic, Ashtavakra, desired the daughter of the great-souled rishi Vadanya, and asked for her. The lady was known by the name of Suprabha and her beauty was unmatched on earth. She was supremely worthy in her qualities, conduct, virtue, character and beauty. A glance of that beautiful-eyed one had robbed him of his heart, just like a beautiful grove adorned with blossoming flowers does so in the spring. The rishi said, 'I will give you my daughter. But listen to me. First, go to the auspicious northern directions, to see what you might find there.'

'"Ashtavakra answered, 'You should tell me what I will see there. I will undertake whatever task you ask me to.'

'"Vadanya said, 'When you pass beyond the dominion of the lord of riches, you will approach the Himalayas and see Rudra's plains, frequented by the siddhas and the charanas. A large number of his cheerful companions will be there. They will possess many kinds of faces and will be engaged in dancing. Their limbs will be smeared with divine paste. There will also be many kinds of pishachas. They will clap their hands and sound musical instruments. The rhythms of their cheerful dancing will be both uneven and smooth. They serve Sharva there. We have heard it said that in that celestial region in the mountains, the god is always present, with his auspicious companions. To obtain Shankara, it was there that the goddess[1159] tormented herself with extremely difficult austerities. It has therefore been said, that region is desired by the god and Uma. There is a cave that is on the great slopes that are to the north of where the god resides. The seasons, the night of destruction[1160] and celestial humans, all assume their own forms to worship the god there. You should cross that region and proceed further. You will see a blue forest that has the complexion of the clouds. You will see a beautiful

[1159]Uma.

[1160]At the time of universal dissolution.

lady there, charming to the mind. The immensely fortunate one is aged and has consecrated herself to asceticism. When you see her there, worship her carefully. When you return after having seen her, you can accept the hand.[1161] If you want to make a true pledge, then undertake a successful journey there.'"'

Chapter 1701(20)

'"Ashtavakra replied, 'There is no doubt that I will undertake a successful journey there, just as you have said. O virtuous one! May you also be truthful in your words.'"

'Bhishma continued, "The illustrious one headed further and further towards the north, to the slopes of the Himalaya mountains, populated by the siddhas and the charanas. The tiger among brahmanas reached the great mountains, the Himalayas. He went to the sacred river of Bahuda, the granter of dharma. He bathed in the clear waters of the tirthas and rendered offerings to the gods. He then spread out a bed of kusha grass and lay down happily. Having spent the night in this way, the brahmana arose in the morning. Having bathed, he followed the rites, kindling a sacrificial fire and offering oblations. He reached the cave known as Rudrani and rested near the lake there. After resting, he awoke and headed towards Kailasa. He saw a golden gate that blazed in its beauty. He saw Mandakini and Nalini, both belonging to the great-souled lord of riches.[1162] There were rakshasas entrusted with the task of protecting that lake full of lotuses and they were led by Manibhadra. On seeing the illustrious one, all of them arose and greeted him. He also honoured those rakshasas, who were terrible in their valour, and told them to quickly inform the lord

[1161]Of the daughter.

[1162]Mandakini is that part of the Ganga which flows through Kailasa. Nalini is a lake, full of lotuses, owned by Kubera.

of riches that he had arrived. O king! At this, the rakshasas told the illustrious one, 'King Vaishravana is himself approaching you. The illustrious one knows the reason for your coming here. Behold. The immensely fortunate one has arrived, blazing in his energy.' Vaishravana approached the unblemished Ashtavakra. He duly asked him about his welfare and told the brahmana rishi, 'May you obtain happiness here. Tell me what you desire from me. O brahmana! Tell me everything. I will do whatever you ask me to. O supreme among brahmanas! If it pleases you, do enter my residence. I will honour you properly. When your task has been accomplished, depart without any obstructions.' Having said this, he took that supreme among brahmanas and led him into his residence. He gave him his own seat, water to wash his feet and a gift.

'"When both of them were seated, Kubera's companions, the yakshas, gandharvas and rakshasas, with Manibhadra leading them, also sat down. When they were seated, the lord of riches spoke these words. 'If they have your permission, the large numbers of apsaras will commence dancing. It is my supreme duty to serve a guest like you.' In a sweet voice, the sage replied that it could commence. Urvara, Mishrakeshi, Rambha, Urvashi, Alambusa, Ghritachi, Chitra, Chitrangada, Ruchi, Manohara, Sukeshi, Sumukhi, Hasini, Prabha, Vidyuta, Prashama, Danta, Vidyota, Rati—these and many other beautiful apsaras started to dance. The gandharvas played on many kinds of musical instruments. The celestial music and dancing started. Without realizing it, the rishi, the extremely great ascetic, found pleasure and spent an entire divine year there. King Vaishravana spoke to the illustrious one. 'O brahmana! Behold. Since you arrived here, more than a year has elapsed. O brahmana! O noble one! This kind of performance is known by the name of gandharva. O brahmana! It shall be as you wish. Shall it continue? You are a guest in my household and a guest must be honoured. All of us will quickly follow your commands. We are supremely devoted to you.' Pleased with Vaishravana, the illustrious one replied, 'O lord of riches! You have honoured me, as is proper. I shall now depart. O lord of riches! I am pleased with you. Everything that you possess is exactly like you. O illustrious one! Through your favours, I must now undertake the task the great-souled rishi[1163] has entrusted me with. May your prosperity become even more prosperous.' The illustrious one emerged and headed in a northward direction. He passed Kailasa, Mandara and all the golden mountains.

'"Beyond this, there is the supreme region, the great mountain known as Kairata. He controlled himself, bowed his head down and circumambulated it. Having descended again on the ground, he thought that he had been purified. Circumambulating the mountain thrice, he proceeded northwards. With joy in his heart, he advanced along the plain ground that extended in front of him. He then saw another beautiful forest. There were roots and fruits that grew in every season and it was full of birds. It was as if the beautiful forest was, here and there, adorned with them. The illustrious one saw a divine hermitage there. There were hills with many kinds of forms, decorated with gold and jewels. Gems were stuck to the ground and there were lakes. He saw many other extremely beautiful things. At this, the maharshi with the cleansed soul was delighted in his mind. There, he saw a celestial and golden house, covered everywhere with jewels. It was extraordinary in form and was superior to the residence of the lord of riches. There were many giant palaces that were like mountains. There were beautiful vimanas and many kinds of gems. The river Mandakini flowed there, covered with *mandara* flowers. There were gems that blazed with their own radiance and the ground was strewn with diamonds. There were many kinds of houses, with colourful jewels on their gates. Nets of pearls were flung around and there were decorations of gems and jewels. It was beautiful everywhere, captivating the mind and the eye, and everything was auspicious. In every direction in that beautiful place, he saw rishis. He began to think about where he might be able to find a residence. He advanced towards a gate. Stationing himself there, he said, 'Let those who dwell here know me to be a guest who has arrived.' At this, several maidens emerged from that house. They had many different forms and all of them were beautiful. O lord! Actually, there were seven maidens. They were so beautiful that, whichever one he looked

[1163]Vadanya.

at, happened to steal his mind. Despite making the best of efforts, he could not control his mind. Finally, the intelligent brahmana resorted to his fortitude and controlled himself. The women said, 'O illustrious one! Enter.' The brahmana was filled with curiosity about the extremely beautiful women in that house and entered the house. There, he saw an aged lady. She was overcome with old age and was dressed in a white garment. Though she was lying down on a bed, she was adorned with every kind of ornament. He spoke words of greeting and the lady reciprocated. She arose and asked the brahmana to be seated.

'"Ashtavakra said, 'Let all these women go to their houses and let only a single one remain. Let the one who remains be extremely wise and extremely tranquil. As they wish, let the others depart.'

'"Thus addressed, the maidens circumambulated the rishi and left the house. The aged lady was the only one who remained. She lay down on a radiant bed and he told her, 'O fortunate one! You should go to sleep. Night is passing.' They were engaged in conversation, but the brahmana put an end to it, himself lying down on a second, extremely radiant bed. After some time, she pretended that her limbs were trembling with the cold and she climbed onto the maharshi's bed. The illustrious one respectfully welcomed her. O bull among men! She was delighted. Stretching out her arms, she embraced the rishi. The rishi was indifferent and was as rigid as a piece of wood. On seeing this, she was miserable and began to converse with the rishi again. 'O brahmana! A man may possess patience, but women are overcome by desire. I am overcome by kama and desire you. You should desire me. O brahmana rishi! Be happy and have intercourse with me. O brahmana! Embrace me. I am severely afflicted with desire for you. This is the revered fruit obtained by your following dharma and observing austerities. As soon as I saw you, I began to desire you. Desire me. All the riches that you see here, all the forests and everything else that you see, are mine. There is no doubt that you will become their lord and also of me. If you find pleasure with me, I will give you every object that you desire. O brahmana! Sport with me in these forests, which grant every fruit that one desires. If you sport with me, I will become obedient to you. We will enjoy all the objects of desire, divine and human. For a woman, there is no task that is superior to that of having intercourse with a man. For us women, that is the supreme fruit. When they are goaded by the god of love, women do whatever they wish. Even if they have to walk over sand that is extremely hot, they do not get burnt.'

'"Ashtavakra replied, 'O fortunate one! I never have intercourse with another man's wife. The sacred texts of dharma have decreed that intercourse with another person's wife is a sin. O fortunate one! I tell you truthfully that I am indeed interested in kama. However, know that I am inexperienced in material objects and am only interested in offspring for the sake of pursuing dharma and artha. There is no doubt that after having obtained a son, I will proceed to those worlds. O fortunate one! Know that this is dharma and that there is nothing superior to this.'

'"The woman said, 'O brahmana! Anila, Agni, Varuna and the other residents of heaven are not loved by women as much as Kama.[1164] Women are addicted to sexual desire. Among thousands of women, even among hundreds of thousands, there will perhaps be only one who is devoted to her husband. They do not care for the father, the lineage, the mother, the brother, the husband, the son or the husband's younger brother.[1165] In the pursuit of pleasure, they destroy the family, just as a great river destroys its banks.[1166] Prajapati himself has spoken about the wicked vices of those evil ones.'"

'Bhishma continued, "The rishi was single-minded and replied to the woman, 'I find no pleasure or desire in you. Tell me what I should do.' The woman said, 'O illustrious one! O immensely wise one! One sees according to the time and the place.[1167] Dwell here and my task will have been accomplished. After that, depart.' O Yudhishthira! The brahmana rishi agreed to this and remained there.

[1164]Kama meaning the god of love. Anila is the god of the wind and Agni is the god of the fire.

[1165]Under the influence of desire.

[1166]There is a pun which the translation misses. *Kula* means both family/lineage and bank.

[1167]There is an implied suggestion that if Ashtavakra remains there, he may find the lady attractive.

He said, 'As long as I am interested in doing so, there is no doubt that I will reside with you.' The rishi glanced at the woman and saw that she was overcome with old age. He thought a lot about this and was tormented. Whenever the brahmana rishi looked at her limbs, he derived no pleasure, because her beauty had been destroyed. 'She is the owner of this house. There is no doubt that her beauty has been destroyed through some curse. I must deduce the reason and not arrive at any hasty conclusion.' He was occupied with these thoughts and desired to know the reason. His mind was anxious and he thought about this, until the day was over. After this, the woman spoke to him. 'O illustrious one! Look at the sun. Its form is now tinged by the evening clouds. What can I possibly do for you?' He told the woman, 'Bring me water for my bath. I will restrain my speech and my senses. Having bathed, I will perform the evening rites.'"'

Chapter 1702(21)

'Bhishma said, "Having been thus addressed, the woman agreed to what the brahmana had said. She brought some divine oil and a garment he would wear during his bath. Having obtained the sage's permission, the woman rubbed the great-souled one's limbs, everywhere, with the oil. She rubbed him gently and then took him to the bathroom. The rishi was made to sit on a colourful, new and excellent seat. When he was seated on that excellent seat, she used her hands to pleasurably and gently wash the rishi all over. She tended to the sage in many divine ways. Because of the pleasure associated with the warm water and because of the pleasure associated with the touch of the hands, the one who was great in his vows did not realize that the entire night had passed in this way. When he arose, the sage was extremely surprised. He saw that in the eastern direction, the sun was rising in the sky. He thought that his intelligence had been confounded. Having worshipped the one with the thousand rays, he asked her what he should do next. She gave the rishi some food that tasted like amrita. Because the food was so delicious, he couldn't eat much. In the course of this, the day passed and it again became evening. The woman requested the illustrious one to go to sleep. Excellent beds were prepared for him and for her.

'"Ashtavakra said, 'O fortunate one! My mind is not interested in intercourse with another person's wife.[1168] O fortunate one! Arise. It is better that you should desist. Go and sleep.'"

'Bhishma continued, "She was thus rebuffed by the brahmana's fortitude. She replied, 'I am independent and you will not commit any deviation from dharma.'[1169]

'"Ashtavakra said, 'There is no independence for women. Women are dependent. It is Prajapati's view that women do not deserve to be independent.'

'"The woman replied, 'O brahmana! I am constrained by the need for intercourse. Behold my devotion to you. O brahmana! You will suffer from adharma if you do not give me delight.'

'"Ashtavakra said, 'If a man is wilful, there are many kinds of sins that lead him astray. O fortunate one! I possess the strength of my fortitude. Go to your own bed.'

'"The woman replied, 'O brahmana! I am bowing down my head before you and you should show me your favours. O unblemished one! I am lying down on the ground before you and have sought refuge with you. O brahmana! I am giving myself to you. If you perceive a sin from congress with another person's wife, then touch me and accept my hand now. There will be no sin associated with this. I am telling you truthfully. Know that I am independent. If there is any adharma, it will vest with me.'[1170]

'"Ashtavakra said, 'O fortunate one! How can you be independent? Tell me the reason. There is no woman in this world who should be regarded as independent. The father protects her when she is a maiden, the husband protects her when she is young

[1168]The Critical edition excises shlokas and there is a break in continuity. As on the previous night, the lady leaves her own bed and comes to Ashtavakra's bed.

[1169]That is, she wasn't anyone else's wife.

[1170]If she has lied about not being married.

and the son protects her when she is aged. There is no woman who deserves to be independent.'

'"The woman replied, 'Since I have been young, I have followed the vow of brahmacharya. There is no doubt that I am a virgin. O brahmana! Do not have a doubt about me. Do not destroy my devotion towards you.'

'"Ashtavakra said, 'Just as you are attracted towards me, I am also attracted towards you.[1171] However, there still remains a doubt. Will the pledge I made to the rishi[1172] not be violated? This is a great wonder. What will bring greater benefit? This maiden has presented herself before me and she was adorned in divine garments and ornaments. How does she possess this supreme beauty and why was she enveloped in that aged appearance earlier? She has assumed the form of a maiden now. Who knows what form she will assume later? However, I should resort to the great strength of my fortitude and never deviate. Deviations do not appeal to me. I will obtain success by resorting to my fortitude.'"'

Chapter 1703(22)

'Yudhishthira asked, "Why was that woman not scared of being cursed by that extremely radiant one? How did the illustrious one return? You should tell me that."

'Bhishma replied, "Ashtavakra asked her, 'How could you change your form? Tell me. You should not wish to utter a falsehood before a brahmana.'

'"The woman said, 'O supreme among brahmanas! O one with truth as his valour! Listen to everything attentively. Whether one is in heaven or on earth, there is desire everywhere. You have witnessed the fickleness of a woman. But know me to be the northern direction. O

[1171]The woman had assumed a beautiful form.

[1172]Vadanya.

one with truth as his valour! You have conquered the worlds through your composure. O unblemished one! I was employed to test you. Even when women are aged, they suffer from the fever of sexual desire. Now, the grandfather and the gods, together with Vasava, are satisfied with you. O illustrious one! That is the reason why you were sent here. O bull among brahmanas! You were sent here by the brahmana who was the father of the maiden. I have done everything so that you might be instructed. Go in peace and you will not suffer from any exhaustion when you head home. O brahmana! You will obtain the maiden and she will bear a son. I tested you through my desire, but you rebuffed me through an appropriate reply. In all the three worlds, this is something that is impossible to overcome. Having accomplished a good deed, depart. What else do you desire to hear? O brahmana rishi! O Ashtavakra! I have told you exactly what occurred. O bull among brahmanas! It was for your sake that I pleased that rishi.[1173] It is to show him honour that I spoke those words to you.'"

'Bhishma said, "On hearing her words, the brahmana stood there, his hands joined in salutation. Having obtained her permission, he returned to his own house again. On reaching his house, he rested and honoured his relatives. O descendant of the Kuru lineage! Following what was proper, he then went to that brahmana. He was asked by that brahmana about the signs that he had seen. With great delight in his heart, the brahmana told the brahmana, 'Having taken your permission, I proceeded towards Gandhamadana. I encountered a great divinity towards the north of that region. It is with her permission that I am recounting this to you. O lord! I have returned home after hearing her words.' The brahmana told him, 'Accept my daughter. Let us follow the conjunction of the nakshatras and the *tithis*.[1174] You are the best groom possible.' O lord! Thus instructed, Ashtavakra agreed and accepted her. The one who was supremely devoted to dharma was delighted with the maiden. He accepted the extremely beautiful maiden as his wife. He was free from all anxiety and dwelt happily in his hermitage."'

[1173]Vadanya.

[1174]For the marriage.

Chapter 1704(23)

'Yudhishthira asked, "O best among the Bharata lineage! Who have the brahmanas always described as the best recipient of a gift? Is it a brahmana with the signs or is it a brahmana without the signs?"[1175]

'Bhishma replied, "O great king! It has been said that one must give to a person who follows his own prescribed conduct, regardless of whether he bears the signs or not, because both are ascetics."

'Yudhishthira asked, "O grandfather! A person may be unclean. Nevertheless, with supreme devotion, he gives to brahmanas. What are the taints associated with such havya, kavya and gifts?"

'Bhishma replied, "O son![1176] There is no doubt that even if a man is impossible to restrain, he is cleansed through devotion. O lord of the earth! He is cleansed in every way. What else is there to say?"

'Yudhishthira said, "A man must not examine a brahmana who is engaged in the tasks of the gods. However, the learned have also said that when it comes to offering kavya, the learning of the brahmana must be tested."[1177]

'Bhishma replied, "Brahmanas do not ensure the success of havya. It is the gods who ensure success. There is no doubt that a person who undertakes a sacrifice is successful in that sacrifice because of the favours of the gods. O best among the Bharata lineage! Brahmanas always speak about the brahman. In ancient times, Markandeya, the most intelligent person in the worlds, said this."

[1175]A brahmana with the signs is someone in the state of brahmacharya or sannyasa. Other brahmanas will not have any obvious signs.

[1176]The word used is tata.

[1177]Havya is offered to the gods and kavya is offered to the ancestors. The learned texts say that before engaging a brahmana in offering havya, the brahmana's qualities need not be tested. However, an examination is needed before offering kavya. Hence, Yudhishthira's question.

'Yudhishthira asked, "A person whom one has not met before, a learned person, a person who is related through marriage, an ascetic and a person who is devoted to sacrifices—why are these regarded as worthy recipients of a gift?"

'Bhishma replied, "Noble lineage, devotion to tasks, learning, non-violence, modesty, uprightness and truthfulness—the foremost recipients possess at least three of these attributes.[1178] O Partha! Listen to the views of four energetic ones—the earth, Kashyapa, Agni and Markandeya.

'"The earth said, 'When a stone is flung into the great ocean, it is destroyed because of that act of flinging. In that way, all evil conduct is destroyed in three kinds of conduct.'[1179]

'"Kashyapa said, 'O king! All the Vedas and the six Vedangas, sankhya, the Puranas and noble birth—if a man deviates from good conduct, none of these can save him from destruction.'

'"Agni said, 'There may be a person who studies and thinks himself to be learned. He may use his learning to destroy the fame of others. Such a brahmana acts as if he has killed a brahmana. All the worlds are destroyed for him.'

'"Markandeya said, 'If one thousand horse sacrifices and truth are weighed on a pair of scales, I do not know whether truth will weigh one and a half times the other.'"

'Bhishma said, "Having said this, those four infinitely energetic ones, the earth, Kashyapa, Agni and Bhargava, with his excellent weapons, quickly went away."[1180]

'Yudhishthira asked, "In this world, there may be a brahmana who follows vows. In order to please brahmanas, if offerings meant

[1178]This isn't a shloka that is easy to understand and we have taken some liberties.

[1179]The text does not tell us what these three are. They are interpreted as teaching, officiating at sacrifices and receiving gifts.

[1180]This entire segment hangs loose. We are not told who these four were asked by, and where they went away from. In addition, though Markandeya was descended from Bhrigu, it is somewhat unusual to find him described as the possessor of weapons. That Bhargava is normally Parashurama.

for gods are eaten by such a brahmana, is that regarded as good conduct?"[1181]

'Bhishma replied, "O Indra among kings! A brahmana may have been instructed and may have become accomplished in the Vedas. However, if he devours what is meant for the brahman, he has deviated from his vows."

'Yudhishthira said, "O grandfather! Learned ones have said that dharma has many end objectives and many doors. Please tell me what has certainly been determined."

'Bhishma replied, "O Indra among kings! Non-violence, truth, lack of anger, lack of injury, self-control and uprightness—these are said to be the certain signs of dharma. There are those who praise dharma and roam around the earth. O lord! However, they may be engaged in wicked conduct, amounting to a confusion of dharma. If a person gives gems, gold, cattle or horses to such a person, then the giver remains in hell for ten years, surviving on excrement. This is also the case if one gives to those who eat human fat and flesh, those who live as outcasts outside habitations and those who are confused by anger and confusion and talk about the undesirable acts that others have performed. O Indra among kings! There may be a brahmana who follows brahmacharya. If a person stupidly gives something meant for the Vishvadevas to such a brahmana, he is made to enjoy inauspicious worlds."

'Yudhishthira asked, "What is superior to brahmacharya? What are the best signs of dharma? What is the best kind of purification? O grandfather! Tell me that."

'Bhishma replied, "O son! The avoidance of liquor and flesh is superior to brahmacharya. The signs of dharma are adherence to strictures, tranquility and purity."

'Yudhishthira asked, "When is the time for pursuing dharma? When is the time for pursuing artha? When is the time for being happy? O grandfather! Tell me that."

[1181]Good conduct by whom? That remains unclear. Evidently, out of reverence for brahmanas, a person performing a sacrifice is giving the offerings to a brahmana.

'Bhishma replied, "There is a time for pursuing artha and that for pursuing dharma comes after that. It is after this that one should pursue kama. But one must not get attached. One must honour brahmanas and worship seniors. One must treat all creatures in a proper way. One must be mild in conduct and pleasant in speech. In a judicial dispute, one must not utter a lie. When one is brought before a king, one must not be deceitful. One must not behave falsely towards a senior. All these are equal to the sin of killing a brahmana. One should not strike a king, nor should one kill a cow. Anyone who does either commits a sin that is equal to that of killing a foetus. One must not abandon the sacrificial fire. One must not abandon the Vedas. Nor should one attack a brahmana. These sins are equal to the sin of killing a brahmana."

'Yudhishthira asked, "What kind of brahmanas are good? Who are the ones to whom one should donate, so as to obtain great fruits? Who are the ones who should be fed? O grandfather! Tell me this."

'Bhishma replied, "Those who are without anger, those who are devoted to dharma, those who are truthful and those who are always self-restrained—these brahmanas are regarded as virtuous. Great fruits are obtained from donating to them. There are those who aren't insolent, withstand everything, are cheerful in pursuing their objectives, have conquered their senses, are engaged in the welfare of all beings and are friendly. Great fruits are obtained from donating to them. There are those who are without avarice, pure, learned, modest, truthful in speech and engaged in their own tasks. Great fruits are obtained from donating to them. There are bulls among brahmanas who have studied the four Vedas and the six Vedangas and have withdrawn from action. The learned have said that they are the best recipients of gifts. Great fruits are obtained from donating to those who have these kinds of qualities. If one gives to a person with these qualities, the giver's own qualities are multiplied one thousand times. Even if there is only one single bull among brahmanas who possesses wisdom and learning and good conduct, he is alone capable of saving an entire lineage.[1182] One should give cattle, horses, riches, food and other objects to such

[1182]Through gifts made to such a brahmana.

a person. In that event, one won't have to grieve after death. Even one brahmana who is excellent is capable of saving an entire lineage. That is the reason one must be selective about choosing the recipient. If one hears that a brahmana who possesses the qualities and is revered by the virtuous lives some distance away, even then, one must honour him and worship him in every possible way."'

Chapter 1705(24)

'Yudhishthira asked, "O grandfather! I desire that you should tell me about the time of a funeral ceremony. What have the gods and the rishis ordained about the gods and about dharma?"

'Bhishma replied, "One must perform rites for the gods in the forenoon and those for the ancestors in the afternoon. This must be done after one has made efforts to purify oneself and has completed the recommended auspicious rites. At an appropriate time towards midday, gifts can be made to men. The learned say that the rakshasas obtain a share of anything that is given at the wrong time. Anything left over, anything licked or touched, anything performed that has been preceded by a discord and anything that has been seen by a woman who is in her season—the learned say that the rakshasas obtain a share of these. O descendant of the Bharata lineage! If there has been public proclamation of a gift, if it has been eaten by someone who doesn't follow vows and if it has been seen or licked by a dog—the learned say that the rakshasas obtain a share of these. If hair or worms are found in food, if someone has sneezed into it, if a dog has looked at it, if drops of tears have fallen into it, or if it is unclean—the learned say that the rakshasas obtain a share in it. O descendant of the Bharata lineage! If food has been tasted by an unworthy person[1183] or by someone who is armed and if food

[1183]A translation cannot do justice to what is intended. The text uses the word *niromkara*, meaning a person who is not worthy to utter the syllable 'Om'.

has been tasted by an evil-souled person—the learned say that the rakshasas obtain a share in it. If food has been tasted by someone else, or if it has been eaten without offerings first being made to the gods and the ancestors—the learned say that the rakshasas always obtain a share in it. If reprehensible or censured food is offered to the gods and the ancestors, or if it is served with anger—the learned say that they don't accept it and that the rakshasas obtain a share. O foremost among men! At funeral ceremonies, if the three varnas serve food without mantras and without rites, the learned say that rakshasas obtain a share in it. If food is served without offerings of clarified butter being made first, or if it has been tasted by wicked people earlier, the learned say that the rakshasas obtain a share in it. O bull among the Bharata lineage! I have spoken to you about the shares that have been stated to be for the rakshasas.

'"I will now tell you how one should determine higher classes of brahmanas. Listen. O king! In rites performed for gods and ancestors, brahmanas who have become outcasts and those who are stupid and mad should never be invited. O king! Nor should one invite and honour one who suffers from white leprosy or leprosy, one who is impotent, one who has been afflicted by tuberculosis, one who suffers from epilepsy or one who is blind. One who is a physician, one who is in a temple, one who practises futile rituals and one who sells soma should never be invited to a funeral ceremony.[1184] A king must never invite those who are singers, dancers, acrobats, players of musical instruments, raconteurs and warriors. A king must never invite those who officiate at the sacrifices of vrishalas,[1185] teaches vrishalas or become the disciples of vrishalas. O descendant of the Bharata lineage! A brahmana who becomes a teacher or a student because of payment should never be invited to a funeral ceremony. They are sellers of the brahman. Even if a brahmana is foremost and is learned in every possible way, if he marries into an inferior varna, a king should never invite him. A brahmana without a sacrificial fire, one who tends to dead

[1184]The emphasis is clearly on payment in certain professions. For instance, the temple bit is about a brahmana who is paid to serve in a temple.

[1185]A vrishala is an inferior person, usually equated with a shudra.

bodies, one who is a thief and one who is an outcaste—a king should never invite such a person. O descendant of the Bharata lineage! One whose earlier antecedents are unknown, one whose tribe is unknown and one who is a *putrika-putra* should never be invited to a funeral ceremony.[1186] A king must never invite a brahmana who earns a living off the interest on loans given to kings, or one who makes a living by selling animals. O bull among the Bharata lineage! A brahmana who was a woman in a former life, one who is the husband of a courtesan, or one who does not perform his meditations, should never be invited to a funeral ceremony. O bull among the Bharata lineage! There are brahmanas who have been recommended for funeral ceremonies and for rites to the gods. They can affectionately give and receive.[1187] Listen. O king! If they observe vows, possess qualities, know about the *savitri* mantra and perform rites, they are capable of being invited, even if they happen to be agriculturists. O son! If a brahmana has been born in a noble lineage, even if he resorts to the dharma of kshatriyas or is a trader, he can be invited to a funeral ceremony. O king! A brahmana who observes the agnihotra sacrifice, resides in a village, is not a thief and tends to guests, can be invited. O bull among the Bharata lineage! O king! One who chants the savitri mantra three times a day, survives by begging for alms and performs the rites can be invited. O king! If a person is rich in the morning and poor in the evening,[1188] if he is non-violent and only has minor faults, he can be invited. O bull among the Bharata lineage! O king! If a brahmana is not mean and is not prone to arguing, if he consciously resorts to begging for alms, he can be invited. There may be one who is devoid of vows, deceitful, a thief, a merchant, or a person who earns a living by selling living

[1186]A putrika-putra son is the outcome of a special kind of contract. The father of a maiden may have a daughter, but no sons. The daughter is married off, with the understanding that the first son will be regarded as her father's son, rather than her own. This son is known as putrika-putra and he has no links with his biological father's family.

[1187]The word affectionately requires explanation. These brahmanas are actually unworthy. However, out of affection towards them, they have been permitted some kind of atonement and become worthy.

[1188]Implying that the wealth has been spent on good purposes.

beings. O king! If he subsequently drinks soma, he can be invited. A person may have earlier earned riches through terrible deeds, or through agriculture. O king! If he subsequently serves the guests, he can be invited. Wealth obtained by selling knowledge, that earned by living off a woman and that earned by living off a eunuch must never be given to the gods and the ancestors. O bull among the Bharata lineage! After a brahmana has officiated at a rite, if he does not speak the words which should be uttered, he commits adharma that is equal to *gavanrita*.[1189] O Yudhishthira! On the day of the new moon, when one has obtained a brahmana, curds, clarified butter and the flesh of wild animals, that is the time for performing a funeral ceremony. When a brahmana's funeral ceremony has been completed, one must say 'svadha'. For a kshatriya, one must say, 'May your ancestors be pleased.' O descendant of the Bharata lineage! For a vaishya, one must say, 'May everything be inexhaustible.' For a shudra, one must say, '*svasti*'. For a brahmana, it is recommended that the sacred word must be pronounced for the gods.[1190] In this way, for a kshatriya, words pronounced for the gods must not have the word 'Om'. For a vaishya, one should say, 'May the gods be pleased.'

'"Listen to what has been decreed about the rites that must be performed, one after the other. O descendant of the Bharata lineage! Those associated with jatakarma[1191] must be performed for all the three varnas. O Yudhishthira! For brahmanas, kshatriyas and vaishyas, these must be performed with the aid of mantras. A brahmana's girdle must be made out munja grass. For someone belonging to the royal family, it will be made out of hemp.[1192] O Yudhishthira! It is dharma that for a vaishya it should be made out of *balbajika*.[1193] O lord! Listen to what is dharma and adharma for

[1189]Gavanrita is a lie about a cow. The sense is that the sin is the same as that when one lies in a dispute over a cow.

[1190]The sacred word is Om.

[1191]Ceremonies at the time of birth.

[1192]The word is *murva*, which means hemp. Since hemp was used to make bowstrings, one could have also translated this as bowstring.

[1193]A type of grass.

the giver and the receiver. If a brahmana utters a lie, that is an act of adharma and he commits a sin. It is said that for a kshatriya, this becomes four times and for a vaishya, it becomes eight times.[1194] If a brahmana has earlier been invited by another brahmana, he should not eat anywhere else. If he does so, he becomes inferior and commits adharma that is equal to causing injury to animals.[1195] If he eats elsewhere after having first been invited by a king or a vaishya, he becomes inferior and commits a sin that is half of what is committed by causing injury to animals. O king! When a sacrifice is performed for the gods, the ancestors, or brahmanas and the other varnas, if a brahmana eats without having bathed first, he commits the adharma of gavanrita. When a sacrifice is performed for kings, brahmanas and the other varnas, and a brahmana eats there out of greed, knowing himself to be impure,[1196] he commits the adharma of gavanrita. O descendant of the Bharata lineage! O Indra among kings! If a person invites someone else to perform a task, because of greed for food or anything else, he is said to commit adharma that is equal to uttering a falsehood. O Yudhishthira! In the three varnas, there may be people who do not observe the vows of the Vedas, are devoid of character and serve without the necessary mantras. They commit adharma that is equal to gavanrita."

'Yudhishthira asked, "O grandfather! There may be things intended for the ancestors and the gods. To obtain great fruits, whom should one give these to? I wish to hear about this."

'Bhishma replied, "O Yudhishthira! Just as farmers wait for excellent rains, there are wives who wait for the leftovers, after their husbands have eaten. Feed them.[1197] There are kings who possess good character. They are emaciated because their subsistence has suffered. Their wealth has disappeared. Great fruits are obtained by giving to them. O king! There are those who are without food,

[1194]The sin from a lie becomes that many multiples of a brahmana's sin.

[1195]Meaning, the futile slaughter of animals, when no sacrifices are intended.

[1196]For instance, for a limited period of time, one is impure when there is a birth or a death in the immediate family.

[1197]That is, feed the husbands.

without homes, without riches and without shelter. When they seek riches, great fruits are obtained by giving to them. O Yudhishthira! There are those who have suffered at the hands of thieves and others and are oppressed by fear. They seek riches so that can obtain food. Great fruits are obtained by giving to them. There are guiltless brahmanas who have made up their minds to beg. When such brahmanas beg, great fruits are obtained by giving to them. There are brahmanas who have lost their possessions and their wives when the country has been flooded. When they desire riches, great fruits are obtained by giving to them. There are learned brahmanas who are mendicants. They resort to rituals and desire riches so that these can be completed. Great fruits are obtained by giving to them. There may be those whose dharma has suffered because of rules enforced by the wicked. Their lives and riches are afflicted. Great fruits are obtained by giving to them. There are innocent people who have been robbed of everything by those who are stronger. They desire some food. Great fruits are obtained by giving to them. There may be ascetics who are devoted to austerities and have resorted to begging for sustenance. When they desire some riches, great fruits are obtained by giving to them. O bull among the Bharata lineage! You have heard about what has been decreed concerning the great fruits from giving.

'"Now hear about what makes one go to hell and what makes one go to heaven. Those who seize other people's wives, those who oppress other people's wives and those who have intercourse with other people's wives go to hell. Those who seize other people's property, those who destroy other people's possessions and those who point out the weaknesses of others go to hell. O descendant of the Bharata lineage! Men who destroy stores of drinking water, assembly houses, roads and apartments go to hell. Men who deceive women without protectors and those who are young, aged, terrified and ascetics, go to hell. O descendant of the Bharata lineage! Those who destroy means of sustenance for others, or their homes or wives, those who destroy other people's hopes and those who cause dissension among friends go to hell. Those who proclaim the weaknesses of others, those who destroy bridges, those who earn a living off others and those who are ungrateful towards friends go to hell. Those who are heretical and censure,[1198] those who censure the ordinances and those who deviate from their beliefs go to hell. Those who cause divisions and take away the shares of those who have accomplished their tasks and are waiting go to hell.[1199] Those who eat without giving shares to wives, fires, servants and guests and those who deviate from making offerings to ancestors and gods go to hell. Those who sell the Vedas,[1200] those who censure the Vedas and those who render the Vedas in writing go to hell. Men who are outside the four ashramas, outside the boundaries of learning and survive through perverse deeds go to hell. O king! Those who sell hair, those who sell poison and those who sell milk go to hell. O Yudhishthira! Those who cause obstructions in the tasks of brahmanas, cattle and women go to hell. O Yudhishthira! Those who sell weapons and make them and those who make stakes and bows go to hell. O bull among the Bharata lineage! Those who cause obstructions along roads, using stakes, pits and holes, go to hell. O bull among the Bharata lineage! Those who abandon preceptors, servants and followers without any valid reason go to hell. Those who make under-age animals work, pierce their noses and tether them go to hell. Having accepted one-sixth of the produce as taxes, those who do not protect, despite being capable, go to hell.[1201] There are people who are forgiving, self-controllled and wise. Despite having associated with such people for a long time, if a person discards them when they are no longer of any use, he goes to hell. Men who eat first, without giving to children, the aged and servants go to hell. All these who have thus been named go to hell. O bull among the Bharata lineage! I will now tell you about the various categories that go to the world of heaven.

'"O descendant of the Bharata lineage! In all the tasks undertaken by brahmanas, where gods are placed at the forefront, if a

[1198]Interpreted as heretical in the sense of not believing in the Vedas.

[1199]This is probably a reference to wages and salaries not being paid to servants.

[1200]Accept payment for teaching the Vedas.

[1201]This is a reference to kings.

person causes hindrances, all his sons and animals are slain.[1202] O Yudhishthira! Men who follow dharma through donations, austerities and truth go to heaven. O descendant of the Bharata lineage! Men who have obtained learning through servitude and austerities and are no longer attached to what they receive go to heaven. Men who act so as to free others from fear, sin, impediments in the way of learning and affliction from disease go to heaven. Men who are forgiving, patient, prone to performing acts of dharma and those who follow auspicious indications go to heaven. Men who refrain from liquour, flesh, intercourse with other people's wives and drinking go to heaven. O descendant of the Bharata lineage! Men who construct hermitages and establish lineages, countries and cities go to heaven. Men who give garments, ornaments, food, drink and grain and those who give to their matrimonial allies go to heaven. Men who refrain from all kinds of violent conduct and withstand everything and men who are refuges to all creatures go to heaven. Men who serve their mothers and fathers, are in control over their senses and are affectionate towards their brothers go to heaven. O descendant of the Bharata lineage! Men who are patient and conquer their senses, despite being rich, powerful and young, go to heaven. Men who are kind towards those who cause injury, men who are mild and affectionate towards their friends and those who gratify and make others happy go to heaven. Despite being surrounded by thousands, men who give to thousands and save thousands go to heaven. O bull among the Bharata lineage! Men who give away gold, cattle, vehicles and mounts go to heaven. O Yudhisthira! Men who give garments to maidens at the time of marriage and to servants go to heaven. Men who construct *viharas*,[1203] houses, gardens, wells, resting-houses, assemblies and *vapras*[1204] go to heaven. O descendant of the Bharata lineage!

[1202]If he doesn't do this, he goes to heaven.

[1203]The word vihara has many meanings, including temple. In this case, a public pleasure ground is probably intended.

[1204]The word vapra has multiple meanings—fortification, embankment, ditch, wall, rampart. All of these fit.

Men who give houses, fields and habitations to those who ask for them go to heaven. O Yudhishthira! Men who give juices, seeds and grain of their own accord go to heaven. Men who are born in noble lineages, have hundreds of children, live for one hundred years, possess compassion and have conquered their anger go to heaven. O descendant of the Bharata lineage! I have told you about the rites that must be performed for the gods and the ancestors. As laid down earlier by the rishis, I have also told you about dharma and adharma concerning gifts."'

Chapter 1706(25)

'Yudhishthira said, "O king! O descendant of the Bharata lineage! You should tell me the truth about this. What kinds of violence are said to be the equal to the sin of actually killing a brahmana?"

'Bhishma replied, "O Indra among kings! On an earlier occasion, I had invited Vyasa to tell me about this. I will tell you the truth about this. Listen with single-minded attention. 'O sage! O one who is fourth from Vasishtha![1205] Tell me the truth about this. What kinds of violence are said to be equal to the sin of actually killing a brahmana?' O great king! Thus asked, Parashara's son told me about the skilful and supreme determination of dharma on this. 'There may be a brahmana who is lean because he lacks a means of subsistence. If a person himself invites him for the sake of giving alms and later says that nothing is available, know that this person has effectively killed a brahmana. O descendant of the Bharata lineage![1206] If an evil-minded person is indifferent and destroys the livelihood of a brahmana who is devoted to learning, know that he is regarded

[1205]Fourth in line, the line being Vasishtha, Shakti, Parashara and Vedavyasa.

[1206]This is actually Vedavyasa speaking to Bhishma. However, Bhishma can also be addressed as a descendant of the Bharata lineage.

as having killed a brahmana. O lord of the earth! When cattle are thirsty and seek to slake their thirst, if a person causes obstructions in this, know him to be guilty of killing a brahmana. The learned texts have been composed by the sages and these sacred texts have been passed down properly. Without knowing them, if a person censures them, know him to be guilty of killing a brahmana. If a person has a beautiful and excellent daughter, but does not bestow the maiden on a groom who is her equal, know him to be guilty of killing a brahmana. If a stupid person is addicted to adharma and, through falsehood, causes affliction and sorrow to brahmanas, know him to be guilty of killing a brahmana. If a person robs all the possessions of someone who is blind, lame or dumb, know him to be guilty of killing a brahmana. Because of delusion, if a person sets fire to a hermitage, a forest, a village or a city, know him to be guilty of killing a brahmana."'

Chapter 1707(26)

'Yudhishthira said, "O bull among the Bharata lineage! O immensely wise one! Visiting the tirthas, bathing in them and hearing about them is said to be superior. I desire to hear the truth about this. You should tell me about all the sacred tirthas on earth. O lord! I have controlled myself and wish to hear about them."

'Bhishma replied, "O immensely radiant one! Angiras spoke about a listing of all the tirthas. O fortunate one! Listen to that and you will obtain supreme dharma. The brave Goutama, rigid in his vows, went to the hermitage of the brahmana and great sage, Angiras, and asked him. 'O illustrious one! I have a doubt about which of the tirthas bring dharma. I wish to hear about all of them. O great sage! Instruct me. O sage! What fruits are obtained by bathing in the waters of these tirthas? What does one get after death? O immensely wise one! Tell me the truth about this.'

'"Angiras said, 'If one fasts for a week and bathes in the waters of the Chandrabhaga or the Vitasta,[1207] which has garlands of waves, then one loses all sense of ego and becomes like a sage. In the circle of rivers that flow through Kashmira, there are many great rivers that flow into the river known as Sindhu.[1208] If one bathes there, one obtains good conduct and goes to heaven. If one bathes in Pushkara, Prabhasa, Naimisha, the waters of the ocean, Devika, Indramarga and Svarnavindu, know that one then ascends a vimana and is served by apsaras.[1209] If one restrains one's agitation and reverentially bathes in Hiranyavindu, Kusheshaya and Devatva, one is cleansed from all sins. If a man controls and purifies himself and then approaches and bathes in Indratoya, which is near Gandhamadana, and in Karatoya, which is in Kuranga, after having fasted for three nights, he obtains the fruits of a horse sacrifice. If one bathes in Gangadvara, Kushavarta, Vilvaka, which is in the Nemi mountains, and in Kankhala,[1210] one is cleansed of sins and goes to heaven. If a person is a brahmachari, conquers his anger, is devoted to the truth and is non-violent, and if he bathes in the lake known as Apa, he obtains the fruits of a vajapeya sacrifice. Bhagirathi Ganga flows in a northern direction, in a spot favoured by Maheshvara. If a man fasts for one month and then bathes there, he can then see the gods themselves. However, even if a man worships at Sapta-Ganga, Tri-Ganga and Indramarga and tastes the water there, he has to be born again.[1211] If a person observes agnihotra, purifies himself, fasts for one month and then bathes in Mahashrama, he obtains success within a month. If a person frees himself from

[1207]Respectively Chenab and Jhelum.

[1208]Indus.

[1209]Pushkara is in Rajasthan, Prabhasa is in Gujarat, by Naimisha one probably means the waters of the Gomati, Devika is in Udhampur, Indramarga and Svarnavindu (also known as Suvarnavindu) are rivers in Kashmir. The identification of most of these is difficult.

[1210]All these places are near Haridwar, Uttarakhand.

[1211]The rivers Ganga, Yamuna, Godavari, Sarasvati, Kaveri, Narmada and Sindhu are known as Sapta-Ganga. By Tri-Ganga, one usually means Bhagirathi, Jahnavi and Alakananda.

avarice, fasts for three nights and bathes in the great lake known as Bhrigutunga,[1212] he is freed from the sin of having killed a brahmana. If one bathes in the waters of Kanyakupa and Balaka, one obtains fame like that of the gods and blazes in that reknown. If a man bathes in the waters of Deshakala and in Lake Sundarika, after death, he obtains beauty and radiance that is like that of the Ashvins. If one fasts for a fortnight and bathes in Mahaganga and Krittikangaraka, one sparkles in heaven. If one bathes in Vaimanika and in the hermitage known as Kinkinika, one obtains greatness and divinity, can roam as one wishes, and dwells with apsaras. If one conquers anger, observes brahmacharya for three nights and bathes in the hermitage of Kalika, in the waters of Vipasha,[1213] one is freed from rebirth. If one bathes in the hermitage of Krittika and worships the ancestors, one satisfies Mahadeva and obtains sparkling heaven. If a man fasts for three nights and bathes in Mahapura, he is freed from fear of all immobile objects and also discards fear of bipeds. If a man purifies himself, fasts for seven nights and bathes in the waters in the forest of Devadaru, he cleanses himself and obtains the world of the gods. If one bathes in the waterfalls in Koushanta, Kushastamba and Dronasharmapada, one is served by large numbers of apsaras. If one fasts and bathes in Chitrakuta, Janasthana[1214] and in the waters of the Mandakini, one obtains royal prosperity. If one goes to the hermitage known as Shyama, fasts and resides there for three nights and bathes there, one dwells in the city of the gandharvas. If one fasts for one month and bathes in the beautiful waters of Gandhatarika, one obtains the powers of disappearing at will. If a man goes to Koushikidvara, casts aside all greed and survives only on air for twenty-one nights, he ascends to heaven. If one bathes in Matanga, one becomes successful in a single night. If one conquers one's senses and bathes in the eternal waters of Analamba, Andhaka, Naimisha or Svargatirtha, within one month, one obtains the fruits

[1212]This is probably Lake Bhrigu, in Kullu district of Himachal Pradesh.

[1213]River Beas.

[1214]Chitrakuta is in Madhya Pradesh and Janasthana has been identified as Nashika (Maharashtra), the capital of the Dandaka kingdom.

of *purushamedha*.[1215] If one bathes in the waters of Gangahrada and Utpalavana for a month, one obtains the fruits of a horse sacrifice. If one bathes in the tirthas that are along the Ganga and the Yamuna and in the sixty lakes that are in Mount Kalanjara,[1216] this is superior to all kinds of donations. O bull among the Bharata lineage! In the month of Magha, ten thousand tirthas and another thirty crore tirthas assemble in Prayaga.[1217] O foremost among the Bharata lineage! If one is controlled, rigid in vows and bathes in Prayaga in the month of Magha, one obtains sparkling heaven. If a man bathes in Marudgana, in the sacred hermitage of the ancestors and in the tirtha of Vaivasvata, he becomes like a tirtha himself. If one goes to Brahmashira and bathes in the waters of the Bhagirathi, after having fasted for one month, one obtains the world of the moon. If a man fasts for twelve days and bathes in the waters of Kapotaka and Ashtavakra, he obtains the fruits of a human sacrifice. If one goes to Munjaprishtha, the divine mountain of Nirriti and Krouchapadi, all three of which are in Gaya, one is freed from the sin of having killed a brahmana.[1218] If one bathes in Kalashya, know that one will obtain a great deal of water. If a man bathes in the city of Agni, in the waters of Vishala and in Devahrada, he becomes radiant and merges with the brahman. If a man is controlled and non-violent and bathes in Purapavartana, Nanda or Mahananda, he goes to Nandana[1219] and is served by apsaras. At the conjunction of Urvashi and Krittika, as is ordained, if one is self-controlled and bathes in the Lohitya, one obtains the fruits of a *pundarika* sacrifice.[1220] If one

[1215]Purushamedha is a sacrifice where human beings were sacrificed.

[1216]In the Bundelkhand region of Uttar Pradesh.

[1217]Prayaga is the confluence of the Ganga and the Yamuna and is in Uttar Pradesh. Magha is January–February. Bathing in Prayaga during the first half of Magha is believed to be extremely auspicious.

[1218]Gaya is in Bihar. The hills around Gaya were formed out of the body of a demon named Gayasura. Since Nirriti means demon, that probably explains Mount Nirriti.

[1219]Indra's pleasure garden.

[1220]Lohitya is the Brahmaputra. Krittika is a nakshatra. But what does the conjunction of Urvashi and Krittika mean? While this is difficult to understand, *urvashi* also means wide.

fasts for twelve days and bathes in Ramahrada and in the waters of Vishala, one is freed from all sins. If a man purifies his mind and bathes in Mahahrada, fasting for one month, he obtains the end got by Jamadagni. If one is non-violent and devoted to the truth, tormenting oneself in Vindhya and standing on one foot for six months, one will be purified within a month. If one fasts for a fortnight and bathes in the waters of Narmada and Surparaka, one becomes a prince. If one goes to Jambumarga and is controlled and self-restrained for three months, one obtains success within a single day and a single night. If one goes to the hermitage of Chandalika and bathes in Kokamukha, subsisting on vegetables and attired in rags, one obtains ten maidens. If one resides in Kanyahrada, one goes to the world of the gods and never goes to Vaivasvata's[1221] abode. O mighty-armed one! If a man is controlled and bathes in Prabhasa on the night of the new moon, when he is reborn, he obtains success within a single night. If one bathes in Ujjanaka, in the hermitages of Arshtishena and Pinga, then, one is freed from all sins. If one purifies oneself and fasts for three nights, bathing in the waters of Kulya and chanting the aghamarshana mantra, one obtains the fruits of a horse sacrifice. If a man fasts for one night and bathes in Pindaraka, then, as soon as night is over, he is purified and obtains the fruits of an *agnishtoma* sacrifice. If one goes to Brahmasara, adorned by the forest known as Dharmaranya, then, as soon as night is over, one is purified and obtains the fruits of a pundarika sacrifice. If one bathes in Mount Mainaka for a month, performing the morning and evening prayers and conquering desire, one then obtains the fruits of all sacrifices. The Himalayas are sacred and famous. They are Shankara's father-in-law. They are a store of all jewels and are frequented by the siddhas and the charanas. There may be a brahmana who knows about Vedanta and knows that life is transient. If he worships the gods, bows to the sages and, following the prescribed rites, fasts and gives up his life there, he obtains divine success. He goes to Brahma's eternal world. There may be a person who dwells in a tirtha, having given up desire, anger

[1221]Yama's.

and avarice. Since he has gone to a tirtha, there is nothing that he cannot obtain. Even if one wishes to go to all the tirthas, some tirthas are inaccessible and difficult to reach. In that case, one should approach them mentally. They are like sacrifices. They make one fortunate. They yield divine bliss. It is a great secret that even the gods purify themselves by bathing there. This secret can be divulged in the hearing of brahmanas, the virtuous, sons, well-wishers and devoted disciples."'

'Bhishma continued, "The great ascetic, Angiras, told Goutama about this, after having obtained the permission of his preceptor, the intelligent Kashyapa.[1222] What the maharshi said is pure and supreme and should be chanted. If one chants it when one wakes up, one is cleansed and obtains heaven. This mystery was obtained from Angiras. If one hears it, one is born in an excellent lineage and remembers one's past life."'

Chapter 1708(27)

Vaishampayana said, 'He was Brihaspati's equal in intelligence and Brahma's equal in forgiveness. He was Shakra's equal in valour and as infinitely energetic as Aditya. Gangeya was extremely radiant and had been brought down in the battle by Arjuna. With his brothers and the others, Yudhishthira worshipped him. The one without decay was waiting for the right time and was lying down on a hero's bed. The maharshis arrived, wishing to see the foremost one among the Bharata lineage. There were Atri, Vasishtha, Bhrigu, Pulastya, Pulaha, Kratu, Angiras, Goutama, Agastya, Sumati, controlled in his soul, Vishvamitra, Sthulashira, Samvarta, Pramati, Dama, Ushanas, Brihaspati, Vyasa, Chyavana, Kashyapa, Dhruva, Durvasa, Jamadagni, Markandeya, Galava,

[1222]The text doesn't say this explicitly. But this is obviously Bhishma continuing.

Bharadvaja, Raibhya, Yavakrita, Trita, Sthulaksha, Shakalaksha, Kanva, Medhatithi, Krisha, Narada, Parvata, Sudhanva, Ekata, Dvita, Nitambhu, Bhuvana, Dhoumya, Shatananda, Kritavrana, Jamadagnya Rama, Kamya, Chetya and others. These great-souled maharshis arrived to see Bhishma. In due order, with his brothers, Yudhishthira worshipped the great-souled ones who had arrived. Having been worshipped, the maharshis seated themselves and began to converse. In extremely gentle tones, which delighted all the senses, they talked about Bhishma. On hearing the words of the rishis, who had cleansed their souls, Bhishma was supremely delighted and satisfied and thought that he was already in heaven. While everyone looked on, taking the leave of Bhishma and the Pandavas, all the rishis vanished. Though those extremely fortunate rishis had disappeared, all the Pandavas continued to repeatedly worship and bow down before them. With cheerful minds, all these supreme Kurus presented themselves before Gangeya, like those who know about mantras presenting themselves before the rising sun. Because of the powers of austerities of the rishis, the Pandavas saw that the directions were ablaze. All of them were quite astounded at this. They thought that the rishis were much more than fortunate. The Pandavas started to converse with Bhishma. When that conversation was over, Yudhishthira, Dharma's son, touched Bhishma's feet with his head and again questioned him about dharma. "O grandfather! Which countries, provinces, hermitages, mountains and rivers are really sacred?"

'Bhishma replied, "In this connection, an ancient history is recounted about a conversation between a person who followed *shilonchhavritti* and one who had obtained success.[1223] A best among bipeds roamed over the entire earth, adorned with mountains. He finally arrived at the house of someone who was best among those who followed *shilavritti*. Once he arrived, he was duly honoured.

[1223]There are grains left after a crop has been harvested, or after grain has been milled. If one subsists on these leftovers, that is known as unchhavritti. *Shila* means gathering the stalks. Shilonchhavritti can be therefore regarded as equivalent to unchhavritti or to shilavritti.

After the ablutions, the guest, who had obtained success, seated himself. Those great-souled ones seated themselves and started to talk about auspicious things, such as what was in the Vedas and in their appendices, and their various attributes. When this conversation was over, the intelligent one who followed shilavritti carefully asked the one who had obtained success to answer the question that you have asked me.

'"Shilavritti asked, 'Which countries, provinces, hermitages, mountains and rivers are really sacred? Tell me that.'

'"The Siddha[1224] replied, 'Countries, provinces, hermitages and mountains are best when Bhagirathi Ganga, supreme among rivers, flows through them. Through austerities, brahmacharya, sacrifices and renunciation, a creature cannot obtain the ends that can be obtained by frequenting the Ganga. If the limbs have been sprinkled with the waters of the Ganga, or if creatures cast aside their bodies there, they are not dislodged from heaven. O brahmana! When embodied creatures perform all their rites in the waters of the Ganga, having left earth, such men are permanently in heaven. Men may have committed sins in the earlier parts of their lives. However, later, if they reside near the Ganga, they advance towards a supreme end. If men control their souls and bathe in the pure waters of the Ganga, they obtain merits that are greater than those obtained through one hundred sacrifices. As long as a man's bones are established in the waters of the Ganga, he obtains greatness in heaven for thousands of years. The run rises in the morning and through its radiance, dispels the terrible darkness. In that way, when washed by the waters of the Ganga, the sins are dispelled and one is radiant. Without the auspicious waters of the Ganga, countries and directions are deprived, like a night without the moon, or a tree without flowers. Without the Ganga, the universe is like sacrifices without soma, or the varna and ashrama system, with everyone deprived of knowledge about his own dharma. There is no doubt that deprived of the Ganga, countries and directions are as deprived as the firmament without the sun, the earth without mountains, or the sky without air. When they obtain

[1224]Literally, the successful one.

the auspicious waters of the Ganga, all the beings in the three worlds are supremely satisified and become content. Drinking water from the Ganga, heated by the sun, is superior to picking out and eating food from the excrement of a cow. To purify one's body, a person may perform one thousand *chandrayana* sacrifices. It is impossible to determine whether this is equal, or unequal, to drinking the water of the Ganga. A man may stand on a single foot for one thousand yugas. It is impossible to determine whether this is equal, or unequal, to standing in a similar way in the Ganga for one month. A man may remain for ten thousand yugas, with his face hanging downwards. However, if one remains on the banks of the Ganga for some time, that is superior. O supreme among brahmanas! When cotton is burnt in a fire, nothing is left. In that way, through submerging in the Ganga, all sins are washed away. The consciousness of all creatures is taken away by misery. If they seek an escape, there is no escape that is equal to the Ganga. On seeing Tarkshya,[1225] a snake loses its poison. In that way, on seeing Ganga, one is freed from all sins. Because of their addiction towards adharma, there are those who are without any status. They obtain refuge, prosperity and protection from the Ganga. There are many who are worst among men, prone to inauspicious deeds and destined for hell. After death, they are saved by the Ganga. Those who always advance towards the Ganga are certainly counted together with the sages and the gods, with Vasava. There are many who are inauspicious and worst among men, devoid of good conduct and humility. O brahmana! When they resort to the Ganga, they become auspicious. The waters of the Ganga are for men what amrita is for the gods, svadha is for the ancestors and *sudha* is for serpents.[1226] Children who are afflicted by hunger seek out their mothers. In that way, embodied beings who desire welfare seek out the Ganga. Svayambhu's region is said to be the best. In that fashion, Ganga is said to be the best among rivers to bathe in. Cattle and the earth are said to be the best means of sustenance for the gods and others. In that way, for all beings on earth, Ganga is the means of sustenance. The

[1225]Garuda.

[1226]Here, sudha is best understood as milk and not as nectar.

gods are established in the sun and the moon and sustain themselves through sacrifices and amrita. For men, the waters of the Ganga are like that. If a man smears himself with sand from the banks of the Jahnavi and arises, he can think of himself as adorned as the gods in heaven. If a person raises up mud from the banks of the Jahnavi and smears it on his head, he becomes radiant, as sparkling and radiant as the sun, the dispeller of darkness. If water mixed with drops of water from the Ganga's waves touches a man, he is instantly cleansed of all sin. If a man is afflicted by hardships and is about to be destroyed, the mere sight of the Ganga cheers him up and dispels those hardships. Swans, ruddy geese and other birds crying on the Ganga challenge the gandharvas and her banks challenge tall mountains. There are swans and many other kinds of birds on the Ganga. There are herds of cattle along the banks. On seeing these, one forgets heaven. The supreme delight obtained by men who reside along the banks of the Ganga is greater than the bliss from residing in heaven, with all one's wishes gratified. There may be a man who has committed the worst of sins in speech, thought and deeds. There is no doubt that on seeing Ganga, he is purified. If a man sees, touches and bathes in the Ganga, he saves seven generations of his ancestors and seven generations of his descendants. In particular, by wishing to hear about the Ganga, seeing it, touching it and drinking its waters, a man rescues both his family lines.[1227] By seeing, touching, drinking and praising the Ganga, hundreds and thousands of sinners become purified. People who desire to make their births, lives and learning successful should go to the Ganga and worship the ancestors and the gods. Through sons, riches and deeds, a man cannot obtain the fruits that can be derived through approaching the Ganga. If a person, though able, does not go and see the sacred and auspicious waters of the Ganga, he is like one born blind, or one who is dead or disabled. The Ganga is worshipped by maharshis who know about the past, the present and the future, and by the gods, together with Indra. Which man will not worship it? Those in vanaprastha and garhasthya, those who are mendicants and brahmacharis and those who have knowledge

[1227]On the father's side and on the mother's side.

and learning resort to the Ganga. Which man will not seek refuge there? When a man is about to give up his breath of life, if he behaves virtuously, controls himself and thinks of the Ganga, he obtains the supreme objective. If a man worships the Ganga at the time of giving up his body, he has no fear from fear and does not suffer from any sin. The extremely sacred goddess fell down from the sky and was held by Maheshvara on his head. It is she who is there in heaven. The three sparkling courses adorn the three worlds.[1228] A man who frequents her waters becomes successful in every possible way. Among the rivers of earth, Ganga is like the lord of the gods[1229] to men, the moon to the ancestors and the sun to the stellar bodies in the firmament. The misery on being separated from a mother, a father, sons, wives or riches is nothing compared to the sorrow on being separated from the Ganga. Through meritorious deeds, sons and the inflow of riches, men do not obtain as much gratification as they do from seeing the Ganga. The hearts of men are delighted on seeing the full moon. On seeing the Ganga, which possesses three flows, hearts rejoice in that fashion. With faith, single-mindedness, devotion and steadfastness, if a devotee worships the Ganga, he becomes her beloved. Creatures who are on earth, in the sky or in heaven, and even those who are higher still, should always bathe in the Ganga. This is a task indicated for the virtuous. Ganga is sacred and is famous in the three worlds. She is illustrious. Sagara's sons, who were reduced to ashes, were conveyed by her to heaven.[1230]

"''Ganga's waves are tall, bright and sparkling and arise, after being driven by winds that make a loud noise. Those who are washed by these are purified and become as radiant as the sun, the one with the one thousand rays. The prosperous waters are swift and difficult to immerse in. They are like the clarified butter generously offered at

[1228]Ganga flows in heaven (as Mandakini), on earth (as Bhagirathi/Ganga) and in the nether regions (as Bhogavati).

[1229]This can also be loosely translated as a lord among men, or king.

[1230]The sage Kapila reduced Sagara's sons to ashes. A descendant, Bhagiratha, brought Ganga down to earth and when those ashes were washed by the waters of the Ganga, Sagara's sons were saved.

sacrifices. Patient men who go to the Ganga and give up their lives there, become like the gods. The Ganga is illustrious and large. The universe is her form. She is worshipped by the sages and by the gods, with Indra at their head. She grants all the objects of desire to those who are blind, dumb and bereft of possessions. Her water is full of energy and is sweet as honey. She is extremely sacred and has three flows. She is the protector of the three worlds. Those who seek refuge with the Ganga, go to heaven. If a mortal person dwells near her and sees her, the gods grant him happiness. He is cleansed by the touch and the sight. The gods grant him auspicious directions. She is large, excellent and accomplished. She is the earth. She is auspicious and like amrita. She is lovely and extremely gracious. She is brilliant and all creatures are established in her. A person who goes to Ganga goes to heaven. Her fame is always known on earth, in the sky and in heaven, and fills the directions and the minor directions. She is supreme among rivers, and by resorting to her waters, all mortal beings accomplish their objectives. This Ganga is always established. She bore the golden Guha in her womb.[1231] She possesses three flows. She has descended as the water of the universe. She is like a flow of clarified butter. If a person bathes in the Ganga in the morning, he is cleansed of all sin. She is a daughter of the mountains and is Hara's wife. She is like an ornament of heaven and earth. She is the radiant one who sustains the earth. O king![1232] Ganga is the purifier of the three worlds. Her flows are as sweet as honey. She is like the clarified butter offered at sacrifices. She is adorned with large waves and with brahmanas. Ganga is like a garland in heaven. She is the daughter of the mountains. She descended from heaven and was held by Bhava on his head. She is the best of wombs. She is radiant and subtle. Fame is granted by her roaring and surging waters. She is the one who protects the universe. Her form is one that confers the greatest benefit. For heaven and for earth, Ganga is the path to follow. In forgiveness, protection and sustenance, brahmanas revere Ganga as the earth's equal. She is like the fire and the sun in her

[1231]Guha is Kartikeya. In the story of Kartikeya's birth, Agni handed over the energy to Ganga, who then deposited it in a clump of reeds.

[1232]Since Shilavritti is being addressed, this is an inconsistency.

radiance. In being gracious towards the brahmanas, she is always like Guha. She is ancient and is praised by the rishis. She emerged from Vishnu's feet. Her waters are extremely auspicious and take one to the worlds one can think of. A person who resorts to Jahnavi with all his soul, goes to Brahma's world. She possesses all the qualities and with all their souls, there are people who worship her, like sons towards their mothers. She is the one who facilitates the restraint of one's soul. If a person desires benefit in Brahma's abode, he should worship Ganga. She is like a pleasant cow that provides her waters to the universe. She is like an ocean of prosperity, as sweet as honey. She is like the amrita desired by the virtuous and is loved by Brahma. Those who seek success in their souls seek refuge with Ganga. Through his fierce austerities, Bhagiratha worshipped the lord and the god,[1233] pleased him and brought down Ganga. Men who go to her can free themselves of all fear, in this world and in the next. Using the best of my intelligence, I have considered and recounted some of her qualities. However, I do not possess the capacity to enumerate and speak about all her qualities. One can enumerate all the jewels in Meru and all the waters that exist in the ocean. But one is incapable of enumerating all the qualities of the waters of the Ganga. Resorting to devotion, one should listen to Jahnavi's supreme qualities and show great faith and reverence, in words, thoughts and deeds. One will then obtain fame and prosperity in the three worlds. One will then obtain the great success, created by Ganga herself, one that is difficult to obtain. In a short while, you will roam around in the desired worlds. She possesses all the great qualities. If we are devoted to our own dharma, may she always turn our intelligence towards her. Ganga is affectionate towards those who seek refuge with her. She grants happiness to those who worship her with faith.'"

'Bhishma continued, "The successful one was radiant. In this way, he expounded the many qualities of the one with the three flows to Shilavritti. Having instructed him in many ways and having told him about the truth of her form, he ascended up into the sky. Shilavritti was awakened by the words of the successful one. In the

[1233]Vishnu.

proper way, he worshipped Ganga and obtained the kind of success that is extremely difficult to obtain. O Kounteya! Therefore, resort to great devotion and always worship Ganga. You will obtain supreme success."'

Vaishampayana said, 'This is the history that Bhishma recounted and Yudhishthira and his brothers were filled with great delight at hearing about Ganga's praise. This is a sacred history, filled with praise about Ganga. Even now, if a person hears it or reads it, he is freed from all sins.'

Chapter 1709(28)

'Yudhishthira said, "You possess wisdom, learning, good conduct and behaviour. You possess all the qualities and are also aged. O supreme among those who uphold dharma! Therefore, I am asking you about dharma. O supreme among kings! If a person is a kshatriya, vaishya or a shudra, you should tell me how he can become a brahmana. O grandfather! Does one become a brahmana through austerities, great deeds or learning? Tell me that."

'Bhishma replied, "O son! O Yudhishthira! For a kshatriya and the others, the three varnas, becoming a brahmana is extremely difficult. For all beings, that is the best state. O son! If one is repeatedly and progressively cooked in the cycle of life, one can then be born as a brahmana. O Yudhishthira! In this connection, there is an ancient history about a conversation between Matanga and a she-ass. O son! There was a brahmana and this lord obtained a son through a varna that was not his equal.[1234] His name was Matanga and he possessed all the qualities. O Kounteya! O scorcher of enemies! Wishing to perform a sacrifice, his father sent him to bring the required objects. He departed on a wagon that travelled

[1234]This will be explained soon.

fast and it was drawn by an ass. O king! The ass was young and it dragged the wagon to its mother. At this, he[1235] repeatedly struck it on the nose. The she-ass loved its son. On seeing those terrible wounds, it said, 'O son! Do not grieve. A chandala is driving you. A brahmana is never terrible. A brahmana is said to be friendly. He is the preceptor of all creatures and their instructor. How can such a person strike? This one is wicked in nature and does not show any compassion, even to someone who is young. By exhibiting his character, he is only exhibiting the nature of his birth.' Matanga heard these terrible words of the she-ass. He descended from the wagon and addressed the she-ass. 'O she-ass! O fortunate one! How was my mother tainted? How do you know that I am a chandala? O she-ass! Instruct me quickly. How was I born as a chandala and how has my status as a brahmana been destroyed? O immensely wise one! Without leaving out anything, tell me everything about this.'

'"The she-ass said, 'There was a brahmana lady who was overcome with desire and you were born through a vrishala who was a barber. That is the reason you have been born as a chandala and the reason why your status as a brahmana has been destroyed.'"

'Bhishma continued, "Having been thus addressed, Matanga returned home. On seeing that he had returned, his father spoke these words. 'I asked you to do some things connected with the sacrifice. How can you return without performing the tasks instructed by your superior? Is everything well with you?'

'"Matanga replied, 'How can someone of uncertain birth, or with the worst possible birth, be well? O father! How can someone with a mother like that be well? O father! I have got to know that though my mother is a brahmana, my father is a vrishala. A superhuman she-ass told me this. Therefore, I must torment myself through great austerities.'"

'Bhishma continued, "Having spoken to his father and having made up his mind, he left for the great forest, to torment himself through great austerities. The gods themselves were tormented by

[1235]Matanga.

the force of these austerities. Through his good conduct, Matanga desired the region that would provide great bliss. While he was thus engaged in austerities, Harivahana[1236] appeared before him and asked, 'O Matanga! Why are you tormenting yourself? Why have you given up the pleasures that men like? I wish to grant you a boon. Tell me about the boon that you desire. Without any delay, tell me about everything that is in your mind.'

'"Matanga replied, 'I have started these austerities with the desire of becoming a brahmana. Having attained this, I will depart from this place. This is the boon sought by me.'"

'Bhishma continued, "On hearing his words, Purandara said, 'You desire the status of a brahmana, but that cannot be obtained by someone whose soul has not been cleansed. This is the best state among all creatures. Therefore, refrain from these austerities. This desire and these fierce austerities will quickly destroy you. Among gods, asuras and mortals, this state is said to be sacred and supreme. Having been born as a chandala, you can never obtain it.'"'

Chapter 1710(29)

'Bhishma said, "O one without decay! Matanga was careful about his vows and in control of his soul. Though he was addressed in this way, he stood on one foot for one hundred years. The immensely illustrious Shakra again appeared before him and said, 'O Matanga! The supreme state that you desire is extremely difficult to obtain. O son! Do not exhibit this futile rashness. This isn't the path of dharma. You cannot obtain what you wish for and will soon be destroyed. O Matanga! I have sought to restrain you from aspiring to obtain that supreme state. If you still desire to perform these austerities, you will be destroyed in every possible

[1236]Indra.

way. Among all the men who are born as inferior[1237] species, only a few are reborn as pulkasa or chandala. O Matanga! Anyone on earth who is seen to have been born as wicked species, will have to whirl around in that state for a long period of time. After having spent one thousand births in this way, one obtains the status of a shudra.[1238] One is whirled around in the state of a shudra for a long period of time. After three thousand births in this way, one obtains the status of a vaishya. One is whirled around in the state of a vaishya for a long period of time. After six thousand births in this way, one obtains the status of a king.[1239] One is whirled around in the state of a king for a long period of time. After six thousand births in this way, one obtains the status of being a friend of a brahmana.[1240] One is whirled around in the state of being a friend of a brahmana for a long period of time. After two thousand births in this way, one obtains the status of a brahmana who earns a living by selling weapons. One is whirled around in the status of a brahmana who earns a living by selling weapons for a long period of time. After three thousand births in this way, one obtains the status of an ordinary brahmana. Having obtained this status, one is whirled around for a long period of time. After four thousand births in this way, one is born as a learned brahmana. One is whirled around in the state of a learned brahmana for a long period of time. O son! In that state, anger, delight, desire, hatred, insolence and argumentation penetrate him and try to make him the worst among brahmanas. When he abandons these enemies, he obtains a virtuous end. However, if they defeat him, he falls down, as if from the top of a palm tree. O Matanga! That is the reason I have spoken to you, restraining you and asking you to ask for some other boon. The status of a brahmana is something that is extremely difficult to obtain.'"'

[1237]Subhuman.

[1238]We have followed non-Critical versions in translating the duration. Non-Critical versions say, ten times one hundred, that is, one thousand. The Critical edition states, ten times. This makes deduction of the duration difficult.

[1239]Meaning a kshatriya.

[1240]That is, a brahmana.

Chapter 1711(30)

'Bhishma said, "Thus addressed, Matanga was overwhelmed by great grief. He went to Gaya and stood on one toe for one hundred years. He performed many kinds of extremely difficult yoga. He became thin and was reduced to veins. The one with dharma in his soul was reduced to nothing but bones and we have heard that he fell down. When he was falling down, Vasava came and seized him. After all, the lord and the granter of boons is engaged in the welfare of all beings.

'"Shakra said, 'O Matanga! You are engaged in trying to obtain the status of a brahmana, but this is a perverse pursuit. Worship what will bring you happiness. Do not worship what will bring you unhappiness. Among all creatures, it is controlled brahmanas who display yoga and kshema. The ancestors and the gods are satisfied through brahmanas. O Matanga! Among all creatures, brahmanas are said to be supreme. It is brahmanas who grant what you are asking for.[1241] O son! One is repeatedly and progressively cooked in the fire of the cycle of life. It is only in rare cases that one can obtain the status of a brahmana.'

'"Matanga replied, 'I am already afflicted by grief. Why are you oppressing me? You are striking me, but I am already like one who is dead. I am not grieving that I have not obtained the radiance that comes about from being a brahmana. O Shatakratu! Among the three varnas, if the status of a brahmana is so difficult to obtain, why do men who have obtained it deviate? An evil person who acts in this way should be regarded as the worst among wicked ones, since he disregards the status of being a brahmana, something that is like getting riches which are extremely difficult to obtain. It is indeed hard to become a brahmana and having become one, it is very difficult to maintain it. Having obtained something that is difficult to get, men do not maintain it. O Shakra! I find pleasure in only one thing.[1242] I

[1241]The implication has to be deduced. Had Matanga been a brahmana, thanks to his powers, he need not have asked for a boon from anyone else. If Matanga needed to ask someone else for a boon, he couldn't be a brahmana.

[1242]His soul.

do not suffer from opposite sentiments. I am devoid of possessions. I am non-violent. I am self-restrained and generous. Why should I not obtain the status of a brahmana? Let me roam around in my own pleasures, just as birds roam around as they will. Without any constraints, let me be revered by both brahmanas and kshatriyas. O Purandara! Let me obtain fame without decay.'

'"Indra said, 'You will become famous as the god of metre and will be worshipped by women.'"[1243]

'Bhishma continued, "Vasava granted this boon to him and disappeared. Having given up his life, Matanga obtained a supreme station. O descendant of the Bharata lineage! Thus, the status of a brahmana is supreme. As indicated in the words of the great Indra, it is extremely difficult to obtain."'

Chapter 1712(31)

'Yudhishthira said, "O extender of the Kuru lineage! I have heard this great account. O supreme among eloquent ones! You have said that the status of a brahmana is extremely difficult to obtain. O excellent one! However, though you have said that it is extremely difficult to obtain, it has been heard that in ancient times, Vishvamitra became a brahmana. I have also heard that rajarshi Vitahavya became a brahmana.[1244] O Gangeya! O lord! I wish to hear everything about this. O supreme among kings! What deeds enabled him to become a brahmana? Was it through a boon or austerities? You should explain this to me in detail."

'Bhishma replied, "O king! Listen. King Vitahavya was greatly illustrious. Though he was a kshatriya, he became a brahmana and was revered by the worlds. O son! The great-souled Manu followed dharma and ruled his subjects. He had a famous son named Sharyati,

[1243]A sage named Matanga was the author of a work (*Brihaddeshi*) on music.

[1244]Vitahavya was a king from the Haihaya dynasty.

who possessed dharma in his soul. O king! Two kings were born in that lineage. O supreme among victorious ones! They were Haihaya and Talajangha and they were the sons of Vatsa. O descendant of the Bharata lineage! Through his ten wives, Haihaya had one hundred brave sons, who did not retreat in battle. They were equal in beauty and power. They were learned and accomplished in fighting. In every way, they completed their learning of *dhanurveda* and of the Vedas. O king! There was a king in Kashi and he was Divodasa's grandfather. He was famous as Haryashva and he was foremost among victorious ones. O bull among men! Because of enmity, in the area between the Ganga and the Yamuna, Vitahavya's sons brought him down in a battle.[1245] Having slain that best of men, the maharathas who were the sons of Haihaya fearlessly returned to their beautiful city in the land of the Vatsas. Haryashva's son became the king of Kashi. His name was Sudeva. He was like a god and he was dharma personified. With dharma in his soul, the descendant of the Kashi lineage ruled the earth. However, because of enmity, Vitahavya's sons again invaded and conquered everything in the battle. Having become victorious in this way, they returned to wherever they had come from. Sudeva's son, Divodasa, was instated as the king of Kashi. Divodasa realized that his great-souled enemies were valorous. On Shakra's instructions, the extremely energetic one rebuilt the fortifications of Varanasi. There were large numbers of brahmanas, kshatriyas, vaishyas and shudras there. There were stores of many kinds of objects and provisions and prosperous shops and stalls. O supreme among kings! The area extended from the northern banks of the Ganga to the southern banks of the Gomati and it was like Shakra's Amaravati. O lord of the earth! The tiger among kings used to dwell there. O descendant of the Bharata lineage! Yet again, the Haihayas advanced and attacked. The immensely radiant Divodasa emerged and fought with them. It was a terrible battle, like that between the gods and the asuras. O great king! He fought against them for one thousand days. However, since his mounts were repeatedly slain, he

[1245]This is cryptic. Vitahavya is another name for Haihaya and the sons of Vitahavya/Haihaya killed Haryashva.

was overcome by distress. O king! The warriors were killed and the king's treasury was exhausted. Abandoning his city, Divodasa fled. He went to the hermitage of the intelligent Bharadvaja. O scorcher of enemies! The king joined his hands in salutation and sought refuge with him.

'"The king said, 'O illustrious one! Vitahavya's sons have destroyed my lineage in battle. I am the only one who has escaped and I have sought refuge with you. O illustrious one! You should protect me, just as you would a disciple. Those performers of wicked deeds have destroyed my lineage.'"

'Bhishma continued, "The powerful and immensely fortunate Bharadvaja replied, 'Do not be frightened. O Sudeva's son! Do not be scared. Dispel your fear. O lord of the earth! So that you can have a son, I will immediately perform a sacrifice. You can use him to strike down thousands on Vitahavya's side.' Desiring a son, the rishi performed a sacrifice. A son was born and he was known as Pratardana. As soon as he was born, he grew up and looked like someone who was thirteen years old. O descendant of the Bharata lineage! He learnt all the Vedas and dhanurveda. The intelligent Bharadvaja immersed himself in yoga. He accumulated all the energy of the worlds and made it penetrate into him.[1246] He was clad in armour and wielded a bow and arrows. He blazed like a fire. Wielding the bow and with his form like that of a monsoon cloud, the archer advanced. On seeing him advance, Sudeva's son was filled with great delight. In his mind, the king thought that Vitahavya's sons had already been consumed. He instated Pratardana as the heir apparent. The king thought that he had already become successful and was full of joy. The king instructed his son Pratardana, the scorcher of enemies, to advance and slay the sons of Vitahavya. On his chariot, the valiant one swiftly crossed the Ganga. The destroyer of enemy cities advanced towards the city of the sons of Vitahavya. The sons of Vitahavya heard the sounds created by that chariot. They emerged on their own chariots, which were like cities, and advanced against the enemy's chariot. They were as swift as tigers. They were colourful

[1246]Into Pratardana.

in fighting. They emerged, attacked Pratardana and showered down arrows and weapons on him. O Yudhishthira! They attacked the king with many kinds of weapons and floods of chariots, like rain clouds showering down on the Himalayas. King Pratardana repulsed their weapons. The immensely energetic one slew them with arrows that were like the vajra or the fire. O king! Hundreds and thousands of broad-headed arrows were used to sever the heads. Flowing with blood, they fell down, like severed *kimshuka* trees. When all of his sons were slain, Vitahavya abandoned his city and fled to Bhrigu's hermitage. King Vitahavya went to Bhrigu and sought refuge with him. Bhrigu offered him shelter, as if to a disciple. Following him, Pratardana swiftly arrived there.

'"Having arrived there, Divodasa's son said, 'O disciples of the great-souled Bhrigu! O those who are in the hermitage! Listen. Please go and tell the sage that I wish to see him.' When he got to know, Bhrigu emerged from the hermitage. Following supreme rites, he honoured him and asked, 'O Indra among kings! What is your purpose with the king?'[1247] O king! He told him the reason why he had come. 'O brahmana! King Vitahavya has come here. Please surrender him. O brahmana! His sons have destroyed my entire lineage. They have devastated the kingdom and the stores of jewels in Kashi. Through my valour, I have slain one hundred of his insolent sons. O brahmana! By killing this one now, I will repay the debt to my father.' Bhrigu, supreme among the upholders of dharma, was overcome by compassion, and replied, 'There is no kshatriya here. Everyone who is here is a brahmana.' Hearing Bhrigu's words, Pratardana thought that this must be the truth. He touched his feet, laughed and gently spoke these words. 'O illustrious one! There is no doubt that I have become successful. Because of my valour, the king will now have to give up the state he was born in. O brahmana! Grant me permission to leave and pronounce your auspicious benedictions on me. O extender of the Bhrigu lineage! Because of you, the king has been forced to give up my varna.' O great king! Having obtained his

[1247]That is, Vitahavya.

permission, King Pratardana departed to where he had come from, like a serpent that has given up its poison. O great king! Thanks to Bhrigu's words alone, Vitahavya became a brahmana rishi and became knowledgable about the brahman. He had a son named Gritsamada, who was Indra's equal in beauty. Once, taking him to be Indra, the daityas oppressed him. O lord of the earth! There is a hymn in the Rig Veda that states, 'Wherever the brahmana Gritsamada goes, the brahmanas regard that place as great.' The illustrious Gritsamada was a brahmana rishi and a brahmachari. Gritsamada had a brahmana son named Suteja.[1248] Suteja's son was Varcha and his son was Vihavya. Vihavya's son was Vitatya. Vitatya's son was Satya and Satya's son was Santa. Santa's son was the rishi Shravas and Shravas had a son named Tama. Tama had a son named Prakasha, who was supreme among brahmanas. Prakasha's son was Vagindra and he was supreme among victorious ones. His son was Pramati, accomplished in the Vedas and the Vedangas. Through Ghritachi, he had a son named Ruru.[1249] Through Pramadvara, Ruru had a son named Shunaka and he was a brahmana rishi. His son was Shounaka. O lord of men! O bull among kshatriyas! O Indra among kings! Thus, though he was a kshatriya, through Bhrigu's favours, Vitahavya became a brahmana. In that way, I have also described Gritsamada's lineage to you in detail. O great king! What else do you wish to ask?"'

Chapter 1713(32)

'Yudhishthira asked, "O bull among the Bharata lineage! Whom should men worship? Who should they bow down to? Tell me this in detail. I am not satisfied with what you have told me."

'Bhishma replied, "In this connection, an ancient history is recounted about a conversation between Narada and Vasudeva.

[1248]The text actually says Sucheta. This should be Suteja and we have corrected it.

[1249]Pramati had a son named Ruru. Ghritachi was an apsara.

On seeing that Narada had joined his hands in salutation and was worshipping bulls among the brahmanas, Keshava asked, 'O illustrious one! Whom are you bowing down to? Whom among these are you revering so much and bowing down to? O supreme among those who know dharma! If possible, I wish to hear this. Tell me.'

'"Narada replied, 'O Govinda! O scorcher of enemies! Listen to whom I am worshipping. Truly, with your exception, which other man in the world is capable of hearing this? O lord! I always worship and bow down before Varuna, Vayu, Aditya, Parjanya, Jataveda,[1250] Sthanu, Skanda, Lakshmi, Vishnu, brahmanas, Vachaspati,[1251] the moon, the water, the earth and Sarasvati. O one who should be revered! O tiger among the Vrishni lineage! I always worship those who are stores of austerities, those who know the Vedas and those who are always devoted to the Vedas. O lord! I bow down before those who perform the tasks of the gods without eating and without boasting about it and those who are content and full of forgiveness. O Yadava! I bow down before those who perform sacrifices well, those who are forgiving, self-controlled and in control of their senses and those who give away grain, riches, land and cattle. O Yadava! I bow down before those who perform austerities in the forest, surviving on roots and fruits, those who do not store anything and those who observe rites. O Yadava! I bow down before those who are fond of maintaining their servants, those who always love the act of tending to guests and those who only eat leftovers, after the gods have eaten. I always worship those who have become unassailable after learning the Vedas, eloquent ones who are knowledgable about the brahman and those who are always engaged in officiating at sacrifices and teaching. I worship those whose hearts are always pleasant towards all creatures and those who study until their backs are heated.[1252] O Yadava! I bow down before those who study by satisfying their preceptors, those who endeavour to be firm in their vows, those who serve and those are without malice. O Yadava! I bow down before

[1250]Agni.

[1251]The lord of speech.

[1252]They study despite their backs being heated by the sun.

sages who are excellent in their vows, brahmanas who are devoted to the truth and offer havya and kavya. O Yadava! I bow down before those who are devoted to subsistence through begging, those who are emaciated, those who live in the houses of their preceptors, those who do not pursue happiness and those who are without riches. There are men without a sense of ownership, without enemies, without shame,[1253] without requirements and without violence, devoted to the truth, self-controlled and devoted to tranquility. O Keshava! I bow down before them. There are those who are householders, devoted to worshipping gods and guests and following the conduct of pigeons.[1254] O Yadava! I always bow down before them. There are those who pursue the three objectives[1255] without deviating from them and are addicted to good conduct. I always bow down before them. In the three worlds, there are brahmanas who pursue the three objectives, without greed, and are devoted to auspicious conduct. O Keshava! I bow down before them. There are those who always subsist on water, air and milk, engaged in many kinds of vows. O Madhava! I bow down before them. I bow down before brahmanas who are celibate, those who aren't celibate but tend to the sacrificial fire, those who are the source of the brahman and those who are the refuge of all creatures. O Krishna! I always bow down before rishis who have created the worlds. They are the eldest in the worlds. Like the sun, they are the dispellers of the darkness of ignorance in the worlds. O Varshneya! Therefore, I always worship those brahmanas. O unblemished one! They confer happiness and deserve to be worshipped. You should also worship them. In this world and in the next, these people are the ones who grant happiness. If you revere them, they will also confer bliss on you. There are those who are always hospitable towards guests and tend to cattle and brahmanas. They are always devoted to the truth and succeed in crossing things that are difficult to traverse. They are always devoted to peace and

[1253]Without a false sense of shame.

[1254]Pigeons pick up grain from the ground. Like that, these people do not accumulate and survive on whatever is available.

[1255]Dharma, artha and kama.

are without malice. They are always devoted to studying and succeed in crossing things that are difficult to traverse. Those who bow down before all the gods, those who resort to even a single god and those who are faithful and controlled succeed in crossing things that are difficult to traverse. Those who bow down before the foremost of brahmanas, are careful in their vows and are addicted to giving succeed in crossing things that are difficult to traverse. Those who follow the rituals, kindle and maintain the sacrificial fire and offer oblations of soma into it succeed in crossing things that are difficult to traverse. O tiger among the Vrishni lineage! A person who is like you and always tends to his mother, his father and his preceptor properly, is always united with bliss. O Kounteya! Therefore, you should also properly tend to ancestors, gods and guests and worship them. You will then obtain a beneficial end.'"'

Chapter 1714(33)

'Yudhishthira asked, "O grandfather! What is the supreme task that has been recommended for a king? For both the worlds,[1256] what are the tasks a king should undertake?"

'Bhishma replied, "O descendant of the Bharata lineage! When a king has been instated, if he desires great happiness, he should worship brahmanas. Learned and aged brahmanas must always be worshipped. There will be extremely learned brahmanas who dwell in the city and in the countryside. They must be comforted, given their shares, revered and worshipped. A king must always look towards this as his supreme task. He must protect them, just as he protects his own self or his sons. When they honour him, he must firmly honour them back. When they are at peace, the kingdom is radiant in every possible way. They must he honoured, revered and protected, like a father. The progress of the worlds depends on this, just as creatures

[1256] This world and the next.

depend on Vasava. They can burn everything down, without leaving any remnants, through their mantras and their energy. Their valour is based on truth and if enraged, they can perform fierce deeds. I do not see anything that can pacify them. When they are enraged, their sight can envelop the directions, like the flames of a forest conflagration. They are learned and courageous and possess excellent qualities. They are like the clear sky, or like pits hidden by grass.[1257] Some are fierce, while others are as mild as cotton. Some are extremely cunning, but others are extreme ascetics. While some are engaged in agriculture and animal husbandry, others earn a living through begging. Some may be thieves and resort to falsehood. Others may be actors and dancers. They are seen to be engaged in all kinds of tasks, superior and inferior. O bull among the Bharata lineage! Brahmanas follow many diverse kinds of conduct. They are engaged in many kinds of tasks. They earn a living through diverse kinds of occupations. Some among them are virtuous and knowledgable about dharma and are always praised. O lord of men! Such immensely fortunate brahmanas officiate as priests for the ancestors, gods, men, serpents and rakshasas. Gods, ancestors, gandharvas, rakshasas, asuras and pishachas are incapable of vanquishing these brahmanas. They can grant divinity to someone who is not divine. They can take away divinity from someone who is divine. If they wish, they can make someone a king. If they dislike someone, they can destroy him. They are skilled in understanding praise and censure and can cause fame and ill repute to people. O king! If inadvertently, a person slanders brahmanas, brahmanas always become enraged with someone who hates them. If brahmanas praise a person, he prospers. If brahmanas censure a person, he is instantly defeated. It is because there are no brahmanas among them that Shakas, Yavanas, Kambojas and other similar kshatriya tribes are regarded as the equals of vrishalas. It is because there are no brahmanas among them that Dramilas, Kalingas, Pulindas, Ushinaras, Kolas, Sarpas, Mahishakas and other similar kshatriya tribes are regarded as the equals of vrishalas. O supreme among victorious ones! It is better to be defeated by them than to

[1257]There qualities cannot be immediately discerned.

defeat them. There is no sin as serious as that of killing a brahmana. The supreme rishis have said that killing a brahmana is a great sin. One must never hear slander about brahmanas. When such words are spoken, one must be silent, with a downcast face. Alternatively, one must arise and walk away. On this earth, there is no one who has been born, or will be born, who can spend a life of happiness after opposing brahmanas. It is impossible to grasp the wind with one's hands. It is impossible to touch the moon with one's hands. It is impossible to hold up the earth on one's head. In this world, it is impossible to vanquish brahmanas."'

Chapter 1715(34)

'Bhishma said, "Brahmanas must always be worshipped reverentially. With Soma as their king, they are the lords of happiness and unhappiness. Just as a king worships and protects his ancestors, they must always be worshipped and revered and offered objects of pleasure, ornaments and whatever else they wish for. The tranquility of the kingdom flows from them, just as all creatures flow from Vasava. Let pure brahmanas, as radiant as the brahman, be born in the kingdom. Maharatha kings,[1258] those who can scorch enemies, are also desired. There may be a brahmana who has been born in a noble lineage, knows about dharma and is rigid in his vows. O king! There is nothing superior to making him dwell in your house. Offerings made to brahmanas are received by the gods. They are the forefathers of all creatures and there is nothing that is superior to them. Aditya, the moon, Vayu, the earth, the water, the sky and the directions—all these enter the body of a brahmana and consume whatever food he eats. When a brahmana does not eat, the ancestors do not consume. When a wicked person hates brahmanas, the gods do not eat with him. When brahmanas are satisfied, the

[1258] Meaning kshatriyas.

ancestors are always delighted. O king! That is the way with gods too and there is no need to think about this. Therefore, when they[1259] are given offerings, the givers are themselves gratified. After death, they aren't destroyed and go to the ultimate destination. Whatever be the proportion in which a man gives offerings to brahmanas, in that proportion, the ancestors and the gods are delighted. All the subjects have originated from brahmanas. They are the origin and after death, they are also the destination. Brahmanas know about the paths to heaven and hell, about both what has happened and about what will occur. They are supreme among bipeds. O foremost among the Bharata lineage! Through his intelligence, a brahmana knows his own dharma. A person who follows them is never defeated. Nor does such a person confront destruction and defeat after death. Great-souled ones who have cleansed their souls and accept the words that issue out of the mouths of brahmanas are never defeated. Kshatriyas scorch through their energy and strength, but are pacified by the energy and strength of brahmanas. The Bhrigus defeated the Talajanghas.[1260] The son of Angiras defeated the Nipas.[1261] O bull among the Bharata lineage! Bharadvaja defeated the Vitahavyas and the Ailas. All these warriors were colourful in fighting. However, those with standards made out of black antelope skins[1262] vanquished them. They are capable of flinging away their water pots, crossing over and striking.[1263] In this world, everything that has been heard of or seen is latent within brahmanas, like a fire concealed inside wood. O bull among the Bharata lineage! In this connection, an ancient history is recounted about a conversation between Vasudeva and the earth.

[1259]Brahmanas.

[1260]This is a reference to Parashurama killing Kartavirya Arjuna.

[1261]The Nipas were a mountainous kingdom. Brahmadatta was the son of Nipa and this may mean the defeat of Brahmadatta by Ayasya, the son of Angiras. Alternatively, there was a king named Nipa in the Bharata lineage too and Parikshit was cursed by a sage who was descended from the Angiras lineage.

[1262]Brahmanas.

[1263]Acting like a kshatriya. This half of the shloka is not very clear and we have taken liberties.

'"Vasudeva asked, 'O mother of all creatures! O beautiful one! I am asking you about a doubt. If a man is a householder, through which acts can be cleanse his sins?'

'"The earth replied, 'The best method of purification is to serve brahmanas. Through serving brahmanas, all kinds of dirt are destroyed. This is the source of prosperity. This is the source of fame. Intelligence is generated by this. This grants superiority over another and is better than the best. If a man is praised by brahmanas, he prospers. If a man slanders brahmanas, he is soon defeated. Just as a lump of earth flung into the great ocean is destroyed, in that way, a performer of wicked deeds faces destruction. Behold the dark marks on the moon and the saline water in the ocean. The great Indra was also marked with the signs of one thousand vaginas. It was through their powers that these were converted into one thousand eyes and Shatakratu obtained peace.[1264] O Madhava! They are like that. O Madhusudana! A man who desires prosperity and fame and the worlds, follow brahmanas and purifies his soul.'"

'Bhishma continued, "Hearing the earth's words, Madhusudana applauded them. Having heard them, he worshipped the earth. O Partha! Since you have heard this, try to always worship the bulls among brahmanas. That is the way you will obtain benefit."'

Chapter 1716(35)

'Bhishma said, "If one is born as a brahmana, one is immensely fortunate. One is revered by all creatures and if one is a guest, one gets to eat first. O son! Brahmanas are well-wishers towards everyone. They have excellent minds and mouths. When they are worshipped, they pronounce auspicious words of benediction. O son!

[1264]Daksha cursed the moon. The sage Koushika cursed the ocean that its water would become salty. The sage Goutama cursed Indra and later changed the one thousand vaginas into one thousand eyes.

There may be those who hate brahmanas and disrespect their birth. When they are not properly worshipped, let them pronounce terrible curses on these. Those who know about the ancient accounts recount a hymn that was sung by Brahma. In ancient times, having created brahmanas, the creator ordained their tasks. 'He[1265] should never do something that has not been properly laid down for him. When they are protected, brahmanas protect. They are the best ornament of any habitation. When a brahmana undertakes his own tasks, there is prosperity. They set the standards for all beings and also restrain them along their paths. A learned brahmana must never undertake tasks recommended for a shudra. If he performs tasks recommended for a shudra, dharma is obstructed. Through studying, he obtains prosperity, intelligence, energy, powers, influence and unadulterated greatness. By offering oblations, they are established in great fortune. Prosperous brahmanas have been thought of as those who deserve to eat even before expectant mothers. If such a person has great faith, is without violence and without greed and is devoted to self-control and studying, he obtains all the objects of desire. Through their austerities, knowledge and humility, they can be successful in obtaining everything that exists in the world of men and gods.' O unblemished one! I have thus recounted to you what Brahma chanted. Out of compassion towards brahmanas, the intelligent one himself stated this. I think that the strength of those who are ascetics is equal to that of those who are kings. They are impossible to assail, fierce, proud and swift in action. There are some virtuous ones who are as spirited as lions. There are others who are as spirited as tigers. There are some who are as spirited as boars or deer. Others are as spirited as elephants. There are some who are as mild as cotton. Others are like *makara*s to the touch. There are some who can destroy those who speak against them. Others can slay with their sight. There are virtuous ones who are like the poison of serpents. But there are also virtuous ones who are mild. O Yudhishthira! Many kinds of conduct are followed by brahmanas. Because there are no brahmanas among

[1265] A brahmana.

them, Mekalas, Dramidas, Kashas, Poundras, Kollagiras, Shoundikas, Daradas, Darvas, Chouras, Shabaras, Barbaras, Kiratas, Yavanas and many other tribes of kshatriyas have been reduced to the status of vrishalas. Having been defeated by brahmanas, asuras had to resort to the depths of the ocean. It is through the favours of brahmanas that gods got to reside in heaven. One is incapable of touching the sky. The Himalaya mountains are incapable of moving. A bridge cannot be constructed over the Ganga. On earth, brahmanas are incapable of being defeated. If one acts counter to brahmanas, one is incapable of ruling the earth. Great-souled brahmanas are like gods among the gods. If you desire to enjoy this entire earth, right up to the girdle of the ocean, always worship them through gifts and servitude. O unblemished one! When they receive gifts, the energy of brahmanas is pacified. O unblemished one! If you wish to protect yourself, do not engage with those who do not receive."'

Chapter 1717(36)

'Bhishma said, "O Yudhishthira! In this connection, an ancient history is recounted, about a conversation between Shakra and Shambara. Listen. Shakra assumed the disguise of an ascetic with matted hair, smeared with dust all over his body. In that distorted form, he presented himself before Shambara and asked, 'O Shambara! What is the conduct through which you have come to be regarded as the foremost one among your relatives? I am asking you. Tell me that.'

'"Shambara replied, 'I never censure brahmanas and Brahma, the grandfather. When brahmanas recite from the sacred texts, I cheerfully honour them. I do not ignore what I have heard, nor do I ever find fault with it. Having grasped the feet of those intelligent ones, I worship and then question them. Since they are always assured by me, they speak to me trustfully. Even if they are distracted, I am attentive. When they are asleep, I am awake. Without any malice, I follow the path indicated by the sacred texts. Like bees use honey in a hive, these brahmanas sprinkle me with knowledge from the sacred texts. I satisfy them and use my intelligence to accept whatever they say. Meditating with my soul, I always think of myself as inferior. I am like one who is licking the juices at the tip of their tongues. That is how I am established amidst my kin, like the moon among nakshatras. The sacred texts that emanate from the mouths of brahmanas are like amrita on earth. If one acts in accordance with this, one obtains supreme benefit. Thus, in ancient times, my father was delighted and amazed to see that this was being used in a battle between the gods and the asuras in ancient times.[1266] On witnessing the greatness of the great-souled brahmanas, my father asked the moon, "How do they become successful?"

"'Soma said, "All the brahmanas become successful through their austerities. Their strength always lies in speech, just as that of kings lies in the valour of their arms. For brahmanas, words are weapons. Wherever he dwells, he should study. If he lives in a place that is extremely difficult to reside in, he must tend to the fire. He must be without anger and without pride. He must be an ascetic who looks upon everything equally. If he is born in a superior lineage, he must dwell in his father's house and study all the Vedas. He must not boast about this learning. Know that this is the sign of an ordinary person. Just as a snake is swallowed up by a hole in the ground, a king who is unwilling to fight and a brahmana who does not dwell far away[1267] are both swallowed. Great insolence destroys prosperity for men who are limited in intelligence. A maiden who conceives is tainted and this is also true of a brahmana who resides at home."'

'"Shambara continued, 'My father heard these extraordinary instructions from Soma. He followed the great vow of worshipping brahmanas and so do I.'"

[1266]Since there was more than one Shambara, it is not obvious which one is meant. The idea clearly is that, in the war, Brihaspati helped the gods and Shukracharya helped the demons.

[1267]Away from home, to study. With the exception of those born in noble lineages, all other brahmanas should go to the houses of their preceptors to study.

'Bhishma said, "On hearing the words that had emanated from the mouth of the Indra among the danavas, Shakra worshipped brahmanas and became the great Indra."'

Chapter 1718(37)

'Yudhishthira asked, "O grandfather! Who is the best recipient for a gift—a stranger, a person with whom one has lived for a long time, or a guest who has come from a long distance away?"

'Bhishma replied, "People follow diverse rites and excellent vows. Everything should be given to whoever asks. However, we have heard that donations that make the various categories of servants suffer must not be undertaken. If the various categories of servants suffer, one's own self suffers. The learned know that all these are proper recipients—a stranger, a person with whom one has lived for a long time, or a guest who has come from a long distance away."

'Yudhishthira said, "One must not give by making the servants suffer or by causing violence to dharma. We must also ascertain the nature of the recipient, so that we do not suffer from the act of giving."

'Bhishma said, "If the officiating priest, the priest, the preceptor, the disciple, matrimonial allies and relatives possess learning and lack tendencies of causing injury, they must all be honoured and worshipped. All those who do not possess these traits do not deserve to be treated virtuously. Therefore, one must always attentively examine men. O descendant of the Bharata lineage! Lack of anger, truthfulness in speech, lack of injury, self-control, uprightness, lack of hatred, lack of excessive pride, modesty, patience, austerities, tranquility and lack of improper deeds—if these signs are seen in a person, he is a deserving recipient and must be honoured. Whether it is someone with whom one has dwelt for a long time, or whether it is someone one has just met, whether it is a stranger or someone one knows, if these signs are present, he is a deserving recipient and must be honoured. A person who questions the proof of the Vedas and transgresses the sacred texts, or a person who questions the ordinances in every way, destroys his own self. O son! There may be a brahmana who thinks himself to be learned but censures the Vedas, who is addicted to the futile knowledge of argumentation and scrutinizes everything in detail, who questions the reasons behind everything and seeks to be triumphant over those who cite reasons, who always speaks against brahmanas and talks too much, who is suspicious of everyone, childish and harsh in speech—the learned know such a man to be the equal of a dog. He barks like a dog, always seeking to bite. The purpose of such speech is to destroy all the sacred texts. Such people are limited in learning and are inferior in arguments. When they are asked, they are seen to be lacking in learning. They may exhibit the signs of knowledge, but they are engaged in detecting weaknesses in those who are learned about shruti, smriti, itihasa, Puranas and the *Aranyaka*s. However, there are also acts that lead to the progress of the worlds and do not cause damage to dharma or one's own self—men who engage in these, obtain prosperity for eternity. The rishis have said that debts to gods, rishis, ancestors, brahmanas and guests, as the fifth, must be repaid.[1268] In due order, if a householder purifies himself and undertakes these tasks that have been laid down, then, his dharma does not suffer."'

Chapter 1719(38)

'Yudhishthira said, "O supreme among the Bharata lineage! I wish to hear about the character of women. O grandfather! Women are the root of all sins and their intelligence is fickle."

'Bhishma replied, "In this connection, an ancient history is recounted about a conversation between Narada and the courtesan

[1268]Debts to gods are paid through sacrifices, to rishis through studying, to ancestors through offspring, to brahmanas through gifts and to guests through hospitality.

Panchachuda. In ancient times, the intelligent devarshi Narada was roaming through the worlds. In Brahma's region, he saw the unblemished apsara, Panchachuda. On seeing all her beautiful limbs, the sage asked the apsara, 'O one with the excellent waist! There is a doubt in my heart. Tell me.' Having been thus addressed, she told the brahmana Narada, 'If you think that I am capable, tell me what the subject is.'

'"Narada said, 'O fortunate one! I will never ask you to do something that you are incapable of. O one with the beautiful face! I wish to hear the truth about the character of women.'"

'Bhishma continued, "On hearing the words of the devarshi, the supreme among apsaras replied, 'Since I am a woman, I am incapable of criticizing women. You know about women and their nature. O devarshi! You should not ask me to answer such a question.' The devarshi said, 'O one with the excellent waist! You have spoken the truth. However, lying is a sin. There is no sin in speaking the truth.' Having been thus addressed, the one with the beautiful smiles made up her mind. She truthfully spoke about the eternal vices of women.

'"Panchachuda said, 'O Narada! Even if a woman belongs to a noble lineage, is beautiful and has a protector, she doesn't follow the restraints. That is a fault among women. There is nothing more evil than women. Women are the root of all sins. You yourself know this. There may be a husband who is famous, prosperous, handsome and obedient. Even then, a woman waits to disregard him. O lord! We women are prone to wickedness and adharma. We abandon our shame and are attracted to evil men. Women like those who approach, desire and serve them. They aren't concerned about not following the restraints. Out of fear of relatives, or injury caused to people, women aren't constrained to follow restraints and stick by their husbands. Women do not find anyone unapproachable, nor do they care about age. They enjoy men, regardless of whether they are handsome or ugly. Because of fear, compassion, riches, kin, family and alliances, women never remain with their husbands. Women of good families also envy independent women who are young and wear beautiful ornaments and garments. There may be beloved wives who are protected and always greatly respected. Even they are attracted to those who are hunchbacked, blind, dumb and dwarves. O devarshi! They are attracted to the disabled and other ugly men. O great sage! There is no one in this world whom women regard as unapproachable. O brahmana! If a man can be obtained in any way, a woman never remains with her husband. If a woman is restrained and protects herself, that is because a man cannot be obtained, out of fear of relatives, or out of fear of being killed or imprisoned. Their nature is fickle. They are difficult to please and difficult to understand. Women are like words spoken by the wise.[1269] Wood never satisfies a fire. The great ocean is never satisfied by rivers. Yama is not satisfied with all creatures. The fair-eyed ones are never satisfied with men. O devarshi! I think that this is a mystery about all women. As soon as she sees a man, a woman's vagina is moistened. Even the best of women are not satisfied with husbands who give them everything that they wish, do whatever they desire and protect them. A woman does not attach as much importance to objects of pleasure, many ornaments and large stores of possessions as she does to the prospect of sexual intercourse. The destroyer, destruction, death, the nether regions, the subterranean fire, the sharpness of a razor, the poison of a snake and the fire—all these collectively exist in a woman. The creator ordained the worlds and the five great elements originated with him. O Narada! When men and women were created, these are the sins that were implanted in women.''''

Chapter 1720(39)

'Yudhishthira said, "In this world, men are extremely attracted to women. O king! They are overcome by great confusion and think that this is because of destiny. In this world, it can be distinctly seen that women are also attracted to men. O descendant of the Kuru lineage! Therefore, a great doubt is circling around in my heart. Why

[1269]In the sense of being difficult to understand.

are men attracted to women? Which are the men who attract and repel women? O tiger among men! How is one capable of protecting them? You should tell me about women and men. They seem to be full of illusion and deceive men. If a man falls into their hands, how can he escape? Like a cow searching out new grass, they seem to seize upon newer and newer men. The learned say that Shambara's maya, Namuchi's maya and that of Bali and Kumbhinasa, all of that exists in a woman. When a man laughs, they laugh.[1270] When a man cries, they weep. By chance, even if a disagreeable person arrives at the house, they greet him with pleasant words. The intelligence of a woman is superior to the sacred texts that Ushanas and Brihaspati know. That being the case, how can men protect themselves? They present falsehood as truth and truth as falsehood. O brave one! That being the case, how can men protect themselves? O slayer of enemies! The purport of the sacred texts seems to have been derived from the essence of feminine intelligence. I think that Brihaspati and others derived their norms of good conduct on that basis. When they are worshipped by men, they turn their minds away from men. O king! Women also agitate the minds of men. How can one protect oneself? I have a great doubt on this score. O mighty-armed one! O extender of the Kuru lineage! Tell me about this. O best among the Kuru lineage! If it is possible, how does one protect oneself against them? How does one do this? Has anyone managed to do this earlier? You should explain this to me."'

Chapter 1721(40)

'Bhishma said, "O mighty-armed one! It is exactly like that. O Kouravya! O lord of men! There is no falsehood in what you have said about women. In this connection, there is an ancient

[1270]The subject is suppressed in the text. We have expanded it, so that the meaning becomes clear.

history about how, earlier, the great-souled Vipula was able to ensure protection. O bull among the Bharata lineage! O son! O lord of the earth! I will also tell you the truth about how and why women were created by Brahma. O son! There is no one who is more evil than women. O lord! A woman is the flame of a fire. She is Maya's maya.[1271] She is the sharp edge of a razor. She is the poison of a snake. A woman is all these, and death, come together. O mighty-armed one! We have heard that these subjects were once devoted to dharma. They themselves obtained divinity. The gods were alarmed at this. O scorcher of enemies! The gods went and met the grandfather. They told him what was in their minds. They stood there silently, with downcast faces. The grandfather discerned what was in the hearts of the gods. For the sake of confusing men, the lord created women. O Kounteya! In an earlier creation, all the women were virtuous. In this creation, Prajapati created those who were wicked. The grandfather gave them desire and, driven by desire, they started to pursue each other. Driven by desire and greed, women tormented the men. The lord, the lord of the gods, also created anger as an aide of desire. Under the subjugation of desire and, anger, all the subjects were submerged. There is no special act of dharma that has been laid down for women. The sacred texts say that they are without senses and without mantras and are prone to falsehood.[1272] Prajapati gave women beds, seats, ornaments, food, drink, ignoble behaviour, immoderation in speech and addiction to desire. Men are incapable of ever restraining them. O son! Even the creator of the universe is incapable of doing that, how can men do it? Words, the prospect of being killed, imprisonment and many kinds of hardships are incapable of keeping women within bounds. They are always without restraints.

'"O tiger among men! However, earlier, I have also heard how, in ancient times, Vipula was able to restrain his preceptor's wife. There was an immensely fortunate and famous rishi by the name of Devasharma. His wife was named Ruchi and her beauty was

[1271]Maya is the architect of the demons.

[1272]They have no rites to follow, including the restraint of the senses.

unmatched on earth. O Indra among kings! All the gods, gandharvas and danavas were attracted to her beauty, in particular, the slayer of Vritra and Paka. The great sage, Devasharma, knew about feminine nature. As best as he could, to the best of his ability, he sought to protect his wife. He knew that Purandara coveted other people's wives. That is the reason he made efforts to protect his wife. O son! On one occasion, the rishi made up his mind to undertake a sacrifice. He began to think about how his wife's protection might be ensured. The immensely ascetic one thought and thought about a method for protection. He summoned his beloved disciple, Vipula, who was from the Bhargava lineage. 'O son! I will depart to undertake a sacrifice. The lord of the gods has always desired Ruchi. You must protect her, to the best of your ability. Be attentive and always watch out for Purandara. O extender of the Bhrigu lineage! He can assume many different kinds of forms.' O king! The ascetic, Vipula, controlled in his senses and always fierce in his austerities, with a resplendence that was like the fire and the sun, was thus addressed. He was knowledgable about dharma and truthful in speech. He signified his assent. O great king! As his preceptor was about to leave, he again asked him, 'O sage! What are the forms in which Shakra appears? What kind of body and energy does he assume? You should explain this to me.' O descendant of the Bharata lineage! The illustrious one described the truth about Shakra's maya to the great-souled Vipula. 'O brahmana rishi! The slayer of Bala and chastiser of Paka has many kinds of maya. Repeatedly, he assumes all these diverse forms. He sports a diadem and wields a vajra or bow. Or he may wear a crown and adorn himself with earrings. In a short instant, he may assume a form like that of a chandala. O son! Yet again, he may have a crest and matted locks and attire himself in rags. His body may be large and thick, or it can again become thin. He can also assume compexions that are fair, dusky or dark. He may be ugly or handsome, young or old. He can be wise, stupid, dumb, short or tall. Shatakratu can appear like a brahmana, a kshatriya, a vaishya or a shudra. He can belong to a superior varna, or an inferior one. He may appear in the form of a parrot or a crow, or in the form of a swan or a cuckoo. He can also assume the form of a lion, a tiger or an elephant. He can appear as a god, a daitya or a king. He may seem to be extremely thin, as if the wind can break down his limbs. He can also appear like a malformed bird. Sometimes, he assumes many forms which are those of quadrupeds. He may also seem to be foolish. He can assume the form of a fly or a mosquito. O Vipula! One is incapable of comprehending the form that he has assumed. O son! The creator of the universe, the one who has created this entire world, cannot understand it. Shakra can also disappear and only be seen with the sight of knowledge. The king of the gods can also transform himself into the form of the wind. O Vipula! Therefore, you must make great efforts in protecting the one with the slender waist. O supreme among the Bhrigu lineage! You must ensure that Indra of the gods does not molest Ruchi. That would be like sacrificial oblations being licked by an evil-minded dog.' Having said this, the sage departed, to undertake the sacrifice. O supreme among the Bharata lineage! The immensely fortunate Devasharma went away.

'"Hearing his preceptor's words, Vipula began to think. 'I will make supreme efforts to protect her from the immensely strong king of the gods. But what can I possibly do to protect my preceptor's wife? Indra of the gods is well versed in maya. He is valiant and unassailable. What efforts will I make to protect her from the chastiser of Paka? He can assume many kinds of forms and enter this cottage. Shakra is capable of assuming the form of the wind to molest my preceptor's wife. Therefore, the best thing I can do now is to penetrate Ruchi's body. In that way, I can protect her through my manliness. The illustrious Harivahana is capable of deception through his many disguises. I will use the strength of my yoga to protect her from the chastiser of Paka. I will penetrate her body with my body and protect her. My preceptor will return and see that his wife, Ruchi, has been defiled. There is no doubt that he will curse me in rage. The great ascetic possesses divine sight. But this lady cannot be protected through techniques adopted by other men. Indra of the gods has the power of maya and I am confronted with a dilemma. I must certainly obey my preceptor's instructions. If I am able to protect her, that will be extraordinary. I will use yoga to penetrate the body of my preceptor's wife. She will be free from taint and no sin will attach to me. On his journey, a traveller seeks shelter in a deserted house. In that way, I will reside in the body of my preceptor's wife. A drop of water moves, but does not touch the lotus leaf that it is on. In that way, I will dwell inside the body, detached.' Knowing everything about the Vedas, this is the way he looked at dharma. Vipula considered his own austerities and those of his preceptor. Having made up his mind, Bhargava resorted to this technique of protection. O king! He made great efforts. Listen. The great ascetic, Vipula, seated himself near his preceptor's wife. When the one with the unblemished limbs was also seated, he distracted her by telling her stories. He fixed his eyes on her eyes and the vision that emerged from him on her vision. Vipula entered her body, like the wind entering the sky. His attributes mixed with her attributes. His face merged into her face. Like an immobile shadow, the sage remained inside her. Vipula numbed the body of his preceptor's wife. He resided there and protected her and she herself didn't get to know. O king! He continued to do this until his great-souled preceptor returned to his house. He protected her for the duration that the sacrifice took."'

Chapter 1722(41)

'Bhishma said, "One day, Indra of the gods assumed a divine form. Sensing an opportunity, he arrived at the hermitage. O lord of men! He assumed a form that was attractive and handsome and in that disguise, he entered the hermitage. He saw that Vipula's body was seated immobile. His eyes were visionless, as if he was a portrait. Ruchi was beautiful in her limbs. Her hips and breasts were full. Her eyes were as large as lotus petals. Her face was like the full moon. She was also seated. On seeing him, she wished to stand up. She was astounded at his form and wished to ask him who he was. O Indra among men! But though she wished to rise, she was restrained by Vipula, who was inside her. She was incapable of movement. In extremely sweet and gentle words, Indra of the gods addressed her. 'O one with the beautiful smiles! Know that I am Indra of the gods and I have come here for you. I am afflicted by the god of love and desire you. O one with the beautiful brows! Therefore, accept me. A long period of time has already elapsed.'[1273] The sage, Vipula, heard Shakra's words. From inside the body of his preceptor's wife, he saw the lord of the gods. O king! However, the unblemished one was incapable of rising. O king! Since Vipula had penetrated her, she was also incapable of speaking. Through the signs, the extender of the Bhrigu lineage understood what his preceptor's wife intended.[1274] O lord! Using his powers of yoga, the immensely energetic one restrained her. Using the bonds of yoga, he tied down all her senses.

'"Seeing that she was indifferent, Shachi's consort addressed her again. O king! Restrained by the strength of yoga, she was ashamed that she couldn't speak. She wished to reply, 'Come to me. Welcome.' However, Vipula restrained the words his preceptor's wife desired to speak. Instead, the words that emerged were, 'Hello. Why have you come here?' From a mouth that was as beautiful as the moon, these refined words emerged.[1275] Under someone else's subjugation, she shame-facedly spoke these words. Purandara was terrified at this and became distracted. O lord of the earth! The king of the gods glanced at her again. The one with the one thousand eyes glanced at her with his divine sight. He thus saw the sage inside her body. Inside the body of the preceptor's wife, he was like an image in a mirror. Purandara saw that he was terrible in his austerities. O lord! Scared of being cursed, he trembled. The immensely great ascetic, Vipula, released his preceptor's wife. He entered his own body and addressed the terrified Shakra. 'O Purandara! You have not conquered your senses. You are wicked in your soul. Gods and men will not worship you for long. O Shakra! Have you forgotten? Is that incident no longer in your mind? You

[1273]Since Devasharma's departure.

[1274]That she was kindly disposed towards Indra.

[1275]Refined words probably means Sanskrit, the implication being that women didn't customarily speak in Sanskrit.

were marked with the signs of vaginas and freed from those because of Goutama. I know that you are foolish in understanding and that you have not cleansed your soul. You are fickle. O stupid one! She is protected by me. O wicked one! Go wherever you have come from. O foolish one! If you do not, I will instantly burn you down with my own energy. O Vasava! It is only out of pity towards you that I am not burning you down. O evil-minded one! My preceptor is intelligent and terrible in his austerities. If he sees you, his eyes will blaze in rage and he will burn you down. O Shakra! Never again, should you disrespect brahmanas in this way. If you do not depart, through the power of brahmanas, your sons and your advisers will be destroyed. You think yourself to be immortal and conduct yourself in this way. But that is not true and there is nothing that cannot be obtained through austerities.' Hearing the great-souled Vipula's words, Shakra did not say anything in reply. Overcome by shame, he disappeared.

'"Soon after Shakra had departed, the great ascetic, Devasharma, returned to his hermitage, having completed the sacrifice he had desired to undertake. O king! Vipula was engaged in doing what brought his preceptor pleasure. As soon as he returned, he handed over his preceptor's unblemished wife, whom he had protected, to him. Devoted to his preceptor and tranquil in his soul, he greeted his preceptor. Without any fear, Vipula greeted him and stood there. When he had rested and was seated with his wife, Vipula told him what Shakra had done. Hearing Vipula's words, the powerful sage was satisfied with his good conduct, austerities and control. The lord saw the Vipula was devoted to his preceptor and was virtuous. On seeing that he was devoted to dharma, he uttered words of praise. The one with dharma in his soul applauded his disciple, who was devoted to dharma. He wished to grant a boon to the one who was devoted to his preceptor. Having obtained his preceptor's permission, he asked that he might be able to perform supreme austerities. From that day, Devasharma, the great ascetic, dwelt there with his wife. In that desolate forest, he no longer had any fear from the slayer of Bala and Vritra."'

Chapter 1723(42)

'Bhishma said, "Having acted in accordance with his preceptor's words, Vipula performed terrible austerities. The valiant one thought that he had accomplished a lot of austerities. O lord of the earth! He rivalled the entire earth in these deeds. He roamed around without any fear. Amongst men, he was regarded as one who had obtained great fame. O Kourvya! The lord Vipula thought that he had conquered both the worlds because of his deeds and austerities. O descendant of the Kuru lineage! After some time had passed, an occasion arose when gifts of riches and grain were to be made to Ruchi's sister. At that time, a celestial damsel was travelling through the sky. Her dazzling beauty was supreme. From her body, some flowers fell down on the ground, not very far from the hermitage. O descendant of the Bharata lineage! Their fragrance was divine. O king! Ruchi, the one with the beautiful eyes, picked them up. Soon, an invitation arrived from the kingdom of Anga. O son! Her elder sister, named Prabhavati, was the wife of the king of Anga, Chitraratha. The beautiful one braided those flowers in her hair. To honour the invitation, Ruchi went to the house of the king of Anga. On seeing those flowers, the queen of the kingdom of Anga, possessing beautiful eyes, asked her sister to get some flowers for her. Ruchi, with the extremely beautiful face, told her husband everything about this. She told the rishi everything that her sister had said.

'"The great ascetic, Devasharma, summoned Vipula. O descendant of the Bharata lineage! He instructed him to go in search of the flowers. Without any hesitation, the great ascetic, Vipula, accepted his preceptor's command. O king! He agreed and went to the spot and the region where those had fallen down from the sky. He saw some other flowers lying there and they were still not faded. He took those divine and beautiful flowers, which were divine in scent. O descendant of the Bharata lineage! He managed to get them because of his own austerities. Having obtained them, he was delighted at having been able to follow his preceptor's words. With that garland of champaka flowers, he quickly left for the city of Champa.[1276] O son! In a desolate forest, he saw a human couple. Holding each other's hands, they were dancing around in a circle. O king! One of them quickly advanced too far ahead and a quarrel ensued between them. One said, 'You moved too fast.' The other said, 'No.' O son! They disagreed and argued with each other. While they debated with each other, each one of them muttered an oath and in the words that each of them mentally spoke, each named Vipula. 'If I have spoken falsely, in the world after death, may I face the end that is destined for the brahmana Vipula.' Hearing this, Vipula's face became cheerless. 'I have undergone terrible austerities and find this difficult to accept. Why has this couple said that I will attain an evil end? Why have they said that my end will be the worst among all creatures?' O supreme among kings! Vipula thought along these lines. He bowed his head down and, distressed, began to think about any wicked deed that he might have committed. As he proceeded, he saw six men gambling with golden and silver dice, so excited that their body hair stood up. They also took oaths just like the ones the couple had uttered and mentioned Vipula in their words. 'If there is anyone among us, who is driven by avarice and plays unfairly, after death, may he obtain the kind of end that Vipula will get.' O Kouravya! Hearing this, Vipula began to think about everything that he had done since birth, but could not remember any transgression of dharma. O king! He was tormented, like a fire burning in the midst of another fire. Because of the curse he had heard, his mind burnt in grief. O son! While he proceeded, he thought about this for many days and nights. He then remembered the way he had protected Ruchi. 'I penetrated her vision with my vision and her face with my face. But I did not narrate the truth to my preceptor.' O Kouravya! This was the wicked deed that Vipula thought of. O immensely fortunate one! He thought that there was

[1276]Champaka is a fragrant flower. The city of Champa is in Chhattisgarh. But this Champa is Champapuri, the capital of Anga. The kingdom of Anga is now what is part of the states of Bihar, Jharkhand and West Bengal.

no doubt that this was the transgression. He went to the city of Champa and gave his preceptor the flowers. Loved by his preceptor, he followed the rites and worshipped his preceptor."'

Chapter 1724(43)

'Bhishma said, "O lord of men! On seeing that his disciple had returned, the immensely energetic Devasharma spoke these words to him. Listen.

'"Devasharma asked, 'O Vipula! What did you see in that great forest? They know about your accomplished soul and about Ruchi.'

'"Vipula said, 'O brahmana rishi! O lord! Who were the couple? Who were those men? They knew about me. You should tell me the truth about this.'

'"Devasharma replied, 'O brahmana! Know that the couple was night and day. Whirling around in a circular way, they knew the truth about your wicked deed. O brahmana! Know that the men who were cheerfully gambling with the dice were the seasons. They too knew about your wicked deed. No one should be comforted that his wicked deed will remain unknown. O brahmana! A man hides his wicked soul and his wicked deed. Even if a man performs a wicked deed secretly, the seasons, night and day are witness to this. They saw that you had not told your preceptor about your deed, but were nevertheless, cheerful. They thought that a learned person like you should be reminded of this. Day and night and the seasons always know the wicked deeds that a man undertakes, the auspicious, as well as the inauspicious deeds. You did not tell me the truth about what you had done, out of fear that you had committed a transgression. O brahmana! Knowing that you had not told me, they spoke to you about it, so that you did not go the worlds that are meant for wicked people. Having committed a deed, you did not tell me about it. O brahmana! You were capable of protecting a woman, whose nature is evil. You did not do anything to cause my displeasure and I am pleased with you. O supreme among brahmanas! Had I thought that you had committed a wicked deed, without thinking about it and in anger, I would have cursed you. Women have intercourse with men and men find this to be an excellent pursuit. However, your intention was to protect her. Otherwise, your end would have been as the recipient of a curse. O son! You protected her and this is known to me. O son! I am pleased with you. You will progress along a path that is comfortable.'"

'Bhishma said, "The great rishi, Devasharma, was pleased and spoke to Vipula in this way. With his wife and his disciple, he cheerfully ascended to heaven. O king! In ancient times, in the course of a conversation on the banks of the Ganga, the great sage, Markandeya, told me about this. O Partha! That is the reason I have said, women must be protected. Both types of women can always be seen, those who are virtuous and those who are evil. The ones who are virtuous are extremely fortunate and are revered as the mothers of the worlds. O king! They hold up this entire earth, with its forests and groves. The ones who are evil are wicked in conduct. Having determined to sin, they destroy the lineage. O king! They can be known through their wicked signs, naturally manifest on their bodies. It is in this fashion that great-souled ones are capable of protecting them. O tiger among kings! There is no other way in which one is capable of protecting women. O tiger among men! They are fierce. They are fierce in their valour. There is nothing that they love more than sexual intercourse with men. O bull among the Bharata lineage! Even when they have agreed to live with one person, they do not act in this way. O descendant of the Pandu lineage! They consort with other men. O lord of men! Men should not act out of affection towards them, nor should they be driven by jealousy. They should be enjoyed regretfully, because that is dharma. O descendant of the Kourava lineage! If a man acts in a contrary way, he will destroy himself. O tiger among men! In every kind of situation, logic is always honoured. That is the single method Vipula used to protect a woman. O king! In this world of men, there is no other way to protect women."'

Chapter 1725(44)

'Yudhishthira said, "O grandfather! Tell me the foundation of all dharma concerning offspring, the home, ancestors, gods and guests."

'Bhishma replied, "O lord of the earth! Those who have thought about dharma have expressed their views about all kinds of dharma associated with the bestowing of a maiden. O Yudhishthira! A virtuous brahmana who is always devoted to dharma bestows his daughter on an excellent groom, after ascertaining his good conduct, learning, birth and deeds. This kind of favourable bestowal is also the eternal dharma of virtuous kshatriyas and is known as a *brahma* form of marriage. O Yudhishthira! When one bestows one's daughter on someone she has herself chosen, ignoring one's own wishes, those who know about dharma speak of this as a gandharva kind of dharma.[1277] O king! When a lot of riches are used to tempt a girl's relatives and purchase her, the learned say that this is an asura kind of dharma. O son! When weeping relatives are slain and their heads severed and a weeping maiden is forcibly abducted from her house, that kind of dharma has the signs of rakshasa. O Yudhishthira! Of these five, three constitute dharma and two are adharma.[1278] The paishacha and asura forms should never be resorted to.[1279] O bull among the Bharata lineage! The brahma, *kshatra* and gandharva forms represent dharma.[1280]

[1277]That is, a gandharva marriage.

[1278]The numbering is a problem, the prajapatya form of marriage not having been mentioned. Had this been included, we would have had the number five and the three acceptable ones would have been brahma, gandharva and prajapatya. The two condemned ones are asura and rakshasa.

[1279]The paishacha form has not been mentioned earlier. This happens when a girl is seduced. If the paishacha is included in the list and prajapatya excluded, the permissible ones are brahma, gandharva and rakshasa. The condemned ones are asura and paishacha.

[1280]Since the kshatra form has not been mentioned earlier, there is another numbering anomaly. The kshatra form is presumably prajapatya. There is a lack of consistency with the eight kinds of marriages listed in the Dharmashastras.

There is no doubt that these should be resorted to, in pure or mixed form.[1281] A brahmana can have three wives, a kshatriya can have two wives. A vaishya should take one from his own varna. The children will be equal.[1282] The brahmana wife will be senior and the kshatriya wife for the kshatriya.[1283] There are people who say that a shudra wife can be accepted for intercourse, but others disagree. The virtuous do not praise the birth of offspring through shudras. If a brahmana has offspring through a shudra, penance is recommended. A man who is thirty years old should wed a girl who is ten years old, known as *nagnika*.[1284] Alternatively, a man who is twenty-one years old should wed a girl who is seven years old. O bull among the Bharata lineage! If a girl has a father, but does not have a brother, she should not be wed, since she might follow the dharma of a *putrika*. When a girl has attained puberty, one should wait for three years. In the fourth year, if she is still not married, she should look for a husband herself. O bull among the Bharata lineage! The offspring of such a girl are not tainted, nor is intercourse with her condemned. If she does not act in this way, Prajapati does not approve of her conduct. One should wed a girl who is not of the same pinda as the mother or the same gotra as the father.[1285] In this way, one follows the dharma that Manu spoke about."

'Yudhishthira said, "Some people offer a bride price and others speak of gifts. Some speak of their bravery, others exhibit their riches. O grandfather! Others accept the hand in marriage. Whom

[1281]Mixed means that a specific wedding can have elements of more than one kind of marriage.

[1282]In the case of more than one wife.

[1283]The three wives permitted for a brahmana might not be brahmana. In such cases, the brahmana wife will be senior. This is the logic for a kshatriya too.

[1284]Nagnika does not mean naked. It means a girl clad in a single piece of garment, that is, a girl who has not yet attained puberty.

[1285]Stated simply, same pinda means the wife should not be the offspring of someone who is related to the groom's mother, going up to three generations. Gotra is when there is a common and unbroken male line, going up to a common male ancestor.

does the maiden belong to?[1286] I wish to ask the truth about this. You are like my sight."

'Bhishma replied, "As long as men remain in their own station, whatever action they undertake is beneficial, regardless of whether it is with mantras or without mantras. However, a lie is a grave sin.[1287] Some people say that if a marriage takes place as the outcome of a falsehood, the wife, the offspring, the officiating priest, the preceptor, the disciple and the instructor, all of these deserve to be punished. But others do not agree. Manu does not approve of intercourse with a person one doesn't desire. This is against fame and against dharma. This is a falsehood that causes violence to dharma.[1288] O descendant of the Bharata lineage! Whether there was a promise to give following dharma, or whether the girl was purchased, in such an instance, there is certainly no sin if the promise to bestow is not adhered to. With the sanction of the relatives, mantras and offerings should be resorted to. Without mantras, an act of bestowal is never successful. When the relatives take a pledge to the accompaniment of mantras, the offspring that are obtained through such a wife are regarded as superior.[1289] It is the injunction of dharma that a husband must regard his wife as having been given to him by the gods. Whether she is a goddess or whether she is human, one must not reject someone who is the victim of a falsehood."[1290]

'Yudhishthira asked, "A bride price may have been obtained for a maiden. Thereafter, one may come across a superior groom. If the father looks at dharma, artha and kama, should he then make his

[1286]These shlokas are cryptic. What is probably meant is that different people might offer different things. But when does the actual act of marriage take place?

[1287]If there has been a promise that a maiden will be bestowed, then breach of contract is a grave sin.

[1288]With some subjectivity in interpretation, this seems to imply that a girl should not marry someone she does not like. Even if a promise has been made, and the girl does not like the groom, going back on the promise is not a sin.

[1289]This is the answer to Yudhishthira's original question. The mantras signify the act of marriage.

[1290]The wife may have gone back on a pledge made by her relatives, without asking her, to bestow her on someone.

words come false? In such instances, whatever one does seems to be inferior. In deciding on what is dharma for all of us, what are the views of those who have thought of dharma? I wish to ask you the truth about this. You are my vision. Therefore, tell me everything. I am not satisfied with what you have recounted."

'Bhishma replied, "One should not be firm in adhering to the bride price and the one who pays it, knows this.[1291] Virtuous ones never bestow their daughters on the basis of a bride price. Relatives desire a bride price only when the groom doesn't possess qualities. Many ornaments are willingly given. When these are given, that's not a price, nor is this a sale. Receiving objects in this way has been eternal dharma. Some say, 'I will bestow this maiden.' Other say nothing. Still others say, 'I will certainly bestow this maiden.' Whether it is said or not said, doesn't matter.[1292] Therefore, there is marriage only when they accept each other's hands. We have heard that earlier, this is the way the Maruts used to bestow their excellent daughters. The rishis have instructed that maidens should not be bestowed on those who are inappropriate. They are the foundation of desire and also the root of offspring. That is my view. Though the practice of purchase and sale of maidens has continued, on scrutiny, it is seen to be associated with many evils and cannot lead to marriage. Listen. Having defeated all the Magadhas, Kashis and Kosalas, I abducted two maidens for Vichitravirya.[1293] He accepted the hand of one, but not the other, because a bride price had been paid through the act of conquest. My father was of the view that even if her hand had been accepted, she should have been released.[1294] Kourava said that one should not marry this maiden. Since I doubted my father's

[1291]This probably means that the payment of a bride price is no guarantee that the maiden will be married to the giver.

[1292]These are references to the girl's father making promises, the point being that such promises don't amount to a marriage.

[1293]Ambika and Ambalika. This account of Vichitravirya marrying one, and not the other, has not been mentioned earlier.

[1294]Subsequent shlokas make it clear that by father, Bhishma means Bahlika, Shantanu's younger brother.

words, I went and asked others, thinking that my father was overly conscious about dharma. O king! Wishing to know the nature of good conduct, I also went to him and repeatedly addressed these words. 'I wish to know the truth about good conduct.' O great king! My father, Bahlika, supreme among the upholders of dharma, spoke to me in these words. 'The issue is whether marriage is contracted when a bride price is accepted, or when the hand is accepted. If one holds that one becomes a husband from the act of acceping a bride price, this is shameless behaviour. The ones who know about dharma have said that there is no such proof in the sacred texts. Marriage results from accepting the hand and not from accepting the bride price. It is known that which is important is the act of bestowal and not purchase and sale. People who respect purchase through a bride price are not those who know about dharma. One should not bestow to those, nor have marriages with their likes. A wife should never be bought or sold. People who think that she can be bought and sold, like a servant-girl, follow the conduct of those who are wicked in intelligence and avaricious.' In this connection, people had asked Satyavan about dharma. 'A person may have paid a bride price for a maiden. But the payer subsequently dies. Can someone else then accept the maiden's hand? We have a doubt on this score about dharma. O immensely wise one! You are revered by the wise. Please dispel our doubt about this. We are asking you about the truth. You are like our sight.' Satyavan spoke these words to all of them. 'She should be bestowed on someone desirable. One should not reflect about this. Since this is true even when the payer is alive, there is no scope for doubt when he is dead.' It is also held that if the girl is a virgin, she can torment herself through great austerities, or marry the husband's[1295] younger brother, follow him and have intercourse with him. Some have written in this way, others have voiced their views strongly. The learned have not spoken firmly about this. Even if all the prenuptial rites have been performed, with all the auspicious

[1295]This is not a continuation of the argument in the earlier sentence and refers to situations where a marriage has taken place.

mantras, there is no sin from uttering a falsehood.[1296] The act of accepting a hand in marriage concludes with the mantras uttered at the seventh step.[1297] The hand of the maiden is offered and accepted as a wife. A brother must give away that maiden and following the rites, there must be circumambulation around the fire. An excellent brahmana must not marry a maiden who is unwilling, or one who is not from a comparable family."'

Chapter 1726(45)

'Yudhishthira asked, "There may be a situation where a bride price has been given for a maiden, but the prospective husband no longer exists.[1298] O grandfather! What should be done then? Tell me that."

'Bhishma replied, "She must be maintained like a son, in case the husband returns. Alternatively, the bride price can be returned. If it is not returned, the maiden belongs to the one who has paid the price. Therefore, she is also capable of having offspring through means that have been sanctioned.[1299] However, no person can use mantras for this purpose.[1300] Instructed by her father, Savitri had herself done this.[1301] Some people who know about dharma have praised this, but not others. There are some who have not acted in this way. There are some who do not hold this to be virtuous. There are those who hold that the best sign of dharma is the conduct of the virtuous. About this kind of conduct, Sukratu spoke the following words. He was the grandson of the king of Videha, the great-souled

[1296]In the sense of going back on the promise to marry.

[1297]Seven steps are taken around the fire.

[1298]The prospective husband may have died, or simply gone away.

[1299]In certain situations, a wife was allowed to have progeny through others, not just her husband.

[1300]As long as she is married to another, she cannot be married again.

[1301]Instructed by her father, Ashvapati, Savitri chose her own husband, Satyavan.

Janaka. 'How can one praise conduct that is along a path followed by the wicked? There should be no questioning or doubt about the conduct of the virtuous. The dharma of the wicked is the confused dharma of asuras. We have not heard of anything like this in the lives of those who have come before us.' The relationship between a wife and a husband is not comparable to mere intercourse between a woman and a man. The latter is the ordinary dharma of desire. This is what that king[1302] said."

'Yudhishthira asked, "What are the rules whereby a man's riches are inherited? For a father's property, a daughter should be no different from a son."

'Bhishma replied, "The son is like one's own self and the daughter is like the son. As long as these offspring are alive, no one else should inherit the riches. Unmarried daughters have a share in their mother's *youtaka*.[1303] If a father dies without leaving any sons, then the daughter's son inherits the ancestral property. He is the one who offers the funeral cakes to both his father and his maternal grandfather. The sacred texts of dharma have said that there is no special difference between a son and a daughter's son. Even if offspring has been generated by someone else,[1304] he is said to be a son. There is no special difference between a son and a daughter's son who has been generated by someone else. However, in cases where a daughter has been sold by the father, I see no reason in dharma that allows a daughter's son to inherit. Such sons are malicious and addicted to adharma. They are deceitful and appropriate other people's possessions. They are the result of an asura form of marriage, a conduct that is contrary to the dictates of dharma. There are those who are knowledgable about the ancient accounts, devoted to dharma and the sacred texts of dharma, binding themselves down to the ordinances of dharma. They recount a chant that was sung by Yama. 'In a desire for riches, if a man sells his own son, or bestows

[1302]Sukratu.

[1303]Youtaka is exclusively the property of a woman. If consists of the dowry, gifts and property she has obtained at the time of marriage.

[1304]Other than the mother's husband.

his daughter through a bride price for the sake of earning a living, he has to progressively pass through seven terrible hells known as Kalasahvya. After death, he feeds on sweat, urine and excrement.' There is a form of marriage called arsha. In this, a cow and a bull are given and some rishis have spoken of this as a bride price. O king! But whether it is small or large, this[1305] should not be regarded as a sale. However, though some people act in this way, it should never be regarded as dharma. Other kinds of marriage are seen, indulged in by those who are greedy. There are some who bring maidens under their subjugation and enjoy them. These are evildoers and have to lie down in hell. A man must never be sold, not to speak of one's own offspring. If riches are obtained with adharma as a foundation, no artha can ever be gained from it."'

Chapter 1727(46)

'Bhishma said, "Those who know about the ancient accounts recite the words of Prachetas. 'Gifts given to relatives cannot be regarded as a sale. Anyone who is not cruel should receive a maiden and, in particular, show her honour by giving the girl gifts.' If they desire a great deal of welfare, the father, brothers, father-in-law and brothers-in-law should honour and sustain her in this way. If the wife does not appeal to a man or does not cause men pleasure, or if a man is not attracted to her, he should not have offspring. O lord of men! A wife must always be honoured and cherished. When women are not honoured, all the rites become unsuccessful. When daughters-in-law grieve, the family is destroyed. O king! When daughters-in-law curse a household, all the performed rites become undone. The houses do not dazzle and grow and their prosperity is destroyed. Before Manu ascended to heaven, he handed over women to men, since they were weak, lightly

[1305]Something that is a gift.

clad, kind and devoted to the truth.[1306] There are others who hold that they are jealous, desire honour, are fierce, lack affection and lack learning. However, women deserve to be honoured and men must show them respect. Dharma is in trusting women, not just in sex and pleasure. Tend to them, honour them and give them what they want. Behold. The generation of offspring, the nurturing of offspring and pleasure in the way of the world—all these are tied to women. By respecting and honouring them, one becomes successful in all the tasks. The daughter of the king of Videha sung a shloka. 'There are no sacrifices for women. There are no funeral ceremonies they have to observe. Their dharma is to serve their husbands and that is the way they conquer heaven. The father protects her when a child, the husband protects her in youth. The son protects her when she is aged. A woman does not deserve to be independent.' A person who desires affluence and prosperity must treat women well. O descendant of the Bharata lineage! Whether she is nurtured or oppressed, a woman is like Shri and this is therefore reflected in one's prosperity."'

Chapter 1728(47)

'Yudhishthira said, "You know the ordinances of all the sacred texts. You know the purport of the dharma of kings. You are famous on earth as someone who can dispel grave doubts. O grandfather! I have a doubt. Explain this to me. When we confront a difficulty, whom shall we ask, other than you? The task of men is to follow eternal dharma. O mighty-armed one! You should explain all of this. O grandfather! Four wives have been recommended for a brahmana—a brahmana, a kshatriya, a vaishya and a shudra, if one desires sexual gratification. O supreme among the Kuru lineage!

[1306]The text uses the word *svalpakoupina*, which translates as lightly clad. The suggestion is that women need to be protected, because they can be easily seduced.

Sons may be born through all of them. In due order, which of these deserves to inherit the father's property? O grandfather! Which of them obtains the father's riches? I wish to hear what has been said about their shares in the sacred texts."

'Bhishma replied, "O Yudhishthira! Brahmanas, kshatriyas and vaishyas—these are the three varnas that are born twice.[1307] It is recommended dharma that a brahmana should marry these. O scorcher of enemies! Through error, greed and desire, a brahmana may marry a shudra, but this is not sanctioned in the sacred texts. If a brahmana lies down in a shudra's bed, he will be afflicted. That is the reason rites of atonement have been laid down for situations like this. O Yudhishthira! If offspring results from this, the penance is doubled. O descendant of the Bharata lineage! I will now tell you about the rules for distributing riches. The son who is born through a brahmana mother will obtain the best auspicious bull and the best vehicle from his father's riches as his share. O Yudhishthira! What is left of the brahmana's property must then be divided into ten parts. From this, the son born through a brahmana mother will obtain four parts as his share of the father's riches. There is no doubt that the son who is born through a kshatriya mother has the same status as a brahmana. However, because the mother is different, he deserves to be given three parts. Though the son born through the vaishya has been born from the third varna, the father was a brahmana. O Yudhishthira! He should be given two parts of the brahmana's property. It has been said that the son born through a brahmana father and a shudra mother should never be given any riches. O descendant of the Bharata lineage! However, a little bit can be given to the son born through the shudra mother.[1308] In this order, the riches are thus divided into ten parts. There may be several sons who have been born through the same varna and they will obtain an equal share in the portion recommended for them. The son who has been born through a shudra mother should not be regarded as a brahmana. Those born through the other three varnas, with a

[1307]The sacred thread ceremony is regarded as a second birth.

[1308]That is, the remaining part.

brahmana father, are regarded as brahmanas. It has been said that there are only four varnas and there is no fifth one. The son born through a shudra will obtain a tenth share in the father's riches. But that share will be given to him if his father has given him the share. If his father has not given it, he will not get it. O descendant of the Bharata lineage! Subject to this, riches must certainly be given to the son of a shudra. Lack of cruelty is supreme dharma and that is the reason he must be given. Whenever there is compassion, it gives rise to good qualities. O descendant of the Bharata lineage! However, irrespective of whether one has sons or does not have sons,[1309] under no circumstances should more than a tenth share be given to the son of a shudra wife. If a brahmana possesses more riches than are required to sustain him for three years, he should faithfully use these to perform sacrifices. Riches must not be acquired without reason. Out of the riches, three thousand coins must be given to the wife. When riches are given to her by her husband, she should enjoy them, without giving them away. When the husband dies without an heir, it has been said that the wife is entitled to enjoy all his riches. However, without asking him, a wife must never take her husband's riches. O Yudhishthira! If a brahmana lady possesses any riches that have been given to her by her father, these are inherited by her daughter, since a daughter is like a son. O king! O descendant of the Kuru lineage! It has been decreed that she is equal to a son. O bull among the Bharata lineage! These are the instructions of dharma. If these instructions of dharma are remembered, any exercise in obtaining riches will not be rendered futile."

'Yudhishthira said, "It has been said that the son of a brahmana father and a shudra mother must be given riches. However, why must a tenth share be specifically given? There is no doubt that a son born through a brahmana father and a brahmana mother is a brahmana. That is also true of a kshatriya mother and a vaishya mother. O supreme among kings! In that case, why is there a differential in shares? After all, the sons of all three varnas have been said to be brahmanas."

[1309]Through wives who are not shudras.

'Bhishma replied, "O scorcher of enemies! All wives in the world are known by the single name of *dara*.[1310] But though they are addressed by the same name, there are great differences between them. Even if a brahmana marries a brahmana wife after having already married three other wives, she is honoured as the eldest and is regarded as the seniormost. Objects for her husband's bath, cosmetics, washing the teeth, collyrium, havya, kavya and everything that is connected with dharma will be kept in her room. When she is present, no one else should think of performing those acts. O Yudhishthira! In the rites, the brahmana wife alone should aid the brahmana. Because she is the foremost, food, drink, garlands, garments and ornaments should be given by the brahmana wife to the husband. O descendant of the Kuru lineage! This has been instructed by Manu in the sacred texts. O great king! Therefore, this has been seen as eternal dharma. O Yudhishthira! Out of desire, if a brahmana acts in a contrary way, it has already been said that he is like a chandala. The son born through a kshatriya wife is equal to the son born through a brahmana wife. O king! But even then, there is a difference in the varnas of the mothers. In this world, that is the reason why sons born through brahmana and kshatriya mothers are unequal. O supreme among kings! The son born through the brahmana mother is the foremost. O Yudhishthira! That is the reason he is regarded as the first in inheriting his father's riches. The sons born through a brahmana mother and a kshatriya mother are not equal. In that way, the sons born through a kshatriya mother and a vaishya mother are not equal. O Yudhishthira! Prosperity, kingdoms and stores of riches have been recommended for kshatriyas. O king! The earth, up to the frontiers of the ocean, are seen to belong to them. If a kshatriya is established in his own dharma, he obtains a great deal of prosperity. The king is the wielder of the rod. O king! There can be no protection without the kshatriya. Brahmanas are extremely fortunate and are like gods among the gods. That is the reason, following the proper way, kings must worship them. Know that this is the eternal and undecaying dharma laid down by the

[1310]The word dara means wife.

rishis. When it decays, by adhering to their own dharma, kshatriyas protect subjects. Riches, wives and all the possessions of all the varnas would have been seized by bandits, had the king not existed as a protector. Thus, there is no doubt that the son of a kshatriya wife is superior to the son of a vaishya wife. O Yudhishthira! That is also the reason he deserves to have a greater share in the father's riches."

'Yudhishthira asked, "O king! O grandfather! You have talked about the rules laid down for brahmanas. What are the rules that have been laid down for the other varnas?"

'Bhishma replied, "O descendant of the Kuru lineage! Two wives have been recommended for a kshatriya. There are instances of a third and shudra wife, but this is not sanctioned by the sacred texts. O Yudhishthira! This is the order that has been laid down for kshatriyas. O Yudhishthira! The property of a kshatriya must be divided into eight parts. The son of a kshatriya wife will obtain four of those parts from the father's riches. He should also take that much from the father's possessions as is required for engaging in warfare. The son of a vaishya will obtain three parts and the son of a shudra will obtain the eighth part. But the son of a shudra should only take what has been given by the father. He should not take what he has not been given. O descendant of the Kuru lineage! A vaishya should only have a single wife. Sometimes, a second shudra wife is seen. But this is not sanctioned by the sacred texts. O bull among the Bharata lineage! O Kounteya! When a vaishya has both a vaishya and a shudra wife, rules have been laid down for a division between the two. O bull among the Bharata lineage! The property of a vaishya must be divided into five parts. O lord of men! I will tell you how this must be divided among the offspring. The son of the vaishya should take four parts from his father's riches. O descendant of the Bharata lineage! The fifth part is the share for the son of the shudra. But the son of a shudra should only take what has been given by the father. He should not take what he has not been given. If the other three varnas have a son through a shudra wife, riches must be given to the son. A shudra can only have a wife from his own varna and not from any other. Even if he has one hundred sons, all of them will have an equal share in the shudra's property. It has also specifically been said that if sons are born through the same varna, irrespective of the varna, all of them will have an equal share in the riches. However, the eldest son is the foremost and the eldest will therefore have one share more than the others. O Partha! This is the law of inheritance, as has been stated by Svayambhu earlier. O king! There is another difference in sons who have been born through the same varna. Especially at the time of marriage, the ones who have been born first must be married first. When the sons are equal, the eldest will obtain one share more. The son in the middle will obtain a medium share and the youngest a smaller share.[1311] Among wives of different varnas, the one who has the same varna as her husband is regarded as the foremost. This is what was stated by maharshi Maricha, the son of Kashyapa."'

Chapter 1729(48)

'Yudhishthira asked, "There is a mixture of the varnas and children of mixed parentage are born out of addiction to wealth, desire, uncertainty about varnas or plain ignorance. What are the rules for children of such mixed parentage? What is their dharma and what are their recommended tasks? O grandfather! Tell me this."

'Bhishma replied, "Earlier, for the sake of performing sacrifices, Prajapati created the four varnas and there were only four kinds of tasks. A brahmana can have four wives and in two of them, he himself is born.[1312] The sons who are born from the two who are lower down are inferior and have the varna of their mothers. The son born through a brahmana father and a shudra mother is known

[1311]What's probably intended is the following. There are special shares for the eldest, the son in the middle and the youngest. After these have been taken away, the rest of the property is divided equally.

[1312]The sons born from the brahmana wife and the kshatriya wife have the status of a brahmana. But the sons born from the vaishya wife and the shudra wife do not have this status.

as a *parashava*, because this is like offspring from a corpse.[1313] He should not give up his own duty of servitude and should serve his own family. He should never abandon that kind of conduct. He must make every kind of effort to hold up the different strands of the family. Even if he is the eldest, he must devote himself to serving the younger ones who are brahmanas. A kshatriya can have three wives and he is himself born in two of these.[1314] The third and shudra wife is inferior and the son born through this is known as *ugra*. A vaishya can have two wives and is himself born in both of these. A shudra can have only one wife and the son obtained through the shudra woman is also a shudra. Any birth outside the pale of the four varnas is condemned by the four varnas. Such a person is especially inferior and will oppress his preceptor's wife. A kshatriya gives birth[1315] to an outcast son known as a *suta*, who is not entitled to sacrifice, but is only entitled to sing praises and eulogies. A vaishya gives birth[1316] to a *vaidehaka*, who earns a living through grass. A shudra gives birth[1317] to a chandala, who is fierce, lives on the outskirts of habitations and acts as an executioner. These sons are born from brahmana mothers and are the worst of their lineages. O best among intelligent ones! O lord! These are the offspring of mixed parentage. The son born through a vaishya is a *bandi* or *magadha*[1318] and earns a living through the use of words. If perversely, a shudra father has a son through a kshatriya mother, the son is known as

[1313]*Param* means no more than and *shava* means corpse. A shudra woman is as defiled as a corpse.

[1314]Through the kshatriya wife and the vaishya wife.

[1315]This is left implicit—the father is a kshatriya and the mother is a brahmana.

[1316]The father is a kshatriya and the mother is a brahmana. The text uses the word *moudgalya* and earning a living through moudgalya. What this means is unclear, though *mudgala* is a kind of grass.

[1317]The father is a shudra and the mother is a brahmana.

[1318]The father is a shudra and the mother is a kshatriya. Bandis and magadhas are synonymous, though bandi is usually gender neutral and magadha is sometimes used for a woman. Both are bards and minstrels. It is possible that bandis recited the compositions of others, while magadhas also composed their own.

a nishada and becomes a fisherman. If a shudra father has a son through a vaishya mother, the son is known as *ayogava* and he dwells in a village or earns a living from the forests. Brahmanas should not accept gifts from them. If those with mixed parentage have offspring through women who are like them in status, the offspring have the same varna. But if the mother's status happens to be inferior, then the offspring that are born are inferior. For the four main varnas, the son has the same status as the father when the mother is of the same varna, or the one immediately below it. However, if the mother's varna is below this too, in general, the offspring is outside the pale of the father's varna. As long as parentage is from the same varna, the offspring also have the same varna. However, where the varnas have intercourse with each other, reprehensible categories are born. For example, a shudra father and a brahmana mother lead to offspring who are outcasts. In this way, those who are outside the four varnas can have offspring with those who are outside the four varnas and this leads to deterioration. There can be such repeated violations of varna, with outcast uniting with outcast. More and more inferior offspring are generated and there are fifteen in number. By having intercourse with someone one should not have intercourse with, a mixture of varnas results. The offspring of *vratya* and magadha are *sairandhra*.[1319] They are servants, earn a living through menial servitude and know about cosmetics and toiletries. The offspring of vratya and ayogava are suta and they earn a living through words. The offspring of *maireyaka* and vaidehaka is *madhuka*. The offspring of nishada and mudgara is *dasha* and they earn a living as boatmen. The offspring of *mritapa* and chandala are shvapaka and they are extremely vile. The offspring of *chatura* and magadha are cruel and earn a living through deceit. They subsist by selling flesh, fragrances, tasty substances and by lending money. Vaidehakas are wicked and cruel and live off their wives. Nishadas give birth to *madranabha*s and they ride on vehicles drawn by asses. Chandalas give birth to pulkasas and they eat the flesh of asses, horses and elephants. These dress themselves in garments stolen from corpses and eat from broken

[1319]The taxonomy given isn't very clear or consistent.

vessels.[1320] Three inferior varnas are born from ayogavas—*kshudra*, vaidehaka and *andhra*. They reside outside the outskirts of a village. *Charmakaras* are born from *karavaras* and nishadas. *Pandusoupakas* are born from chandalas and they make objects of use from stripped cane. Nishadas and vaidehakas give birth to *ahindakas*. Chandalas and *soupakas* give birth to those who earn a living through moudgalya. Nishadas and chandalas have sons who live outside human habitations. These sons live in cremation grounds and are exiled outside. Depending on the transgressions of the father and the mother, many such children of mixed parentage are born. Whether they disclose this or do not disclose this, they should know their own tasks. There is no dharma other than that for the four varnas. There are no indications about dharma for those who are outside the four varnas. They have been born out of wilfulness. They are outside the pale of virtue and no sacrifices have been recommended for them. Outcastes and more outcastes hae been born. They can dwell where they please and earn a living as they please. They reside at crossroads, in cremation grounds, in mountains, and even in trees. They wear ornaments and use many kinds of implements. There is no doubt that they act for the welfare of cattle and brahmanas. They have traits of non-violence, compassion, truthfulness in speech and forgiveness. O tiger among men! There is no doubt that by giving up their own lives to protect others, they can ensure success. I have recounted the instructions about how the intelligent ones have thought about men having offspring. One should not have offspring through a woman from a wrong varna. That would be like a stone sinking into the water. Irrespective of whether a man possesses intelligence or does not possess intelligence, he must not come under the subjugation of desire and anger and walk along an ignoble path. It is the nature of women to taint men. That is the reason learned people are not attracted to women."

'Yudhishthira asked, "There may be a man who is born of a wicked lineage, but his varna is unknown. O king! How does one discern whether he is noble or ignoble?"

[1320]Those discarded by others.

'Bhishma replied, "Those who are born of mixed parentage have many different kinds of conduct. The purity of birth can be discerned from one's virtuous acts. Ignoble conduct, contrary behaviour, cruelty and not practising the rites—in this world, these are the signs of a man being born in a wicked lineage. A son inherits his father's conduct, his mother's conduct, or both. He will never be able to conceal his narrow nature. One is born with a form that is like that of the mother or the father. Just as a tiger's stripes reveal, a man will be constrained by his own nature. Even if the origin of the lineage is hidden, if one is born of mixed parentage, a man will reveal himself, depending on whether his good conduct is a lot or is limited. To achieve some purpose, one may walk along a path and adopt a conduct that is apparently noble. However, adherence to good conduct will enable one to determine whether that person is from a superior varna or an inferior varna. People have many kinds of conduct and undertake many kinds of deeds. But in this world, there is nothing as important as good birth and good conduct. A man is affected by his body and his spirit. The spirit can be superior, middling or inferior. Depending on the spirit, one decides on what brings one pleasure. If a person has high birth, but lacks good conduct, he is not worshipped. And if a shudra has good conduct, he is worshipped by those who know about dharma. A man makes himself known through his own deeds. He shows his character through his conduct, good or bad. A man can destroy himself and his lineage, but he also makes it resplendent through his own deeds. That is the reason learned people avoid all those different kinds of women, where they are themselves not born."'[1321]

Chapter 1730(49)

'Yudhishthira said, "O foremost among the Kuru lineage! Tell us about the different kinds of sons who are born in separate

[1321] As was mentioned earlier, if the wife is from one of the sanctioned varnas, the husband is himself born, in the sense of granting his status to his son.

varnas. What kinds of sons are these? Who are they? Whose sons are they? We have heard that there have been many disagreements about these sons. O king! We are confused about this. You should sever our doubts."

'Bhishma replied, "Know that an *anantaraja* son is like one's own self.[1322] Know that a son who has been obtained through *niyukta* is called *prasritaja*.[1323] When a husband unites with his wife, despite knowing that she has gone astray, the son obtained in this fashion is known as *vadhyuda*. There are six kinds of sons known as *apadhvamsaja* and also the one known as *kanina*.[1324] O descendant of the Bharata lineage! Know that these are the kinds that have been mentioned."

'Yudhishthira asked, "Who are the six kinds of sons known as apadhvamsaja? Who is the one known as an *apasada*? You should explain the truth about all this to me."

'Bhishma replied, "O Yudhishthira! O descendant of the Bharata lineage! The sons that a brahmana obtains through the three lower varnas, the sons that a king obtains through the two lower varnas and the sons that a vaishya obtains through the lower varna are understood to be apadhvamsajas. Now hear about apasadas. Chandala, vratya and *vena*—these are seen to be the three kinds of apasadas and are respectively born through a shudra father and a brahmana, kshatriya or vaishya mother. A vaishya father is seen to have magadha or *vamaka* sons, depending respectively on whether the mother is a brahmana or a kshatriya. When a kshatriya father is seen to have a son through a brahmana mother, the offspring is known as suta. These are said to be apasadas. O lord of men! One is incapable of falsely asserting that these kinds of sons aren't really sons."

[1322]The term anantaraja son is used for a brahmana, kshatriya or vaishya father, when the mother is of the same varna, or is only one varna below.

[1323]Niyukta is when someone other than the husband, for specific reasons, is invited to have a son through the wife.

[1324]Apadhvamsaja sons are of mixed parentage. An unmarried maiden has a kanina child.

'Yudhishthira asked, "Some say that the son is *kshetraja*. Others say that he is *shukraja*.[1325] Are both of these the same? Whom does the son belong to? O grandfather! Tell me this."

'Bhishma replied, "The son is said to be both shukraja[1326] and kshetraja. Listen to me. The sole exception to this principle is *adhyuda*."[1327]

'Yudhishthira asked, "We know that the son is shukraja. How can the son become kshetraja? We know about the one called adhyuda. However, in a violation of an agreement, why does the father abandon him?"

'Bhishma replied, "He may have obtained another son, or there may be some other reason. In any event, ownership does not come from the seed, but from the field. O lord of the earth! The field is the proof. When a person desires to marry for the sake of a son and has a son, that son is his own. O bull among the Bharata lineage! But in other cases,[1328] the son is said to be kshetraja. The son cannot conceal his biological traits. They can be discerned.[1329] The son is sometimes known as the son of the father who has given him birth, or the one who has reared him. O Yudhishthira! Therefore, neither the seed, nor the field, is the complete proof."

'Yudhishthira asked, "When is a son regarded as that of the biological father and when is he regarded as the son of the one who has reared him? O descendant of the Bharata lineage! When is the seed, or the field, taken to be the proof?"

[1325]We have deliberately retained the Sanskrit words. Kshetra means field, signifying the mother. Kshetraja means someone born from the mother. Shukra means semen/seed, signifying the father. Shukraja means someone born from the father.

[1326]The text uses the word *retaja*, but retaja and shukraja mean the same thing.

[1327]This is a situation where the women become pregnant before marriage and the biological father does not marry her. In such instances, the son belongs to the mother.

[1328]When the biological father does not marry the mother.

[1329]Even when the mother has married someone else.

'Bhishma replied, "A son may be found abandoned on the road by the mother and the father. Unable to find the mother and the father, someone may rear him. In this case, since he is no one's son, he becomes the son of the person who has reared him. Just as a son obtains the varna of the person who has given him birth, this son obtains the varna of the person who has reared him."

'Yudhishthira asked, "How are the sacraments[1330] of such a person performed? Who undertakes them? What kind of girl should he be married to? O grandfather! Tell me this."

'Bhishma replied, "The person who rears him should himself perform the sacraments. Having been abandoned by the mother and the father, it is his varna that the son has adopted. O undecaying one! The sacraments should be performed in accordance with the foster-father's gotra and varna. O Yudhishthira! The maiden bestowed on him should thus be of the same varna. Such sacraments are performed without knowing the biological mother's gotra and varna. Kanina and adhyuda are known to be tainted sons. Despite this, it has been determined that sacraments should be performed for them. Brahmanas and others should use the same kinds of sacraments for kshetrajas, apasadas and adhyudas as they would for themselves. The sacred texts of dharma have determined injunctions for the different varnas. I have recounted all of this. What else do you wish to hear?"'

Chapter 1731(50)

'Yudhishthira asked, "O grandfather! What kind of affection results from seeing someone or dwelling together? What is the great fortune that is associated with cattle? O grandfather! Tell me this."

'Bhishma replied, "O immensely radiant one! I will tell you an ancient account, about a conversation between Nahusha and

[1330]Samskaras.

maharshi Chyavana. O bull among the Bharata lineage! In ancient times, maharshi Chyavana, from the Bhargava lineage, decided to observe an extremely great vow, characterized by residing in water. He destroyed his pride, anger, joy and sorrow. Firm in his vows, the sage dwelt in water for twelve years. He offered all the creatures there great and auspicious reassurances. To the creatures who lived in the water, the lord was like cool rays. He purified himself and was like a pillar. He bowed down before the gods. He entered the water at the confluence of the Ganga and the Yamuna. The currents of the Ganga and the Yamuna flowed with a loud and terrible roar. The force was as swift as that of the wind, but he received all this on his head. The Ganga and the Yamuna, and the other rivers that followed and flowed into them, passed by the rishi and did not cause him any affliction. The great sage was like a piece of wood and happily slept inside the water. O bull among the Bharata lineage! Sometimes, the intelligent one stood upright. The creatures that lived in the water thought that he was agreeable to look at. Cheerful in their minds, the fish sniffed at him. Thus, a long period of time elapsed. O immensely radiant one! On one occasion, some fishermen arrived at the spot, with fishing nets in their hands. Those many nishadas had made up their minds to catch fish. They were brave, strong and broad and were not scared of the water. They arrived at that spot, determined to cast their nets. O lord of men! O supreme among the Bharata lineage! They tied all their nets together and readied themselves to catch fish in the water. Desiring to catch fish, those *kaivartas*[1331] arrived at the banks of the Ganga and the Yamuna and covered a part of the water with nets that were joined together. These nets were made of new strands and covered a large space. They cast this large net at an appropriate place in the water. With great force, all of them then began to draw the net in from every side. They were cheerful and without fear and listened to each other. Many fish and other aquatic creatures got enmeshed. Chyavana, descendant of the Bhrigu lineage, was surrounded by the fish. O great king! As they dragged in the net, as they wished, he too got enmeshed. His limbs

[1331]Fishermen.

were covered with moss. His beard and matted hair were tawny. Large numbers of conch shells and other kinds of shells had attached themselves to his body and made it multicoloured. As they dragged in the net, they saw the one who was accomplished in the Vedas. All those lower classes joined their hands in salutation, bowed their heads and prostrated themselves on the ground. When the net had been dragged in, the fish were distressed at having been brought in contact with the ground. They were terrified and lamented. The sage saw the carnage that had been done to the fish. He was overcome by compassion and sighed repeatedly.

'"The nishadas said, 'In our ignorance, we have committed this sin.[1332] Show us your favours. O great king![1333] What can we do to please you? Tell us.'"

'Bhishma continued, "Chyavana was thus addressed in the midst of the fish and spoke these words. 'Listen with single-minded attention to my supreme desire now. Whether I have to give up my life, or whether I am sold, I wish to remain with the fish now. I have dwelt with them for a long time and cannot abandon them now.' Having been thus addressed, the nishadas trembled in great fear. All their faces were distressed and they went and told Nahusha what had happened."'

Chapter 1732(51)

'Bhishma said, "Hearing this, with his advisers and his priest, Nahusha swiftly arrived at the spot where Chyavana was. As is proper, the king purified himself, joined his hands in salutation and presented himself before the great-souled Chyavana. O lord of the earth! The king's priest worshipped the one who was truthful in his vows, immensely fortunate and the equal of a god.

[1332]Of dragging Chyavana up.

[1333]Since this is not being addressed to Yudhishthira, this is an inconsistency.

'"Nahusha said, 'You should tell me in detail what agreeable task I can perform for you. O illustrious one! I will do everything for you, even if it is something that is extremely difficult to accomplish.'

'"Chyavana replied, 'These kaivartas earn a living through fish and have made great efforts. Pay them a price for selling me and the fish.'

'"Nahusha said, 'Let the priest give one thousand coins to the nishadas as a price for purchasing such an illustrious one as the descendant of the Bhrigu lineage.'

'"Chyavana replied, 'O king! I am worth more than one thousand coins. What do you think? Use your own intelligence to determine the appropriate price that should be given.'

'"Nahusha said, 'Let one hundred thousand coins quickly be given to the nishadas. Perhaps that is the appropriate price for you. What do you think?'

'"Chyavana replied, 'O bull among kings! I should not be purchased with one hundred thousand coins. Give an appropriate price. Think. Consult your ministers and decide.'

'"Nahusha said, 'Let the priest give one crore coins to the nishadas. If you do not agree to this, let more be given to them.'

'"Chyavana replied, 'O king! O immensely radiant one! I do not deserve to be purchased with one crore coins, or even more. Give an appropriate price. Think. Consult with the brahmanas and decide.'

'"Nahusha said, 'Let one half of my kingdom, or all of it, be given to the nishadas. I think that this should be a right price. O brahmana! Do you think differently?'

'"Chyavana replied, 'O king! I do not deserve to be purchased with one half of the kingdom, or with all of it. Give an appropriate price. Think. Consult with the rishis and decide.'"

'Bhishma continued, "Hearing the maharshi's words, Nahusha was afflicted by grief. He began to think, consulting his ministers and his priest. At that time, a forest dweller who survived on roots and fruits arrived before Nahusha. He was a sage, but had been born from a cow. The supreme among brahmanas addressed the king. 'I will ensure that the brahmana is satisfied. I do not utter a lie, even in jest. How can it be otherwise? Without any doubts, you should do exactly what I tell you.'

'"Nahusha said, 'O illustrious one! Tell me a price that is appropriate for the maharshi descended from the Bhrigu lineage. Save me, my kingdom and my lineage. If the illustrious one is angry, he can destroy the three worlds, not to speak of someone like me, who is devoid of austerities and only possesses the valour of his arms. With my advisers and my officiating priest, I have now been submerged in fathomless waters. O maharshi! Become my boat and determine the price.'"

'Bhishma continued, "Hearing Nahusha's words, the powerful one who had been born from a cow spoke, thereby delighting all the advisers and the king. 'O great king! Brahmanas are supreme among varnas and there can be no price for them. O lord of the earth! However, cows are also priceless. Suggest a cow as a price.' O king! Hearing the maharshi's words, Nahusha, and his advisers and his priest, were filled with great delight. They went to Chyavana, the descendant of the Bhrigu lineage, who was devoted to his vows. Wishing to satisfy him, the king spoke these words. 'Arise. O brahmana rishi! Get up. O Bhargava! I have purchased you with a cow. O supreme among those who uphold dharma! I think that this is your price.'

'"Chyavana replied, 'O Indra among kings! I am getting up. O unblemished one! You have indeed purchased me properly. O one without decay! I do not see any riches that are equal to a cow. O king! O brave one! Talking about, hearing about, giving and seeing cattle is praised. This is auspicious and cleanses all sins. Cows are always the foundation of prosperity. There are no sins in cattle. Cows are like food and represent the supreme oblation that can be offered to gods. Cows are always established in sounds of "svaha" and "vashatkara". Cows are the ones who convey sacrifices. They are the mouth of a sacrifice. The undecaying and divine milk is borne by them and flows from them. It is like amrita. They are stores of amrita and are honoured by all the worlds. In energy and form, cows are like a fire on earth. Cows represent great energy and bring happiness to beings. When they are in a cow pen and can breathe without fear, that country is resplendent and sins are not attracted to it. Cows represent the ladder to heaven. Cows are worshipped in heaven. Cows are like goddesses that yield every object of desire. It is said that there is nothing superior to a cow. O bull among kings! I have thus recounted the greatness of cattle. I can only state some of the qualities and am not capable of repeating them in their entirety.'

'"The nishadas said, 'O sage! You have seen us and have spoken to us. O lord! The virtuous say that seven steps taken together lead to friendship. Show us your favours. The fire consumes all the oblations that are offered into it. O one with dharma in one's soul! In that way, you are a man who is as powerful as the fire. O learned one! We are bowing down before you. Show us your favours. To show us your grace, take this cow back from us.'

'"Chyavana replied, 'The sight of a sage is like virulent poison and can burn down a niggardly person from his roots, just as a fire consumes dead wood. O kaivartas! I have accepted the cow. You have been freed from all sin. Swiftly go to heaven, with all the fish that have been caught in the net.'"

'Bhishma continued, "Because of the favours of the maharshi with the cleansed soul and because of his words, the nishadas and the fish went to heaven. O bull among the Bharata lineage! On seeing the fishermen ascend to heaven with the fish, King Nahusha was amazed. The sage born from the cow and Chyavana, extender of the Bhrigu lineage, delighted the king by giving him comparable boons, until he said enough. O supreme among the Bharata lineage! The immensely valorous King Nahusha, lord of the earth, was supremely delighted. The king was Indra's equal and following dharma, received these. In great joy, he honoured the rishis back. Having completed his vow, Chyavana returned to his hermitage. The immensely energetic sage, descended from a cow, also returned to his hermitage. O lord of men! With the fish, the nishadas went to heaven. Having received the boons, Nahusha went to his own city. O son! O Yudhishthira! I have thus told you what you had asked me about, the affection that results from sight and from dwelling together. It is also the determination of dharma that cows are extremely fortunate. O brave one! What will I speak about next? What does your heart want to know?"'

Chapter 1733(52)

'Yudhishthira said, "O immensely wise one! I have a doubt that is as large as the great ocean. Listen. O mighty-armed one! Having heard, you should explain this to me. O lord! I have a great curiosity about Jamadagni's son, Rama, foremost among the upholders of dharma. You should explain this to me. How was Rama, with truth as his valour, born? Despite being born in a lineage of brahmana rishis, how did he come to practise the dharma of kshatriyas? O king! The entire world also recounts the story of Koushika. Despite being born in a lineage of kshatriyas, how did he become a brahmana? O tiger among men! The power of those two extremely great-souled ones, Rama and Vishvamitra, was exceedingly great. What sins skipped their sons and afflicted their grandsons? How did that happen? You should explain this to me."

'Bhishma replied, "O descendant of the Bharata lineage! In this connection, the ancient history of a conversation between Chyavana and Kushika is recounted. Bhargava Chyavana, immensely intelligent and a bull among sages, foresaw in advance a sin that would descend on his own lineage. He mentally thought about all its good and bad aspects, its strength and weaknesses. The store of austerities desired to burn down the entire Kushika lineage.[1334] Chyavana went to Kushika and spoke these words to him. 'O unblemished one! I desire to dwell with you for some time.'

'"Kushika said, 'O illustrious one! The learned ones have held that the act of dwelling together is a dharma that should be practised only when a daughter has been given away in marriage. That is what learned people have always said. O store of austerities! Otherwise, the door to dharma will be barred. However, with your permission, I should do what you have asked me to.'"

'Bhishma continued, "Kushika instructed that a seat should be offered to the great sage, Chyavana. With his wife, he went and stood before the sage. The king took a vessel and offered him water

[1334]As will be told, the Kushika lineage would be responsible for the sin.

to wash his feet. The great-souled one ensured that all the rites were observed. Following the prescribed rites, the king offered Chyavana madhuparka. He anxiously waited for the great-souled one, rigid in his vows, to accept this. Having shown the brahmana honour in this way, he spoke these words. 'O illustrious one! We are waiting for your instructions. What should we do for you? O one who is rigid in vows! Is it the kingdom, riches, cattle or objects given in sacrifices? Tell us. I will give you everything. This house, this kingdom and this seat of dharma are yours. You are the king of everything, with the servants. Rule everything. I am also dependent on you.' Having been thus addressed by Kushika in these words, Bhargava Chyavana was filled with great joy. He replied, 'O king! I do not desire the kingdom, riches, women, cattle, the country, or objects offered at sacrifices. If it pleases both of you, I desire to observe a vow. While I am observing it, you should tend to me, without any doubts.' Thus addressed, the couple was delighted. O descendant of the Bharata lineage! They told the rishi that it would be that way. Cheerfully, the king led him to an excellent part of the palace, to a beautiful apartment and showed it to him. 'O illustrious one! This is your bed. Live here, as you please. O store of austerities! We should do our best to please you.' While they were conversing in this way, the sun set and the rishi instructed that food and drink should be brought. King Kushika bowed down and asked, 'What kind of food do you desire? What will I present before you?' O descendant of the Bharata lineage! Filled with great delight, he told the king, 'Offer me appropriate food that is ready.' Hearing these words, the king honoured him and agreed. The lord of men offered him appropriate food. Having eaten, the illustrious one, knowledgable about dharma, told the couple, 'O lord! I wish to sleep now. Sleep is getting in the way.' The illustrious one, supreme among rishis, went to his bedchamber. The king and the queen also entered and waited. Bhargava said, 'Do not wake me up while I am asleep. Remain awake and press my feet throughout the night.' Kushika knew about dharma. Without doubting this, he agreed. Without waking him, they waited for night to be over. As they had been instructed by the maharshi, they tended to him in an excellent way. O great king! The couple tried its best to do this. As he had told the king, the illustrious brahmana slept. He did not turn in his sleep and slept for twenty-one days. O descendant of the Kuru lineage! The king and his wife remained without food. They cheerfully remained engaged in tending to him and serving him. Eventually, Bhargava, the store of austerities, himself awoke. Without saying anything to them, the great ascetic left the house. The two of them were hungry and overcome with exhaustion. Husband and wife followed him. But the best among sages did not even glance at them. While they looked on, the extender of the Bhargava lineage vanished. O Indra among kings! At this, the king fell down on the ground. However, the immensely radiant one arose in a short while. With his queen, he made great efforts to again search for him everywhere."'

Chapter 1734(53)

'Yudhishthira asked, "When the brahmana disappeared, what did the king do? What did his immensely fortunate wife do? O grandfather! Tell me this."

'Bhishma replied, "When the rishi could no longer be seen, the king and his wife were tired. Ashamed and bereft of their senses, they returned. In distress, they entered the city and did not say anything. They only thought about what Chyavana had done. With an empty mind, the king entered his house and saw that the descendant of the Bhrigu lineage was lying down on his bed. They were amazed at seeing this and thought about this marvel. The sight of the sage removed their exhaustion. They remained in their places and again began to tend to him. However, this time, the great sage was sleeping on his other side. The valiant one arose after the same time span. Though they were scared, they did not display any of their agitation. O lord of the earth! O descendant of the Bharata lineage! Having awoken, the sage said, 'Give me some oil for my limbs. I wish to have a bath.' Despite being hungry and afflicted by exhaustion, they agreed. They presented him with some extremely expensive oil that had been boiled one hundred times. When the rishi was happily seated, they controlled their words and rubbed him with the oil, until the immensely great ascetic, Bhargava, said that he had had enough. Bhargava noticed that they seemed to be indifferent. He suddenly arose and entered the bathroom. Everything required for taking a bath, befitting a king, had been kept there. Ignoring all this, while the king looked on, the sage disappeared again.

'"O bull among the Bharata lineage! However, the couple was not disturbed at this. Kushika and his wife then saw the illustrious lord, the descendant of the Bhrigu lineage, seated on the throne, after having taken his bath. Cheerfully, King Kushika and his wife offered the sage some food that had been cooked, feigning complete indifference. The sage had told the king that food should be brought, and with his wife, the king served it. There were many kinds of meat and many kinds of vegetables. There were spices and condiments, and light drinks were served. There were succulent biscuits, colourful cakes and confectionery. There were many kinds of tasty items, including wild fare that sages feed on. There were varied kinds of fruit and piles of good. There were jujubes, *inguda* nuts, *kashmari* nuts and cashew nuts. There was food meant for householders and for forest dwellers. Fearing the sage's curse, the king offered all kinds of food. All of this was brought and placed before Chyavana. Once this had been brought, a bed and a seat were offered to the sage. The food was placed in vessels and covered with white cloth. But Chyavana, the descendant of the Bhrigu lineage, burnt all this down to ashes. Engaged in their great vow, the couple did not exhibit any rage at this. While they looked on, he disappeared again. For the entire night, the rajarshi stood there, with his wife. The prosperous one did not say anything. Nor did he allow rage to penetrate him. Every day, in the king's abode, he was honoured with many kinds of mantras, given the best of beds and all the expensive requirements for having a bath. There were large piles of garments that were offered. Chyavana was incapable of detecting any change in their behaviour.

'"The brahmana rishi again spoke to King Kushika. 'You and your wife get yoked to a chariot and quickly bear me to wherever I ask you to.' Without showing any doubt, the king agreed to what the store of austerities had said. He only asked, 'Should it be a chariot for pleasure or a chariot for fighting?' The king cheerfully spoke these words to the sage. Chyavana cheerfully replied to the destroyer of enemy cities. 'Swiftly prepare a chariot that is used for warfare. Equip it with weapons, flags, spears, spikes and staffs. Let it roar with hundreds of bells. Stock it with javelins. Let it also be stocked with clubs and swords and armed with the best of weapons.' He agreed and prepared a giant chariot. His wife was yoked to the left and he was himself yoked to the right. A three-pointed goad was placed on the chariot. It was as hard as the vajra and as sharp as a needle. Having equipped it in this way, the king spoke these words. 'O illustrious one! The chariot is ready. Where does the descendant of the Bhrigu lineage want it to go? O brahmana rishi! The chariot will go wherever you ask it to.' The illustrious one told the king, 'Let it proceed one step at a time, gently. The two of you should drag it so that I am not exhausted and the rhythm does not break. While all the people look on, I should be borne pleasantly. If any passer-by approaches me, I will give him riches. Along the way, there may be brahmanas who desire riches. Without retaining anything, I will give them all the riches and the gems. O king! Without any reflection, act entirely in this way.' Hearing these words, the king summoned his servants and said, 'Without any doubts, give the sage everything that he has asked for.' Many kinds of riches, women, pairs of sheep, raw and polished gold, large elephants that were like elephants and all the king's advisers were made to follow the rishi's chariot. Lamentations arose from every part of the afflicted city. The king and the queen were violently struck on their backs and flanks by the pointed goad. However, they displayed no signs of agitation. They trembled, because they were hungry and had not eaten for fifty nights. But the brave couple managed to drag along that excellent chariot. They were severely struck in many places and blood began to flow from their wounds. O great king! They looked like flowering kimshuka trees. On seeing them, the citizens were overcome by great grief. However, afraid of being cursed, no one said anything. They gathered in groups of two and said,

'Behold the strength of austerities. Though we are angry, we are incapable of looking at the best of sages. Great is the valour of the illustrious maharshi, who has cleansed his soul. But also behold the fortitude of the king and his wife. They are exhausted and afflicted. Nevertheless, they are dragging the chariot along. The descendant of the Bhrigu lineage cannot detect any signs of agitation in them.' The extender of the Bhrigu lineage saw that they were indifferent. As if he was Vaishravana,[1335] he began to give away the riches. Despite this, the king remained cheerful in his soul and did all that he was asked to do.

'"The illustrious one, supreme among sages, was pleased. He descended from the best of chariots and released the couple. Having released them in the proper way, he spoke these words. O descendant of the Bharata lineage! Bhargava was extremely happy and spoke these gentle and deep words. He said, 'I wish to grant you the best of boons.' The learned one, the best of sages, rubbed their delicate bodies with his hands. O supreme among the Bharata lineage! The touch of his affection was like that of amrita. The king spoke these words. 'We have not suffered from any exhaustion.' Their exhaustion was dispelled through Bhargava's powers. Cheerfully, the illustrious one said, 'I have never spoken a falsehood. What I say will happen. This is an auspicious and beautiful spot on the banks of the Ganga. O king! Devoted to my vow, I will dwell here for some time. O son! You are exhausted. Return to your own city. O lord of men! Come here with your wife tomorrow and you will see me. You should not yield to rage. A beneficial time is imminent. Everything that is in your heart will be accomplished.' Thus addressed, Kushika was cheerful in his mind. He spoke these words, which were full of purport, to the tiger among sages. 'O immensely fortunate one! I have no anger. O illustrious one! We have been purified by you. Our bodies have become young and strong. I and my wife no longer see any of the wounds that were caused by the goad on our bodies. With my wife, I am hale. O sage! I see that this queen looks like a divine apsara.

[1335]Kubera.

She possesses great beauty, just as I have seen her in earlier times. O great sage! All of this has become possible because of your favours. O illustrious one! O one with truth as one's valour! There is no marvel in your having accomplished this.' Thus addressed, Chyavana told Kushika, 'O lord of men! With your wife, come here tomorrow.' Hearing this, the rajarshi honoured him and took his permission. With a body that was like that of the king of the gods, he returned to the city. The advisers and priests came out to meet him. So did all the soldiers, the courtesans and the ordinary people. King Kushika blazed in his supreme prosperity and they surrounded him. He happily entered his city and was praised by the bards. Having entered the city, he performed all the ablutions. With his wife, the king ate and spent the night. They looked at each other. Their old age was gone and it was as if their youth had just bloomed. They were like immortals. They were delighted with these new bodies and went to sleep. Because of the boon granted by the brahmana, they had become extremely handsome. The rishi was an extender of the fame of the lineage of the Bhrigus. The store of austerities changed that forest into a prosperous spot. The learned one adorned it with many kinds of jewels. This was a beauty that Shatakratu's abode didn't possess."'

Chapter 1735(54)

'Bhishma said, "When night was over, the extremely intelligent king awoke. Having performed the morning ablutions, with his wife, he headed for the forest. There, the king saw a palace that was completely made out of gold. There were a thousand pillars covered with jewels and it was like a city of the gandharvas. Kushika saw that everything seemed to have been divinely designed. There were hills with beautiful peaks and valleys. There were lilies and lotuses. O descendant of the Bharata lineage! There were galleries with many kinds of gates. The ground was verdant, as if the fields were made out of gold. There were blossoming *sahakaras*, *ketakas*, *uddalakas*, *dhavas*, ashokas, *muchukundas*, flowering *atimuktas*, champakas, *tilakas*, *bhavyas*, panasas, *vanjulas* and flowering karnikaras.[1336] This is what he saw there, here and there. There were dark *varanapushpas* and *ashtapadika* creepers. The king saw that these had been properly trimmed. There were trees on which there were lotuses and lilies and there were flowers from every season. He saw many mansions that were as beautiful as celestial vehicles and mountains. O descendant of the Bharata lineage! Some of the water was cool and some was warm. There were colourful seats and the best of beds. The beds were made completely out of gold and were strewn with expensive covers and cushions. Large quantities of food and drink had been prepared and were properly laid out. There were parrots that spoke, she-parrots, fork-tailed shrikes, cuckoos, woodpeckers, lapwings, wild cocks, peacocks, domestic cocks, *putrakas*,[1337] partridges, Greek partridges, monkeys, swans, cranes and ducks. There were beautiful sounds and sights on every side. O king! In some places, there were large numbers of apsaras and gandharvas. He saw that they were sporting with their loved ones. Sometimes, the king was able to see them and sometimes, he was unable to see them. There was the extremely beautiful sound of singing and also the sounds of teaching going on. The king also heard the melodious sound of geese. On seeing this extraordinary sight, the king began to think. 'This must be a dream. Perhaps my mind has gone. Is this for real? In my body, have I attained the supreme end? This must be the sacred land of Uttara Kuru or Amaravati. What is this wonder that I have seen?' He thought in this way.

[1336]A sahakara is a mango tree, ketaka is the crew pine, uddalaka is probably a typo for *uddanaka* (mimosa), dhava is the axle-wood tree, ashoka is *Saraca indica*, muchukunda is the cork-leaved bayur tree, atimukta is the Indian rosewood, champaka is the sampangi flower, tilaka is the bleeding-heart plant, bhavya is starfruit, panasa is jackfruit, vanjula is similar to ashoka, karnikara is the Indian laburnum, varanapushpa is a kind of plant and ashtapadika is the bread-flower tree.

[1337]Since there is no bird with this name, this is probably a typo.

'"While he was thinking, he saw the bull among the sages. He was in a celestial vehicle made out of gold and its pillars were encrusted with jewels. The descendant of the Bhrigu lineage was lying down on an expensive and divine bed. With great delight, the king and his wife approached him. Chyavana would be seen to disappear and would then appear again. He next saw him in a part of the forest. He was seated on a mat made out of kusha grass and was meditating, engaged in a great vow. Through his powers of yoga, the brahmana confounded the king. In an instant, the forest, the large numbers of apsaras, the gandharvas and the trees—all of these vanished. O king! The banks of the Ganga became silent again. As had been the case earlier, it was again covered with kusha grass and termite hills. King Kushika and his wife were supremely astounded at these deeds. They thought it was a great wonder that everything had disappeared. Kushika was filled with delight and spoke to his wife. 'O fortunate one! Behold. The colourful sight that we have witnessed is extremely difficult to see. This is because of the favours of the foremost one of the Bhrigu lineage. Other than the strength of austerities, what can this be? These things can be obtained through austerities, not merely by wishing for them. Austerities are superior to the kingdoms of the three worlds. The store of austerities has tormented himself with extremely great austerities and is sporting. Through the valour of his austerities, he is even capable of creating other worlds. Brahmanas are born to perform auspicious deeds and use their intelligence. Who other than Chyavana could have endeavoured to do this? A kingdom is very easy for a man to obtain. However, in this world, the status of a brahmana is extremely difficult to obtain. It is because of the brahmana's powers that we were yoked to the chariot, like beasts of burden.' Chyavana got to know about these thoughts of his. He glanced at the king and said, 'Come here quickly.' Thus addressed, he and his wife advanced towards the great sage. The king bowed his head down and they worshipped the one who should be revered. The sage pronounced a benediction over the king. O bull among men! The intelligent one comforted him and asked him to be seated. O king! Assuming his natural form, Bhargava comforted the king.

O descendant of the Bharata lineage! To reassure him, he spoke these gentle words. 'O king! You have properly controlled the five senses, the five organs of action and the sixth sense of the mind. That is the reason you have escaped from the hardship. O supreme among eloquent ones! O son! You have honoured me properly. I have not been able to detect the slightest bit of taint in you. O king! With your permission, I will now return to wherever I had come from. O Indra among kings! I am pleased with you. Accept a boon from me.'

'"Kushika replied, 'O illustrious one! In your presence, I have been like one who is in the midst of a fire. O tiger among the Bhrigu lineage! It is sufficient that my lineage and I have not been burnt down. O descendant of the Bhrigu lineage! This is the best of boons and I have already obtained it. O unblemished one! If you are pleased with me, let the conduct of my lineage be auspicious. O brahmana! If you grant me this, the purpose of my life will have been accomplished. This is the fruit of my kingdom and this is my supreme austerity. O descendant of the Bhrigu lineage! However, I have a doubt. If you are pleased with me, you should explain this to me.'"'

Chapter 1736(55)

'"Chyavana said, 'Accept a boon from me. What is the doubt in your heart? O foremost among men! Tell me what it is and I will explain everything to you.'

'"Kushika said, 'O illustrious one! O Bhargava! If you are pleased with me, tell me something. I wish to hear the reason why you decided to reside with me. What was the reason for sleeping on the bed for twenty-one days, without changing sides? O bull among sages! Why did you depart, without saying anything? Why did you suddenly disappear and again reveal yourself? O brahmana! You again slept for twenty-one days. After having been rubbed with oil, you left my house, without having eaten. There were many kinds of food that were brought, but you burnt them down with fire. Why did you suddenly and swiftly depart on a chariot? Why did you give away the riches? Why did you show us the forest? O great sage! There were many golden palaces there. You showed us beds where the bed posts were decorated with jewels. Then you made them disappear again. I wish to hear the reason for this. I am extremely confused by this and have thought about this day and night. But I have been unable to understand anything about this. O store of austerities! I wish to hear the entire truth about this.'

'"Chyavana replied, 'Listen in detail to all the reasons. O king! Since you have asked me, I cannot refuse to tell you. Earlier, in an assembly of the gods, the grandfather said something. O king! I heard that and will tell you. Listen. Because of a conflict between a brahmana and a kshatriya, my lineage will become mixed up and tainted. O king! Your grandson will be full of energy and valour. That is the reason I have come to you, to save my lineage. O Kushika! I desired to exterminate and burn down your lineage. O lord of the earth! Earlier, that is the reason I came to you and said, "I am observing a vow. You should serve me. However, while I resided in your house, I could not detect any signs of wicked conduct. O rajarshi! That is the reason you are still alive. Otherwise, you would no longer have been here. That is the reason I decided to sleep for twenty-one days. O king! I was hoping that someone would wake me up. But you and your wife allowed me to sleep and did not wake me. O supreme among kings! That is when my mind became pleased with you. O lord of the earth! O lord! I awoke and departed. I was hoping that you would restrain me, so that I could curse you. I repeatedly disappeared in your house. For twenty-one days, I again immersed myself in yoga. O lord of men! You were hungry and exhausted and I was hoping that you would show your anger. That is the reason I afflicted you with hunger. O king! However, I could not detect the slightest bit of anger in your mind. O best among men! I became pleased with you and your wife. When I had the food brought and burnt it down, I was hoping that you would be overcome by anger. But you tolerated that. O lord of men! That is when I ascended the chariot and told you and your wife to drag me along. But you did what I had asked you to. O lord of men! You did not show any doubts and I was pleased with you. You were not overcome with rage when I gave away the riches. O king! O lord of men! While I was pleased with you, for you and your wife, I created the forest that you saw. To please you, I showed you heaven. O king! In that forest, you saw some signs of heaven. O king! You saw a little bit of heaven in your physical body. O king! O supreme among kings! For a short while, you and your wife witnessed that. O lord of men! This was to demonstrate to you the dharma of austerities. O king! I am aware of the desire that there is in your heart. O lord of the earth! Through your austerities, you desire to obtain the status of a brahmana. O king! You have no interest in being a king on earth or being a king of the gods. O son! However, the status of a brahmana will be extremely difficult for you to obtain. Having become a brahmana, it is difficult to become a rishi. Having become a rishi, it is difficult to become an ascetic. O Kushika! But your desire will come true. There will be a Koushika[1338] who will become a brahmana. He will be third in descent from you and he will obtain the status of a brahmana. O best among kings! He will be born in your lineage, but he will possess the energy of the Bhrigus. Your grandson will become a brahmana. He will be an ascetic, with the resplendence of the fire. He will be one who will cause fright to gods and men and to the three worlds. I tell you this truthfully. O rajarshi! Ask for the boon that is in your mind. A long period of time has elapsed and I wish to proceed on a visit to the tirthas.'

'"Kushika said, 'O great sage! This is enough of a boon, since you are pleased with me. O unblemished one! Let my grandson become a brahmana through his austerities. O illustrious one! Grant me the boon that my lineage should always have that status. O illustrious one! Once again, I wish to ask you about this in detail. O descendant of the Bhrigu lineage! How will my lineage obtain the status of a brahmana? Who will be my relative? Whom will I honour?'"'

[1338]Vishvamitra.

Chapter 1737(56)

'"Chyavana said, 'O bull among men! I should certainly tell you this. O lord of men! That is the reason I came here, wishing to exterminate your lineage. O lord of men! Kshatriyas always have the assistance of the Bhrigus in the performance of sacrifices. However, because of reasons determined by destiny, there will be conflict between them. O lord of men! The kshatriyas will slay all the Bhrigus. Struck by the rod of destiny, they will not even spare those who are in the wombs. Then, in our lineage, a person will be born to extend the line. His name will be Ourva and he will be greatly energetic. His resplendence will be like that of the blazing fire. The flames of his anger will be such that they will be capable of destroying the three worlds. He will be capable of reducing the earth, with its mountains and oceans, to ashes. He will control the fire of his anger for some time. That supreme of sages will hurl it into the ocean, in the form of the subterranean fire. However, the descendant of the Bhrigu lineage will have an immensely fortunate son named Richika. O unblemished one! The entire dhanurveda will present itself before him. Because of reasons determined by destiny, so as to destroy the kshatriyas, he will receive it and pass it on to his son, Jamadagni, who will be immensely fortunate and will clease his soul through austerities. But that tiger among the Bhrigu lineage will still hold that knowledge. O supreme among kings! The one with dharma in his soul will unite with a maiden from your lineage, for spreading that knowledge on. The great ascetic will obtain your granddaughter and Gadhi's daughter. He will give birth to Rama, who will be a brahmana, but will follow the dharma of kshatriyas. In your lineage will be born Visvamitra, as Gadhi's son. He will be extremely devoted to dharma and will be like Brihaspati in his energy. He will be a kshatriya, but will follow the dharma of brahmanas. O immensely radiant one! Gadhi will have this son, who will be devoted to great austerities. There will be a mixing up because of women.[1339]

[1339]The charus were mixed up, a story that has already been told.

This has been determined by the grandfather. It will happen and there can be no reversal. In the third generation from you, there will be a brahmana. The Bhrigus, cleansed in their souls, will be your matrimonial allies.'"

'Bhishma continued, "Hearing the words of the sage, the great-souled Chyavana, Kushika was delighted. The king, with dharma in his soul, replied in the following words. 'Let it be this way.' O supreme among the Bharata lineage! The greatly energetic Chyavana again spoke to the king. He urged the king to ask for a boon, who said, 'O great king! I will accept it and let my desire truly come true through you. Let my lineage have the status of brahmanas and let their minds always be fixed on dharma.' The sage, Chyavana, replied that it would indeed be this way. Having taken the king's permission, he then departed for a visit to the tirthas. O king! I have told you everything, exactly as it occurred. This is the reason for the matrimonial alliance between the Bhrigus and the Kushikas. O king! Everything happened exactly as the sage had said. The births of Rama and the sage, Vishvamitra, occurred in that way."'

Volume 9 ends here. Section 87 will be concluded in Volume 10.

The final volume ends the instructions of the Anushasana Parva. The horse sacrifice is held, and Dhritarashtra, Gandhari, Kunti, Vidura and Sanjaya leave for the forest. Krishna and Balarama die as the Yadavas fight among themselves. The Pandavas leave on the great journey with the famous companion—Dharma disguised as a dog. Refusing to abandon the dog, Yudhishthira goes to heaven in his physical body and sees all the Kurus and the Pandavas are already there.

About the Translator

Bibek Debroy is a member of NITI Aayog, the successor to the Planning Commission. He is an economist who has published popular articles, papers and books on economics. Before NITI Aayog, he has worked in academic institutes, industry chambers and for the government. Bibek Debroy also writes on Indology and Sanskrit. Penguin published his translation of the Bhagavad Gita in 2006 and *Sarama and Her Children: The Dog in Indian Myth* in 2008. The 10-volume unabridged translation of the Mahabharata was sequentially published between 2010 and 2014 and he is now translating the Hari Vamsha, to be published in 2016. Bibek Debroy was awarded the Padma Shri in 2015.